The Best of Both Worlds

WITH DESIGNS BY PAUL BACON

The Best of

AN ANTHOLOGY OF STORIES

Both Worlds

FOR ALL AGES

COMPILED BY

Georgess McHargue

OUBLEDAY & COMPANY, INC. • GARDEN CITY, NEW YORK

Grateful acknowledgment is made for the use of the following:

"By the Waters of Babylon" from *Selected Works of Stephen Vincent Benet*, published by Holt, Rinehart and Winston, Inc. Copyright 1937 by Stephen Vincent Benét; copyright renewed 1964, by Thomas C. Benét, Stephanie B. Mahin and Rachel Benét Lewis. Reprinted by permission of Brandt & Brandt.

"The Fifty-First Dragon" from *Seeing Things at Night* by Heywood Broun. Reprinted by permission of Mrs. Heywood Broun.

Chapter I from *Five Children and It* by E. Nesbit. Reprinted by permission of Coward-McCann, Inc.

"Motion Study Tonsils" from *Cheaper by the Dozen* by Frank B. Gilbreth, Jr., and Ernestine Gilbreth Carey. Copyright © 1963, 1948 by Frank B. Gilbreth, Jr., and Ernestine Gilbreth Carey. Reprinted by permission of Thomas Y. Crowell Company.

"A, B, & C: The Human Element in Mathematics" from *Literary Lapses* by Stephen Leacock. Reprinted by permission of Dodd, Mead & Company and McClelland and Stewart Limited.

"The Serial Garden" from *Armitage, Armitage, Fly Away Home* by Joan Aiken. Copyright © 1966 by Macmillan & Co., Ltd. Reprinted by permission of Doubleday & Company, Inc. and Macmillan Co. of Canada, Ltd.

The Small Miracle by Paul Gallico, copyright 1950 by Paul Gallico; "Hearts and Hands" from *Waifs and Strays* by O. Henry; "The Colt" from *Fierce and Gentle Warriors: Three Stories by Mikhail Sholokhov*, translated by Miriam Morton, copyright © 1967 by Miriam Morton; and excerpt from *Mary Jane* by Dorothy Sterling, copyright © 1959 by Dorothy Sterling. All reprinted by permission of Doubleday & Company, Inc.

Excerpt from *We Are Seven* by Una Troy. Copyright © 1957 by Una Troy. Reprinted by permission of E. P. Dutton & Co., Inc. and David Higham Associates.

Chapter 7 from *Ring of Bright Water* by Gavin Maxwell. Copyright © 1960 by Gavin Maxwell. Reprinted by permission of E. P. Dutton & Co., Inc. and Longmans, Green & Co., Limited.

"Charles" from *The Lottery* by Shirley Jackson, copyright 1948, 1949 by Shirley Jackson. Reprinted by permission of Farrar, Straus & Giroux, Inc.

Excerpt from *Abe Lincoln Grows Up* by Carl Sandburg, copyright 1926, 1928 by Harcourt, Brace & World, Inc., renewed 1954, 1956 by Carl Sandburg; Chapters 1–4 from *The Borrowers* by Mary Norton, copyright 1952, 1953 by Mary Norton; "The Circus" from *My Name is Aram* by William Saroyan, copyright © 1937, 1938, 1939, 1940,

To the memory of
Seth M. Agnew
whose concern for
editorial excellence
is continuously in
the minds of those
who knew him

Table of Contents

VIII QUESTS AND DISCOVERIES

Editor's Note

It is common talk among parents and educators that the last decades have seen a pronounced change in reading habits among children of high school and junior high school age. No longer are teens and young teens reading only books written exclusively for them. In fact, the whole distinction between adult and juvenile reading is becoming more and more vague. In preparing this anthology it has seemed to me that if there are many teens who will enjoy reading Hemingway, there are many adults who will enjoy STUART LITTLE with equal zest. It was for these individuals (of whatever age) that this book was compiled.

G. McH. 1968

The Best of Both Worlds

I

Adventures and Mishaps

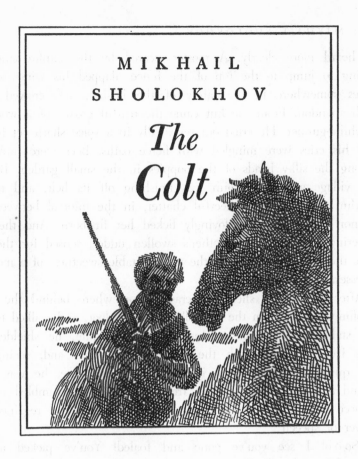

MIKHAIL
SHOLOKHOV

The
Colt

He struggled out of his mother's body in broad daylight, head first. His spindly front legs stretched out near a pile of manure buzzing with emerald flies, and the first thing he saw was the dove-gray puff of a shrapnel explosion melting overhead. The roar of a cannon split the air and threw his little wet body under his mother's legs. Terror was the first feeling he knew on this earth.

An ill-smelling hail of grapeshot rattled on the tiled roof of the stable and sprinkled the ground below. The frightened mother jumped to her feet and with a shrill neigh dropped down again, her sweating flank resting against the sheltering dung heap.

She was soldier Trofim's mare.

In the sultry silence that followed, the buzzing of the flies could be heard more clearly. A rooster, scared by the gunfire and not daring to jump to the top of the fence, flapped his wings several times somewhere in the safety of the bushes, and crowed there with abandon. From the hut came the tearful groans of a wounded machine-gunner. He cried out repeatedly in a voice sharp yet hoarse, and his cries were mingled with fierce oaths. Bees were humming among the silky heads of the poppies in the small garden. Beyond the village a machine gun was finishing off its belt, and to the rhythm of its weirdly cheerful chatter, in the interval between the cannon shots, the mare lovingly licked her firstborn. And the colt, lowering himself to his mother's swollen udder, sensed for the first time the fullness of life and the unforgettable sweetness of a mother's caresses.

After the second shell had crashed somewhere behind the barn, Trofim emerged from the hut, slammed the door, and walked toward the stable. As he was passing the manure pile, he shielded his eyes from the sun with the palm of his hand and, seeing the colt quiver with the strain of sucking at his mare, he was spellbound and dumfounded. With trembling hands he fumbled for his tobacco pouch. After rolling himself a cigarette, he regained his power of speech:

"So-o-o! I see you've gone and foaled! You've picked a fine time, I must say!" There was a bitter note of injury in his last remark.

Scrub grass and dry dung clung to the mare's shaggy flanks. She looked indecently thin and loose, but her eyes beamed with a proud joy touched with weariness, and her satiny upper lip curled back in a grin. Or so at least it seemed to Trofim. He led his mare into the stable. She snorted as she shook the bag of grain he hung from her head. Trofim leaned against the doorpost and, looking crossly at the colt, asked his mother dryly:

"What the devil am I going to do with him?"

The sound of grain being crunched could be heard in the dimness and stillness of the stable. A crooked sunbeam, like a column of golden dust, shed its light through a chink in the closed door and shone on Trofim's cheek. His whiskers and the brush of his beard were tinged with a reddish hue. The lines around his mouth curved in dark furrows. The colt stood on its thin, downy legs like a wooden toy horse.

"Will I have to kill him?" Trofim said, pointing his tobacco-stained forefinger in the direction of the newborn.

The mare rolled her bloodshot eyeballs, blinked, and gave her master a sidelong, mocking glance.

That evening, inside the best room of the hut, Trofim had a conversation with the Squadron Commander:

". . . I could tell my mare was in foal, she couldn't trot, I couldn't get her to canter, and she kept getting short of breath. I had taken a good look at her one day and it turned out she was in foal. And what care she took of it! Such care! You know, the colt is a sort of bay color . . . That's how . . ." Trofim told his story, hesitating between the details.

The Squadron Commander clutched the copper mug of tea in his fist as he would clutch a sabre hilt before going into battle, and kept staring at the lamp with tired eyes. Above the yellow flame moths flew about in a frenzy. They had flown in through the open window and were burning themselves against the lamp's glass chimney, one after another.

"It makes no difference—bay or black—it's all the same. Shoot it! With a colt around we'll be like a gypsy camp, not a cavalry squadron," the Commander said.

Trofim muttered something.

"What? . . . That's what I said, just like gypsies. And if the Chief were to show up, what then? There he'll be, reviewing the regiment, and the colt will come prancing out with its tail up. . . . The whole Red Army will be shamed and disgraced. I don't understand how you could have allowed such a thing, Trofim. Here we are, at the very height of the Civil War, and suddenly, there is this kind of thing going on. Why, it's downright disgraceful! Give the hostlers the strictest orders to keep the stallions away from the mares."

Next morning Trofim came out of the hut carrying his rifle. The sun hadn't yet fully risen. The grass was sparkling with roseate dew. The meadow, marked with traces of the infantry's boots and dug up for trenches, reminded one of a girl's tear-stained, sorrowful face. The cooks were bustling around the field kitchen. On the porch of the hut the Commander was sitting in a threadbare undershirt. As he sat there, shaping a ladle out of wood, his fingers, now more accustomed to the chilly touch of a revolver, were awkward at this task. The feel and fragrance of the damp wood brought back to him the forgotten past of village life.

As Trofim went by he asked, with a show of interest:

"Making a dumpling ladle?"

The Commander finished off the handle and said through his teeth:

"That woman, that pest of a housekeeper, kept after me: 'Do, please make me one. . . .' At one time I was good at this sort of thing, but now somehow it doesn't come out right."

"No, on the contrary . . . I think it's quite good," Trofim praised his Commander's handiwork.

He brushed the chips off his knees and asked Trofim:

"Going to shoot the colt?"

Trofim waved his hand and said nothing. After a moment's pause he walked on toward the stable.

With head bent, the Commander waited for the sound of the shot. A minute passed, then another, but he heard nothing. Trofim reappeared from around the corner of the stable. He looked distressed.

"Well?"

"Something must be wrong with the hammer of the rifle. It won't strike the percussion cap."

"Let me have a look at it."

Trofim reluctantly handed over his rifle. The Commander pulled the bolt back and forth, and screwed up his eyes.

"You have no bullets in it."

"Can't be!" Trofim exclaimed.

"I tell you it's empty."

"Guess I must have dropped them somewhere . . . maybe behind the stable."

The Commander laid the rifle aside and spent some time turning over the new ladle in his hands. The scent of the moist wood was so strong that his nostrils quickened to the fragrance of flowering alders and of newly plowed earth. He thought longingly of past toil almost forgotten in the endless conflagration of war.

"All right! The devil with him! Let him stay near his mother. For the time being let him live . . . then we'll see. When the war is over, he may yet be of some use—maybe for plowing. . . .

And if anything goes wrong, the Chief will understand that the colt is a suckling and must be allowed to nurse . . . the Chief was once a suckling himself . . . and we have nursed too . . . and since it is the way of nature, that's all there is to it! But, there's nothing whatever wrong with your rifle."

It so happened that a month later, not far from the village of Ust-Khopersk, Trofim's squadron was engaged in battle with a company of enemy Cossacks. The two sides opened fire at twilight. It was getting dark as they rode into attack, sabres bared. Halfway in the charge Trofim had fallen behind his platoon. Neither the whip nor the bit, which Trofim pulled so hard that his mare's mouth bled, could get her to break into a gallop. Tossing her head high, she neighed hoarsely and stamped the ground until the colt, waving his tail, caught up with her. Trofim leaped from his saddle, thrust his sabre into its scabbard, and, his face contorted with rage, tore the rifle from his shoulder. The men on the right flank were already in hand-to-hand combat with the enemy. Near a cliff a group of fighters was moving back and forth as if swayed by a strong wind. They brandished their sabres in silence. Only the dull thud of the horses' hoofs could be heard. Trofim glanced in their direction for a second, then aimed at the colt's narrow head. His hand may have trembled in his exasperation, or perhaps there was some other reason for it, but he missed his aim. After the shot the colt merely kicked up his heels stupidly, neighed in a thin voice and, throwing up clumps of gray dirt, circled around and came to a standstill a little way off. Trofim fired several more bullets at the little devil. Then, convinced that the shots had caused neither injury nor the death of his mare's offspring, he leaped on to her back, and swearing monstrously, rode off at a jogtrot to where bearded, red-faced Cossacks were pressing his Squadron Commander and three other Red Army men toward a gully.

The squadron spent that night in the steppe, near a shallow gully. The men smoked little. They didn't unsaddle the horses. A reconnaissance returning from the Don reported that considerable enemy forces had gathered to prevent the Reds from crossing the river.

As Trofim lay dozing, his feet wrapped in the folds of a rubber cloak, he could not stop thinking of the events of the past day.

Before dawn, the Commander came over and squatted down beside him in the darkness.

"Trofim, are you asleep?"

"Just dozing."

Looking up at the fading stars, the Commander said:

"Get rid of that colt. He's causing trouble in battle. When I look at him my hand shakes. . . . I can't use my sabre. It's all because he reminds us of home . . . and we can't have that sort of thing in war . . . it turns the soldier's heart from stone to a limp rag. And, besides, when the horses went into attack the scamp got between their legs and they wouldn't tread on him." The Commander was silent a moment, then smiled sadly. But Trofim did not see the smile. "Do you understand, Trofim?" he continued. "That colt's tail . . . seeing that tail . . . the way he puts it over his back, kicks up his heels . . . and his tail is just like a fox's. . . . It's a marvelous tail! . . ."

Trofim remained silent. He drew his coat over his head and, shivering in the dewey dampness, fell asleep with astonishing speed.

Opposite a certain ancient monastery, the Don strikes against projecting cliffs and dashes past them with reckless swiftness. At the bend the water spins in little whirlpools, and the green, white-maned waves rush to fling themselves against the chalk rocks scattered into the river by the spring floods.

The enemy had occupied the shore where the current was weaker and the river broader and calmer. They were on the right bank. They were now aiming their fire at the foothills across from their vantage point. To avoid the line of fire, the Squadron Commander could not do otherwise than have his men cross the rushing river opposite the monastery. He rode down from the sandbank beneath the cliffs and led the way into the water with his bay horse. The rest of the squadron followed him with a thunderous splash— one hundred and eight half-naked swimmers and the same number of horses of varied colors. The saddles were piled into three canoes. Trofim was steering one of them. He had entrusted his mare to the platoon leader, Nechepurenko. From the middle of the river Trofim could see the leading horses wading deeply, forced to gulp water. Their riders urged them on. In less than a minute, some one hundred and fifty feet from the shore, the water was thickly dotted with horses' heads, snorting in a variety of sounds. The men swam at their sides, clinging to their manes, clothes and knapsacks tied to rifles which they held above their heads.

Throwing his oar into the boat, Trofim rose to his full height and, screwing up his eyes against the sun, looked anxiously for his mare's head among the swimming horses. The squadron resembled a gaggle of geese scattered over the sky by hunters' shots. Right in front was the Squadron Commander's bay, his glossy back rising high out of the water. Behind it was a dark cloud of animals and, last of all, falling more and more behind the others, as Trofim could see, came platoon leader Nechepurenko's bristling head, with the pointed ears of Trofim's mare on his left. Straining his eyes, Trofim also caught sight of the colt. He was swimming in spurts, rising high out of the water, then sinking till his nostrils were barely visible.

And then the wind passing over the Don carried to Trofim's ears a plaintive neigh, as thin as a spider's thread.

The cry sounded over the water as sharp and keen as the point of a sabre. It struck right at Trofim's heart, and something extraordinary happened to the man: he had gone through five years of war, death had gazed like a temptress into his eyes again and again, and who knows what else. But now he went pale under his red bushy beard, turning the color of ashes. Snatching up the oar, he sent the boat back against the current, toward the spot where the exhausted colt was spinning in a whirlpool. And some sixty feet away, Nechepurenko was struggling with the mare but could not hold her back. She was swimming toward that whirlpool, whinnying in distress. Trofim's friend, Steshka Yefremov, sitting on a pile of saddles in another canoe, shouted to him:

"Don't take a fool's chances. Make for the shore. Look! There they are—the Cossacks!"

"I'll shoot him!" Trofim cried, his breath coming hard as he tugged at his rifle strap.

The current had carried the colt to where the squadron was crossing. The small whirlpool swung him around and around smoothly, lapping against him with its green, foam-capped waves. Trofim worked his oar desperately as the boat lurched violently. He could see the Cossacks rushing out of a ravine on the right shore. A Maxim gun began its rapid drumming. The bullets hissed as they smacked into the water. An enemy officer in a torn canvas shirt shouted something, waving his rifle.

The colt whinnied more and more rarely, the short, piercing cry grew fainter and fainter. And that cry sounded so much like the cry of an infant that it sent a chill of horror through all who heard it.

Nechepurenko, abandoning the mare, easily swam back to the left shore. Trembling, Trofim seized his rifle and fired, aiming just below the small head being sucked down by the whirlpool. Then he kicked off his boots and, stretching out his arms dived into the river with a dull moan.

On the right bank the officer in the canvas shirt bellowed: "Cease fire!"

Within five minutes Trofim reached the colt. With his left hand he supported his chilled body, and panting and coughing in spasms, made for the left shore. Not a shot was fired from the opposite side.

Sky, forest, sand—all glowingly green, transparent. . . . With one last tremendous effort Trofim's feet felt the ground. He dragged the colt's slippery body onto the shore, and, sobbing, spat up the green water as he groped over the sand with his hands. From the forest across the Don came the muffled voices of his squadron that had made the crossing. Somewhere beyond the sandbank on the opposite side rifle shots rang out. The mare stood at Trofim's side, shaking herself and licking her colt. From her tail a rainbow stream was dripping, making small holes in the sand.

Swaying, Trofim rose to his feet, took a few steps, then sprang into the air and dropped on his side. He felt as though a hot arrow had pierced his chest. He heard the shot as he fell. A single shot in the back, from the opposite shore. There the officer in the torn canvas shirt casually rattled his carbine lock ejecting the smoking cartridge case, while on the sand, two paces from the colt, Trofim twitched and his rough blue lips, which for five years had not kissed a child, smiled for the last time.

1926

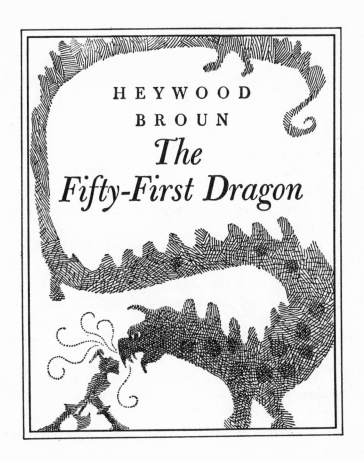

HEYWOOD
BROUN
The
Fifty-First Dragon

O f all the pupils at the knight school Gawaine le Cœur-Hardy
was among the least promising. He was tall and sturdy, but his
instructors soon discovered that he lacked spirit. He would hide
in the woods when the jousting class was called, although his
companions and members of the faculty sought to appeal to his
better nature by shouting to him to come out and break his neck
like a man. Even when they told him that the lances were padded,
the horses no more than ponies and the field unusually soft for
late autumn, Gawaine refused to grow enthusiastic. The Headmaster
and the Assistant Professor of Pleasaunce were discussing the case
one spring afternoon and the Assistant Professor could see no remedy
but expulsion.

"No," said the Headmaster, as he looked out at the purple hills which ringed the school, "I think I'll train him to slay dragons."

"He might be killed," objected the Assistant Professor.

"So he might," replied the Headmaster brightly, but he added, more soberly, "we must consider the greater good. We are responsible for the formation of this lad's character."

"Are the dragons particularly bad this year?" interrupted the Assistant Professor. This was characteristic. He always seemed restive when the head of the school began to talk ethics and the ideals of the institution.

"I've never known them worse," replied the Headmaster. "Up in the hills to the south last week they killed a number of peasants, two cows and a prize pig. And if this dry spell holds there's no telling when they may start a forest fire simply by breathing around indiscriminately."

"Would any refund on the tuition fee be necessary in case of an accident to young Cœur-Hardy?"

"No," the principal answered, judicially, "that's all covered in the contract. But as a matter of fact he won't be killed. Before I send him up in the hills I'm going to give him a magic word."

"That's a good idea," said the Professor. "Sometimes they work wonders."

From that day on Gawaine specialized in dragons. His course included both theory and practice. In the morning there were long lectures on the history, anatomy, manners and customs of dragons. Gawaine did not distinguish himself in these studies. He had a marvelously versatile gift for forgetting things. In the afternoon he showed to better advantage, for then he would go down to the South Meadow and practice with a battle-ax. In this exercise he was truly impressive, for he had enormous strength as well as speed and grace. He even developed a deceptive display of ferocity. Old alumni say that it was a thrilling sight to see Gawaine charging across the field toward the dummy paper dragon which had been set up for his practice. As he ran he would brandish his ax and shout "A murrain on thee!" or some other vivid bit of campus slang. It never took him more than one stroke to behead the dummy dragon.

Gradually his task was made more difficult. Paper gave way to papier-mâché and finally to wood, but even the toughest of these dummy dragons had no terrors for Gawaine. One sweep of the ax always did the business. There were those who said that when the practice was protracted until dusk and the dragons threw long, fantastic shadows across the meadow Gawaine did not charge so impetuously nor shout so loudly. It is possible there was malice in this charge. At any rate, the Headmaster decided by the end of June that it was time for the test. Only the night before a dragon had come close to the school grounds and had eaten some of the lettuce from the garden. The faculty decided that Gawaine was ready. They gave him a diploma and a new battle-ax and the Headmaster summoned him to a private conference.

"Sit down," said the Headmaster. "Have a cigarette."

Gawaine hesitated.

"Oh, I know it's against the rules," said the Headmaster. "But after all, you have received your preliminary degree. You are no longer a boy. You are a man. Tomorrow you will go out into the world, the great world of achievement."

Gawaine took a cigarette. The Headmaster offered him a match, but he produced one of his own and began to puff away with a dexterity which quite amazed the principal.

"Here you have learned the theories of life," continued the Headmaster, resuming the thread of his discourse, "but after all, life is not a matter of theories. Life is a matter of facts. It calls on the young and the old alike to face these facts, even though they are hard and sometimes unpleasant. Your problem, for example, is to slay dragons."

"They say that those dragons down in the south wood are five hundred feet long," ventured Gawaine, timorously.

"Stuff and nonsense!" said the Headmaster. "The curate saw one last week from the top of Arthur's Hill. The dragon was sunning himself down in the valley. The curate didn't have an opportunity to look at him very long because he felt it was his duty to hurry back to make a report to me. He said the monster, or shall I say, the big lizard?—wasn't an inch over two hundred feet. But the size has nothing at all to do with it. You'll find the big ones even easier than the little ones. They're far slower on their feet and less aggressive, I'm told. Besides, before you go I'm going to equip you in such fashion that you need have no fear of all the dragons in the world."

"I'd like an enchanted cap," said Gawaine.

"What's that?" answered the Headmaster, testily.

"A cap to make me disappear," explained Gawaine.

The Headmaster laughed indulgently. "You mustn't believe all those old wives' stories," he said. "There isn't any such thing. A cap to make you disappear, indeed! What would you do with it? You haven't even appeared yet. Why, my boy, you could walk from here to London, and nobody would so much as look at you. You're nobody. You couldn't be more invisible than that."

Gawaine seemed dangerously close to a relapse into his old habit of whimpering. The Headmaster reassured him: "Don't worry; I'll give you something much better than an enchanted cap. I'm going to give you a magic word. All you have to do is to repeat this magic charm once and no dragon can possibly harm a hair of your head. You can cut off his head at your leisure."

He took a heavy book from the shelf behind his desk and began to run through it. "Sometimes," he said, "the charm is a whole phrase or even a sentence. I might, for instance, give you 'To make the'—No, that might not do. I think a single word would be best for dragons."

"A short word," suggested Gawaine.

"It can't be too short or it wouldn't be potent. There isn't so much hurry as all that. Here's a splendid magic word: 'Rumplesnitz.' Do you think you can learn that?"

Gawaine tried and in an hour or so he seemed to have the word well in hand. Again and again he interrupted the lesson to inquire, "And if I say 'Rumplesnitz' the dragon can't possibly hurt me?" And always the Headmaster replied, "If you only say 'Rumplesnitz,' you are perfectly safe."

Toward morning Gawaine seemed resigned to his career. At daybreak the Headmaster saw him to the edge of the forest and pointed him to the direction in which he should proceed. About a mile away to the southwest a cloud of steam hovered over an open meadow in the woods and the Headmaster assured Gawaine that under the steam he would find a dragon. Gawaine went forward slowly. He wondered whether it would be best to approach the dragon on the run as he did in his practice in the South Meadow or to walk slowly toward him, shouting "Rumplesnitz" all the way.

The problem was decided for him. No sooner had he come to the fringe of the meadow than the dragon spied him and began to charge. It was a large dragon and yet it seemed decidedly aggressive in spite of the Headmaster's statement to the contrary. As the dragon charged it released huge clouds of hissing steam through its nostrils. It was almost as if a gigantic teapot had gone mad. The dragon came forward so fast and Gawaine was so frightened that he had time to say "Rumplesnitz" only once. As he said it, he swung his battle-ax and off popped the head of the dragon. Gawaine had to admit that it was even easier to kill a real dragon than a wooden one if only you said "Rumplesnitz."

Gawaine brought the ears home and a small section of the tail. His schoolmates and faculty made much of him, but the Headmaster wisely kept him from being spoiled by insisting that he go on with his work. Every clear day Gawaine rose at dawn and went out to kill dragons. The Headmaster kept him at home when it rained, because he said the woods were damp and unhealthy at such times and that he didn't want the boy to run needless risks. Few good days passed in which Gawaine failed to get a dragon. On one particularly fortunate day he killed three, a husband and wife and a visiting relative. Gradually he developed a technique. Pupils who sometimes watched him from the hilltops a long way off said that he often allowed the dragon to come within a few feet before he said "Rumplesnitz." He came to say it with a mocking sneer. Occasionally he did stunts. Once when an excursion party from London was watching him he went into action with his right hand tied behind his back. The dragon's head came off just as easily.

As Gawaine's record of killings mounted higher the Headmaster found it impossible to keep him completely in hand. He fell into the habit of stealing out at night and engaging in long drinking bouts at the village tavern. It was after such a debauch that he rose a little before dawn one fine August morning and started out after his fiftieth dragon. His head was heavy and his mind sluggish. He was heavy in other respects as well, for he had adopted the somewhat vulgar practice of wearing his medals, ribbons and all, when he went out dragon hunting. The decorations began on his chest and ran all the way down to his abdomen. They must have weighed at least eight pounds.

Gawaine found a dragon in the same meadow where he had killed the first one. It was a fair-sized dragon, but evidently an old one. Its face was wrinkled and Gawaine thought he had never seen so hideous a countenance. Much to the lad's disgust, the monster refused to charge and Gawaine was obliged to walk toward him. He whistled as he went. The dragon regarded him hopelessly, but craftily. Of course it had heard of Gawaine. Even when the lad raised his battle-ax the dragon made no move. It knew that there was no salvation in the quickest thrust of the head, for it had been informed that this hunter was protected by an enchantment. It merely waited, hoping something would turn up. Gawaine raised the battle-ax and suddenly lowered it again. He had grown very pale and he trembled violently. The dragon suspected a trick. "What's the matter?" it asked, with false solicitude.

"I've forgotten the magic word," stammered Gawaine.

"What a pity," said the dragon. "So that was the secret. It doesn't seem quite sporting to me, all this magic stuff, you know. Not cricket, as we used to say when I was a little dragon; but after all, that's a matter of opinion."

Gawaine was so helpless with terror that the dragon's confidence rose immeasurably and it could not resist the temptation to show off a bit.

"Could I possibly be of any assistance?" it asked. "What's the first letter of the magic word?"

"It begins with an 'r,'" said Gawaine weakly.

"Let's see," mused the dragon, "that doesn't tell us much, does it? What sort of a word is this? Is it an epithet, do you think?"

Gawaine could do no more than nod.

"Why, of course," exclaimed the dragon, "reactionary Republican." Gawaine shook his head.

"Well, then," said the dragon, "we'd better get down to business. Will you surrender?"

With the suggestion of a compromise Gawaine mustered up enough courage to speak.

"What will you do if I surrender?" he asked.

"Why, I'll eat you," said the dragon.

"And if I don't surrender?"

"I'll eat you just the same."

"Then it doesn't make any difference, does it?" moaned Gawaine.

"It does to me," said the dragon with a smile. "I'd rather you didn't surrender. You'd taste much better if you didn't."

The dragon waited for a long time for Gawaine to ask "Why?" but the boy was too frightened to speak. At last the dragon had to give the explanation without his cue line. "You see," he said, "if you don't surrender you'll taste better because you'll die game."

This was an old and ancient trick of the dragon's. By means of some such quip he was accustomed to paralyze his victims with laughter and then to destroy them. Gawaine was sufficiently paralyzed as it was, but laughter had no part in his helplessness. With the last word of the joke the dragon drew back his head and struck. In that second there flashed into the mind of Gawaine the magic word "Rumplesnitz," but there was no time to say it. There was time only to strike and, without a word, Gawaine met the onrush of the dragon with a full swing. He put all his back and shoulders into it. The impact was terrific and the head of the dragon flew away almost a hundred yards and landed in a thicket.

Gawaine did not remain frightened very long after the death of the dragon. His mood was one of wonder. He was enormously puzzled. He cut off the ears of the monster almost in a trance. Again and again he thought to himself, "I didn't say 'Rumplesnitz'!" He was sure of that and yet there was no question that he had killed the dragon. In fact, he had never killed one so utterly. Never before had he driven a head for anything like the same distance. Twenty-five yards was perhaps his best previous record. All the way back to the knight school he kept rumbling about in his mind seeking an explanation for what had occurred. He went to the Headmaster immediately and after closing the door told him what had happened. "I didn't say 'Rumplesnitz,'" he explained with great earnestness.

The Headmaster laughed. "I'm glad you've found out," he said. "It makes you ever so much more of a hero. Don't you see that?

Now you know that it was you who killed all these dragons and not that foolish little word 'Rumplesnitz.'"

Gawaine frowned. "Then it wasn't a magic word after all?" he asked.

"Of course not," said the Headmaster, "you ought to be too old for such foolishness. There isn't any such thing as a magic word."

"But you told me it was magic," protested Gawaine. "You said it was magic and now you say it isn't."

"It wasn't magic in a literal sense," answered the Headmaster, "but it was much more wonderful than that. The word gave you confidence. It took away your fears. If I hadn't told you that you might have been killed the very first time. It was your battle-ax did the trick."

Gawaine surprised the Headmaster by his attitude. He was obviously distressed by the explanation. He interrupted a long philosophic and ethical discourse by the Headmaster with, "If I hadn't of hit 'em all mighty hard and fast any one of 'em might have crushed me like a, like a——" He fumbled for a word.

"Egg shell," suggested the Headmaster.

"Like a egg shell," assented Gawaine, and he said it many times. All through the evening meal people who sat near him heard him muttering, "Like a egg shell, like a egg shell."

The next day was clear, but Gawaine did not get up at dawn. Indeed, it was almost noon when the Headmaster found him cowering in bed, with the clothes pulled over his head. The principal called the Assistant Professor of Pleasaunce, and together they dragged the boy toward the forest.

"He'll be all right as soon as he gets a couple more dragons under his belt," explained the Headmaster.

The Assistant Professor of Pleasaunce agreed. "It would be a shame to stop such a fine run," he said. "Why, counting that one yesterday, he's killed fifty dragons."

They pushed the boy into a thicket above which hung a meager cloud of steam. It was obviously quite a small dragon. But Gawaine did not come back that night or the next. In fact, he never came back. Some weeks afterward brave spirits from the school explored the thicket, but they could find nothing to remind them of Gawaine except the metal part of his medals. Even the ribbons had been devoured.

The Headmaster and the Assistant Professor of Pleasaunce agreed that it would be just as well not to tell the school how Gawaine had achieved his record and still less how he came to die. They held that it might have a bad effect on school spirit. Accordingly, Gawaine has lived in the memory of the school as its greatest hero. No visitor succeeds in leaving the building today without seeing a great shield which hangs on the wall of the dining hall. Fifty pairs of dragons' ears are mounted upon the shield and underneath in gilt letters is "Gawaine le Cœur-Hardy," followed by the simple inscription, "He killed fifty dragons." The record has never been equaled.

F. SCOTT
FITZGERALD

*The
Freshest
Boy*

It was a hidden Broadway restaurant in the dead of the night, and
a brilliant and mysterious group of society people, diplomats and
members of the underworld were there. A few minutes ago the
sparkling wine had been flowing and a girl had been dancing gaily
upon a table, but now the whole crowd were hushed and breathless.
All eyes were fixed upon the masked but well-groomed man in the
dress suit and opera hat who stood nonchalantly in the door.

"Don't move, please," he said, in a well-bred, cultivated voice that
had, nevertheless, a ring of steel in it. "This thing in my hand might
—go off."

His glance roved from table to table—fell upon the malignant man higher up with his pale saturnine face, upon Heatherly, the suave secret agent from a foreign power, then rested a little longer, a little more softly perhaps, upon the table where the girl with dark hair and dark tragic eyes sat alone.

"Now that my purpose is accomplished, it might interest you to know who I am." There was a gleam of expectation in every eye. The breast of the dark-eyed girl heaved faintly and a tiny burst of subtle French perfume rose into the air. "I am none other than that elusive gentleman, Basil Lee, better known as the Shadow."

Taking off his well-fitting opera hat, he bowed ironically from the waist. Then, like a flash, he turned and was gone into the night.

"You get up to New York only once a month," Lewis Crum was saying, "and then you have to take a master along."

Slowly, Basil Lee's glazed eyes returned from the barns and bill-boards of the Indiana countryside to the interior of the Broadway Limited. The hypnosis of the swift telegraph poles faded and Lewis Crum's stolid face took shape against the white slip-cover of the opposite bench.

"I'd just duck the master when I got to New York," said Basil.

"Yes, you would!"

"I bet I would."

"You try it and you'll see."

"What do you mean saying I'll see, all the time, Lewis? What'll I see?"

His very bright dark-blue eyes were at this moment fixed upon his companion with boredom and impatience. The two had nothing in common except their age, which was fifteen, and the lifelong friend-ship of their fathers—which is less than nothing. Also they were bound from the same Middle-Western city for Basil's first and Lewis' second year at the same Eastern school.

But, contrary to all the best traditions, Lewis the veteran was mis-erable and Basil the neophyte was happy. Lewis hated school. He had grown entirely dependent on the stimulus of a hearty vital mother, and as he felt her slipping farther and farther away from him, he plunged deeper into misery and homesickness. Basil, on the other hand, had lived with such intensity on so many stories of boarding-school life that, far from being homesick, he had a glad feeling of recognition and familiarity. Indeed, it was with some sense of doing the appropriate thing, having the traditional rough-house, that he had thrown Lewis' comb off the train at Milwaukee last night for no reason at all.

To Lewis, Basil's ignorant enthusiasm was distasteful—his instinctive attempt to dampen it had contributed to the mutual irritation.

"I'll tell you what you'll see," he said ominously. "They'll catch you smoking and put you on bounds."

"No, they won't, because I won't be smoking. I'll be in training for football."

"Football! Yeah! Football!"

"Honestly, Lewis, you don't like anything, do you?"

"I don't like football. I don't like to go out and get a crack in the eye." Lewis spoke aggressively, for his mother had canonized all his timidities as common sense. Basil's answer, made with what he considered kindly intent, was the sort of remark that creates life-long enmities.

"You'd probably be a lot more popular in school if you played football," he suggested patronizingly.

Lewis did not consider himself unpopular. He did not think of it in that way at all. He was astounded.

"You wait!" he cried furiously. "They'll take all that freshness out of you."

"Clam yourself," said Basil, coolly plucking at the creases of his first long trousers. "Just clam yourself."

"I guess everybody knows you were the freshest boy at the Country Day!"

"Clam yourself," repeated Basil, but with less assurance. "Kindly clam yourself."

"I guess I know what they had in the school paper about you—"

Basil's own coolness was no longer perceptible.

"If you don't clam yourself," he said darkly, "I'm going to throw your brushes off the train too."

The enormity of this threat was effective. Lewis sank back in his seat, snorting and muttering, but undoubtedly calmer. His reference had been to one of the most shameful passages in his companion's life. In a periodical issued by the boys of Basil's late school there had appeared, under the heading Personals:

> "If someone will please poison young Basil, or find some other means to stop his mouth, the school at large and myself will be much obliged."

The two boys sat there fuming wordlessly at each other. Then, resolutely, Basil tried to re-inter this unfortunate souvenir of the past. All that was behind him now. Perhaps he had been a little fresh, but he was making a new start. After a moment, the memory passed and with it the train and Lewis' dismal presence—the breath of the East came sweeping over him again with a vast nostalgia. A voice called him out of the fabled world; a man stood beside him with a hand on his sweater-clad shoulder.

"Lee!"

"Yes, sir."

"It all depends on you now. Understand?"

"Yes, sir."

"All right," the coach said, "go in and win."

Basil tore the sweater from his stripling form and dashed out on the field. There were two minutes to play and the score was 3 to 0 for the enemy, but at the sight of young Lee, kept out of the game all year by a malicious plan of Dan Haskins, the school bully, and Weasel Weems, his toady, a thrill of hope went over the St. Regis stand.

"33-12-16-22!" barked Midget Brown, the diminutive little quarterback.

It was his signal——

"Oh, gosh!" Basil spoke aloud, forgetting the late unpleasantness. "I wish we'd get there before tomorrow."

II

St. Regis School, Eastchester,
November 18, 19—

"Dear Mother: There is not much to say today, but I thought I would write you about my allowance. All the boys have a bigger allowance than me, because there are a lot of little things I have to get, such as shoe laces, etc. School is still very nice and am having a fine time, but football is over and there is not much to do.

I am going to New York this week to see a show. I do not know yet what it will be, but probably the Quacker Girl or little boy Blue as they are both very good. Dr. Bacon is very nice and there's a good phycission in the village. No more now as I have to study Algebra.

> "Your Affectionate Son,
> "BASIL D. LEE."

As he put the letter in its envelope, a wizened little boy came into the deserted study hall where he sat and stood staring at him.

"Hello," said Basil, frowning.

"I been looking for you," said the little boy, slowly and judicially. "I looked all over—up in your room and out in the gym, and they said you probably might of sneaked off in here."

"What do you want?" Basil demanded.

"Hold your horses, Bossy."

Basil jumped to his feet. The little boy retreated a step.

"Go on, hit me!" he chirped nervously. "Go on, hit me, cause I'm just half your size—Bossy."

Basil winced. "You call me that again and I'll spank you."

"No, you won't spank me. Brick Wales said if you ever touched any of us—"

"But I never did touch any of you."

"Didn't you chase a lot of us one day and didn't Brick Wales—"

"Oh, what do you want?" Basil cried in desperation.

"Doctor Bacon wants you. They sent me after you and somebody said maybe you sneaked in here."

Basil dropped his letter in his pocket and walked out—the little boy and his invective following him through the door. He traversed a long corridor, muggy with that odor best described as the smell of stale caramels that is so peculiar to boys' schools, ascended a stairs and knocked at an unexceptional but formidable door.

Doctor Bacon was at his desk. He was a handsome, redheaded Episcopal clergyman of fifty whose original real interest in boys was now tempered by the flustered cynicism which is the fate of all headmasters and settles on them like green mould. There were certain preliminaries before Basil was asked to sit down—gold-rimmed glasses had to be hoisted up from nowhere by a black cord and fixed on Basil to be sure that he was not an impostor; great masses of paper on the desk had to be shuffled through, not in search of anything but as a man nervously shuffles a pack of cards.

"I had a letter from your mother this morning—ah—Basil." The use of his first name had come to startle Basil. No one else in school had yet called him anything but Bossy or Lee. "She feels that your marks have been poor. I believe you have been sent here at a certain amount of—ah—sacrifice and she expects—"

Basil's spirit writhed with shame, not at his poor marks but that his financial inadequacy should be so bluntly stated. He knew that he was one of the poorest boys in a rich boys' school.

Perhaps some dormant sensibility in Doctor Bacon became aware of his discomfort; he shuffled through the papers once more and began on a new note.

"However, that was not what I sent for you about this afternoon. You applied last week for permission to go to New York on Saturday, to a matinée. Mr. Davis tells me that for almost the first time since school opened you will be off bounds tomorrow."

"Yes, sir."

"That is not a good record. However, I would allow you to go to New York if it could be arranged. Unfortunately, no masters are available this Saturday."

Basil's mouth dropped ajar. "Why, I—why, Doctor Bacon, I know two parties that are going. Couldn't I go with one of them?"

Doctor Bacon ran through all his papers very quickly. "Unfortunately, one is composed of slightly older boys and the other group made arrangements some weeks ago."

"How about the party that's going to the *Quaker Girl* with Mr. Dunn?"

"It's that party I speak of. They feel that their arrangements are complete and they have purchased seats together."

Suddenly Basil understood. At the look in his eye Doctor Bacon went on hurriedly:

"There's perhaps one thing I can do. Of course there must be several boys in the party so that the expenses of the master can be divided up among all. If you can find two other boys who would like to make up a party, and let me have their names by five o'clock, I'll send Mr. Rooney with you."

"Thank you," Basil said.

Doctor Bacon hesitated. Beneath the cynical incrustations of many years an instinct stirred to look into the unusual case of this boy and find out what made him the most detested boy in school. Among boys and masters there seemed to exist an extraordinary hostility toward him, and though Doctor Bacon had dealt with many sorts of schoolboy crimes, he had neither by himself nor with the aid of trusted sixth-formers been able to lay his hands on its underlying cause. It was probably no single thing, but a combination of things; it was most probably one of those intangible questions of personality. Yet he remembered that when he first saw Basil he had considered him unusually prepossessing.

He sighed. Sometimes these things worked themselves out. He wasn't one to rush in clumsily. "Let us have a better report to send home next month, Basil."

"Yes, sir."

Basil ran quickly downstairs to the recreation room. It was Wednesday and most of the boys had already gone into the village of Eastchester, whither Basil, who was still on bounds, was forbidden to follow. When he looked at those still scattered about the pool tables and piano, he saw that it was going to be difficult to get anyone to go with him at all. For Basil was quite conscious that he was the most unpopular boy at school.

It had begun almost immediately. One day, less than a fortnight after he came, a crowd of the smaller boys, perhaps urged on to it, gathered suddenly around him and began calling him Bossy. Within the next week he had two fights, and both times the crowd was vehemently and eloquently with the other boy. Soon after, when he was merely shoving indiscriminately, like every one else, to get into the dining room, Carver, the captain of the football team, turned about and, seizing him by the back of the neck, held him and dressed him down savagely. He joined a group innocently at the piano and was told, "Go on away. We don't want you around."

After a month he began to realize the full extent of his unpopularity. It shocked him. One day after a particularly bitter humiliation he went up to his room and cried. He tried to keep out of the way for a while, but it didn't help. He was accused of sneaking off here and there, as if bent on a series of nefarious errands. Puzzled and wretched, he looked at his face in the glass, trying to discover there the secret of their dislike—in the expression of his eyes, his smile.

He saw now that in certain ways he had erred at the outset—he had boasted, he had been considered yellow at football, he had pointed out people's mistakes to them, he had shown off his rather extraordinary fund of general information in class. But he had tried to do better and couldn't understand his failure to atone. It must be too late. He was queered forever.

He had, indeed, become the scapegoat, the immediate villain, the sponge which absorbed all malice and irritability abroad—just as the most frightened person in a party seems to absorb all the others' fear, seems to be afraid for them all. His situation was not helped by the fact, obvious to all, that the supreme self-confidence with which he had come to St. Regis in September was thoroughly broken. Boys taunted him with impunity who would not have dared raise their voices to him several months before.

This trip to New York had come to mean everything to him—surcease from the misery of his daily life as well as a glimpse into the long-awaited heaven of romance. Its postponement for week after week due to his sins—he was constantly caught reading after lights, for example, driven by his wretchedness into such vicarious escapes from reality—had deepened his longing until it was a burning hunger. It was unbearable that he should not go, and he told over the short list of those whom he might get to accompany him. The possibilities were Fat Gaspar, Treadway, and Bugs Brown. A quick journey to their rooms showed that they had all availed themselves of the Wednesday permission to go into Eastchester for the afternoon.

Basil did not hesitate. He had until five o'clock and his only chance was to go after them. It was not the first time he had broken bounds, though the last attempt had ended in disaster and an extension of his confinement. In his room, he put on a heavy sweater—an overcoat was a betrayal of intent—replaced his jacket over it and hid a cap in his back pocket. Then he went downstairs and with an elaborately careless whistle struck out across the lawn for the gymnasium. Once there, he stood for a while as if looking in the windows, first the one close to the walk, then one near the corner of the building. From here he moved quickly, but not too quickly, into a grove of lilacs. Then he dashed around the corner, down a long stretch of lawn that was blind from all windows and, parting the strands of a wire fence, crawled through and stood upon the grounds of a neighboring estate. For the moment he was free. He put on his cap against the chilly November wind, and set out along the half-mile road to town.

Eastchester was a suburban farming community, with a small shoe factory. The institutions which pandered to the factory workers were the ones patronized by the boys—a movie house, a quick-lunch wagon on wheels known as the Dog and the Bostonian Candy Kitchen. Basil tried the Dog first and happened immediately upon a prospect.

This was Bugs Brown, a hysterical boy, subject to fits and strenuously avoided. Years later he became a brilliant lawyer, but at that time he was considered by the boys of St. Regis to be a typical lunatic because of his peculiar series of sounds with which he assuaged his nervousness all day long.

He consorted with boys younger than himself, who were without the prejudices of their elders, and was in the company of several when Basil came in.

"Who-ee!" he cried. "Ee-ee-ee!" He put his hand over his mouth and bounced it quickly, making a wah-wah-wah sound. "It's Bossy Lee! It's Bossy Lee! It's Boss-Boss-Boss-Boss-Bossy Lee!"

"Wait a minute, Bugs," said Basil anxiously, half afraid that Bugs would go finally crazy before he could persuade him to come to town. "Say, Bugs, listen. Don't, Bugs—wait a minute. Can you come up to New York Saturday afternoon?"

"Whe-ee-ee!" cried Bugs to Basil's distress. "Whee-ee-ee!"

"Honestly, Bugs, tell me, can you? We could go up together if you could go."

"I've got to see a doctor," said Bugs, suddenly calm. "He wants to see how crazy I am."

"Can't you have him see about it some other day?" said Basil without humor.

"Whee-ee-ee!" cried Bugs.

"All right then," said Basil hastily. "Have you seen Fat Gaspar in town?"

Bugs was lost in shrill noise, but someone had seen Fat: Basil was directed to the Bostonian Candy Kitchen.

This was a gaudy paradise of cheap sugar. Its odor, heavy and sickly and calculated to bring out a sticky sweat upon an adult's palms, hung suffocatingly over the whole vicinity and met one like a strong moral dissuasion at the door. Inside, beneath a pattern of flies, material as black point lace, a line of boys sat eating heavy dinners of banana splits, maple nut, and chocolate marshmallow nut sundaes. Basil found Fat Gaspar at a table on the side.

Fat Gaspar was at once Basil's most unlikely and most ambitious quest. He was considered a nice fellow—in fact he was so pleasant that he had been courteous to Basil and had spoken to him politely all fall. Basil realized that he was like that to everyone, yet it was just possible that Fat liked him, as people used to in the past, and he was driven desperately to take a chance. But it was undoubtedly a presumption, and as he approached the table and saw the stiffened faces which the other two boys turned toward him, Basil's hope diminished.

"Say, Fat—" he said, and hesitated. Then he burst forth suddenly. "I'm on bounds, but I ran off because I had to see you. Doctor Bacon told me I could go to New York Saturday if I could get two other boys to go. I asked Bugs Brown and he couldn't go, and I thought I'd ask you."

He broke off, furiously embarrassed, and waited. Suddenly the two boys with Fat burst into a shout of laughter.

"Bugs wasn't crazy enough!"

Fat Gasper hesitated. He couldn't go to New York Saturday and ordinarily he would have refused without offending. He had nothing against Basil; nor, indeed, against anybody; but boys have only a certain resistance to public opinion and he was influenced by the contemptuous laughter of the others.

"I don't want to go," he said indifferently. "Why do you want to ask *me?*"

Then, half in shame, he gave a deprecatory little laugh and bent over his ice cream.

"I just thought I'd ask you," said Basil.

Turning quickly away, he went to the counter and in a hollow and unfamiliar voice ordered a strawberry sundae. He ate it mechanically, hearing occasional whispers and snickers from the table behind. Still in a daze, he started to walk out without paying his check, but the clerk called him back and he was conscious of more derisive laughter.

For a moment he hesitated whether to go back to the table and hit one of those boys in the face, but he saw nothing to be gained. They would say the truth—that he had done it because he couldn't get anybody to go to New York. Clenching his fists with impotent rage, he walked from the store.

He came immediately upon his third prospect, Treadway. Treadway had entered St. Regis late in the year and had been put in to room with Basil the week before. The fact that Treadway hadn't witnessed his humiliations of the autumn encouraged Basil to behave naturally toward him, and their relations had been, if not intimate, at least tranquil.

"Hey, Treadway," he cried, still excited from the affair in the Bostonian, "can you come up to New York to a show Saturday afternoon?"

He stopped, realizing that Treadway was in the company of Brick Wales, a boy he had had a fight with and one of his bitterest enemies. Looking from one to the other, Basil saw a look of impatience in Treadway's face and a faraway expression in Brick Wales', and he realized what must have been happening. Treadway, making his way into the life of the school, had just been enlightened as to the status of his roommate. Like Fat Gaspar, rather than acknowledge himself eligible to such an intimate request, he preferred to cut their friendly relations short.

"Not on your life," he said briefly. "So long." The two walked past him into the candy kitchen.

Had these slights, so much the bitterer for their lack of passion, been visited upon Basil in September, they would have been unbearable. But since then he had developed a shell of hardness which, while it did not add to his attractiveness, spared him certain delicacies of torture. In misery enough, and despair and self-pity, he went the other way along the street for a little distance until he could control the violent contortions of his face. Then, taking a roundabout route, he started back to school.

He reached the adjoining estate, intending to go back the way he had come. Half-way through a hedge, he heard footsteps approaching along the sidewalk and stood motionless, fearing the proximity of masters. Their voices grew nearer and louder; before he knew it he was listening with horrified fascination:

"—so, after he tried Bugs Brown, the poor nut asked Fat Gasper to go with him and Fat said, 'What do you ask me for?' It serves him right if he couldn't get anybody at all."

It was the dismal but triumphant voice of Lewis Crum.

III

Up in his room, Basil found a package lying on his bed. He knew its contents and for a long time he had been eagerly expecting it, but such was his depression that he opened it listlessly. It was a series of eight color reproductions of Harrison Fisher girls "on glossy paper, without printing or advertising matter and suitable for framing."

The pictures were named Dora, Marguerite, Babette, Lucille, Gretchen, Rose, Katherine and Mina. Two of them—Marguerite and Rose—Basil looked at, slowly tore up and dropped in the wastebasket, as one who disposes of the inferior pups from a litter. The other six he pinned at intervals around the room. Then he lay down on his bed and regarded them.

Dora, Lucille and Katherine were blonde; Gretchen was medium; Babette and Mina were dark. After a few minutes, he found that he was looking oftenest at Dora and Babette and, to a lesser extent, at Gretchen, though the latter's Dutch cap seemed unromantic and precluded the element of mystery. Babette, a dark little violet-eyed beauty in a tight-fitting hat, attracted him most; his eyes came to rest on her at last.

"Babette," he whispered to himself—"Beautiful Babette."

The sound of the word, so melancholy and suggestive, like "Vilia" or "I'm happy at Maxim's" on the phonograph, softened him and, turning over on his face, he sobbed into the pillow. He took hold of the bed rails over his head and, sobbing and straining, began to talk to himself brokenly—how he hated them and whom he hated—he listed a dozen—and what he would do to them when he was great and powerful. In previous moments like these he had always rewarded Fat Gaspar for his kindness, but now he was like the rest. Basil set upon him, pummeling him unmercifully, or laughed sneeringly when he passed him blind and begging on the street.

He controlled himself as he heard Treadway come in, but did not move or speak. He listened as the other moved about the room, and after a while became conscious that there was an unusual opening of closets and bureau drawers. Basil turned over, his arm concealing his tear-stained face. Treadway had an armful of shirts in his hand.

"What are you doing?" Basil demanded.

His roommate looked at him stonily. "I'm moving in with Wales," he said.

"Oh!"

Treadway went on with his packing. He carried out a suitcase full, then another, took down some pennants and dragged his trunk into the hall. Basil watched him bundle his toilet things into a towel and take one last survey about the room's new barrenness to see if there was anything forgotten.

"Good-by," he said to Basil, without a ripple of expression on his face.

"Good-by."

Treadway went out. Basil turned over once more and choked into the pillow.

"Oh, poor Babette!" he cried huskily. "Poor little Babette! Poor little Babette!"

Babette, svelte and piquant, looked down at him coquettishly from the wall.

IV

Doctor Bacon, sensing Basil's predicament and perhaps in the extremity of his misery, arranged it that he should go into New York, after all. He went in the company of Mr. Rooney, the football coach and history teacher. At twenty Mr. Rooney had hesitated for some time between joining the police force and having his way paid through a small New England college; in fact he was a hard specimen and Doctor Bacon was planning to get rid of him at Christmas. Mr. Rooney's contempt for Basil was founded on the latter's ambiguous and unreliable conduct on the football field during the past season—he had consented to take him to New York for reasons of his own.

Basil sat meekly beside him on the train, glancing past Mr. Rooney's bulky body at the Sound and the fallow fields of Westchester County. Mr. Rooney finished his newspaper, folded it up and sank into a moody silence. He had eaten a large breakfast and the exigencies of time had not allowed him to work it off with exercise. He remembered that Basil was a fresh boy, and it was time he did something fresh and could be called to account. This reproachless silence annoyed him.

"Lee," he said suddenly, with a thinly assumed air of friendly interest, "why don't you get wise to yourself?"

"What sir?" Basil was startled from his excited trance of this morning.

"I said why don't you get wise to yourself?" said Mr. Rooney in a somewhat violent tone. "Do you want to be the butt of the school all your time here?"

"No, I don't." Basil was chilled. Couldn't all this be left behind for just one day?

"You oughtn't to get so fresh all the time. A couple of times in history class I could just about have broken your neck." Basil could think of no appropriate answer. "Then out playing football," continued Mr. Rooney "—you didn't have any nerve. You could play better than a lot of 'em when you wanted, like that day against the Pomfret seconds, but you lost your nerve."

"I shouldn't have tried for the second team," said Basil. "I was too light. I should have stayed on the third."

"You were yellow, that was all the trouble. You ought to get wise to yourself. In class, you're always thinking of something else. If you don't study, you'll never get to college."

"I'm the youngest boy in the fifth form," Basil said rashly.

"You think you're pretty bright, don't you?" He eyed Basil ferociously. Then something seemed to occur to him that changed his attitude and they rode for a while in silence. When the train began to run through the thickly clustered communities near New York, he spoke again in a milder voice and with an air of having considered the matter for a long time:

"Lee, I'm going to trust you."

"Yes, sir."

"You go and get some lunch and then go on to your show. I've got some business of my own I got to attend to, and when I've finished I'll try to get to the show. If I can't, I'll anyhow meet you outside." Basil's heart leaped up. "Yes, sir."

"I don't want you to open your mouth about this at school—I mean, about me doing some business of my own."

"No, sir."

"We'll see if you can keep your mouth shut for once," he said, making it fun. Then he added, on a note of moral sternness, "And no drinks, you understand that?"

"Oh, no, sir!" The idea shocked Basil. He had never tasted a drink, nor even contemplated the possibility, save the intangible and non-alcoholic champagne of his café dreams.

On the advice of Mr. Rooney he went for luncheon to the Manhattan Hotel, near the station, where he ordered a club sandwich, French fried potatoes and a chocolate parfait. Out of the corner of his eye he watched the nonchalant, debonair, blasé New Yorkers at neighboring tables, investing them with a romance by which these possible fellow citizens of his from the Middle West lost nothing. School had fallen from him like a burden; it was no more than an unheeded clamor, faint and far away. He even delayed opening the letter from the morning's mail which he found in his pocket, because it was addressed to him at school.

He wanted another chocolate parfait, but being reluctant to bother the busy waiter any more, he opened the letter and spread it before him instead. It was from his mother:

> "Dear Basil: This is written in great haste, as I didn't want to frighten you by telegraphing. Grandfather is going abroad to take the waters and he wants you and me to come too. The idea is that you'll go to school at Grenoble or Montreux for the rest of the year and learn the languages and we'll be close by. That is, if you want to. I know how you like St. Regis and playing football and baseball, and of course there would be none of that; but on the other hand, it would be a nice change, even if it postponed your entering Yale by an extra year. So, as usual, I want you to do just as you like. We will be leaving home almost as soon as you get this and will come to the Waldorf in New York, where you can come in and see us for a few days, even if you decide to stay. Think it over, dear.
> "With love to my dearest boy,
> "Mother."

Basil got up from his chair with a dim idea of walking over to the Waldorf and having himself locked up safely until his mother came. Then, impelled to some gesture, he raised his voice and in one of his first basso notes called boomingly and without reticence for the waiter. No more St. Regis! No more St. Regis! He was almost strangling with happiness.

"Oh, gosh!" he cried to himself. "Oh, golly! Oh, gosh! Oh, gosh!" No more Doctor Bacon and Mr. Rooney and Brick Wales and Fat Gaspar. No more Bugs Brown and on bounds and being called Bossy. He need no longer hate them, for they were impotent shadows in the stationary world that he was sliding away from, sliding past, waving his hand. "Good-by!" he pitied them. "Good-by!"

It required the din of Forty-second Street to sober his maudlin joy. With his hand on his purse to guard against the omnipresent pickpocket, he moved cautiously toward Broadway. What a day! He would tell Mr. Rooney—Why, he needn't ever go back! Or perhaps it would be better to go back and let them know what he was going to do, while they went on and on in the dismal, dreary round of school.

He found the theater and entered the lobby with its powdery feminine atmosphere of a matinée. As he took out his ticket, his gaze was caught and held by a sculptured profile a few feet away. It was that of a well-built blond young man of about twenty with a strong chin and direct gray eyes. Basil's brain spun wildly for a moment and then came to rest upon a name—more than a name—upon a legend, a sign in the sky. What a day! He had never seen the young man before, but from a thousand pictures he knew beyond the possibility of a doubt that it was Ted Fay, the Yale football captain, who had almost singlehanded beaten Harvard and Princeton last fall. Basil felt a sort of exquisite pain. The profile turned away; the crowd revolved; the hero disappeared. But Basil would know all through the next hours that Ted Fay was here too.

In the rustling, whispering, sweet-smelling darkness of the theater he read the program. It was the show of all shows that he wanted to see, and until the curtain actually rose the program itself had a curious sacredness—a prototype of the thing itself. But when the curtain rose it became waste paper to be dropped carelessly to the floor.

ACT I. *The Village Green of a Small Town near New York.*

It was too bright and blinding to comprehend all at once, and it went so fast that from the very first Basil felt he had missed things; he would make his mother take him again when she came—next week—tomorrow.

An hour passed. It was very sad at this point—a sort of gay sadness, but sad. The girl—the man. What kept them apart even now? Oh, those tragic errors and misconceptions. So sad. Couldn't they look into each other's eyes and *see?*

In a blaze of light and sound, of resolution, anticipation and imminent trouble, the act was over.

He went out. He looked for Ted Fay and thought he saw him leaning rather moodily on the plush wall at the rear of the theater, but he could not be sure. He bought cigarettes and lit one, but fancying at the first puff that he heard a blare of music he rushed back inside.

ACT II. *The Foyer of the Hotel Astor.*

Yes, she was, indeed, like that song—a Beautiful Rose of the Night. The waltz buoyed her up, brought her with it to a point of aching beauty and then let her slide back to life across its last bars as a leaf slants to earth across the air. The high life of New York! Who could blame her if she was carried away by the glitter of it all, vanishing into the bright morning of the amber window borders or into distant and entrancing music as the door opened and closed that led to the ballroom? The toast of the shining town.

Half an hour passed. Her true love brought her roses like herself and she threw them scornfully at his feet. She laughed and turned to the other, and danced—danced madly, wildly. Wait! That delicate treble among the thin horns, the low curving note from the great strings. There it was again, poignant and aching, sweeping like a great gust of emotion across the stage, catching her again like a leaf helpless in the wind:

"Rose—Rose—Rose of the night,
    When the spring moon is bright you'll be fair—"

A few minutes later, feeling oddly shaken and exalted, Basil drifted outside with the crowd. The first thing upon which his eyes fell was the almost forgotten and now curiously metamorphosed specter of Mr. Rooney.

Mr. Rooney had, in fact, gone a little to pieces. He was, to begin with, wearing a different and much smaller hat than when he left Basil at noon. Secondly, his face had lost its somewhat gross aspect and turned a pure and even delicate white, and he was wearing his necktie and even portions of his shirt on the outside of his unaccountably wringing-wet overcoat. How, in the short space of four hours, Mr. Rooney had got himself in such shape is explicable only by the pressure of confinement in a boys' school upon a fiery outdoor spirit. Mr. Rooney was born to toil under the clear light of heaven and, perhaps half consciously, he was headed toward his inevitable destiny.

"Lee," he said dimly, "you ought to get wise to y'self. I'm going to put you wise y'self."

To avoid the ominous possibility of being put wise to himself in the lobby, Basil uneasily changed the subject.

"Aren't you coming to the show?" he asked, flattering Mr. Rooney by implying that he was in any condition to come to the show. "It's a wonderful show."

Mr. Rooney took off his hat, displaying wringing-wet matted hair. A picture of reality momentarily struggled for development in the back of his brain.

"We got to get back to school," he said in a somber and unconvinced voice.

"But there's another act," protested Basil in horror. "I've got to stay for the last act."

Swaying, Mr. Rooney looked at Basil, dimly realizing that he had put himself in the hollow of this boy's hand.

"All righ'," he admitted. "I'm going to get somethin' to eat. I'll wait for you next door."

He turned abruptly, reeled a dozen steps and curved dizzily into a bar adjoining the theater. Considerably shaken, Basil went back inside.

Act III. *The Roof Garden of Mr. Van Astor's House. Night.*

Half an hour passed. Everything was going to be all right, after all. The comedian was at his best now, with the glad appropriateness of laughter after tears, and there was a promise of felicity in the bright tropical sky. One lovely plaintive duet, and then abruptly the long moment of incomparable beauty was over.

Basil went into the lobby and stood in thought while the crowd passed out. His mother's letter and the show had cleared his mind of bitterness and vindictiveness—he was his old self and he wanted to do the right thing. He wondered if it was the right thing to get Mr. Rooney back to school. He walked toward the saloon, slowed up as he came to it and, gingerly opening the swinging door, took a quick peer inside. He saw only that Mr. Rooney was not one of those drinking at the bar. He walked down the street a little way, came back and tried again. It was as if he thought the doors were teeth to bite him, for he had the old-fashioned Middle-Western boy's horror of the saloon. The third time he was successful. Mr. Rooney was sound asleep at a table in the back of the room.

Outside again Basil walked up and down, considering. He would give Mr. Rooney half an hour. If, at the end of that time, he had not come out, he would go back to school. After all, Mr. Rooney had laid for him even since football season—Basil was simply washing his hands of the whole affair, as in a day or so he would wash his hands of school.

He had made several turns up and down, when, glancing up an alley that ran beside the theater his eye was caught by the sign, Stage Entrance. He could watch the actors come forth.

He waited. Women streamed by him, but those were the days before Glorification and he took these drab people for wardrobe women or something. Then suddenly a girl came out and with her a man, and Basil turned and ran a few steps up the street as if afraid they would recognize him—and ran back, breathing as if with a heart attack—for the girl, a radiant little beauty of nineteen, was Her and the young man by her side was Ted Fay.

Arm in arm, they walked past him, and irresistibly Basil followed. As they walked, she leaned toward Ted Fay in a way that gave them a fascinating air of intimacy. They crossed Broadway and turned into the Knickerbocker Hotel, and twenty feet behind them Basil followed, in time to see them go into a long room set for afternoon tea. They sat at a table for two, spoke vaguely to a waiter, and then, alone at last, bent eagerly toward each other. Basil saw that Ted Fay was holding her gloved hand.

The tea room was separated only by a hedge of potted firs from the main corridor. Basil went along this to a lounge which was almost up against their table and sat down.

Her voice was low and faltering, less certain than it had been in the play, and very sad: "Of course I do, Ted." For a long time, as their conversation continued, she repeated "Of course I do" or "But I do, Ted." Ted Fay's remarks were too low for Basil to hear.

"——says next month, and he won't be put off any more. . . . I do in a way, Ted. It's hard to explain, but he's done everything for mother and me. . . . There's no use kidding myself. It was a fool-proof part and any girl he gave it to was made right then and there. . . . He's been awfully thoughtful. He's done everything for me."

Basil's ears were sharpened by the intensity of his emotion; now he could hear Ted Fay's voice too:

"And you say you love me."

"But don't you see I promised to marry him more than a year ago."

"Tell him the truth—that you love me. Ask him to let you off."

"This isn't musical comedy, Ted."

"That was a mean one," he said bitterly.

"I'm sorry, dear, Ted darling, but you're driving me crazy going on this way. You're making it so hard for me."

"I'm going to leave New Haven, anyhow."

"No, you're not. You're going to stay and play baseball this spring. Why, you're an ideal to all those boys! Why, if you——"

He laughed shortly. "You're a fine one to talk about ideals."

"Why not? I'm living up to my responsibility to Beltzman; you've got to make up your mind just like I have—that we can't have each other."

"Jerry! Think what you're doing! All my life, whenever I hear that waltz——"

Basil got to his feet and hurried down the corridor, through the lobby and out of the hotel. He was in a state of wild emotional confusion. He did not understand all he had heard, but from his clandestine glimpse into the privacy of these two, with all the world that his short experience could conceive of at their feet, he had gathered that life for everybody was a struggle, sometimes magnificent from a distance, but always difficult and surprisingly simple and a little sad.

They would go on. Ted Fay would go back to Yale, put her picture in his bureau drawer and knock out home runs with the bases full this spring—at 8:30 the curtain would go up and She would miss something warm and young out of her life, something she had had this afternoon.

It was dark outside and Broadway was a blazing forest fire as Basil walked slowly along toward the point of brightest light. He looked up at the great intersecting planes of radiance with a vague sense of approval and possession. He would see it a lot now, lay his restless heart upon this greater restlessness of a nation—he would come whenever he could get off from school.

But that was all changed—he was going to Europe. Suddenly Basil realized that he wasn't going to Europe. He could not forego the molding of his own destiny just to alleviate a few months of pain. The conquest of the successive worlds of school, college and New York—why, that was his true dream that he had carried from boyhood into adolescence, and because of the jeers of a few boys he had been about to abandon it and run ignominiously up a back alley! He shivered violently, like a dog coming out of the water, and simultaneously he was reminded of Mr. Rooney.

A few minutes later he walked into the bar, past the quizzical eyes of the bartender and up to the table where Mr. Rooney still sat asleep. Basil shook him gently, then firmly. Mr. Rooney stirred and perceived Basil.

"G'wise to yourself," he muttered drowsily. "G'wise to yourself an' let me alone."

"I am wise to myself," said Basil. "Honest, I am wise to myself, Mr. Rooney. You got to come with me into the washroom and get cleaned up, and then you can sleep on the train again, Mr. Rooney. Come on, Mr. Rooney, please——"

V

It was a long hard time. Basil got on bounds again in December and wasn't free again until March. An indulgent mother had given him no habits of work and this was almost beyond the power of anything but life itself to remedy, but he made numberless new starts and failed and tried again.

He made friends with a new boy named Maplewood after Christmas, but they had a silly quarrel; and through the winter term, when a boys' school is shut in with itself and only partly assuaged from its natural savagery by indoor sports, Basil was snubbed and slighted a good deal for his real and imaginary sins, and he was much alone. But on the other hand, there was Ted Fay, and Rose of the Night on the phonograph—"All my life whenever I hear that waltz"—and the remembered lights of New York, and the thought of what he was going to do in football next autumn and the glamorous mirage of Yale and the hope of spring in the air.

Fat Gaspar and a few others were nice to him now. Once when he and Fat walked home together by accident from downtown they had a long talk about actresses—a talk that Basil was wise enough not to presume upon afterward. The smaller boys suddenly decided that they approved of him, and a master who had hitherto disliked him put his hand on his shoulder walking to a class one day. They would all forget eventually—maybe during the summer. There would be new fresh boys in September; he would have a clean start next year.

One afternoon in February, playing basketball, a great thing happened. He and Brick Wales were at forward on the second team and in the fury of the scrimmage the gymnasium echoed with sharp slapping contacts and shrill cries.

"Here yar!"

"Bill! Bill!"

Basil had dribbled the ball down the court and Brick Wales, free, was crying for it.

"Here yar! Lee! Hey! Lee-y!"

Lee-y!

Basil flushed and made a poor pass. He had been called by a nickname. It was a poor makeshift, but it was something more than the stark bareness of his surname or a term of derision. Brick Wales went on playing, unconscious that he had done anything in particular or that he had contributed to the events by which another boy was saved from the army of the bitter, the selfish, the neurasthenic and the unhappy. It isn't given to us to know those rare moments when people are wide open and the lightest touch can wither or heal. A moment too late and we can never reach them any more in this world. They will not be cured by our most efficacious drugs or slain with our sharpest swords.

Lee-y! It could scarcely be pronounced. But Basil took it to bed with him that night, and thinking of it, holding it to him happily to the last, fell easily to sleep.

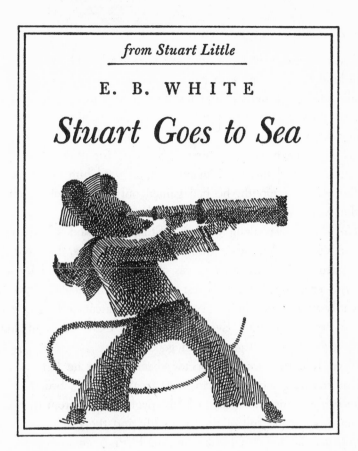

from Stuart Little

E. B. WHITE

Stuart Goes to Sea

When Mrs. Frederick C. Little's second son was born, everybody noticed that he was not much bigger than a mouse. The truth of the matter was, the baby looked very much like a mouse in every way. He was only about two inches high; and he had a mouse's sharp nose, a mouse's tail, a mouse's whiskers, and the pleasant, shy manner of a mouse. Before he was many days old he was not only looking like a mouse but acting like one, too—wearing a gray hat and carrying a small cane. Mr. and Mrs. Little named him Stuart, and Mr. Little made him a tiny bed out of four clothespins and a cigarette box.

Unlike most babies, Stuart could walk as soon as he was born. When he was a week old he could climb lamps by shinnying up the cord. Mrs. Little saw right away that the infant clothes she had provided were unsuitable, and she set to work and made him a fine little blue worsted suit with patch pockets in which he could keep his handkerchief, his money, and his keys. Every morning, before Stuart dressed, Mrs. Little went into his room and weighed him on a small scale which was really meant for weighing letters. At birth Stuart could have been sent by first class mail for three cents, but his parents preferred to keep him rather than send him away; and when, at the age of a month, he had gained only a third of an ounce, his mother was so worried she sent for the doctor.

The doctor was delighted with Stuart and said that it was very unusual for an American family to have a mouse. He took Stuart's temperature and found that it was 98.6, which is normal for a mouse. He also examined Stuart's chest and heart and looked into his ears solemnly with a flashlight. (Not every doctor can look into a mouse's ear without laughing.) Everything seemed to be all right, and Mrs. Little was pleased to get such a good report.

"Feed him up!" said the doctor cheerfully, as he left.

One morning when the wind was from the west, Stuart put on his sailor suit and his sailor hat, took his spyglass down from the shelf, and set out for a walk, full of the joy of life and the fear of dogs. With a rolling gait he sauntered along toward Fifth Avenue, keeping a sharp lookout.

Whenever he spied a dog through his glass, Stuart would hurry to the nearest doorman, climb his trouser-leg, and hide in the tails of his uniform. And once, when no doorman was handy, he had to crawl into a yesterday's paper and roll himself up in the second section till danger was past.

At the corner of Fifth Avenue there were several people waiting for the uptown bus, and Stuart joined them. Nobody noticed him, because he wasn't tall enough to be noticed.

"I'm not tall enough to be noticed," thought Stuart, "yet I'm tall enough to want to go to Seventy-second Street."

When the bus came into view, all the men waved their canes and briefcases at the driver, and Stuart waved his spyglass. Then, knowing that the step of the bus would be too high for him, Stuart seized hold of the cuff of a gentleman's pants and was swung aboard without any trouble or inconvenience whatever.

Stuart never paid any fare on buses, because he wasn't big enough to carry an ordinary dime. The only time he had ever attempted to carry a dime, he had rolled the coin along like a hoop while he raced along beside it; but it had got away from him on a hill and had been snatched up by an old woman with no teeth. After that experience Stuart contented himself with the tiny coins which his father made for him out of tin foil. They were handsome little things, although rather hard to see without putting on your spectacles.

When the conductor came around to collect the fares, Stuart fished in his purse and pulled out a coin no bigger than the eye of a grasshopper.

"What's that you're offering me?" asked the conductor.

"It's one of my dimes," said Stuart.

"Is it, now?" said the conductor. "Well, I'd have a fine time explaining that to the bus company. Why, you're no bigger than a dime yourself."

"Yes I am," replied Stuart angrily. "I'm more than twice as big as a dime. A dime only comes up to here on me." And Stuart pointed to his hip. "Furthermore," he added, "I didn't come on this bus to be insulted."

"I beg pardon," said the conductor. "You'll have to forgive me, for I had no idea that in all the world there was such a small sailor."

"Live and learn," muttered Stuart, tartly, putting his change purse back in his pocket.

When the bus stopped at Seventy-second Street, Stuart jumped out and hurried across to the sailboat pond in Central Park. Over the pond the west wind blew, and into the teeth of the west wind sailed the sloops and schooners, their rails well down, their wet decks gleaming. The owners, boys and grown men, raced around the cement shores hoping to arrive at the other side in time to keep the boats from bumping. Some of the toy boats were not as small as you might think, for when you got close to them you found that their mainmast was taller than a man's head, and they were beautifully made, with everything shipshape and ready for sea. To Stuart they seemed enormous, and he hoped he would be able to get aboard one of them and sail away to the far corners of the pond. (He was an adventurous little fellow and loved the feel of the breeze in his face and the cry of the gulls overhead and the heave of the great swell under him.)

As he sat cross-legged on the wall that surrounds the pond, gazing out at the ships through his spyglass, Stuart noticed one boat that seemed to him finer and prouder than any other. Her name was Wasp. She was a big, black schooner flying the American flag. She had a clipper bow, and on her foredeck was mounted a three-inch cannon. She's the ship for me, thought Stuart. And the next time she sailed in, he ran over to where she was being turned around.

"Excuse me, sir," said Stuart to the man who was turning her, "but are you the owner of the schooner Wasp?"

"I am," replied the man, surprised to be addressed by a mouse in a sailor suit.

"I'm looking for a berth in a good ship," continued Stuart, "and I thought perhaps you might sign me on. I'm strong and I'm quick."

"Are you sober?" asked the owner of the Wasp.

"I do my work," said Stuart, crisply.

The man looked sharply at him. He couldn't help admiring the trim appearance and bold manner of this diminutive seafaring character.

"Well," he said at length, pointing the prow of the Wasp out toward the center of the pond, "I'll tell you what I'll do with you. You see that big racing sloop out there?"

"I do," said Stuart.

"That's the Lillian B. Womrath," said the man, "and I hate her with all my heart."

"Then so do I," cried Stuart, loyally.

"I hate her because she is always bumping into my boat," continued the man, "and because her owner is a lazy boy who doesn't understand sailing and who hardly knows a squall from a squid."

"Or a jib from a jibe," cried Stuart.

"Or a luff from a leech," bellowed the man.

"Or a deck from a dock," screamed Stuart.

"Or a mast from a mist," yelled the man. "But hold on, now, no more of this! I'll tell you what we'll do. The Lillian B. Womrath has always been able to beat the Wasp sailing, but I believe that if my schooner were properly handled it would be a different story. Nobody knows how I suffer, standing here on shore, helpless, watching the Wasp blunder along, when all she needs is a steady hand on her helm. So, my young friend, I'll let you sail the Wasp across the pond and back, and if you can beat that detestable sloop I'll give you a regular job."

"Aye, aye, sir!" said Stuart, swinging himself aboard the schooner and taking his place at the wheel. "Ready about!"

"One moment," said the man. "Do you mind telling me *how* you propose to beat the other boat?"

"I intend to crack on more sail," said Stuart.

"Not in *my* boat, thank you," replied the man quickly. "I don't want you capsizing in a squall."

"Well, then," said Stuart, "I'll catch the sloop broad on, and rake her with fire from my forward gun."

"Foul means!" said the man. "I want this to be a boat race, not a naval engagement."

"Well, then," said Stuart cheerfully, "I'll sail the Wasp straight and true, and let the Lillian B. Womrath go yawing all over the pond."

"Bravo!" cried the man, "and good luck go with you!" And so saying, he let go of the Wasp's prow. A puff of air bellied out the schooner's headsails and she paid off and filled away on the port tack, heeling gracefully over to the breeze while Stuart twirled her wheel and braced himself against a deck cleat.

"By the by," yelled the man, "you haven't told me your name."

"Name is Stuart Little," called Stuart at the top of his lungs. "I'm the second son of Frederick C. Little, of this city."

"*Bon voyage*, Stuart," hollered his friend, "take care of yourself and bring the Wasp home safe."

"That I will," shouted Stuart. And he was so proud and happy, he let go of the wheel for a second and did a little dance on the sloping deck, never noticing how narrowly he escaped hitting a tramp steamer that was drifting in his path, with her engines disabled and her decks awash.

When the people in Central Park learned that one of the toy sailboats was being steered by a mouse in a sailor suit, they all came running. Soon the shores of the pond were so crowded that a policeman was sent from headquarters to announce that everybody would have to stop pushing, but nobody did. People in New York like to push each other. The most excited person of all was the boy who owned the Lillian B. Womrath. He was a fat, sulky boy of twelve, named LeRoy. He wore a blue serge suit and a white necktie stained with orange juice.

"Come back here!" he called to Stuart. "Come back here and get on *my* boat. I want you to steer *my* boat. I will pay you five dollars a week and you can have every Thursday afternoon off and a radio in your room."

"I thank you for your kind offer," replied Stuart, "but I am happy aboard the Wasp—happier than I have ever been before in all my life." And with that he spun the wheel over smartly and headed his schooner down toward the starting line, where LeRoy was turning his boat around by poking it with a long stick, ready for the start of the race.

"I'll be the referee," said a man in a bright green suit. "Is the Wasp ready?"

"Ready, sir!" shouted Stuart, touching his hat.

"Is the Lillian B. Womrath ready?" asked the referee.

"Sure, I'm ready," said LeRoy.

"To the north end of the pond and back again!" shouted the referee. "On your mark, get set, GO!"

"Go!" cried the people along the shore.

"Go!" cried the owner of the Wasp.

"Go!" yelled the policeman.

And away went the two boats for the north end of the pond, while the seagulls wheeled and cried overhead and the taxicabs tooted and honked from Seventy-second Street and the west wind (which had come halfway across America to get to Central Park) sang and whistled in the rigging and blew spray across the decks, stinging Stuart's cheeks with tiny fragments of flying peanut shell tossed up from the foamy deep. "This is the life for me!" Stuart murmured to himself. "What a ship! What a day! What a race!"

Before the two boats had gone many feet, however, an accident happened on shore. The people were pushing each other harder and harder in their eagerness to see the sport, and although they really didn't mean to, they pushed the policeman so hard they pushed him right off the concrete wall and into the pond. He hit the water in a sitting position, and got wet clear up to the third button of his jacket. He was soaked.

This particular policeman was not only a big, heavy man, but he had just eaten a big, heavy meal, and the wave he made went curling outward, cresting and billowing, upsetting all manner of small craft and causing every owner of a boat on the pond to scream with delight and consternation.

When Stuart saw the great wave approaching he jumped for the rigging, but he was too late. Towering above the Wasp like a mountain, the wave came crashing and piling along the deck, caught Stuart up and swept him over the side and into the water, where everybody supposed he would drown. Stuart had no intention of drowning. He kicked hard with his feet, and thrashed hard with his tail, and in a minute or two he climbed back aboard the schooner, cold and wet but quite unharmed. As he took his place at the helm, he could hear people cheering for him and calling, "Atta mouse, Stuart! Atta mouse!" He looked over and saw that the wave had capsized the Lillian B. Womrath but that she had righted herself and was sailing on her course, close by. And she stayed close alongside till both boats reached the north end of the pond. Here Stuart put the Wasp about and LeRoy turned the Lillian around with his stick, and away the two boats went for the finish line.

"This race isn't over yet," thought Stuart.

The first warning he had that there was trouble ahead came when he glanced into the Wasp's cabin and observed that the barometer had fallen sharply. That can mean only one thing at sea—dirty weather. Suddenly a dark cloud swept across the sun, blotting it out and leaving the earth in shadow. Stuart shivered in his wet clothes. He turned up his sailor blouse closer around his neck, and when he spied the Wasp's owner among the crowd on shore he waved his hat and called out:

"Dirty weather ahead, sir! Wind backing into the south-west, seas confused, glass falling."

"Never mind the weather!" cried the owner. "Watch out for flotsam dead ahead!"

Stuart peered ahead into the gathering storm, but saw nothing except gray waves with white crests. The world seemed cold and ominous. Stuart glanced behind him. There came the sloop, boiling along fast, rolling up a bow wave and gaining steadily.

"Look out, Stuart! Look out where you're going!"

Stuart strained his eyes, and suddenly, dead ahead, right in the path of the Wasp, he saw an enormous paper bag looming up on the surface of the pond. The bag was empty and riding high, its open end gaping wide like the mouth of a cave. Stuart spun the wheel over but it was too late: the Wasp drove her bow-sprit straight into the bag and with a fearful *whooosh* the schooner slowed down and came up into the wind with all sails flapping. Just at this moment Stuart heard a splintering crash, saw the bow of the Lillian plow through his rigging, and felt the whole ship tremble from stem to stern with the force of the collision.

"A collision!" shouted the crowd on shore.

In a jiffy the two boats were in a terrible tangle. Little boys on shore screamed and danced up and down. Meanwhile the paper bag sprang a leak and began to fill.

The Wasp couldn't move because of the bag. The Lillian B. Womrath couldn't move because her nose was stuck in the Wasp's rigging.

Waving his arms, Stuart ran forward and fired off his gun. Then he heard, above the other voices on shore, the voice of the owner of the Wasp yelling directions and telling him what to do.

"Stuart! Stuart! Down jib! Down staysail!"

Stuart jumped for the halyards, and the jib and the forestaysail came rippling down.

"Cut away all paper bags!" roared the owner.

Stuart whipped out his pocketknife and slashed away bravely at the soggy bag until he had the deck cleared.

"Now back your foresail and give her a full!" screamed the owner of the Wasp.

Stuart grabbed the foresail boom and pulled with all his might. Slowly the schooner paid off and began to gather headway. And as she heeled over to the breeze she rolled her rail out from under the Lillian's nose, shook herself free, and stood away to the southard. A loud cheer went up from the bank. Stuart sprang to the wheel and answered it. Then he looked back, and to his great joy he perceived that the Lillian had gone off in a wild direction and was yawing all over the pond.

Straight and true sailed the Wasp, with Stuart at the helm. After she had crossed the finish line, Stuart brought her alongside the wall, and was taken ashore and highly praised for his fine seamanship and daring. The owner was delighted and said it was the happiest day of

his life. He introduced himself to Stuart, said that in private life he
was Dr. Paul Carey, a surgeon-dentist. He said model boats were his
hobby and that he would be delighted to have Stuart take command of
his vessel at any time. Everybody shook hands with Stuart—everybody, that is, except the policeman, who was too wet and mad to
shake hands with a mouse.

When Stuart got home that night, his brother George asked him
where he had been all day.

"Oh, knocking around town," replied Stuart.

EVELYN WAUGH

*The Man Who
Liked Dickens*

Although Mr Todd had lived in Amazonas for nearly sixty years, no one except a few families of Pie-wie Indians was aware of his existence. His house stood in a small savannah, one of those little patches of sand and grass that crop up occasionally in that neighbourhood, three miles or so across, bounded on all sides by forest.

The stream which watered it was not marked on any map; it ran through rapids, always dangerous and at most seasons of the year impassable, to join the upper waters of the river where Dr Messinger had come to grief. None of the inhabitants of the district, except Mr Todd, had ever heard of the governments of Brazil or Dutch Guiana, both of which from time to time claimed its possession.

Mr Todd's house was larger than those of his neighbours, but similar in character—a palm thatch roof, breast-high walls of mud and wattle, and a mud floor. He owned the dozen or so head of puny cattle which grazed in the savannah, a plantation of cassava, some banana and mango trees, a dog and, unique in the neighbourhood, a single-barrelled, breech-loading shot gun. The few commodities which he employed from the outside world, came to him through a long succession of traders, passed from hand to hand, bartered for in a dozen languages at the extreme end of one of the longest threads in the web of commerce that spreads from Manáos into the remote vastness of the forest.

One day while Mr Todd was engaged in filling some cartridges, a Pie-wie came to him with the news that a white man was approaching through the forest, alone and very sick. He closed the cartridge and loaded his gun with it, put those that were finished into his pocket and set out in the direction indicated.

The man was already clear of the bush when Mr Todd reached him, sitting on the ground, clearly in a very bad way. He was without hat or boots, and his clothes were so torn that it was only by the dampness of his body that they adhered to it; his feet were cut and grossly swollen; every exposed surface of skin was scarred by insect and bat bites; his eyes were wild with fever. He was talking to himself in delirium but stopped when Todd approached and addressed him in English.

'You're the first person who's spoken to me for days,' said Tony. 'The others won't stop. They keep bicycling by . . . I'm tired . . . Brenda was with me at first but she was frightened by a mechanical mouse, so she took the canoe and went off. She said she would come back that evening but she didn't. I expect she's staying with one of her new friends in Brazil . . . You haven't seen her, have you?'

'You are the first stranger I have seen for a very long time.'

'She was wearing a top hat when she left. You can't miss her.' Then he began talking to someone at Mr Todd's side, who was not there.

'Do you see that house over there? Do you think you can manage to walk to it? If not, I can send some Indians to carry you.'

Tony squinted across the savannah at Mr Todd's hut.

'Architecture harmonizing with local character,' he said, 'indigenous material employed throughout. Don't let Mrs Beaver see it or she will cover it with chromium plating.'

'Try and walk.' Mr Todd hoisted Tony to his feet and supported him with a stout arm.

'I'll ride your bicycle. It *was* you I passed just now on a bicycle, wasn't it? . . . except that your beard is a different colour. His was green . . . green as mice.'

Mr Todd led Tony across the hummocks of grass towards the house.

'It is a very short way. When we get there I will give you something to make you better.'

'Very kind of you . . . rotten thing for a man to have his wife go away in a canoe. That was a long time ago. Nothing to eat since.' Presently he said, 'I say, you're English. I'm English too. My name is Last.'

'Well, Mr Last, you aren't to bother about anything more. You're ill and you've had a rough journey. I'll take care of you.'

Tony looked round him. 'Are you all English?'

'Yes, all of us.'

'That dark girl married a Moor . . . It's very lucky I met you all. I suppose you're some kind of cycling club?'

'Yes.'

'Well, I feel too tired for bicycling . . . never liked it much . . . you fellows ought to get motor bicycles, you know, much faster and noisier . . . Let's stop here.'

'No, you must come as far as the house. It's not very much farther.'

'All right . . . I suppose you would have some difficulty getting petrol here.'

They went very slowly, but at length reached the house.

'Lie there in the hammock.'

'That's what Messinger said. He's in love with John Beaver.'

'I will get something for you.'

'Very good of you. Just my usual morning tray—coffee, toast, fruit. And the morning papers. If her Ladyship has been called I will have it with her . . .'

Mr Todd went into the back room of the house and dragged a tin canister from under a heap of skins. It was full of a mixture of dried leaf and bark. He took a handful and went outside to the fire. When he returned, his guest was bolt upright astride the hammock, talking angrily.

'. . . You would hear better and it would be more polite if you stood still when I addressed you instead of walking round in a circle. It is for your own good that I am telling you . . . I know you are friends of my wife and that is why you will not listen to me. But be careful. She will say nothing cruel, she will not raise her voice, there will be no hard words. She hopes you will be great friends afterwards as before. But she will leave you. She will go away quietly during the night. She will take her hammock and her rations of farine . . . Listen to me. I know I am not clever but that is no reason why we should forget all courtesy. Let us kill in the gentlest manner. I will tell you what I have learned in the forest, where time is different. There is no City. Mrs Beaver has covered it with chromium plating and converted it into flats. Three guineas a week, each with a separate bathroom. Very suitable for base love. And Polly will be there. She and Mrs Beaver under the fallen battlements . . .'

Mr Todd put a hand behind Tony's head and held up the concoction of herbs in the calabash. Tony sipped and turned away his head.

'Nasty medicine,' he said, and began to cry.

Mr Todd stood by him holding the calabash. Presently Tony drank some more, screwing up his face and shuddering slightly at the bitterness. Mr Todd stood beside him until the draught was finished; then he threw out the dregs on to the mud floor. Tony lay back in the hammock sobbing quietly. Soon he fell into a deep sleep.

Tony's recovery was slow. At first, days of lucidity alternated with delirium; then his temperature dropped and he was conscious even when most ill. The days of fever grew less frequent, finally occurring in the normal system of the tropics, between long periods of comparative health. Mr Todd dosed him regularly with herbal remedies.

'It's very nasty,' said Tony, 'but it does do good.'

'There is medicine for everything in the forest,' said Mr Todd; 'to make you well and to make you ill. My mother was an Indian and she taught me many of them. I have learned others from time to time from my wives. There are plants to cure you and give you fever, to kill you and send you mad, to keep away snakes, to intoxicate fish so that you can pick them out of the water with your hands like fruit from a tree. There are medicines even I do not know. They say that it is possible to bring dead people to life after they have begun to stink, but I have not seen it done.'

'But surely you are English?'

'My father was—at least a Barbadian. He came to Guiana as a missionary. He was married to a white woman but he left her in Guiana to look for gold. Then he took my mother. The Pie-wie women are ugly but very devoted. Most of the men and women living in this savannah are my children. That is why they obey—for that reason and because I have the gun. My father lived to a great age. It is not twenty years since he died. He was a man of education. Can you read?'

'Yes, of course.'

'It is not everyone who is so fortunate. I cannot.'

Tony laughed apologetically. 'But I suppose you haven't much opportunity here.'

'Oh yes, that is just it. I have a *great* many books. I will show you when you are better. Until five years ago there was an Englishman— at least a black man, but he was well educated in Georgetown. He died. He used to read to me every day until he died. You shall read to me when you are better.'

'I shall be delighted to.'

'Yes, you shall read to me,' Mr Todd repeated, nodding over the calabash.

During the early days of his convalescence Tony had little conversation with his host. He lay in the hammock staring up at the thatched roof and thinking about Brenda. The days, exactly twelve hours each, passed without distinction. Mr Todd retired to sleep at sundown, leaving a little lamp burning—a handwoven wick drooping from a pot of beef fat—to keep away vampire bats.

The first time that Tony left the house Mr Todd took him for a little stroll around the farm.

'I will show you the black man's grave,' he said, leading him to a mound between the mango trees. 'He was very kind. Every afternoon until he died, for two hours, he used to read to me. I think I will put up a cross—to commemorate his death and your arrival—a pretty idea. Do you believe in God?'

'I suppose so. I've never really thought about it much.'

'I have thought about it a great deal and still I do not know . . . Dickens did.'

'I suppose so.'

'Oh yes, it is apparent in all his books. You will see.'

That afternoon Mr Todd began the construction of a headpiece for the negro's grave. He worked with a large spokeshave in a wood so hard that it grated and rang like metal.

At last when Tony had passed six or seven consecutive nights without fever, Mr Todd said, 'Now I think you are well enough to see the books.'

At one end of the hut there was a kind of loft formed by a rough platform erected in the eaves of the roof. Mr Todd propped a ladder against it and mounted. Tony followed, still unsteady after his illness. Mr Todd sat on the platform and Tony stood at the top of the ladder looking over. There was a heap of bundles there, tied up with rag, palm leaf and raw hide.

'It has been hard to keep out the worms and ants. Two are practically destroyed. But there is an oil the Indians make that is useful.'

He unwrapped the nearest parcel and handed down a calf bound book. It was an early American edition of *Bleak House.*

'It does not matter which we take first.'

'You are fond of Dickens?' .

'Why, yes, of course. More than fond, far more. You see, they are the only books I have ever heard. My father used to read them and then later the black man . . . and now you. I have heard them all several times by now but I never get tired; there is always more to be learned and noticed, so many characters, so many changes of scene, so many words . . . I have all Dickens's books here except those that the ants devoured. It takes a long time to read them all—more than two years.'

'Well,' said Tony lightly, 'they will well last out my visit.'

'Oh, I hope not. It is delightful to start again. Each time I think I find more to enjoy and admire.'

They took down the first volume of *Bleak House* and that afternoon Tony had his first reading.

He had always rather enjoyed reading aloud and in the first year of marriage had shared several books in this way with Brenda, until one day, in a moment of frankness, she remarked that it was torture to her. He had read to John Andrew, late in the afternoon, in winter, while the child sat before the nursery fender eating his supper. But Mr Todd was a unique audience.

The old man sat astride his hammock opposite Tony, fixing him throughout with his eyes, and following the words, soundlessly, with his lips. Often when a new character was introduced he would say, 'Repeat the name, I have forgotten him,' or 'Yes, yes, I remember her well. She dies, poor woman.' He would frequently interrupt with questions; not as Tony would have imagined about the circumstances of the story—such things as the procedure of the Lord Chancellor's Court or the social conventions of the time, though they must have been unintelligible, did not concern him—but always about the characters. 'Now, why does she say that? Does she really mean it? Did she feel faint because of the heat of the fire or of something in that paper?' He laughed loudly at all the jokes and at some passages which did not seem humorous to Tony, asking him to repeat them two or three times, and later at the description of the sufferings of the outcasts in 'Tom-all-alone's' tears ran down his cheeks into his beard. His comments on the story were usually simple. 'I think that Dedlock is a very proud man,' or, 'Mrs Jellyby does not take enough care of her children.'

Tony enjoyed the readings almost as much as he did.

At the end of the first day the old man said, 'You read beautifully, with far better accent than the black man. And you explain better. It is almost as though my father were here again.' And always at the end of a session he thanked his guest courteously. 'I enjoyed that *very* much. It was an extremely distressing chapter. But, if I remember it rightly, it will all turn out well.'

By the time that they were in the second volume, however, the novelty of the old man's delight had begun to wane and Tony was feeling strong enough to be restless. He touched more than once on the subject of his departure, asking about canoes and rains and the possibility of finding guides. But Mr Todd seemed obtuse and paid no attention to these hints.

One day, running his thumb through the pages of *Bleak House* that remained to be read, Tony said, 'We still have a lot to get through. I hope I shall be able to finish it before I go.'

'Oh, yes,' said Mr Todd. 'Do not disturb yourself about that. You will have time to finish it, my friend.'

For the first time Tony noticed something slightly menacing in his host's manner. That evening at supper, a brief meal of farine and dried beef, eaten just before sundown, Tony renewed the subject.

'You know, Mr Todd, the time has come when I must be thinking about getting back to civilization. I have already imposed myself on your hospitality far too long.'

Mr Todd bent over the plate, crunching mouthfuls of farine, but made no reply.

'How soon do you think I shall be able to get a boat? . . . I said, how soon do you think I shall be able to get a boat? I appreciate all your kindness to me more than I can say, but . . .'

'My friend, any kindness I may have shown is amply repaid by your reading of Dickens. Do not let us mention the subject again.'

'Well, I'm very glad you have enjoyed it. I have, too. But I really must be thinking of getting back . . .'

'Yes,' said Mr Todd. 'The black man was like that. He thought of it all the time. But he died here . . .'

Twice during the next day Tony opened the subject, but his host was evasive. Finally, he said, 'Forgive me, Mr Todd, but I really must press the point. When can I get a boat?'

'There is no boat.'

'Well, the Indians can build one.'

'You must wait for the rains. There is not enough water in the river now.'

'A month . . . two months . . .'

They had finished *Bleak House* and were nearing the end of *Dombey and Son* when the rain came.

'Now it is the time to make preparations to go.'

'Oh, that is impossible. The Indians will not make a boat during the rainy season—it is one of their superstitions . . .'

'You might have told me.'

'Did I not mention it? I forgot.'

Next morning Tony went out alone while his host was busy, and, looking as aimless as he could, strolled across the savannah to the group of Indian houses. There were four or five Pie-wies sitting in one of the doorways. They did not look up as he approached them. He addressed them in the few words of Macushi he had acquired during the journey but they made no sign whether they understood him or not. Then he drew a sketch of a canoe in the sand, he went through some vague motions of carpentry, pointed from them to him, then made motions of giving something to them and scratched out the outlines of a gun and a hat and a few other recognizable articles of trade. One of the women giggled but no one gave any sign of comprehension, and he went away unsatisfied.

At their midday meal Mr Todd said. 'Mr Last, the Indians tell me that you have been trying to speak with them. It is easier that you say anything you wish through me. You realize, do you not, that they would do nothing without my authority? They regard themselves, quite rightly in many cases, as my children.'

'Well, as a matter of fact, I was asking them about a canoe.'

'So they gave me to understand . . . and now if you have finished your meal perhaps we might have another chapter. I am quite absorbed in the book.'

They finished *Dombey and Son;* nearly a year had passed since Tony had left England, and his gloomy foreboding of permanent exile became suddenly acute when, between the pages of *Martin Chuzzlewit,* he found a document written in pencil in irregular characters.

> Year 1919.
> I James Todd of Brazil do swear to Barnabas Washington of Georgetown that if he finish this book in fact Martin Chuzzlewit I will let him go away back as soon as finished.

There followed a heavy pencil X and after it: *Mr Todd made this mark signed Barnabas Washington.*

'Mr Todd,' said Tony, 'I must speak frankly. You saved my life, and when I get back to civilization I will reward you to the best of my ability. I will give you anything within reason. But at present you are keeping me here against my will. I demand to be released.'

'But, my friend, what is keeping you? You are under no restraint. Go when you like.'

'You know very well that I can't get away without your help.'

'In that case you must humour an old man. Read me another chapter.'

'Mr Todd, I swear by anything you like that when I get to Manáos I will find someone to take my place. I will pay a man to read to you all day.'

'But I have no need of another man. You read so well.'

'I have read for the last time.'

'I hope not,' said Mr Todd politely.

That evening at supper only one plate of dried meat and farine was brought in and Mr Todd ate alone. Tony lay without speaking, staring at the thatch.

Next day at noon a single plate was put before Mr Todd but with it lay his gun, cocked, on his knee, as he ate. Tony resumed the reading of *Martin Chuzzlewit* where it had been interrupted.

Weeks passed hopelessly. They read *Nicholas Nickleby* and *Little Dorrit* and *Oliver Twist*. Then a stranger arrived in the savannah, a half-caste prospector, one of that lonely order of men who wander for a lifetime through the forests, tracing the little streams, sifting the gravel, and ounce by ounce, filling the little leather sack of gold dust, more often than not dying of exposure and starvation with five hundred dollars worth of gold hung round their necks. Mr Todd was vexed at his arrival, gave him farine and *tasso* and sent him on his journey within an hour of his arrival, but in that hour Tony had time to scribble his name on a slip of paper and put it into the man's hand.

From now on there was hope. The days followed their unvarying routine; coffee at sunrise, a morning of inaction while Mr Todd pottered about on the business of the farm, farine and *tasso* at noon, Dickens in the afternoon, farine and *tasso* and sometimes some fruit for supper, silence from sunset to dawn with the small wick glowing in the beef fat and the palm thatch overhead dimly discernible; but Tony lived in quiet confidence and expectation.

Sometime, this year or the next, the prospector would arrive at a Brazilian village with news of his discovery. The disasters of the Messinger expedition would not have passed unnoticed. Tony could imagine the headlines that must have appeared in the popular press; even now, probably, there were search parties working over the country he had crossed; any day English voices must sound over the savannah and a dozen friendly adventurers come crashing through the bush. Even as he was reading, while his lips mechanically followed the printed pages, his mind wandered away from his eager, crazy host opposite, and he began to narrate to himself incidents of his home-coming—the gradual re-encounters with civilization (he shaved and bought new clothes at Manáos, telegraphed for money, received wires of congratulation; he enjoyed the leisurely river journey to Belem, the big liner to Europe; savoured good claret and fresh meat and spring vegetables; he was shy at meeting Brenda and uncertain how to address her . . . 'Darling, you've been much longer than you said. I quite thought you were lost . . .'

And then Mr Todd interrupted. 'May I trouble you to read that passage again? It is one I particularly enjoy.'

The weeks passed; there was no sign of rescue but Tony endured the day for hope of what might happen on the morrow; he even felt a slight stirring of cordiality towards his jailer and was therefore quite willing to join him when, one evening after a long conference with an Indian neighbour, he proposed a celebration.

'It is one of the local feast days,' he explained, 'and they have been making privari. You may not like it but you should try some. We will go across to this man's home tonight.'

Accordingly after supper they joined a party of Indians that were assembled round the fire in one of the huts at the other side of the savannah. They were singing in an apathetic, monotonous manner and passing a large calabash of liquid from mouth to mouth. Separate bowls were brought for Tony and Mr Todd, and they were given hammocks to sit in.

'You must drink it all without lowering the cup. That is the etiquette.'

Tony gulped the dark liquid, trying not to taste it. But it was not unpleasant, hard and muddy on the palate like most of the beverages he had been offered in Brazil, but with a flavour of honey and brown bread. He leant back in the hammock feeling unusually contented. Perhaps at that very moment the search party was in camp a few hours' journey from them. Meanwhile he was warm and drowsy. The cadence of song rose and fell interminably, liturgically. Another calabash of pivari was offered him and he handed it back empty. He lay full length watching the play of shadows on the thatch as the Pie-wies began to dance. Then he shut his eyes and thought of England and Hetton and fell asleep.

He awoke, still in the Indian hut, with the impression that he had outslept his usual hour. By the position of the sun he knew it was late afternoon. No one else was about. He looked for his watch and found to his surprise that it was not on his wrist. He had left it in the house, he supposed, before coming to the party.

'I must have been tight last night,' he reflected. 'Treacherous drink that.' He had a headache and feared a recurrence of fever. He found when he set his feet to the ground that he stood with difficulty; his walk was unsteady and his mind confused as it had been during the first weeks of his convalescence. On the way across the savannah he was obliged to stop more than once, shutting his eyes and breathing deeply. When he reached the house he found Mr Todd sitting there.

'Ah, my friend, you are late for the reading this afternoon. There is scarcely another half hour of light. How do you feel?'

'Rotten. That drink doesn't seem to agree with me.'

'I will give you something to make you better. The forest has remedies for everything; to make you awake and to make you sleep.'

'You haven't seen my watch anywhere?'

'You have missed it?'

'Yes. I thought I was wearing it. I say, I've never slept so long.'

'Not since you were a baby. Do you know how long? Two days.'

'Nonsense. I can't have.'

'Yes, indeed. It is a long time. It is a pity because you missed our guests.'

'Guests?'

'Why, yes. I have been quite gay while you were asleep. Three men from outside. Englishmen. It is a pity you missed them. A pity for them, too, as they particularly wished to see you. But what could I do? You were so sound asleep. They had come all the way to find you, so— I thought you would not mind—as you could not greet them yourself, I gave them a little souvenir, your watch. They wanted something to take back to England where a reward is being offered for news of you. They were very pleased with it. And they took some photographs of the little cross I put up to commemorate your coming. They were pleased with that, too. They were very easily pleased. But I do not suppose they will visit us again, our life here is so retired . . . no pleasures except reading . . . I do not suppose we shall ever have visitors again . . . well, well, I will get you some medicine to make you feel better. Your head aches, does it not? . . . We will not have any Dickens today . . . but tomorrow, and the day after that, and the day after that. Let us read *Little Dorrit* again. There are passages in that book I can never hear without the temptation to weep.'

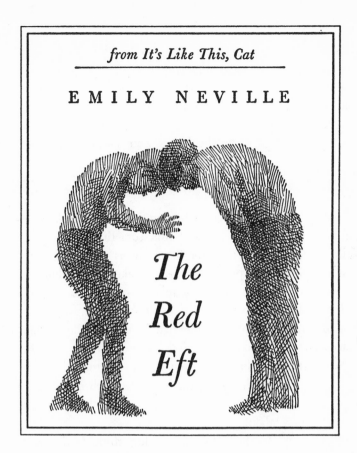

from It's Like This, Cat

EMILY NEVILLE

*The
Red
Eft*

Ben and I both take biology, and the first weekend assignment we get, right after Rosh Hashanah, is to find and identify an animal native to New York City and look up its family and species and life cycle.

"What's a species?" says Ben.

"I don't know. What's a life cycle?"

We both scratch our heads, and he says, "What animals do we know?"

I say, "Cat. And dogs and pigeons and squirrels."

"That's dull. I want to get some animal no one else knows about."

"Hey, how about a praying mantis? I saw one once in Gramercy Park."

Ben doesn't even know what it is, so I tell him about this one I saw. For an insect, it looks almost like a dragon, about four or five inches long and pale green. When it flies, it looks like a baby helicopter in the sky. We go into Gramercy Park to see if we can find another, but we can't.

Ben says, "Let's go up to the Bronx Zoo Saturday and see what we can find."

"Stupid, they don't mean you to do lions and tigers. They're not native."

"Stupid, yourself. They got other animals that are. Besides, there's lots of woods and ponds. I might find something."

Well, it's as good an idea for Saturday as any, so I say O.K. On account of both being pretty broke, we take lunch along in my old school lunchbox. Also six subway tokens—two extras for emergencies. Even I would be against walking home from the Bronx.

Of course there are plenty of native New York City animals in the zoo—raccoons and woodchucks and moles and lots of birds—and I figure we better start home not too late to get out the encyclopedias for species and life cycles. Ben still wants to catch something wild and wonderful. Like lots of city kids who haven't been in the country much, he's crazy about nature.

We head back to the subway, walking through the woods so he can hunt. We go down alongside the pond and kick up rocks and dead trees to see if anything is under them.

It pays off. All of a sudden we see a tiny red tail disappearing under a rotten log. I push the log again and Ben grabs. It's a tiny lizard, not more than two or three inches long and brick red all over. Ben cups it in both hands, and its throat pulses in and out, but it doesn't really try to get away.

"Hey, I love this one!" Ben cries. "I'm going to take him home and keep him for a pet, as well as do a report on him. You can't keep cats and dogs in Peter Cooper, but there's nothing in the rules about lizards."

"How are you going to get him home?"

"Dump the lunch. I mean—we'll eat it, but I can stab a hole in the top of the box and keep Redskin in it. Come on, hurry! He's getting tired in my hand I think!"

Ben is one of those guys who is very placid most of the time, but he gets excitable all of a sudden when he runs into something brand-new to him, and I guess he never caught an animal to keep before. Some people's parents are very stuffy about it.

I dump the lunch out, and he puts the lizard in and selects some particular leaves and bits of dead log to put in with him to make him feel at home. Without even asking me, he takes out his knife and makes holes in the top of my lunchbox. I sit down and open up a sandwich, but Ben is still dancing around.

"What do you suppose he is? He might be something very rare! How'm I going to find out? You think we ought to go back and ask one of the zoo men?"

"Umm, nah," I say, chewing. "Probably find him in the encyclopedia."

Ben squats on a log, and the log rolls. As he falls over backward I see two more lizards scuttle away. I grab one. "Hey, look! I got another. This one's bigger and browner."

Ben is up and dancing again. "Oh, boy, oh, boy! Now I got two! Now they'll be happy! Maybe they'll have babies, huh?"

He overlooks the fact that I caught this one. Oh, well, I don't want a lizard, anyway. Cat'd probably eat it.

Ben takes it from me and slips it in the lunchbox. "I'm going to call this one Big Brownie."

Finally he calms down enough to eat lunch, taking peeks at his catch between mouthfuls. As soon as he's finished eating, he starts hustling to get home so he can make a house for them. He really acts like a kid.

We get on the subway. It's aboveground—elevated—up here in the Bronx. After a while I see Yankee Stadium off to one side, which is funny because I don't remember seeing it when we were coming up. Pretty soon the train goes underground. I remember then. Coming up, we changed trains once. Ben has his eye glued to the edge of the lunchbox and he's talking to Redskin, so I figure there's no use consulting him. I'll just wait and see where this train seems to come out. It's got to go downtown. We go past something called Lenox Avenue, which I think is in Harlem, then Ninety-sixth Street, and then we're at Columbus Circle.

"Hey, Ben, we're on the West Side subway," I say.

"Yeah?" He takes a bored look out the window.

"We can just walk across town from Fourteenth Street."

"With you I always end up walking. Hey, what about those extra tokens?"

"Aw, it's only a few blocks. Let's walk."

Ben grunts, and he goes along with me. As we get near Union Square, there seem to be an awful lot of people around. In fact they're jamming the sidewalk and we can hardly move. Ben frowns at them and says, "Hey, what goes?"

I ask a man, and he says, "Where you been, sonny? Don'tcha know there's a parade for General Sparks?"

I remember reading about it now, so I poke Ben. "Hey, push along! We can see Sparks go by!"

"Quit pushing and don't try to be funny."

"Stupid, he's a general. Test pilot, war hero, and stuff. Come on, push."

"QUIT PUSHING! I got to watch out for these lizards!"

So I go first and edge us through the crowd to the middle of the block, where there aren't so many people and we can get up next to the police barrier. Cops on horseback are going back and forth, keeping the street clear. No sign of any parade coming yet, but people are throwing rolls of paper tape and handfuls of confetti out of upper-story windows. The wind catches the paper tape and carries it up and around in all kinds of fantastic snakes. Little kids keep scuttling under the barrier to grab handfuls of ticker tape that blow to the ground. Ben keeps one eye on the street and one on Redskin and Brownie.

"How soon you think they're coming?" he asks fretfully.

People have packed in behind us, and we couldn't leave now if we wanted to. Pretty soon we can see a helicopter flying low just a little ways downtown, and people all start yelling, "That's where they are! They're coming!"

Suddenly a bunch of motorcycle cops zoom past, and then a cop backing up a police car at about thirty miles an hour, which is a very surprising-looking thing. Before I've hardly got my eyes off that, the open cars come by. This guy Sparks is sitting up on the back of the car, waving with both hands. By the time I see him, he's almost past. Nice-looking, though. Everyone yells like crazy and throws any kind of paper they've got. Two little nuts beside us have a box of Wheaties, so they're busy throwing Breakfast of Champions. As soon as the motorcade is past, people push through the barriers and run in the street.

Ben hunches over to protect his precious animals and yells, "Come on! Let's get out of this!"

We go into my house first because I'm pretty sure we've got a wooden box. We find it and take it down to my room, and Ben gets extra leaves and grass and turns the lizards into it. He's sure they need lots of fresh air and exercise. Redskin scoots out of sight into a corner right away. Big Brownie sits by a leaf and looks around.

"Let's go look up what they are," I say.

The smallest lizard they show in the encyclopedia is about six inches long, and it says lizards are reptiles and have scales and claws and should not be confused with salamanders, which are amphibians and have thin moist skin and no claws. So we look up salamanders.

This is it, all right. The first picture on the page looks just like Redskin, and it says he's a Red Eft. The Latin name for his species is *Triturus viridescens,* or in English just a common newt.

"Hey, talk about life cycles, listen to this," says Ben, reading. "'It hatches from an egg in the water and stays there during its first summer as a dull-green larva. Then its skin becomes a bright orange, it absorbs its gills, develops lungs and legs, and crawls out to live for about three years in the woods. When fully mature, its back turns dull again, and it returns to the water to breed.'"

Ben drops the book. "Brownie must be getting ready to breed! What'd I tell you? We got to put him near water!" He rushes down to my room.

We come to the door and stop short. There's Cat, poised on the edge of the box.

I grab, but no kid is as fast as a cat. Hearing me coming, he makes his grab for the salamander. Then he's out of the box and away, with Big Brownie's tail hanging out of his mouth. He goes under the bed.

Ben screams, "Get him! Kill him! He's got my Brownie!" He's in a frenzy, and I don't blame him. It does make you mad to see your pet get hurt. I run for a broom to try to poke Cat out, but it isn't any use. Meanwhile, Ben finds Redskin safe in the box, and he scoops him back into the lunchbox.

Finally, we move the bed, and there is Cat poking daintily with his paw at Brownie. The salamander is dead. Ben grabs the broom and bashes Cat. Cat hisses and skids down the hall. "That rotten cat! I wish I could kill him! What'd you ever have him for?"

I tell Ben I'm sorry, and I get him a little box so he can bury Brownie. You can't really blame Cat too much—that's just the way a cat is made, to chase anything that wiggles and runs. Ben calms down after a while, and we go back to the encyclopedia to finish looking up about the Red Eft.

"I don't think Brownie was really ready to lay eggs, or he would have been in the pond already," I say. "Tell you what. We could go back some day with a jar and try to catch one in the water."

That cheers Ben up some. He finishes taking notes for his report and tracing a picture, and then he goes home with Redskin in the lunchbox. I pull out the volume for C.

Cat. Family, *Felidae*, including lions and tigers. Species, *Felis domesticus*. I start taking notes: "'The first civilized people to keep cats were the Egyptians, thirteen centuries before Christ. . . . Fifty million years earlier the ancestor of the cat family roamed the earth, and he is the ancestor of all present-day carnivores. The Oligocene cats, thirty million years ago, were already highly specialized, and the habits and physical characteristics of cats have been fixed since then. This may explain why house cats remain the most independent of pets, with many of the instincts of their wild ancestors.'"

I call Ben up to read him this, and he says, "You and your lousy carnivore! *My* salamander is an amphibian, and amphibians are the ancestors of *all* the animals on earth, even you and your Cat, you sons of toads!"

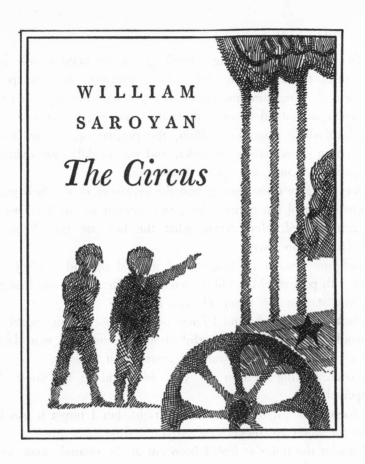

WILLIAM
SAROYAN

The Circus

A ny time a circus came to town, that was all me and my old pal
Joey Emerian needed to make us run hog-wild, as the saying is.
All we needed to do was see the signs on the fences and in the empty
store windows to start going to the dogs and neglecting our educa-
tions. All we needed to know was that a circus was on its way to
town for me and Joey to start wanting to know what good a little
education ever did anybody anyway.

After the circus *reached* town we were just no good at all. We
spent all our time down at the trains, watching the gang unload the
animals, walking out Ventura Avenue with the lions and tigers in
their golden wagons, and hanging around the grounds, trying to win
the favor of the animal men, the acrobats, and the clowns.

The circus was everything everything else we knew wasn't. It was adventure, travel, danger, skill, grace, romance, comedy, peanuts, popcorn, chewing-gum, and soda-water. We used to carry water to the elephants and stand around afterwards and try to seem associated with the whole magnificent affair, the putting up of the big tent, the getting of everything in order, and the worldly-wise waiting for the people to come and spend their money.

One day Joey came tearing into the classroom of the fifth grade at Emerson School ten minutes late, and without so much as removing his cap shouted, Hey, Aram, what the hell are you doing here? The circus is in town.

And sure enough I'd forgotten. I jumped up and ran out of the room with poor old Miss Flibety screaming after me, Aram Garoghlanian, you stay in this room. Do you hear me?

I heard her all right and I knew what my not staying would mean. It would mean another powerful strapping from old man Dawson. But I couldn't help it. I was just crazy about a circus.

I been looking all over for you, Joey said in the street. What happened?

I forgot. I knew it was coming all right, but I forgot it was today. How far along are they?

I was at the trains at five. I been out at the grounds since seven. I had breakfast at the circus table, with the gang.

How are they?

Great, the same as ever. Couple more years, they told me, and I'll be ready to go away with them.

As what? Lion-tamer, or something like that?

I guess maybe not as a lion-tamer, Joey said. I figure more like a workman in the gang till I learn about being a clown or something. I don't figure I could work with lions right away.

We were out on Ventura Avenue, headed for the circus grounds, out near the County Fairgrounds, just north of the County Hospital.

What a breakfast! Joey said. Hot-cakes, ham and eggs, sausages, coffee. Boy.

Why didn't you tell me?

I thought you knew. I thought you'd be down at the trains same as last year. I would have told you if I knew you'd forgotten. What made you forget?

I don't know. Nothing, I guess.

I was wrong there, but I didn't know it at the time. I hadn't really forgotten. What I'd done was *remembered*. I'd gone to work and remembered the strapping Dawson gave me last year for staying out of school the day the circus was in town. That was the thing that had kind of kept me sleeping after four-thirty in the morning when by rights I should have been up and dressing and on my way to the trains. It was the memory of that strapping old man Dawson had given me, but I didn't know it at the time. We used to take the strappings kind of for granted, me and Joey, on account of we wanted to be fair and square with the Board of Education and if it was against the rules to stay out of school when you weren't sick, and if you were supposed to get strapped for doing it, well, there we were, we'd done it, so let the Board of Education balance things the best way they knew how. They did that with a strapping. They used to threaten to send me and Joey to Reform School but they never did it.

Circus? old man Dawson used to say. Well, bend down, boy.

So we'd bend down and old man Dawson would get some powerful shoulder exercise while we tried not to howl. We wouldn't howl for five or six licks, but after that we'd howl like Indians coming. They used to be able to hear us all over the school and old man Dawson, after our visits got to be kind of regular, urged us politely to try to make a little less noise, inasmuch as it was a school and people were trying to study.

It ain't fair to the others, he said. They're trying to learn something for themselves.

We can't help it, Joey said. It hurts.

That I know, but it seems to me there's such a thing as modulation. I believe a lad can overdo his howling if he ain't thoughtful of others. Just try to modulate that awful howl a little. I think you can do it.

He gave Joey a strapping of twenty and Joey tried his best not to howl so loud. After the strapping Joey's face was red and old man Dawson was very tired.

How was that? Joey said.

By far the most courteous you've managed yet.

I did my best.

I'm grateful to you, old man Dawson said.

He was tired and out of breath. I moved up to the chair in front of him that he furnished during these matters to help us suffer the stinging pain. I got in the right position and he said, Wait a minute, Aram. Give a man a chance to catch his breath. I'm not twenty-three years old. I'm *sixty*-three. Let me rest a minute.

All right, but I sure would like to get this over with.

So would I, but don't howl so loud. Folks passing by in the street are liable to think this is a veritable chamber of tortures. Does it really hurt that much?

You can ask Joey.

How about it, Joey? Aren't you lads exaggerating just a little? Perhaps to impress someone in your room? Some girl, perhaps?

We don't howl to impress anybody, Mr. Dawson. Howling makes us feel ashamed, doesn't it, Aram?

It's embarrassing to go back to our seats after howling that way. We'd rather not howl if we could help it.

Well, I'll not be unreasonable. I'll only ask you to try to modulate it a little.

I'll do my best, Mr. Dawson. Catch your breath?

Give me just a moment longer.

When he got his breath back he gave me my twenty and I howled a little louder than Joey and then we went back to class. It was awfully embarrassing. Everybody was looking at us.

Well, Joey said to the class, what did you expect? You'd fall down and die if *you* got twenty. You wouldn't *howl a little,* you'd die.

That'll be enough out of you, Miss Flibety said.

Well, it's true, Joey said. They're all scared. A circus comes to town and what do they do? They come to school.

That'll be enough.

Who do they think they are, giving us dirty looks?

Miss Flibety lifted her hand, hushing Joey.

Now the circus was back in town, another year had gone by, it was April again, and we were on our way out to the grounds. Only this time it was worse than ever because they'd seen us at school and *knew* we were going out to the circus.

Do you think they'll send Stafford after us? I said.

Stafford was truant officer.

We can always run, Joey said. If he comes, I'll go one way, you go another. He can't chase *both* of us.

When we got out to the grounds a couple of the little tents were up, and the big one was going up. We stood around and watched. It was great the way they did it. Just a handful of guys who looked like tramps doing work you'd think no less than a hundred men could do. Doing it with style, too.

All of a sudden a man everybody called Red hollered at me and Joey.

Here, you Arabs, give us a hand.

Me and Joey ran over to him.

Yes sir, I said.

He was a small man with very broad shoulders and very big hands. You didn't feel that he was small, because he seemed so powerful and because he had so much thick red hair on his head. You thought he was practically a giant.

He handed me and Joey a rope. The rope was attached to some canvas that was lying on the ground.

This is easy, Red said. As the boys lift the pole and get it in place you keep pulling the rope, so the canvas will go up with the pole.

Yes sir, Joey said.

Everybody was busy when we saw Stafford.

We can't run now, I said.

Let him come, Joey said. We told Red we'd give him a hand and we're going to do it.

We'll tell him we'll go with him after we get the canvas up; then we'll run.

All right, Joey said.

Stafford was a big fellow in a business suit who had a beef-red face and looked as if he ought to be a lawyer or something. He came over and said, All right, you hooligans, come along with me.

We promised to give Red a hand, Joey said. We'll come just as soon as we get this canvas up.

We were pulling for all we were worth, slipping and falling. The men were all working hard. Red was hollering orders, and then the whole thing was over and we had done our part.

We didn't even get a chance to find out what Red was going to say to us, or if he was going to invite us to sit at the table for lunch, or what.

Joey busted loose and ran one way and I ran the other and Stafford came after *me*. I heard the circus men laughing and Red hollering, Run, boy, run. He can't catch *you*. He's soft. Give him a good run. He needs the exercise.

I could hear Stafford, too. He was very sore and he was cussing.

I got away, though, and stayed low until I saw him drive off in his Ford. Then I went back to the big tent and found Joey.

We'll get it this time, he said.

I guess it'll be Reform School.

No, it'll be thirty, and that's a lot of whacks even if he *is* sixty-three years old.

Thirty? That's liable to make me cry.

Me too, maybe, Joey said. Seems like ten can make you cry, then you hold off till it's eleven, then twelve, howling so you *won't* cry, and you think you'll start crying on the next one, but you don't. We haven't so far, anyway. Maybe we will when it's thirty, though.

Oh, well, that's tomorrow.

Red gave us some more work to do around the grounds and let us sit next to him at lunch. It was beef stew and beans, all you could eat. We talked to some acrobats who were Spanish, and to a family of Italians who worked with horses. We saw both shows, the afternoon one and the evening one, and then we helped with the work, taking the circus to pieces again; then we went down to the trains, and then home. I got home real late. In the morning I was sleepy when I had to get up for school.

They were waiting for us. Miss Flibety didn't even let us sit down for the roll call. She just told us to go to the office. Old man Dawson was waiting for us, too. Stafford was there, too, and very angry.

I figured, Well, here's where we go to Reform School.

Here they are, Mr. Dawson said to Stafford. Take them away, if you like.

It was easy to tell they'd been talking for some time and hadn't been getting along too well.

In *this* school, old man Dawson said, I do any punishing that's got to be done. Nobody else. I can't stop you from taking them to Reform School, though.

Stafford didn't say anything. He just gave old man Dawson a very dirty look and left the office.

Well, lads, old man Dawson said. How was it?

We had lunch with them, Joey said.

Good. But now down to business. What offense is this, the sixteenth or the seventeenth?

It ain't that many, Joey said. Must be eleven or twelve.

Well, I'm sure of one thing. This is the time I'm supposed to make it thirty.

I think the next one is the one you're supposed to make thirty, Joey said.

No, we've lost track somewhere, but I'm sure this is the time it goes up to thirty. Who's going to be first?

Me.

All right, Aram. Take a good hold on the chair, brace yourself, and try to modulate your howl.

Yes sir. I'll do my best, but thirty's an awful lot.

Well, a funny thing happened. He gave me thirty all right and I howled all right, but it *was* a modulated howl. It was the most modulated howl I ever howled; because it was the *easiest* strapping I ever got. I counted them and there were thirty all right, but they didn't hurt, so I didn't cry, as I was afraid I might.

It was the same with Joey. We stood together waiting to be dismissed.

I'm awfully grateful to you boys, old man Dawson said, for modulating your howls so nicely this time. I don't want people to think I'm killing you.

We wanted to thank him for giving us such easy strappings, but we didn't know how. I think he knew the way we felt, though, because he kind of laughed when he told us to go back to class.

It was a proud and happy moment for both of us because we knew everything would be all right till the County Fair opened in September.

The End of the Party

GRAHAM GREENE

Peter Morton woke with a start to face the first light. Through the window he could see a bare bough dropping across a frame of silver. Rain tapped against the glass. It was January the fifth.

He looked across a table, on which a night-light had guttered into a pool of water, at the other bed. Francis Morton was still asleep, and Peter lay down again with his eyes on his brother. It amused him to imagine that it was himself whom he watched, the same hair, the same eyes, the same lips and line of cheek. But the thought soon palled, and the mind went back to the fact which lent the day importance. It was the fifth of January. He could hardly believe that a year had passed since Mrs. Henne-Falcon had given her last children's party.

Francis turned suddenly upon his back and threw an arm across his face, blocking his mouth. Peter's heart began to beat fast, not with pleasure now but with uneasiness. He sat up and called across the table, "Wake up." Francis's shoulders shook and he waved a clenched fist in the air, but his eyes remained closed. To Peter Morton the whole room seemed suddenly to darken, and he had the impression of a great bird swooping. He cried again, "Wake up," and once more there was silver light and the touch of rain on the windows.

Francis rubbed his eyes. "Did you call out?" he asked.

"You are having a bad dream," Peter said with confidence. Already experience had taught him how far their minds reflected each other. But he was the elder, by a matter of minutes, and that brief extra interval of light, while his brother still struggled in pain and darkness, had given him self-reliance and an instinct of protection towards the other who was afraid of so many things.

"I dreamed that I was dead," Francis said.

"What was it like?" Peter asked with curiosity.

"I can't remember," Francis said, and his eyes turned with relief to the silver of day, as he allowed the fragmentary memories to fade.

"You dreamed of a big bird."

"Did I?" Francis accepted his brother's knowledge without question, and for a little the two lay silent in bed facing each other, the same green eyes, the same nose tilting at the tip, the same firm lips parted, and the same premature modeling of the chin. The fifth of January, Peter thought again, his mind drifting idly from the image of cakes to the prizes which might be won. Egg-and-spoon races, spearing apples in basins of water, blindman's buff.

"I don't want to go," Francis said suddenly. "I suppose Joyce will be there . . . Mabel Warren." Hateful to him, the thought of a party shared with those two. They were older than he. Joyce was eleven and Mabel Warren thirteen. Their long pigtails swung superciliously to a masculine stride. The sex humiliated him, as they watched him fumble with his egg, from under lowered scornful lids. And last year . . . he turned his face away from Peter, his cheeks scarlet.

"What's the matter?" Peter asked.

"Oh, nothing. I don't think I'm well. I've got a cold. I oughtn't to go to the party."

Peter was puzzled. "But, Francis, is it a bad cold?"

"It will be a bad cold if I go to the party. Perhaps I shall die."

"Then you mustn't go," Peter said with decision, prepared to solve all difficulties with one plain sentence, and Francis let his nerves relax in a delicious relief, ready to leave everything to Peter. But though he was grateful he did not turn his face towards his brother. His cheeks still bore the badge of a shameful memory, of the game of hide-and-seek last year in the darkened house, and of how he had screamed when Mabel Warren put her hand suddenly upon his arm. He had not heard her coming. Girls were like that. Their shoes never squeaked. No boards whined under their tread. They slunk like cats on padded claws. When the nurse came in with hot water Francis lay tranquil, leaving everything to Peter. Peter said, "Nurse, Francis has got a cold."

The tall starched woman laid the towels across the cans and said, without turning, "The washing won't be back till tomorrow. You must lend him some of your handkerchiefs."

"But, Nurse," Peter asked, "hadn't he better stay in bed?"

"We'll take him for a good walk this morning," the nurse said. "Wind'll blow away the germs. Get up now, both of you," and she closed the door behind her.

"I'm sorry," Peter said, and then, worried at the sight of a face creased again by misery and foreboding, "Why don't you just stay in bed? I'll tell mother you felt too ill to get up." But such a rebellion against destiny was not in Francis's power. Besides, if he stayed in bed they would come up and tap his chest and put a thermometer in his mouth and look at his tongue, and they would discover that he was malingering. It was true that he felt ill, a sick empty sensation in his stomach and a rapidly beating heart, but he knew that the cause was only fear, fear of the party, fear of being made to hide by himself in the dark, uncompanioned by Peter and with no night-light to make a blessed breach.

"No, I'll get up," he said, and then with sudden desperation, "but I won't go to Mrs. Henne-Falcon's party. I swear on the Bible I won't." Now surely all would be well, he thought. God would not allow him to break so solemn an oath. He would show him a way. There was all the morning before him and all the afternoon until four o'clock. No need to worry now when the grass was still crisp with the early frost. Anything might happen. He might cut himself or break his leg or really catch a bad cold. God would manage some-how.

He had such confidence in God that when at breakfast his mother said, "I hear you have a cold, Francis," he made light of it. "We should have heard more about it," his mother said with irony, "if there was not a party this evening," and Francis smiled uneasily, amazed and daunted by her ignorance of him. His happiness would have lasted longer if, out for a walk that morning, he had not met Joyce. He was alone with his nurse, for Peter had leave to finish a rabbit-hutch in the woodshed. If Peter had been there he would have cared less; the nurse was Peter's nurse also, but now it was as though she were employed only for his sake, because he could not be trusted to go for a walk alone. Joyce was only two years older and she was by herself.

She came striding towards then, pigtails flapping. She glanced scornfully at Francis and spoke with ostentation to the nurse. "Hello, Nurse. Are you bringing Francis to the party this evening? Mabel and I are coming." And she was off again down the street in the direction of Mabel Warren's home, consciously alone and self-sufficient in the long empty road. "Such a nice girl," the nurse said. But Francis was silent, feeling again the jump-jump of his heart, realizing how soon the hour of the party would arrive. God had done nothing for him, and the minutes flew.

They flew too quickly to plan any evasion, or even to prepare his heart for the coming ordeal. Panic nearly overcame him when, all unready, he found himself standing on the doorstep, with coat-collar turned up against a cold wind, and the nurse's electric torch making a short luminous trail through the darkness. Behind him were the lights of the hall and the sound of a servant laying the table for dinner, which his mother and father would eat alone. He was nearly overcome by a desire to run back into the house and call out to his mother that he would not go to the party, that he dared not go. They could not make him go. He could almost hear himself saying those final words, breaking down for ever, as he knew instinctively, the barrier of ignorance that saved his mind from his parents' knowledge. "I'm afraid of going. I won't go. I daren't go. They'll make me hide in the dark, and I'm afraid of the dark. I'll scream and scream and scream." He could see the expression of amazement on his mother's face, and then the cold confidence of a grown-up's retort. "Don't be silly. You must go. We've accepted Mrs. Henne-Falcon's invitation."

But they couldn't make him go; hesitating on the doorstep while the nurse's feet crunched across the frost-covered grass to the gate, he knew that. He would answer, "You can say I'm ill. I won't go. I'm afraid of the dark." And his mother, "Don't be silly. You know there's nothing to be afraid of in the dark." But he knew the falsity of that reasoning; he knew how they taught also that there was nothing to fear in death, and how fearfully they avoided the idea of it. But they couldn't make him go to the party. "I'll scream. I'll scream."

"Francis, come along." He heard the nurse's voice across the dimly phosphorescent lawn and saw the small yellow circle of her torch wheel from tree to shrub and back to tree again. "I'm coming," he called with despair, leaving the lighted doorway of the house; he couldn't bring himself to lay bare his last secrets and end reserve between his mother and himself, for there was still in the last resort a further appeal possible to Mrs. Henne-Falcon. He comforted himself with that, as he advanced steadily across the hall, very small, towards her enormous bulk. His heart beat unevenly, but he had control now over his voice, as he said with meticulous accent, "Good evening, Mrs. Henne-Falcon. It was very good of you to ask me to your party." With his strained face lifted towards the curve of her breasts, and his polite set speech, he was like an old withered man. For Francis mixed very little with other children. As a twin he was in many ways an only child. To address Peter was to speak to his own image in a mirror, an image a little altered by a flaw in the glass, so as to throw back less a likeness of what he was than of what he wished to be, what he would be without his unreasoning fear of darkness, footsteps of strangers, the flight of bats in dusk-filled gardens.

"Sweet child," said Mrs. Henne-Falcon absent-mindedly, before, with a wave of her arms, as though the children were a flock of chickens, she whirled them into her set programme of entertainments: egg-and-spoon races, three-legged races, the spearing of apples, games which held for Francis nothing worse than humiliation. And in the frequent intervals when nothing was required of him and he could stand alone in corners as far removed as possible from Mabel Warren's scornful gaze, he was able to plan how he might avoid the approaching terror of the dark. He knew there was nothing to fear until after tea, and not until he was sitting down in a pool of yellow radiance cast by the ten candles on Colin Henne-Falcon's birthday cake did he become fully conscious of the imminence of what he feared. Through the confusion of his brain, now assailed suddenly by a dozen contradictory plans, he heard Joyce's high voice down the table. "After tea we are going to play hide-and-seek in the dark."

"Oh, no," Peter said, watching Francis's troubled face with pity and an imperfect understanding, "don't let's. We play that every year."

"But it's on the programme," cried Mabel Warren. "I saw it myself. I looked over Mrs. Henne-Falcon's shoulder. Five o'clock, tea. A quarter to six to half-past, hide-and-seek in the dark. It's all written down in the programme."

Peter did not argue, for if hide-and-seek had been inserted in Mrs. Henne-Falcon's programme, nothing which he could say could avert it. He asked for another piece of birthday cake and sipped his tea slowly. Perhaps it might be possible to delay the game for a quarter of an hour, allow Francis at least a few extra minutes to form a plan, but even in that Peter failed, for children were already leaving the table in twos and threes. It was his third failure, and again, the reflection of an image in another's mind, he saw a great bird darken his brother's face with its wings. But he upbraided himself silently for his folly, and finished his cake encouraged by the memory of that adult refrain, "There's nothing to fear in the dark." The last to leave the table, the brothers came together to the hall to meet the mustering and impatient eyes of Mrs. Henne-Falcon.

"And now," she said, "we will play hide-and-seek in the dark."

Peter watched his brother and saw, as he had expected, the lips tighten. Francis, he knew, had feared this moment from the beginning of the party, had tried to meet it with courage and had abandoned the attempt. He must have prayed desperately for cunning to evade the game, which was now welcomed with cries of excitement by all the other children. "Oh, do let's." "We must pick sides." "Is any of the house out of bounds?" "Where shall home be?"

"I think," said Francis Morton, approaching Mrs. Henne-Falcon, his eyes unwaveringly on her exuberant breasts, "it will be no use my playing. My nurse will be calling for me very soon."

"Oh, but your nurse can wait, Francis," said Mrs. Henne-Falcon absent-mindedly, while she clapped her hands together to summon to her side a few children who were already straying up the wide staircase to upper floors. "Your mother will never mind."

That had been the limit of Francis's cunning. He had refused to believe that so well prepared an excuse could fail. All that he could say now, still in the precise tone which other children hated, thinking it a symbol of conceit, was, "I think I had better not play." He stood motionless, retaining, though afraid, unmoved features. But the knowledge of his terror, or the reflection of the terror itself, reached his brother's brain. For the moment, Peter Morton could have cried aloud with the fear of bright lights going out, leaving him alone in an island of dark surrounded by the gentle lapping of strange footsteps. Then he remembered that the fear was not his own, but his brother's. He said impulsively to Mrs. Henne-Falcon, "Please. I don't think Francis should play. The dark makes him jump so." They were the wrong words. Six children began to sing, "Cowardly, cowardly custard," turning torturing faces with the vacancy of wide sunflowers towards Francis Morton.

Without looking at his brother, Francis said, "Of course I will play. I am not afraid. I only thought . . ." But he was already forgotten by his human tormentors and was able in loneliness to contemplate the approach of the spiritual, the more unbounded, torture. The children scrambled round Mrs. Henne-Falcon, their shrill voices pecking at her with questions and suggestions. "Yes, anywhere in the house. We will turn out all the lights. Yes, you can hide in the cupboards. You must stay hidden as long as you can. There will be no home."

Peter, too, stood apart, ashamed of the clumsy manner in which he had tried to help his brother. Now he could feel, creeping in at the corners of his brain, all Francis's resentment of his championing. Several children ran upstairs, and the lights on the top floor went out. Then darkness came down like the wings of a bat and settled on the landing. Others began to put out the lights at the edge of the hall, till the children were all gathered in the central radiance of the chandelier, while the bats squatted round on hooded wings and waited for that, too, to be extinguished.

"You and Francis are on the hiding side," a tall girl said, and then the light was gone, and the carpet wavered under his feet with the sibilance of footfalls, like small cold draughts, creeping away into corners.

"Where's Francis?" he wondered. "If I join him he'll be less frightened of all these sounds." "These sounds" were the casing of silence. The squeak of a loose board, the cautious closing of a cupboard door, the whine of a finger drawn along polished wood.

Peter stood in the center of the dark deserted floor, not listening but waiting for the idea of his brother's whereabouts to enter his brain. But Francis crouched with fingers on his ears, eyes uselessly closed, mind numbed against impressions, and only a sense of strain could cross the gap of dark. Then a voice called "Coming," and as though his brother's self-possession had been shattered by the sudden cry, Peter Morton jumped with fear. But it was not his own fear. What in his brother was a burning panic, admitting no ideas except those which added to the flame, was in him an altruistic emotion that left the reason unimpaired. "Where, if I were Francis, should I hide?" Such, roughly, was his thought. And because he was, if not Francis himself, at least a mirror to him, the answer was immediate. "Between the oak bookcase on the left of the study door and the leather settee." Peter Morton was unsurprised by the swiftness of the response. Between the twins there could be no jargon of telepathy. They had been together in the womb, and they could not be parted.

Peter Morton tiptoed towards Francis's hiding place. Occasionally a board rattled, and because he feared to be caught by one of the soft questers through the dark, he bent and untied his laces. A tag struck the floor and the metallic sound set a host of cautious feet moving in his direction. But by that time he was in his stockings and would have laughed inwardly at the pursuit had not the noise of someone stumbling on his abandoned shoes made his heart trip in the reflection of another's surprise. No more boards revealed Peter Morton's progress. On stockinged feet he moved silently and unerringly towards his object. Instinct told him that he was near the wall, and, extending a hand, he laid the fingers across his brother's face.

Francis did not cry out, but the leap of his own heart revealed to Peter a proportion of Francis's terror. "It's all right," he whispered, feeling down the squatting figure until he captured a clenched hand. "It's only me. I'll stay with you." And grasping the other tightly, he listened to the cascade of whispers his utterance had caused to fall. A hand touched the bookcase close to Peter's head and he was aware of how Francis's fear continued in spite of his presence. It was less intense, more bearable, he hoped, but it remained. He knew that it was his brother's fear and not his own that he experienced. The dark to him was only an absence of light; the groping hand that of a familiar child. Patiently he waited to be found.

He did not speak again, for between Francis and himself touch was the most intimate communion. By way of joined hands thought could flow more swiftly than lips could shape themselves round words. He could experience the whole progress of his brother's emotion, from the leap of panic at the unexpected contact to the steady pulse of fear, which now went on and on with the regularity of a heart-beat. Peter Morton thought with intensity, "I am here. You needn't be afraid. The lights will go on again soon. That rustle, that movement is nothing to fear. Only Joyce, only Mabel Warren." He bombarded the drooping form with thoughts of safety, but he was conscious that the fear continued. "They are beginning to whisper together. They are tired of looking for us. The lights will go on soon. We shall have won. Don't be afraid. That was only someone on the stairs. I believe it's Mrs. Henne-Falcon. Listen. They are feeling for the lights." Feet moving on a carpet, hands brushing a wall, a curtain pulled apart, a clicking handle, the opening of a cupboard door. In the case above their heads a loose book shifted under a touch. "Only Joyce, only Mabel Warren, only Mrs. Henne-Falcon," a crescendo of reassuring thought before the chandelier burst, like a fruit tree, into bloom.

The voices of the children rose shrilly into the radiance. "Where's Peter?" "Have you looked upstairs?" "Where's Francis?" but they were silenced again by Mrs. Henne-Falcon's scream. But she was not the first to notice Francis Morton's stillness, where he had collapsed against the wall at the touch of his brother's hand. Peter continued to hold the clenched fingers in an arid and puzzled grief. It was not merely that his brother was dead. His brain, too young to realize the full paradox, yet wondered with an obscure self-pity why it was that the pulse of his brother's fear went on and on, when Francis was now where he had been always told there was no more terror and no more darkness.

II

Families and Other People

from Cheaper by the Dozen

FRANK GILBRETH and ERNESTINE GILBRETH CAREY

Motion Study Tonsils

[*Having a family of twelve presents many difficulties. To Father Gilbreth in the 1920s, it was simply a matter of promoting efficiency in the home just as he did in the factories and businesses that consulted him. He even believed the family's health could be managed with careful planning.*]

D ad thought the best way to deal with sickness in the family was simply to ignore it.

"We don't have time for such nonsense," he said. "There are too many of us. A sick person drags down the performance of the entire group. You children come from sound pioneer stock. You've been given health, and it's your job to keep it. I don't want any excuses. I want you to stay well."

Except for measles and whooping cough, we obeyed orders. Doctors' visits were so infrequent we learned to identify them with Mother's having a baby.

Dad's mother, who lived with us for awhile, had her own secret for warding off disease. Grandma Gilbreth was born in Maine, where she said the seasons were Winter, July and August. She claimed to be an expert in combatting cold weather and in avoiding head colds.

Her secret prophylaxis was a white bag, filled and saturated with camphor, which she kept hidden in her bosom. Grandma's bosom offered ample hiding space not only for camphor, but for her eyeglasses, her handkerchief, and, if need be, for the bedspread she was crocheting.

Each year, as soon as the first frost appeared, she made twelve identical, white, camphor-filled bags for each of us.

"Mind what Grandma says and wear these all the time," she told us. "Now if you bring home a cold it will be your own blessed fault, and I'll skin you alive."

Grandma always was threatening to skin someone alive, or draw and quarter him, or scalp him like a red Indian, or spank him till his bottom blistered.

Grandma averred she was a great believer in "spare the rod and spoil the child." Her own personal rod was a branch from a lilac bush, which grew in the side lawn. She always kept a twig from this bush on the top of her dresser.

"I declare, you're going to catch it now," she would say. "Your mother won't spank you and your father is too busy to spank you, but your grandma is going to spank you till your bottom blisters."

Then she would swing the twig with a vigor which belied her years. Most of her swings were aimed so as merely to whistle harmlessly through the air. She'd land a few light licks on our legs, though, and since we didn't want to hurt her feelings we'd scream and holler as if we were receiving the twenty-one lashes from a Spanish inquisitor. Sometimes she'd switch so vigorously at nothing that the twig would break.

"Ah, you see? You were so bad that I had to break my whip on you. Now go right out in the yard and cut me another one for next time. A big, thick one that will hurt even more than this one. Go along now. March!"

On the infrequent occasions when one of us did become sick enough to stay in bed, Grandma and Dad thought the best treatment was the absent treatment.

"A child abed mends best if left to himself," Grandma said, while Dad nodded approval. Mother said she agreed, too, but then she proceeded to wait on the sick child hand and foot.

"Here, darling, put my lovely bed jacket around your shoulders," Mother would tell the ailing one. "Here are some magazines, and scissors and paste. Now how's that? I'm going down to the kitchen and fix you a tray. Then I'll be up and read to you."

A cousin brought measles into the house, and all of us except Martha were stricken simultaneously. Two big adjoining bedrooms upstairs were converted into hospital wards—one for the boys and the other for the girls. We suffered together for two or three miserable, feverish, itchy days, while Mother applied cocoa butter and ice packs. Dr. Burton, who had delivered most of us, said there was nothing to worry about. He was an outspoken man, and he and Dad understood each other.

"I'll admit, Gilbreth, that your children don't get sick very often," Dr. Burton said, "but when they do it messes up the public health statistics for the entire state of New Jersey."

"How come, Mr. Bones?" Dad asked.

"I have to turn in a report every week on the number of contagious diseases I handle. Ordinarily, I handle a couple of cases of measles a week. When I report that I had eleven cases in a single day, they're liable to quarantine the whole town of Montclair and close up every school in Essex County."

"Well, they're probably exceptionally light cases," Dad said. "Pioneer stock, you know."

"As far as I'm concerned, measles is measles, and they've got the measles."

"Probably even pioneers got the measles," Dad said.

"Probably so. Pioneers had tonsils, too, and so do your kids. Really ugly tonsils. They ought to come out."

"I never had mine out."

"Let me see them," Dr. Burton ordered.

"There's nothing the matter with them."

"For God's sake don't waste my time," said Dr. Burton. "Open your mouth and say 'Ah'."

Dad opened his mouth and said, "Ah."

"I thought so," Dr. Burton nodded. "Yours ought to come out too. Should have had them taken out years ago. I don't expect you to admit it, but you have sore throats, don't you? You have one right this minute, haven't you?"

"Nonsense," said Dad. "Never sick a day in my life."

"Well, let yours stay in if you want. You're not hurting anybody but yourself. But you really should have the children's taken out."

"I'll talk it over with Lillie," Dad promised.

Once the fever from the measles had gone, we all felt fine, although we still had to stay in bed. We sang songs, told continued stories, played spelling games and riddles, and had pillow fights. Dad spent considerable time with us, joining in the songs and all the games except pillow fights, which were illegal. He still believed in letting sick children alone, but with all of us sick—or all but Martha, at any rate—he became so lonesome he couldn't stay away.

He came into the wards one night after supper, and took a chair over in a corner. We noticed that his face was covered with spots.

"Daddy," asked Anne, "what's the matter with you? You're all broken out in spots."

"You're imagining things," said Dad, smirking. "I'm all right."

"You've got the measles."

"I'm all right," said Dad. "I can take it."

"Daddy's got the measles, Daddy's got the measles." Dad sat there grinning, but our shouts were enough to bring Grandma on the run.

"What's the matter here?" she asked. And then to Dad. "Mercy sakes, Frank, you're covered with spots."

"It's just a joke," Dad told his mother, weakly.

"Get yourself to bed. A man your age ought to know better. Shame on you."

Grandma fumbled down her dress and put on her glasses. She peered into Dad's face.

"I declare, Frank Gilbreth," she told him, "sometimes I think you're more trouble than all of your children. Red ink! And you think it's a joke to scare a body half to death. Red ink!"

"A joke," Dad repeated.

"Very funny," Grandma muttered as she stalked out of the room. "I'm splitting my sides."

Dad sat there glumly.

"Is it red ink, Daddy?" we asked, and we agreed with him that it was, indeed, a very good joke. "Is it? You really had us fooled."

"You'll have to ask your grandma," Dad sulked. "She's a very smart lady. She knows it all."

Martha, who appeared immune to measles, nevertheless, wasn't allowed to come into the wards. She couldn't go to school, since the house was quarantined, and the week or two of being an "only child" made her so miserable that she lost her appetite. Finally, she couldn't stand it any more, and sneaked into the sick rooms to visit us.

"You know you're not allowed in here," said Anne. "Do you want to get sick?"

Martha burst into tears. "Yes," she sobbed. "Oh, yes."

"Don't tell us you miss us? Why I should think it would be wonderful to have the whole downstairs to yourself, and to be able to have Mother and Dad all by yourself at dinner."

"Dad's no fun any more," said Mart. "He's nervous. He says the quiet at the table is driving him crazy."

"Tell him that's not of general interest," said Ern.

It was shortly after the measles epidemic that Dad started applying motion study to surgery to try to reduce the time required for certain operations.

"Surgeons really aren't much different from skilled mechanics," Dad said, "except that they're not so skilled. If I can get to study their motions, I can speed them up. The speed of an operation often means the difference between life and death."

At first, the surgeons he approached weren't very cooperative.

"I don't think it will work," one doctor told him. "We aren't dealing with machines. We're dealing with human beings. No two human beings are alike, so no set of motions could be used over and over again."

"I know it will work," Dad insisted. "Just let me take some moving pictures of operations and I'll show you."

Finally he got permission to set up his movie equipment in an operating room. After the film was developed he put it in the projector which he kept in the parlor and showed us what he had done.

In the background was a cross-section screen and a big clock with "GILBRETH" written across its face and a hand which made a full revolution every second. Each doctor and nurse was dressed in white, and had a number on his cap to identify him. The patient was on an operating table in the foreground. Off to the left, clad in a white sheet, was something that resembled a snow-covered Alp. When the Alp turned around, it had a stopwatch in its hand. And when it smiled at the camera you could tell through the disguise that it was Dad.

It seemed to us, watching the moving pictures, that the doctors did a rapid, business-like job of a complicated abdominal operation. But Dad, cranking the projector in back of us, kept hollering that it was "stupidity incorporated."

"Look at that boob—the doctor with No. 3 on his cap. Watch what he's going to do now. Walk all the way around the operating table. Now see him reach way over there for that instrument? And then he decides that he doesn't want that one after all. He wants this one. He should call the instrument's name, and that nurse—No. 6, she's his caddy—should hand it to him. That's what she's there for. And look at his left hand—dangling there at his side. Why doesn't he use it? He could work twice as fast."

The result of the moving picture was that the surgeons involved managed to reduce their ether time by fifteen per cent. Dad was far from satisfied. He explained that he needed to take moving pictures of five or six operations, all of the same type, so that he could sort out the good motions from the wasted motions. The trouble was that most patients refused to be photographed, and hospitals were afraid of law suits.

"Never mind, dear," Mother told him. "I'm sure the opportunity will come along eventually for you to get all the pictures that you want."

Dad said that he didn't like to wait; that when he started a project, he hated to put it aside and pick it up again piecemeal whenever he found a patient, hospital, and doctor who didn't object to photographs. Then an idea hit him, and he snapped his fingers.

"I know," he said. "I've got it. Dr. Burton has been after me to have the kids' tonsils out. He says they really have to come out. We'll rig up an operating room in the laboratory here, and take pictures of Burton."

"It seems sort of heartless to use the children as guinea pigs," Mother said doubtfully.

"It does for a fact. And I won't do it unless Burton says it's perfectly all right. If taking pictures is going to make him nervous or anything we'll have the tonsils taken out without the motion study."

"Somehow or other I can't imagine Dr. Burton being nervous," Mother said.

"Me either. I'm going to call him. And you know what? I feel a little guilty about this whole deal. So, as conscience balm, I'm going to let the old butcher take mine out, too."

"I feel a little guilty about the whole deal, too," said Mother. "Only thank goodness I had mine taken out when I was a girl."

Dr. Burton agreed to do the job in front of a movie camera.

"I'll save you for the last, Old Pioneer," he told Dad. "The best for the last. Since the first day I laid eyes on your great, big, beautiful tonsils, I knew I wouldn't be content until I got my hands on them."

"Stop drooling and put away your scalpel, you old flatterer you," said Dad. "I intend to be the last. I'll have mine out after the kids get better."

Dr. Burton said he would start with Anne and go right down the ladder, through Ernestine, Frank, Bill and Lillian.

Martha alone of the older children didn't need to have her tonsils out, the doctor said, and the children younger than Lillian could wait awhile.

The night before the mass operation, Martha was told she would sleep at the house of Dad's oldest sister, Aunt Anne.

"I don't want you underfoot," Dad informed her. "The children who are going to have their tonsils out won't be able to have any supper tonight or breakfast in the morning. I don't want you around to lord it over them."

Martha hadn't forgotten how we neglected her when she finally came down with the measles. She lorded it over us plenty before she finally departed.

"Aunt Anne always has apple pie for breakfast," she said, which we all knew to be perfectly true, except that sometimes it was blueberry instead of apple. "She keeps a jar of doughnuts in the pantry and she likes children to eat them." This, too, was unfortunately no more than the simple truth. "Tomorrow morning, when you are awaiting the knife, I will be thinking of you. I shall try, if I am not too full, to dedicate a doughnut to each of you."

She rubbed her stomach with a circular motion, and puffed out her cheeks horribly as if she were chewing on a whole doughnut. She opened an imaginary doughnut jar and helped herself to another, which she rammed into her mouth.

"My goodness, Aunt Anne," she said, pretending that that lady was in the room, "those doughnuts are even more delicious than usual." . . . "Well, why don't you have another, Martha?" . . . "Thanks, Aunt Anne, I believe I will." . . . "Why don't you take two or three, Martha?" . . . "I'm so full of apple pie I don't know whether I could eat two more, Aunt Anne. But since it makes you happy to have people eat your cooking, I will do my best."

"Hope you choke, Martha, dear," we told her.

The next morning, the five of us selected to give our tonsils for motion study assembled in the parlor. As Martha had predicted, our stomachs were empty. They growled and rumbled. We could hear beds being moved around upstairs, and we knew the wards were being set up again. In the laboratory, which adjoined the parlor, Dad, his movie cameraman, a nurse, and Dr. Burton were converting a desk into an operating table, and setting up the cross-section background and lights.

Dad came into the parlor, dressed like an Alp again. "All right, Anne, come on." He thumped her on the back and smiled at the rest of us. "There's nothing to it. It will be over in just a few minutes. And think of the fun we'll have looking at the movies and seeing how each of you looks when he's asleep."

As he and Anne went out, we could see that his hands were trembling. Sweat was beginning to pop through his white robe. Mother came in and sat with us. Dad had wanted her to watch the operations, but she said she couldn't. After awhile we heard

Dad and a nurse walking heavily up the front stairs, and we knew Anne's operation was over and she was being carried to bed.

"I know I'm next, and I won't say I'm not scared," Ernestine confided. "But I'm so hungry all I can think of is Martha and that pie. The lucky dog."

"And doughnuts," said Bill. "The lucky dog."

"Can we have pie and doughnuts after our operations?" Lill asked Mother.

"If you want them," said Mother, who had had her tonsils out.

Dad came into the room. His robe was dripping sweat now. It looked as if a spring thaw had come to the Alps.

"Nothing to it," he said. "And I know we got some great movies. Anne slept just like a baby. All right, Ernestine, girl. You're next; let's go."

"I'm not hungry any more," she said. "Now I'm just scared."

A nurse put a napkin saturated with ether over Ern's nose. The last thing she remembered was Mr. Coggin, Dad's photographer, grinding away at the camera. "He should be cranking at two revolutions a second," she thought. "I'll count and see if he is. And one and two and three and four. That's the way Dad says to count seconds. You have to put the 'and' in between the numbers to count at the right speed. And one and two and three . . ." She fell asleep.

Dr. Burton peered into her mouth.

"My God, Gilbreth," he said. "I told you I didn't want Martha."

"You haven't got Martha," Dad said. "That's Ernestine."

"Are you sure?"

"Of course I'm sure, you jackass. Don't you think I know my own children?"

"You must be mistaken," Dr. Burton insisted. "Look at her carefully. There, now, isn't that Martha?"

"You mean to say you think I can't tell one child from another?"

"I don't mean to say anything, except if that isn't Martha we've made a horrible mistake."

"We?" Dad squealed. "We? I've made no mistake. And I hope I'm wrong in imagining the sort of a mistake you've made."

"You see, all I know them by is their tonsils," said Dr. Burton.

"I thought these tonsils were Martha. They were the only pair that didn't have to come out."

"No," moaned Dad. "Oh, no!" Then growing indignant: "Do you mean to tell me you knocked my little girl unconscious for no reason at all?"

"It looks as if I did just that, Gilbreth. I'm sorry, but it's done. It was damned careless. But you do have an uncommon lot of them, and they all look just alike to me."

"All right, Burton," Dad said. "Sorry I lost my temper. What do we do?"

"I'm going to take them out anyway. They'd have to come out eventually at any rate, and the worst part of an operation is dreading it before hand. She's done her dreading, and there's no use to make her do it twice."

As Dr. Burton leaned over Ernestine, some reflex caused her to knee him in the mouth.

"Okay, Ernestine, if that's really your name," he muttered. "I guess I deserved that."

As it turned out, Ernestine's tonsils were recessed and bigger than the doctor had expected. It was a little messy to get at them, and Mr. Coggin, the movie cameraman, was sick in a waste basket.

"Don't stop cranking," Dad shouted at him, "or your tonsils will be next. I'll pull them out by the roots, myself. Crank, by jingo, crank."

Mr. Coggin cranked. When the operation was over, Dad and the nurse carried Ernestine upstairs.

When Dad came in the parlor to get Frank, he told Mother to send someone over to Aunt Anne's for Martha.

"Apple pie, doughnuts or not, she's going to have her tonsils out," he said. "I'm not going to go through another day like this one again in a hurry."

Frank, Bill, and Lillian had their tonsils out, in that order. Then Martha arrived, bawling, kicking, and full of pie and doughnuts.

"You said I didn't have to have my tonsils out, and I'm not going to have my tonsils out," she screamed at the doctor. Before he could get her on the desk which served as the operating table, she kicked him in the stomach.

"The next time I come to your house," he said to Dad as soon as he could get his breath, "I'm going to wear a chest protector and a catcher's mask." Then to the nurse: "Give some ether to Martha, if that's really her name."

"Yes, I'm Martha," she yelled through the towel. "You're making a mistake."

"I told you she was Martha," Dad said triumphantly.

"I know," Dr. Burton said. "Let's not go into that again. She's Martha, but I've named her tonsils Ernestine. Open your mouth, Martha, you sweet child, and let me get Ernestine's tonsils. Crank on Mr. Coggin. Your film may be the first photographic record of a man slowly going berserk."

All of us felt terribly sick that afternoon, but Martha was in agony.

"It's a shame," Grandma kept telling Martha, who was named for her and was her especial pet. "They shouldn't have let you eat all that stuff and then brought you back here for the butchering. I don't care whether it was the doctor's fault or your father's fault. I'd like to skin them both alive and then scalp them like red Indians."

While we were recuperating, Dad spent considerable time with us, but minimized our discomforts, and kept telling us we were just looking for sympathy.

"Don't tell me," he said. "I saw the operations, didn't I? Why there's only the little, tiniest cut at the back of your throat. I don't understand how you can do all that complaining. Don't you remember the story about the Spartan boy who kept his mouth shut while the fox was chewing on his vitals?"

It was partly because of our complaining, and the desire to show us how the Spartan boy would have his tonsils out, that Dad decided to have only a local anesthetic for his operation. Mother, Grandma, and Dr. Burton all advised against it. But Dad wouldn't listen.

"Why does everyone want to make a mountain out of a molehill over such a minor operation?" he said. "I want to keep an eye on Burton and see that he doesn't mess up the job."

The first day that we children were well enough to get up, Dad and Mother set out in the car for Dr. Burton's office. Mother had urged Dad to call a taxi. She didn't know how to drive, and she said Dad probably wouldn't feel like doing the driving on the way home. But Dad laughed at her qualms.

"We'll be back in about an hour," Dad called to us as he tested his three horns to make sure he was prepared for any emergency. "Wait lunch for us. I'm starving."

"You've got to hand it to him," Anne admitted as the Pierce Arrow bucked up Wayside Place. "He's the bee's knees, all right. We were all scared to death before our operations. And look at him. He's looking forward to it."

Two hours later, a taxicab stopped in front of the house, and the driver jumped out and opened the door for his passengers. Then Mother emerged, pale and red-eyed. She and the driver helped a crumpled mass of moaning blue serge to alight. Dad's hat was rumpled and on sideways. His face was gray and sagging. He wasn't crying, but his eyes were watering. He couldn't speak and he couldn't smile.

"He's sure got a load on all right, Mrs. Gilbreth," said the driver enviously. "And still early afternoon, too. Didn't even know he touched the stuff, myself."

We waited for the lightning to strike, but it didn't. The seriousness of Dad's condition may be adjudged by the fact that he contented himself with a withering look.

"Keep a civil tongue in your head," said Mother, in one of the sharpest speeches of her career. "He's deathly ill."

Mother and Grandma helped Dad up to his room. We could hear him moaning, all the way downstairs.

Mother told us all about it that night, while Dad was snoring under the effects of sleeping pills. Mother had waited in Dr. Burton's ante-room while the tonsillectomy was being performed. Dad had felt wonderful while under the local anesthetic. When the operation was half over, he had come out into the ante-room, grinning and waving one tonsil in a pair of forceps.

"One down and one to go, Lillie," he had said. "Completely painless. Just like rolling off a log."

After what had seemed an interminable time, Dad had come out into the waiting room again, and reached for his hat and coat. He was still grinning, only not so wide as before.

"That's that," he said. "Almost painless. All right, boss, let's go. I'm still hungry."

Then, as Mother watched, his high spirits faded and he began to fall to pieces.

"I'm stabbed," he moaned. "I'm hemorrhaging. Burton, come here. Quick. What have you done to me?"

Dr. Burton came out of his office. It must be said to his credit that he was sincerely sympathetic. Dr. Burton had had his own tonsils out.

"You'll be all right, Old Pioneer," he said. "You just had to have it the hard way."

Dad obviously couldn't drive, so Mother had called the taxi. A man from the garage towed Foolish Carriage home later that night.

"I tried to drive it home," the garage man told Mother, "but I couldn't budge it. I got the engine running all right, but it just spit and bucked every time I put it in gear. Durndest thing I ever saw."

"I don't think anyone but Mr. Gilbreth understands it," Mother said.

Dad spent two weeks in bed, and it was the first time any of us remembered his being sick. He couldn't smoke, eat, or talk. But he could glare, and he glared at Bill for two full minutes when Bill asked him one afternoon if he had had his tonsils taken out like the Spartans used to have theirs removed.

Dad didn't get his voice back until the very day that he finally got out of bed. He was lying there, propped up on pillows, reading his office mail. There was a card from Mr. Coggin, the photographer.

"Hate to tell you, Mr. Gilbreth, but none of the moving pictures came out. I forgot to take off the inside lens cap. I'm terribly sorry. Coggin. P.S. I quit."

Dad threw off the covers and reached for his bathrobe. For the first time in two weeks, he spoke:

"I'll track him down to the ends of the earth," he croaked. "I'll take a blunt button hook and pull his tonsils out by the by jingoed roots, just like I promised him. He doesn't quit. He's fired."

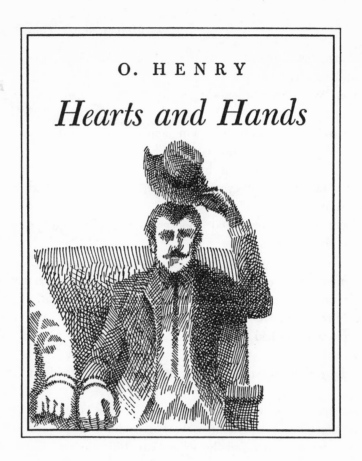

O. HENRY

Hearts and Hands

At Denver there was an influx of passengers into the coaches on the eastbound B. & M. express. In one coach there sat a very pretty young woman dressed in elegant taste and surrounded by all the luxurious comforts of an experienced traveler. Among the newcomers were two young men, one of handsome presence with a bold, frank countenance and manner; the other a ruffled, glum-faced person, heavily built and roughly dressed. The two were handcuffed together.

As they passed down the aisle of the coach the only vacant seat offered was a reversed one facing the attractive young woman. Here the linked couple seated themselves. The young woman's glance fell upon them with a distant, swift disinterest; then with a lovely smile brightening her countenance and a tender pink tingeing her rounded cheeks, she held out a little gray-gloved hand. When she spoke her voice, full, sweet, and deliberate, proclaimed that its owner was accustomed to speak and be heard.

"Well, Mr. Easton, if you *will* make me speak first, I suppose I must. Don't you ever recognize old friends when you meet them in the West?"

The younger man roused himself sharply at the sound of her voice, seemed to struggle with a slight embarrassment which he threw off instantly, and then clasped her fingers with his left hand.

"It's Miss Fairchild," he said, with a smile. "I'll ask you to excuse the other hand; it's otherwise engaged just at present."

He slightly raised his right hand, bound at the wrist by the shining "bracelet" to the left one of his companion. The glad look in the girl's eyes slowly changed to a bewildered horror. The glow faded from her cheeks. Her lips parted in a vague, relaxing distress. Easton, with a little laugh, as if amused, was about to speak again when the other forestalled him. The glum-faced man had been watching the girl's countenance with veiled glances from his keen, shrewd eyes.

"You'll excuse me for speaking, miss, but, I see you're acquainted with the marshal here. If you'll ask him to speak a word for me when we get to the pen he'll do it, and it'll make things easier for me there. He's taking me to Leavenworth prison. It's seven years for counterfeiting."

"Oh!" said the girl, with a deep breath and returning color. "So that is what you are doing out here? A marshal!"

"My dear Miss Fairchild," said Easton, calmly, "I had to do something. Money has a way of taking wings unto itself, and you know it takes money to keep step with our crowd in Washington. I saw this opening in the West, and—well, a marshalship isn't quite as high a position as that of ambassador, but——"

"The ambassador," said the girl, warmly, "doesn't call any more. He needn't ever have done so. You ought to know that. And so now you are one of these dashing Western heroes, and you ride and shoot and go into all kinds of dangers. That's different from the Washington life. You have been missed from the old crowd."

The girl's eyes, fascinated, went back, widening a little, to rest upon the glittering handcuffs.

"Don't you worry about them, miss," said the other man. "All marshals handcuff themselves to their prisoners to keep them from getting away. Mr. Easton knows his business."

"Will we see you again soon in Washington?" asked the girl.

"Not soon, I think," said Easton. "My butterfly days are over, I fear."

"I love the West," said the girl, irrelevantly. Her eyes were shining softly. She looked away out the car window. She began to speak truly and simply, without the gloss of style and manner: "Mamma and I spent the summer in Denver. She went home a week ago because father was slightly ill. I could live and be happy in the West. I think the air here agrees with me. Money isn't everything. But people always misunderstand things and remain stupid——"

"Say, Mr. Marshal," growled the glum-faced man. "This isn't quite fair. I'm needin' a drink, and haven't had a smoke all day. Haven't you talked long enough? Take me in the smoker now, won't you? I'm half dead for a pipe."

The bound travelers rose to their feet, Easton with the same slow smile on his face.

"I can't deny a petition for tobacco," he said, lightly. "It's the one friend of the unfortunate. Good-bye, Miss Fairchild. Duty calls, you know." He held out his hand for a farewell.

"It's too bad you are not going East," she said, reclothing herself with manner and style. "But you must go on to Leavenworth, I suppose?"

"Yes," said Easton, "I must go on to Leavenworth."

The two men sidled down the aisle into the smoker.

The two passengers in a seat near by had heard most of the conversation. Said one of them: "That marshal's a good sort of chap. Some of these Western fellows are all right."

"Pretty young to hold an office like that, isn't he?" asked the other.

"Young!" exclaimed the first speaker, "why——Oh! didn't you catch on? Say—did you ever know an officer to handcuff a prisoner to his *right* hand?"

from Harriet the Spy

LOUISE FITZHUGH

The Dancing Spy

[*Harriet Welsch had one special ambition—she wanted to know everything about everybody she met. Whenever she found out something particularly interesting she wrote it down in her notebook. Harriet was going to be the world's greatest spy, just as her best friend Janie was going to be the world's greatest scientist and blow everyone up.*]

Harriet decided to go see Janie awhile. Janie lived in the garden duplex of a renovated brownstone off East End Avenue on Eighty-fourth Street. Harriet rang the outside bell and pushed the door when it buzzed back. Janie was standing inside at her doorway and she was in a foul mood. Harriet could tell just by looking at her. Janie always looked terribly cheerful when she was in her most angry mood. Harriet figured it had to be that way because Janie's normal face was one of sheer rage. Today she smiled happily and sang out winningly, "Hello, there, Harriet Welsch." Things couldn't be worse.

Harriet walked toward her tentatively, as one would toward a mad dog, trying to see Janie's eyes more clearly, but Janie whipped inside the door. Harriet followed her in.

"What's the matter?" Harriet whispered. They were standing in the little foyer off the living room.

"They're after me," whispered Janie, still smiling wildly.

"Who?"

"The Rat Pack." This was what Janie called her mother, her father, her brother, and her grandmother who lived with them.

"Why?"

"My mother says I'm going to blow us all up and that I have to go to dancing school. Come past here, then they won't see us." Janie was hissing through her outrageous smile as she led them up the back steps to what she called her lab but which was really her room.

One corner of her room had been stripped bare. The rug had been pulled back, exposing one corner where Janie had started to cut off the excess to get it out of the way, but which she had been stopped from doing by her mother in an hysterical fit. At that time there had been a large fight through which Janie grinned broadly, and her mother let her know that it didn't make a whit of difference if they didn't ordinarily have rugs in labs ("They catch fire," Janie had said, which had set her mother off again), that Janie had a rug in her room that was going to stay there, and that the very best she could hope for was to have it rolled back. So it lay there in a roll at the end of the room.

The lab itself was very complex and frightened Harriet whenever she looked at it, although she never would have admitted this to Janie. It consisted of rows and rows of shelves filled with bottles, all filled with suspicious fluids and looking as though you would turn into Mr. Hyde if you drank them. Only Janie understood anything whatever about them, and she wouldn't explain but instead called everyone a cretin who asked her. The maids wouldn't go near Janie's room, so years ago she had had to learn to clean it herself.

Harriet stood staring at all the equipment while Janie rushed over to something boiling furiously on a Bunsen burner. She fiddled with it and turned it lower, then turned back to Harriet. "This time I may really get it," she said thoughtfully and went over and flopped on her bed.

"You mean . . ."

"Yes. They may take it *all* away."

"Oh, they couldn't."

"There have been people before me who have been misunderstood. They could." And the way Janie said this, with her smile dropped and her eyes boring into Harriet's, made shivers run up Harriet's back.

"What would you do?"

"Leave. Of course." One thing about Janie, thought Harriet, she never has a moment's hesitation about anything.

"What is this about dancing school?"

"Just wait, buddy. They're going to get you too. I heard my mother talking to your mother. Who ever heard of Pasteur going to dancing school? Or Madame Curie or Einstein?" Janie spit out the names.

Harriet couldn't think of any spies who went to dancing school either. This was a bad development. "Whether they know it or not, I'm not going," Harriet said firmly.

"They will *never get me*," Janie said very loudly. Then in a different tone, "Hey, Harriet, I've got to finish this experiment."

"That's all right. I've got some things to put in my notebook. Go ahead." Janie got up briskly and went over to her lab table. "If I don't do it now, this thing will curdle."

"What are you making?"

There was no answer. There was never any answer when you asked Janie this, but Harriet did it every now and then just to be polite. It was something explosive. That much was perfectly clear. Harriet sat looking around her for a while, at Janie's back bent attentively over her work, at the sunlight coming in the window— the late afternoon sun which looked sad and pleasant at the same time and which reminded her abruptly of New Year's Day last year. There hadn't been anything important about that day. She had just happened to look at the sun in the same way. She leaned back on the bed. It would be nice to be here or somewhere like this every day.

> Maybe when I grow up I can have an office. On the door it can say "Harriet the Spy" in gold letters. And then it can have office hours like the dentist's door has and underneath it can say *Any Spy Work Undertaken*. I guess I won't put the price on the door. Then they'll have to come in and ask me. I can go there every day from eleven to four and write in my notebook. People will come in and tell me who to go and spy on and I can do that outside of office hours. I wonder if I will get any murder cases. I would have to have a gun and follow people but I bet it would be at night and I wouldn't be allowed out.

"Hey, Janie, if you were going to slit somebody's throat, wouldn't you do it in the dead of night?"

"I'd poison them." Janie didn't even turn around.

I bet you would, thought Harriet. "But, Janie, they'd just trace the poison."

"Not the one I've got."

"Did you make a new one?"

"Yes."

Harriet went back to her notebook.

> Well, maybe there's something to this chemistry after all. I could poison Pinky and no one would ever know it. I bet they need some new poisons. But Ole Golly says that in Washington they've already got a little tube with a spoonful of something in it that will blow up the whole world, maybe the whole universe. What would happen? Would we fly through the air? In space you just float around. I would be lonely.

"Oh, *boy*, is that maddening." Janie stormed away from the lab table and sat down with her arms folded.

"What happened?" Harriet looked up.

"I goofed," Janie said. "If I'd done it right, it would have made a terrific noise."

"What would your mother have done?"

"That's who the noise was for, silly. If they think I'll set foot in a dancing school, they're off their rockers."

"Why don't you blow up the dancing school?" Harriet asked sensibly.

"Oh, they'd just find another place to have it. I know this kind of thing. Once they get this kind of thing in their heads, forget it. The only way out is to absolutely refuse. My mother hates to spend money, that's one thing; so if she can make a joke out of my not wanting to, then I'm in the clear because then she can save the money."

Harriet knew what she meant. Mrs. Gibbs tried to make a bad joke out of everything. Mrs. Welsch always spoke of Janie's mother as "that smart nose, Mabel Gibbs." Harriet thought to herself that one thing she couldn't stand was the kind of person who thought she was funny when she wasn't.

"See, if she can get across to her friends the idea that I'm an impossible eccentric, then it won't be her fault I'm not in dancing school," Janie went on. "And as for me, I couldn't care less if I learn to dance. I've got a big picture of Newton learning the Charleston."

Janie had a definite mind. That was one thing you could say for her. Harriet admired it.

There was a knock on the door. "Oh, brother," Janie said and got up to answer it.

It was Janie's mother. She gave her big horse laugh as she came into the room. "Well, well, how's Dr. Caligari?" she boomed out and laughed again raucously.

It's a good thing *she* laughs, thought Harriet, because no one else ever does. Janie looked at her mother stony-faced. Harriet did the same.

"That's my kid, a bundle of fun," and so saying Mrs. Gibbs slapped Janie on the back with such a wallop that Janie almost fell to the floor. Recovering herself, she glared again, a hideous smile beginning to creep across her face.

"'Yes, sir, that's my baby. No, sir, don't mean maybe,'" Mrs. Gibbs began to sing in her rollicking way while Harriet and Janie looked at the floor in a state of acute embarrassment. Noticing finally that she had no audience, Mrs. Gibbs stopped. "Well, Harriet," she hollered, "haven't seen you in a long time. Have a nice summer?" Mrs. Gibbs never waited for an answer from children, thinking they were too shy to speak (which they always were around her), but zoomed on with her shouts. "Talked to your mother the other day. Has Janie told you about dancing school? Your mother's all for it and I am too. You girls need a few graces, you know, turning into young women any day now, don't want to be clumps on the dance floor, nothing more embarrassing than a wallflower. Your mother's worried about the way you move, Harriet." And she suddenly focused on Harriet, waking her out of a reverie.

"Fast," Harriet said, "that's the way I move, fast. What's wrong with that?"

Mrs. Gibbs stared at her. Janie went back to her lab table. Mrs. Gibbs, not having any idea how to take Harriet's comment, decided, as she always did, that the best thing was to laugh it off. She gave an enormous whoop of laughter. Harriet saw Janie's shoulders go up in a quick little embarrassed cringe.

"Well, now, aren't you something. Wait'll I tell Harry that. You're as bad as Janie." She laughed a lot more for good measure. "Well, we'll just see about that. I think you girls have something to learn. I think you have to find out you're girls. I think we might just get together, all us mothers, and blast a little sense into your heads" —her hand was on the doorknob—"and I don't mean *your* kind of blast, Dr. Jekyll." She started to open the door and at that moment there was a terrific noise. Something on the lab table flew straight up into the air, and Mrs. Gibbs went through the door like a shot.

Janie turned around and they both looked at the door through which came several different screams and feet clattering as Mrs. Gibbs tore down the steps, screeching, "Harry Gibbs, she's done it. Harry, come here, Harry, that maniac will kill us all, Harry Gibbs, come here, she's blown up the house!"

They listened to a whispered colloquy in the downstairs hall after Harry had run out, saying, "WHAT! WHAT? What's happened?"

After the whispers there was an ominous silence during which they must have realized that the house was still standing. Then Harry's voice—"I'll go speak to her"—and his feet beginning the climb.

Harriet had no desire to watch Mr. Gibbs's tiny perspiring face as he tried to cope with his daughter. It would only make it worse for him if she was there.

"I think I'll just go down the back steps," she said gently, going toward the door.

"I guess you better." Janie sounded tired.

"Don't give up," Harriet whispered as she left.

"Never," Janie whispered back.

*   *   *

That night at dinner everything was going along as usual, that is, Mr. and Mrs. Welsch were having an interminable, rambling conversation about nothing in particular while Harriet watched it all like a tennis match, when suddenly Harriet leaped to her feet as though she had just then remembered, and screamed, "I'll be *damned* if I'll go to dancing school."

"Harriet!" Mrs. Welsch was appalled. "How dare you use words like that at the table."

"Or any other place, dear," interjected Mr. Welsch calmly.

"All right, I'll be FINKED if I'll go to dancing school." Harriet stood and screamed this solidly. She was throwing a fit. She only threw fits as a last resort, so that even as she did it she had a tiny feeling in the back of her brain that she had already lost. She wouldn't, however, have it said that she went down without a try.

"Where in the world did you learn a word like that?" Mrs. Welsch's eyebrows were raised almost to her hairline.

"It's not a verb, anyway," said Mr. Welsch. They both sat looking at Harriet as though she were a curiosity put on television to entertain them.

"I *will not*, I *will not*, I *will not*," shouted Harriet at the top of her lungs. She wasn't getting the right reaction. Something was wrong.

"Oh, but you will," said Mrs. Welsch calmly. "It really isn't so bad. You don't even know what it's like."

"I hated it," said Mr. Welsch and went back to his dinner.

"I *do so* know what it's like." Harriet was getting tired of standing up and screaming. She wished she could sit down but it wouldn't have done. It would have looked like giving up. "I went there once on a visit with Beth Ellen because she had to go and I was spending the night, and you have to wear party dresses and all the boys are too short and you feel like a *hippopotamus.*" She said this all in one breath and screamed "hippopotamus."

Mr. Welsch laughed. "An accurate description, you must admit."

"Darling, the boys get taller as you go along."

"I just *won't.*" Somehow, indefinably, Harriet felt she was losing ground all the time.

"It isn't so bad." Mrs. Welsch went back to her dinner.

This was too much. The point wasn't coming across at all. They had to be roused out of their complacency. Harriet took a deep breath, and in as loud a voice as she could, repeated, "I'll be *damned* if I'll go!"

"All right, that does it." Mrs. Welsch stood up. She was furious. "You're getting your mouth washed out with soap, young lady. Miss Golly, Miss Golly, step in here a minute." When there was no response, Mrs. Welsch rang the little silver dinner bell and in a moment Cook appeared.

Harriet stood petrified. *Soap!*

"Cook, will you tell Miss Golly to step in here a minute." Mrs. Welsch stood looking at Harriet as though she were a worm, as Cook departed. "Now Harriet, to your room. Miss Golly will be up shortly."

"But . . ."

"Your *room,*" said Mrs. Welsch firmly, pointing to the door.

Feeling rather like an idiot, Harriet left the dining room. She thought for half a second about waiting around and listening outside but decided it was too risky.

She went up to her room and waited. Ole Golly came in a few minutes later.

"Well, now, what is this about dancing school?" she asked amiably.

"I'm not going," Harriet said meekly. There was something that made her feel ridiculous when she shouted at Ole Golly. Maybe because she never got the feeling with Ole Golly that she did with her parents that they never heard anything.

"Why not?" Ole Golly asked sensibly.

Harriet thought a minute. The other reasons weren't really it. It was that the thought of being in dancing school somehow made her feel undignified. Finally she had it. "*Spies* don't go to dancing school," she said triumphantly.

"Oh, but they do," said Ole Golly.

"They do *not*," said Harriet rudely.

"Harriet"—Ole Golly took a deep breath and sat down—"have you ever thought about how spies are trained?"

"Yes. They learn languages and guerrilla fighting and everything about a country so if they're captured they'll know all the old football scores and things like that."

"That's *boy* spies, Harriet. You're not thinking."

Harriet hated more than anything else to be told by Ole Golly that she wasn't thinking. It was worse than any soap. "What do you mean?" she asked quietly.

"What about *girl* spies? What are they taught?"

"The same things."

"The same things and a few more. Remember that movie we saw about Mata Hari one night on television?"

"Yes . . ."

"Well, think about that. Where did she operate? Not in the woods guerrilla fighting, right? She went to parties, right? And remember that scene with the general or whatever he was—she was dancing, right? Now how are you going to be a spy if you don't know how to dance?"

There must be some answer to this, thought Harriet as she sat there silently. She couldn't think of a thing. She went "Hmmmph" rather loudly. Then she thought of something. "Well, do I have to wear those silly dresses? Couldn't I wear my spy clothes? They're better to learn to dance in anyway. In school we wear our gym suits to learn to dance."

"Of course not. Can you see Mata Hari in a gym suit? First of all, if you wear your spy clothes everyone knows you're a spy, so what have you gained? No, you have to look like everyone else, then you'll get by and no one will suspect you."

"That's true," said Harriet miserably. She couldn't see Mata Hari in a gym suit either.

"Now"—Ole Golly stood up—"you better march downstairs and tell them you changed your mind."

"What'll I say?" Harriet felt embarrassed.

"Just say you've changed your mind."

Harriet stood up resolutely and marched down the steps to the dining room. Her parents were having coffee. She stood in the doorway and said in a loud voice, "I've changed my mind!" They looked at her in a startled way. She turned and left the doorway abruptly. There was nothing further to be said. As she went back up the steps she heard them burst out laughing and then her father say, "Boy, that Miss Golly is magic, sheer magic. I wonder where we'd be without her?"

Harriet didn't know how to approach Janie about her defection, but she decided she must. At lunch Sport and Janie sat laughing over the new edition of *The Gregory News* which had just come out. *The Gregory News* was the school paper. There was a page reserved for every grade in the Middle School and every grade in the Upper School. The Lower School were such idiots they didn't need a page.

"Look at that. It's ridiculous." Janie was talking about Marion Hawthorne's editorial about candy wrappers everywhere.

"She just did that because Miss Whitehead talked about them on opening day," Harriet sneered.

"Well, what else? She hasn't got the sense to think of anything original." Sport bit into a hard-boiled egg. Sport made his own lunch and it was usually hard-boiled eggs.

"But it's so dumb and boring," Harriet said. "Listen to this: 'We must not drop our candy wrappers on the ground. They must be put into the wastebaskets provided for this purpose.' It's not even news; we hear it practically every day."

"I'll put *her* in a wastebasket," said Janie with satisfaction.

"My father says you have to catch the reader's attention right at first and then hold it," said Sport.

"Well, she just lost it," said Harriet.

"You oughta write it, Harriet, you're a writer," said Sport.

"I wouldn't do it now if they paid me. They can have their dumb paper." Harriet finished her sandwich with a frown.

"They should be blown up," said Janie.

They ate in silence for a moment.

"Janie . . ." Harriet hesitated so long that they both looked up at her. "I think they've got me," she said sadly.

"What? Was that sandwich poisoned?" Janie stood up. The egg fell right out of Sport's mouth.

"No," Harriet said quickly. Now it was anticlimactic. "I mean dancing school," Harriet said grimly.

Janie sat down and looked away as though Harriet had been impolite.

"Dancing school?" Sport squeaked, picking the egg out of his lap.

"Yes," said Janie grimly.

"Oh, boy, am I glad. My father never even *heard* of that." Sport grinned around his egg.

"Well," said Harriet sadly, "it looks like I'm gonna have to if I'm gonna be a spy."

"Who ever heard of a dancing spy?" Janie was so furious she wouldn't even look at Harriet.

"Mati Hari," Harriet said quietly; then when Janie didn't turn around she added very loudly, "I can't *help* it, Janie."

Janie turned and looked at her. "I know," she said sadly, "I'm going too."

It was all right then, and Harriet ate her other tomato sandwich happily.

ERNEST HEMINGWAY
Indian Camp

At the lake shore there was another rowboat drawn up. The two
Indians stood waiting.

Nick and his father got in the stern of the boat and the Indians
shoved it off and one of them got in to row. Uncle George sat in
the stern of the camp rowboat. The young Indian shoved the
camp boat off and got in to row Uncle George.

The two boats started off in the dark. Nick heard the oarlocks
of the other boat quite a way ahead of them in the mist. The
Indians rowed with quick choppy strokes. Nick lay back with his
father's arm around him. It was cold on the water. The Indian
who was rowing them was working very hard, but the other boat
moved further ahead in the mist all the time.

"Where are we going, Dad?" Nick asked.

"Over to the Indian camp. There is an Indian lady very sick."

"Oh," said Nick.

Across the bay they found the other boat beached. Uncle George was smoking a cigar in the dark. The young Indian pulled the boat way up on the beach. Uncle George gave both the Indians cigars.

They walked up from the beach through a meadow that was soaking wet with dew, following the young Indian who carried a lantern. Then they went into the woods and followed a trail that led to the logging road that ran back into the hills. It was much lighter on the logging road as the timber was cut away on both sides. The young Indian stopped and blew out his lantern and they all walked on along the road.

They came around a bend and a dog came out barking. Ahead were the lights of the shanties where the Indian barkpeelers lived. More dogs rushed out at them. The two Indians sent them back to the shanties. In the shanty nearest the road there was a light in the window. An old woman stood in the doorway holding a lamp.

Inside on a wooden bunk lay a young Indian woman. She had been trying to have her baby for two days. All the old women in the camp had been helping her. The men had moved off up the road to sit in the dark and smoke out of range of the noise she made. She screamed just as Nick and the two Indians followed his father and Uncle George into the shanty. She lay in the lower bunk, very big under a quilt. Her head was turned to one side. In the upper bunk was her husband. He had cut his foot very badly with an ax three days before. He was smoking a pipe. The room smelled very bad.

Nick's father ordered some water to be put on the stove, and while it was heating he spoke to Nick.

"This lady is going to have a baby, Nick," he said.

"I know," said Nick.

"You don't know," said his father. "Listen to me. What she is going through is called being in labor. The baby wants to be born and she wants it to be born. All her muscles are trying to get the baby born. That is what is happening when she screams."

"I see," Nick said.

Just then the woman cried out.

"Oh, Daddy, can't you give her something to make her stop screaming?" asked Nick.

"No. I haven't any anæsthetic," his father said. "But her screams are not important. I don't hear them because they are not important."

The husband in the upper bunk rolled over against the wall.

The woman in the kitchen motioned to the doctor that the water was hot. Nick's father went into the kitchen and poured about half of the water out of the big kettle into a basin. Into the water left in the kettle he put several things he unwrapped from a handkerchief.

"Those must boil," he said, and began to scrub his hands in the basin of hot water with a cake of soap he had brought from the camp. Nick watched his father's hands scrubbing each other with the soap. While his father washed his hands very carefully and thoroughly, he talked.

"You see, Nick, babies are supposed to be born head first but sometimes they're not. When they're not they make a lot of trouble for everybody. Maybe I'll have to operate on this lady. We'll know in a little while."

When he was satisfied with his hands he went in and went to work.

"Pull back that quilt, will you, George?" he said. "I'd rather not touch it."

Later when he started to operate Uncle George and three Indian men held the woman still. She bit Uncle George on the arm and Uncle George said, "Damn!" and the young Indian who had rowed Uncle George over laughed at him. Nick held the basin for his father. It all took a long time.

His father picked the baby up and slapped it to make it breathe and handed it to the old woman.

"See, it's a boy, Nick," he said. "How do you like being an interne?"

Nick said, "All right." He was looking away so as not to see what his father was doing.

"There. That gets it," said his father and put something into the basin.

Nick didn't look at it.

"Now," his father said, "there's some stitches to put in. You can watch this or not, Nick, just as you like. I'm going to sew up the incision I made."

Nick did not watch. His curiosity had been gone for a long time.

His father finished and stood up. Uncle George and the three Indian men stood up. Nick put the basin out in the kitchen.

Uncle George looked at his arm. The young Indian smiled reminiscently.

"I'll put some peroxide on that, George," the doctor said.

He bent over the Indian woman. She was quiet now and her eyes were closed. She looked very pale. She did not know what had become of the baby or anything.

"I'll be back in the morning," the doctor said, standing up. "The nurse should be here from St. Ignace by noon and she'll bring everything we need."

He was feeling exalted and talkative as football players are in the dressing room after a game.

"That's one for the medical journal, George," he said. "Doing a Cæsarian with a jack-knife and sewing it up with nine-foot, tapered gut leaders."

Uncle George was standing against the wall, looking at his arm.

"Oh, you're a great man, all right," he said.

"Ought to have a look at the proud father. They're usually the worst sufferers in these little affairs," the doctor said. "I must say he took it all pretty quietly."

He pulled back the blanket from the Indian's head. His hand came away wet. He mounted on the edge of the lower bunk with the lamp in one hand and looked in. The Indian lay with his face toward the wall. His throat had been cut from ear to ear. The blood had flowed down into a pool where his body sagged the bunk. His head rested on his left arm. The open razor lay, edge up, in the blankets.

"Take Nick out of the shanty, George," the doctor said.

There was no need of that. Nick, standing in the door of the kitchen, had a good view of the upper bunk when his father, the lamp in one hand, tipped the Indian's head back.

It was just beginning to be daylight when they walked along the logging road back toward the lake.

"I'm terribly sorry I brought you along, Nickie," said his father, all his post-operative exhilaration gone. "It was an awful mess to put you through."

"Do ladies always have such a hard time having babies?" Nick asked.

"No, that was very, very exceptional."

"Why did he kill himself, Daddy?"

"I don't know, Nick. He couldn't stand things, I guess."

"Do many men kill themselves, Daddy?"

"Not very many, Nick."

"Do many women?"

"Hardly ever."

"Don't they ever?"

"Oh, yes. They do sometimes."

"Daddy?"

"Yes."

"Where did Uncle George go?"

"He'll turn up all right."

"Is dying hard, Daddy?"

"No, I think it's pretty easy, Nick. It all depends."

They were seated in the boat, Nick in the stern, his father rowing. The sun was coming up over the hills. A bass jumped, making a circle in the water. Nick trailed his hand in the water. It felt warm in the sharp chill of the morning.

In the early morning on the lake sitting in the stern of the boat with his father rowing, he felt quite sure that he would never die.

SHIRLEY JACKSON

Charles

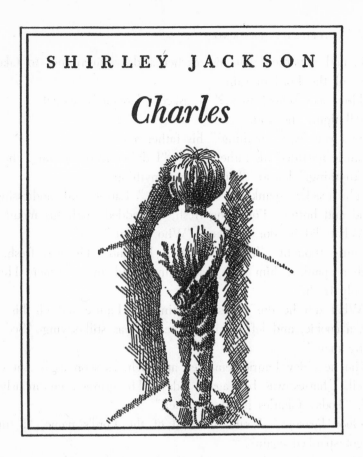

The day my son Laurie started kindergarten he renounced corduroy overalls with bibs and began wearing blue jeans with a belt; I watched him go off the first morning with the older girl next door, seeing clearly that an era of my life was ended, my sweet-voiced nursery-school tot replaced by a long-trousered, swaggering character who forgot to stop at the corner and wave good-bye to me.

He came home the same way, the front door slamming open, his cap on the floor, and the voice suddenly become raucous shouting, "Isn't anybody *here?*"

At lunch he spoke insolently to his father, spilled his baby sister's milk, and remarked that his teacher said we were not to take the name of the Lord in vain.

"How *was* school today?" I asked, elaborately casual.

"All right," he said.

"Did you learn anything?" his father asked.

Laurie regarded his father coldly. "I didn't learn nothing," he said.

"Anything," I said. "Didn't learn anything."

"The teacher spanked a boy, though," Laurie said, addressing his bread and butter. "For being fresh," he added, with his mouth full.

"What did he do?" I asked. "Who was it?"

Laurie thought. "It was Charles," he said. "He was fresh. The teacher spanked him and made him stand in a corner. He was awfully fresh."

"What did he do?" I asked again, but Laurie slid off his chair, took a cookie, and left, while his father was still saying, "See here, young man."

The next day Laurie remarked at lunch, as soon as he sat down, "Well, Charles was bad again today." He grinned enormously and said, "Today Charles hit the teacher."

"Good heavens," I said, mindful of the Lord's name, "I suppose he got spanked again?"

"He sure did," Laurie said. "Look up," he said to his father.

"What?" his father said, looking up.

"Look down," Laurie said. "Look at my thumb. Gee, you're dumb." He began to laugh insanely.

"Why did Charles hit the teacher?" I asked quickly.

"Because she tried to make him color with red crayons," Laurie said. "Charles wanted to color with green crayons so he hit the teacher and she spanked him and said nobody play with Charles but everybody did."

The third day—it was Wednesday of the first week—Charles bounced a see-saw on to the head of a little girl and made her bleed, and the teacher made him stay inside all during recess. Thursday Charles had to stand in a corner during story-time because he kept pounding his feet on the floor. Friday Charles was deprived of blackboard privileges because he threw chalk.

On Saturday I remarked to my husband, "Do you think kindergarten is too unsettling for Laurie? All this toughness, and bad grammar, and this Charles boy sounds like such a bad influence."

"It'll be all right," my husband said reassuringly. "Bound to be people like Charles in the world. Might as well meet them now as later."

On Monday Laurie came home late, full of news. "Charles," he shouted as he came up the hill; I was waiting anxiously on the front steps. "Charles," Laurie yelled all the way up the hill, "Charles was bad again."

"Come right in," I said, as soon as he came close enough. "Lunch is waiting."

"You know what Charles did?" he demanded, following me through the door. "Charles yelled so in school they sent a boy in from first grade to tell the teacher she had to make Charles keep quiet, and so Charles had to stay after school. And so all the children stayed to watch him."

"What did he do?" I asked.

"He just sat there," Laurie said, climbing into his chair at the table. "Hi, Pop, y'old dust mop."

"Charles had to stay after school today," I told my husband. "Everyone stayed with him."

"What does this Charles look like?" my husband asked Laurie. "What's his other name?"

"He's bigger than me," Laurie said. "And he doesn't have any rubbers and he doesn't ever wear a jacket."

Monday night was the first Parent-Teachers meeting, and only the fact that the baby had a cold kept me from going; I wanted passionately to meet Charles's mother. On Tuesday Laurie remarked suddenly, "Our teacher had a friend come to see her in school today."

"Charles's mother?" my husband and I asked simultaneously.

"Naaah," Laurie said scornfully. "It was a man who came and made us do exercises, we had to touch our toes. Look." He climbed down from his chair and squatted down and touched his toes. "Like this," he said. He got solemnly back into his chair and said, picking up his fork, "Charles didn't even *do* exercises."

"That's fine," I said heartily. "Didn't Charles want to do exercises?"

"Naaah," Laurie said. "Charles was so fresh to the teacher's friend he wasn't *let* do exercises."

"Fresh again?" I said.

"He kicked the teacher's friend," Laurie said. "The teacher's friend told Charles to touch his toes like I just did and Charles kicked him."

"What are they going to do about Charles, do you suppose?" Laurie's father asked him.

Laurie shrugged elaborately. "Throw him out of school, I guess," he said.

Wednesday and Thursday were routine; Charles yelled during story hour and hit a boy in the stomach and made him cry. On Friday Charles stayed after school again and so did all the other children.

With the third week of kindergarten Charles was an institution in our family; the baby was being a Charles when she cried all afternoon; Laurie did a Charles when he filled his wagon full of mud and pulled it through the kitchen; even my husband, when he caught his elbow in the telephone cord and pulled telephone, ashtray, and a bowl of flowers off the table, said, after the first minute, "Looks like Charles."

During the third and fourth weeks it looked like a reformation in Charles; Laurie reported grimly at lunch on Thursday of the third week, "Charles was so good today the teacher gave him an apple."

"What?" I said, and my husband added warily, "You mean Charles?"

"Charles," Laurie said. "He gave the crayons around and he picked up the books afterward and the teacher said he was her helper."

"What happened?" I asked incredulously.

"He was her helper, that's all," Laurie said, and shrugged.

"Can this be true, about Charles?" I asked my husband that night. "Can something like this happen?"

"Wait and see," my husband said cynically. "When you've got a Charles to deal with, this may mean he's only plotting."

He seemed to be wrong. For over a week Charles was the teacher's helper; each day he handed things out and he picked things up; no one had to stay after school.

"The P.T.A. meeting's next week again," I told my husband one evening. "I'm going to find Charles's mother there."

"Ask her what happened to Charles," my husband said. "I'd like to know."

"I'd like to know myself," I said.

On Friday of that week things were back to normal. "You know what Charles did today?" Laurie demanded at the lunch table, in a voice slightly awed. "He told a little girl to say a word and she said it and the teacher washed her mouth out with soap and Charles laughed."

"What word?" his father asked unwisely, and Laurie said, "I'll have to whisper it to you, it's so bad." He got down off his chair and went around to his father. His father bent his head down and Laurie whispered joyfully. His father's eyes widened.

"Did Charles tell the little girl to say *that?*" he asked respectfully.

"She said it *twice,*" Laurie said. "Charles told her to say it *twice.*"

"What happened to Charles?" my husband asked.

"Nothing," Laurie said. "He was passing out the crayons."

Monday morning Charles abandoned the little girl and said the evil word himself three or four times, getting his mouth washed out with soap each time. He also threw chalk.

My husband came to the door with me that evening as I set out for the P.T.A. meeting. "Invite her over for a cup of tea after the meeting," he said. "I want to get a look at her."

"If only she's there," I said prayerfully.

"She'll be there," my husband said. "I don't see how they could hold a P.T.A. meeting without Charles's mother."

At the meeting I sat restlessly, scanning each comfortable matronly face, trying to determine which one hid the secret of Charles. None of them looked to me haggard enough. No one stood up in the meeting and apologized for the way her son had been acting. No one mentioned Charles.

After the meeting I identified and sought out Laurie's kindergarten teacher. She had a plate with a cup of tea and a piece of chocolate cake; I had a plate with a cup of tea and a piece of marshmallow cake. We maneuvered up to one another cautiously, and smiled.

"I've been so anxious to meet you," I said. "I'm Laurie's mother."

"We're all so interested in Laurie," she said.

"Well, he certainly likes kindergarten," I said. "He talks about it all the time."

"We had a little trouble adjusting, the first week or so," she said primly, "but now he's a fine little helper. With occasional lapses, of course."

"Laurie usually adjusts very quickly," I said. "I suppose this time it's Charles's influence."

"Charles?"

"Yes," I said, laughing, "you must have your hands full in that kindergarten, with Charles."

"Charles?" she said. "We don't have any Charles in the kindergarten."

from Dead Man in the Silver Market

C. AUBREY MENEN

My Grandmother and the Dirty English

[*Young Aubrey Menen's father was Indian, his mother Irish, but until he met his Indian grandmother his life had been shaped mainly by English schools. Only in Malabar did he learn that European ways were neither universally imitated nor even admired.*]

My grandmother, like Michelangelo, had *terribilita*. She had a driving will; she would not be balked and whatever she did was designed to strike the spectator with awe. She was also something of a stick. She rarely spoke to anyone who was not of her own social station and she received them formally: that is to say, with her breasts completely bare. Even in her time women were growing lax about this custom in Malabar. But my grandmother insisted on it. She thought that married women who wore blouses and pretty *saris* were Jezebels; in her view, a wife who dressed herself above her waist could only be aiming at adultery.

When I was twelve she demanded that I be brought and shown to her. I was incontinently taken half across the earth, from London to South beyond the town of Calicut. My mother came with me.

The last part of the journey was made by dugout canoe (there being no railways and no good roads near our family estate) and in this we were poled on a moonlit night up the Ponnani River. The river was lined with palm trees and crocodiles.

My mother taking fright at these beasts, I sang to keep them away from the boat. I sang a song I had been taught at school called "Drake's Drum." This had been written in the reign of Queen Victoria and told how, if the Spaniards should embark on the unlikely project of attacking nineteenth century England, Drake would come back to life and drum them up the Channel "as he drummed them long ago." I had been taught many songs of similar sentiments but this was the noisiest. I sang it with a will because my young heart (especially in such very foreign parts) glowed with the sentiment. The crocodiles yawned and, like the Spaniards in the Victorian age, showed no signs of attacking.

This singing marked a stage in my life. Shortly afterwards I lost my innocence. My grandmother took me in hand and I never thought the English were perfect again.

When our boat journey was done, servants with flaming torches led us along narrow paths between tall trees, and finally conducted us to a house. This house was large and smelt of paint. It was (my father said) not my ancestral roof.

When my grandmother had heard that my mother intended to make the visit as well as myself, she had given orders for a special house to be put in repair for my mother's accommodation. It was on the furthest confines of the family property. This was her solution of a difficult problem. My mother was ritually unclean, and therefore whenever she entered my family house, she would defile it. The house would have to be purified and so would every caste Hindu in it. It followed logically that if my mother stayed in the house, it would be permanently in a state of defilement and permanently in a state of being ritually cleaned. Since this ceremony involved drums and conch shells, my mother's visit foreshadowed a prolonged uproar. All this was avoided by my grandmother's decision to put her up in a separate building.

I cannot say that my grandmother was ever rude to my mother. She never referred to her by name but always as "the Englishwoman." This was not necessarily an insulting expression, but my mother had Irish blood and what with this, and the house, and some other pin-pricks, her temper rose. She ordered a quantity of medical stores from Calicut, and when they arrived she set up a free dispensary on the verandah, to which the peasants flocked. It was an admirably devised answer. My grandmother had shut the door in my mother's face: she now had the galling experience of seeing my mother industriously cleaning up the doorstep. As my mother well knew, each drop of iodine that she dispensed stung not only the grateful patient, but also my grandmother's conscience.

My grandmother brooded on this for a while and then sent my mother a bag of golden sovereigns. My mother, taking this to be a bribe at the worst, or at the best, a tip, sent it back. But she was wrong. It was a peace offering. It was sent again next day, accompanied by the family goldsmith who sat, slept and ate on the verandah for a week while he made the sovereigns (with tweezers and a charcoal fire) into a great gold collar which my mother still, on occasions, wears.

When, fourteen years before my trip, my father had written from England to say that he was getting married to a white woman, my grandmother had been far from giving the union her blessing. But it would be wrong to say that she had objected to it. If an American boy of twenty-two wrote home from foreign parts to say that he had taken to cannibalism, his parents would not object. They would be so revolted that a mere objection would never meet the case. So with my grandmother.

She had never met the English but she knew all about them. She knew they were tall, fair, given to strong drink, good soldiers and that they had conquered her native country. She also knew that they were incurably dirty in their personal habits. She respected them but wished they would keep their distance. It was very much the way that a Roman matron looked upon the Goths.

My eldest uncle had been to England for two years and he spoke up for the English. He said that while the Hindus were undoubtedly the most civilised race on earth and had been civilised a thousand years before the English, nevertheless, the English were now the masters of the Hindus. My grandmother's reply to this was that the English were masters of the Hindus only because "nobody would listen to *us*." By this she meant that our family along with others of the same caste had strongly objected to Vasco da Gama being allowed to land in Calicut. They had, in fact, done their best to get him and his sailors massacred. But the country was not behind them and he escaped. Everything, my grandmother argued (and not without some reason), had started with that.

But her chief complaint was that the English were so dirty, and this was rather a poser for my uncle. When my grandmother asked if, like decent people, they took a minimum of two baths a day, my uncle, who could not lie to his mother without committing a disgraceful sin, said that, well, no: but a few took one bath and the habit was spreading. He could go no further than that. But he added that my grandmother should remember that England had a cold climate. This she loyally did, and when she discussed the matter with me, she was able to treat the matter lightly, as one does the disgusting but rational liking of the Eskimos for eating blubber.

As for the question of eating, she did not have the expected prejudices. She did not think it strange that the English ate ham and beef. The outcaste hill-tribes (called *Todas*) who made the family straw mats and cleaned the latrines, ate anything. She was not disturbed either, about their religion, because my uncle assured her that they had practically none. Their manners, however, she abominated. If she did not mind them eating meat, she considered their way of eating it beyond the pale of decent society. In my family home, each person eats his meal separately, preferably in a secluded corner. The thought that English people could sit opposite each other and watch each other thrust food into their mouths, masticate, and swallow it, made her wonder if there was anything that human beings would not do, when left to their own devices.

She was not surprised to hear, after this, that in England a woman could have more than one husband, particularly (and this was the crowning paradox) if she had been a widow. To the day of her death my grandmother could never understand how people could call themselves civilised and yet allow widows to marry again. For her the very foundation-stone of society was that a child should have one father, and obey him. Nobody ever dared her wrath sufficiently to explain the position of women in English society. She was intensely proud of the standards of her house and she permitted no lewd talk to defile them—certainly never in her presence.

With this background, then, my grandmother's peace offering of a bag of sovereigns was a considerable victory for my mother, particularly since the gold collar which the goldsmith had been told to make from them was the characteristic jewellery of a Malabar bride.

The way was now open for me. I could go and see her. I had waited about three weeks.

I had many meetings with her. I used to visit her in considerable state. The distance from our home—the isolation wing, so to speak—to the main family mansion was too far for walking in the Malabar sun. I used to go by palanquin. It was a hammock of red cloth with rather worn embroidery of gold thread, and it was swung on a black pole which had silver ornaments at either end. Four virtually naked men, two in front and two behind, carried the palanquin at a swift trot. There was considerable art in this. If the four men trotted just as they pleased, the hammock would swing in a growing arc until it tipped the passenger out on to the road. To prevent this, the men trotted in a complicated system that I never really understood: watching them and trying to trace it out was as difficult as trying to determine the order in which a horse puts its hoofs down. They kept their rhythm by chanting. I used to fall asleep on the way, listening to them. It must have presented an interesting spectacle—a red palanquin, the sweating men, and a sleeping schoolboy wearing an English blazer with its pocket sewn with a badge gained by infantile prowess at some sport that I do not now remember.

The family house was vast and cool and in my view, unfurnished. But to my grandmother's eye it was very elegant. There was nothing but the floor to sit on. She disliked chairs and thought them vulgar. What use were they, except for ostentation? She approved of beds but insisted that the mattress be made of taut string—nothing else was considered clean. She also had a taste for handsome brass-bound boxes. So beds, boxes, and oil-lamps were the sole furniture of the innumerable rooms of the house. There were no tables and no table-cloths. In my grandmother's house, if anybody dared eat in any fashion but off a fresh plantain-leaf, his next meal would have been served in the kitchen, where the servants were allowed to eat without ceremony.

My grandmother usually received me sitting by her favourite box in her boudoir. She made an unforgettable picture. She had great black eyes, a shock of white hair and lips as lush and curved as a girl of eighteen. The skin of her bosom, bare as I have said, was quite smooth. I used to sit on the floor in front of her in my school blazer and since my father had never taught me Malayalam (wishing me to be brought up like any other English schoolboy), we talked through one of my uncles.

The things my grandmother told me were a puzzle at the time. But I have come to understand them better. Much as she looked down on the English, I think that had she met some of them, had she overcome her well-bred fastidiousness and actually mixed with them, she would have found she and they had much in common. Her riding passion, like theirs, was racial pride. She believed —and this made her character—that she belonged to the cleverest family of the cleverest people on earth. According to Lord Russell, this was also the firm faith of Mrs. Beatrice Webb, who used to repeat it to herself in moments when, otherwise, she might have felt inferior, such as when she made her entry into a distinguished party. Though my grandmother never went to parties I'm sure that she, too, repeated the formula as a stiffener of her already formidable morale.

She felt that she was born of a superior race and she had all the marks of it. For instance, she deplored the plumbing of every other nation but her own. She would often say to me, through my uncle:

"Never take a bath in one of those contraptions in which you sit in dirty water like a buffalo. Always bathe in running water.

If you have servants to pour it over you, that's best. But otherwise you must stand under a tap or pour the water over yourself. A really nice person does not even glance at his own bath water much less sit in it." Here she would laugh to herself, while my uncle translated; not an unkind laugh, but a pitying one, as she thought of the backwardness of the white man's bathroom.

Another mark—and I have met it in many nations—was that she believed that English sexual morals permitted and encouraged all sorts of abominations from which a civilised person shrank. She spoke to me with great freedom on this point: I was after all at puberty. I could not always follow the drift of her remarks, but I did gather that she felt strongly on one point. Why, if the English wanted their offspring to grow up decently and not lewdly, did they omit to marry them off when they were children? There was something sinister in the neglect. A child should grow up knowing quite well that all that side of his life was settled according to the best available advice and in the best possible manner for his welfare. When he was eighteen or twenty the marriage would be consummated. Till then, he did not have to worry his head about women—or if he did worry, he knew he was morally slipping.

History, I have discovered, is on my grandmother's side. The great majority of civilised peoples have always agreed with her. Romance and love and such things were, in antiquity, things for slaves. Respectable families arranged their marriages as my grandmother arranged those of her offspring. To take a single example, my grandmother and Brutus would fully have understood each other. She felt hurt that she had not been consulted over my father's marriage: while among the many sidelights that we have on that honourable man who assassinated Julius Caesar in a letter in which he complains at being left out of the bargaining that went on during the betrothal of "my dear little Attica," who was nine years old.

But a grandson was a grandson, even though her permission had not been sought to bring him into the world, and she set about being a mother as well as a grandmother to me. She knew that soon I would go back among the heathen to finish my education and she wanted me to go back knowing who and what I was. On one of my visits she gave me a small book in which was written all my duties and privileges as a member of my class. The book was written on dried palm-leaves, strung together with a cord between two covers of wood. It began with a prayer to God thanking Him for creating us—our caste, that is—so much superior in every respect to the great majority of other human beings.

My grandmother explained what followed several times and with much emphasis, for she wanted to imprint it on my memory. Our family belongs to the caste—or class—called Nayars. The Nayars of Malabar are as old as Indian history and therefore, it can be assumed, a good deal older. My grandmother told me that traditionally we had two obligations to society. We were warriors when there was fighting to do: and when there was not, we had the duty, on certain holy days, of carrying flowers to the temple.

I remember that I thought this very romantic at the time and could not understand why my grandmother took it so prosaically: to me, warriors, flowers and temples conjured up a picture of some Oriental Round Table. But my grandmother was right. Our caste is a commonplace: it exists everywhere. In England it is scattered all over the countryside. The men are what is called "Army" and the women take not only flowers, but fruit to the temple on the occasion of the Harvest Festival. It is curious, and inexplicable, that the combination of these two activities, whether in the Shires or in the coconut groves of Malabar, produces the most ferocious snobs.

My grandmother explained to me that as a Nayar, I should always be very careful to keep my dignity when dealing with Brahmins: Brahmins are priests. The priests who have the cure of souls of my family are treated as domestic chaplains. Since their temples are on our property my grandmother had several "living," so to speak at her disposal, this side of religious affairs always being left in the hands of the older women. Priests were therefore expected to make themselves agreeable, in return for which they were regularly fed. They were expected to mind their own business, which was to perform the weekly ceremonies and to direct their preaching at the lower orders, particularly the servants. The Anglican Settlement in England was much more elaborate but reduced to what it meant to the average priest-in-the-vestry, it came much to the same thing, and provides one more reason why I wish my grandmother had visited the country of my birth.

But my grandmother was quite ignorant of these striking resemblances and begged me when moving among the English to remember myself. "They will look up to you, as a Nayar, to set an example," she used to say. "They know that you have two thousand years of advantage over them and they will be willing to learn. Show them this book. They will be very interested. It was written when they still went about naked. And I will give you some trinkets which you can hand out as gifts: some amulets which we use and some things made of sandalwood, which is very rare in England so I am told, and much sought after. They will help you make friends. But remember, it is your *example* which will count more than anything."

She gave me all the things she promised and as she had foretold, they were much admired. Some of them, I believe, are still in my school museum. She also gave me her blessing, which was what I had been brought across the world to get.

I thought over her advice but I was in some confusion. My headmaster, wishing me good by and good-luck when I had set out on my trip had said much the same thing. "Let them see," he had said, "by your example that you have been trained in an *English* school. Wherever you go, it is for *you* to set the tone." He did not give me any sandalwood, but I was very impressed. I was also very greatly impressed with what my grandmother had said.

In my dilemma I remembered that I had another grandmother. She had been born, as I have said, in Killarney, but had come to England to live—briefly enough, for she had died before I was born. I asked my mother about her. She told me many things but one stood out in my mind above all others.

"My mother," she said, "was never really happy among the English. She longed to go back to Killarney. Sometimes when things had become unbearably tiresome, she would heave a long, deep sigh, shake her head and gently close her eyes."

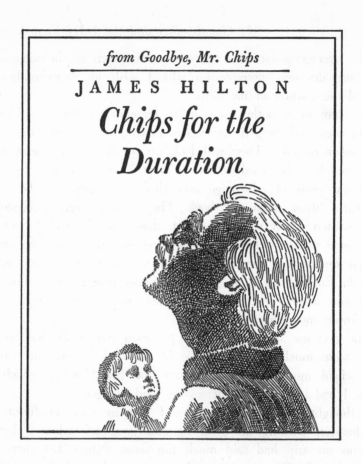

from *Goodbye, Mr. Chips*

JAMES HILTON

Chips for the Duration

[*On the eve of the First World War in England, when Mr. Chipping retired to live across the road from the school where he had taught all his life, he had little idea that a visit from Mr. Chatteris, the Headmaster, would show him that his days of teaching at Brookfield were far from over.*]

The War years.

The first shock, and then the first optimism. The Battle of the Marne, the Russian steam-roller, Kitchener.

"Do you think it will last long, sir?"

Chips, questioned as he watched the first trial game of the season, gave quite a cheery answer. He was, like thousands of others, hopelessly wrong; but, unlike thousands of others, he did not afterward conceal the fact. "We ought to have—um—finished it—um—by

Christmas. The Germans are already beaten. But why? Are you thinking of—um—joining up, Forrester?"

Joke—because Forrester was the smallest new boy Brookfield had ever had—about four feet high above his muddy football boots. (But not so much a joke, when you came to think of it afterward; for he was killed in 1918—shot down in flames over Cambrai.) But one didn't guess what lay ahead. It seemed tragically sensational when the first Old Brookfeldian was killed in action—in September. Chips thought, when that news came: A hundred years ago boys from the school were fighting *against* the French. Strange, in a way, that the sacrifices of one generation should so cancel out those of another. He tried to express this to Blades, the Head of School House; but Blades, eighteen years old and already in training for a cadetship, only laughed. What had all that history stuff to do with it, anyhow? Just old Chips with one of his queer ideas, that's all.

1915. Armies clenched in deadlock from the sea to Switzerland. The Dardanelles. Gallipoli. Military camps springing up quite near Brookfield; soldiers using the playing fields for sports and training; swift developments of Brookfield O.T.C. Most of the younger masters gone or in uniform. Every Sunday night, in the Chapel after evening service, Chatteris read out the names of old boys killed, together with short biographies. Very moving; but Chips, in the back pew under the gallery, thought: They are only names to him; he doesn't see their faces as I do. . . .

1916. . . . The Somme Battle. Twenty-three names read out one Sunday evening.

Toward the close of that catastrophic July, Chatteris talked to Chips one afternoon at Mrs. Wickett's. He was overworked and overworried and looked very ill. "To tell you the truth, Chipping, I'm not having too easy a time here. I'm thirty-nine, you know, and unmarried, and lots of people seem to think they know what I ought to do. Also, I happen to be diabetic, and couldn't pass the blindest M.O., but I don't see why I should pin a medical certificate on my front door."

Chips hadn't known anything about this; it was a shock to him, for he liked Chatteris.

The latter continued: "You see how it is. Ralston filled the place up with young men—all very good, of course—but now most of them have joined up and the substitutes are pretty dreadful, on the whole. They poured ink down a man's neck in prep one night last week—silly fool—got hysterical. I have to take classes myself, take prep for fools like that, work till midnight every night, and get cold-shouldered as a slacker on top of everything. I can't stand it much longer. If things don't improve next term I shall have a breakdown."

"I do sympathize with you," Chips said.

"I hoped you would. And that brings me to what I came here to ask you. Briefly, my suggestion is that—if you felt equal to it and would care to—how about coming back here for a while? You look pretty fit, and, of course, you know all the ropes. I don't mean a lot of hard work for you—you needn't take anything strenuously—just a few odd jobs here and there, as you choose. What I'd like you for more than anything else is not for the actual work you'd do—though that, naturally, would be very valuable—but for your help in other ways—in just *belonging* here. There's nobody ever been more popular than you were, and are still—you'd help to hold things together if there were any danger of them flying to bits. And perhaps there *is* that danger. . . ."

Chips answered, breathlessly and with a holy joy in his heart: "I'll come. . . ."

He still kept on his rooms with Mrs. Wickett; indeed, he still lived there; but every morning, about half-past ten, he put on his coat and muffler and crossed the road to the School. He felt very fit, and the actual work was not taxing. Just a few forms in Latin and Roman History—the old lessons—even the old pronunciation. The same joke about the Lex Canuleia—there was a new generation that had not heard it, and he was absurdly gratified by the success it achieved. He felt a little like a music-hall favorite returning to the boards after a positively last appearance.

They all said how marvelous it was that he knew every boy's name and face so quickly. They did not guess how closely he had kept in touch from across the road.

He was a grand success altogether. In some strange way he did, and they all knew and felt it, help things. For the first time in his life he felt *necessary*—and necessary to something that was nearest his heart. There is no sublimer feeling in the world, and it was his at last.

He made new jokes, too—about the O.T.C. and the food-rationing system and the anti-air-raid blinds that had to be fitted on all the windows. There was a mysterious kind of rissole that began to appear on the School menu on Mondays, and Chips called it *abhorrendum*—"meat to be abhorred." The story went round—heard Chips's latest?

Chatteris fell ill during the winter of '17, and again, for the second time in his life, Chips became Acting Head of Brookfield. Then in April Chatteris died, and the Governors asked Chips if he would carry on "for the duration." He said he would, if they would refrain from appointing him officially. From that last honor, within his reach at last, he shrank instinctively, feeling himself in so many ways unequal to it. He said to Rivers: "You see, I'm not a young man and I don't want people to—um—expect a lot from me. I'm like all these new colonels and majors you see everywhere—just a war-time fluke. A ranker—that's all I am really."

1917. 1918. Chips lived through it all. He sat in the headmaster's study every morning, handling problems, dealing with plaints and requests. Out of vast experience had emerged a kindly, gentle confidence in himself. To keep a sense of proportion, that was the main thing. So much of the world was losing it; as well keep it where it had, or ought to have, a congenial home.

On Sundays in Chapel it was he who now read out the tragic list, and sometimes it was seen and heard that he was in tears over it. Well, why not, the School said; he was an old man; they might have despised anyone else for the weakness.

One day he got a letter from Switzerland, from friends there; it was heavily censored, but conveyed some news. On the following Sunday, after the names and biographies of old boys, he paused a moment and then added:—

"Those few of you who were here before the War will remember Max Staefel, the German master. He was in Germany, visiting his home, when war broke out. He was popular while he was here, and made many friends. Those who knew him will be sorry to hear that he was killed last week, on the Western Front."

He was a little pale when he sat down afterward, aware that

he had done something unusual. He had consulted nobody about it, anyhow; no one else could be blamed. Later, outside the Chapel, he heard an argument:—

"On the Western Front, Chips said. Does that mean he was fighting for the Germans?"

"I suppose it does."

"Seems funny, then, to read his name out with all the others. After all, he was an *enemy*."

"Oh, just one of Chips's ideas, I expect. The old boy still has 'em."

Chips, in his room again, was not displeased by the comment. Yes, he still had 'em—those ideas of dignity and generosity that were becoming increasingly rare in a frantic world. And he thought: Brookfield will take them, too, from me; but it wouldn't from anyone else.

Once, asked for his opinion of bayonet practice being carried on near the cricket pavilion, he answered, with that lazy, slightly asthmatic intonation that had been so often and so extravagantly imitated: "It seems—to me—umph—a very vulgar way of killing people." The yarn was passed on and joyously appreciated—how Chips had told some big brass hat from the War Office that bayonet fighting was vulgar. Just like Chips. And they found an adjective for him— an adjective just beginning to be used: he was pre-War.

And once, on a night of full moonlight, the air-raid warning was given while Chips was taking his lower fourth in Latin. The guns began almost instantly, and, as there was plenty of shrapnel falling about outside, it seemed to Chips that they might just as well stay where they were, on the ground floor of School House. It was pretty solidly built and made as good a dugout as Brookfield could offer; and as for a direct hit, well, they could not expect to survive that, wherever they were.

So he went on with his Latin, speaking a little louder amid the reverberating crashes of the guns and the shrill whine of anti-aircraft shells. Some of the boys were nervous; few were able to be attentive. He said, gently: "It may possibly seem to you, Robertson—at this particular moment in the world's history—umph—that the affairs of Caesar in Gaul some two thousand years ago—are—umph—of somewhat secondary importance—and that—umph—the irregular conjugation of the verb *tollo* is—umph—even less important still. But believe me—umph—my dear Robertson—that is not really the case." Just then there came a particularly loud explosion—quite near. "You cannot—umph—judge the importance of things—umph—by the noise they make. Oh dear me, no." A little chuckle. "And these things—umph—that have mattered—for thousands of years—are not going to be—snuffed out—because some stink merchant—in his laboratory—invents a new kind of mischief." Titters of nervous laughter; for Buffles, the pale, lean, and medically unfit science master, was nicknamed the Stink Merchant. Another explosion—nearer still. "Let us —um—resume our work. If it is fate that we are soon to be—umph—interrupted, let us be found employing ourselves in something—umph—really appropriate. Is there anyone who will volunteer to construe?"

Maynard, chubby, dauntless, clever, and impudent, said: "I will, sir."

"Very good. Turn to page forty and begin at the bottom line."

The explosions still continued deafeningly; the whole building shook as if it were being lifted off its foundations. Maynard found the page, which was some way ahead, and began, shrilly:—

"*Genus hoc erat pugnae*—this was the kind of fight—*quo se Germani exercuerant*—in which the Germans busied themselves. Oh, sir, that's good—that's really very funny indeed, sir—one of your very best—"

Laughing began, and Chips added: "Well—umph—you can see—now—that these dead languages—umph—can come to life again—sometimes—eh? Eh?"

Afterward they learned that five bombs had fallen in and around Brookfield, the nearest of them just outside the School grounds. Nine persons had been killed.

The story was told, retold, embellished. "The dear old boy never turned a hair. Even found some old tag to illustrate what was going on. Something in Caesar about the way the Germans fought. You wouldn't think there were things like that in Caesar, would you? And the way Chips laughed . . . you know the way he *does* laugh . . . the tears all running down his face . . . never seen him laugh so much. . . ."

He was a legend.

With his old and tattered gown, his walk that was just beginning to break into a stumble, his mild eyes peering over the steel-rimmed spectacles, and his quaintly humorous sayings, Brookfield would not have had an atom of him different.

November 11, 1918.

News came through in the morning; a whole holiday was decreed for the School, and the kitchen staff were implored to provide as cheerful a spread as war-time rationing permitted. There was much cheering and singing, and a bread fight across the Dining Hall. When Chips entered in the midst of the uproar there was an instant hush, and then wave upon wave of cheering; everyone gazed on him with eager, shining eyes, as on a symbol of victory. He walked to the dais, seeming as if he wished to speak; they made silence for him, but he shook his head after a moment, smiled, and walked away again.

It had been a damp, foggy day, and the walk across the quadrangle to the Dining Hall had given him a chill. The next day he was in bed with bronchitis, and stayed there till after Christmas. But already, on that night of November 11, after his visit to the Dining Hall, he had sent in his resignation to the Board of Governors.

When school reassembled after the holidays he was back at Mrs. Wickett's. At his own request there were no more farewells or presentations, nothing but a handshake with his successor and the word "acting" crossed out on official stationery. The "duration" was over.

III

Three Wishes and More

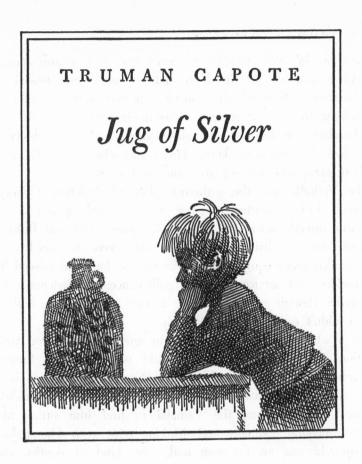

TRUMAN CAPOTE

Jug of Silver

After school I used to work in the Valhalla drugstore. It was owned by my uncle, Mr. Ed Marshall. I call him Mr. Marshall because everybody, including his wife, called him Mr. Marshall. Nevertheless he was a nice man.

This drugstore was maybe old-fashioned, but it was large and dark and cool: during summer months there was no pleasanter place in town. At the left, as you entered, was a tobacco-magazine counter behind which, as a rule, sat Mr. Marshall: a squat, square-faced, pink-fleshed man with looping, manly, white mustaches. Beyond this counter stood the beautiful soda fountain. It was very antique and made of fine, yellowed marble, smooth to the touch but without a trace of cheap glaze. Mr. Marshall bought it at an auction in New Orleans in 1910 and was plainly proud of it. When you sat on the high, delicate stools and looked across the fountain you could see yourself reflected softly, as though by candlelight, in a row of ancient, mahogany-framed mirrors. All general merchandise was displayed in glass-doored, curio-like cabinets that were locked with brass keys. There was always in the air the smell of syrup and nutmeg and other delicacies.

The Valhalla was the gathering place of Wachata County till a certain Rufus McPherson came to town and opened a second drugstore directly across the courthouse square. This old Rufus Mc-Pherson was a villain; that is, he took away my uncle's trade. He installed fancy equipment such as electric fans and colored lights; he provided curb service and made grilled-cheese sandwiches to order. Naturally, though some remained devoted to Mr. Marshall, most folks couldn't resist Rufus McPherson.

For a while, Mr. Marshall chose to ignore him: if you were to mention McPherson's name he would sort of snort, finger his mustaches and look the other way. But you could tell he was mad. And getting madder. Then one day toward the middle of October I strolled into the Valhalla to find him sitting at the fountain playing dominoes and drinking wine with Hamurabi.

Hamurabi was an Egyptian and some kind of dentist, though he didn't do much business as the people hereabouts have unusually strong teeth, due to an element in the water. He spent a great deal of his time loafing around the Valhalla and was my uncle's chief buddy. He was a handsome figure of a man, this Hamurabi, being dark-skinned and nearly seven feet tall; the matrons of the town kept their daughters under lock and key and gave him the eye themselves. He had no foreign accent whatsoever, and it was always my opinion that he wasn't any more Egyptian than the man in the moon.

Anyway, there they were swigging red Italian wine from a gallon jug. It was a troubling sight, for Mr. Marshall was a renowned teetotaler. So naturally, I thought: Oh, golly, Rufus McPherson has finally got his goat. That was not the case, however.

"Here, son," said Mr. Marshall, "come have a glass of wine."

"Sure," said Hamurabi, "help us finish it up. It's store-bought, so we can't waste it."

Much later, when the jug was dry, Mr. Marshall picked it up and said, "Now we shall see!" And with that disappeared out into the afternoon.

"Where's he off to?" I asked.

"Ah," was all Hamurabi would say. He liked to devil me.

A half-hour passed before my uncle returned. He was stooped and grunting under the load he carried. He set the jug atop the fountain and stepped back, smiling and rubbing his hands together. "Well, what do you think?"

"Ah," purred Hamurabi.

"Gee . . ." I said.

It was the same wine jug, Gods knows, but there was a wonderful difference; for now it was crammed to the brim with nickels and dimes that shone dully through the thick glass.

"Pretty, eh?" said my uncle. "Had it done over at the First National. Couldn't get in anything bigger-sized than a nickel. Still, there's lotsa money in there, let me tell you."

"But what's the point, Mr. Marshall?" I said. "I mean, what's the idea?"

Mr. Marshall's smile deepened to a grin. "This here's a jug of silver, you might say. . . ."

"The pot at the end of the rainbow," interrupted Hamurabi.

". . . and the idea, as you call it, is for folks to guess how much money is in there. For instance, say you buy a quarter's worth of stuff—well, then you get to take a chance. The more you buy, the more chances you get. And I'll keep all guesses in a ledger till Christmas Eve, at which time whoever comes closest to the right amount will get the whole shebang."

Hamurabi nodded solemnly. "He's playing Santa Claus—a mighty crafty Santa Claus," he said. "I'm going home and write a book: *The Skillful Murder of Rufus McPherson.*" To tell the truth, he sometimes did write stories and send them out to the magazines. They always came back.

It was surprising, really like a miracle, how Wachata County took to the jug. Why, the Valhalla hadn't done so much business since Station Master Tully, poor soul, went stark raving mad and claimed to have discovered oil back of the depot, causing the town to be overrun with wildcat prospectors. Even the pool-hall bums who never spent a cent on anything not connected with whiskey or women took to investing their spare cash in milk shakes. A few elderly ladies publicly disapproved of Mr. Marshall's enterprise as a kind of gambling, but they didn't start any trouble and some even found occasion to visit us and hazard a guess. The school kids were crazy about the whole thing, and I was very popular because they figured I knew the answer.

"I'll tell you why all this is," said Hamurabi, lighting one of the Egyptian cigarettes he bought by mail from a concern in New York City. "It's not for the reason you may imagine; not, in other words, avidity. No. It's the mystery that's enchanting. Now you look at those nickels and dimes and what do you think: ah, *so* much! No, no. You think: ah, *how* much? And that's a profound question, indeed. It can mean different things to different people. Understand?"

And oh, was Rufus McPherson wild! When you're in trade, you count on Christmas to make up a large share of your yearly profit, and he was hard pressed to find a customer. So he tried to imitate the jug; but being such a stingy man he filled his with pennies. He also wrote a letter to the editor of *The Banner*, our weekly paper, in which he said that Mr. Marshall ought to be "tarred and feathered and strung up for turning innocent little children into confirmed gamblers and sending them down the path to Hell!" You can imagine what kind of laughing stock he was. Nobody had anything for McPherson but scorn. And so by the middle of November he just stood on the sidewalk outside his store and gazed bitterly at the festivities across the square.

At about this time Appleseed and sister made their first appearance.

He was a stranger in town. At least no one could recall ever having seen him before. He said he lived on a farm a mile past Indian Branches; told us his mother weighed only seventy-four pounds and that he had an older brother who would play the fiddle at anybody's wedding for fifty cents. He claimed that Appleseed was the only name he had and that he was twelve years old. But his sister, Middy, said he was eight. His hair was straight and dark yellow. He had a tight, weather-tanned little face with anxious green eyes that had a very wise and knowing look. He was small and puny and high-strung; and he wore always the same outfit: a red sweater, blue denim britches and a pair of man-sized boots that went clop-clop with every step.

It was raining that first time he came into the Valhalla; his hair was plastered round his head like a cap and his boots were caked with red mud from the country roads. Middy trailed behind as he swaggered like a cowboy up to the fountain where I was wiping some glasses.

"I hear tell you folks got a bottle fulla money you fixin' to give 'way," he said, looking me square in the eye. "Seein' as you-all are givin' it away, we'd be obliged iffen you'd give it to us. Name's Appleseed, and this here's my sister, Middy."

Middy was a sad, sad-looking kid. She was a good bit taller and older-looking than her brother: a regular bean pole. She had tow-colored hair that was chopped short, and a pale pitiful little face. She wore a faded cotton dress that came way up above her bony knees. There was something wrong with her teeth, and she tried to conceal this by keeping her lips primly pursed like an old lady.

"Sorry," I said, "but you'll have to talk with Mr. Marshall."

So sure enough he did. I could hear my uncle explaining what he would have to do to win the jug. Appleseed listened attentively, nodding now and then. Presently he came back and stood in front of the jug and, touching it lightly with his hand, said, "Ain't it a pretty thing, Middy?"

Middy said, "Is they gonna give it to us?"

"Naw. What you gotta do, you gotta guess how much money's inside there. And you gotta buy two bits' worth so's even to get a chance."

"Huh, we ain't got no two bits. Where you 'spec we gonna get us two bits?"

Appleseed frowned and rubbed his chin. "That'll be the easy part, just leave it to me. The only worrisome thing is: I can't just take a chance and guess. . . . I gotta *know*."

Well, a few days later they showed up again. Appleseed perched on a stool at the fountain and boldly asked for two glasses of water, one for him and one for Middy. It was on this occasion that he gave out the information about his family: ". . . then there's Papa Daddy, that's my mama's papa, who's a Cajun, an' on accounta that he don't speak English good. My brother, the one what plays the fiddle, he's been in jail three times. . . . It's on accounta him we had to pick up and leave Louisiana. He cut a fella bad in a razor fight over a woman ten years older'n him. She had yellow hair."

Middy, lingering in the background, said nervously, "You oughtn't to be tellin' our personal private fam'ly business thataway, Appleseed."

"Hush now, Middy," he said, and she hushed. "She's a good little gal," he added, turning to pat her head, "but you can't let her get away with much. You go look at the picture books, honey, and stop frettin' with your teeth. Appleseed here's got some figurin' to do."

This figuring meant staring hard at the jug, as if his eyes were trying to eat it up. With his chin cupped in his hand, he studied it for a long period, not batting his eyelids once. "A lady in Louisiana told me I could see things other folks couldn't see 'cause I was born with a caul on my head."

"It's a cinch you aren't going to see how much there is," I told him. "Why don't you just let a number pop into your head, and maybe that'll be the right one."

"Uh, uh," he said, "too darn risky. Me, I can't take no sucha chance. Now, the way I got it figured, there ain't but one sure-fire thing and that's to count every nickel and dime."

"Count!"

"Count what?" asked Hamurabi, who had just moseyed inside and was settling himself at the fountain.

"This kid says he's going to count how much is in the jug," I explained.

Hamurabi looked at Appleseed with interest. "How do you plan to do that, son?"

"Oh, by countin'," said Appleseed matter-of-factly.

Hamurabi laughed. "You better have X-ray eyes, son, that's all I can say."

"Oh, no. All you gotta do is be born with a caul on your head. A lady in Louisiana told me so. She was a witch; she loved me and when my ma wouldn't give me to her she put a hex on her and now my ma don't weigh but seventy-four pounds."

"Ve-ry in-ter-esting," was Hamurabi's comment as he gave Appleseed a queer glance.

Middy sauntered up, clutching a copy of *Screen Secrets*. She pointed out a certain photo to Appleseed and said: "Ain't she the nicest-lookin' lady? Now you see, Appleseed, you see how pretty her teeth are? Not a one outa joint."

"Well, don't you fret none," he said.

After they left Hamurabi ordered a bottle of orange Nehi and drank it slowly, while smoking a cigarette. "Do you think maybe that kid's o.k. upstairs?" he asked presently in a puzzled voice.

Small towns are best for spending Christmas, I think. They catch the mood quicker and change and come alive under its spell. By the first week in December house doors were decorated with wreaths, and store windows were flashy with red paper bells and snowflakes of glittering isinglass. The kids hiked out into the woods and came back dragging spicy evergreen trees. Already the women were busy baking fruitcakes, unsealing jars of mincemeat and opening bottles of blackberry and scuppernong wine. In the courthouse square a huge tree was trimmed with silver tinsel and colored electric bulbs that were lighted up at sunset. Late of an afternoon you could hear the choir in the Presbyterian church practicing carols for their annual pageant. All over town the japonicas were in full bloom.

The only person who appeared not the least touched by this heartwarming atmosphere was Appleseed. He went about his declared business of counting the jug-money with great, persistent care. Every day now he came to the Valhalla and concentrated on the jug, scowling and mumbling to himself. At first we were all fascinated, but after a while it got tiresome and nobody paid him any mind whatsoever. He never bought anything, apparently having never been able to raise the two bits. Sometimes he'd talk to Hamurabi, who had taken a tender interest in him and occasionally stood treat to a jawbreaker or a penny's worth of licorice.

"Do you still think he's nuts?" I asked.

"I'm not so sure," said Hamurabi. "But I'll let you know. He doesn't eat enough. I'm going to take him over to the Rainbow Café and buy him a plate of barbecue."

"He'd appreciate it more if you'd give him a quarter."

"No. A dish of barbecue is what he needs. Besides, it would be better if he never was to make a guess. A high-strung kid like that, so unusual, I wouldn't want to be the one responsible if he lost. Say, it would be pitiful."

I'll admit that at the time Appleseed struck me as being just funny. Mr. Marshall felt sorry for him, and the kids tried to tease him, but had to give it up when he refused to respond. There you could see him plain as day sitting at the fountain with his forehead puckered and his eyes fixed forever on that jug. Yet he was so withdrawn you sometimes had this awful creepy feeling that, well, maybe he didn't exist. And when you were pretty much convinced of this he'd wake up and say something like, "You know, I hope a 1913 buffalo nickel's in there. A fella was tellin' me he saw where a 1913 buffalo nickel's worth fifty dollars." Or, "Middy's gonna be a big lady in the picture shows. They make lotsa money, the ladies in the picture shows do, and then we ain't gonna never eat another collard green as long as we live. Only Middy says she can't be in the picture shows 'less her teeth look good."

Middy didn't always tag along with her brother. On those occasions when she didn't come, Appleseed wasn't himself; he acted shy and left soon.

Hamurabi kept his promise and stood treat to a dish of barbecue at the café. "Mr. Hamurabi's nice, all right," said Appleseed afterward, "but he's got peculiar notions: has a notion that if he lived in this place named Egypt he'd be a king or somethin'."

And Hamurabi said, "That kid has the most touching faith. It's a beautiful thing to see. But I'm beginning to despise the whole business." He gestured toward the jug. "Hope of this kind is a cruel thing to give anybody, and I'm damned sorry I was ever a party to it."

Around the Valhalla the most popular pastime was deciding what you would buy if you won the jug. Among those who participated were: Solomon Katz, Phoebe Jones, Carl Kuhnhardt, Puly Simmons, Addie Foxcroft, Marvin Finkle, Trudy Edwards and a colored man named Erskine Washington. And these were some of their answers: a trip to and a permanent wave in Birmingham, a second-hand piano, a Shetland pony, a gold bracelet, a set of *Rover Boys* books and a life insurance policy.

Once Mr. Marshall asked Appleseed what he would get. "It's a secret," was the reply, and no amount of prying could make him tell. We took it for granted that whatever it was, he wanted it real bad.

Honest winter, as a rule, doesn't settle on our part of the country till late January, and then is mild, lasting only a short time. But in the year of which I write we were blessed with a singular cold spell the week before Christmas. Some still talk of it, for it was so terrible: water pipes froze solid; many folks had to spend the days in bed snuggled under their quilts, having neglected to lay in enough kindling for the fireplace; the sky turned that strange dull gray as it does just before a storm, and the sun was pale as a waning moon. There was a sharp wind: the old dried-up leaves of last fall fell on the icy ground, and the evergreen tree in the courthouse square was twice stripped of its Christmas finery. When you breathed, your breath made smoky clouds. Down by the silk mill where the very poor people lived, the families huddled together in the dark at night and told tales to keep their minds off the cold. Out in the country the farmers covered their delicate plants with gunny sacks and prayed; some took advantage of the weather to slaughter their hogs and bring the fresh sausage to town. Mr. R. C. Judkins, our town drunk, outfitted himself in a red cheesecloth suit and played Santa Claus at the five 'n' dime. Mr. R. C. Judkins was the father of a big family, so everybody was happy to see him sober enough to earn a dollar. There were several church socials, at one of which Mr. Marshall came face to face with Rufus Mc-Pherson: bitter words were passed but not a blow was struck.

Now, as has been mentioned, Appleseed lived on a farm a mile below Indian Branches; this would be approximately three miles from town; a mighty long and lonesome walk. Still, despite the cold, he came every day to the Valhalla and stayed till closing time which, as the days had grown short, was after nightfall. Once in a while he'd catch a ride partway home with the foreman from the silk mill, but not often. He looked tired, and there were worry lines about his mouth. He was always cold and shivered a lot. I don't think he wore any warm drawers underneath his red sweater and blue britches.

It was three days before Christmas when out of the clear sky, he announced: "Well, I'm finished. I mean I know how much is in the bottle." He claimed this with such grave, solemn sureness it was hard to doubt him.

"Why, say now, son, hold on," said Hamurabi, who was present. "You can't know anything of the sort. It's wrong to think so: you're just heading to get yourself hurt."

"You don't need to preach to me, Mr. Hamurabi. I know what I'm up to. A lady in Louisiana, she told me . . ."

"Yes yes yes—but you got to forget that. If it were me, I'd go home and stay put and forget about this goddamned jug."

"My brother's gonna play the fiddle at a wedding over in Cherokee City tonight and he's gonna give me the two bits," said Appleseed stubbornly. "Tomorrow I'll take my chance."

So the next day I felt kind of excited when Appleseed and Middy arrived. Sure enough, he had his quarter: it was tied for safekeeping in the corner of a red bandanna.

The two of them wandered hand in hand among the showcases, holding a whispery consultation as to what to purchase. They decided finally on a thimble-sized bottle of gardenia cologne which Middy promptly opened and partly emptied on her hair. "It smells like . . . Oh, darlin' Mary, I ain't never smelled nothin' as sweet. Here, Appleseed, honey, let me douse some on your hair." But he wouldn't let her.

Mr. Marshall got out the ledger in which he kept his records, while Appleseed strolled over to the fountain and cupped the jug between his hands, stroking it gently. His eyes were bright and his cheeks flushed from excitement. Several persons who were in the drugstore at that moment crowded close. Middy stood in the background quietly scratching her leg and smelling the cologne. Hamurabi wasn't there.

Mr. Marshall licked the point of his pencil and smiled. "Okay, son, what do you say?"

Appleseed took a deep breath. "Seventy-seven dollars and thirty-five cents," he blurted.

In picking such an uneven sum he showed originality, for the run-of-the-mill guess was a plain round figure. Mr. Marshall repeated the amount solemnly as he copied it down.

"When'll I know if I won?"

"Christmas Eve," someone said.

"That's tomorrow, huh?"

"Why, so it is," said Mr. Marshall, not surprised. "Come at four o'clock."

During the night the thermometer dropped even lower, and toward dawn there was one of those swift, summerlike rainstorms, so that the following day was bright and frozen. The town was like a picture postcard of a Northern scene, what with icicles sparkling whitely on the trees and frost flowers coating all windowpanes. Mr. R. C. Judkins rose early and, for no clear reason, tramped the streets ringing a supper bell, stopping now and then to take a swig of whiskey from a pint which he kept in his hip pocket. As the day was windless, smoke climbed lazily from various chimneys straightway to the still, frozen sky. By mid-morning the Presbyterian choir was in full swing; and the town kids (wearing horror masks, as at Hallowe'en) were chasing one another round and round the square, kicking up an awful fuss.

Hamurabi dropped by at noon to help us fix up the Valhalla. He brought along a fat sack of Satsumas, and together we ate every last one, tossing the hulls into a newly installed potbellied stove (a present from Mr. Marshall to himself) which stood in the middle of the room. Then my uncle took the jug off the fountain, polished and placed it on a prominently situated table. He was no help after that whatsoever, for he squatted in a chair and spent his time tying and retying a tacky green ribbon around the jug. So Hamurabi and I had the rest to do alone: we swept the floor and washed the mirrors and dusted the cabinets and strung streamers of red and green crepe paper from wall to wall. When we were finished it looked very fine and elegant.

But Hamurabi gazed sadly at our work, and said: "Well, I think I better be getting along now."

"Aren't you going to stay?" asked Mr. Marshall, shocked.

"No, oh, no," said Hamurabi, shaking his head slowly. "I don't want to see that kid's face. This is Christmas and I mean to have a rip-roaring time. And I couldn't, not with something like that on my conscience. Hell, I wouldn't sleep."

"Suit yourself," said Mr. Marshall. And he shrugged, but you could see he was really hurt. "Life's like that—and besides, who knows, he might win."

Hamurabi sighed gloomily. "What's his guess?"

"Seventy-seven dollars and thirty-five cents," I said.

"Now I ask you, isn't that fantastic?" said Hamurabi. He slumped in a chair next to Mr. Marshall and crossed his legs and lit a cigarette. "If you got any Baby Ruths I think I'd like one; my mouth tastes sour."

As the afternoon wore on, the three of us sat around the table feeling terribly blue. No one said hardly a word and, as the kids had deserted the square, the only sound was the clock tolling the hour in the courthouse steeple. The Valhalla was closed to business, but people kept passing by and peeking in the window. At three o'clock Mr. Marshall told me to unlock the door.

Within twenty minutes the place was jam full; everyone was wearing his Sunday best, and the air smelled sweet, for most of the little silk-mill girls had scented themselves with vanilla flavoring. They scrunched up against the walls, perched on the fountain, squeezed in wherever they could; soon the crowd had spread to the sidewalk and stretched into the road. The square was lined with team-drawn wagons and Model T Fords that had carted farmers and their families into town. There was much laughter and shouting and joking—several outraged ladies complained of the cursing and the rough, shoving ways of the younger men, but nobody left. At the side entrance a gang of colored folks had formed and were having the most fun of all. Everybody was making the best of a good thing. It's usually so quiet around here: nothing much ever happens. It's safe to say that nearly all of Wachata County was present but invalids and Rufus McPherson. I looked around for Appleseed but didn't see him anywhere.

Mr. Marshall harumphed, and clapped for attention. When things quieted down and the atmosphere was properly tense, he raised his voice like an auctioneer, and called: "Now listen, everybody, in this here envelope you see in my hand"—he held a manila envelope above his head—"well, in it's the *answer*—which nobody but God and the First National Bank knows up to now, ha, ha. And in this book"—he held up the ledger with his free hand—"I've got written down what you folks guessed. Are there any questions?" All was silence. "Fine. Now, if we could have a volunteer . . ."

Not a living soul budged an inch: it was as if an awful shyness had overcome the crowd, and even those who were ordinarily natural-born show-offs shuffled their feet, ashamed. Then a voice, Appleseed's, hollered, "Lemme by . . . Outa the way, please, ma'am." Trotting along behind as he pushed forward were Middy and a lanky, sleepy-eyed fellow who was evidently the fiddling brother. Appleseed was dressed the same as usual, but his face was scrubbed rosy clean, his boots polished and his hair slicked back skin tight with Stacomb. "Did we get here in time?" he panted.

But Mr. Marshall said, "So you want to be our volunteer?"

Appleseed looked bewildered, then nodded vigorously.

"Does anybody have an objection to this young man?"

Still there was dead quiet. Mr. Marshall handed the envelope to Appleseed who accepted it calmly. He chewed his under lip while studying it a moment before ripping the flap.

In all that congregation there was no sound except an occasional cough and the soft tinkling of Mr. R. C. Judkins' supper bell. Hamurabi was leaning against the fountain, staring up at the ceiling; Middy was gazing blankly over her brother's shoulder, and when he started to tear open the envelope she let out a pained little gasp.

Appleseed withdrew a slip of pink paper and, holding it as though it was very fragile, muttered to himself whatever was written there. Suddenly his face paled and tears glistened in his eyes.

"Hey, speak up, boy," someone hollered.

Hamurabi stepped forward and all but snatched the slip away. He cleared his throat and commenced to read when his expression changed most comically. "Well, Mother o' God . . ." he said.

"Louder! Louder!" an angry chorus demanded.

"Buncha crooks!" yelled Mr. R. C. Judkins, who had a snootful by this time. "I smell a rat and he smells to high heaven!" Whereupon a cyclone of catcalls and whistling rent the air.

Appleseed's brother whirled round and shook his fist. "Shuddup, shuddup 'fore I bust every one a your goddamn heads together so's you got knots the size a musk melons, hear me?"

"Citizens," cried Mayor Mawes, "citizens—I say, this is Christmas . . . I say . . ."

And Mr. Marshall hopped up on a chair and clapped and stamped till a minimum of order was restored. It might as well be noted here that we later found out Rufus McPherson had paid Mr. R. C. Judkins to start the rumpus. Anyway, when the outbreak was quelled, who should be in possession of the slip but me . . . don't ask how.

Without thinking, I shouted, "Seventy-seven dollars and thirty-five cents." Naturally, due to the excitement, I didn't at first catch the meaning; it was just a number. Then Appleseed's brother let forth with his whooping yell, and so I understood. The name of the winner spread quickly, and the awed, murmuring whispers were like a rainstorm.

Oh, Appleseed himself was a sorry sight. He was crying as though he was mortally wounded, but when Hamurabi lifted him onto his shoulders so the crowd could get a gander, he dried his eyes with the cuffs of his sweater and began grinning. Mr. R. C. Judkins yelled, "Gyp! Lousy gyp!" but was drowned out by a deafening round of applause.

Middy grabbed my arm. "My teeth," she squealed. "Now I'm gonna get my teeth."

"Teeth?" said I, kind of dazed.

"The false kind," says she. "That's what we're gonna get us with the money—a lovely set of white false teeth."

But at that moment my sole interest was in how Appleseed had known. "Hey, tell me," I said desperately, "tell me, how in God's name did he know there was just exactly seventy-seven dollars and thirty-five cents?"

Middy gave me this *look*. "Why, I thought he told you," she said, real serious. "He counted."

"Yes, but how—how?"

"Gee, don't you even know how to count?"

"But is that all he did?"

"Well," she said, following a thoughtful pause, "he did do a little praying, too." She started to dart off, then turned back and called, "Besides, he was born with a caul on his head."

And that's the nearest anybody ever came to solving the mystery. Thereafter, if you were to ask Appleseed "How come?" he would smile strangely and change the subject. Many years later he and his family moved to somewhere in Florida and were never heard from again.

But in our town his legend flourishes still; and, till his death a year ago last April, Mr. Marshall was invited each Christmas Day to tell the story of Appleseed to the Baptist Bible class. Hamurabi once typed up an account and mailed it around to various magazines. It was never printed. One editor wrote back and said that "If the little girl really turned out to be a movie star, then there might be something to your story." But that's not what happened, so why should you lie?

LUDWIG
BEMELMANS

*Little
Bit
and
the
America*

"Look, what a lovely day we have for sailing," I said, pointing my pen toward the lit-up greenery outside the open window. The birds sang in the trees, and the sun shone on a deck of brightly colored luggage tags which I was filling out. Under "S.S. *America*" I had carefully lettered my name, and I answered the gay question of "Destination?" with "Cherbourg."

I was about to fill out a new tag when I noticed Barbara's silence. She was standing at the window, staring at me. I saw clearly the symptoms of wanting something, symptoms long known to me and always the same. I remembered that the day before she had said something about a dog, but I had been called away before I could talk about it at length.

For the most part, Barbara is a sweet and normal child; when she wants something, she changes. The child is then under great stress. A trembling of the lower lip precedes the filling of the beautiful eyes with tears. I am allowed to see these hopeless eyes for a moment, and then, as a spotlight moves from one place to another, she averts her gaze and slowly turns, folds her arms, and looks into the distance, or if there is no distance, at the wall. The crisis is approaching. She swallows, but her throat is constricted; finally, with the urgency of a stammerer, and with her small hands clenched, she manages to convey a few dry words. The small voice is like a cold trumpet. The last word is a choking sound. There is a long, cold silence.

On the morning of sailing I recognized the first stage of this painful condition that overcomes her from time to time. I could tell it by her eyes, her mouth, the position she stood in, the peculiar angles of her arms and legs. She was twisted in an unhappy pose of indecision. Not that she didn't know precisely what she wanted: she was undecided about how to broach the subject.

After the tears, the gaze into the distance, the silence, Barbara blurted out, "You promised I could have a dog."

I steeled myself and answered, "Yes, when we get back from Europe you can have a dog."

An answer like that is worse than an outright no. The mood of "I wish I was dead" descended on Barbara. She stared coldly out of the window, and then she turned and limply dragged herself down the corridor to her room, where she goes at times of crisis. She closed the door not by slamming it, but with a terrible, slow finality. One can see from the corridor how she lets go of the handle inside—in unspeakably dolorous fashion; slowly the handle rises, and there is the barely audible click of the mechanism. There is then the cutting off of human relations, a falling off of appetite, and nothing in the world of joy or disaster matters.

Ordinarily the comatose state lasts for weeks. In this case, however, Barbara was confronted with a deadline, for the ship was sailing at five that afternoon and it was now eleven in the morning. I usually break down after three or four weeks of resistance. The time limit for this operation was five hours.

She decided at first to continue with standard practice, the manual of which I know as well as I do the alphabet.

From the door at the end of the corridor came the sound of heartbreaking sobs. Normally these sobs last for a good while, and then, the crisis ebbing off, there follows an hour or two of real or simulated sleep, in which she gathers strength for renewed efforts. This time, however, the sobs were discontinued ahead of schedule and were followed by a period of total silence, which I knew was taken up with plotting at the speed of calculating machinery. This took about ten minutes. As the door had closed, so it opened again, and fatefully and slowly, as the condemned walk to their places of execution, the poor child, handkerchief in hand, dragged along the corridor past my room into the kitchen. I never knew until that morning that the pouring of milk into a glass could be a bitter and hopeless thing to watch.

I am as hardened against the heartbreak routine as a coroner is to postmortems. I can be blind to tears and deaf to the most urgent pleading. I said, "Please be reasonable. I promise you that the moment we get back you can have a dog."

I was not prepared for what followed—the new slant, the surprise attack.

She leaned against the kitchen doorjamb and drank the last of the milk. Her mouth was ringed with white. She said in measured and accusing tones, "You read in the papers this morning what they did in Albany."

"I beg your pardon?"

"They passed a law that all institutions like the A.S.P.C.A. are to be forced to turn dogs over to hospitals, for vivisection—and you know what will happen. They'll get her and then they'll cut her open and sew her up again over and over until she's dead."

"What has that got to do with me?"

"It has to do with the dog you promised me."

"What dog?"

"The dog that Frances wants to give me."

Frances is a red-headed girl who goes to school with Barbara. "I didn't know Frances had a dog."

Barbara raised her eyebrows. "You never listen," she said, and as if talking to an idiot and with weary gestures she recited, "Poppy,

I told you all about it a dozen times. Doctor Lincoln, that's Frances's father, is going to Saudi Arabia to work for an oil company, and he had to sign a paper agreeing not to take a dog, because it seems the Arabs don't like dogs. So the dog has to be got rid of. So Doctor Lincoln said to Frances, 'If you don't get rid of her, I will.' Now you know how doctors are—they have no feelings whatever for animals. He'll give her to some hospital for experiments."

I resumed filling out baggage tags. When I hear the word "dog" I see in my mind a reasonably large animal of no particular breed, uncertain in outline, like a Thurber dog, and with a rough, dark coat. This image was hovering about when I asked, "What kind of a dog is it?"

"Her name is Little Bit."

"What?"

"Little *BIT*—that's her name. She's the dearest, sweetest, snow-white, itsy-bitsy tiny little toy poodle you have ever seen. Can I have her, please?"

I almost let out a shrill bark.

"Wait till you see her and all the things she's got—a special little wicker bed with a mattress, and a dish with her picture on it, and around it is written 'Always faithful' in French. You see, Poppy, they got Little Bit in Paris last year, and she's the uniquest, sharpest little dog you've ever seen, and naturally she's housebroken, and Frances says she's not going to give her to anybody but me."

I was playing for time. I would have settled for a Corgi, a Yorkshire, a Weimaraner, even a German boxer or a Mexican hairless, but Little Bit was too much. I knew that Doctor Lincoln lived some thirty miles out of the city, and that it would be impossible to get the dog to New York before the ship sailed.

"Where is the dog now?" I asked with faked interest.

"She'll be here any minute, Poppy. Frances is on the way now—and oh, wait till you see, she has the cutest little boots for rainy weather, and a cashmere sweater, sea green, and several sets of leashes and collars—you won't have to buy a thing."

"All right," I said, "you can have the dog. We'll put her in a good kennel until we return."

The symptoms, well known and always the same, returned again. The lower lip trembled. "Kennel," she said—and there is no actress on stage or screen who could have weighted this word with more reproach and misery.

"Yes, kennel," I said and filled out the baggage tag for my portable typewriter.

"Poppy—" she started, but I got up and said, "Now look, Barbara, the ship leaves in a few hours, and to take a dog aboard you have to get a certificate from a veterinary, and reserve a place for him, and buy a ticket."

To my astonishment, Barbara smiled indulgently. "Well, if that's all that's bothering you—first of all, we're going to France; the French, unlike the English, have no quarantine for dogs, and they don't even ask for a health certificate. Second, you can make all the arrangements for the dog's passage on board ship, after it sails. Third, there is plenty of room in the kennels. I know all this because Frances and I went down to the U. S. Lines and got the information day before yesterday."

I stared into the distance. At such times I feel a great deal for the man who's going to marry Barbara. With all hope failing I said, "But we'll have to get a traveling bag or something to put the dog in."

"She has a lovely little traveling bag with her name lettered on it, 'Little Bit.'"

The name stung like a whip. "All right then." I wrote an extra baggage tag to be attached to the dog's bag.

Barbara wore the smug smile of success. "Wait till you see her," she said and ran out of the room. In a moment she returned with Frances, who, I am sure, had been sitting there waiting all the while. The timing was perfect.

Little Bit had shoebutton eyes and a patent-leather nose and a strawberry-colored collar; she was fluffy from the top of her head to her shoulders and then shorn like a miniature Persian lamb. At the end of a stub of a tail was a puff of fluff, and other puffs on the four legs. She wore a pale blue ribbon, and bell on the collar. I thought that if she were cut open most probably sawdust would come out.

A real dog moves about a room and sniffs its way into corners. It inspects furniture and people, and makes notes of things. Little Bit stood with cocksparrow stiffness on four legs as static as her stare. She was picked up and brought over to me. I think she knew exactly what I thought of her, for she lifted her tiny lip on the left side of her face over her mouse teeth and sneered. She was put down, and she danced on stilts, with the motion of a mechanical toy, back to Frances.

I was shown the traveling bag, which was like one of the pocketbooks that WAC colonels carry.

"We don't need that tag," said Barbara. "I'll carry her in this. Look." The pocketbook, which had a circular opening with a wire screen on each end for breathing purposes, was opened; Little Bit jumped into it, and it was closed. "You see, she won't be any bother whatever."

The bag was opened again. With a standing jump Little Bit hurdled the handles of the bag and started toward me. Tilting her head a little, she stood looking up, and then she again lifted her lip over her small fangs.

"Oh, look, Barbara!" said Frances. "Little Bit likes your father— she's smiling at him."

I had an impulse to sneer back, but I took the baggage tags and began to attach them to the luggage. Then I left the room, for Frances showed signs of crisis; her eyes were filling, and the heartbreak was too much for me. Little Bit was less emotional. She ate a hearty meal from her *Toujours fidèle* dish and inspected the house, tinkling about with the small bell that hung from her collar.

It was time to go to the boat. The luggage was taken to a taxi, and Little Bit hopped into her bag. On the way I thought about the things I had forgotten to take care of, and also about Little Bit. It is said that there are three kinds of books that are always a success: a book about a doctor, a book about Lincoln, and a book about a dog. Well, here was Doctor Lincoln's dog, but it didn't seem to hold the elements of anything except chagrin. I wondered if Lincoln had ever had a dog, or a doctor, or if Lincoln's doctor had had a dog. I wondered if that side of Lincoln, perhaps the last remaining side, had been investigated as yet or was still open.

We arrived with Doctor Lincoln's dog at the customs barrier, and our passports were checked. The baggage was brought aboard.

In our cabin we found some friends waiting. Frances and Barbara, with Little Bit looking out of her bag, inspected the ship. The gong sounded, and the deck steward sang out, "All ashore that's going ashore!" The passengers lined up to wave their farewells. The last of those that were going ashore slid down the gangplank. Good-by, good-by—and then the engine bells sounded below, and the tugs moaned and hissed, and the ship backed out into the river.

There are few sights in the world as beautiful as a trip down the Hudson and out to sea, especially at dusk. I was on deck until we passed the Ambrose Lightship, and then I went down to the cabin.

Little Bit was lying on a blotter, on the writing desk, and watching Barbara's hand. Barbara was already writing a letter to Frances, describing the beauty of travel and Little Bit's reactions. "Isn't she the best traveling dog we've ever had, Poppy?"

The cabins aboard the *America* are the only ones I have ever been in that don't seem to be aboard ship. They are large—more like rooms in a country home—a little chintzy in decoration, and over the portholes are curtains. In back of these one suspects screened doors that lead out to a porch and a Connecticut lawn rather than the ocean.

I put my things in place and changed to a comfortable jacket. I said, "I guess I better go up and get this dog business settled."

"It's all attended to, Poppy. I took care of it," said Barbara and continued writing.

"Well, then you'd better take her upstairs to the kennels. It's almost dinnertime."

"She doesn't have to go to the kennels."

"Now, look, Barbara—"

"See for yourself, Poppy. Just ring for the steward, or let me ring for him."

"Yes, sir," said the steward, smiling.

"Is it all right for the dog to stay in the cabin?" I asked. The steward had one of the most honest and kind faces I have ever seen. He didn't fit on a ship either. He was more like a person that works around horses, or a gardener. He had bright eyes and squint lines, a leathery skin, and a good smile.

He closed his eyes and announced, "Dog? I don't see no dog in here, sir." He winked like a burlesque comedian and touched one finger to his head in salute. "My name is Jeff," he said. "If you want anything—" And then he was gone.

"You see?" said Barbara. "And besides, you save fifty dollars, and coming back another fifty, makes a hundred."

I am sure that Little Bit understood every word of the conversation. She stood up on the blotter and tilted her head, listening to Barbara, who said to her, "You know, Little Bit, you're not supposed to be on this ship at all. You mustn't let anybody see you. Now you hide, while we go down to eat."

There was a knock at the door. Silently Little Bit jumped to the floor and was out of sight.

It was the steward. He brought a little raw meat mixed with string beans on a plate covered with another plate. "Yes, sir," was all he said.

Barbara was asleep when the first rapport between me and Little Bit took place. I was sitting on a couch, reading, when she came into my cabin. By some magic trick, like an elevator going up a building shaft, she rose and seated herself next to me. She kept a hand's width of distance, tilted her head, and then lifted her lip over the left side of her face. I think I smiled back at her in the same fashion. I looked at her with interest for the first time— she was embarrassed. She looked away and then suddenly changed position, stretching her front legs ahead and sitting down flat on her hind legs. She made several jerky movements but never uttered a sound.

Barbara's sleepy voice came from the other room. "Aren't you glad we have Little Bit with us?"

"Yes," I said, "I am." I thought about the miracles of nature, how this tough little lion in sheep's pelt functioned as she did; with a brain that could be no larger than an olive, she had memory, understanding, tact, courage, and no doubt loyalty, and she was completely self-sufficient. She smiled once more, and I smiled back: the relationship was established. Life went on as steadily as the ship.

On the afternoon of the third day out, as I lay in my deck

chair reading, Barbara came running. "Little Bit is gone," she stammered with trembling lower lip.

We went down to the cabin. The steward was on all fours, looking under the beds and furniture. "Somebody musta left the door open," he said, "or it wasn't closed properly and swung open, and I suppose she got lonesome here all by herself and went looking for you. You should have taken her up to the movies with you, Miss."

"She's a smart dog," said Barbara. "Let's go to every spot on board where she might look for us."

So we went to the dining room, to the smoking room, the theater, the swimming pool, up the stairs, up on all the decks and around them, and to a secret little deck we had discovered between second and third class at the back of the ship, where Little Bit was taken for her exercise mornings and evenings and could run about freely while I stood guard.

A liner is as big as a city. She was nowhere.

When we got back the steward said, "I know where she is. You see, anybody finds a dog naturally takes it up to the kennels, and that's where she is. And there she stays for the rest of the trip. Remember, I never saw the dog, I don't know anything about her. The butcher—that's the man in charge of the kennels—he's liable to report me if he finds out I helped hide her. He's mean, especially about money. He figures that each passenger gives him ten bucks for taking care of a dog, and he doesn't want any of us to snatch. There was a Yorkshire stowing away trip before last; he caught him at the gangplank as the dog was leaving the ship—the passenger had put him on a leash. Well, the butcher stopped him from getting off. He held up everything for hours, the man had to pay passage for the dog, and the steward who had helped hide him was fired. Herman Haegeli is his name, and he's as mean as they come. You'll find him on the top deck, near the aft chimney, where it says 'Kennels.'"

At such moments I enjoy the full confidence and affection of my child. Her nervous little hand is in mine, she willingly takes direction, her whole being is devotion, and no trouble is too much. She loved me especially then, because she knows that I am larcenous at heart and willing to go to the greatest lengths to beat a game and especially a meany.

"Now remember," I said, "if you want that dog back we have to be very careful. Let's first go and case the joint."

We climbed up into the scene of white and red ventilators, the sounds of humming wires, and the swish of the water. In yellow and crimson fire, the ball of the sun had half sunk into the sea, precisely at the end of the avenue of foam that the ship had plowed through the ocean. We were alone. We walked up and down, like people taking exercise before dinner, and the sea changed to violet and to indigo and then to that glossy gunmetal hue that it wears on moonless nights. The ship swished along to the even pulse of her machinery.

There was the sign. A yellow light shone from a porthole. I lifted Barbara, and inside, in one of the upper cages, was Little Bit, behind bars. There was no lock on her cage.

No one was inside. The door was fastened by a padlock. We walked back and forth for a while, and then a man came up the stairs, carrying a pail. He wore a gray cap, a towel around his neck, and a white coat such as butchers work in.

"That's our man," I said to Barbara.

Inside the kennels he brought forth a large dish that was like the body of a kettledrum. The dogs were barking.

"Now listen carefully, Barbara. I will go in and start a conversation with Mr. Haegeli. I will try to arrange it so that he turns his back on Little Bit's cage. At that moment, carefully open the door of the cage, grab Little Bit, put her under your coat, and then don't run—stand still, and after a while say, 'Oh, please let's get out of here.' I will then say good evening and we both will leave very slowly. Remember to act calmly, watch the butcher, but don't expect a signal from me. Decide yourself when it is time to act. It might be when he is in the middle of work, or while he is talking."

"Oh, please, Poppy, let's get out of here," Barbara rehearsed.

I opened the door to the kennel and smiled like a tourist in appreciation of a new discovery. "Oh, that's where the dogs are kept," I said. "Good evening."

Mr. Haegeli looked up and answered with a grunt. He was mixing dog food.

"My, what nice food you're preparing for them. How much do they charge to take a dog across?"

"Fifty dollars," said Mr. Haegeli in a Swiss accent. There are all kinds of Swiss, some with French, some with Italian, and some with German accents. They all talk in a singing fashion. The faces are as varied as the accents. The butcher didn't look like a butcher—a good butcher is fat and rosy. Mr. Haegeli was thin-lipped, thin-nosed, his chin was pointed. In the light he didn't look as mean as I expected; he looked rather fanatic, and frustrated.

"How often do you feed them?"

"They eat twice a day and as good as anybody on board," said Mr. Haegeli. "All except Rolfi there—he belongs to an actor, Mr. Kruger, who crosses twice a year and brings the dog's food along." He pointed to the cage where a large police dog was housed. "Rolfi, he is fed once a day, out of cans." He seemed to resent Rolfi and his master.

"You exercise them?"

"Yes, of course—all except Rolfi. Mr. Kruger comes up in the morning and takes him around with him on the top deck and sits with him there on a bench. He doesn't leave him alone. There is such a thing as making too much fuss over a dog."

I said that I agreed with him.

"He tried to keep him in his cabin—he said he'd pay full fare for Rolfi, like a passenger. He'll come up any minute now to say good night to Rolfi. Some people are crazy about dogs." Mr. Haegeli was putting chopped meat, vegetables, and cereal into the large dish. "There are other people that try to get away with something—they try and smuggle dogs across, like that one there." He pointed at Little Bit. "But we catch them," he said in his Swiss accent. "Oh yes, we catch them. They think they're smart, but they don't get away with it—not with me on board they don't. I have ways of finding out. I track them down." The fires of the fanatic burned in his eyes. "I catch them every time." He sounded as if he turned them over to the guillotine after he caught them. "Ah, here comes Mr. Kruger," he said and opened the door.

Kurt Kruger, the actor, said good evening and introduced himself.

He spoke to Mr. Haegeli in German—and Mr. Haegeli turned his back on Little Bit's cage to open Rolfi's. The entire place was immediately deafened with barking from a dozen cages. The breathless moment had arrived. Barbara was approaching the door, but the dog-lover Kruger spotted Little Bit and said, "There's a new one." He spoke to Little Bit, and Little Bit, who had behaved as if she had been carefully rehearsed for her liberation, turned away with tears in her eyes.

Mr. Kruger and his dog disappeared.

Mr. Haegeli wiped his hands on his apron and went back to mixing the dog food. The chances for rescuing Little Bit were getting slim.

"Where do you come from, Mr. Haegeli?"

"Schaffhausen. You know Schaffhausen?"

"Yes, yes," I said in German, *"Wunderbar."*

"Ja, ja, beautiful city."

"And the waterfall!"

"You know the Haegeli Wurstfabrik there?"

"No, I'm sorry."

"Well, it's one of the biggest sausage factories in Switzerland—liverwurst, salami, cervelat, frankfurters, boned hams—a big concern, belongs to a branch of my family. I'm sort of a wanderer. I like to travel—restless, you know—I can't see myself in Schaffhausen." He looked up. He was mixing food with both hands, his arms rotating.

"I understand."

"Besides, we don't get along, my relatives and I. All they think about is money, small money—I think in large sums. I like a wide horizon. Schaffhausen is not for me."

"How long have you been traveling?"

"Oh, I've been two years on this ship. You see, I'm not really a butcher but an inventor."

"How interesting! What are you working on?"

At last Mr. Haegeli turned his back on the cage in which Little Bit waited. "Well, it's something tremendous. It's, so to say, revolutionary."

"Oh?"

"There's a friend of mine, a Swiss, who is a baker, but you

know, like I'm not a real butcher, he is not exactly a baker—I mean, he knows his trade but he has ambition to make something of himself—and together we have created something that we call a frankroll." He waited for the effect.

"What is a frankroll?"

"It's a frankfurter baked inside a roll. We've got everything here to experiment with, the material and the ovens. I make the franks and he makes the rolls. We've tried it out on the passengers. Mr. Kruger, for example, says it's a marvelous idea. I might add that the experimental stage is over. Our product is perfect. Now it is a question of selling the patent, or licensing somebody—you know the way that is done. You make much more that way."

"Have you tried?"

Mr. Haegeli came close, the inventor's excitement in his eyes now. "That is where the hitch comes in. On the last trip I saw the biggest frankfurter people in America—they're in New York. Well, the things you find out! They were very nice. The president received us and looked at the product and tasted it. He liked it, because he called for his son and a man who works close to him. 'I think you've got something there,' said the old man. I think with him we would have had clear sailing, but he had one of these wisenheimers for a son."

As Haegeli talked he forgot completely about the dogs. He gesticulated with hands that were sticky with hash, using them as a boxer does when he talks with his gloves on. Standing close to me, he held them away lest dog food soil my clothes. He stood exactly right, with his back turned to the spot where Barbara was slowly reaching to the door of Little Bit's cage. It was all foiled again by the return of Mr. Kruger and Rolfi. Mr. Kruger kissed his dog good night and stood waiting while Rolfi slowly walked into his cage. He said to Rolfi that it was only for two more nights that he had to be here, he wished us a good night, also, and after a final good night to his dog he went.

"Where was I?" said the butcher.

"With the frankroll, the old man, and the wise-guy son."

"Right. Well, the son was looking at our product with a mixture of doubt, so he took a bite out of it, and in the middle of it he stopped chewing. 'Mmmm,' he said. 'Not bad, not bad at all.

But—' He paused a long time, and then he said, 'What about the mustard, gentlemen?'

"I said, 'All right, what about the mustard?'

"So the wise guy says, 'I'm a customer. I'm buying. I'm at a hotdog stand. I watch the man in the white jacket. He picks up the frankfurter roll that's been sliced and placed face down on the hot plate—he picks it up in a sanitary fashion—and he takes the skinless frank with his prong and puts it in the roll and hands it to me. Now, I dip into the mustard pot, or maybe I decide on a little kraut, or maybe I want some condiments or relish. Anyway, I put that on the frank—' He held out his hand.

"So I said, 'What's all that got to do with our frankroll?'

"So Junior says, 'A lot. Let me explain. It's got no appeal. Practical maybe, but to put the mustard on the hot dog the customer would have to slice the frankfurter bun first, and that leads us straight back to the old-fashioned frankfurter and the old-fashioned roll. The frankroll may be practical, but it's got no sizzle to it. No eye appeal, no nose appeal—it's no good.'

"Well, the old man was confused, and he got up and said that he'd like to think about it, and then he said he'd like to show us the factory. Well, you'd never think how important a thing a frankfurter is. There are two schools of thought about frankfurters, the skin frank and the skinless. These people specialize in skinless ones—because the American housewife prefers them without the skin—but did you know that the skinless come with skins and have to be peeled? This factory is spotless. There is a vast hall, and at long tables sit hundreds of women, and music plays, and they all have in their left hand a frankfurter, and in the right a paring knife, and all day long they remove the skins from frankfurters—an eight-hour day. And at the end of the room is a first-aid station, because at the speed at which they work there is a great deal of laceration. The man in charge—"

"Oh, please, Poppy, let's get out of here!" Barbara broke in.

"The man in charge explained that in spite of elaborate safety precautions there was a great deal of absenteeism on account of carelessness. They had people who were working on a machine to skin the frankfurters. 'Now if you could invent a frankfurter-skinning device,' said the old man to me, 'you'd be a millionaire overnight.' Well, we're not licked yet. The beauty of working on a ship is that you have everything on board. One of the engineers is working with us on a skinning machine, and I have another outfit lined up for the frankroll."

The light in Mr. Haegeli's eyes faded. He wiped his hand again on his apron, and I shook it, and slowly we walked out on deck and down the first flight of stairs to A deck. I said to Barbara, "Run for your life, for by now he has discovered that Little Bit is gone."

We got to the cabin. Little Bit smiled on both sides of her face, and she bounced from floor to chair to dresser. There was a knock on the door—the thrill of the game of cops and robbers had begun. Little Bit vanished.

Barbara asked innocently, "Who is it?"

It was the steward. "Did you find her?"

Barbara smiled.

"You got her back?"

Barbara nodded.

"Well, for heaven's sake, keep her out of sight. That crazy butcher is capable of anything—and I got a wife and family."

"From now on the dog must not be left," I said to Barbara. "She must go with us wherever we go, to the dining room, on deck, to the lounge, and to the movies. And you can't carry her in that bag—you have to cover her with a scarf or have her inside your coat."

Barbara started going about as if she carried her arm in a sling. The steward averted his eyes whenever he met us, and he didn't bring any more dog food.

Mr. Kruger said, "The kennel man suspects you of having removed the dog from the kennel."

"We did."

"Good," said the actor. "Anything I can do, I will."

"Well, act as if you didn't know anything about it. How is Rolfi?"

"Oh, Rolfi is fine. You know, he's never bitten anybody in his life except that kennel man."

Mr. Kruger offered to get Little Bit off the boat. He had a wicker basket in which he carried some of Rolfi's things, and he would empty that, except for Rolfi's coat, and in that he would carry Little Bit off the *America*, for the butcher would follow us and watch us closely, and if he didn't find the dog before he'd catch us at the customs.

"Isn't he a nice man—Mr. Kruger? People always say such mean things about movie actors," said Barbara.

Camouflaged in a scarf, Little Bit rested on Barbara's lap during meals. On the deck chair she lay motionless between my feet, covered by a steamer rug. She traveled about under Barbara's coat, and she took her exercise on the secret afterdeck, while I watched from above.

After the morning walk, the next day, the steward knocked. He looked worried. "The butcher was here," he said, "and went all over the room. He found the dish with those French words and the dog's picture on it, on the bathroom floor."

"How could we be so careless?" I said, my professional pride hurt.

"And of course he saw the bag with 'Little Bit' printed on it. I said I didn't know nothing about any dog."

We doubled our precautions. Little Bit's mouth was down at the edges with worry. I contemplated what to do. After all, there were only two more days, and if the worst happened we could sit upstairs with Little Bit, the way Mr. Kruger sat with Rolfi. I said to Barbara, "Perhaps it would be best to pay the passage and have it over with."

The symptoms were back. "No, you can't do that. Think of the poor steward and his family!"

"Well, we could settle that, I think, with the butcher. I don't like to cheat the line—"

"Well, Poppy, you can send them a check afterward, if that worries you, or drink a few extra bottles of champagne, or buy something in the shop."

Knock on the door.

"Who is it?"

"The purser, sir."

"Please come in."

The door opened. Behind the purser stood Mr. Haegeli.

"Just wanted to look and see if everything is all right. Are you comfortable, sir?"

"Everything is fine."

"By the way, sir, we're looking for a small white dog that's been lost. We wondered if by any chance it's in here."

"Come in and look for yourself."

"That's quite all right, sir. Excuse the intrusion. Good evening." The purser closed the door.

"What a nice man!" said Barbara.

The butcher was excluded from pursuing us in the public rooms of the ship; he couldn't follow us to the movies or the dining room. But he seemed to have spies. "What a lovely scarf you have there, Miss," said the elevator boy, and after that we used the stairs. The butcher came on deck in a fatigue uniform and followed us on the evening promenade around the deck, during which Little Bit sat inside my overcoat, held in place by my right hand in a Napoleonic pose. We made four turns around the deck. I leaned against the railing once, holding Little Bit in place, so that I could stretch my arms; Barbara was skipping rope, and the maneuver fooled him. He ran downstairs, and we caught him as he emerged from near our cabin—he had made another search. We saw his shadow on the wall near the stairs several times. He seemed to be nearing a nervous breakdown. Mr. Kruger told us that he had sworn we had the dog and meant to find it at any cost. There was one more night to go, and the next day the ship would dock.

At ten Barbara would deliver Little Bit to Mr. Kruger, and we would fill the bag in which she traveled with paper tissue, tobacco, soap, extra toothbrushes, razor blades, dental floss, and other things, which can all be bought in Europe but which for some droll reason one always takes along.

Little Bit was fed from luncheon trays which we ordered for ourselves in the cabin instead of going down to lunch.

The steward was shaking. "I don't know," he said, "when that guy butchers, or when he takes care of the other dogs. He's hanging around here all the time. I hope you get off all right."

On the last afternoon on board I became careless. Some passengers and a bearded ship's officer were watching the last game of the deck-tennis tournament, and others were lying this way and that in their deck chairs, forming a protective barricade. Barbara had checked on the butcher—he was busy aft, airing some of his charges.

I thought it safe to take Little Bit out of my coat and place her on deck, so that we all could relax a bit. She had been there but a moment when I heard a cry. "Ha," it went. It was the "Ha" of accusation and discovery, chagrin and triumph, and it had been issued by Mr. Haegeli, who stood with both arms raised. Fortunately he was not a kangaroo and was therefore unable to jump over the occupied deck chairs. I gathered up Little Bit, and we were safe for a few seconds. By now I knew the ship's plan as well as the man who designed her. We went down two decks on outside stairs, entered through a serving pantry, climbed one inside service stair, and then nonchalantly walked to the bar. I sat down and rang for the steward. I ordered something to drink. In a little while Barbara, with her lemonade in hand, said, "He's watching us through the third window!"

I swept my eyes over the left side of the room, and his face was pressed against the glass, pale and haunting. He kept watch from the outside, and ran back and forth as we moved around inside.

We went down to dinner. When we came back I got a cigar. He was outside the bar. As I went to the saloon to have coffee he was outside that window.

"Don't give Little Bit any sugar," Barbara said. "He's watching us."

The floor was cleared for dancing, and we got up to walk back to the library. There is a passage between the main saloon and the library off which are various pantries and side rooms, and it has no window. In a corner of it is the shop, and on this last evening people stood there in numbers buying cartons of cigarettes, film, small sailor hats, miniature lifebelts and ship models with "S.S. America" written on them. Here I suddenly realized the miraculous solution of our problem. It was in front of me, on a shelf. Among stuffed Mickey Mice, Donald Ducks, and teddy bears of various sizes stood the exact replica of Little Bit—the same button eyes and patent-leather nose, the fluff, the legs like sticks, the pompom at the end of the tail, and the blue ribbon in its hair.

"How much is that dog?" I asked the young lady.

"Two ninety-five."

"I'll take it."

"Shall I wrap it up, sir?"

"No, thanks, I'll take it as is."

"What are we going to do now, Poppy?"

"Now you keep Little Bit hidden, and I'll take the stuffed dog, and we'll go into the library."

There we sat down. I placed the stuffed dog at my side and spoke to it. The butcher was on the far side of the ship, but he almost went through the window. He disappeared and ran around to the other side. I had arranged the toy dog so that it seemed to be asleep at my side, partly covered by Barbara's scarf. I told her to take Little Bit down to the cabin and then come back, and we'd have some fun with the butcher.

When she came back Barbara took the toy dog and fixed its hair and combed the fluff. Then I said, "Please give me the dog." We walked the length of the ship on the inside. The butcher was sprinting outside, his face flashing momentarily in the series of windows.

At the front of the ship we went out on deck. I held the dog so that the pompom stuck out in back, and I wiggled it a little, to give it the illusion of life. It took the butcher a while to catch up. He walked fast—we walked faster. He almost ran— we ran. He shouted, "Mister!" I continued running. As we came toward the stern I asked Barbara, "Can you let out a terrible scream?"

"Yes, of course," said Barbara.

"One—two—three—*now.*"

She screamed, and I threw the dog in a wide curve out into the sea. The butcher, a few feet away, gripped the railing and looked below, where the small white form was bobbing up and down in the turbulent water. Rapidly it was washed away in the wake of the *America.*

We turned to go back into the saloon.

We left the butcher paralyzed at the stern. He wasn't at the gangplank the next day.

Little Bit landed in France without further incident.

from **An Episode of Sparrows**

RUMER GODDEN

Bomb-Ruin Garden

[*Left by her mother to board with Mrs. Combie in a slum district of London, Lovejoy Mason conceived a secret project which led her to steal a packet of seeds from the little boy Sparkey. Now it was three weeks later . . .*]

Before going down into the bomb-ruin, Lovejoy cast her usual wary look up and down the Street, and there was Sparkey, in an overcoat and muffler, being led away by his mother from the newspaper stand for his tea. She crossed over to speak to them.

"Where's Sparkey been?" she asked.

"Having his spring bronchitis," said Sparkey's mother. Lovejoy nodded; that was an annual fixture. Sparkey's mother looked gaunt and tired and had black marks under her eyes, while Sparkey was more than ever thin and transparent-looking, but they had not forgotten the packet. Sparkey put out his tongue, and, "You leave him alone," said his mother.

"Of course," said Lovejoy distantly and walked away.

Sparkey's mother went on towards Garden Row, but presently Sparkey slipped his hand and came, dodging from one portico to another, back to his step. He watched Lovejoy go through the gap; then he stood up on tiptoe to see more.

I haven't been for three weeks, Lovejoy was thinking, and she realized what an interference her mother and Uncle Francis had been. Well, he has gone, she thought comfortably, and her mother was back with the Blue Moons where she belonged. Lovejoy felt as if dozens of tight threads that had been sewn tightly into her were being loosened one by one.

As she came across the rubble, she noticed that there were rather more nettles and weeds between the walls; it had been raining, there were puddles on the ground, but the sun was drying them up. There was the usual smell of rubbish and soot and cess. Lovejoy sniffed it as she looked round carefully; then she bent and scuttled between the walls, behind the pyramids, till she came round her own two walls to the garden.

There she stood still.

The packet had said that the seeds would come up; Mr. Isbister had said that too; when Lovejoy had planted them she supposed she had believed it, but it had been more hope than belief. Now, on the patch of earth under the net, had come a film of green; when she bent down and looked closely, she could see that it was made of countless little stalks as fine as hairs, some so fine that she could scarcely see their colour, others vividly showing their new green. They're *blades*, thought Lovejoy, blades of grass! In the borders were what she thought at first were tiny weeds, until she saw real weeds among them. The weeds were among the grass too; she could tell them because they were bigger, a different pattern, and when she looked again the borders were peopled with myriad heads, all alike, each head made of two flat leaves, no bigger than pinheads, on a stalk; they were so many and so all the same that she knew they were meant; no weed seeded like that. They must come from a sowing—my sowing, thought Lovejoy suddenly, the seeds I planted.

She knelt down, carefully lifted the net away, and very gently, with her palm, she brushed the hair blades; they seemed to move as if they were not quite rooted, but rooted they were; when she held one in her thumb and finger it did not come away. "It's like— earth's fur," said Lovejoy. She said it aloud in her astonishment, and the sound of her own voice made her jump and look up. It was then she heard the whistle.

It was the kind of whistle that is made by blowing on fingers in the corners of the mouth, a boy's whistle. Boys! Lovejoy crouched down, tense and still.

* * *

Lovejoy thought the bomb-ruin was deserted, but there was a camp there and it belonged to Tip Malone.

Sparkey knew why the gang had not been to the camp all this time; just as the girls had suddenly taken to skipping—three months ago not a skipping-rope was to be seen in the Street—now the boys were playing baseball; Tony Zassi, the little American, had taught them. Sparkey knew where they played in the park across the river; they had been there every day all the holidays. "Well, you can't go," said Sparkey's mother. "It's too far and the ball's too hard." Sparkey trembled in case any boy heard her.

But now school had begun and the boys were back, and as Sparkey stood straining to see, while his mother called him, he heard the familiar rabble sound of voices, of scuffling, and the boys came into view, walking and twisting together in a huddle of jeans, corduroy trousers, and shorts, old darned sweaters and jackets, cropped heads, short-cut hair, and weapons, knives and catapults; it was the gang, and in the middle walked Tip. All the Malones were big, and Tip was a head above the other boys; he was carrying a bat—it was not his but Tony's. Tip was swinging it and talking in his big Irish voice. Sparkey stood up on his step; his eyes glittered so that if his mother had seen them she would have thought he was feverish again and taken him in, but a neighbour had come up to talk to her. Sparkey was husky with emotion as he called, "Tip. Tip Malone. Tip."

One of the boys, Puggy, glanced across the pavement but when he saw it was only Sparkey he took no notice.

"Tip," croaked Sparkey. "Tip."

In a pause in his stream of talk, Tip heard; unlike Puggy, when he saw it was only Sparkey he stopped. The other boys, even Puggy, stopped too. "Well, young 'un?" said Tip.

Sparkey's bowels could have melted within him at Tip's kindness but he held firm. He had an end in view. "I know something you don't," he said.

"Blimey. What cheek!" said John.

"I do," said Sparkey.

"What do you know?" asked Tip, amused at this strange little creature with owl eyes and spindly legs.

"'F I tell you kin I be in the gang?" Sparkey flushed as the boys guffawed. They all guffawed but Tip. Tip looked down at Sparkey and said, much as Sparkey's mother had done, "But you can only be six—or seven," said Tip as a compliment.

"Aw, c'mon," said Rory, and Puggy twitched Tip's sleeve, but Sparkey looked so miserable that Tip was moved to ask, "What do you know?"

"'F I tell can I be in the gang?"

"He *can't* know anything," said Jimmy Howes.

"I do." Sparkey forgot to croak; his voice was so shrill that it carried right down the Street.

"Ssh," said Tip. "D'you want everyone to hear?"

There were murmurs from the gang because Tip was taking this seriously. "C'mon," "Le's-go," "*Aw, c'mon,*" they said, but Tip was a dictator. "Shut your mouths," he said. "This may be important."

Sparkey swelled with joy and hope; he almost told there and then but he wanted to make his bargain. "'F I tell—" he began when Tip interrupted.

"You can't be *in* the gang," he said reasonably. "You couldn't keep up; you're too small, you'd get knocked about, but I tell you what: we'll keep a place open for you and for now you can be our look-out, our spy."

"A—spy!" said Sparkey. His bronchitis had left him weak and he nearly fainted from joy. "I'll do anything for you, Tip," he said huskily.

"Well, tell us what you've got to tell us, if it *is* anything," said Puggy impatiently.

Sparkey drew himself up; he felt twice as big and as important as he had a minute ago.

"I'll tell Tip," he said, "not you," and he looked at Tip. "There's a girl," he said, "on your ruin."

There was silence while they all turned and looked at the bomb-ruin, where nothing, no life, stirred. "Don't be bloody silly," said Tip.

"There is. It's Lovejoy Mason." As he told that Sparkey felt an immense satisfaction. Now he was even with her for the packet. "She goes in and out," he said.

"What for?" asked Rory.

A garden had not crossed Sparkey's mind, and, "I think she's building herself a camp," he said.

"A *camp?*" They were outraged.

"What d'you know about that!" said Ginger, flabbergasted.

"Blasted cheek," said John.

Tip's camp was the best-hidden for miles; screened by a bit of an old wall, it was like an igloo built of rubble; there was only a little hole, close to the ground, by which to go in and out; even the smallest of the boys had to lie down and wriggle. Outside it looked just another pile of bricks and stones; inside it had bunks made of orange boxes, an old meat safe for keeping things in, and an older cooking stove in which it was possible to light a fire or heat up a sausage or soup over a candle; drinks were kept in a hot-water bottle. "It's real drink, sometimes it's beer," whispered Sparkey—he always whispered when he spoke of the camp—and sometimes the boys had cigarettes.

"Do you have to smoke?" Mrs. Malone asked Tip when, for the tenth time, he was sick.

"Yes, I have to," said Tip desperately. "They wouldn't think anything of me, else."

The gang had thought the camp completely secret, but, "She's there now," said Sparkey breathlessly. "I just seen her go in."

For a moment they stood still, then Tip put his two little fingers in the corners of his mouth and whistled. The next moment they were through the gap, down the bank, and in the bomb-ruin. There was a violent noise of boots on stones, of hoots and cries, as they hunted among the walls; then they found, and Lovejoy was surrounded.

One minute the garden was there, its stones arranged, the cornflowers growing, the grass green; the next there were only boots. To Lovejoy they were boots, though most of the boys wore shoes, but boys' shoes with heavy steel tips to the soles and heels. She crouched where she was, while the boots smashed up the garden, trampled down the grass, and kicked away the stones; the cornflower earth was scattered, the seedlings torn out and pulled in bits. In a minute no garden was left, and Tip picked up the trowel and fork and threw them far away across the rubble. "Now get out," said Tip to Lovejoy.

Lovejoy stood up; she felt as if she were made of stone she was so cold and hard; then, in a boy's hand, she saw an infinitesimal bit of green; he was rolling a cornflower between his finger and thumb; suddenly her chin began to tremble.

"D'you know what we do to girls who come on our land?" said Puggy. "We take their pants off and send 'em home without them."

The boys guffawed again. "Shut up," said Tip. "I'm talking."

Tip had seen two things the other boys had not; being in front as they attacked, he had seen the garden whole; he had not had time to look properly but he had a vision of something laid out, green and alive, carefully edged with stones; the other thing he had seen, and saw now, only he did not want to look, was the trembling of Lovejoy's chin. She had not uttered a sound, not screamed or cried or protested; the Malones were vociferous, Tip connected females with screams and cries, and here was only this small trembling. It made him feel uncomfortable; he remembered how a puppy's legs, when he had seen it run over and killed, had trembled like that.

"Get out," he said to Lovejoy but less fiercely. As she still seemed dazed he put his hand on her shoulder to turn her, but he should have known better than to touch her; this was Lovejoy, who had thrown the potato knife, who had spat at Angela; she turned her head and bit Tip's hand.

She bit as hard as she could, and ran.

When she came through the gap, the boys after her, Sparkey looked down at his shoes and smiled.

* * *

One of the things that has to be learned is that even sorrow cannot be had in peace, because other people have sorrows too; no boy could catch Lovejoy, and she had had only one thought as she ran, to get to Mrs. Combie, but when she got home Vincent and Mrs. Combie were quarrelling.

Lovejoy heard Mrs. Combie weeping and took herself out of the way upstairs.

It was an hour or two later that Cassie burst into the Masons' room. She never knocked. One does not knock for children.

"There's a boy wants to see you," she told Lovejoy.

"I don't want to see a boy," said Lovejoy.

"Hoity-toity!" said Cassie. "Well, I'm making poor Mrs. Combie a cup of tea. You'd better come down and have yours now."

"I don't want any tea."

"Don't you feel well?" asked curious Cassie.

"Quite well," said Lovejoy but she felt neither well nor ill; she felt nothing, nothing at all; she might have been dead. "You can come down or go to bed," said Cassie.

Lovejoy came down, but in the kitchen they had started again. "The whole of Dad's money gone!" said Cassie.

"We'll get it back," Vincent shouted at her.

"There's a place called Queer Street," said Cassie.

Lovejoy left the kitchen so that she would not have to hear any more. Her fingers, gripped in her pocket, found the pillbox. Thoughtfully she took it outside and emptied it down the gutter.

The seeds fell down like rain; she wondered if they would stick in the gutter and grow, and she thought of nasturtiums flowering on the pavement edges and at once the familiar feeling stirred in her, the garden feeling. But what's the use of that now? Lovejoy was thinking wearily when a boy came up from the shadow by the side door. It was Tip.

Lovejoy stiffened. "What do you want?" she said, backing against the house wall.

Tip did not see why she should flinch and back away like that. He had not hurt her, while she had left a half-circle of bleeding little purple marks on his hand; "The first thing she ever did for me she bit me," he was to say afterwards. The bite ached still. Nor did he at all understand why he was doing what he did now. "I came to bring you this," he said and held out the garden fork. "I couldn't find the trowel," said Tip, "but we've got a little old shovel you could use."

Lovejoy made no attempt to hold the fork; as she walked away to the edge of the pavement she let it drop from her hand into the gutter; then she sat down on the curb and began to cry.

Tip was one of those boys who are so big and strong that people do not really look at them; they look at their boots, their big young knees and shoulders, their jaws, perhaps, but not at them. "What a young tough," people said of Tip, but Mrs. Malone, who knew him better than anyone else, said, "He's not tough. He's gentle." Few people divined this. Yet Lovejoy divined it, at once.

To Lovejoy, Tip was a bitter-enemy boy, the biggest and worst of the ones who had smashed her garden, and yet she, who never cried in front of anyone, who had not cried then, was moved to cry now, in front of him. He did not jeer at her, nor did he go away embarrassed; he picked up the fork and sat down on the curb beside her.

The curb of a busy street may seem a poor place to talk but on an early May evening, almost warm enough for summer, when people are taking their ease outside, there is something relaxed about it; if the street is familiar it can even be peaceful. The stone Tip and Lovejoy were sitting on was warm, it was the right height from the gutter to be comfortable. Scraps of conversation fell into their talk as people passed, but that only made it seem more private; a Sister of Charity came by with her quiet skirt and noisy beads and she smiled down on them; the man with the two dogs passed on the opposite side of the road; a gang of big boys stayed, shouting and laughing on the corner at a group of girls. A little farther up the Street, Yvette and Susie Romney were practising handstands against a wall. Pooh! I could show them, thought Lovejoy. The pink and white of their thighs flashed each time their legs went up and their skirts fell back. One of Mrs. Cleary's and Miss Arnot's cats—not Istanbul but a white blear-eyed cat—

came down the Street, arching its back against every pillar, and mewing as it stalked the smell of the fried fish and chips that two big girls were eating out of a newspaper as they walked. A few smaller children, up late, were playing hopscotch. Lovejoy heard all this and saw it as if she were in a dream; she was too tired, too dead to think or feel or care for herself or Vincent or Mrs. Combie, but she felt Tip beside her and she noticed him acutely.

She saw the shabby blue jeans, the way his wrists came far out of his grey-coloured sweater—it was halfway up his arms—the way his shoes were rubbed and the heels worn down. He did not seem to mind any of these things; she thought that her plimsolls, the threadbare plaid of her coat might seem to him entirely natural and that gave her a feeling of ease. She noticed other things: how hard and bony Tip's arms were, where hers showed round and soft; the funny look of his cheek that was bony too and freckled, freckles all over it, thought Lovejoy; his hair was rough; Lovejoy's head only came up to his shoulder, and when he turned to look at her his eyes were dark blue. A boy with blue eyes? thought Lovejoy, surprised. She had never thought of a boy's eyes as having a particular colour before; for Lovejoy that made him seem suddenly human.

As for Tip, he only stole glances at her but she seemed to him small and curiously clean, and he noticed that her hair was beautifully brushed.

They sat together and the tears dried on Lovejoy's cheeks; fixing her eyes on the hopscotch, watching it without seeing it, she told Tip about the garden, beginning with the packet of cornflower seeds and going on to the buying of the fork and trowel—she left out the candle box—but Tip did not seem to be listening.

"Who brushes your hair?" asked Tip.

"I brush it." Tip, thinking of the screams and protests of his young sisters Josephine and Bridget when his mother brought out the family hairbrush, marvelled, but Lovejoy was telling him about Mr. Isbister and the grass seed, and the net—leaving out how she took it; she told about the seeds—leaving out how she stole them from Woolworth's—and of how the grass and the cornflowers had come up. There she stopped.

Tip listened, hitting his leg thoughtfully with the fork. Boys have to hit something, thought Lovejoy irritably. "That's how I made the garden," she said, staring across the road. "My garden," and she gave a little hiccup of misery.

"Make another."

It sounded so unsympathetic that Lovejoy sat up indignantly until she saw Tip was better than sympathetic, he was interested. "You were silly to make it there," he said. "Make another somewhere else."

That was what Mr. Isbister was to say. He was quite angry. "Catford Street?" he said. "What d'you expect? Cats—boys, frost, drought—or a dang—great thunderstorm. Make a garden, you're in for it. Then don't come mewling here," said Mr. Isbister.

"But is it any good? Do things ever grow?" asked Lovejoy.

Mr. Isbister grunted and said, "Look." He had been putting in cuttings of geraniums, plain little pieces of plants with three or four leaves.

"They haven't got a root," said Lovejoy.

"They make one," said Mr. Isbister. "Stick 'em in the ground, they grow."

"Just bits of plant?" asked Lovejoy incredulously.

"Bits of plant," said Mr. Isbister, poking at them with his finger. "That's earth," he said, "and not boys, cats—hailstones—can—beat that, all the time." And he said what Tip said now. "Make another."

"You were silly to make it there," said Tip.

"But *where* else can I make it?" Lovejoy's voice was as sharp and irritated as Cassie's. "There isn't anywhere," she said scornfully. "Nowhere that boys don't spoil. It wasn't a very good garden," she said, "not what I wanted but—" Her voice trembled as if she were going to cry again.

"What kind of garden do you want?" asked Tip hastily. He only asked to divert her but it brought an answer from Lovejoy, an answer she had not dreamed of before.

"I want an Italian garden," said Lovejoy.

There was one walk she had been with Vincent—long ago, while I was still looking for a garden, thought Lovejoy now. It was a street along the river, with gardens, embankment gardens, thought

Lovejoy, in front. Its houses were dark red. "What is it called?" she had asked Vincent.

"Cheyne Walk," said Vincent.

Most of the houses had small private gardens. "That's what I want," Lovejoy had said, looking into them, "a small private garden."

Those in Cheyne Walk were not very private; they could be looked into easily; Lovejoy had thought, I'd want mine to be more private than that. They were all different; some had small lawns, edged with coloured cobbles; some had clipped bushes, in some there were beds of daffodils and wallflowers; one had a rock garden built of rough stone; one or two had round beds with rosebushes cut back; some had empty beds, ready for planting or sowing—in April, thought Lovejoy. She had stopped to study one of these carefully; the soil was finely raked and black-looking. "Is that good garden earth?" she asked.

"I suppose it is," said Vincent. "Come along."

Then they had found a garden they both liked.

It was different from the others. It was worked out in stone and it was shapely; in the middle was a small stone urn filled with earth and standing on a pedestal; round the pedestal was a square of grass, clipped smooth and green, and this was bordered with narrow flowerbeds that were edged with fluted stone.

"The flowerbeds in the Square Gardens don't have stone edges," said Lovejoy.

"The Square Gardens are ordinary gardens," said Vincent with scorn. "*This* is Italian."

Vincent had schooled Lovejoy into thinking that everything superbly good was Italian, that everything Italian was superbly good, and she looked at the garden with awe.

"Italian gardens," said Vincent, who had never seen one, "are stone and green, with fountains and vases and walks, not just flowers."

This instant, as she sat beside Tip on the curb, that came into Lovejoy's mind.

"I want a garden with stone," she said. "With a vase in the middle and walks—"

When she said "stone" Tip looked up. He stopped beating his leg with the fork. "I know where," he said.

* * *

"But we're going into the church," said Lovejoy and stopped. She was wary of going into Our Lady of Sion now.

"That's all right, it's my church," said Tip serenely.

"Yours?" Lovejoy was astounded.

"Yes," said Tip firmly, "where I go."

"Go to *church?*"

"Yes. Don't you?"

"I've never been," said Lovejoy, and she looked at him as if he were a phenomenon. "I've never known anyone who went to church," she said.

Tip was suddenly moved to take her hand. "C'mon," he said.

Lovejoy followed him up the church steps to the landing where the rusty bell was; Father Lambert had put it into a cage because the boys slipped in and rang it.

"Look," said Tip, and, going to the top of the opposite flight that led down into the church, he hoisted himself up, in the footholds made by the broken bricks, till he was sitting on the wall above. "Can you do that?" he asked.

"Of course," said Lovejoy and came up after him, more nimble than he.

"Turn yourself round," said Tip, "and come down." He disappeared behind the wall. "Slide down," he said. "Feel with your toes." There were some broken bits like ledges in the wall. "You kin put your feet on them," whispered Tip. "Gimme your foot and I'll show you. No, the other one. Now down. Hold on tight." It was hard to hold to a ledge, hanging by a hand while the other groped for the next ledge; below was a heap of sharp rubble and stone that would hurt if one fell on them, but Lovejoy came on down. "Steady! Let yourself down now. You're there!" whispered Tip and she dropped lightly beside him. "Good girl," he said. "Bridget wouldn't have done that, but that's what you have to do, see? Look carefully, and when no one's there, get over the wall. It's difficult going back; you have to climb up by the bricks."

"I can do it," said Lovejoy.

She looked round. They were in a space behind the church

that once, long ago, had been a graveyard. At one side was the Priest's House, but the two windows that looked on it were blank and curtained. "It's Father Lambert's bedroom," whispered Tip. "He's only in it at night, and the room above's a storeroom; I know. I've carried books up there." At the back a long blank wall ran the length of the graveyard. "That's Potter's garage," whispered Tip, "and that's the dairy." He nodded towards a wall on the third side with high gratings. "Nobody can get up there to look," he said, "and nobody comes here. Most people don't even know it's here. They don't look over the wall. They don't think of it because it's the church, see, but you could make a garden here, if you kin find a place," he added—the space was piled with rubble and debris. "There's a lot of stone," said Tip, looking at it.

There was more stone than Lovejoy had ever seen, bits of broken pillars, cornices; a great tombstone with cherubs on it—"Supernatural babies," whispered Lovejoy—had been laid against the wall. There were flutings and chippings and pieces, bits of faces, and hands and wings, and flowers. "They're from the old church," whispered Tip— instinctively they whispered here. "One day they're going to build it new."

"The aeroplane isn't nearly up," said Lovejoy comfortably. She was quite alive again. She could see already that this was a much better place for a garden. Protected by the church, it would be safe. Lovejoy had never heard the word "sanctuary" but she knew she had found a safe place. She felt like Christopher Columbus when he had landed on the shores of the Bahamas, and perhaps to have discovered in Catford Street a quiet, empty place for a garden was a feat almost as unlikely.

She took two steps over the rubble, and then stood still. The last sun was slanting exactly where she needed to look; at the back of the church hut, between stumps where a second row of the old pillars had been, was a space, empty and sunny; it was strewn with chips of glass and stone but it was earth; she could see its darkness. It was perhaps seven feet by four, the size of a hearthrug, but big enough, and at one end, as if it had been placed in readiness, was, not a vase but a bit of a small broken-off column, whiter than the stumps of the big pillars—"Pure marble," whispered Tip, who had come up; marble and fluted, "Like a piece of Edinburgh Rock," whispered

Lovejoy, and, as if to prove the ground was fertile, up the little column grew a stem with green leaves, broad and shining, in the shape of hearts. "What is it?" Lovejoy was to ask Mr. Isbister when she took him a leaf.

"You never seen ivy?" asked Mr. Isbister incredulously. Lovejoy could not remember that she had.

But now it did not matter to her what the stem was; she simply gazed.

*   *   *

When Lovejoy looked at the plot, measuring it with her eye, considering what to do with it, she found out a surprising thing; where before she had groped uncertainly, now she knew something about gardens; she began searching among the stone until at last she picked up a piece of fluted carving. "We must edge the beds with stone like this," she said.

"That's a bit of grave," objected Tip.

"The grave's all smashed," said Lovejoy, unconcerned, "and look." She had found another broken grave spread with fine marble chips. "We can make paths with this," she said.

She had said "we." Tip began to feel uneasy. He had shown her where she could make a garden, that was enough. "You do what you like," said Tip. "'S your garden, not mine."

"We'll make a lawn here," said Lovejoy as if he had not spoken, "and flowerbeds here, between the stone edges and the grass. Let's clear some of the bits." She squatted down and began picking up the stones. "We mustn't make a noise so don't throw anything, put it down gently," she commanded. Tip did not move. "Help me," said Lovejoy.

"Who d'you think I am?" said Tip. Lovejoy did not answer.

"I'm not going to make no sissy garden," said Tip. "I showed you where it was, what else do you want?" And he turned to go back to the wall.

He expected an outcry; when anyone crossed Bridget or Josephine Malone—or Clara or Margaret or Mary, any of his five sisters—there was always an outcry; that was a good name for it, a howling, it might almost have been called a bawling, that could be heard right down the Street; but Lovejoy said nothing. She stayed where she was, picking up the stones, only her head sank lower and the two sides of her hair swung forward, hiding her face and showing her neck; with her finger she poked in the earth.

The effect was curiously powerful. Tip went a few steps and looked back; the silence tugged at him; she seemed so small and solitary among the stones that he could not bear it; he tried to go, he went a step more, then he came back. "All right, then, I'll help you," said Tip angrily.

She kept him till it grew cold and eerie in the graveyard. "My mum'll lam me," he said.

"Does she lam you?" asked Lovejoy wistfully.

"Don't they care how late you are?" he asked.

"No," said Lovejoy briefly and worked on. Tip began to think there were advantages in being Lovejoy; she could stay out as late as she liked, she was free of church; he began to look at her with a mixture of disapproval and respect.

They worked on; he had to admire the way she did it, soundlessly moving and clearing the stone and glass. "Keep any little bits that will do for edging," she said, but to almost every bit Tip found she said, "No, that won't do." It was hard work. Tip's back had begun to ache when at last she stopped. "You've got spunk, I'll say that for you," said Tip, when she stood stiffly up.

"It isn't nearly done," was all she said. "You'll come tomorrow?"

"Me? No fear," said Tip.

She looked at him.

"I've things to do," said Tip loftily.

Lovejoy bent her head again in that quivering silence.

"I promised the others," said Tip not quite as loftily.

"I was going to move that big stone there an' I can't by myself," said Lovejoy sorrowfully. "An' that iron bar, I can't get that up." It was a lament. "*You* told me to make another garden," said Lovejoy. "How can I all alone? It was going to be so lo-ve-ly." In the darkness her whisper seemed to go on and on like a sad little ghost. Tip tried to shut it out but he could not.

"Oh, all right," he said crossly, "I'll come for a little while."

He was soon to learn his mistake. Lovejoy was a tyrant.

"I only came to tell you I can't come," he would begin. "We're meeting down by the river." But mysteriously he stayed, and missed the meeting. "Come straight after school," begged Lovejoy. Her begging was almost as compelling as her silence.

On the second day the patch was cleared, and now began the work of finding the stone. Schooled by Vincent, Lovejoy was meticulous. "That doesn't match," she said to most of Tip's efforts.

"Why does it have to have a stone edging?" asked Tip rebelliously. "Other gardens don't."

"This is an *Italian* garden," said Lovejoy, "a real Italian garden."

from *We Are Seven*

UNA TROY

*Pansy
and the
Film
Magnate*

The film magnate had come at last. He wasn't merely a hopeful dream this time; he was really and truly there. The moment she heard the news Pansy dressed herself and Jennifer in their best, rubbed geranium petals to her cheeks and to Jennifer's, and set off to him.

Three miles on a hot summer's day is tiring for a small child but Pansy's pace never slackened. Only just outside Ballybay did she pause to take out pocket mirror and piece of broken comb, rearrange her hair, curl up her eyelashes with a moistened forefinger, and then she pressed on. She stopped the first man she met in the village.

"Where," she said, "are the picture people?"

To Pansy's surprise, the man regarded her with extreme disfavor.

For the past three nights he had tried to sleep with six of his children, all under eight years of age, in his room, four of them actually in his bed. He was fond of his family but not so fond as all that. He had now an aching head and a general dislike of children.

"Those ones?" he said. He spat, almost at Pansy's feet. "They're all over the place," he said and slouched glumly by her.

Pansy stood stock still on the road. Then, hurriedly, she pulled out the mirror and took a reassuring glance. No, she looked all right; it wasn't that. She dismissed the oddly disagreeable person from her mind, gazed around (despite what he had said, there was no one in sight) and then walked determinedly towards the little post office.

There was a very old woman behind the counter. From her Pansy bought a bottle of lemonade and drank it in a droughty, exhausted fashion. She put down the empty bottle with a weak smile.

"That was very nice. I was very thirsty."

"It's thirsty kind of weather."

"I had a long walk," Pansy explained. "From Doon."

"From Doon? Now, who would you be, I wonder?"

"My name is Monaghan. Pansy Monaghan."

"Is that so, now?" The old woman's attention quickened. "Now, what Monaghans would you be? Would you be——?" She paused. "Would your mother's name be Bridget Monaghan?" she asked, delicately.

"Yes." Pansy saw that her questioner was eager for information and judged the moment opportune to move slowly towards the door. "I must be going. I came to look at the picture people and Mammy will be angry if I'm not back for tea."

"The picture people, is it? They're down by the slip—it's only round the turn of the street. You'll know when you're come to them easy enough by the crowd around them." The old woman sniffed contemptuously. Then, as Pansy neared the threshold, she said in desperation: "Won't you have another bottle of lemonade?"

Pansy's finger fondled the shilling in her pocket.

"I've no more money," she said, sadly.

She paid for her second bottle of lemonade with information—much of it erroneous but all of it apparently enthralling to her listener—about herself and her family and then, sternly averting her eyes from jars of sweets and tins of biscuits, she made her way directly towards her goal.

A crowd of sightseers lined the wall above the little harbor. Pansy eeled her way between knobby elbows and yielding sides, and looked down. The small bay was formed by a natural shelf of rock on one side and on the other by a concrete slip shelving down to the sea. On the crescent of hard yellow sand between, figures were grouped in irregular formation and, to the right of them, Pansy saw, with one of her few impacts of genuine emotion, the cameras.

For fully a quarter of an hour, she gazed in mute and selfless adoration. Then, realizing that this was getting her nowhere, she began to look around.

It was difficult to know which was the magnate. On such a hot day, he could not, unfortunately, be identified by his fur-collared coat. She narrowed her eyes, searching for a cigar, but nothing but cigarettes dangled from fingers or lips. The only thing to do was to go down and inquire. She removed her elbow from its nicely adjusted pressure on the hip of the woman nearest her and asked politely: "How do I get down to the strand, please?"

"Eh?" Freed from the sharp jab of Pansy's determined joint, the woman stirred comfortably and seemed to flow over her. "You can't go down there. No one's allowed down."

She settled herself in a better position, obliterating Pansy's view and almost smothering her. But, even as she had spoken, Pansy had noticed a small girl sitting alone on the edge of the rocks beside the beach. Where that child could go, Pansy Monaghan certainly could. Like a ruthless porcupine this time (for she disliked being smothered) Pansy went through the yielding crowd, leaving behind her a scatter of sore flesh and bone and muttered curses. She had a good sense of direction which did not fail her now. She went purposefully towards the right until she found herself alone on a grassy cliff top, climbed down a perilous goat path to a strip of shingle, turned to the left and scrambled over a belt of rocks (once she fell but, luckily, on top of Jennifer) and finally arrived, with only one small scratch on her knee as a mark of her dangerous journey, by that child.

She sat down boldly beside the child. She looked at her. Mellowed by the successful conclusion of her enterprise, she said: "Hallo!" though, ordinarily, this was not at all the type of child to whom

Pansy would deign to make advances. This little girl was dressed in a very ragged green skirt, with bare patches of skin showing through the holes in her ragged red jersey. Her fair hair hung down limply without clasp or ribbon. Her feet were bare.

She looked at Pansy and frowned. Pansy said: "Hallo!" again, more loudly but still kindly. The child turned her head away. She said, in a high, chill English accent. "What are you doing here?"

Pansy nearly fell off her rock into the pool below. She had heard this accent, often on the films, occasionally from the fox-hunting county hacking through Doon, and she knew what it connoted. She studied the surprising child more carefully. She noticed now that, despite the rags, there was no single speck of dirt visible and the untrammeled hair was sleek and gleaming. She said, cautiously: "I came to look on."

The strange child turned that imperious frown on her again.

"You can't stay here. Don't you know that nobody's supposed to come down here while they're shooting?"

"*You're* here," Pansy said.

The child laughed scornfully.

"I'm Maybella Merton." Pansy stared. The child said, very sharply: "Don't you know me?"

"No," Pansy said.

Maybella Merton shrugged her shoulders and looked wearily out to sea.

"Of course, there wouldn't *be* any films in a place like this."

"There are. At least, there are in Kilmuc. I often go there."

"Really?" The child raised her eyebrows. "And have you seen *The Loaded Bough?*"

"I don't think so."

The child seemed unutterably bored.

"That was my latest."

For perhaps the first time in her life, Pansy was bereft of speech. At last she said, slowly: "Do you mean you *act* in pictures?"

"Naturally. I told you I was Maybella Merton."

There was a long silence. Maybella stared at the horizon and Pansy stared at Maybella. At last Pansy drew a deep breath.

"It's—it's wonderful to meet you."

With a faint semblance of interest, Maybella ceased studying the horizon.

"I suppose anything unusual is exciting in a place like this."

"Oh, no, not *anything*," Pansy said. "There are lots of unusual things that mightn't be a bit exciting. But meeting *you* is. Meeting a famous film star!"

Maybella was almost smirking now.

"You can't know much about me if you've never seen my films."

"Oh, but I do. Not seeing your films—not yet—but reading all about you. In the magazines. They said you were wonderful and very famous. I just didn't catch your name the first time you said it," Pansy explained, glibly, "but of course I know all about you. Even to look at you, anyone would know you were famous."

Maybella smirked outright.

"I suppose I *am* fairly well known."

Pansy ploughed on.

"Of course, you're well known. Everywhere. Probably now you thought that a child like me mightn't have heard of you, but you see I have. We've often talked of you at home," said Pansy, feeling that the creature was insatiable, "looking at pictures of you and—that sort of thing. Often and often." Pansy paused and sighed. She waited for a moment and then asked, meekly: "Would it matter if I stayed here? Just keeping quiet, you know. Just to be with you."

"It will probably be all right. I shouldn't think they'll get around to my scenes today."

With a sigh of relief, Pansy relaxed. She wiggled to a less spiky position on the rock and settled Jennifer beside her. Secure and at ease, she scanned the intermingling and apparently chaotic company on the beach so near now that she could distinguish the players by their peculiarly painted faces. But she couldn't find the magnate. She had to ask Maybella.

"Who's making this picture, Maybella?"

"How do you mean, making it? All of us, of course."

"But who's the head one?"

"Do you mean Alan Horton? He's over there!"

Mr. Horton was talking earnestly to a girl dressed in a green shawl and red skirt, almost as tattered as Maybella's, and a fat little priest, whose round hat was pushed to the back of his head. All three were gesticulating freely with cigarettes. Mr. Horton wore a khaki shirt, brown corduroy trousers and sandals. He was a small man and looked worried. Pansy felt a vague sense of disappointment and loss. But there, such as he was, was the magnate, and she fixed him with a vulture eye.

"I," said Maybella, "am playing her when she's young."

She pointed to the green-shawled girl.

"Oh! Is that why your clothes are torn, too?"

"We're fisher folk."

Pansy had never seen any fisherman's families dressed in such slattern brightness. She said, earnestly: "It seems queer you not mending your clothes when you're her. She'd be old enough to mend her clothes. And even her when she's you would have a mother or someone to mend them."

Maybella shrugged her shoulders.

"Irish, you know."

Pansy felt worried.

"But I'm Irish and——"

"Sh-h-h!" said Maybella, fiercely. "They're making a take."

The crowd had withdrawn from the girl and the priest, leaving them standing together by a beached boat. The girl sprang into the boat and out again. She was very wild. She looked passionately at the sea and made a speech that Pansy could not hear. The priest backed a pace, took off his round hat and made a sweeping sign of the cross on himself. The girl tossed her head in a madcap fashion and flung out her arms.

"Och! yer riverince," she said, loudly enough now for Pansy to catch the words, "'tis how I must be going towards the bright lights beyant. 'Tis afther dyin' I'd be," said the head-strong girl, "an' I to be stayin' any longer here by the waves an' the lonely places." She dropped to her knees. "Let you be afther givin' me yer blessin', yer riverince, an' I to be settin' out on me way!"

The obliging clergyman gave her a generous blessing and then all the people on the strand surged together again.

Maybella yawned.

"They've done that three times already. They'll probably keep on at it all afternoon. She's not much good, really."

Pansy knew it was safe to agree wholeheartedly.

"They've queer voices."

"Irish," said Maybella.

"Why did she call him 'yer riverince'?" Pansy asked, vastly puzzled by this novel form of address.

"Irish, of course."

"Oh!" Pansy hesitated. "And why did he bless himself so big?"

"You ought to know. Aren't you a Roman?"

Pansy swelled with pride. She had heard Sissy and Willie discussing the Romans. Some were Emperors and some fought on bridges and they were all very noble. Obviously, because of her smart and fashionable condition, Maybella, with her odd preconceptions, had mistaken her nationality. She said: "Well, 'smatter of fact, I am, but——"

Maybella reached over and pulled Jennifer from her obscure position.

"Your doll is nicely dressed. Matches you, doesn't she?" She tilted her head. "It seems rather a waste to bother dressing up such an old doll, though, doesn't it?"

"All my new dolls," said Pansy, brilliantly, "are well dressed already. I just thought I'd give that old one an outing." A beautifully applicable phrase from a song she had heard came to her. "For old time's sake."

"I know." Maybella looked sentimental. "I have a favorite old doll, too. Very old."

"I thought you'd have so many dolls, you wouldn't have any favorite ones."

"I'm a very simple child," Maybella said, angrily. "I average eighty pounds a week, less income tax, and I only get half-a-crown for pocket money. That's how simple I am."

Privately, Pansy, whose weekly income from a reluctant parent now far exceeded this, thought it very simple indeed. She watched Maybella languidly dandling Jennifer. At last she said, without a single maternal pang: "You can keep my doll, if you like."

"No, thank you!" Coldly Maybella replaced Jennifer on the rock. "She's rather too old."

Pansy longed to hit her. Instead she said, in a small, simpering voice: "I'd love to see you acting."

"You may tomorrow, if they don't have too many retakes."

"Oh! Will you be here again tomorrow? Here on the rocks? And can I sit with you again tomorrow?"

"Yes," said Maybella, graciously, "if you keep quiet."

"I'll keep quiet. I did today, didn't I? And I'll bring sweets. What kind of sweets do you like?"

Maybella looked angry again.

"I'm not allowed sweets except two before I brush my teeth at night. *They* say they're bad for my teeth."

Pansy hesitated.

"If," she began, at length, feeling her way, "if you were allowed to eat the sweets I'll bring tomorrow, what kind would you like?"

"I like chocolates best. Ones with jelly inside and pink cream."

"Those are the kind I'll be bringing tomorrow." The cameras on the beach were being dismantled now. Pansy stood up to go. "Would there be a place for another child in this picture?" she asked, casually.

"Of course not. I'm the only child in it."

"I see."

Pansy gave her a strange, dark look.

Half a mile beyond Ballybay, a bread van overtook her. She looked so small and lost that the driver gave her a lift to the turn of the road near her home. She hardly spoke to him at all, apart from thanking him, politely, if absent-mindedly, as she got out. She was too busy thinking to talk.

She was up very early next morning. She set out at once for Kilmuc and was again fortunate in getting a lift, this time in a creamery cart. She made straight for Darmody's, where Mary opened the door to her. Mary was surprised, and rather alarmed, at this unexpected visit of her small sister.

"What brings you here, love? Nothing wrong at home, is there?"

"No. At least, not 'xactly wrong. But Tommy's bike got broken and he has to get it mended and he sent me for a loan of yours until his is fixed because you won't be wanting it these days when you're staying here altogether for the present." Pansy drew a much needed breath. "Please, he said."

Sedately, she wheeled off Mary's new bicycle, nodding her head gravely at reiterated admonitions not to cycle on it herself on the main road.

"Because you know, love, when your legs aren't long enough to let you sit on the saddle, you can't have any proper balance. So you will promise me not to cycle, won't you?"

"I promise," Pansy said. "Besides," she added, virtuously, "even if you hadn't told me, I wouldn't have cycled. I'd be afraid something might happen to your lovely new bike."

Her incorrigibly foolish sister kissed and hugged her.

"And you'll go straight home, won't you, love? You won't—you won't go talking to anyone in Kilmuc?"

"Of course I'll go straight home. I promised Mammy."

*　　*　　*

William Bates never gave a glad reception to any of the Monaghans but he kept the best chocolates. Pansy bought two pound boxes of the most expensive, which took fourteen of her last twenty shillings, tied her parcel carefully to the bicycle carrier and set out for home with all her business expeditiously concluded.

She carried in her parcel secretly. She did not attempt to conceal the bicycle but told her mother that Mary having no immediate use for it, had lent it, "because," said Pansy, "she thought I'd be tired doing messages," and her trusting mother nodded and smiled.

Then Pansy went to dress. This took a long time. She found a blue jersey of Tommy's, in fair condition but shrunk too small for him and thus carefully darned and washed and laid aside for Willie, and Sissy's white Confirmation dress, also laid aside to await Pansy's reception of that grave sacrament. She cut holes in these garments and put them on, the jersey over the dress. The effect was good, but the feet were still wrong. She took off her socks, scratched the uppers of her shoes against the soles and rubbed ashes well into them. Nothing remained now but to pull off her hair ribbon and comb her hair down over her right eye. She gazed critically at the final result in the mirror and was satisfied. She looked Irish. Not so Irish as Maybella, but Irish, all the same.

Jennifer's toilet presented what seemed insurmountable difficulties. It was obviously impossible, at such short notice, to have a matching

Irish Jennifer. Pansy considered leaving her behind, but she had carried the troublesome doll so long and faithfully that Jennifer had become a habit and Pansy felt incomplete without her. Finally, with that happy inspiration which never failed her, she stripped Jennifer naked and decided that the battered canvas body, with fantastically lolling limbs denuded of any exterior support, looked quite Irish enough.

Now she was correctly attired, she had what would surely prove an irresistible bait for Maybella, she had a means of swift and easy transport. She went on her way.

Maybella finished all the soft chocolates, leaving the toffees and the stony centers for Pansy. Pansy chewed and crunched, grimly pleased.

"I'm bringing another box tomorrow."

"Are you?" Maybella was torpid with the effects of over three-quarters of a pound of greedily swallowed chocolate. "I expect I'll be busy all day tomorrow. They've got to get my scenes finished, because I'm due back in London next week. I've only been lent to this crowd."

Valiantly Pansy continued to do her nauseating best.

"Probably your own crowd—the ones that lent you—are much better than these?"

"My dear!" said Maybella. "What do you think!"

She took up a toffee, bit it tentatively, wrinkled her nose and threw the toffee away. With an unrestrainable yelp of anguish, Pansy saw it plop into the sea. She gave a hollow cough. Instantly, Maybella edged away from her.

"Have you got a cold? Because if you have, you must go away. I catch colds very easily. Even if I get my feet wet, I catch a cold. I have to be very, very careful," said Maybella, solemnly, "because I'm not very strong."

"I haven't a cold but I'm not strong either. I spit blood."

"Anyone can do that. I did, at Christmas, when my tooth fell out."

But Pansy had resigned from this competitive frailty. She was meditating.

"It's a pity you're not strong. Probably if you got wet all over, you'd get a bad cold. Probably then," said Pansy, slowly, "you wouldn't be able to do what you have to do in this picture, would you?"

"My dear! I certainly wouldn't. I'd just *die!*"

"Tomorrow," said Pansy, "I'll be bringing a special kind of sweets. They're a new kind. Special. I'll be here early tomorrow. There's a lovely place along the rocks that I want to show you. A place with a pool of colored fish. Special place. I'll bring you there tomorrow and you can look at the fish and eat the special sweets."

At the moment, Maybella was too full of chocolate to respond enthusiastically to this lure.

"I'll be working tomorrow."

"I'll come early. The fish are most 'strordinary in that pool. Red and green and——" Fortunately, caution prevailed. "Well, 'strordinary fish."

Maybella poked Jennifer disgustedly.

"She looks horrible like that."

"She's sun-bathing. It's good for her."

Maybella said nothing. She looked at Pansy's carefully tattered garments. It was only too obvious that she approved neither of Pansy nor her doll today. It was also obvious that she was bored. She stood up and yawned.

"I must go now. They'll be wanting me soon."

As she strolled off, Pansy called after her.

"But you'll be here tomorrow?"

"Perhaps."

A stony Medusa, Pansy sat on her rock and watched the innocent Maybella perform before the cameras. Maybella ran lightheartedly across the strand, paddled ankle-deep in the waveless tide (and here the proceedings had to be halted while her feet were carefully dried by a woman in a black linen coat and skirt), jumped in and out of the boat (apparently the Irish heroine had formed the habit young) and spoke in that peculiar accent. She did nothing that Pansy could not have done better.

Pansy was, within limits, a kind child. She would not willingly choose harsh methods if easier would prevail. As the cameras were being packed up, she walked boldly across the strand to where the fussy man in the corduroy trousers and sandals was giving some loud-voiced instructions for tomorrow and addressed him directly.

"Can I act in this picture?"

He took no notice of her. Nobody took any notice of her.

"I can act as well as Maybella. I can act better. Everyone says I can."

The voices went on uninterruptedly above her. She stood still, while a slow rage mounted in her, and then she grabbed him by the shirt and tugged.

"Can I act in your picture?"

He uttered an old English word, very common in Doon.

"It's bad enough being in the mess we're in without having the natives pinching bits out of me! Here, you, clear off."

Pansy's injured pride almost induced her to leave his shilling lying where he had flung it.

She left the house next morning before anyone else was awake. She carried an empty box, neatly wrapped in brown paper. There was no more need to waste luxuries on Maybella.

She had been waiting for two hours before Maybella joined her. She led the way over the rocks out towards the sea, with her victim scrambling awkwardly in her wake. Several times the grumbling Maybella faltered and stopped but Pansy urged her on until they were safely hidden away together, with quarter of a mile of sheltering rocks behind them, the empty ocean in front, and a deep pool at their feet.

"There!" said Pansy, and pointed downwards.

Maybella was very hot and very tired. Peevishly, she looked at the black, seaweed-fringed depths.

"I don't see any fish."

"They're hidden by the seaweed. Throw this stone in and lean over!"

Maybella threw the stone in and leaned over and Pansy pushed her into the pool.

Never, even in her most justly irritated moments, had Pansy intended Maybella to drown, but this is what Maybella appeared to be doing. The pool, although narrow, was four and a half feet in the center to Maybella's four, and Pansy's strength and endurance were well tested before Maybella was out on the rocks again, choking and gasping and crying.

Pansy regarded her with satisfaction. She was thoroughly wet, inside and out. She was sick, too. Pansy sat and watched but at last even this spectacle began to pall.

"We'd better go back."

Maybella gasped and wailed.

"I can't move. I'm dying. You murdered me."

"I saved you," Pansy said, indignantly.

"You pushed me in."

"I slipped. Anyone could slip. These are very slippy rocks."

Maybella uttered a strangled shriek of pure anguish.

"I'm cold. I'm dying."

"So am I cold. I got all wet from saving you. Any ordinary polite person would be thanking me for saving your life." She paused but Maybella showed no disposition towards gratitude. "*I'm* going back, anyway, and you can stay here if you like."

She began to clamber away from the wretched Maybella, who, appalled by the prospect of being left to die, alone and marooned, shrieked louder than ever. But Pansy was tired of her. She kept on, giving only one backward glance to see Maybella in the distance crawling weakly after her.

The strand was crowded and the confusion was even worse than usual. The woman in the black coat and skirt was rushing around, shrieking almost as loudly as Maybella.

"She came down here. I know she did. She said she wanted to look at the sea."

"If you're looking for Maybella, she's over there." Pansy pointed at the rocks. "She fell into a pool." She paused. "I pulled her out."

But no one thanked her this time either. Everyone spoke together and ran around and shouted until at last Maybella was carried into their midst, clinging to the woman in black.

"I was drowning, Momma. She tried to drown me."

"Yes, yes, darling. You're all right now."

Pansy stood squarely.

"I pulled her out."

"She—she pushed——"

Maybella choked and gurgled. Then she suddenly fell silent and began slowly to turn blue. The woman in black swung around to Mr. Horton and spoke in a clipped, crisp voice.

"I'm taking her straight home. We'll get a plane from Dublin."

"But, good heavens you can't——"

"She must be under Dr. Denvan's care immediately. She's in one of her bad attacks of asthma."

"But, good heavens, woman! Don't fuss! Can't you get a doctor here? Maybe she'll be all right tomorrow."

"It will be at least two weeks before the child is able to work. *If* she escapes pneumonia."

"But, look here, Mrs. Merton——"

"And if you're thinking of your picture," said Maybella's mother, viciously, "it couldn't be worse than it is, could it? And it certainly would have added nothing to Maybella's reputation."

Equally viciously, Mr. Horton said: "Your contract!"

"Act of God," said Mrs. Merton, and, blue and silent, Maybella was borne away.

There was a deadly quiet.

"That does it!" said Mr. Horton. With an awful calm, he lit a cigarette. "What do we do now, boys and girls? Pick up and go home?"

There was a babble of suggestions. Then someone said: "But, really I mean to say, couldn't we get a brat somewhere?"

"Who?"

Nobody seemed to know. But someone else suggested, feebly: "Well, couldn't we *try* the agencies?"

Mr. Horton was apparently engrossed in the delicate shades of smoke curling from his cigarette tip.

"We're supposed to be back to do the London sequences on Tuesday," he said, still with that terrifying calm. "We had three days to take that kid's scenes. Are we supposed to stay on here in this Godforsaken spot, while the agencies are being scoured? Damn! Damn! Damn!" roared Mr. Horton and threw away his cigarette.

"I knew this place was unlucky," said a long-haired man. "As soon as we arrived, I felt it. The aura——"

"Aw!" said Mr. Horton and made a very rude remark.

Pansy judged the moment opportune to come forward. She said, in a polite, distinct voice: "If you want a child, wouldn't I do?"

"For Chrissake!" said Mr. Horton. "It's the little brat that pinched me yesterday." His eyes flashed with joy at this legitimate and very small object on which to vent his fury. "Clear away, you little so-and-so!"

"I can act," said Pansy. "I can act very well. I can do everything that poor Maybella does."

Without giving him time to reply, she proceeded to prove it. She jumped in and out of the boat. She ran to the sea and splashed there, laughing. She came to the priest and said, wistfully: "It's how I'm sad to think that mebbe one day I'll not be wantin' to run and play no more but mebbe be quiet like an' old." (Pansy had an excellent memory.) "Would you say that the angels are quiet, or would there be small ones like me that might be afther wantin' to play, too?" For good measure, she added: "Yer riverince!"

Because they had nothing else to do, they had watched her. And now Mr. Horton lit another cigarette, and said, slowly, while Pansy stood in front of him with her hands tightly clasped on Jennifer, her heart throbbing and all the sincerity she had in her wide anxious eyes: "I don't see that she's any worse than the other."

There was a relieved murmur of agreement.

"A damn' pretty kid."

"Voice all right, too."

"The other," said the long-haired man, "was a little beast. So is her mother."

"You know, it might be an idea." Mr. Horton was musing, staring through Pansy as if she were invisible. "Film unit discovers new child actress." Hastily he corrected himself. "Well-known director discovers new child actress. From the lonely little village of Ballybay on the barren Atlantic-swept Waterford coast, a new light has shone on the film horizon. A simple little colleen—and all the rest of that piffle. Might give the thing a boost—and heaven knows it needs it! Besides," he said and frowned in a puzzled way at Pansy, "she's not bad. At least I suppose she *is*, but it doesn't hit you in the eye. Since we're stuck anyway, there's no harm in trying her out. We can run it through tonight and then decide what to do. And she's not *bad.*" He wheeled around. "Well, chaps, what are we waiting for?"

Pansy spent a busy day. At the end of it, she was driven home in the magnate's car by the magnate himself. She talked to him all through the short journey. He said little, but looked at her very often. She led him confidently into her house and presented him to her bewildered mother. He was very polite and kind and patient with Bridget Monaghan though it took her unduly long to grasp the significance of what had occurred. Before he left, he gave her a five-pound note.

"If we use Pansy for the next few days, that will be another ten pounds. Will that be all right?"

Bridget Monaghan could only nod a weak assent.

"Of course, we can't know until we run her scenes through. If the result is satisfactory, I'll call for her at nine tomorrow morning."

Pansy ushered him to the door.

"I'll be ready at nine. I'm very punctual."

"But you understand, don't you, Pansy, that——"

"I'll be ready at nine," Pansy said calmly.

He looked at her again with that queer puzzled frown and laughed.

"By God! you know," he said, "maybe I've got something, at last. Maybe I have!"

Out of the overflowing gladness of her heart, Pansy shared the box of chocolates that had been spared from Maybella with her family. That night she slept the dreamless sleep of the successful unjust. At nine o'clock she and Jennifer were at the gate when the car arrived.

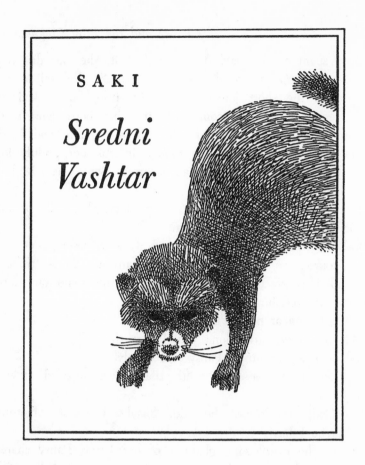

SAKI

Sredni Vashtar

Conradin was ten years old, and the doctor had pronounced his
professional opinion that the boy would not live another five
years. The doctor was silky and effete, and counted for little,
but his opinion was endorsed by Mrs. De Ropp, who counted for
nearly everything. Mrs. De Ropp was Conradin's cousin and guardian,
and in his eyes she represented those three-fifths of the world that
are necessary and disagreeable and real; the other two-fifths, in
perpetual antagonism to the foregoing, were summed up in himself
and his imagination. One of these days Conradin supposed he
would succumb to the mastering pressure of wearisome necessary
things—such as illnesses and coddling restrictions and drawnout

dulness. Without his imagination, which was rampant under the spur of loneliness, he would have succumbed long ago.

Mrs. De Ropp would never, in her honestest moments, have confessed to herself that she disliked Conradin, though she might have been dimly aware that thwarting him "for his good" was a duty which she did not find particularly irksome. Conradin hated her with a desperate sincerity which he was perfectly able to mask. Such few pleasures as he could contrive for himself gained an added relish from the likelihood that they would be displeasing to his guardian, and from the realm of his imagination she was locked out—an unclean thing, which should find no entrance.

In the dull, cheerless garden, overlooked by so many windows that were ready to open with a message not to do this or that, or a reminder that medicines were due, he found little attraction. The few fruit-trees that it contained were set jealously apart from his plucking, as though they were rare specimens of their kind blooming in an arid waste; it would probably have been difficult to find a market-gardener who would have offered ten shillings for their entire yearly produce. In a forgotten corner, however, almost hidden behind a dismal shrubbery, was a disused tool-shed of respectable proportions, and within its walls Conradin found a haven, something that took on the varying aspects of a playroom and a cathedral. He had peopled it with a legion of familiar phantoms, evoked partly from fragments of history and partly from his own brain, but it also boasted two inmates of flesh and blood. In one corner lived a ragged-plumaged Houdan hen, on which the boy lavished an affection that had scarcely another outlet. Further back in the gloom stood a large hutch, divided into two compartments, one of which was fronted with close iron bars. This was the abode of a large polecat-ferret, which a friendly butcher-boy had once smuggled, cage and all, into its present quarters, in exchange for a long-secreted hoard of small silver. Conradin was dreadfully afraid of the lithe, sharp-fanged beast, but it was his most treasured possession. Its very presence in the tool-shed was a secret and fearful joy, to be kept scrupulously from the knowledge of the Woman, as he privately dubbed his cousin. And one day, out of Heaven knows what material, he spun the beast a wonderful name, and from that moment it grew into a god and a religion. The Woman indulged in religion once a week at a church near by, and took Conradin with her, but to him the church service was an alien rite in the House of Rimmon. Every Thursday, in the dim and musty silence of the tool-shed, he worshipped with mystic and elaborate ceremonial before the wooden hutch where dwelt Sredni Vashtar, the great ferret. Red flowers in their season and scarlet berries in the winter-time were offered at his shrine, for he was a god who laid some special stress on the fierce impatient side of things, as opposed to the Woman's religion, which, as far as Conradin could observe, went to great lengths in the contrary direction. And on great festivals powdered nutmeg was strewn in front of his hutch, an important feature of the offering being that the nutmeg had to be stolen. These festivals were of irregular occurrence, and were chiefly appointed to celebrate some passing event. On one occasion, when Mrs. De Ropp suffered from acute toothache for three days, Conradin kept up the festival during the entire three days, and almost succeeded in persuading himself that Sredni Vashtar was personally responsible for the toothache. If the malady had lasted for another day the supply of nutmeg would have given out.

The Houdan hen was never drawn into the cult of Sredni Vashtar. Conradin had long ago settled that she was an Anabaptist. He did not pretend to have the remotest knowledge as to what an Anabaptist was, but he privately hoped that it was dashing and not very respectable. Mrs. De Ropp was the ground plan on which he based and detested all respectability.

After a while Conradin's absorption in the tool-shed began to attract the notice of his guardian. "It is not good for him to be pottering down there in all weathers," she promptly decided, and at breakfast one morning she announced that the Houdan hen had been sold and taken away overnight. With her short-sighted eyes she peered at Conradin, waiting for an outbreak of rage and sorrow, which she was ready to rebuke with a flow of excellent precepts and reasoning. But Conradin said nothing: there was nothing to be said. Something perhaps in his white set face gave her a momentary qualm, for at tea that afternoon there was toast on the table, a delicacy which she usually banned on the ground that it was bad for him; also because the making of it "gave trouble," a deadly offence in the middle-class feminine eye.

"I thought you liked toast," she exclaimed, with an injured air, observing that he did not touch it.

"Sometimes," said Conradin.

In the shed that evening there was an innovation in the worship of the hutch-god. Conradin had been wont to chant his praises, tonight he asked a boon.

"Do one thing for me, Sredni Vashtar."

The thing was not specified. As Sredni Vashtar was a god he must be supposed to know. And choking back a sob as he looked at that other empty corner, Conradin went back to the world he so hated.

And every night, in the welcome darkness of his bedroom, and every evening in the dusk of the tool-shed, Conradin's bitter litany went up: "Do one thing for me, Sredni Vashtar."

Mrs. De Ropp noticed that the visits to the shed did not cease, and one day she made a further journey of inspection.

"What are you keeping in that locked hutch?" she asked. "I believe it's guinea-pigs. I'll have them all cleared away."

Conradin shut his lips tight, but the Woman ransacked his bedroom till she found the carefully hidden key, and forthwith marched down to the shed to complete her discovery. It was a cold afternoon, and Conradin had been bidden to keep to the house. From the furthest window of the dining-room the door of the shed could just be seen beyond the corner of the shrubbery, and there Conradin stationed himself. He saw the Woman enter, and then he imagined her opening the door of the sacred hutch and peering down with her short-sighted eyes into the thick straw bed where his god lay hidden. Perhaps she would prod at the straw in her clumsy impatience. And Conradin fervently breathed his prayer for the last time. But he knew as he prayed that he did not believe. He knew that the Woman would come out presently with that pursed smile he loathed so well on her face, and that in an hour or two the gardener would carry away his wonderful god, a god no longer, but a simple brown ferret in a hutch. And he knew that the Woman would triumph always as she triumphed now, and that he would grow ever more sickly under her pestering and domineering and superior wisdom, till one day nothing would matter much more with him, and the doctor would be proved right. And in the sting and misery of his defeat, he began to chant loudly and defiantly the hymn of his threatened idol:

Sredni Vashtar went forth,
His thoughts were red thoughts and his teeth were white.
His enemies called for peace, but he brought them death.
Sredni Vashtar the Beautiful.

And then of a sudden he stopped his chanting and drew closer to the window-pane. The door of the shed still stood ajar as it had been left, and the minutes were slipping by. They were long minutes, but they slipped by nevertheless. He watched the starlings running and flying in little parties across the lawn; he counted them over and over again, with one eye always on that swinging door. A sour-faced maid came in to lay the table for tea, and still Conradin stood and waited and watched. Hope had crept by inches into his heart, and now a look of triumph began to blaze in his eyes that had only known the wistful patience of defeat. Under his breath, with a furtive exultation, he began once again the paean of victory and devastation. And presently his eyes were rewarded: out through that doorway came a long, low, yellow-and-brown beast, with eyes a-blink at the waning daylight, and dark wet stains around the fur of jaws and throat. Conradin dropped on his knees. The great polecat-ferret made its way down to a small brook at the foot of the garden, drank for a moment, then crossed a little plank bridge and was lost to sight in the bushes. Such was the passing of Sredni Vashtar.

"Tea is ready," said the sour-faced maid; "where is the mistress?"

"She went down to the shed some time ago," said Conradin.

And while the maid went to summon her mistress to tea, Conradin fished a toasting-fork out of the sideboard drawer and proceeded to toast himself a piece of bread. And during the toasting of it and the buttering of it with much butter and the slow enjoyment of eating it, Conradin listened to the noises and silences which fell in quick spasms beyond the dining-room door. The loud foolish screaming of the maid, the answering chorus of wondering ejaculations from the kitchen region, the scuttering footsteps and hurried embassies for outside help, and then, after a lull, the scared sobbings and the shuffling tread of those who bore a heavy burden into the house.

"Whoever will break it to the poor child? I couldn't for the life of me!" exclaimed a shrill voice. And while they debated the matter among themselves, Conradin made himself another piece of toast.

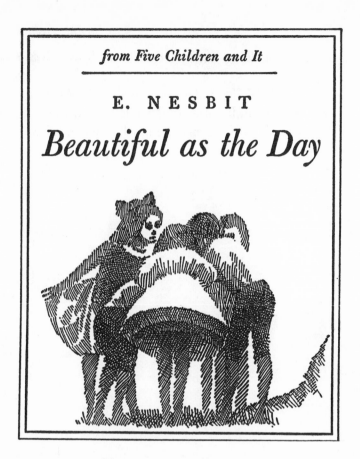

from Five Children and It

E. NESBIT

Beautiful as the Day

T he house was three miles from the station, but before the dusty hired fly had rattled along for five minutes the children began to put their heads out the carriage window and to say, "Aren't we nearly there?" And every time they passed a house, which was not very often, they all said, "Oh, *is* this it?" But it never was, till they reached the very top of the hill, just past the chalk-quarry and before you come to the gravel-pit. And then there was a white house with a green garden and an orchard beyond, and mother said, "Here we are!"

"How white the house is," said Robert.

"And look at the roses," said Anthea.

"And the plums," said Jane.

"It is rather decent," Cyril admitted.

The Baby said, "Wanty go walky"; and the fly stopped with a last rattle and jolt.

Everyone got its legs kicked or its feet trodden on in the scramble to get out of the carriage that very minute, but no one seemed to mind. Mother, curiously enough, was in no hurry to get out; and even when she had come down slowly and by the step, and with no jump at all, she seemed to wish to see the boxes carried in, and even to pay the driver, instead of joining in that first glorious rush round the garden and the orchard and the thorny, thistly, briery, brambly wilderness beyond the broken gate and the dry fountain at the side of the house. But the children were wiser, for once. It was not really a pretty house at all; it was quite ordinary, and mother thought it was rather inconvenient, and was quite annoyed at there being no shelves, to speak of, and hardly a cupboard in the place. Father used to say that the ironwork on the roof and coping was like an architect's nightmare. But the house was deep in the country, with no other house in sight, and the children had been in London for two years, without so much as once going to the seaside even for a day by an excursion train, and so the White House seemed to them a sort of Fairy Palace set down in an Earthly Paradise. For London is like prison for children, especially if their relations are not rich.

Of course there are the shops and the theatres, and Maskelyne and Cook's, and things, but if your people are rather poor you don't get taken to the theatres, and you can't buy things out of the shops; and London has none of those nice things that children may play with without hurting the things or themselves—such as trees and sand and woods and waters. And nearly everything in London is the wrong sort of shape—all straight lines and flat streets, instead of being all sorts of odd shapes, like things are in the country. Trees are all different, as you know, and I am sure some tiresome person must have told you that there are no two blades of grass exactly alike. But in streets where the blades of grass don't grow, everything is like everything else. This is why so many children who live in towns are so extremely naughty. They do not know what is the matter with them, and no more do their fathers and mothers, aunts, uncles, cousins, tutors, governesses, and nurses;

but I know. And so do you now. Children in the country are naughty sometimes, too, but that is for quite different reasons.

The children had explored the gardens and the outhouses thoroughly before they were caught and cleaned for tea, and they saw quite well that they were certain to be happy at the White House. They thought so from the first moment, but when they found the back of the house covered with jasmine, all in white flower, and smelling like a bottle of the most expensive scent that is ever given for a birthday present; and when they had seen the lawn, all green and smooth, and quite different from the brown grass in the gardens at Camden Town; and when they had found the stable with a loft over it and some old hay still left, they were almost certain; and when Robert had found the broken swing and tumbled out of it and got a lump on his head the size of an egg, and Cyril had nipped his finger in the door of a hutch that seemed made to keep rabbits in, if you ever had any, they had no longer any doubts whatever.

The best part of it all was that there were no rules about not going to places and not doing things. In London almost everything is labelled "You mustn't touch," and though the label is invisible it's just as bad, because you know it's there, or if you don't you jolly soon get told.

The White House was on the edge of a hill, with a wood behind it—and the chalk-quarry on one side and the gravel-pit on the other. Down at the bottom of the hill was a level plain, with queer-shaped white buildings where people burnt lime, and a big red brewery and other houses; and when the big chimneys were smoking and the sun was setting, the valley looked as if it was filled with golden mist, and the limekilns and oast-houses glimmered and glittered till they were like an enchanted city out of the *Arabian Nights*.

Now that I have begun to tell you about the place, I feel that I could go on and make this into a most interesting story about all the ordinary things that the children did,—just the kind of things you do yourself, you know,—and you would believe every word of it; and when I told about the children's being tiresome, as you are sometimes, your aunts would perhaps write in the margin of the story with a pencil, "How true!" or "How like life!" and you would see it and very likely be annoyed. So I will only tell you the really astonishing things that happened, and you may leave the book about quite safely, for no aunts and uncles either are likely to write "How true!" on the edge of the story. Grown-up people find it very difficult to believe really wonderful things, unless they have what they call proof. But children will believe almost anything, and grown-ups know this. That is why they tell you that the earth is round like an orange, when you can see perfectly well that it is flat and lumpy; and why they say that the earth goes round the sun, when you can see for yourself any day that the sun gets up in the morning and goes to bed at night like a good sun as it is, and the earth knows its place, and lies as still as a mouse. Yet I daresay you believe all that about the earth and the sun, and if so you will find it quite easy to believe that before Anthea and Cyril and the others had been a week in the country they had found a fairy. At least they called it that, because that was what it called itself; and of course it knew best, but it was not at all like any fairy you ever saw or heard of or read about.

It was at the gravel-pits. Father had to go away suddenly on business, and mother had gone away to stay with Granny, who was not very well. They both went in a great hurry, and when they were gone the house seemed dreadfully quiet and empty, and the children wandered from one room to another and looked at the bits of paper and string on the floors left over from the packing, and not yet cleared up, and wished they had something to do. It was Cyril who said—

"I say, let's take our Margate spades and go and dig in the gravel-pits. We can pretend it's seaside."

"Father said it was once," Anthea said; "he says there are shells there thousands of years old."

So they went. Of course they had been to the edge of the gravel-pit and looked over, but they had not gone down into it for fear father should say they mustn't play there, and the same with the chalk-quarry. The gravel-pit is not really dangerous if you don't try to climb down the edges, but go the slow safe way round by the road, as if you were a cart.

Each of the children carried its own spade, and took it in turns to carry the Lamb. He was the baby, and they called him that because "Baa" was the first thing he ever said. They called Anthea "Panther," which seems silly when you read it, but when you say it it sounds a little like her name.

The gravel-pit is very large and wide, with grass growing round the edges at the top, and dry stringy wildflowers, purple and yellow. It is like a giant's wash-hand basin. And there are mounds of gravel, and holes in the sides of the basin where gravel has been taken out, and high up in the steep sides there are the little holes that are the little front doors of the little sand-martins' little houses.

The children built a castle, of course, but castle-building is rather poor fun when you have no hope of the swishing tide ever coming in to fill up the moat and wash away the drawbridge, and, at the happy last, to wet everybody up to the waist at least.

Cyril wanted to dig out a cave to play smugglers in, but the others thought it might bury them alive, so it ended in all spades going to work to dig a hole through the castle to Australia. These children, you see, believed that the world was round, and that on the other side the little Australian boys and girls were really walking wrong way up, like flies on the ceiling, with their heads hanging down into the air.

The children dug and they dug and they dug, and their hands got sandy and hot and red, and their faces got damp and shiny. The Lamb had tried to eat the sand, and had cried so hard when he found that it was not, as he had supposed, brown sugar, that he was now tired out, and was lying asleep in a warm fat bunch in the middle of the half-finished castle. This left his brothers and sisters free to work really hard, and the hole that was to come out in Australia soon grew so deep that Jane, who was called Pussy for short, begged the others to stop.

"Suppose the bottom of the hole gave way suddenly," she said, "and you tumbled out among the little Australians, all the sand would get in their eyes."

"Yes," said Robert; "and they would hate us, and throw stones at us, and not let us see the kangaroos, or opossums, or blue-gums, or Emu Brand birds, or anything."

Cyril and Anthea knew that Australia was not quite so near as all that, but they agreed to stop using their spades and go on with their hands. This was quite easy, because the sand at the bottom of the hole was very soft and fine and dry, like sea-sand. And there were little shells in it.

"Fancy it having been wet sea here once, all sloppy and shiny," said Jane, "with fishes and conger-eels and coral and mermaids."

"And masts of ships and wrecked Spanish treasure. I wish we could find a gold doubloon, or something," Cyril said.

"How did the sea get carried away?" Robert asked.

"Not in a pail, silly," said his brother. "Father says the earth got too hot underneath, like you do in bed sometimes, so it just hunched up it shoulders, and the sea had to slip off like the blankets do off us, and the shoulder was left sticking out, and turned into dry land. Let's go and look for shells; I think that little cave looks likely; and I see something sticking out there like a bit of wrecked ship's anchor, and it's beastly hot in the Australian hole."

The others agreed, but Anthea went on digging. She always liked to finish a thing when she had once begun it. She felt it would be a disgrace to leave that hole without getting through to Australia.

The cave was disappointing, because there were no shells, and the wrecked ship's anchor turned out to be only the broken end of a pickaxe handle, and the cave party were just making up their minds that sand makes you thirstier when it is not by the seaside, and someone had suggested going home for lemonade, when Anthea suddenly screamed:

"Cyril! Come here! Oh, come quick! It's alive! It'll get away! Quick!"

They all hurried back.

"It's a rat, I shouldn't wonder," said Robert. "Father says they infest old places—and this must be pretty old if the sea was here thousands of years ago."

"Perhaps it is a snake," said Jane, shuddering.

"Let's look," said Cyril, jumping into the hole. "I'm not afraid of snakes. I like them. If it's a snake I'll tame it, and it will follow me everywhere, and I'll let it sleep round my neck at night."

"No, you won't," said Robert firmly. He shared Cyril's bedroom. "But you may if it's a rat."

"Oh, don't be silly!" said Anthea; "it's not a rat, it's *much* bigger. And it's not a snake. It's got feet; I saw them; and fur! No—not the spade. You'll hurt it! Dig with your hands."

"And let *it* hurt *me* instead! That's so likely, isn't it?" said Cyril, seizing a spade.

"Oh, don't!" said Anthea. "Squirrel, *don't*. I—it sounds silly, but it said something. It really and truly did."

"What?"

"It said, 'You let me alone'."

But Cyril merely observed that his sister must have gone off her nut, and he and Robert dug with spades while Anthea sat on the edge of the hole, jumping up and down with hotness and anxiety. They dug carefully, and presently everyone could see that there really was something moving in the bottom of the Australian hole.

Then Anthea cried out. "*I'm* not afraid. Let me dig," and fell on her knees and began to scratch like a dog does when he has suddenly remembered where it was that he buried his bone.

"Oh, I felt fur," she cried, half laughing and half crying. "I did indeed! I did!" when suddenly a dry husky voice in the sand made them all jump back, and their hearts jumped nearly as fast as they did.

"Let me alone," it said. And now everyone heard the voice and looked at the others to see if they had too.

"But we want to see you," said Robert bravely.

"I wish you'd come out," said Anthea, also taking courage.

"Oh, well—if that's your wish," the voice said, and the sand stirred and spun and scattered, and something brown and furry and fat came rolling out into the hole, and the sand fell off it, and it sat there yawning and rubbing the ends of its eyes with its hands.

"I believe I must have dropped asleep," it said, stretching itself.

The children stood round the hole in a ring, looking at the creature they had found. It was worth looking at. Its eyes were on long horns like a snail's eyes, and it could move them in and out like telescopes; it had ears like a bat's ears, and it's tubby body was shaped like a spider's and covered with thick soft fur; its legs and arms were furry too, and it had hands and feet like a monkey's.

"What on earth is it?" Jane said. "Shall we take it home?"

The thing turned its long eyes to look at her, and said: "Does she always talk nonsense, or is it only the rubbish on her head that makes her silly?"

It looked scornfully at Jane's hat as it spoke.

"She doesn't mean to be silly," Anthea said gently; "we none of us do, whatever you may think! Don't be frightened; we don't want to hurt you, you know."

"Hurt *me!*" it said. "*Me* frightened! Upon my word! Why, you talk as if I were nobody in particular." All its fur stood out like a cat's when it is going to fight.

"Well," said Anthea, still kindly, "perhaps if we knew who you are in particular we could think of something to say that wouldn't make you cross. Everything we've said so far seems to have. Who are you? And don't get angry! Because really we don't know."

"You don't know?" it said. "Well, I knew the world had changed —but—well, really—do you mean to tell me seriously you don't know a Psammead when you see one?"

"A Sammyadd? That's Greek to me."

"So it is to everyone," said the creature sharply. "Well, in plain English, then, a *Sand-fairy*. Don't you know a Sand-fairy when you see one?"

It looked so grieved and hurt that Jane hastened to say, "Of course I see you are, *now*. It's quite plain now one comes to look at you."

"You came to look at me several sentences ago," it said crossly, beginning to curl up again in the sand.

"Oh—don't go away again! Do talk some more," Robert cried. "I didn't know you were a Sandy-fairy, but I knew directly I saw you that you were much the wonderfullest thing I'd ever seen."

The Sandy-fairy seemed a shade less disagreeable after this.

"It isn't talking I mind," it said, "as long as you're reasonably civil. But I'm not going to make polite conversation for you. If you talk nicely to me, perhaps I'll answer you, and perhaps I won't. Now say something."

Of course no one could think of anything to say, but at last Robert thought of "How long have you lived here?" and he said it at once.

"Oh, ages—several thousand years," replied the Psammead.

"Tell us all about it. Do."

"It's all in books."

"*You* aren't!" Jane said. "Oh, tell us everything you can about yourself! We don't know anything about you, and you *are* so nice."

The Sand-fairy smoothed his long rat-like whiskers and smiled between them.

"Do please tell!" said the children all together.

It is wonderful how quickly you get used to things, even the most astonishing. Five minutes before, the children had had no more idea than you that there was such a thing as a sand-fairy in the world, and now they were talking to it as though they had known it all their lives.

It drew its eyes in and said:

"How very sunny it is—quite like old times. Where do you get your Megatheriums from now?"

"What?" said the children all at once. It is very difficult always to remember that "what" is not polite, especially in moments of surprise or agitation.

"Are Pterodactyls plentiful now?" the Sand-fairy went on.

The children were unable to reply.

"What do you have for breakfast?" the Fairy said impatiently, "and who gives it you?"

"Eggs and bacon, and bread-and-milk, and porridge and things. Mother gives it us. What are Mega-what's-its-names and Ptero-what-do-you-call-thems? And does anyone have them for breakfast?"

"Why, almost everyone had Pterodactyl for breakfast in my time! Pterodactyls were something like crocodiles and something like birds —I believe they were very good grilled. You see it was like this: of course there were heaps of sand-fairies then, and in the morning early you went out and hunted for them, and when you'd found one it gave you your wish. People used to send their little boys down to the seashore early in the morning before breakfast to get the day's wishes, and very often the eldest boy in the family would be told to wish for a Megatherium, ready jointed for cooking. It was as big as an elephant, you see, so there was a good deal of meat on it. And if they wanted fish, the Ichthyosaurus was asked for,—he was twenty to forty feet long, so there was plenty of him. And for poultry there was the Plesiosaurus; there were nice pickings on that too. Then the other children could wish for other things. But when people had dinner-parties it was nearly always Megatheriums; and Ichthyosaurus, because his fins were a great delicacy and his tail made soup."

"There must have been heaps and heaps of cold meat left over," said Anthea, who meant to be a good housekeeper some day.

"Oh no," said the Psammead, "that would never have done. Why, of course at sunset what was left over turned into stone. You find the stone bones of the Megatherium and things all over the place even now, they tell me."

"Who tell you?" asked Cyril; but the Sand-fairy frowned and began to dig very fast with its furry hands.

"Oh, don't go!" they all cried; "tell us more about it when it was Megatheriums for breakfast! Was the world like this then?"

It stopped digging.

"Not a bit," it said; "it was nearly all sand where I lived, and coal grew on trees, and the periwinkles were as big as tea-trays—you find them now; they're turned into stone. We sand-fairies used to live on the seashore, and the children used to come with their little flint-spades and flint-pails and make castles for us to live in. That's thousands of years ago, but I hear that children still build castles on the sand. It's difficult to break yourself of a habit."

"But why did you stop living in the castles?" asked Robert.

"It's a sad story," said the Psammead gloomily. "It was because they *would* build moats to the castles, and the nasty wet bubbling sea used to come in, and of course as soon as a sand-fairy got wet it caught cold, and generally died. And so there got to be fewer and fewer, and, whenever you found a fairy and had a wish, you used to wish for a Megatherium, and eat twice as much as you wanted, because it might be weeks before you got another wish."

"And did *you* get wet?" Robert inquired.

The Sand-fairy shuddered. "Only once," it said; "the end of the twelfth hair of my top left whisker—I feel the place still in damp weather. It was only once, but it was quite enough for me. I went away as soon as the sun had dried my poor dear whisker. I scurried away to the back of the beach, and dug myself a house deep in warm dry sand, and there I've been ever since. And the sea changed its lodgings afterwards. And now I'm not going to tell you another thing."

"Just one more, please," said the children. "Can you give wishes now?"

"Of course," said it, "didn't I give you yours a few minutes ago? You said, 'I wish you'd come out,' and I did."

"Oh, please, mayn't we have another?"

"Yes, but be quick about it. I'm tired of you."

I daresay you have often thought what you would do if you had three wishes given you, and have despised the old man and his wife in the black-pudding story, and felt certain that if you had the chance you could think of three really useful wishes without a moment's hesitation. These children had often talked this matter over, but, now the chance had suddenly come to them, they could not make up their minds.

"Quick," said the Sand-fairy crossly. No one could think of anything, only Anthea did manage to remember a private wish of her own and Jane's which they had never told the boys. She knew the boys would not care about it—but still it was better than nothing.

"I wish we were all as beautiful as the day," she said in a great hurry.

The children looked at each other, but each could see that the others were not any better-looking than usual. The Psammead pushed out its long eyes, and seemed to be holding its breath and swelling itself out till it was twice as fat and furry as before. Suddenly it let its breath go in a long sigh.

"I'm really afraid I can't manage it," it said apologetically, "I must be out of practice."

The children were horribly disappointed.

"Oh, *do* try again!" they said.

"Well," said the Sand-fairy, "the fact is, I was keeping back a little strength to give the rest of you your wishes with. If you'll be contented with one wish a day amongst the lot of you I daresay I can screw myself up to do it. Do you agree to that?"

"Yes, oh yes!" said Jane and Anthea. The boys nodded. They did not believe the Sand-fairy could do it. You can always make girls believe things much easier than you can boys.

It stretched out its eyes farther than ever, and swelled and swelled and swelled.

"I do hope it won't hurt itself," said Anthea.

"Or crack its skin," Robert said anxiously.

Everyone was very much relieved when the Sand-fairy, after getting so big that it almost filled up the hole in the sand, suddenly let out its breath and went back to its proper size.

"That's all right," it said, panting heavily. "It'll come easier to-morrow."

"Did it hurt much?" asked Anthea.

"Only my poor whisker, thank you," said he, "but you're a kind and thoughtful child. Good day."

It scratched suddenly and fiercely with its hands and feet, and disappeared in the sand. Then the children looked at each other, and each child suddenly found itself alone with three perfect strangers, all radiantly beautiful.

They stood for some moments in perfect silence. Each thought that its brothers and sisters had wandered off, and that these strange children had stolen up unnoticed while it was watching the swelling form of the Sand-fairy. Anthea spoke first—

"Excuse me," she said very politely to Jane, who now had enormous blue eyes and a cloud of russet hair, "but have you seen two little boys and a little girl anywhere about?"

"I was just going to ask you that," said Jane. And then Cyril cried:

"Why, it's *you!* I know the hole in your pinafore! You *are* Jane, aren't you? And you're the Panther; I can see your dirty handkerchief that you forgot to change after you'd cut your thumb! Crikey! The wish has come off, after all. I say, am I as handsome as you are?"

"If you're Cyril, I liked you much better as you were before," said Anthea decidedly. "You look like the picture of the young chorister, with your golden hair; you'll die young, I shouldn't wonder. And if that's Robert, he's like an Italian organ-grinder. His hair's all black."

"You two girls are like Christmas cards, then—that's all—silly Christmas cards," said Robert angrily. "And Jane's hair is simply carrots."

It was indeed of that Venetian tint so much admired by artists.

"Well, it's no use finding fault with each other," said Anthea; "let's get the Lamb and lug it home to dinner. The servants will admire us most awfully, you'll see."

Baby was just waking when they got to him, and not one of the children but was relieved to find that he at least was not as beautiful as the day, but just the same as usual.

"I suppose he's too young to have wishes naturally," said Jane. "We shall have to mention him specially next time."

Anthea ran forward and held out her arms.

"Come to own Panther, ducky," she said.

The Baby looked at her disapprovingly, and put a sandy pink thumb in his mouth. Anthea was his favourite sister.

"Come then," she said.

"G'way long!" said the Baby.

"Come to own Pussy," said Jane.

"Wants my Panty," said the Lamb dismally, and his lip trembled.

"Here, come on, Veteran," said Robert, "come and have a yidey on Yobby's back."

"Yah, narky narky boy," howled the Baby, giving way altogether. Then the children knew the worst. *The Baby did not know them!*

They looked at each other in despair, and it was terrible to each, in this dire emergency, to meet only the beautiful eyes of perfect strangers, instead of the merry, friendly, commonplace, twinkling, jolly little eyes of its own brothers and sisters.

"This is most truly awful," said Cyril when he had tried to lift up the Lamb, and the Lamb had scratched like a cat and bellowed like a bull. "We've got to *make friends* with him! I can't carry him home screaming like that. Fancy having to make friends with our own baby!—it's too silly."

That, however, was exactly what they had to do. It took over an hour, and the task was not rendered any easier by the fact that the Lamb was by this time as hungry as a lion and as thirsty as a desert.

At last he consented to allow these strangers to carry him home by turns, but as he refused to hold on to such new acquaintances he was a dead weight, and most exhausting.

"Thank goodness, we're home!" said Jane, staggering through the iron gates to where Martha, the nursemaid, stood at the front door shading her eyes with her hand and looking out anxiously. "Here! Do take Baby!"

Martha snatched the Baby from her arms.

"Thanks be, *he's* safe back," she said. "Where are the others, and whoever to goodness gracious are all of you?"

"We're *us*, of course," said Robert.

"And who's *us*, when you're at home?" asked Martha scornfully.

"I tell you it's *us*, only we're beautiful as the day," said Cyril. "I'm Cyril, and these are the others, and we're jolly hungry. Let us in, and don't be a silly idiot."

Martha merely dratted Cyril's impudence and tried to shut the door in his face.

"I know we *look* different, but I'm Anthea, and we're so tired, and it's long past dinner-time."

"Then go home to your dinners, whoever you are; and if our children put you up to this play-acting you can tell them from me they'll catch it, so they know what to expect!" With that she did bang the door. Cyril rang the bell violently. No answer. Presently cook put her head out of a bedroom window and said:

"If you don't take yourself off, and that precious sharp, I'll go and fetch the police." And she slammed down the window.

"It's no good," said Anthea. "Oh, do, do come away before we get sent to prison!"

The boys said it was nonsense, and the law of England couldn't put you in prison for just being as beautiful as the day, but all the same they followed the others out into the lane.

"We shall be our proper selves after sunset, I suppose," said Jane.

"I don't know," Cyril said sadly; "it mayn't be like that now—things have changed a good deal since Megatherium times."

"Oh," cried Anthea suddenly, "perhaps we shall turn into stone at sunset, like the Megatheriums did, so that there mayn't be any of us left over for the next day."

She began to cry, so did Jane. Even the boys turned pale. No one had the heart to say anything.

It was a horrible afternoon. There was no house near where the children could beg a crust of bread or even a glass of water. They were afraid to go to the village, because they had seen Martha go down there with a basket, and there was a local constable. True, they were all as beautiful as the day, but that is a poor comfort when you are as hungry as a hunter and as thirsty as a sponge.

Three times they tried in vain to get the servants in the White House to let them in and listen to their tale. And then Robert went alone, hoping to be able to climb in at one of the back windows and so open the door to the others. But all the windows were out of reach, and Martha emptied a toilet-jug of cold water over him from a top window, and said:

"Go along with you, you nasty little Eyetalian monkey."

It came at last to their sitting down in a row under the hedge, with their feet in a dry ditch, waiting for sunset, and wondering whether, when the sun *did* set, they would turn into stone, or only into their own old natural selves; and each of them still felt lonely and among strangers and tried not to look at the others, for, though their voices were their own, their faces were so radiantly beautiful as to be quite irritating to look at.

"I don't believe we *shall* turn to stone," said Robert, breaking a long miserable silence, "because the Sand-fairy said he'd give us another wish to-morrow, and he couldn't if we were stone, could he?"

The others said "No," but they weren't at all comforted.

Another silence, longer and more miserable, was broken by Cyril's suddenly saying, "I don't want to frighten you girls, but I believe it's beginning with me already. My foot's quite dead. I'm turning to stone, I know I am, and so will you in a minute."

"Never mind," said Robert kindly, "perhaps you'll be the only stone one, and the rest of us will be all right, and we'll cherish your statue and hang garlands on it."

But when it turned out that Cyril's foot had only gone to sleep through his sitting too long with it under him, and when it came to life in an agony of pins and needles, the others were quite cross.

"Giving us such a fright for nothing!" said Anthea.

The third and miserablest silence of all was broken by Jane. She said: "If we *do* come out of this all right we'll ask the Sammyadd to make it so that the servants don't notice anything different, no matter what wishes we have."

The others only grunted. They were too wretched even to make good resolutions.

At last hunger and fright and crossness and tiredness—four very nasty things—all joined together to bring one nice thing, and that was sleep. The children lay asleep in a row, with their beautiful eyes shut and their beautiful mouths open. Anthea woke first. The sun had set, and the twilight was coming on.

Anthea pinched herself very hard, to make sure, and when she found she could still feel pinching she decided that she was not stone, and then she pinched the others. They, also, were soft.

"Wake up," she said, almost in tears for joy; "it's all right, we're not stone. And oh, Cyril, how nice and ugly you do look, with your old freckles and your brown hair and your little eyes. And so do you all!" she added, so that they might not feel jealous.

When they got home they were very much scolded by Martha, who told them about the strange children.

"A good-looking lot, I must say, but that impudent."

"I know," said Robert, who knew by experience how hopeless it would be to try to explain things to Martha.

"And where on earth have you been all this time, you naughty little things, you?"

"In the lane."

"Why didn't you come home hours ago?"

"We couldn't because of *them*," said Anthea.

"Who?"

"The children who were as beautiful as the day. They kept us there till after sunset. We couldn't come back till they'd gone. You don't know how we hated them! Oh, do, do give us some supper—we are so hungry."

"Hungry! I should think so," said Martha angrily; "out all day like this. Well, I hope it'll be a lesson to you not to go picking up with strange children—down here after measles, as likely as not. Now mind, if you see them again, don't speak to them—not one word nor so much as a look—but come straight away and tell me. I'll spoil their beauty for them!"

"If ever we *do* see them again we'll tell you," Anthea said; and Robert, fixing his eyes fondly on the cold beef that was being brought in on a tray by cook, added in heartfelt undertones—

"And we'll take jolly good care we never *do* see them again."

And they never have.

PAUL GALLICO

The
Small Miracle

Approaching Assisi via the chalky, dusty road that twists its way up Monte Subasio, now revealing, now concealing the exquisite little town, as it winds its way through olive and cypress groves, you eventually reach a division where your choice lies between an upper and a lower route.

If you select the latter, you soon find yourself entering Assisi through the twelfth-century archway of the denticulated door of St. Francis. But if, seduced by the clear air, the wish to mount even closer to the canopy of blue Italian sky and expose still more of the delectable view of the rich Umbrian valley below, you choose the upper way, you and your vehicle eventually become inextricably entangled in the welter of humanity, oxen, goats, bawling calves, mules, fowl, children, pigs, booths and carts gathered at the market place outside the walls.

It is here you would be most likely to encounter Pepino, with his donkey Violetta, hard at work, turning his hand to anything whereby a small boy and a strong, willing beast of burden could win for themselves the crumpled ten and twenty lira notes needed to buy food and pay for lodging in the barn of Niccolo the stableman.

Pepino and Violetta were everything to each other. They were a familiar sight about Assisi and its immediate environs—the thin brown boy, ragged and barefooted, with the enormous dark eyes, large ears, and close-cropped, upstanding hair, and the dust-colored little donkey with the Mona Lisa smile.

Pepino was ten years old and an orphan, his father, mother and near relatives having been killed in the war. In self-reliance, wisdom and demeanor he was, of course, much older, a circumstance aided by his independence, for Pepino was an unusual orphan in that having a heritage he need rely on no one. Pepino's heritage was Violetta.

She was a good, useful and docile donkey, alike as any other with friendly, gentle eyes, soft taupe-colored muzzle, and long, pointed brown ears, with one exception that distinguished her. Violetta had a curious expression about the corners of her mouth, as though she was smiling gently over something that amused or pleased her. Thus, no matter what kind of work, or how much she was asked to do, she always appeared to be performing it with a smile of quiet satisfaction. The combination of Pepino's dark lustrous eyes and Violetta's smile was so harmonious that people favored them and they were able not only to earn enough for their keep but, aided and advised by Father Damico, the priest of their parish, to save a little as well.

There were all kinds of things they could do—carry loads of wood or water, deliver purchases carried in the panniers that thumped against Violetta's sides, hire out to help pull a cart mired in the mud, aid in the olive harvest, and even, occasionally, help some citizen who was too encumbered with wine to reach his home on foot, by means of a four-footed taxi with Pepino walking beside to see that the drunkard did not fall off.

But this was not the only reason for the love that existed between boy and donkey, for Violetta was more than just the means of his livelihood. She was mother to him, and father, brother, playmate, companion, and comfort. At night, in the straw of Niccolo's stable, Pepino slept curled up close to her when it was cold, his head pillowed on her neck.

Since the mountainside was a rough world for a small boy, he was sometimes beaten or injured, and then he could creep to her for comfort and Violetta would gently nuzzle his bruises. When there was joy in his heart, he shouted songs into her waving ears; when he was lonely and hurt, he could lean his head against her soft, warm flank and cry out his tears.

On his part, he fed her, watered her, searched her for ticks and parasites, picked stones from her hoofs, scratched and groomed and curried her, lavished affection on her, particularly when they were alone, while in public he never beat her with the donkey stick more than was necessary. For this treatment Violetta made a god of Pepino, and repaid him with loyalty, obedience and affection.

Thus, when one day in the early spring Violetta fell ill, it was the most serious thing that had ever happened to Pepino. It began first with an unusual lethargy that would respond neither to stick nor caresses, nor the young, strident voice urging her on. Later Pepino observed other symptoms and a visible loss of weight. Her ribs, once so well padded, began to show through her sides. But most distressing, either through a change in the conformation of her head, due to growing thinner, or because of the distress of the illness, Violetta lost her enchanting and lovable smile.

Drawing upon his carefully hoarded reserves of lira notes and parting with several of the impressive denomination of a hundred, Pepino called in Dr. Bartoli, the vet.

The vet examined her in good faith, dosed her, and tried his best; but she did not improve and, instead, continued to lose weight and grow weaker. He hummed and hawed then and said, "Well, now, it is hard to say. It might be one thing, such as the bite of a fly new to this district, or another, such as a germ settling in the intestine." Either way, how could one tell? There had been a similar case in Foligno and another in a far-away town. He recommended resting the beast and feeding her lightly. If the illness passed from her and

God willed, she might live. Otherwise, she would surely die and there would be an end to her suffering.

After he had gone away, Pepino put his cropped head on Violetta's heaving flank and wept unrestrainedly. But then, when the storm, induced by the fear of losing his only companion in the world, had subsided, he knew what he must do. If there was no help for Violetta on earth, the appeal must be registered above. His plan was nothing less than to take Violetta into the crypt beneath the lower church of the Basilica of St. Francis, where rested the remains of the Saint who had so dearly loved God's creations, including all the feathered and the four-footed brothers and sisters who served Him. There he would beg St. Francis to heal her. Pepino had no doubt that the Saint would do so when he saw Violetta.

These things Pepino knew from Father Damico, who had a way of talking about St. Francis as though he were a living person who might still be encountered in his frayed cowl, bound with a hemp cord at the middle, merely by turning a corner of the Main Square in Assisi or by walking down one of the narrow, cobbled streets.

And besides, there was a precedent. Giani, his friend, the son of Niccolo the stableman, had taken his sick kitten into the crypt and asked St. Francis to heal her, and the cat had got well—at least half well, anyway, for her hind legs still dragged a little; but at least she had not died. Pepino felt that if Violetta were to die, it would be the end of everything for him.

Thereupon, with considerable difficulty, he persuaded the sick and shaky donkey to rise, and with urgings and caresses and minimum use of the stick drove her through the crooked streets of Assisi and up the hill to the Basilica of St. Francis. At the beautiful twin portal of the lower church he respectfully asked Fra Bernard, who was on duty there, for permission to take Violetta down to St. Francis, so that she might be made well again.

Fra Bernard was a new monk, and, calling Pepino a young and impious scoundrel, ordered him and his donkey to be off. It was strictly forbidden to bring livestock into the church, and even to think of taking an ass into the crypt of St. Francis was a desecration. And besides, how did he imagine she would get down there when the narrow, winding staircase was barely wide enough to accommodate humans in single file, much less four-footed animals? Pepino must be a fool as well as a shiftless rascal.

As ordered, Pepino retreated from the portal, his arm about Violetta's neck, and bethought himself of what he must do next to succeed in his purpose, for while he was disappointed at the rebuff he had received, he was not at all discouraged.

Despite the tragedy that had struck Pepino's early life and robbed him of his family, he really considered himself a most fortunate boy, compared with many, since he had acquired not only a heritage to aid him in earning a living but also an important precept by which to live.

This maxim, the golden key to success, had been left with Pepino, together with bars of chocolate, chewing gum, peanut brittle, soap, and other delights, by a corporal in the United States Army who had, in the six months he had been stationed in the vicinity of Assisi, been Pepino's demigod and hero. His name was Francis Xavier O'Halloran, and what he told Pepino before he departed out of this life forever was, "If you want to get ahead in this world, kid, don't never take no for an answer. Get it?" Pepino never forgot this important advice.

He thought now that his next step was clear; nevertheless, he went first to his friend and adviser, Father Damico, for confirmation.

Father Damico, who had a broad head, lustrous eyes, and shoulders shaped as though they had been especially designed to support the burdens laid upon them by his parishioners, said, "You are within your rights, my son, in taking your request to the lay Supervisor and it lies within his power to grant or refuse it."

There was no malice in the encouragement he thus gave Pepino, but it was also true that he was not loath to see the Supervisor brought face to face with an example of pure and innocent faith. For in his private opinion that worthy man was too much concerned with the twin churches that formed the Basilica and the crypt as a tourist attraction. He, Father Damico, could not see why the child should not have his wish, but, of course, it was out of his jurisdiction. He was, however, curious about how the Supervisor would react, even though he thought he knew in advance.

However, he did not impart his fears to Pepino and merely called after him as he was leaving, "And if the little one cannot be got in from above, there is another entrance from below, through the old church, only it has been walled up for a hundred years. But it could be opened. You might remind the Supervisor when you see him. He knows where it is."

Pepino thanked him and went back alone to the Basilica and the monastery attached to it and asked permission to see the Supervisor.

This personage was an accessible man, and even though he was engaged in a conversation with the Bishop, he sent for Pepino, who walked into the cloister gardens where he waited respectfully for the two great men to finish.

The two dignitaries were walking up and down, and Pepino wished it were the Bishop who was to say yea or nay to his request, as he looked the kindlier of the two, the Supervisor appearing to have more the expression of a merchant. The boy pricked up his ears, because, as it happened, they were speaking of St. Francis, and the Bishop was just remarking with a sigh, "He has been gone too long from this earth. The lesson of his life is plain to all who can read. But who in these times will pause to do so?"

The Supervisor said, "His tomb in the crypt attracts many to Assisi. But in a Holy Year, relics are even better. If we but had the tongue of the Saint, or a lock of his hair, or a fingernail."

The Bishop had a far-away look in his eyes, and he was shaking his head gently. "It is a message we are in need of, my dear Supervisor, a message from a great heart that would speak to us across the gap of seven centuries to remind us of The Way." And here he paused and coughed, for he was a polite man and noticed that Pepino was waiting.

The Supervisor turned also and said, "Ah yes, my son, what is it that I can do for you?"

Pepino said, "Please, sir, my donkey Violetta is very sick. The Doctor Bartoli has said he can do nothing more and perhaps she will die. Please, I would like permission to take her into the tomb of Saint Francis and ask him to cure her. He loved all animals, and particularly little donkeys. I am sure he will make her well."

The Supervisor looked shocked. "A donkey. In the crypt. However did you come to that idea?"

Pepino explained about Giani and his sick kitten, while the Bishop turned away to hide a smile.

But the Supervisor was not smiling. He asked, "How did this Giani succeed in smuggling a kitten into the tomb?"

Since it was all over, Pepino saw no reason for not telling, and replied, "Under his coat, sir."

The Supervisor made a mental note to warn the brothers to keep a sharper eye out for small boys or other persons with suspicious-looking lumps under their outer clothing.

"Of course we can have no such goings on," he said. "The next thing you know, everyone would be coming, bringing a sick dog, or an ox, or a goat, or even a pig. And then where should we end up? A veritable sty."

"But, sir," Pepino pleaded, "no one need know. We would come and go so very quickly."

The Supervisor's mind played. There was something touching about the boy—the bullet head, the enormous eyes, the jug-handle ears. And yet, what if he permitted it and the donkey then died, as seemed most likely if Dr. Bartoli had said there was no further hope? Word was sure to get about, and the shrine would suffer from it. He wondered what the Bishop was thinking and how *he* would solve the problem.

He equivocated: "And besides, even if we were to allow it, you would never be able to get your donkey around the turn at the bottom of the stairs. So, you see, it is quite impossible."

"But there is another entrance," Pepino said. "From the old church. It has not been used for a long time, but it could be opened just this once—couldn't it?"

The Supervisor was indignant. "What are you saying—destroy church property? The entrance has been walled up for over a century, ever since the new crypt was built."

The Bishop thought he saw a way out and said gently to the boy, "Why do you not go home and pray to Saint Francis to assist you? If you open your heart to him and have faith, he will surely hear you."

"But it wouldn't be the same," Pepino cried, and his voice was shaking with the sobs that wanted to come. "I must take her where Saint Francis can see her. She isn't like any other old donkey—

Violetta has the sweetest smile. She does not smile any more since she has been so ill. But perhaps she would, just once more for Saint Francis. And when he saw it he would not be able to resist her, and he would make her well. I know he would!"

The Supervisor knew his ground now. He said, "I am sorry, my son, but the answer is no."

But even through his despair and the bitter tears he shed as he went away, Pepino knew that if Violetta was to live he must not take no for an answer.

"Who is there, then?" Pepino asked of Father Damico later. "Who is above the Supervisor and my lord the Bishop who might tell them to let me take Violetta into the crypt?"

Father Damico's stomach felt cold as he thought of the dizzying hierarchy between Assisi and Rome. Nevertheless, he explained as best he could, concluding with, "And at the top is His Holiness, the Pope himself. Surely his heart would be touched by what has happened if you were able to tell him, for he is a great and good man. But he is busy with important weighty affairs, Pepino, and it would be impossible for him to see you."

Pepino went back to Niccolo's stable, where he ministered to Violetta, fed and watered her and rubbed her muzzle a hundred times. Then he withdrew his money from the stone jar buried under the straw and counted it. He had almost three hundred lire. A hundred of it he set aside and promised to his friend Giani if he would look after Violetta, while Pepino was gone, as if she were his own. Then he patted her once more, brushed away the tears that had started again at the sight of how thin she was, put on his jacket, and went out on the high road, where, using his thumb as he had learned from Corporal Francis Xavier O'Halloran, he got a lift in a lorry going to Foligno and the main road. He was on his way to Rome to see the Holy Father.

Never had any small boy looked quite so infinitesimal and forlorn as Pepino standing in the boundless and almost deserted, since it was early in the morning, St. Peter's Square. Everything towered over him—the massive dome of St. Peter's, the obelisk of Caligula, the Bernini colonnades. Everything contrived to make him look pinched and miserable in his bare feet, torn trousers, and ragged jacket. Never was a boy more overpowered, lonely, and frightened, or carried a greater burden of unhappiness in his heart.

For now that he was at last in Rome, the gigantic proportions of the buildings and monuments, their awe and majesty, began to sap his courage, and he seemed to have a glimpse into the utter futility and hopelessness of his mission. And then there would arise in his mind a picture of the sad little donkey who did not smile any more, her heaving flanks and clouded eyes, and who would surely die unless he could find help for her. It was thoughts like these that enabled him finally to cross the piazza and timidly approach one of the smaller side entrances to the Vatican.

The Swiss guard, in his slashed red, yellow, and blue uniform, with his long halberd, looked enormous and forbidding. Nevertheless, Pepino edged up to him and said, "Please, will you take me to see the Pope? I wish to speak to him about my donkey Violetta, who is very ill and may die unless the Pope will help me."

The guard smiled, not unkindly, for he was used to these ignorant and innocent requests, and the fact that it came from a dirty, ragged little boy, with eyes like ink pools and a round head from which the ears stood out like the handles on a cream jug, made it all the more harmless. But, nevertheless, he was shaking his head as he smiled, and then said that His Holiness was a very busy man and could not be seen. And the guard grounded his halberd with a thud and let it fall slantwise across the door to show that he meant business.

Pepino backed away. What good was his precept in the face of such power and majesty? And yet the memory of what Corporal O'Halloran had said told him that he must return to the Vatican yet once again.

At the side of the piazza he saw an old woman sitting under an umbrella, selling little bouquets and nosegays of spring flowers— daffodils and jonquils, snowdrops and white narcissus, Parma violets and lilies of the valley, vari-colored carnations, pansies, and tiny sweetheart roses. Some of the people visiting St. Peter's liked to place these on the altar of their favorite saint. The flowers were crisp and fresh from the market, and many of them had glistening drops of water still clinging to their petals.

Looking at them made Pepino think of home and Father Damico

and what he had said of the love St. Francis had for flowers. Father Damico had the gift of making everything he thought and said sound like poetry. And Pepino came to the conclusion that if St. Francis, who had been a holy man, had been so fond of flowers, perhaps the Pope, who according to his position was even holier, would love them, too.

For fifty lire he bought a tiny bouquet in which a spray of lilies of the valley rose from a bed of dark violets and small red roses crowded next to yellow pansies all tied about with leaf and feather fern and paper lace.

From a stall where postcards and souvenirs were sold, he begged pencil and paper, and laboriously composed a note:

> Dear and most sacred Holy Father:
> These flowers are for you. Please let me see you and tell you about my donkey Violetta who is dying, and they will not let me take her to see Saint Francis so that he may cure her. I live in the town of Assisi, but I have come all the way here to see you
> Your loving Pepino.

Thereupon, he returned to the door, placed the bouquet and the note in the hand of the Swiss guard, and begged, "Please take these up to the Pope. I am sure he will see me when he receives the flowers and reads what I have written."

The guard had not expected this. The child and the flowers had suddenly placed him in a dilemma from which he could not extricate himself in the presence of those large and trusting eyes. However, he was not without experience in handling such matters. He had only to place a colleague at his post, go to the Guard Room, throw the flowers and the note into the wastepaper basket, absent himself for a sufficient length of time, and then return to tell the boy that His Holiness thanked him for the gift of the flowers and regretted that press of important business made it impossible for him to grant him an audience.

This little subterfuge the guard put into motion at once; but when he came to completing the next-to-last act in it, he found to his amazement that somehow he could not bring himself to do it. There was the wastepaper basket, yawning to receive the offering, but the little nosegay seemed to be glued to his fingers. How gay, sweet, and cool the flowers were. What thoughts they brought to his mind of spring in the green valleys of his far-off canton of Luzern. He saw again the snow-capped mountains of his youth, the little gingerbread houses, the gray, soft-eyed cattle grazing in the blossom-carpeted meadows, and he heard the heart-warming tinkling of their bells.

Dazed by what had happened to him, he left the Guard Room and wandered through the corridors, for he did not know where to go or what to do with his burden. He was eventually encountered by a busy little Monsignor, one of the vast army of clerks and secretaries employed in the Vatican, who paused, astonished at the sight of the burly guard helplessly contemplating a tiny posy.

And thus occurred the minor miracle whereby Pepino's plea and offering crossed the boundary in the palace that divided the mundane from the spiritual, the lay from the ecclesiastical.

For to the great relief of the guard, the Monsignor took over the burning articles that he had been unable to relinquish; and this priest they touched, too, as it is the peculiar power of flowers that while they are universal and spread their species over the world, they invoke in each beholder the dearest and most cherished memories.

In this manner, the little bouquet passed on and upward from hand to hand, pausing briefly in the possession of the clerk of the Apostolic Chamber, the Privy Almoner, the Papal Sacristan, the Master of the Sacred Palaces, the Papal Chamberlain. The dew vanished from the flowers; they began to lose their freshness and to wilt, passing from hand to hand. And yet they retained their magic, the message of love and memories that rendered it impossible for any of these intermediaries to dispose of them.

Eventually, then, they were deposited with the missive that accompanied them on the desk of the man for whom they had been destined. He read the note and then sat there silently contemplating the blossoms. He closed his eyes for a moment, the better to entertain the picture that arose in his mind of himself as a small Roman boy taken on a Sunday into the Alban Hills, where for the first time he saw violets growing wild.

When he opened his eyes at last, he said to his secretary, "Let the child be brought here. I will see him."

Thus it was that Pepino at last came into the presence of the Pope, seated at his desk in his office. Perched on the edge of a chair next to him, Pepino told the whole story about Violetta, his need to take her into the tomb of St. Francis, about the Supervisor who was preventing him, and all about Father Damico, too, and the second entrance to the crypt, Violetta's smile, and his love for her—everything, in fact, that was in his heart and that now poured forth to the sympathetic man sitting quietly behind the desk.

And when, at the end of half an hour, he was ushered from the presence, he was quite sure he was the happiest boy in the world. For he had not only the blessing of the Pope, but also, under his jacket, two letters, one addressed to the lay Supervisor of the Monastery of Assisi and the other to Father Damico. No longer did he feel small and overwhelmed when he stepped out on to the square again past the astonished but delighted Swiss guard. He felt as though he could give one leap and a bound and fly back to his Violetta's side.

Nevertheless, he had to give heed to the more practical side of transportation. He enquired his way to a bus that took him to where the Via Flaminia became a country road stretching to the north, then plied his thumb backed by his eloquent eyes, and before nightfall of that day, with good luck, was home in Assisi.

After a visit to Violetta had assured him that she had been well looked after and at least was no worse than she had been before his departure, Pepino proudly went to Father Damico and presented his letters as he had been instructed to do.

The Father fingered the envelope for the Supervisor and then, with a great surge of warmth and happiness, read the one addressed to himself. He said to Pepino, "Tomorrow we will take the Supervisor's letter to him. He will summon masons and the old door will be broken down and you will be able to take Violetta into the tomb and pray there for her recovery. The Pope himself has approved it."

The Pope, of course, had not written the letters personally. They had been composed with considerable delight and satisfaction by the Cardinal-Secretary, backed by Papal authority, who said in his missive to Father Damico:

> Surely the Supervisor must know that in his lifetime the blessed Saint Francis was accompanied to chapel by a little lamb that used to follow him about Assisi. Is an *asinus* any less created by God because his coat is rougher and his ears longer?

And he wrote also of another matter, which Father Damico imparted to Pepino in his own way.

He said, "Pepino, there is something you must understand before we go to see the Abbot. It is your hope that because of your faith in St. Francis he will help you and heal your donkey. But had you thought, perhaps, that he who dearly cared for all of God's creatures might come to love Violetta so greatly that he would wish to have her at his side in Eternity?"

A cold terror gripped Pepino as he listened. He managed to say, "No, Father, I had not thought——" The priest continued: "Will you go to the crypt only to ask, Pepino, or will you also, if necessary, be prepared to give?"

Everything in Pepino cried out against the possibility of losing Violetta, even to someone as beloved as St. Francis. Yet when he raised his stricken face and looked into the lustrous eyes of Father Damico, there was something in their depths that gave him the courage to whisper, "I will give—if I must. But, oh, I hope he will let her stay with me just a little longer."

The clink of the stonemason's pick rang again and again through the vaulted chamber of the lower church, where the walled-up door of the passageway leading to the crypt was being removed. Nearby waited the Supervisor and his friend the Bishop, Father Damico, and Pepino, large-eyed, pale, and silent. The boy kept his arms about the neck of Violetta and his face pressed to hers. The little donkey was very shaky on her legs and could barely stand.

The Supervisor watched humbly and impassively while broken bricks and clods of mortar fell as the breach widened and the freed current of air from the passage swirled the plaster dust in clouds. He was a just man for all his weakness and had invited the Bishop to witness his rebuke.

A portion of the wall proved obstinate. The mason attacked the archway at the side to weaken its support. Then the loosened masonry began to tumble again. A narrow passageway was effected, and through the opening they could see the distant flicker of the candles placed at the altar wherein rested the remains of St. Francis.

Pepino stirred towards the opening. Or was it Violetta who had moved nervously, frightened by the unaccustomed place and noises?

Father Damico said, "Wait," and Pepino held her; but the donkey's uncertain feet slipped on the rubble and then lashed out in panic, striking the side of the archway where it had been weakened. A brick fell out. A crack appeared.

Father Damico leaped and pulled boy and animal out of the way as, with a roar, the side of the arch collapsed, laying bare a piece of the old wall and the hollow behind it before everything vanished in a cloud of dust.

But when the dust settled, the Bishop, his eyes starting from his head, was pointing to something that rested in a niche of the hollow just revealed. It was a small, gray, leaden box. Even from there they could see the year 1226, when St. Francis died, engraved on the side, and the large initial "F."

The Bishop's breath came out like a sigh. "Ah, could it be? The legacy of Saint Francis! Fra Leo mentions it. It was hidden away centuries ago, and no one had ever been able to find it since."

The Supervisor said hoarsely, "The contents! Let us see what is inside—it may be valuable!"

The Bishop hesitated. "Perhaps we had best wait. For this is in itself a miracle, this finding."

But Father Damico, who was a poet and to whom St. Francis was a living spirit, cried, "Open it, I beg of you! All who are here are humble. Surely Heaven's plan has guided us to it."

The Abbot held the lantern. The mason with his careful, honest workman's hands deftly loosed the bindings and pried the lid of the airtight box. It opened with an ancient creaking of its hinge and revealed what had been placed there more than seven centuries before.

There was a piece of hempen cord, knotted as though, perhaps, once it had been worn about the waist. Caught in the knot, as fresh as though it had grown but yesterday, was a single sprig of wheat. Dried and preserved, there lay, too, the stem and starry flower of a mountain primrose and, next to it, one downy feather from a tiny meadow bird.

Silently the men stared at these objects from the past to try to read their meaning, and Father Damico wept, for to him they brought the vivid figure of the Saint, half-blinded, worn and fragile, the cord knotted at his waist, singing, striding through a field of wheat.

The flower might have been the first discovered by him after a winter's snow, and addressed as "Sister Cowslip," and praised for her tenderness and beauty. As though he were transported there, Father Damico saw the little field bird fly trustingly to Francis' shoulder and chirrup and nestle there and leave a feather in his hand. His heart was so full he thought he could not bear it.

The Bishop, too, was close to tears as, in his own way, he interpreted what they had found. "Ah, what could be clearer than the message of the Saint? Poverty, love, and faith. This is his bequest to all of us."

Pepino said, "Please, lords and sirs, may Violetta and I go into the crypt now?"

They had forgotten him. Now they started up from their contemplation of the touching relics.

Father Damico cleared the tears from his eyes. The doorway was freed now, and there was room for boy and donkey to pass. "Ah, yes," he said. "Yes, Pepino. You may enter now. And may God go with you."

The hoofs of the donkey went sharply *clip-clop, clip-clop* on the ancient flagging of the passageway. Pepino did not support her now, but walked beside, hand just resting lightly and lovingly on her neck. His round, cropped head with the outstanding ears was held high, and his shoulders were bravely squared.

And to Father Damico it seemed, as they passed, whether because of the uneven light and the dancing shadows, or because he wished it so, that the ghost, the merest wisp, the barest suspicion of a smile had returned to the mouth of Violetta.

Thus the watchers saw boy and donkey silhouetted against the flickering oil lamps and altar candles of the crypt as they went forward to complete their pilgrimage of faith.

IV

Long Ago
and
Far Away

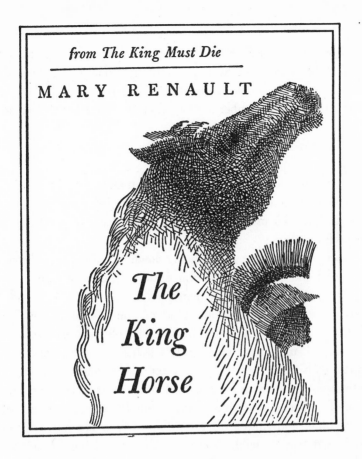

from *The King Must Die*

MARY RENAULT

The King Horse

[*Greece, the second millenium B.C.*]

The Citadel of Troizen, where the Palace stands, was built by
giants before anyone remembers. But the Palace was built by
my great-grandfather. At sunrise, if you look at it from Kalauria across
the strait, the columns glow fire-red and the walls are golden. It
shines bright against the dark woods on the mountainside.

Our house is Hellene, sprung from the seed of Ever-Living Zeus.
We worship the Sky Gods before Mother Dia and the gods of earth.
And we have never mixed our blood with the blood of the Shore
People, who had the land before us.

My grandfather had about fifteen children in his household, when
I was born. But his queen and her sons were dead, leaving only my

mother born in wedlock. As for my father, it was said in the Palace that I had been fathered by a god. By the time I was five, I had perceived that some people doubted this. But my mother never spoke of it; and I cannot remember a time when I should have cared to ask her.

When I was seven, the Horse Sacrifice came due, a great day in Troizen.

It is held four-yearly, so I remembered nothing of the last one. I knew it concerned the King Horse, but thought it was some act of homage to him. To my mind, nothing could have been more fitting. I knew him well.

He lived in the great horse field, down on the plain. From the Palace roof I had often watched him, snuffing the wind with his white mane flying, or leaping on his mares. And only last year I had seen him do battle for his kingdom. One of the House Barons, seeing from afar the duel begin, rode down to the olive slopes for a nearer sight, and took me on his crupper. I watched the great stallions rake the earth with their forefeet, arch their necks, and shout their war cries; then charge in with streaming manes and teeth laid bare. At last the loser foundered; the King Horse snorted over him, threw up his head neighing, and trotted off toward his wives. He had never been haltered, and was as wild as the sea. Not the King himself would ever throw a leg across him. He belonged to the god.

His valor alone would have made me love him. But I had another cause as well. I thought he was my brother.

Poseidon, as I knew, can look like a man or like a horse, whichever he chooses. In his man shape, it was said, he had begotten me. But there were songs in which he had horse sons too, swift as the north wind, and immortal. The King Horse, who was his own, must surely be one of these. It seemed clear to me, therefore, that we ought to meet. I had heard he was only five years old. "So," I thought, "though he is the bigger, I am the elder. It is for me to speak first."

Next time the Master of the Horse went down to choose colts for the chariots, I got him to take me. While he did his work, he left me with a groom; who presently drew in the dust a gambling board, and fell to play with a friend. Soon they forgot me. I climbed the palisade, and went seeking the King Horse.

The horses of Troizen are pure-bred Hellene. We have never

crossed them with the little strain of the Shore People, whom we took
the land from. When I was in with them, they looked very tall. As
I reached up to pat one, I heard the Horse Master shout behind me;
but I closed my ears. "Everyone gives me orders," I thought. "It
comes of having no father. I wish I were the King Horse; no one
gives them to him." Then I saw him, standing by himself on a little
knoll, watching the end of the pasture where they were choosing
colts. I went nearer, thinking, as every child thinks once for the first
time, "Here is beauty."

He had heard me, and turned to look. I held out my hand, as I did
in the stables, and called, "Son of Poseidon!" On this he came
trotting up to me, just as the stable horses did. I had brought a lump
of salt, and held it out to him.

There was some commotion behind me. The groom bawled out, and
looking round I saw the Horse Master beating him. My turn would
be next, I thought; men were waving at me from the railings, and
cursing each other. I felt safer where I was. The King Horse was so
near that I could see the lashes of his dark eyes. His forelock fell
between them like a white waterfall between shining stones. His
teeth were as big as the ivory plates upon a war helm; but his lip,
when he licked the salt out of my palm, felt softer than my mother's
breast. When the salt was finished, he brushed my cheek with his,
and snuffed at my hair. Then he trotted back to his hillock, whisking
his long tail. His feet, with which as I learned later he had killed a
mountain lion, sounded neat on the meadow, like a dancer's.

Now I found myself snatched from all sides, and hustled from the
pasture. It surprised me to see the Horse Master as pale as a sick
man. He heaved me on his mount in silence, and hardly spoke all the
way home. After so much to-do, I feared my grandfather himself
would beat me. He gave me a long look as I came near; but all he
said was, "Theseus, you went to the horse field as Peiros' guest. It was
unmannerly to give him trouble. A nursing mare might have bitten
your arm off. I forbid you to go again."

This happened when I was six years old; and the Horse Feast
fell next year.

It was the chief of all feasts at Troizen. The Palace was a week
getting ready. First my mother took the women down to the river
Hyllikos, to wash the clothes. They were loaded on mules and brought

down to the clearest water, the basin under the fall. Even in drought
the Hyllikos never fails or muddies; but now in summer it was low.
The old women rubbed light things at the water's edge, and beat them
on the stones; the girls picked up their petticoats and trod the heavy
mantles and blankets in midstream. One played a pipe, which they
kept time to, splashing and laughing.

On the feast day I woke at dawn. My old nurse dressed me in my
best: my new doeskin drawers with braided borders, my red belt
rolled upon rope and clasped with crystal, and my necklace of gold
beads. When she had combed my hair, I went to see my mother
dressing. She was just out of her bath, and they were dropping her
petticoat over her head. The seven-tiered flounces, sewn with gold
drops and pendants, clinked and glittered as she shook them out.
When they clipped together her gold-worked girdle and her bodice
waist, she held her breath in hard and let it out laughing.

They took her hair out of the crimping-plaits (it was darker than
mine, about the color of polished bronze) and began to comb it.
I ran outside on the terrace, which runs all round the royal rooms,
for they stand on the roof of the Great Hall. Morning was red,
and the crimson-painted columns burned in it. I could hear, down
in the courtyard, the House Barons assembling in their war dress.
This was what I had waited for.

They came in by twos and threes, the bearded warriors talking,
the young men laughing and scuffling, shouting to friends, or
feinting at each other with the butts of their spears. They had on
their tall-plumed leather helmets, circled with bronze or strengthened
with rolls of hide. Their broad breasts and shoulders, sleekly oiled,
shone russet in the rosy light; their wide leather drawers stood
stiffly out from the thigh, making their lean waists, pulled in with
the thick rolled sword-belts, look slenderer still. They waited, ex-
changing news and chaff, and striking poses for the women, the
young men lounging with the tops of their tall shields propping
their left armpits, their right arms stretched out grasping their spears.
Their upper lips were all fresh shaved, to make their new beards
show clearer. I scanned the shield devices, birds or fish or serpents
worked upon the hide, picking out friends to hail, who raised their
spears in greeting. Seven or eight of them were uncles of mine.
My grandfather had got them in the Palace on various women of

good blood, prizes of his old wars, or gifts of compliment from neighbor kings.

The land barons were coming in from their horses or their chariots; they too bare to the waist, for the day was warm, but wearing all their jewels; even their boot tops had golden tassels. The sound of men's voices grew louder and deeper and filled the air above the courtyard. I squared back my shoulders, and nipped my belt in; gazed at a youth whose beard was starting, and counted years on my fingers.

Talaos came in, the War Leader; a son of my grandfather's youth, got upon a chief's wife taken in battle. He had on his finest things: his prize helmet from the High King of Mycenae's funeral games, all plated, head and cheeks, with the carved teeth of boars, and both his swords, the long one with the crystal pommel which he sometimes let me draw, the short one with a leopard hunt inlaid in gold. The men touched their spear shafts to their brows; he numbered them off with his eye, and went in to tell my grandfather they were ready. Soon he came out, and standing on the great steps before the king-column that carried the lintel, his beard jutting like a warship's prow, shouted, "The god goes forth!"

They all trooped out of the courtyard. As I craned to see, my grandfather's body servant came and asked my mother's maid if the Lord Theseus was ready to go with the King.

I had supposed I should be going with my mother. So I think had she. But she sent word that I was ready whenever her father wished.

She was Chief Priestess of Mother Dia in Troizen. In the time of the Shore People before us, that would have made her sovereign queen; and if we ourselves had been sacrificing at the Navel Stone, no one would have walked before her. But Poseidon is husband and lord of the Mother, and on his feast day the men go first. So, when I heard I was going with my grandfather, I saw myself a man already.

I ran to the battlements, and looked out between their teeth. Now I saw what god it was the men were following. They had let loose the King Horse, and he was running free across the plain.

The village too, it seemed, had turned out to welcome him. He went through standing corn in the common fields, and no one raised a hand to stop him. He crossed the beans and the barley, and would have gone up to the olive slopes; but some of the men were there and he turned away. While I was watching, down in the empty court a chariot rattled. It was my grandfather's; and I remembered I was to ride in it. By myself on the terrace I danced for joy.

They fetched me down. Eurytos the charioteer was up already, standing still as an image in his short white tunic and leather greaves, his long hair bound in a club; only his arm muscles moved, from holding in the horses. He lifted me in, to await my grandfather. I was eager to see him in his war things, for in those days he was tall.

He came out, after all, in his priestly robe and fillet, with a scepter instead of a spear. He heaved himself in by the chariot rail, set his feet in the bracers, and gave the word to go. As we clattered down the cobbled road, you could not have taken him for anything but a warrior, fillet or no. He rode with the broad rolling war straddle a man learns driving cross-country with weapons in his hands. Whenever I rode with him, I had to stand on his left; it would have set his teeth on edge to have anything in front of his spear arm. Always I seemed to feel thrown over me the shelter of his absent shield.

Seeing the road deserted, I was surprised, and asked him where the people were. "At Sphairia," he said, grasping my shoulder to steady me over a pothole. "I am taking you to see the rite, because soon you will be waiting on the god there, as one of his servants."

This news startled me. I wondered what service a horse god wanted, and pictured myself combing his forelock, or putting ambrosia before him in golden bowls. But he was also Poseidon Bluehair, who raises storms; and the great black Earth Bull whom, as I had heard, the Cretans fed with youths and girls. After some time I asked my grandfather, "How long shall I stay?"

He looked at my face and laughed, and ruffled my hair with his big hand. "A month at a time," he said. "You will only serve the shrine, and the holy spring. It is time you did your duties to Poseidon, who is your birth-god. So today I shall dedicate you, after the sacrifice. Behave respectfully, and stand still till you are told; remember, you are with me."

We had reached the shore of the strait, where the ford was. I had looked forward to splashing through it in the chariot; but a boat was waiting, to save our best clothes. On the other side we mounted again, and skirted for a while the Kalaurian shore, looking across at Troizen. Then we turned inward, through pines. The horses' feet drummed on a wooden bridge and stopped. We had come to the little holy island at the big one's toe; and kings must walk in the presence of the gods.

The people were waiting. Their clothes and garlands, the warriors' plumes, looked bright in the clearing beyond the trees. My grandfather took my hand and led me up the rocky path. On either side a row of youths was standing, the tallest lads of Troizen and Kalauria, their long hair tied up to crest their heads like manes. They were singing, stamping the beat with their right feet all together, a hymn to Poseidon Hippios. It said how the Horse Father is like the fruitful earth; like the seaway whose broad back bears the ships safe home; his plumed head and bright eye are like daybreak over the mountains, his back and loins like the ripple in the barley field; his mane is like the surf when it blows streaming off the wave crests; and when he stamps the ground, men and cities tremble, and kings' houses fall.

I knew this was true, for the roof of the sanctuary had been rebuilt in my own lifetime; Poseidon had overthrown its wooden columns, and several houses, and made a crack in the Palace walls. I had not felt myself that morning; they had asked me if I was sick, at which I only cried. But after the shock I was better. I had been four years old then, and had almost forgotten.

Our part of the world had always been sacred to Earth-Shaker; the youths had many of his deeds to sing about. Even the ford, their hymn said, was of his making; he had stamped in the strait, and sea had sunk to a trickle, then risen to flood the plain. Up till that time, ships had passed through it; there was a prophecy that one day he would strike it with his fish-spear, and it would sink again.

As we walked between the boys, my grandfather ran his eye along them, for likely warriors. But I had seen ahead, in the midst of the sacred clearing, the King Horse himself, browsing quietly from a tripod.

He had been hand-broken this last year, not for work but for this occasion, and today he had had the drugged feed at dawn. But without knowing this, I was not surprised he should put up with the people round him; I had been taught it was the mark of a king to receive homage with grace.

The shrine was garlanded with pine boughs. The summer air bore scents of resin and flowers and incense, of sweat from the horse and the young men's bodies, of salt from the sea. The priests came forward, crowned with pine, to salute my grandfather as chief priest of the god. Old Kannadis, whose beard was as white as the King Horse's forelock, laid his hand on my head nodding and smiling. My grandfather beckoned to Diokles, my favorite uncle; a big young man eighteen years old, with the skin of a leopard, which he had killed himself, hanging on his shoulder. "Look after the boy," said my grandfather, "till we are ready for him."

Diokles said, "Yes, sir," and led me to the steps before the shrine, away from where he had been standing with his friends. He had on his gold snake arm-ring with crystal eyes, and his hair was bound with a purple ribbon. My grandfather had won his mother at Pylos, second prize in the chariot race, and had always valued her highly; she was the best embroidress in the Palace. He was a bold gay youth, who used to let me ride on his wolfhound. But today he looked at me solemnly, and I feared I was a burden to him.

Old Kannadis brought my grandfather a pine wreath bound with wool, which should have been ready, but had been found after some delay. There is always some small hitch at Troizen; we do not do these things with the smoothness of Athens. The King Horse munched from the tripod, and flicked off flies with his tail.

There were two more tripods; one bowl held water, the other water and wine. In the first my grandfather washed his hands, and a young server dried them. The King Horse lifted his head from the feed, and it seemed they looked at one another. My grandfather set his hand on the white muzzle, and stroked down hard; the head dipped, and rose with a gentle toss. Diokles leaned down to me and said, "Look, he consents."

I looked up at him. This year his beard showed clearly against the light. He said, "It means a good omen. A lucky year." I nodded, thinking the purpose of the rite accomplished; now we would go home. But my grandfather sprinkled meal on the horse's back from a golden dish; then took up a little knife bright with grinding, and cut a lock from his mane. He gave a small piece to Talaos, who was standing near, and some to the first of the barons. Then he turned my way, and beckoned. Diokles' hand on my shoulder pushed me forward. "Go up," he whispered. "Go and take it."

I stepped out, hearing men whisper, and women coo like mating pigeons. I knew already that the son of the Queen's own daughter ranked before the sons of the Palace women; but I had never had it noticed publicly. I thought I was being honored like this because the King Horse was my brother.

Five or six strong white hairs were put in my hand. I had meant to thank my grandfather; but now I felt come out of him the presence of the King, solemn as a sacred oak wood. So, like the others, I touched the lock to my brow in silence. Then I went back, and Diokles said, "Well done."

My grandfather raised his hands and invoked the god. He hailed him as Earth-Shaker, Wave-Gatherer, brother of King Zeus and husband of the Mother; Shepherd of Ships, Horse-Lover. I heard a whinny from beyond the pine woods, where the chariot teams were tethered, ready to race in honor of the god. The King Horse raised his noble head, and softly answered.

The prayer was long, and my mind wandered, till I heard by the note that the end was coming. "Be it so, Lord Poseidon, according to our prayer; and do you accept the offering." He held out his hand, and someone put in it a great cleaver with a bright ground edge. There were tall men standing with ropes of oxhide in their hands. My grandfather felt the cleaver's edge and, as in his chariot, braced his feet apart.

It was a good clean killing. I myself, with all Athens watching, am content to do no worse. Yet, even now, I still remember. How he reared up like a tower, feeling his death, dragging the men like children; the scarlet cleft in the white throat, the rank hot smell; the ruin of beauty, the fall of strength, the ebb of valor; and the grief, the burning pity as he sank upon his knees and laid his bright head in the dust. That blood seemed to tear the soul out of my breast, as if my own heart had shed it.

As the newborn babe, who has been rocked day and night in his soft cave knowing no other, is thrust forth where the harsh air pierces him and the fierce light stabs his eyes, so it was with me. But between me and my mother, where she stood among the women, was the felled carcass twitching in blood, and my grandfather with the crimson cleaver. I looked up; but Diokles was watching the death-throe, leaning easily on his spear. I met only the empty eye-slits of the leopardskin, and the arm-snake's jewelled stare.

My grandfather dipped a cup into the offering bowl, and poured the wine upon the ground. I seemed to see blood stream from his hand. The smell of dressed hide from Diokles' shield, and the man's smell of his body, came to me mixed with the smell of death. My grandfather gave the server the cup, and beckoned. Diokles shifted his spear to his shield arm, and took my hand. "Come," he said. "Father wants you. You have to be dedicated now."

I thought, "So was the King Horse." The bright day rippled before my eyes, which tears of grief and terror blinded. Diokles swung around his shield on its shoulder sling to cover me like a house of hide, and wiped his hard young hand across my eyelids. "Behave," he said. "The people are watching. Come, where's the warrior? It's only blood."

He took the shield away; and I saw the people staring.

At the sight of all their eyes, memories came back to me. "Gods' sons fear nothing," I thought. "Now they will know, one way or the other." And though within me was all dark and crying, yet my foot stepped forward.

Then it was that I heard a sea-sound in my ears; a pulse and a surging, going with me, bearing me on. I heard it then for the first time.

I moved with the wave, as if it broke down a wall before me; and Diokles led me forward. At least, I know that I was led; by him, or one who took his shape as the Immortals may. And I know that having been alone, I was alone no longer.

My grandfather dipped his finger in the blood of the sacrifice, and made the sign of the trident on my brow. Then he and old Kannadis took me under the cool thatch that roofed the holy spring, and dropped in a votive for me, a bronze bull with gilded horns. When we came out, the priests had cut off the god's portion from the carcass, and the smell of burned fat filled the air. But it was not till I got home, and my mother asked, "What is it?" that at last I wept.

Between her breasts, entangled in her shining hair, I wept as if to purge away my soul in water. She put me to bed, and sang to me, and said when I was quiet, "Don't grieve for the King Horse; he has gone to the Earth Mother, who made us all. She has a thousand thousand children, and knows each one of them. He was too good for anyone here to ride; but she will find him some great hero, a child of the sun or the north wind, to be his friend and master; they will gallop all day, and never be tired. Tomorrow you shall take her a present for him, and I will tell her it comes from you."

Next day we went down together to the Navel Stone. It had fallen from heaven long ago, before anyone remembers. The walls of its sunken court were mossy, and the Palace noises fell quiet around. The sacred House Snake had his hole between the stones; but he only showed himself to my mother, when she brought him his milk. She laid my honey-cake on the altar, and told the Goddess whom it was for. As we went, I looked back and saw it lying on the cold stone, and remembered the horse's living breath upon my hand, his soft lip warm and moving.

I was sitting among the house dogs, at the doorway end of the Great Hall, when my grandfather passed through, and spoke to me in greeting.

I got up, and answered; for one did not forget he was the King. But I stood looking down, and stroking my toe along a crack in the flagstones. Because of the dogs, I had not heard him coming, or I would have been gone. "If he could do this," I had been thinking, "how can one trust the gods?"

He spoke again, but I only said "Yes," and would not look at him. I could feel him high above me, standing in thought. Presently he said, "Come with me."

I followed him up the corner stairs to his own room above. He had been born there, and got my mother and his sons, and it was the room he died in. Then I had been there seldom; in his old age he lived all day in it, for it faced south, and the chimney of the Great Hall went through to warm it. The royal bed at the far end was seven feet long by six feet wide, made of polished cypress, inlaid and carved. The blue wool cover with its border of flying cranes had taken my grandmother half a year on the great loom. There was a bronze-bound chest by it, for his clothes; and for his jewels an ivory coffer on a painted stand. His arms hung on the wall: shield, bow, longsword and dagger, his hunting knife, and his tall-plumed helmet of quilted hide, lined with crimson leather the worse for wear. There was not much else, except the skins on the floor and a chair. He sat, and motioned me to the footstool.

Muffled up the stairway came the noises of the Hall: women scrubbing the long trestles with sand, and scolding men out of their way; a scuffle and a laugh. My grandfather's head cocked, like an old dog's at a footstep. Then he rested his hands on the chair-arms carved with lions, and said, "Well, Theseus? Why are you angry?"

I looked up as far as his hand. His fingers curved into a lion's open mouth; on his forefinger was the royal ring of Troizen, with the Mother being worshipped on a pillar. I pulled at the bearskin on the floor, and was silent.

"When you are a king," he said, "you will do better than we do here. Only the ugly and the base shall die; what is brave and beautiful shall live for ever. That is how you will rule your kingdom?"

To see if he was mocking me, I looked at his face. Then it was as if I had only dreamed the priest with the cleaver. He reached out and drew me in against his knees, and dug his fingers in my hair as he did with his dogs when they came up to be noticed.

"You knew the King Horse; he was your friend. So you know if it was his own choice to be King, or not." I sat silent, remembering the great horse-fight and the war calls. "You know he lived like a king, with first pick of the feed, and any mare he wanted; and no one asked him to work for it."

I opened my mouth, and said, "He had to fight for it."

"Yes, that is true. Later, when he was past his best, a younger stallion would have come, and won the fight, and taken his kingdom. He would have died hard, or been driven from his people and his wives to grow old without honor. You saw that he was proud."

I asked, "Was he so old?"

"No." His big wrinkled hand lay quietly on the lion mask. "No older for a horse than Talaos for a man. He died for another cause. But if I tell you why, then you must listen, even if you do not understand. When you are older, if I am here, I will tell it to you again; if not you will have heard it once, and some of it you will remember."

While he spoke, a bee flew in and buzzed among the painted rafters. To this day, that sound will bring it back to me.

"When I was a boy," he said, "I knew an old man, as you know me. But he was older; the father of my grandfather. His strength was gone, and he sat in the sun or by the hearthside. He told me this tale, which I shall tell you now, and you, perhaps, will tell one day to your son." I remember I looked up then, to see if he was smiling.

"Long ago, so he said, our people lived in the northland, beyond Olympos. He said, and he was angry when I doubted it, that they never saw the sea. Instead of water they had a sea of grass, which stretched as far as the swallow flies, from the rising to the setting sun. They lived by the increase of their herds, and built no cities; when the grass was eaten, they moved where there was more. They did not grieve for the sea, as we should, or for the good things earth brings forth with tilling; they had never known them; and they had few skills, because they were wandering men. But they saw a wide sky, which draws men's mind to the gods; and they gave their firstfruits to Ever-Living Zeus, who sends the rain.

"When they journeyed, the barons in their chariots rode round about, guarding the flocks and the women. They bore the burden of danger, then as now; it is the price men pay for honor. And to this very day, though we live in the Isle of Pelops and build walls, planting olives and barley, still for the theft of cattle there is always blood. But the horse is more. With horses we took these lands from the Shore People who were here before us. The horse will be the victor's sign, as long as our blood remembers.

"The folk came south by little and little, leaving their first lands. Perhaps Zeus sent no rain, or the people grew too many, or they were pressed by enemies. But my great-grandfather said to me that they came by the will of All-Knowing Zeus, because this was the place of their moira."

He paused in thought. I said to him, "What is that?"

"Moira?" he said. "The finished shape of our fate, the line drawn round it. It is the task the gods allot us, and the share of glory they allow; the limits we must not pass; and our appointed end. Moira is all these."

I thought about this, but it was too big for me. I asked, "Who told them where to come?"

"The Lord Poseidon, who rules everything that stretches under the sky, the land and the sea. He told the King Horse; and the King Horse led them."

I sat up; this I could understand.

"When they needed new pastures, they let him loose; and he, taking care of his people as the god advised him, would smell the air seeking food and water. Here in Troizen, when he goes out for the god, they guide him round the fields and over the ford. We do it in memory. But in those days he ran free. The barons followed him, to give battle if his passage was disputed; but only the god told him where to go.

"And so, before he was loosed, he was always dedicated. The god only inspires his own. Can you understand this, Theseus? You know that when Diokles hunts, Argo will drive the game to him; but he would not do it for you, and by himself he would only hunt small game. But because he is Diokles' dog, he knows his mind.

"The King Horse showed the way; the barons cleared it; and the King led the people. When the work of the King Horse was done, he was given to the god, as you saw yesterday. And in those days, said my great-grandfather, as with the King Horse, so with the King."

I looked up in wonder; and yet, not in astonishment. Something within me did not find it strange. He nodded at me, and ran down his fingers through my hair, so that my neck shivered.

"Horses go blindly to the sacrifice; but the gods give knowledge to men. When the King was dedicated, he knew his moira. In three years, or seven, or nine, or whenever the custom was, his term would end and the god would call him. And he went consenting, or else he was no king, and power would not fall on him to lead the people. When they came to choose among the Royal Kin, this was his sign: that he chose short life with glory, and to walk with the god, rather than live long, unknown like the stall-fed ox. And the custom changes, Theseus, but this token never. Remember, even if you do not understand."

I wanted to say I understood him. But I was silent, as in the sacred oak wood.

"Later the custom altered. Perhaps they had a King they could not spare, when war or plague had thinned the Kindred. Or perhaps Apollo showed them a hidden thing. But they ceased to offer the King at a set time. They kept him for the extreme sacrifice, to appease the gods in their great angers, when they had sent no rain, or the cattle died, or in a hard war. And it was no one's place to say to him, 'It is time to make the offering.' He was the nearest to the god, because he consented to his moira; and he himself received the god's commandment."

He paused; and I said, "How?"

"In different ways. By an oracle, or an omen, or some prophecy being fulfilled; or, if the god came close to him, by some sign between them, something seen, or a sound. And so it is still, Theseus. We know our time."

I neither spoke nor wept, but laid my head against his knee. He saw that I understood him.

"Listen, and do not forget, and I will show you a mystery. It is not the sacrifice, whether it comes in youth or age, or the god remits it; it is not the bloodletting that calls down power. It is the consenting, Theseus. The readiness is all. It washes heart and mind from things of no account, and leaves them open to the god. But one washing does not last a lifetime; we must renew it, or the dust returns to cover us. And so with this. Twenty years I have ruled in Troizen, and four times sent the King Horse to

Poseidon. When I lay my hand on his head to make him nod, it is not only to bless the people with the omen. I greet him as my brother before the god, and renew my moira."

He ceased. Looking up, I saw him staring out between the red pillars of the window, at the dark-blue line of the sea. We sat some while, he playing with my hair as a man will scratch his dog to quiet it, lest its importunities disturb his thoughts. But I had no word to say to him. The seed is still, when first it falls into the furrow.

At last he sat up with a start, and looked at me. "Well, well, child, the omens said I should reign long. But sometimes they talk double; and too early's better than too late. All this is heavy for you. But the man in you challenged it, and the man will bear it." He got up rather stiffly from his chair, and stretched, and strode to the doorway; his shout echoed down the twisted stair. Presently Diokles running up from below said, "Here I am, sir."

"Look at this great lad here," my grandfather said, "growing out of his clothes, and nothing to do but sit with the house dogs, scratching. Take him away, and teach him to ride."

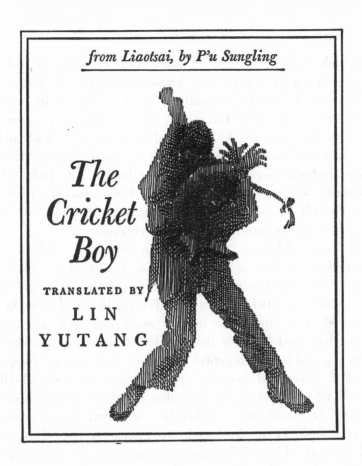

from Liaotsai, by P'u Sungling

The
Cricket
Boy

TRANSLATED BY
LIN
YUTANG

When Kiti, a boy of eleven, came home with his father after a day's fruitless search for crickets, he had a most wonderful feeling—the discovery of his father as a play companion. Kiti was an extremely impressionable child. Once, when he was five, his father held a stick to punish him for something, and Kiti's face turned so pale with fright that his father let the stick drop out of his hand. He had always had a great fear of his father, a taciturn man of forty-five.

He was small for his age, about the size of other children of nine or ten, and the jacket which his mother had made for him a year ago, thinking he would grow up quickly, still seemed ample and long. His slim, childish figure was accentuated by a disproportionately large head and a pair of big, black, playful eyes and plump round cheeks. He jumped and skipped, rather than walked normally, and he was still very much a child in his emotions. When his brother was Kiti's age, he was already a great help to his mother, but not Kiti. Now the brother was dead and his only sister was married into a family in another town. Kiti was perhaps pampered by his mother, a sad but strongly built woman, who could be made to smile only by Kiti's unusual pranks and wiles. He still retained many childish ways in his looks and smiles, and in the intense joys and sorrows of childhood.

Kiti loved crickets as only boys can love, and, with a child's keen enthusiasm and poetic imagination, he found in the beauty and delicacy of the insect something utterly perfect, noble, and strong. He admired the cricket's complicated mandibles and thought that no animal of a larger size in this world had such a lacquered, armored body and legs. He thought that if an animal the size of a dog or pig had such a beautiful outfit—no, there was no comparable animal. Crickets had been his passion since his early childhood. Like all village children, he had played with them and had come to know the worth of a cricket by the sound of its creak, the size and angle of its legs, and the proportion and shape of its head and body. There was a northern window in his room, adjoining a back garden, and as he lay in bed listening to the song of the crickets, it seemed to him the most pleasing music in the world. It represented to him all that was good and strong and beautiful in this world. Confucius and Mencius he learned quickly from his teacher, who was now his own father, and forgot just as quickly; but this song of the crickets he understood and remembered. He had heaped a pile of bricks and stones under the window for the purpose of attracting them. No grown-up seemed to understand this— certainly not his cold and severe father—but today for the first time, he had come out with Kiti and run over the mountainside to look for a champion fighter.

There had been a memorable incident when Kiti was six. He had brought a cricket to the classroom, and the teachers discovered it and crushed it. Kiti was so furious that when the teacher turned his back, Kiti leaped from his chair, saddled on his back and pummeled the teacher with all the strength of his small fists, to the amusement of the students, until the teacher had to shake him down.

That afternoon, he had watched his father silently making a hand net with a bamboo handle for catching crickets. When the net was made, his father had said to him, "Kiti, bring that bamboo box. We will go to the southern hills." It was beneath the scholar's dignity to announce that he was going to catch crickets.

But Kiti understood. He went out with his father and felt as if he were on a New Year holiday. It was like an answer to a child's prayer. He had gone out to catch crickets, but had never had the luxury of a proper net. Furthermore, he had never been allowed to go to the southern hills, about a mile and a half away, where he knew there were plenty of crickets.

It was July and the day was hot. The father and child, net in hand, ran all over the foothill slopes, making their way through thickets, jumping over ditches, turning over and peeping under stones, listening for that most important sound, the clear, metallic chirp of a good champion. They had found no worthy champion, but they had found each other as companions. That was a wonderful new sensation for Kiti. He had seen his father's eyes shine when they heard a clear, sharp note, and heard him curse under his breath when they lost one in the underbrush. On their way back, his father was still uttering sighs of regret over missing the beautiful one. For the first time, his father had become human, and he loved his father then.

His father had not bothered to explain why he suddenly took an interest in crickets, and Kiti, though secretly delighted, saw no reason to ask. But when they got home he saw his mother standing at the door, waiting for them to return for supper.

"Did you catch any?" asked his mother anxiously.

"No!" The father's reply was solemn and heavy with disappointment.

Kiti wondered greatly about it. That night he asked his mother, when they were alone, "Tell me, Mother, does Father love crickets, too? I thought I was the only one."

"No, he does not. He has to do it."

"Why? For whom?"

"For the emperor. Your father is the head of the village. He received an order from the magistrate to catch a good fighter. Who dares disobey the emperor?"

"I do not understand." Kiti was still more puzzled.

"Nor do I. But your father has to catch a good one within the next ten days, or he will lose his job and be fined. We are too poor to pay, and he may have to go to jail if he fails."

Kiti gave up trying to understand and asked no more questions. He only knew that it was something of terrible importance.

At this time, there was a great craze for cricket fights among the ladies of the court, with heavy betting going on, and culminating in the annual mid-autumn championship contests. It was perhaps an old tradition at the court, for the last premier of Sung Dynasty was known to have been watching his cricket fights when the armies of Genghis Khan marched into the capital. The district of Hwayin where Mr. Cheng lived was not known for producing the best fighters, but a year ago, an alert magistrate of the province had obtained a good champion and sent it to the court. A prince had written a letter to the governor of the province asking him to send more champions for the annual mid-autumn contest, and the governor had issued an order to all his magistrates to send their choicest selections from the districts to him. What had been a private request from a prince had become an edict of the emperor, as far as the common people were concerned. The price of good crickets skyrocketed and one magistrate was known to have offered as much as a hundred dollars for a good champion. Cricket fights had also become a popular pastime among the local people, and those who had champions were reluctant to part with them for any price.

Some heads of villages had taken the occasion to extort money from the people to buy crickets for the emperor, calling it the "crickets' levy." Mr. Cheng could have collected one or two hundred dollars from the villagers, pocketed half of it, and with the other half bought a cricket from the town. He, however would do nothing of the kind. If it was his duty to submit a champion, he would go and catch it himself.

Kiti shared his father's anxiety and felt important because his child's pastime had now become a dignified, grown-up affair. He watched his father's expression, as they were taking a rest in the cool shade. His father took out his pipe, lighted it, and his eyebrows danced a little as he puffed. He seemed to want to say something but paused and puffed away at his pipe, opened his mouth and then stopped to puff again. Finally, he said with an almost guilty expression on his face, "Kiti, you can catch a good champion for me. It is worth a lot of money."

"How, Father?"

"You see, son, there is a national championship at the imperial palace on mid-autumn festival. The winner will be awarded a big prize by the emperor."

"Really—by the emperor himself?" exclaimed Kiti. "Does the emperor love crickets, too?"

"Yes," replied the father reluctantly, as if a shameful confession had been forced from his lips.

"Hey, Father, we might catch a good fighter and win the national championship!" Kiti was greatly excited. "Will you be able to see the emperor?"

"No, I will send the cricket through the magistrate, and then through the governor, if it is good enough. It has got to be good. There is a big award in silver for the champion owner."

"Father, we will catch one, and we will be rich!"

It was difficult to repress the child's enthusiasm. But the father, having told him an important secret, looked serious once more. They got up and continued the search. Kiti now felt it was his responsibility to catch a champion fighter for his father, and for his mother as well because he had often heard her complain about being poor.

"I will catch one and fight and fight till we win," said the child.

The father was now glad that Kiti knew so much about crickets and was able to help him. For three days, they could not find a champion, but on the fourth day, they had a streak of good luck. They had gone over the top of the hill and descended on the farther side where there was a deep thicket and heavy underbrush. Far down the slope was an ancient tomb site. The outline of the tomb, some fifty feet across, was clearly visible. Kiti suggested going down to the tomb where they might catch some good crickets, especially because the sand there was reddish yellow. They followed a small brook and reached the site where a great many stone slabs lay about, showing the outlines of the ancient tomb. Their hope was justified. The crickets were singing on that July afternoon, not a few, but dozens of them in concert. Kiti's senses were sharpened. A frog suddenly leaped from the grass under his feet and disappeared into a hole, from which sprang out a big, beautiful insect, hopping away in long, powerful strides. The big cricket disappeared into an underground hole protected by stone slabs. The father and son crouched down and listened with bated breath to the rich, resonant chirp. Kiti took a long blade of grass and tried to stir the insect out of the hole, but it stopped its singing. They were sure now that the prize champion was in that hole, but the crack was too small even for the child's small hands to reach down through it. The father tried to smoke it out without success. Then Kiti went to fetch some water to pour down the hole, while the father held the net in readiness outside the entrance.

In a few seconds, the cricket sprang neatly into their net. He was a beauty, of the kind called "blackneck," with wide jaws, slender body, and powerful legs bent at a high angle. His whole body was of a fine and deep reddish-brown lacquer finish. Their labor was rewarded.

They returned home happily and placed their prize in an earthen jar on a table in the father's room, carefully covered with a sheet of copper wire netting. Mr. Cheng would take it to town the next day to present it to the magistrate. He instructed his wife to guard it carefully against neighbors' cats, and he went out to get some chestnut meat to feed it. Nobody was to touch it while he was away.

Kiti was excited beyond measure. He could not help coming into the room to listen to the insect's chirp and stare at it in sheer joy.

Then a tragedy happened. There was for a time no noise whatever in the jar. Kiti tapped it and still there was no sign of a movement. The cricket was apparently gone. He could not see into the dark jar, so he took it near the window and removed the wire net slowly to look when out hopped the cricket and landed on a book shelf. Kiti was desperate. He closed the window quickly and started to chase the insect around the room. In his excitement he neglected to use the net, and by the time he had caught the cricket under his palm, he had crushed its neck and broken one of its legs.

Kiti was pale with terror. His mouth was dry and he was without tears. He had destroyed what had promised to be a national champion.

"You accumulated debt of ten generations!" scolded his mother. "You are going to die! When your father returns, I do not know what he will do to you!"

Kiti's face was deathly white. He finally broke into sobs and ran away from the house.

At supper time Kiti still had not returned. His father was enraged and mortified, and threatened to give him a sound thrashing when he returned. The parents thought that he was hiding away, afraid to return, but believed that he would come home when he was hungry.

Toward ten o'clock, there was still no sign of Kiti, and the anger of the parents had turned into anxiety for him. They went out with a lantern into the night to search for him; and toward midnight they found Kiti's body at the bottom of a well.

When the child was brought out, he was apparently lifeless. There was a big wound on his head, but a trickle of fresh blood was still oozing from a cut on his forehead. It was a shallow well, but his whole body was drenched. They dried him and bandaged him, laying him on the bed, and were glad to find that his heart was still beating. Only a feeble breath indicated that the child was still alive. The shock was apparently so great that Kiti remained unconscious for a whole day, hovering between life and death. That evening they heard him mumbling in his sleep, "I have killed the champion—the blackneck, the blackneck!"

The next morning, Kiti could take some soup, but he was a changed child. All life seemed to have gone out of him. He could not recognize his father and mother. His sister, hearing of the incident, came to visit him, and he made no sign of recognition. An old doctor told them that he had been badly frightened and that his illness was too deep to be cured by medicines. The only coherent words Kiti said were, "I have killed him!"

Happy that Kiti was at least alive, and hopeful of an eventual recovery, Mr. Cheng remembered that he had still four more days in which to catch another fighter. He had a faint hope that if he could catch a good one and show it to Kiti, it might help to cure him. After all, there were plenty of crickets in the ancient tomb site. He slept lightly and at dawn he heard a chirp in his house. He got up and traced the sound to the kitchen, where he saw a small cricket resting high up on the wall.

A strange thing now happened. As the father stood looking at it, he thought how small and probably useless it was for such a loud chirp. But with three loud chirps the little one hopped down onto his sleeve, as if asking to be caught.

The father captured it and examined it slowly. It had a long neck and a plum-flower design on its wings. It might be a good fighter, but it was so small. He would not dare to offer it to the magistrate.

A neighboring young man had a local champion which had won every bout in the village. He had put a high price on it, but he had found no buyer, so he brought it to Mr. Cheng's house, intending to sell it to him.

When Mr. Cheng suggested a match, the young man took a look at the little cricket and covered his mouth in laughter. The two insects were placed inside a cage, and Cheng felt ashamed of his cricket and wanted to withdraw. The young man insisted on a fight to show his insect's prowess, and Cheng, thinking it would be no great sacrifice if the little one should be killed or maimed, yielded. The two insects now stood facing each other inside a basin. The little one stood still while the big one opened its fangs and glowered as if eagar for combat. The young man teased the little one with a pig's bristle to provoke it, but it remained unmoved. Again he prodded it, repeatedly, and suddenly the little fellow sprang into action, and the two insects fell at each other. In an instant, they saw the small cricket tilt its tail, raise its feelers, and with a powerful leap, sink its jaws into the opponent's neck. The young man quickly lifted the cage and called the fight off in the hope of saving his pet. The little cricket raised its head and chirped triumphantly.

Cheng was greatly pleased and amazed, but while he was admiring his new find, along with his family, a cock came along unnoticed by them, and pecked at the prize. The little cricket hopped away, chased by the cock, and in immediate reach of its claws. Cheng thought all was lost. Then he saw the cock shaking its head repeatedly, and observed that the little cricket had perched safely on the cock's neck and was harassing it from that position. They were all astounded and delighted.

Now confident of the little cricket's fighting power, Cheng decided to present it to the magistrate, telling him the story. The magistrate was far from impressed and was very skeptical, but he gave the insect a trial. The cricket won every fight over others collected in his office. He tried it again on a cock, and the little "plum-flower-wing" repeated his tactic of landing on the cock's neck, to everybody's astonishment. Satisfied with the district champion, the magistrate put it in a copper-wire cage and sent it to the governor. It was already the last day of July, and he dispatched it on horseback.

The father waited and hoped; one cricket had brought on his son's illness, another one might cure him. Then he heard that the little cricket had become the provincial champion, and his hopes went higher. It would take probably a month before he heard the results of the national championship match.

"Huh!" said Kiti's mother to her husband when she was told of the little cricket's fighting tactics. "Is it not just like Kiti riding on the teacher's back and pommeling him from behind?"

Kiti did not recover from his shock. Most of the time he was asleep and his mother had to force food down his mouth with a spoon. The first few days, his muscles twitched and he perspired heavily. The doctor came again and after hearing the symptoms announced that Kiti had burst his gall bladder in fright, and said that his *yang-yin* system of internal secretions had turned backwards. His three spiritual and seven animal spirits had been frightened away. It would take a long and slow cure to restore his vitality.

After three days, Kiti suffered another fit of paroxysms. Then his head seemed clearer for a day—it was the last day of July, his mother remembered clearly—and he could even smile when he said to his mother, "I have won!" His eyes stared vacantly.

"You have what?"

"I have won."

"Won what?"

"I do not know. I must win." He seemed to be still in a delirium.

Then his spirit left him again, and he fell into a profound coma for half a month.

At dawn, on the morning of August the eighteenth, Kiti's mother heard him calling, "Mother, I am hungry!"

It was the first time Kiti had called his mother since the incident. She jumped out of bed, called her husband, and they went in together to see their boy.

"Mother, I am hungry."

"My darling child, you are well again!" The mother wiped her eyes with the hem of her jacket.

"How are you feeling?" asked the father.

"I am feeling fine, Father."

"You have slept a long time."

"Have I? How long?"

"About three weeks. You scared us."

"Was it that long? I did not know anything. Father, I did not mean to hurt that champion. I was trying to capture him for you." Kiti's voice was perfectly normal, and he spoke as if the incident had happened only a day ago.

"Do not worry, Kiti," said the father. "While you were ill, I caught a better champion. He was small, but a terribly good fighter. The magistrate accepted it and sent it to the governor. I hear that he has won every fight."

"Then you have forgiven me?"

"Of course I have. Do not worry, son. That plucky little fighter may be a national champion yet. Now put your mind at rest, and soon you will be able to get up."

The family was happy once more. Kiti had a good appetite and only complained that his thighs were sore.

"That is very strange," said his mother.

"I feel, Mother, as if I had run and jumped hundreds of miles."

His mother massaged his legs, while Kiti kept on saying that his thighs were stiff.

In a day, Kiti was able to get up and walk a few steps. On the third day after his recovery, father, mother, and the boy were sitting by the lamp after supper, eating chestnuts.

"This is like the chestnut meat I had at the palace," Kiti remarked casually.

"Where?"

"At the imperial palace," Kiti replied, not knowing how strange his words must have sounded in his parents' ears.

"You must have been dreaming."

"No, Mother, I was there. Now I remember. All the ladies were dressed in red and blue and gold, when I came out of my golden cage."

"Did you dream that when you were ill?"

"No, it was true. Believe me, Mother, I was there."

"What did you see?"

"There were men with long beards and there was one I thought must be the emperor. They had come to see me. I only thought of Father and said to myself that I must win. When I was let out of the cage, I saw a big fellow. He had very long feelers and I got frightened, until the fight started. Night after night, I fought with only one idea that I must win for Father. On the last night, I met a redhead. He was fearful to look at. I was not afraid any more. I went at him, but when he came at me, I leaped away. I was in perfect form and felt very light and alert. I tore at his tail and bit off one of his front legs. He got mad and came at me with open fangs. I thought I was done for, but I bit him somewhere. Then he became confused. I saw his eye was bleeding. I sprang on his neck and finished him."

Kiti told all this so realistically that his parents listened in silence, knowing that he was perfectly sincere in describing what he had seen in his dreams.

"And you have won the national championship?" asked the father.

"I think I did. I wanted to so much. I only thought of you, Father."

The parents did not know whether to believe his story or not. The child was not lying, they knew. They would wait and see.

The little cricket, sent in a golden cage by the imperial system, had reached the capital just one day before the contests began. The governor was risking a great deal in submitting such a small cricket to the prince. If the insect gave a good account of itself, well and good, but if it failed, he stood a chance of being ridiculed for being in his dotage. He trembled at the thought. The official document of three thousand words accompanying the cricket was something unusual, both apologetic and bombastic at the same time.

"My friend is mad," said the prince, after reading his letter.

"Why not give it a trial?" remarked his wife, the emperor's daughter.

The plucky little fighter fought with supercricket powers. As far as they could see, he had shown no fear when put in a basin opposite the other provincial champions.

After the first night in which he felled a champion almost twice his size, the little plum-flower-wing was regarded as a marvel and became the talk of the court.

Night after night, the little one won. It was true that he had the advantage of lightness and agility. While no champion could get at him, he always harassed the big fellows by his lightning attacks and bit the opponent here and there before he came in with deadly accuracy for a crushing bite. His accomplishments seemed incredible.

The contests lasted five nights from August fourteenth to August eighteenth. On the last night he became the champion. The next morning, the little champion had completely disappeared from his cage.

When the news reached Kiti's family, the father wept, and they were all overjoyed. The father put on his best gown and took Kiti along to the magistrate. He was told that he would be made an honorary member of the district college with monthly stipends for his support.

The family fortunes turned, and Kiti eventually was able to go to college. Kiti not only felt embarrassed to have his story told, but he stopped watching cricket fights altogether. He could not stand it.

Later he became a *hanlin* and was able to support his parents in ease and comfort in their old age. Mr. Cheng, now a proud grandfather, never tired of telling the story of his son, which grew better and better every time, and he always ended with the words, "There are many ways of showing filial piety. When one's heart is good, the spirits of heaven and earth will show mercy to them that love their parents."

DYLAN THOMAS

A Conversation about Christmas

SMALL BOY: Years and years ago, when you were a boy . . .

SELF: When there were wolves in Wales, the birds the colour of red-flannel petticoats whisked past the harp-shaped hills, when we sang and wallowed all night and day in caves that smelt like Sunday afternoons in damp front farmhouse parlours, and chased, with the jawbones of deacons, the English and the bears . . .

SMALL BOY: You are not so old as Mr. Beynon Number Twenty-Two who can remember when there were no motors. Years and years ago, when you were a boy . . .

SELF: Oh, before the motor even, before the wheel, before the duchess-faced horse, when we rode the daft and happy hills bareback . . .

SMALL BOY: You're not so daft as Mrs. Griffiths up the street, who says she puts her ear under the water in the reservoir and listens to the fish talk Welsh. When you were a boy, what was Christmas like?

SELF: It snowed.

SMALL BOY: It snowed last year, too. I made a snowman and my brother knocked it down and I knocked my brother down and then we had tea.

SELF: But that was not the same snow. Our snow was not only shaken in whitewash buckets down the sky, I think it came shawling out of the ground and swam and drifted out of the arms and hands and bodies of the trees; snow grew overnight on the roofs of the houses like a pure and grandfather moss, minutely ivied the walls, and settled on the postman, opening the gate, like a dumb, numb thunderstorm of white, torn Christmas cards.

SMALL BOY: Were there postmen, then, too?

SELF: With sprinkling eyes and wind-cherried noses, on spread, frozen feet they crunched up to the doors and mittened on them manfully. But all that the children could hear was a ringing of bells.

SMALL BOY: You mean that the postman went rat-a-tat-tat, and the doors rang?

SELF: The bells that the children could hear were inside them.

SMALL BOY: I only hear thunder sometimes, never bells.

SELF: These were church bells, too.

SMALL BOY: Inside them?

SELF: No, no, no, in the bat-black, snow-white belfries, tugged by bishops and storks. And they rang their tidings over the bandaged town, over the frozen foam of the powder and ice-cream hills, over the crackling sea. It seemed that all the churches boomed, for joy, under my window; and the weathercocks crew for Christmas, on our fence.

SMALL BOY: Get back to the postmen.

SELF: They were just ordinary postmen, fond of walking, and dogs, and Christmas, and the snow. They knocked on the doors with blue knuckles . . .

SMALL BOY: Ours has got a black knocker . . .

SELF: And then they stood on the white welcome mat in the

little, drifted porches, and clapped their hands together, and huffed and puffed, making ghosts with their breath, and jogged from foot to foot like small boys wanting to go out.

SMALL BOY: And then the Presents?

SELF: And then the Presents, after the Christmas box. And the cold postman, with a rose on his buttonnose, tingled down the teatray-slithered run of the chilly glinting hill. He went in his ice-bound boots like a man on fishmonger's slabs. He wagged his bag like a frozen camel's hump, dizzily turned the corner on one foot, and, by God, he was gone.

SMALL BOY: Get back to the Presents.

SELF: There were the Useful Presents: engulfing mufflers of the old coach days, and mittens made for giant sloths; zebra scarves of a substance like silky gum that could be tug-o'-warred down to the goloshes; blinding tam-o'-shanters like patchwork tea-cosies, and bunny-scutted busbies and balaclavas for victims of head-shrinking tribes; from aunts who always wore wool next to the skin, there were moustached and rasping vests that made you wonder why the aunties had any skin left at all; and once I had a little crocheted nosebag from an aunt now, alas, no longer whinnying with us. And pictureless books in which small boys, though warned, with quotations, not to, *would* skate on Farmer Garge's pond, and did, and drowned; and books that told me everything about the wasp, except why.

SMALL BOY: Get on to the Useless Presents.

SELF: On Christmas Eve I hung at the foot of my bed Bessie Bunter's black stocking, and always, I said, I would stay awake all the moonlit, snowlit night to hear the roof-alighting reindeer and see the hollied boot descend through soot. But soon the sand of the snow drifted into my eyes, and, though I stared towards the fireplace and around the flickering room where the black sack-like stocking hung, I was asleep before the chimney trembled and the room was red and white with Christmas. But in the morning, though no snow melted on the bedroom floor, the stocking bulged and brimmed: press it, it squeaked like a mouse-in-a-box; it smelt of tangerine; a furry arm lolled over, like the arm of a kangaroo out of its mother's belly; squeeze it hard in the middle, and something squelched; squeeze it again—squelch again. Look out of the frost-scribbled window: on the great loneliness of the small hill, a blackbird was silent in the snow.

SMALL BOY: Were there any sweets?

SELF: Of course there were sweets. It was the marshmallows that squelched. Hardboileds, toffee, fudge and allsorts, crunches, cracknels, humbugs, glaciers, and marzipan and butterwelsh for the Welsh. And troops of bright tin soldiers who, if they would not fight, could always run. And Snakes-and-Families and Happy Ladders. And Easy Hobbi-Games for Little Engineers, complete with Instructions. Oh, easy for Leonardo! And a whistle to make the dogs bark to wake up the old man next door to make him beat on the wall with his stick to shake our picture off the wall. And a packet of cigarettes: you put one in your mouth and you stood at the corner of the street and you waited for hours, in vain, for an old lady to scold you for smoking a cigarette and then, with a smirk, you ate it. And, last of all, in the toe of the stocking, sixpence like a silver corn. And then downstairs for breakfast under the balloons!

SMALL BOY: Were there Uncles, like in our house?

SELF: There are always Uncles at Christmas. The same Uncles. And on Christmas mornings, with dog-disturbing whistle and sugar fags, I would scour the swathed town for the news of the little world, and find always a dead bird by the white Bank or by the deserted swings: perhaps a robin, all but one of his fires out, and that fire still burning on his breast. Men and women wading and scooping back from church or chapel, with taproom noses and wind-smacked cheeks, all albinos, huddled their stiff black jarring feathers against the irreligious snow. Mistletoe hung from the gas in all the front parlours; there was sherry and walnuts and bottled beer and crackers by the dessertspoons; and cats in their fur-abouts watched the fires; and the high-heaped fires crackled and spat, all ready for the chestnuts and the mulling pokers. Some few large men sat in the front parlours, without their collars, Uncles almost certainly, trying their new cigars, holding them out judiciously at arm's-length, returning them to their mouths, coughing, then holding them out again as though waiting for the explosion; and some few small aunts, not wanted in the kitchen, nor anywhere else for that matter, sat on the very edges of their chairs, poised and brittle, afraid to break, like faded cups and saucers. Not many those mornings trod the piling streets: an old man always, fawn-bowlered, yellow-gloved, and, at this time of year, with spats of snow, would take his constitutional to the white bowling-green, and back, as he would take it wet or fine on Christmas Day or Doomsday; sometimes two hale young men, with big pipes blazing, no overcoats, and windblown scarves, would trudge, unspeaking, down to the forlorn sea, to work up an appetite, to blow away the fumes, who knows, to walk into the waves until nothing of them was left but the two curling smoke clouds of their inextinguishable briars.

SMALL BOY: Why didn't you go home for Christmas dinner?

SELF: Oh, but I did, I always did. I would be slap-dashing home, the gravy smell of the dinners of others, the bird smell, the brandy, the pudding and mince, weaving up my nostrils, when out of a snow-clogged side-lane would come a boy the spit of myself, with a pink-tipped cigarette and the violet past of a black eye, cocky as a bullfinch, leering all to himself. I hated him on sight and sound, and would be about to put my dog-whistle to my lips and blow him off the face of Christmas when suddenly he, with a violent wink, put *his* whistle to *his* lips and blew so stridently, so high, so exquisitely loud, that gobbling faces, their cheeks bulged with goose, would press against their tinselled windows, the whole length of the white echoing street.

SMALL BOY: What did you have for Dinner?

SELF: Turkey, and blazing pudding.

SMALL BOY: Was it nice?

SELF: It was not made on earth.

SMALL BOY: What did you do after dinner?

SELF: The Uncles sat in front of the fire, took off their collars, loosened all buttons, put their large moist hands over their watch-chains, groaned a little, and slept. Mothers, aunts, and sisters scuttled to and fro, bearing tureens. The dog was sick. Auntie Beattie had to have three aspirins, but Auntie Hannah, who liked port, stood in the middle of the snowbound backyard, singing like a big-bosomed thrush. I would blow up balloons to see how big they would blow up to; and, when they burst, which they all did, the Uncles jumped and rumbled. In the rich and heavy afternoon, the Uncles breathing like dolphins and the snow descending, I would sit in the front room, among festoons and Chinese lanterns, and nibble at dates, and try to make a model man-o'-war, following the Instructions for Little Engineers, and produce what might be mistaken for a sea-going tram. And then, at Christmas tea, the recovered Uncles would be jolly over their mince-pies; and the great iced cake loomed in the centre of the table like a marble grave. Auntie Hannah laced her tea with rum, because it was only once a year. And in the evening, there was Music. An uncle played the fiddle, a cousin sang Cherry Ripe, and another uncle sang Drake's Drum. It was very warm in the little house. Auntie Hannah, who had got on to the parsnip wine, sang a song about Rejected Love, and Bleeding Hearts, and Death, and then another in which she said that her Heart was like a Bird's Nest; and then everybody laughed again, and then I went to bed. Looking through my bedroom window, out into the moonlight and the flying, unending, smoke-coloured snow, I could see the lights in the windows of all the other houses on our hill, and hear the music rising from them up the long, steadily falling night. I turned the gas down, I got into bed. I said some words to the close and holy darkness, and then I slept.

SMALL BOY: But it all sounds like an ordinary Christmas.

SELF: It was.

SMALL BOY: But Christmas when you were a boy wasn't any different to Christmas now.

SELF: It was, it was.

SMALL BOY: Why was Christmas different then?

SELF: I mustn't tell you.

SMALL BOY: Why mustn't you tell me? Why is Christmas different for me?

SELF: I mustn't tell you.

SMALL BOY: Why can't Christmas be the same for me as it was for you when you were a boy?

SELF: I mustn't tell you. I mustn't tell you because it is Christmas now.

from Johnny Tremain

E S T H E R   F O R B E S

The Lyte Cup

[*Johnny Tremain enjoyed his work as apprentice to silversmith Silas Lapham—until he burned his hand in an accident and lost all hope of becoming a craftsman. Now, as an orphan, he must find other work. Only if all else failed would he consider trying to trace his family through the silver cup his mother had left him.*]

September was ending. A large part of every day Johnny spent doing what he called 'looking for work.' He did not really want to follow any trade but his own. He looked down on soap-boilers, leather-dressers, ropemakers, and such. He did not begin his hunt along Hancock's Wharf and Fish Street, where he and his story were well known and the masters would have been apt to employ him from pity. He went to the far ends of Boston.

Mr. Lapham had told him to stand about and watch the different artisans at their trades until he was sure it was work he could do. Then he was to address the master politely, explain about his bad hand, and ask to be taken on. But Johnny was too impatient, too unthinking and too scornful. He barged into shop after shop along the great wharves and up and down Cornhill and Orange, Ann, and Ship Streets, Dock Square, King and Queen Streets—'Did the master want another boy?'—keeping his hand hidden in his pocket.

His quickness and address struck everyone favorably, and so an old clockmaker eagerly agreed to take him on—especially when he told him that he had already served Mr. Lapham two years.

'But why, my boy, is Mr. Lapham ready to part with you, now that you must be of value to him?'

'I've a bad hand.'

'Let me see it.'

He did not want to show his hand, but the masters always insisted. He would take it out of the pocket where he always kept it, with a flourish, display it to the sickening curiosity of the master, apprentices, journeymen, lady customers. After such an experience he would sometimes loiter and swim for the rest of the day. Sometimes he would grit his teeth and plunge headlong into the next shop.

He barely bothered to look at the signs over the door which indicated what work was done inside. A pair of scissors for a tailor, a gold lamb for a wool weaver, a basin for a barber, a painted wooden book for a bookbinder, a large swinging compass for an instrument-maker. Although more and more people were learning how to read, the artisans still had signs above their shops, not wishing to lose a possible patron merely because he happened to be illiterate.

Having been told by one clockmaker he would not suit, Johnny walked in on two more and got the same answer.

A butcher (his sign was a gilded ox skull) would have employed him, but the idea of slaughtering animals sickened him. He was a fine craftsman to the tips of his fingers—even to the tips of his maimed hand.

Now he never came home for the hearty midday dinner. Mrs. Lapham, Madge, and Dorcas were always pointing out how much he ate and how little he did. He knew Mrs. Lapham was looking around for a grown-up silversmith who would come in as a partner for Grandpa, and she had said (looking straight at Johnny) she would not ask him to sleep in the attic with the two boys. He was to have the birth and death room. 'I declare,' she said one day, 'no business can be run with just a feeble old man and three of the most worthless boys in Boston—eating their heads off.'

Seems she was negotiating with a Mr. Tweedie—newly arrived from Baltimore. He had arrived alone, but she must make sure he really was a bachelor or a widower. Obviously, whatever partner she found for her father-in-law must marry one of her 'poor fatherless girls.' The shop must stay in the family.

So Johnny ate as little as he could, and did not come home at noon. But someone would usually slip a piece of hard bread, cheese, jerked beef, or salt fish and johnnycake in the pocket of his jacket as it hung on its hook. He knew it was Cilla, but he never spoke to her about it. His unhappiness was so great he felt himself completely cut off from the rest of the world.

But sometimes, as he lay in the sun on Beacon Hill or Copp's Hill (among the graves), or curled himself upon a coil of rope along a wharf, eating the food she had managed to get for him, he would dream of the great things he would do for her—when he was man-grown. There were three things she longed for—a gold necklace; a gray pony with a basket cart; a little sailboat. He dreamed of himself as successful—rich. Never as the ditchdigger and ragpicker Mrs. Lapham was always suggesting to him.

Some days there was no food in his pocket. Then he went hungry.

On one such day, he was strolling up Salt Lane. Here about him and on Union Street were printing offices. It was noon, and all over Boston work had stopped and everyone, except himself, had either gone home for dinner or to one of the famous taverns. Above one tiny shop he saw a sign that attracted him. It was a little man in bright blue coat and red breeches, solemnly gazing at Salt Lane through a spyglass. So this was where the *Boston Observer* was published. The Laphams took no newspaper, but he had heard Mr. Lapham speak of the wicked *Observer* and how it was trying to stir up discontent in Boston, urging the people to revolt against the mild rule of England. The comical little painted man looked so genial, so ready to welcome anyone, that Johnny stepped in.

He might have guessed he would waste his time. Of course the master would be off for dinner, but because he had liked the painted sign, he went in. He had not even stopped to consider whether or not a printer's work was something that he could do.

He saw the squat, buglike printing press, the trays of type, the strings on which printed sheets were hung to dry like clothes on a line. On a workbench was a smaller press for notifications, proclamations, broadsides, trade cards. Everything smelled of printers' ink.

A boy, larger than himself and probably a few years older, was standing at a counter talking with a stout marketwoman in a frayed red skirt. Her pig had strayed from her yard. She wished to advertise it. The boy wrote down what she said.

'Lost—a spotted sow from Whitebread Alley,' the boy repeated.

'She was the *dearest* pig,' said the woman—'would come for a whistle like a dog. My children taught her to play "dead pig." We don't ever think to eat her—only her increase. We called her Myra.'

The boy did not write that down. He lifted his dark face, indolent dark eyes. The lashes flickered. He was interested.

'Was she hard to teach, ma'am?'

'Oh, no! Pigs are clever.'

'I never knew that. How do they compare with dogs?'

Then the old lady began to talk. She talked about pigs in general and her Myra in particular.

The printer's boy, unruffled, unhurried, heard her through. He was tall and powerfully built. There was something a little sluggish in his casual movements, in his voice—almost as though he was saving himself for emergencies, not wasting himself on every casual encounter.

The woman was delighted with so good a listener and his few intelligent questions. Johnny, standing at the door, forgot his own errand. He had no idea that either pigs or old marketwomen could be so interesting. It was the apprentice, standing at the counter in his leather apron and full white shirt, his thoughtful face framed in hair, black and straight as an Indian's, who had cast a spell over the old gossip and her subject.

Although the boy had nodded casually as Johnny came in, he did not speak to him until after the woman was gone and he had set up the few lines of type. There was nothing rude about this seeming neglect. It was almost as if they were friends of long standing. The strange boy had none of the bustling smartness of the usual Boston apprentice. Johnny had seen enough of them in the last month, apprentices who knew what you wanted and that you would not suit, and you were out on the street again in three minutes.

Having set the advertisement, the boy took a covered basket from under the counter, put it on a table, and drew up two stools.

'Why don't you sit down?' he said, 'and eat. My master's wife— she's my aunt—always sends over more than I can manage.'

Seemingly he had sized up everything with only half a glance from the lazy, dark eyes. He had known Johnny was hungry without once really looking at him and had also known that he was someone he himself liked. He was both friendly and aloof. Nonchalantly he took out his claspknife, cut hunks of bread from the long loaf. There were also cheese, apples, and ham.

The ham seemed to remind the printer's boy of the gossip and her pig.

'I grew up on a farm,' he said, 'but I never knew you could teach a pig tricks. Help yourself to more bread?'

Johnny hesitated. So far he had not taken his bad hand out of his pocket since entering the shop. Now he must, or go hungry. He took the claspknife in his left hand and stealthily drew forth the maimed hand to steady the loaf. It was hard to saw through the crusty loaf with a left hand, but he managed to do it. It took him a long time. The other boy said nothing. He did not, thank God, offer to help him. Of course he had seen the crippled hand, but at least he did not stare at it. Asked no questions. Seemingly he saw everything and said nothing. Because of this quality in him, Johnny said:

'I'm looking for some sort of work I think I could do well in . . . even with a bad hand.'

'That's quite a recent burn.' It was the first intelligent remark any man, woman, or child had made about Johnny's hand in any shop he had been in.

'I did it last July. I am . . . I *was* apprenticed to a silversmith. I burned it on hot silver.'

'I see. So everything you are trained for is out?'

'Yes. I wouldn't mind so much being a clockmaker or instrument-maker. But I can't and I *won't* be a butcher nor a soap-boiler.'

'No.'

'I've *got* to do something I like, or . . . or . . .'

The dark boy put the question to him he had not been able to ask himself.

'Or what?'

Johnny lifted his thin, fair face. His lips parted before he spoke. 'I just don't know. I can't think.'

Apparently the printer's boy did not know either. All he said was, 'More cheese?'

Then Johnny began to talk. He told all about the Laphams and how he somehow couldn't seem even to thank Cilla for the food she usually got to him. How cross and irritable he had become. How rude to people who told him they were sorry for him. And he admitted he had used no sense in looking for a new job. He told about the burn, but with none of the belligerent arrogance with which he had been answering the questions kind people had put to him. As he talked to Rab (for the boy had told him this was his name), for the first time since the accident he felt able to stand aside from his problems—see himself.

Mr. Lorne, Rab's uncle by marriage, came back. He was a scholarly young man with a face as sharp and bright as a fox's. Rab did not immediately spring into action to make a good show of his industry before his master. He had none of the usual 'yes, sir,' 'no, sir,' 'please, sir.' He went on calmly eating bread and cheese.

On Mr. Lorne's heels came two little boys in big aprons—the Webb twins. Seemingly they went back to their master's house across Salt Lane for dinner, while the nephew ate out of a basket and minded the shop.

The Webbs were set to work. Mr. Lorne began to ink a pad. Johnny felt he must go. Rab walked with him to the door. He was still eating bread and cheese.

'I don't know how you'll make out,' said Rab. 'Of course you can get work—if you'll take it.'

'I know . . . unskilled work.'

'Yes, work you don't want.'

'But'—the dinner had raised Johnny's hopes—'I feel sure I'll get something.'

Overhead the little man with the spyglass and the red breeches was swinging in the wind—observing Boston from a variety of angles.

Rab said: 'There is some work here you could do. Not the sort that teaches a boy a skilled trade. Just riding for us—delivering papers all over Boston and around. Nothing you'd want. But if you can't find anything else, you come back.'

'I'll come back all right—but not until I can tell you what a good job I've found myself.'

'You haven't any folks?'

'None at all.'

'I've got lots of relatives,' said Rab, 'but my parents are dead.'

'Oh.'

'Come again.'

'I'll come.'

It wasn't the food alone that so raised Johnny's hopes. It was Rab himself; an ease and confidence flowed out and supported those around him. The marketwoman had felt better about losing her Myra after she had talked with Rab. He was the first person to whom Johnny Tremain had confided his own story.

The coming of Mr. Percival Tweedie, journeyman silversmith of Baltimore, cast a longer and longer shadow over the Lapham household and conversation. While the terms of partnership were being drawn up, he stayed at a cheap lodging house on Fish Street. Johnny left right after breakfast and often did not return until dark. He did not meet Mr. Tweedie for a long time and he got tired of hearing about him. Mr. Tweedie was ready to sign the contract of partnership Mrs. Lapham had had drawn up—and Mr. Tweedie would not sign. When Mr. Tweedie came to the shop it was Dorcas he seemed to fancy—no, it was Madge. Although almost forty, he was still a bachelor—Mrs. Lapham had asked him about that.

Johnny already hated the very sound of his name, and then one morning, before breakfast, he met him. Mr. Tweedie was diffidently standing about in the shop, hoping Mrs. Lapham would ask him to breakfast. He was fingering a pocketbook sent in for a new clasp, and his stomach was rolling from hunger.

'Heh!' said Johnny rudely. The timid creature jumped like a shot rabbit and dropped the pocketbook.

'What are you doing here?' the boy demanded, pretending he had caught a thief.

Mr. Tweedie swallowed twice, his Adam's apple rising and falling with emotion, but said nothing.

'Are you a thief or are you that Tweedie man I've heard tell of?'

'I'm Tweedie.'

'I'm Johnny Tremain.'

'You don't say.'

'I'll tell Mrs. Lapham you're here—for breakfast.'

'I just happened by—just thought I'd come in.' He had a queer, squeaky voice. Johnny disliked him even more than he had expected. Such impotence, such timidity in a grown man irritated the boy.

'Oh, come out with it flat,' he said. 'You've been getting your dinners here free for two weeks and now you're feeling out for breakfast. I don't care, not me. But I'll warn the women to put on an extra plate.'

The man said nothing, but he looked at Johnny and the look of bleak hatred amazed the boy. He had not guessed Mr. Tweedie had that much gumption in him.

Mrs. Lapham came thumping down the stairs. It was her second trip to the foot of the attic ladder and she still wasn't sure Dove and Dusty were out of bed. Everything had gone wrong. Breakfast was late. Madge had a felon on her finger and wasn't good for anything and Dorcas was complaining because there was no butter for breakfast. She had slapped Dorcas, who had gone out back to cry. How easily, smoothly everything had gone in the old days before Johnny got hurt! Then the household went like clockwork and the shop had earned money for butter and butcher's meat once or twice a week. The sight of Johnny Tremain standing there in the lower hall doing nothing, good for nothing, irritated her.

'Hurry,' she snorted and waddled into the kitchen, Johnny on her heels. The fire was smoking and she knelt down to mend it. Johnny might have done that while she was upstairs.

Although Johnny was now looked upon as something of a black sheep and Mrs. Lapham was no longer telling him he would end up picking rags, but on the gallows, he thought it behooved him to tell her just what he thought of Mr. Tweedie.

'I can see why that Tweedie has never been a master smith. He hasn't the force of character. As a man he's no good—if he is a man, which I doubt. I think he is somebody's spinster aunt dressed up in men's clothes.'

Mrs. Lapham heaved herself to her knees and brushed back her streaming hair with a red forearm.

'You don't say!' Her voice showed her exasperation. She had found Mr. Tweedie herself. She was trying to nurse him along, to get the wary creature to sign her contract and marry one of her girls.

'Yep, I do say,' said Johnny. 'I've just been talking with him. He's no good and——'

'He's here now?'

'Yep. In the shop. That squeak-pig is trying to horn in on breakfast.'

The doors were all open. Anyone in the shop could have heard Johnny's insults.

Slowly, like a great sow pulling out of a wallow, Mrs. Lapham got to her feet, glaring down at Johnny, her enormous bosom heaving.

'And I'm going to tell you what I think of that squeak-pig.' Without a word and before he could finish his remarks or dodge, Mrs. Lapham gave him a resounding cuff on the ear.

'Sometimes actions do speak louder than words,' she said, 'and this is one of them times. You get right out of here, Johnny Tremain. That tongue of yours isn't going to do any more damage in *my* house.'

Johnny grabbed his jacket (Cilla had not yet put food in it), pulled his tattered hat over his eyes, and stalked out.

Since his accident he had unconsciously taken to wearing his hat at a rakish angle. This, and the way he always kept his right hand thrust into his breeches pocket, gave him a slightly arrogant air. The arrogance had always been there, but formerly it had come out in pride in his work—not in the way he wore his hat and walked. He told no one what he did all day and Mrs. Lapham was convinced that he had taken to, or was about to take to, 'evil ways.' He did look, at times, both shabby and desperate; in other words, a potential criminal. Sometimes he looked so proud and fine people thought he must be a great gentleman's son in misfortune. One thing he did not look like any more was a smart, industrious Boston apprentice.

He walked down Fish Street to Ann, crossed Dock Square with Faneuil Hall on his left. It was market day. He picked his way about the farm carts, the piles of whitish green cabbages, baskets of yellow corn, rows of plump, pale, plucked turkeys, orange pumpkins, country cheeses—big as a baby's head. Some of the market folk, men and women, children and black slaves, called to him, seeing in the shabby, proud boy a possible rich customer, but others counted the pats of butter on their tables after he had passed by.

Without heeding anyone, he crossed Dock Square and in a moment's time stood beside the brick Town House at the head of King Street. The lower floor of the Town House was an open promenade and here every day the merchants gathered 'on 'change.' Not a merchant in sight. They did not rise as early as market folk. Suddenly Johnny had an idea. Although seemingly he had tried every shop in Boston in search of a new master, he had not tried the merchants. From where he sat on the steps of the Town House, he could look the brief length of King Street which quickly and imperceptibly turned into Long Wharf, running for half a mile into the sea. It was the only wharf in Boston larger than Hancock's. There was not another wharf in all America so large, so famous, so rich.

As at his own wharf, one side was built up solidly with counting houses, warehouses, sail lofts, stores. The other side was left open for the ships. Already sailors, porters, riggers, and such were at work. He waited—it seemed to him for a long time—and then the clerks began to arrive, counting-house doors were unlocked, warehouses were unchained.

At last the merchants came, some striding down King Street, rosy-faced, double-chinned, known and greeted by everyone, apparently knowing and greeting everyone in return. Some came in chaises, gigs. Some had sour, gimlet-eyed faces; some had not yet lost the rolling gait of sea captains. Johnny saw the same gray horse and gig, with the arms upon the door, that had carried John Hancock to the Laphams' last July, trot quickly down King Street onto Long Wharf. Although Mr. Hancock had recently bought Hancock's Wharf, his principal place of business was on Long.

Mr. Hancock has on a cherry-red coat, Johnny thought. He drives the horse himself, but now he is getting out, telling that dressed-up doll of a black boy to put his horse up for him. Johnny decided he would start at the top of the merchants and work down, only, of course, skipping Merchant Lyte. He'd go first to John Hancock.

From where he sat he could see that a great ship was slowly warping in—no coaster this, no mere sugar boat from the Sugar Isles. A number of fashionably dressed young men, as well as the usual dockhands and porters, were crowding about to welcome her.

There was the heavy clatter of a great coach almost beside him and a coachman was bawling to lesser folk, 'Make way, make way.' Black horses in glittering, silver-mounted harnesses, the rumble and rattle of a ruby coach on cobbles, and on the door panel the familiar crest—a rising eye. Half-seen inside, Merchant Jonathan Lyte. Evidently he had just heard his ship was in and had come down from his mansion on Beacon Hill in a hurry. He was still struggling with the lace about his throat.

Johnny left his seat and strolled down the wharf to watch. No one had ever told him not to watch the Lytes, but he always felt guilty when he did. From afar he knew them all. He knew, for instance, that Mr. Lyte had a broken front tooth. He knew Mrs. Lyte was dead and two sons had been drowned as boys, and girls had died in infancy—this he could read upon the slate gravestones of Copp's Hill. He knew that besides the town house on Beacon Hill there was a county seat at Milton. And he knew that Lavinia Lyte had spent the last summer in London. Now she was back in Boston once more.

She was very tall for a woman, slender and graceful, and moved slowly down the gangplank with the stately self-consciousness which happened to be the fashionable gait for a lady at the moment. A hundred times before, Johnny had stopped on the streets of Boston, or before her house, to watch her: he but one more gaping face in a crowd, she the accepted reigning belle. He admired her odd, strong beauty which, unlike her regal gait, was not of the fashionable type. To begin with, she was too tall, and golden curls, pink-and-white skin were the mode. She was a black-haired woman, and only for balls and such was she powdered and curled. In contrast, her skin was dead white. Her features were clear-cut enough to justify the poems written to her in London and even here in Boston, comparing her to a classic goddess.

There was only one flaw to her marble beauty. Between the low-sweeping black brows was a tiny perpendicular line. Once, and once only, the master hand that carved her face had let the chisel slip. This blemish was odd enough for a young lady still in her twenties. It boded no good for the peace of mind of those about her—nor for her own. Now she was all glitter and smiles, greeting the young gentlemen who had come to meet her. Johnny did not notice what she wore, but the mantua-makers, dressmakers, milliners, glovers, and jewelers all knew that whatever Lavinia Lyte brought back from London would set Boston styles for the winter.

'Oh, Papa! Papa!' she suddenly exclaimed. There was an urgency in her voice, a soft flash in her eyes none of the young men's faces had called forth. Like any country girl, merely glad to be home again, she flung herself into her father's arms.

Spiritually Johnny shrugged, determined to be neither overimpressed nor envious. That overdressed moppet. That lean beanpole— for Miss Lavinia was lean in comparison to Madge and Dorcas, who had always been held up to Johnny as the end-all of feminine beauty. Bad-tempered, too. *I hope she kills herself overeating cakes and plum pudding, turkeys with stuffing and gravy, hot white rolls.* His stomach was gnawing at him. He forgot Lavinia Lyte as he thought of the wonderful things it was her privilege to overeat if she wished.

Surely by now enough time had passed since John Hancock's arrival at his counting house so that he would be ready to talk to a likely boy looking for work. His hand might be good enough for a cabin boy.

Johnny found one does not step into a great merchant's counting house and see the merchant as easily as one steps into a shop and sees the master artisan. Although he had made up his mind that he would begin his conversation with Mr. Hancock by explaining he had a burned hand, he did not see any reason why he should explain to the clerk who stopped him in the outer office. All he said was that he wanted work.

The clerk asked him if he could read and write.

He said he could.

The thin, weak-eyed gentleman gave him a mortgage and told him to read that. This he read well.

Then Mr. Hancock, who had been sitting alone over his little hearth fire in the back office, came out. He had been attracted by the quality of the boy's voice, for, although Johnny often spoke in the rougher, slurring manner of Hancock's Wharf, in reading he reverted to the cleaner speech his mother had taught him.

Mr. Hancock did not recognize him as the apprentice of Mr. Lapham who had rashly promised a sugar basin in time for his Aunt Lydia's birthday. And then the old man had been forced at the last to admit he could not do it.

'Add this, my lad,' he said, handing Johnny an invoice he held in his hand.

Johnny added easily. He was given a few more simple sums which he did in his head.

The clerk and merchant exchanged glances.

Mr. Hancock said: 'If your handwriting is as good as your reading and ciphering, I promise you a place right here in my counting house. I've been put to it to find just the right boy. Your writing . . .'

'I've been taught to write.' But Johnny was suddenly frightened.

The clerk put a piece of paper before him and inked a pen. 'Write John Hancock, Esquire.'

Johnny stubbornly stared at the paper. At last he had found a place where he wanted to be. And he knew that ever and again boys who started working for great merchants became great merchants themselves. Surely, surely, if only he tried hard enough he could do it. He could write for the length of just 'John Hancock, Esquire.' His hand shot out of his pocket, grasped the pen. The letters were as clumsy as though written with a left hand.

The clerk laughed. 'Mr. Hancock, I've never seen worse writing.'

The merchant said, 'My boy, you must have been rattled. Surely you can do better than that.'

Johnny stared at his miserable scratches. 'God help me,' he whispered. 'It is the best I can do.'

'Why, the lad has a crippled hand—look, Mr. Hancock.'

Mr. Hancock quickly averted his fine eyes.

'Run away, boy, run away. You knew you could not do the work and yet you came and took up my valuable time and . . .'

'But I thought maybe you could ship me as a cabin boy.'

'And carry the captain's grog? And be brisk and useful to him? No, no, my captains want whole boys. So now—go away . . . please.'

Johnny wandered off. 'I burned my hand making you a silver basin . . . Now, it is "go away, please."'

He flung himself down in the shadow of a sail loft, for the late September day was warm as summer. He could hear the tap of shipwright's hammers, the creak of wooden wheels, a boatswain's whistle. Everywhere boys and men were at work. Only he was idle.

He saw picking his way delicately around barrels of molasses, bales, ox teams, a familiar, fantastic figure. It was Mr. Hancock's little black slave, Jehu. He was looking from side to side. When he saw Johnny, he went to him and said like a parrot, 'My master, Mr. John Hancock, Esquire, has commanded me to give this purse to the poor work-boy in the broken shoes who just left his counting house, and to tell him that he wishes him well.'

Johnny took the purse. It was heavy. That much copper would provide him with food for days. He opened it. It was not copper, but silver. John Hancock had not been able to look at the crippled hand—nor could he help but make this handsome present.

The thought of Lavinia Lyte gorging herself to death (if it pleased her) on fine foods had started the gastric juices in his stomach an hour ago. He had had no breakfast and for supper the night before only one salt alewife and a mug of milk. It was noontime and he craved food—not the mere coarse bread, cheese, ale, and apples which had always made up the large part of his diet, but rare and interesting things such as he had smelled cooking in rich people's houses and the best taverns, but had never tasted.

First he tormented his hunger by going from one tavern kitchen to the next to see which smelled the best. At the Bunch of Grapes a maid was basting a roast of beef. A spicy pudding was bubbling on the hearth. At the King's Coffee House a suckling pig was so crisp and brown it was fairly bursting. He almost drooled at this pig, but walked on. And everywhere he smelled chocolate and coffee. He had never in his life tasted either. He stopped in the kitchen of the Afric Queen. What he saw there made him feel he had swallowed a small live kitten, but he could almost enjoy these pangs, for in his pocket was Mr. Hancock's silver. Any minute he could assuage that kitten. And so to the Cromwell Head and back again to Union Street. His mind was made up. He would dine at the Afric Queen. For here he had seen maids roasting innumerable small squabs, each stuffed with fragrant dressing and wrapped in bacon. And he had seen pastries—apple, mince, pumpkin, plum tarts—coming out of the brick oven. The crust on them was an inch thick and so short and flaky it looked like scorched tissue paper.

'Well, kitten,' he said contentedly to his stomach as he took his seat humbly in the kitchen where grooms and such were fed while their betters ate in the dining rooms, 'you're going to have more than a saucer of milk today. How'd you like, say, five of those little squabs?"

But when he began to give his order to the serving maid, she giggled and ran off for the landlady.

"Now, boy,' this lady said to him firmly, 'you just show me the color of your money.'

Satisfied, she grunted, and told the maid to serve 'the little master.' This young girl was hardly older than Cilla. She could not help laughing at the things he ordered. The five little squabs, three of each kind of pastry, a wreath of jellied eels (because she said it was a specialty of the house), a tipsy parson—white bread tied into little knots, buttered and baked. And a pot of coffee and another of chocolate. When Johnny saw a dish being prepared in the kitchen for some diner in the other room, he would call for 'some of that,' and she giggled again and fetched it for him.

There was only one disappointment. The smell of coffee had always attracted him. He was disappointed at the bitter taste. The chocolate, however, was even better than he had dared to hope.

But when he came to pay, he was chagrined to find so much of his money had gone to fill and overfill his stomach. The kitten was no longer gnawing inside him, trying to get out. In fact, it was no longer a kitten. 'I feel as if I had swallowed a Newfoundland dog and it had died on me.'

What a fool he had been! He thought suddenly of Rab: that Rab wouldn't have let himself go so; and for the first time, standing in the cobbled stable yard behind the inn, he realized that the back of the little building he saw beyond the Afric Queen stables was the printing shop of the *Boston Observer* on Salt Lane. He wanted to cross through the back yards—go to see that Rab—but thought better of it. Not until he came as a friend and equal—not as a beggar. No.

He decided he would buy himself some shoes. His own flapped as he walked. His toes showed, but he hadn't liked it when Jehu had referred to him as 'a boy with broken shoes.'

As he left the cobbler's, his new shoes squeaking on his feet, he saw a peddler pushing a barrow of limes up Cornhill.

'Fine lemons and limes—lemons and limes.'

There was nothing in the world Isannah so craved as limes and Mrs. Lapham could not buy them for her. They were too dear. But sometimes sailors from the Indies or storekeepers would give her one—because she was so beautiful and would hug and kiss anyone who gave her a lime.

Johnny filled the pockets of his jacket and breeches with limes. Now for Cilla. He could not buy her a gray pony, a gold necklace, nor a little sailboat. He went to a stationer's. There he found a book with the most wonderful pictures of Calvinistic martyrs, dying horrible but prayerful deaths. He glanced at the text. With his help she would soon be able to read it. Next he bought pastel crayons, but he passionately regretted all those squabs. He had no money left to get her drawing paper.

His new shoes fitted to a nicety. If the Newfoundland dog was a heavier tenant in his stomach than the kitten, it was more restful. His pockets were full of fine gifts. He whistled as he walked, and entered the Lapham kitchen ready to tell of his adventure with Mr. Hancock.

The womenfolk had spent all day paring apples, threading them on strings preparing to dry them for the winter. Even Mrs. Lapham looked tired. The lazy apprentice bursting in, happy for the first time in two months, irritated her. Then she saw his new shoes.

'Johnny Tremain,' she cried, 'what have you been up to?'

'What?'

'You wicked, wicked boy! Oh, I declare, you are going to bring disgrace on us all.'

He did not understand.

'Them shoes!' she roared. 'You never got them honestly. You've taken to thieving. I'm going to tell your master. He'll call a constable and then see if you darest not tell where you stole them. You've just gone from worse to worse. You're going to get whipped for this—set in the stocks. You're going to jail. You'll end up on the gallows.'

He let her scold, shake her wattles at him. As she flounced out of the room, Madge and Dorcas saw their chance to escape for a moment. All afternoon Frizel, Junior, the leather-dresser, had been standing outside on the street waiting for one or the other to come out. Frizel, Junior, was an accepted suitor, but no one knew whether it was Madge or Dorcas he was after. Mrs. Lapham didn't know. The girls didn't know. Frizel, Junior, himself did not seem to know. Both Madge and Dorcas were now wild to get out and after him. It looked as though whichever one was not Mrs. Frizel would end up Mrs. Tweedie.

Johnny stood before Cilla and Isannah, who had huddled together in a corner of the settle like frightened little animals as their mother accused Johnny of theft. He smiled and they smiled. He was so happy about his gifts that he forgot his misfortunes.

Cilla said happily, 'I know you didn't steal.'

'Of course not. Look, girl . . . I've got crayons for you.' He put them on the table.

'For me?'

'And a book with pictures. Now, Cil, the printing is so easy I think you can almost teach yourself to read.'

'Oh, Johnny, look, *look* at that funny little man. See, he's got tiny little buttons on his coat. Oh, I never thought to own a book with pictures.'

He began fishing limes out of his frayed pockets. Isannah jumped about him like a puppy. 'Limes, limes!' she cried. They began to fall on the floor, rolling in all directions. All three children went down after them. Cilla was almost happier over Isannah's pleasure than her own. Johnny was happiest of all. For the first time he completely forgot his crippled hand. It was all as if nothing had happened and he and Cilla and Isannah were all one again.

He was pretending not to give the limes to the little girl. He was going to put them back in his pockets. But she knew they were for her. She wrapped herself about him, hugging him, kissing the front of his shirt (this was as far as she could reach). He started to pick her up in his arms, hold her over his head until she said, 'Please pretty.'

Suddenly Isannah's delighted cries changed to hysterical screams. 'Don't touch me! Don't touch me with that dreadful hand!'

Johnny stopped. It was the worst thing anyone had said to him. He stood like stone, his hand thrust back into his pocket. Cilla froze too—half under the kitchen table, a lime in her hand. 'Oh, *Isannah!* How could you?'

The nervous child went on screaming. 'Go away, Johnny, go away! I hate your hand.' Cilla slapped her and she burst into tears.

So he went away.

Now he was sure that what they all felt Isannah had been young enough to say. He felt his heart was broken. Once again he started to walk until he was so tired he could not think. The long, late-September night had already begun before he reached the town gates on the Neck. Beyond him, in the semi-darkness, running across mud flats, was the one road which connected Boston with the mainland. And here the gallows—on which Mrs. Lapham promised him to end. He turned back from the lonely place. The gallows and the graves of suicides frightened him a little. He wandered about through the salt marshes at the foot of the Common, circling until he came out on Beacon Hill. There he sat in an orchard for quite a while. It was either Mr. Lyte's or Mr. Hancock's, for the houses stood side by side. He saw the glitter of candles throughout the great mansions, guests coming and going, heard the music of a spinet. Isannah's words rang in his ears. He who had struggled hard never to cry now wished that he could. Then he walked off into sparsely settled West Boston. Behind the pesthouse by lantern light men were digging a hurried grave. He left West Boston and, skirting dirty Mill Cove, came at last into his own North Boston. On Hull Street he heard the staves of the town watch and the feet of the watchmen clumping on cobbles. By law no apprentice was allowed out so late. He slipped into Copp's Hill graveyard to hide until they were gone.

'One o'clock and a warm fair night,' called the watch.

It was indeed warm and fair and no hardship to spend such a night out under the moon and stars. Around about him everywhere lay the dead worthies of Boston. Their slate stones stood shoulder to shoulder. This was the highest land in Boston, next only to Beacon Hill.

Here, close to Hull Street, his mother was buried in an unmarked grave. He had not forgotten where and flung himself down beside the spot. Then he began to cry. He had not been able to cry before. It was as if Isannah's words had broken down the last strength in him. He cried half for himself and half because he knew how sorry his mother would be for him if she knew. I can't do decent work. I can't ever be a silversmith—not even a watchmaker. My friends don't want me to touch them with my dreadful hand.

Seemingly neither the moon nor the stars above him nor the dead about him cared.

Then he lay face down, sobbing and saying over and over that God had turned away from him. But his frenzied weeping had given him some release. He must have slept.

He sat up suddenly wide awake. The moon had seemingly come close and closer to him. He could see the coats of arms, the winged death's heads, on the slate stones about him. He was so wide awake he felt someone must have called his name. His ears were straining to hear the next words. What was it his mother had said so long ago? If there was nothing left and God Himself had turned away his face, then, and only then, Johnny was to go to Mr. Lyte. In his ears rang his mother's sweet remembered accents. Surely for one second, between sleeping and waking, he had seen her dear face, loving, gentle, intelligent, floating toward him through the moonlight on Copp's Hill.

He sat a long time with his arms hugging his knees. Now he knew what to do. This very day he would go to Merchant Lyte. When at last he lay down, he slept heavily, without a dream and without a worry.

*   *   *

It was past dawn when he woke, his feeling of contentment still in him. He was no longer his own problem but Merchant Lyte's. Tomorrow at this time what would he be calling him? 'Uncle

Jonathan?' 'Cousin Lyte?' Perhaps 'Grandpa,' and he laughed out loud.

Only imagine how Mrs. Lapham would come running, dropping nervous curtsies, when he drove up in that ruby coach! How Madge and Dorcas would stare! First thing he did would be to take Cilla for a drive. He'd not even invite Isannah. But how she would bawl when left behind! And then . . . his imagination jumped ahead.

At the Charlestown ferry slip he washed in the cold sea water, and because the sun was warm sunned himself as he did what he could to make his shabby clothes presentable. He combed his lank, fair hair with his fingers, cleaned his nails with his teeth. Of course now he could buy Cilla that pony and cart. And Grandpa Lapham . . . oh, he'd buy him a Bible with print an inch high in it. Mrs. Lapham? Not a thing, madam, not one thing.

Christ's Church said ten o'clock. He got up and started for Long Wharf where his great relative had his counting house. On his way he passed down Salt Lane. There was the comical little painted man observing Boston through his tiny spyglass. Johnny wanted to stop—tell that fellow—that Rab—of his great connections, but decided to wait until he was sure of his welcome into the Lyte family. Although half of him was leaping ahead imagining great things for himself, the other half was wary. It was quite possible he would get no welcome at all—and he knew it.

He walked the length of Long Wharf until he saw carved over a door the familiar rising eye. The door was open, but he knocked. None of the three clerks sitting on their high stools with their backs to him, scratching in ledgers, looked up, so he stepped inside. Now that he had to speak, he found there was a barrier across his throat, something that he would have to struggle to get his voice over. He was more excited than he had realized. But he was scornful too. These three clerks would not even look up when he came in today, but tomorrow what would it be? 'Good morning, little master; I'll tell your uncle—cousin—grandfather that you are here, sir.'

Finally a well-fed, rosy youth, keeping one finger in his ledger, swung around and asked him what he wanted.

'It is a personal matter between myself and Mr. Lyte.'

'Well,' said the young man pleasantly, 'even if it is personal, you'd better tell me what it is.'

'It is a family matter. I cannot, in honor, tell anyone except Mr. Lyte.'

'Hum . . .'

One of the elderly clerks laughed in a mean way. 'Just another poor suitor for the hand of Miss Lavinia.'

The young clerk flushed. Johnny had seen enough of Madge and Dorcas and their suitors to know that the gibe about poor boys aspiring to Miss Lavinia had gone home.

'Tell him,' snickered the other ancient spider of a clerk, 'that Mr. Lyte is—ah—sensible of the great honor—ah—and regrets to say he has formed other plans for his daughters' future. Ah!' Evidently he mimicked Mr. Lyte.

The young clerk was scarlet. He flung his pen. 'Can't you ever forget that?' he protested. 'Here, kid,' and turned to Johnny. 'Mr. Lyte's closeted behind that door with two of his sea captains. When they leave, you just walk in.'

Johnny sat modestly on a stool, his arrogant shabby hat in his good hand, and looked about him. The three backs were bent once more over the ledgers. The quill pens scratched. He heard the gritting of sand as they blotted their pages. There was a handsome half-model of a ship on the wall. Sea chests, doubtless full of charts, maps, invoices, were under the desks.

The door opened. Two ruddy men with swaying walks stepped out and Mr. Lyte himself was shaking hands, bidding them success on their voyaging, and God's mercy. As he turned to go back to his sanctuary, Johnny followed him.

Mr. Lyte sat himself in a red-leather armchair beside an open window. Through that window he could watch his *Western Star* graving in the graving dock. He would have been a handsome man, with his fine dark eyes, bushy black brows, contrasting smartly with the white tie-wig he wore, except for the color and quality of his flesh. It was as yellow as tallow. Seemingly it had melted and run down. The lids were heavy over the remarkable eyes. The melted flesh made pouches beneath them. It hung down along his jawbone, under his jutting chin.

'What is it?' he demanded. 'Who let you in? What do you want, and who, for Heaven's sake, are you?'

'Sir,' said Johnny, 'I'm Jonathan Lyte Tremain.'

There was a long pause. The merchant's glittering black eyes did not waver, nor the tallow cheeks redden. If the name meant anything to him, he did not show it.

'Well?"

'My mother, sir.' The boy's voice shook slightly. 'She told me . . . she always said . . .'

Mr. Lyte opened his jeweled snuffbox, took snuff, sneezed and blew his nose.

'I can go on from there, boy. Your mother on her deathbed told you you were related to the rich Boston merchant?'

Johnny was sure now Mr. Lyte knew of the relationship. 'Yes, sir, she did, but I didn't know you'd know.'

'*Know?* I didn't need to *know*. It is a very old story—a very old trick, and will you be gone—or shall I have you flung out?'

'I'll stay,' Johnny said stubbornly.

'Sewall.' The merchant did not raise his voice, but instantly the young clerk was on his threshold. 'Show him out, Sewall, and happens he lands in the water, you—ah! can baptize him with my name—ah . . . ha, ha!'

Mr. Lyte took up a handful of papers. The incident was over.

Sewall looked at Johnny and Johnny at Sewall. The young man was as kind as his cherubic face suggested.

'I can prove to you one thing, Mr. Lyte. My name is Jonathan Lyte Tremain.'

'What of it? Any back-alley drabtail can name her child for the greatest men in the colony. There should be a law against it, but there is none.'

Johnny's temper began to go.

'You flatter yourself. What have you ever done except be rich? Why, I doubt even a monkey mother would name a monkey child after you.'

Mr. Lyte gave a long whistle. 'That was quite a mouthful. Sewall!'

'Yes, sir.'

'You just take this monkey child of a monkey mother out, and drown it.'

'Yes, sir.'

Sewall put a soft hand on the boy's shoulder, but Johnny fiercely shook himself free.

'I don't want your money,' he said, more proudly than accurately. 'Now that I've met you face to face, I don't much fancy you as kin.'

'Your manners, my boy, are a credit to your mother.'

'But facts are facts, and I've a cup with your arms on it to prove what I say is true.'

The merchant's unhealthy, brilliant eyes quivered and glittered. 'You've got a cup of mine?'

'No, of *mine*.'

'So . . . so you've got a cup. Will you describe it?'

Johnny described it as only a silversmith could.

'Why, Mr. Lyte, that must be . . .' Sewall began, but Mr. Lyte hushed him. Evidently not only Mr. Lyte, but his clerks had heard of this cup. Johnny was elated.

'My boy,' said the merchant, 'you have—ah—brought me great news. I must see your cup.'

'Any time you say, sir.'

'My long-lost cup returned to me by my long-lost little—ha-ha—whatever you are—kerchoo!' He had taken more snuff. 'Bring your cup to me tonight. You know my Beacon Hill house.'

'Yes, sir.'

'And we'll kill the fatted calf—you long-lost whatever-you-are. Come an hour after candles are lit. Prodigal Son, what? Got a cup, has he?'

Although Johnny might have been more cordially received by Merchant Lyte, he was satisfied enough with his welcome to build up air castles. He really knew they were air castles, for at bottom he was hard-headed, not easily taken in even by his own exuberant imagination. Still, as he trudged up Fish Street, turned in at the Laphams' door, in his mind he was in that ruby coach. Money, and a watch in his pocket.

He had hoped to slip to the attic and fetch away his cup without being noticed, but Mrs. Lapham saw him enter and called him into the kitchen. She said nothing about his shoes. Evidently the girls had told her his story and she had believed it.

'Johnny, you come set a moment. No, girls, you needn't leave. I want you to hear what I'm going to say.'

Johnny looked a little smug. Had he not (almost) arrived in the Lyte coach?

'Grandpa says as long as he lives you are to have a place to sleep. But you've got to go back to the attic. Mr. Tweedie's to have the birth and death room, and you can have a little somewhat to eat. I've agreed that's all right. I'll manage *somehow.*'

'Don't fret . . . I'm going for good.'

'I'll believe that when I see it. Now, mind. I've two things to say to you.'

The four girls were all sitting about, hands folded as though they were at meeting.

'First. You shan't insult Mr. Tweedie—least, not until he has signed the contract. No more talk of his being a spinster aunt dressed up in men's clothes. And NO MORE SQUEAK-PIGS. He's sensitive. You hurt his feelings horribly. He almost took ship then and there back to Baltimore.'

'I'm sorry.'

'Secondly. There's to be no more talk of you and Cilla. Don't you ever *dare* to lift your eyes to one of my girls again.'

'*Lift* my eyes? I can't see that far down into the dirt even to know they are there.'

'Now, you saucebox, you hold that tongue of yours. You're not to go hanging 'round Cilla—giving her presents—and dear knows how you got the money. I've told her to keep shy of you. Now I'm telling you. You mark my words . . .'

'Ma'am, I wouldn't marry that sniveling, goggle-eyed frog of a girl even though you gave her to me on a golden platter. Fact is, I don't like girls—nor'—with a black look at his mistress—'women either—and that goes for Mr. Tweedie too.'

He left to go upstairs for his cup.

When he came down, the more capable women of the household were out in the yard hanging up the wash. Cilla was paring apples in that deft, absent-minded way she did such things. Isannah was eating the parings. She'd be sick before nightfall.

Cilla lifted her pointed, translucent little face. Her hazel eyes, under their veil of long lashes, had a greenish flash to them. There never was a less goggle-eyed girl.

'Johnny's mad,' she said sweetly.

'His ears are red! He's mad!' Isannah chanted.

These words sounded wonderful to him. He was happy because once more they were insulting him. They were not pitying him or being afraid of him because he had had an accident.

'Goggle-eyed, sniveling frogs!'

With his silver cup in its flannel bag, he set off to kill time until he might take it to Mr. Lyte.

He spent a couple of hours dreaming of his rosy future. And the tears in Merchant Lyte's unhealthy, brilliant black eyes—the tremor in his pompous 'ah-ha-ha' manner of speech as he clutched his 'long-lost whatever-you-are' to his costly waistcoat. Even if he did not like women, Miss Lavinia, he decided, was to kiss him on the brow. Through this dreaming he felt enough confidence in his good fortune at last to stop in to see 'that Rab.' There had not been a day since the first meeting that he had not wanted to.

Rab showed no surprise either over his return or the strange story that he proceeded to pour out. It was nightfall and, as Johnny hoped, Uncle Lorne and the little Webbs were gone. Rab was waiting for the ink to dry on the *Observer* so he could fold it. He sat with his long legs stretched before him, his hands clasped behind his neck.

'Lyte's crooked, you know,' he said at last.

'I've heard that before.'

'He's sly. When the merchants agreed not to import any English goods until the Stamp Act was repealed, he was one of the first to sign—then imported secretly. Sold through another name. Made more money. Sam Adams spoke to him privately—scared him. He says he won't do that again. He's trying to ride two horses—Whig and Tory.'

Johnny's life with the Laphams had been so limited he knew little of the political strife which was turning Boston into two armed camps. The Whigs declaring that taxation without representation is tyranny. The Tories believing all differences could be settled with time, patience, and respect for government.

Rab obviously was a Whig. 'I can stomach some of the Tories,' he went on, 'men like Governor Hutchinson. They honestly think we're better off to take anything from the British Parliament—let them break us down, stamp in our faces, take all we've got by taxes, and never protest. They say we American colonies are too weak to get on without England's help and guidance. But Governor Hutchinson's a good man. Of course we'll destroy him. We've marked him down. Sam Adams is already greasing the ways under him. But I can't stand men like Lyte, who care nothing for anything except themselves and their own fortune. Playing both ends against the middle.'

'I'd never have picked him for a relative. But beggars can't be choosers—and happens I'm a beggar. It's on to time to get ready to go to him.'

Understanding Johnny's unspoken desire not to appear too meanly before the great gentleman, Rab went to the attic above the shop where he slept and came down with a clean shirt of finest white linen and a fawn-colored corduroy jacket with silver buttons.

'It's too small for me. Ought to about fit you.'

It did.

Almost miraculously—for Johnny had not seen where it came from—bread and cheese were on the counter. It was his first food since yesterday's gorging.

With the straight, fair hair well brushed and tied behind with taffeta, the handsome jacket, the frilled, immaculate shirt, Johnny did cut a very presentable figure.

By the printing-shop clock the sun had been set for almost an hour. Rab was folding newspapers.

'You can sleep here,' he said, 'if they don't offer you anything. But . . . good luck, bold fellow.'

Standing on Beacon Hill, so far removed from the hurly-burly of the wharves, shops, markets of town, Johnny hesitated. Should he, as a poor out-of-work apprentice, go around back, or should he, as a long-lost something-or-other, raise that gleaming brass knocker on the paneled front door? The silver buttons and Rab's 'bold fellow' heartened him. The knocker fell, and instantly a maid was bidding him enter, curtsying, asking his name.

'I'm Jonathan Lyte Tremain.'

The front hall was very large. From it rose a flight of stairs, taking their time in their rising, taking all the space they needed. Along the walls were portraits: Merchant Lyte in his handsome, healthy youth; Lavinia, painted long before in London, as regal a child as now she was a young woman. Time blackened old things, already a hundred years old. Was it their long dried blood which now ran red and living in Johnny's veins?

To the left was the drawing room. The tinkle of a spinet, low voices, laughter. Could it be they were laughing because the maid was announcing him? He wished he had called himself merely Johnny Tremain.

'Ah-ha-ha.' That was Merchant Lyte. 'Fetch him in, Jenny. Just a little family party. All want to see him, eh?'

Johnny's first impression was of dozens of wax candles lighting the long, dove-colored and lavender-and-yellow room. They were reflected in mirrors, silver, gleaming floors and mahogany. A dozen people were gathered together in the far end of the room.

Johnny stood a moment, anxious to do nothing wrong, conscious that the new shoes he had been so proud of did not much resemble the little black buckled pumps on the gentlemen.

'Well,' said Mr. Lyte, rising, but not approaching him. 'So . . . here we are?'

'Yes, sir.'

'Lavinia, Cousin Talbot, Aunt Best, how do you like his looks?'

Aunt Best, a horrifyingly ugly, cross old woman with two gold-headed canes, vowed through her whiskers and toothless gums that he looked just as bad as she had expected.

Lavinia turned from the spinet. She had on a stiff, turquoise-blue dress that suited her marvelously. She looked at the boy with her head tipped sidewise as Johnny had seen other ladies look at silver teapots before they bought.

'At least, Papa, he's a deal handsomer than most of my relatives. Isn't he, Cousin Sewall?' It was the rosy clerk, lovelorn Sewall, who was turning her music for her.

'Yes, daughter.' Mr. Lyte's eyes flickered over Johnny. 'Quite the little gentleman—from the waist up. Silver buttons, eh? Ruffled shirt?'

His eyes slid over his 'little family party.' He addressed them in so low a voice he seemed to ignore Johnny standing at the far upper end of the long room.

He had been expecting some such apparition from the past ever since last August. In spite of family efforts to keep certain things dark, he had reason to believe certain things were well known, even among the—ah—lower classes. Then he called to Johnny.

'Now, boy, you brought your cup?'

'It is here—in this bag.'

'Very good. Will you—and all of you—please to step into the dining room?' This took some time, for Aunt Best had to be pulled in front and pushed from behind before she was balanced on her two gold-headed canes. She scolded, muttered, and shook her whiskers at everyone, including her famous nephew.

Only Lavinia, still at the spinet, and Cousin Sewall bending over her, did not go into the dining room.

There on the sideboard were three standing cups. They were identical with Johnny's. Silently he took his from its bag, set it with the other three, then stood back to look at the silken, be-jeweled, perfumed folk crowding about him.

Mr. Lyte took up the cup, studied it, compared it with one of his own. Silently he handed it to a plainly dressed, thick-set gentleman who thus far had said nothing.

'I think,' said Mr. Lyte quietly, 'all of you ladies and gentlemen will agree that this cup our—ah, cousin, is it?—has brought back tonight is one of this set?'

There was a murmur of assent. Johnny could hear the tiny tinkle, seemingly far away, of Miss Lavinia's spinet.

'It is perfectly obvious that this cup now stands where it belongs. The question is how was it ever separated from its fellows?'

Johnny felt that everyone there except himself knew the answer to this question.

'In fact,' the merchant's voice was smooth as oil, 'I declare this to be the very cup which was stolen from me by thieves. They broke through yonder window on the twenty-third of last August. Sheriff, I order you to arrest this boy for burglary.'

The thick-set plain man whom Johnny had already noticed, put a heavy hand on his shoulder. His formal words flowed over him.

'Johnny Tremain, alias Jonathan Lyte Tremain . . . apprentice to Ephraim Lapham . . . name of King and Bay Colony . . . standing cup . . . taken away the twenty-third day . . . month . . . year of our Lord one thousand seven hundred and seventy-three.'

'This is not true,' Johnny said.

'You can explain to the Judge.'

'Very well, I can and will.' The full horror of the accusation (for a boy might be hanged for stealing a silver cup) froze him into seeming nonchalance. This coolness made a bad impression. Aunt Best was poking at him with one of her canes. She hoped she'd live long enough to see him hanged. He was a perfect little viper—and he looked it. A florid woman was flapping a pink feather fan. She thought he had one of those falsely innocent little faces that are such an aid to evil boys.

'No,' someone else was saying, 'he has a shifty eye.'

Aunt Best croaked, 'Look at those silver buttons on his coat. I'm sure he stole them.'

Mr. Lyte said, 'Boy, where did you get that coat?'

'It was lent me.'

'Lent you? By whom, pray?'

'A printer's boy. I don't know his last name. Down at the *Observer* office . . . He's called Rab.'

'That coat is worth money. Do you think someone whose last name you admit you don't know would *lend* you a coat?'

'It doesn't sound likely—but happens it's true.'

'Sheriff, look into this.'

'I certainly will, Mr. Lyte.'

'I sent Sewall over to the Laphams—a very respectable, humble, pious, poor sort of folk. Mrs. Lapham swore this boy never owned a thing but the clothes he stood in. As for his name, she showed Sewall the papers of his indenture, signed by his dead mother. She put him down as Johnny Tremain, no Jonathan Lyte about it. And Mrs. Lapham believed that lately he had taken to evil ways—stealing shoes and little things. She swore he never owned a cup. And Mr. Tweedie, a partner of Mr. Lapham, said the boy was a notorious liar, and of most evil report.'

The sheriff was taking out handcuffs, snapping them on Johnny's wrist and his own.

'Soon's I get this scamp locked up, I'll be back for that bowl of punch you promised, Mr. Lyte,' he called cheerfully as he left. The last sound Johnny heard was the fairy tinkle of the spinet.

The chain clanked. The sheriff said nothing until they had reached the stone jail in Prison Lane. Then, as the jailer was writing down Johnny's name in his book, the sheriff said kindly:

'Now, boy, you've got some rights. Who do you want notified? Got any kin except the Lytes, eh? How about old Mr. Lapham?'

'He's my master no more. He dismissed me months ago.'

'Relatives? Parents?'

'I've nothing. But will you please tell that boy down at the *Observer?* He's a tall boy, and dark—all I know is that his name is Rab.'

'The one you stole the coat off, hey? I was going to look him up tonight.'

Oddly enough, Johnny slept well on his straw pallet in the jail. The night before, lying and weeping among the graves of Copp's Hill, he had reached bottom. He could not go lower than that. No matter what happened, he could not help but now go up. He knew Isannah's childish squeals were nothing compared to the serious charge Mr. Lyte had brought against him, but the squeals had just about broken his heart. The accusation of burglary he could take. He felt tough enough and hard enough to take anything. But he could not help but think of the gallows, just beyond the town gates, how they had loomed up at him through the dark of the night like a warning.

Before he had finished his breakfast of corn gruel, Rab arrived. Johnny had known he would come. He brought blankets, books, food. Seemingly by the nonchalance of his manner, nothing was more usual than to find one's friends in jail. About his muscular, brown throat Johnny could see a medal hung upon a string. On it was engraved a Tree of Liberty. So Rab was one of the semi-secret famous Sons of Liberty, those carefully organized 'mobs' who often took justice into their own hands. They frightened royal officers out of Boston, stopped British admirals from impressing Yankee seamen, as they were impressed in England. They could at will paralyze trade, courts, government. Many a night Johnny had heard their whistles, conch shells, and cries of 'town-born, turn out,' the running of their feet. And next day had seen the effigies they had hung, the Tory fences they had torn down or windows broken, and heard that Royal Commissioner So-and-So had been frightened out of Boston. Or such-and-such a merchant had wept when haled before the Liberty Tree and sworn never to do trade with England until all grievances had been righted. The Laphams had hated such lawless seizure of government by the Sons of Liberty. Johnny had not thought much about it. Seeing the medal at Rab's throat made him think it might be fun to be out with them.

The medal did its work, for both the turnkey and the jailer were also 'Sons.' Johnny was given a neat, private room on the ground floor. Such rooms were usually reserved for gentlemen jailed for debt.

Here he told Rab his entire story. Rab had already found out that the case would come up on the following Tuesday, before Mr. Justice Dana. If Mr. Justice thought there was not sufficient evidence to hold him for a higher court and a jury trial, he would immediately release him. Then he asked if Johnny had shown his cup to any living soul sometime before August twenty-third. Such a witness would prove that Johnny had owned a cup, before Mr. Lyte's had been stolen.

'Why, of course—Cilla Lapham. That was July. Come to think, it was the very day Mr. Hancock ordered his sugar basin. It was the second day of July—that was a Tuesday.'

'That's all you'll need. Mr. Lyte was a fool to bring so flimsy a charge against you.'

'What do you suppose he meant when he said he had expected something like me turning up as soon as that cup was stolen?'

'I don't know what goes on in that clever, bad head, but perhaps he thinks you are an impostor and stole the cup first to back up some claim of kinship. Of course Cilla will come to court for you?'

'She will. If her mother will let her.'

'Would Mrs. Lapham give you a good character?'

'No. She thinks these days I'm bad enough to steal a wig off a parson's head.'

Next day Rab was back at the same time. He was a little perturbed. Mr. Lyte himself had been to the Laphams (in the ruby coach) and ordered a dozen silver spoons, a tea caddy, and, *if all went well*, would order a silver tankard a foot high.

'A bribe?'

'Cilla says he paid in advance. Then it was Mrs. Lapham said she would not have her girl mixed up in such a disgraceful case. She promised Cilla would spend next Tuesday under lock and key.'

'I could hang first?'

'And she is determined to please that Mr. Tweedie too. If he won't sign that contract and get right to work, she can't get Mr. Lyte's silver made. Poor old Mr. Lapham won't do anything but read his Bible. Says he hasn't long to prepare to meet his Maker. By the way, Mr. Tweedie just about hates you. Says you called him a squeak-pig. He didn't like it.'

'Of course, I called him a squeak-pig. Don't see why he cares.'

'Well—you go around calling people squeak-pigs and you've just about got to take it when they hit back. Not with their tongues—mostly they're not quick enough—but like this. Tweedie saw his chance to get back at you. He says if Mrs. Lapham lets Cilla testify for you, he'll take a ship back to Baltimore. Says he's sensitive and a great artist and he can't be upset by thieves and brawlers. Well . . . never mind. But I don't see the point of going around and . . .'

'Oh, forget those squeak-pigs, for Heaven's sake.' Johnny was sulky.

'Now for a lawyer. I've talked to Josiah Quincy. He often writes for the *Observer*. He says if you want him, he's ready.'

'Josiah Quincy? But . . . Rab, you tell him not to . . .'

'You don't want him? He's the best young lawyer in Boston.'

'I could never pay him.'

'You don't understand. He'll give you his time for nothing. He's coming to see you this afternoon. And I'm meeting Cilla, sort of behind her mother's back, to make plans.'

'It all depends on Cilla, doesn't it?'

'Well . . . pretty much.'

'And Mrs. Lapham and the squeak—I mean Tweedie—say they'll lock her up?'

'Lock her up so I can't get her out? Boy, I could get her out of this jail. Get her out of the Tower of London. And that girl would testify for you, even if it cost her her life. What's her real name?'

'Priscilla.'

'Well, may Priscilla be on my side if ever I'm accused of anything. What about the little girl—is she really as bright as she looks?'

'No, I don't think so. She's just sort of a parrot. She's always going around repeating what Cilla or anyone else says to her as if she had thought it all up herself.'

Mr. Justice Dana was a stout and florid man, dressed in a black silk robe and a great woolly white wig.

Johnny sat close to Mr. Quincy, watching the Justice's nervous, taut hands, listening to his 'What have we heres' and quick questions to the men and women shoved up before him. Some people he dismissed, some he ordered fined, or whipped, or set in the stocks, or held for a higher court. Johnny knew when his own case would soon be called because he heard the Justice tell a beadle to run down to Long Wharf and tell Merchant Lyte to present himself in half an hour.

Once again Johnny squirmed about, studying every face in the courtroom. Rab and Cilla were not there and he was frightened.

Mr. Quincy whispered to him.

'Rab said he'd get her here by eleven. Rab's never slipped yet.'

Johnny liked his young lawyer. A frail man, flushed with fever. His cough was prophetic of an early death. That was how Johnny's mother had died—burned up by fever, coughing herself to death. The man had a mobile, passionate face, handsome except for one wall eye.

Mr. Lyte arrived, escorted by his poor relative and clerk, Sewall. He entered as though he owned the court, calling a cheery good morning to Mr. Justice, interrupting the mumbled explanation of a shabby bakeress accused of selling mouldy bread. Next there was a rattle of light gig wheels, a jingle of horse gear, and to the intense pleasure of everyone Miss Lavinia Lyte entered and, as modestly as she was able, took a seat near the door.

Even the Justice straightened the bands at his throat. Sewall blushed. The bakeress forgot what she was saying as she turned to gape at the beautiful, dark woman, darkly dressed. Restless, easily bored, Miss Lyte often did unexpected things.

'Jonathan Lyte *versus* Johnny Tremain, alias Jonathan Lyte Tremain.'

Mr. Quincy gave him a secret pat on the knee. Johnny knew he must now step forward, take his oath on the Bible to tell the truth, the whole truth—so help him God. He was frightened, for as he stepped forward he was conscious that these might be the first steps toward those gallows—waiting in the dark beyond the town gates.

Next Mr. Lyte was called and was taking the same oath. Mr. Quincy's one good eye caught Johnny's. He was forming words on his lips. The clock had indeed struck eleven and there, standing in the doorway, were Rab and Cilla. Rab, enigmatical, dark, capable, looked as always. Cilla had on a hood that half-covered her face.

Mr. Lyte was talking as informally as though he and Mr. Dana were alone together, sitting at a tavern, cracking walnuts, drinking Madeira. He told how his great-grandfather, Jonathan Lyte, Mayor of Causeway, Kent, England, had had six identical cups made— one for each of his sons. Four of these cups had come to this country and these he himself had owned until last August. On the night of the twenty-third, a thief or thieves had broken a pane out of his dining-room window. The space was too small to admit a grown man, so it was a half-grown boy who had slipped in and taken only one of the famous cups.

Then he snapped his fingers at Sewall, who stepped forward and set four silver cups on the table before the Justice.

'This is the stolen cup,' Mr. Lyte said confidently. 'I've tied a red ribbon on it.' Then he went on to tell, with considerable humor and a bright sparkle in his slippery black eyes, about Johnny's visit to his shop, his claims of kinship, and how he had lured him to his house with the stolen cup.

The Justice said: 'Mr. Lyte, could it not be possible that this boy is related to you? Could his story be true?'

No, no, it was impossible. Would Mr. Justice Dana be so good as to glance at this indenture—which the boy's erstwhile master, Mr. Lapham, had been so kind as to lend him? The name was put down as Johnny Tremain—nothing about Lyte. Undoubtedly older heads than this boy's had egged him on to this wretched, scurvy trick, but Mr. Lyte had no wish to go into the matter beyond the recovery of his own property. He did not wish to suggest in any way that the Laphams had any part in the imposture—they were very humble, honest, pious folk. He believed that the case of the theft, all that interested him at the moment, was 'dead open and shut against the boy.' And might he ask the death penalty? There was too much thieving going on in Boston. Poor apprentices were getting out of hand. The gallows had been too long empty.

'That's for the court to say,' said the Justice sourly. He took snuff and Mr. Lyte took snuff. They sneezed together.

Mr. Quincy led Johnny on to tell his own story. The boy spoke confidently, now that Rab and Cilla were there. He had never had an audience before and he felt the courtroom hanging on his words, believing him. He spoke better and better. He told how his mother had given him the cup, the little that she had told him. She had bidden him not to part with the cup—ever. Nor ever go to the Lytes unless he had come to the end of everything. Then he spoke simply and easily of his accident, his hunt for work, his despair—and arrest. There was a murmur almost of applause.

'Johnny,' said Mr. Quincy, 'did you obey your mother—never show your cup to anyone?'

'Once I disobeyed. It was the second day of last July. I forgot —or didn't heed. I told my master's daughter, Priscilla Lapham, what my mother said was my true name, and about the cup. She wanted to see it. It was just dawn—that is, the dawn of the third of July. Tuesday it was.'

Cilla was called. Johnny had always thought her a shy girl, but she stood up straight before the Judge, speaking in her clear, low voice. He was proud of her. And he had always thought her a skinny, plain girl. She looked at the moment just about beautiful to him.

As she finished, there was a sensation in the courtroom that outweighed the arrival of Mr. Lyte and even his handsome daughter.

Isannah, her bright curls in wild array, flew into the courtroom, seeming, like a mouse, to run without feet. She stopped for no oath, no formalities, but flung herself upon Mr. Justice Dana, telling over again Cilla's story. Johnny knew she had been sound asleep when he had told Cilla. She had even been in bed when he had actually shown the cup to her older sister. He was amazed at the vividness of her jumbled recital and touched by the virtues she attributed to himself. Yet she was making it all up.

In vain Mr. Justice Dana's 'What have we here?' and 'I cannot accept this as testimony,' and Cilla's attempts to quiet her. She was so enchanting, so seemingly come from another world, she had her say.

'Bless me!' said Mr. Justice, blowing his nose. 'And how old might you be?'

'Eight, sir, going on for nine.'

'There now—be a good girl—here, you take this piece of licorice I have in my pocket and sit down quietly and eat it. There!"

Almost immediately he dismissed the case. There was not the slightest evidence, the Justice was saying, that the accused had stolen a cup, nor that the cup with the red ribbon, now illegally in the possession of Mr. Lyte, was the same one as was stolen from his house last August. Evidence was against that. For these young Lapham misses had proved to his satisfaction (and might he point out to Mr. Lyte his own testimony about the high character of honesty and piety the Laphams enjoyed?) that, unlikely as it might seem, the apprentice had possession of a silver cup, undoubtedly one of the original six ordered by the Mayor of Causeway, Kent. He bade Johnny Tremain take the one with the red ribbon. It was his own. If he liked, he might even bring a suit against Mr. Lyte. Didn't recommend it—Mr. Lyte was too powerful.

Johnny took the cup. In a moment he and Mr. Quincy, Rab and Cilla, were standing in the sunshine of the street outside the courthouse. They were so happy they could only laugh. The lawyer said now they would all go together, as his guests, to a tavern, to eat at their leisure, and drink a health to Johnny from the cup. But where was Isannah?

She was standing with a tiny hand in one of Miss Lyte's gloved ones, gazing up at her in adoration.

Cilla called her crossly. Miss Lyte stepped up into her high gig. It was a long step, but she was a lithe, long-legged woman.

'She said,' panted Isannah, 'she had never seen anything like me . . . not even in some lane in London.'

'Drury Lane,' said young Mr. Quincy dryly. 'I was thinking of that myself.'

'Rab,' said the little girl, 'was I really all right?'

'Just about perfect. Only some of it you put in the first person, so it wasn't quite the truth, but . . . you'll never starve.'

Then she tried to kiss Johnny, but he thought it beneath his dignity to be kissed on the street.

'You're too mussed up with licorice,' he said.

She bent and kissed his burned hand.

He said nothing. He was suddenly afraid he might cry.

from *Abe Lincoln Grows Up*
CARL SANDBURG

Barefoot in Yellow Clay

During the year 1817, little Abe Lincoln, eight years old, going on nine, had an ax put in his hands and helped his father cut down trees and notch logs for the corners of their new cabin, forty yards from the pole-shed where the family was cooking, eating, and sleeping.

Wild turkey, ruffed grouse, partridge, coon, rabbit, were to be had for the shooting of them. Before each shot Tom Lincoln took a rifle-ball out of a bag and held the ball in his left hand; then with his right hand holding the gunpowder horn he pulled the stopper with his teeth, slipped the powder into the barrel, followed with the ball; then he rammed the charge down the barrel with a hickory ramrod held in both hands, looked to his trigger, flint, and feather in the touch-hole—and he was ready to shoot—to kill for the home skillet.

Having loaded his rifle just that way several thousand times in his life, he could do it in the dark or with his eyes shut. Once Abe took the gun as a flock of wild turkeys came toward the new log cabin, and, standing inside, shot through a crack and killed one of the big birds; and after that, somehow, he never felt like pulling the trigger on game-birds. A mile from the cabin was a salt lick where deer came; there the boy could have easily shot the animals, as they stood rubbing their tongues along the salty slabs or tasting of a saltish ooze. His father did the shooting; the deer killed gave them meat for Nancy's skillet; and the skins were tanned, cut, and stitched into shirts, trousers, mitts, moccasins. They wore buckskin; their valley was called the Buckhorn Valley.

After months the cabin stood up, four walls fitted together with a roof, a one-room house eighteen feet square, for a family to live in. A stick chimney plastered with clay ran up outside. The floor was packed and smoothed dirt. A log-fire lighted the inside; no windows were cut in the walls. For a door there was a hole cut to stoop through. Bedsteads were cleated to the corners of the cabin; pegs stuck in the side of a wall made a ladder for young Abe to climb up in a loft to sleep on a hump of dry leaves; rain and snow came through chinks of the roof onto his bearskin cover. A table and three-legged stools had the top sides smoothed with an ax, and the bark-side under, in the style called "puncheon."

A few days of this year in which the cabin was building, Nancy told Abe to wash his face and hands extra clean; she combed his hair, held his face between her two hands, smacked him a kiss on the mouth, and sent him to school—nine miles and back—Abe and Sally hand in hand hiking eighteen miles a day. Tom Lincoln used to say Abe was going to have "a real eddication," explaining, "You air a-goin' to larn readin', writin', and cipherin'."

He learned to spell words he didn't know the meaning of, spelling the words before he used them in sentences. In a list of "words of eight syllables accented upon the sixth," was the word "incomprehensibility." He learned that first, and then such sentences as "Is he to go in?" and "Ann can spin flax."

Some neighbors said, "It's a pore make-out of a school," and Tom complained it was a waste of time to send the children nine miles just to sit with a lot of other children and read out loud all day in a "blab" school. But Nancy, as she cleaned Abe's ears in corners where he forgot to clean them, and as she combed out the tangles in his coarse, sandy black hair, used to say, "Abe, you go to school now, and larn all you kin." And he kissed her and said, "Yes, Mammy," and started with his sister on the nine-mile walk through timberland where bear, deer, coon, and wildcats ran wild.

Fall time came with its early frost and they were moved into the new cabin, when horses and a wagon came breaking into the clearing one day. It was Tom and Betsy Sparrow and their seventeen-year-old boy, Dennis Hanks, who had come from Hodgenville, Kentucky, to cook and sleep in the pole-shed of the Lincoln family till they could locate land and settle. Hardly a year had passed, however, when both Tom and Betsy Sparrow were taken down with the "milk sick," beginning with a whitish coat on the tongue. Both died and were buried in October on a little hill in a clearing in the timbers near by.

Soon after, there came to Nancy Hanks Lincoln that white coating of the tongue; her vitals burned; the tongue turned brownish; her feet and hands grew cold and colder, her pulse slow and slower. She knew she was dying, called for her children, and spoke to them her last choking words. Sarah and Abe leaned over the bed. A bony hand of the struggling mother went out, putting its fingers into the boy's sandy black hair; her fluttering guttural words seemed to say he must grow up and be good to his sister and father.

So, on a bed of poles cleated to the corner of the cabin, the body of Nancy Hanks Lincoln lay, looking tired . . . tired . . . with a peace settling in the pinched corners of the sweet, weary mouth, silence slowly etching away the lines of pain and hunger drawn around the gray eyes where now the eyelids closed down in the fine pathos of unbroken rest, a sleep without interruption settling about the form of the stooped and wasted shoulder-bones, looking to the children who tiptoed in, stood still, cried their tears of want and longing, whispered "Mammy, Mammy," and heard only their own whispers answering, looking to these little ones of her brood as though new secrets had come to her in place of the old secrets given up with the breath of life.

And Tom Lincoln took a log left over from the building of the cabin, and he and Dennis Hanks whipsawed the log into planks, planed the planks smooth, and made them of a measure for a box to bury the dead wife and mother in. Little Abe, with a jackknife, whittled pine-wood pegs. And then, while Dennis and Abe held the planks, Tom bored holes and stuck the whittled pegs through the bored holes. This was the coffin, and they carried it the next day to the same little timber clearing near by, where a few weeks before they had buried Tom and Betsy Sparrow. It was in the way of the deer-run leading to the saltish water; light feet and shy hoofs ran over those early winter graves.

So the woman, Nancy Hanks, died, thirty-six years old, a pioneer sacrifice, with memories of monotonous, endless everyday chores, of mystic Bible verses read over and over for their promises, and with memories of blue wistful hills and a summer when the crab-apple blossoms flamed white and she carried a boy-child into the world.

She had looked out on fields of blue-blossoming flax and hummed "Hey, Betty Martin, tiptoe, tiptoe"; she had sung of bright kingdoms by and by and seen the early frost leaf its crystals on the stalks of buttonweed and redbud; she had sung:

> You may bury me in the east,
> You may bury me in the west,
> And we'll all rise together in that morning.

* * *

Some weeks later, when David Elkin, elder of the Methodist church, was in that neighborhood, he was called on to speak over the grave of Nancy Hanks. He had been acquainted with her in Kentucky, and to the Lincoln family and a few neighbors he spoke of good things she had done, sweet ways she had of living her life in this Vale of Tears, and her faith in another life yonder past the River Jordan.

The "milk sick" took more people in that neighborhood the same year, and Tom Lincoln whipsawed planks for more coffins. One settler lost four milch cows and eleven calves. The nearest doctor for people or cattle was thirty-five miles away. The wilderness is careless.

Lonesome and dark months came for Abe and Sarah. Worst of all were the weeks after their father went away, promising to come back.

Elizabethtown, Kentucky, was the place Tom Lincoln headed for.

As he footed it through the woods and across the Ohio River, he was saying over to himself a speech—the words he would say to Sarah Bush Johnston, down in Elizabethtown. Her husband had died a few years before, and she was now in Tom's thoughts.

He went straight to the house where she was living in Elizabethtown, and, speaking to her as "Miss Johnston," he argued: "I have no wife and you no husband. I came a-purpose to marry you. I knowed you from a gal and you knowed me from a boy. I've no time to lose; and if you're willin' let it be done straight off."

Her answer was, "I got debts." She gave him a list of the debts; he paid them; a license was issued; and they were married on December 2, 1819.

He could write his name; she couldn't write hers. Trying to explain why the two of them took up with each other so quickly, Dennis Hanks at a later time said, "Tom had a kind o' way with women, an' maybe it was somethin' she took comfort in to have a man that didn't drink an' cuss none."

Little Abe and Sarah, living in the lonesome cabin on Little Pigeon Creek, Indiana, got a nice surprise one morning when four horses and a wagon came into their clearing, and their father jumped off, then Sarah Bush Lincoln, the new wife and mother, then John, Sarah, and Matilda Johnston, Sarah Bush's three children by her first husband. Next off the wagon came a feather mattress, feather pillows, a black walnut bureau, a large clothes-chest, a table, chairs, pots and skillets, knives, forks, spoons.

Abe ran his fingers over the slick wood of the bureau, pushed his fist into the feather pillows, sat in the new chairs, and wondered to himself, because this was the first time he had touched such fine things, such soft slick things.

"Here's your new mammy," his father told Abe as the boy looked up at a strong, large-boned, rosy woman, with a kindly face and eyes, with a steady voice, steady ways. The cheek-bones of her face stood out and she had a strong jaw-bone; she was warm and friendly for Abe's little hands to touch, right from the beginning. As one of her big hands held his head against her skirt he felt like a cold chick warming under the soft feathers of a big wing. She took the cornhusks Abe had been sleeping on, piled them in the yard and said they would be good for a pig-pen later on; and Abe sunk his head and bones that night in a feather pillow and a feather mattress.

Ten years pass with that cabin on Little Pigeon Creek for a home, and that farm and neighborhood the soil for growth. There the boy Abe grows to be the young man, Abraham Lincoln.

Ten years pass and the roots of a tree spread out finding water to carry up to branches and leaves that are in the sun; the trunk thickens, the forked limbs shine wider in the sun, they pray with their leaves in the rain and the whining wind; the tree arrives, the mystery of its coming, spreading, growing, a secret not even known to the tree itself; it stands with its arms stretched to the corners the four winds come from, with its murmured testimony, "We are here, we arrived, our roots are in the earth of these years," and beyond that short declaration, it speaks nothing of the decrees, fates, accidents, destinies, that made it an apparition of its particular moment.

Abe Lincoln grows up. His father talks about the waste of time in "eddication"; it is enough "to larn readin', writin', cipherin'"; but the stanch, yearning stepmother, Sarah Bush Lincoln, comes between the boy and the father. And the father listens to the stepmother and lets her have her way.

* * *

When he was eleven years old, Abe Lincoln's young body began to change. The juices and glands began to make a long, tall boy out of him. As the months and years went by, he noticed his lean wrists getting longer, his legs too, and he was now looking over the heads of other boys. Men said, "Land o' Goshen, that boy air a-growin'!"

As he took on more length, they said he was shooting up into the air like green corn in the summer of a good corn-year. So he grew. When he reached seventeen years of age, and they measured him, he was six feet, nearly four inches, high, from the bottoms of his moccasins to the top of his skull.

These were years he was handling the ax. Except in spring plowing-time and the fall fodder-pulling, he was handling the ax nearly all the time. The inside of his hands took on callus thick as leather. He cleared openings in the timber, cut logs and puncheons, split fire-wood, built pig-pens.

He learned how to measure with his eye the half-circle swing of the ax so as to nick out the deepest possible chip from off a tree-trunk. The trick of swaying his body easily on the hips so as to throw the heaviest possible weight into the blow of the ax—he learned that.

On winter mornings he wiped the frost from the ax-handle, sniffed sparkles of air into his lungs, and beat a steady cleaving of blows into a big tree—till it fell—and he sat on the main log and ate his noon dinner of corn bread and fried salt pork—and joked with the gray squirrels that frisked and peeped at him from high forks of near-by walnut trees.

He learned how to make his ax flash and bite into a sugar-maple or a sycamore. The outside and the inside look of black walnut and black oak, hickory and jack oak, elm and white oak, sassafras, dogwood, grapevines, sumac—he came on their secrets. He could guess close to the time of the year, to the week of the month, by the way the leaves and branches of trees looked. He sniffed the seasons.

Often he worked alone in the timbers, all day long with only the sound of his own ax, or his own voice speaking to himself, or the crackling and swaying of branches in the wind, and the cries and whirs of animals, of brown and silver-gray squirrels, of partridges, hawks, crows, turkeys, sparrows, and the occasional wildcats.

The tricks and whimsies of the sky, how to read clear skies and cloudy weather, the creeping vines of ivy and wild grape, the recurrence of dogwood blossoms in spring, the ways of snow, rain, drizzle, sleet, the visitors of sky and weather coming and going hour by hour—he tried to read their secrets, he tried to be friendly with their mystery.

So he grew, to become hard, tough, wiry. The muscle on his bones and the cords, tendons, cross-weaves of fiber, and nerve centers, these became instruments to obey his wishes. He found with other men he could lift his own end of a log—and more too. One of the neighbors said he was strong as three men. Another said, "He can sink an ax deeper into wood than any man I ever saw." And another, "If you heard him fellin' trees in a clearin', you would say there was three men at work by the way the trees fell."

He was more than a tough, long, rawboned boy. He amazed men with his man's lifting power. He put his shoulders under a new-built corncrib one day and walked away with it to where the farmer wanted it. Four men, ready with poles to put under it and carry it, didn't need their poles. He played the same trick with a chicken house; at the new, growing town of Gentryville near by, they said the chicken house weighed six hundred pounds, and only a big boy with a hard backbone could get under it and walk away with it.

A blacksmith shop, a grocery, and a store had started up on the crossroads of the Gentry farm. And one night after Abe had been helping thresh wheat on Dave Turnham's place, he went with Dennis Hanks, John Johnston, and some other boys to Gentryville where the farm-hands sat around with John Baldwin, the blacksmith, and Jones, the storekeeper, passed the whisky jug, told stories, and talked politics and religion and gossip. Going home late that night, they saw something in a mud puddle alongside the road. They stepped over to see whether it was a man or a hog. It was a man—drunk—snoring—sleeping off his drunk—on a frosty night outdoors in a cold wind.

They shook him by the shoulders, doubled his knees to his stomach, but he went on sleeping, snoring. The cold wind was getting colder. The other boys said they were going home, and they went away leaving Abe alone with the snoring sleeper in the mud puddle. Abe stepped into the mud, reached arms around the man, slung him over his shoulders, carried him to Dennis Hanks's cabin, built a fire, rubbed him warm and left him sleeping off the whisky.

And the man afterward said Abe saved his life. He told John Hanks, "It was mighty clever of Abe to tote me to a warm fire that night."

So he grew, living in that Pigeon Creek cabin for a home, sleeping in the loft, climbing up at night to a bed just under the roof, where sometimes the snow and the rain drove through the cracks, eating sometimes at a table where the family had only one thing to eat—potatoes. Once at the table, when there were only potatoes, his father spoke a blessing to the Lord for potatoes; the boy murmured, "Those are mighty poor blessings." And Abe made jokes once when company came and Sally Bush Lincoln brought out raw potatoes, gave the visitors a knife apiece, and they all peeled raw potatoes, and talked about the crops, politics, religion, gossip.

Days when they had only potatoes to eat didn't come often. Other days in the year they had "yaller-legged chicken" with gravy, and corn dodgers with shortening, and berries and honey. They tasted of bear meat, deer, coon, quail, grouse, prairie turkey, catfish, bass, perch.

Abe knew the sleep that comes after long hours of work outdoors, the feeling of simple food changing into blood and muscle as he worked in those young years clearing timberland for pasture and corn crops, cutting loose the brush, piling it and burning it, splitting rails, pulling the crosscut saw and the whipsaw, driving the shovel-plow, harrowing, planting, hoeing, pulling fodder, milking cows, churning butter, helping neighbors at house-raisings, log-rollings, corn-huskings.

He found he was fast, strong, and keen when he went against other boys in sports. On farms where he worked, he held his own at scuffling, knocking off hats, wrestling. The time came when around Gentryville and Spencer County he was known as the best "rassler" of all, the champion. In jumping, foot-racing, throwing the maul, pitching the crowbar, he carried away the decisions against the lads of his own age always, and usually won against those older than himself.

He earned his board, clothes, and lodgings, sometimes working for a neighbor farmer. He watched his father, while helping make cabinets, coffins, cupboards, window frames, doors. Hammers, saws, pegs, cleats, he understood first-hand, also the scythe and the cradle for cutting hay and grain, the corn-cutter's knife, the leather piece to protect the hand while shucking corn, and the horse, the dog, the cow, the ox, the hog. He could skin and cure the hides of coon and deer. He lifted the slippery two-hundred-pound hog carcass, head down, holding the hind hocks up for others of the gang to hook, and swung the animal clear of the ground. He learned where to stick a hog in the under side of the neck so as to bleed it to death, how to split it in two, and carve out the chops, the parts for sausage grinding, for hams, for "cracklings."

Farmers called him to butcher for them at thirty-one cents a day, this when he was sixteen and seventeen years old. He could "knock a beef in the head," swing a maul and hit a cow between the eyes, skin the hide, halve and quarter it, carve out the tallow, the steaks, kidneys, liver.

And the hiding-places of fresh spring water under the earth crust had to be in his thoughts; he helped at well-digging; the wells Tom Lincoln dug went dry one year after another; neighbors said Tom was always digging a well and had his land "honey-combed"; and the boy, Abe, ran the errands and held the tools for the well-digging.

When he was eighteen years old, he could take an ax at the end of the handle and hold it out in a straight horizontal line, easy and steady—he had strong shoulder muscles and steady wrists early in life. He walked thirty-four miles in one day, just on an errand, to please himself, to hear a lawyer make a speech. He could tell his body to do almost impossible things, and the body obeyed.

Growing from boy to man, he was alone a good deal of the time. Days came often when he was by himself all the time except at breakfast and supper hours in the cabin home. In some years more of his time was spent in loneliness than in the company of other people. It happened, too, that this loneliness he knew was not like that of people in cities who can look from a window on streets where faces pass and repass. It was the wilderness loneliness he became acquainted with, solved, filtered through body, eye, and brain, held communion with in his ears, in the temples of his forehead, in the works of his beating heart.

He lived with trees, with the bush wet with shining raindrops, with the burning bush of autumn, with the lone wild duck riding a north wind and crying down on a line north to south, the faces of open sky and weather, the ax which is an individual one-man instrument, these he had for companions, books, friends, talkers, chums of his endless changing soliloquies.

His moccasin feet in the winter-time knew the white spaces of snowdrifts piled in whimsical shapes against timber slopes or blown in levels across the fields of last year's cut corn stalks; in the summer-time his bare feet toughened in the gravel of green streams while he laughed back to the chatter of bluejays in the red-haw trees or while he kept his eyes ready in the slough quack-grass for the cow-snake, the rattler, the copperhead.

He rested between spells of work in the springtime when the upward push of the coming out of the new grass can be heard, and in autumn weeks when the rustle of a single falling leaf lets go a whisper that a listening ear can catch.

He found his life thrown in ways where there was a certain chance for a certain growth. And so he grew. Silence found him; he met silence. In the making of him as he was, the element of silence was immense.

* * *

It was a little country of families living in one-room cabins. Dennis Hanks said at a later time, "We lived the same as the Indians, 'ceptin' we took an interest in politics and religion."

Cash was scarce; venison, hams, bacon slabs, and barrels of whisky served as money; there were seasons when storekeepers asked customers, "What kind of money have you today?" because so many sorts of wildcat dollar bills were passing around. In sections of timberland, wild hogs were nosing out a fat living on hickory nuts, walnuts, acorns; it was said the country would be full of wild hogs if the wolves didn't find the litters of young pigs a few weeks old and kill them.

Farmers lost thirty and forty sheep in a single wolf raid. Toward the end of June came "fly time," when cows lost weight and gave less milk because they had to fight flies. For two or three months at the end of summer, horses weakened, unless covered with blankets, under the attacks of horse-flies; where one lighted on a horse, a drop of blood oozed; horses were hitched to branches of trees that gave loose rein to the animals, room to move and fight flies.

Men and women went barefoot except in the colder weather; women carried their shoes in their hands and put them on just before arrival at church meetings or at social parties.

Rains came, loosening the top soil of the land where it was not held by grass roots; it was a yellow clay that softened to slush; in this yellow slush many a time Abe Lincoln walked ankle-deep; his bare feet were intimate with the clay dust of the hot dog-days, with the clay mud of spring and fall rains; he was at home in clay. In the timbers with his ax, on the way to chop, his toes, heels, soles, the balls of his feet, climbed and slid in banks and sluices of clay. In the corn-fields, plowing, hoeing, cutting, and shucking, again his bare feet spoke with the clay of the earth; it was in his toenails and stuck on the skin of his toe-knuckles. The color of clay was one of his own colors.

In the short and simple annals of the poor, it seems there are people who breathe with the earth and take into their lungs and blood some of the hard and dark strength of its mystery. During six and seven months each year in the twelve fiercest formative years of his life, Abraham Lincoln had the pads of his foot-soles bare against clay of the earth. It may be the earth told him in her own tough gypsy slang one or two knacks of living worth keeping. To be organic with running wildfire and quiet rain, both of the same moment, is to be the carrier of wave-lines the earth gives up only on hard usage.

*   *   *

He took shape in a tall, long-armed cornhusker. When rain came in at the chinks of the cabin loft where he slept, soaking through the book Josiah Crawford loaned him, he pulled fodder two days to pay for the book, made a clean sweep, till there wasn't a blade left on a cornstalk in the field of Josiah Crawford.

His father was saying the big boy looked as if he had been roughhewn with an ax and needed smoothing with a jack-plane. "He was the ganglin'est, awkwardest feller that ever stepped over a ten-rail snake fence; he had t' duck to git through a door; he 'peared to be all j'ints."

His stepmother told him she didn't mind his bringing dirt into the house on his feet; she could scour the floor; but she asked him to keep his head washed or he'd be rubbing the dirt on her nice whitewashed rafters. He put barefoot boys to wading in a mud-puddle near the horsetrough, picked them up one by one, carried

them to the house upside down, and walked their muddy feet
across the ceiling. The mother came in, laughed an hour at the
foot-tracks, told Abe he ought to be spanked—and he cleaned the
ceiling so it looked new.

The mother said, "Abe never spoke a cross word to me in his
life since we lived together." And she said Abe was truthful;
when Tilda Johnston leaped onto Abe's back to give him a scare
on a lonely timber path, she brought the big axman to the ground
by pulling her hands against his shoulders and pressing her knee
into his backbone. The ax-blade cut her ankle, and strips from
Abe's shirt and Tilda's dress had to be used to stop the blood.
By then she was sobbing over what to tell her mother. On Abe's
advice she told her mother the whole truth.

As time went by, the stepmother of Abe became one of the rich,
silent forces in his life. Besides keeping the floors, pots, pans,
kettles, and milk-crocks spick and span, weaving, sewing, mending,
and managing with sagacity and gumption, she had a massive,
bony, human strength backed with an elemental faith that the
foundations of the world were mortised by God with unspeakable
goodness of heart toward the human family. Hard as life was, she
was thankful to be alive.

Once she told Abe how her brother Isaac, back in Hardin County,
had hot words with a cowardly young man who shot Isaac without
warning. The doctors asked Isaac if they could tie him down while
they cut his flesh and took out the bullet. He told them he didn't
need to be tied down; he put two lead musket-balls in between his
teeth and ground his teeth on them while the doctors cut a slash
nine inches long and one inch deep till they found the bullet
and brought it out. Isaac never let out a moan or a whimper;
he set his teeth into the musket-balls, ground them into flat sheets,
and spat them from his mouth when he thanked the doctors.

Sally Bush, the stepmother, was all of a good mother to Abe.
If he broke out laughing when others saw nothing to laugh at,
she let it pass as a sign of his thoughts working their own way.
So far as she was concerned he had a right to do unaccountable
things; since he never lied to her, why not? So she justified him.
When Abe's sister, Sarah, married Aaron Grigsby and a year after
died with her newborn child, it was Sally Bush who spoke comfort

to the eighteen-year-old boy of Nancy Hanks burying his sister and the wraith of a child.

A neighbor woman sized him up by saying, "He could work when he wanted to, but he was no hand to pitch in like killing snakes." John Romine made the remarks: "Abe Lincoln worked for me, but was always reading and thinking. I used to get mad at him for it. I say he was awful lazy. He would laugh and talk—crack his jokes and tell stories all the time; didn't love work half as much as his pay. He said to me one day that his father taught him to work, but he never taught him to love it."

A misunderstanding came up one time between Abe Lincoln and William Grigsby. It ended with Grigsby so mad he challenged Abe to a fight. Abe looked down at Grigsby, smiled, and said the fight ought to be with John Johnston, Abe's stepbrother. The day was set for the fight; each man was there with his seconds; the mauling began, with the two fighters stripped to the waist, beating and bruising each other with bare knuckles.

A crowd stood around, forming a ring, cheering, yelling, hissing, till after a while they saw Johnston getting the worst of it. Then the ring of people forming the crowd was broken as Abe Lincoln shouldered his way through, stepped out, took hold of Grigsby and threw that fighter out of the center of the fight-ring.

Then Abe Lincoln called out, "I'm the big buck of this lick." And looking around so his eyes swept the circle of the crowd he let loose the challenge, "If any of you want to try it, come on and whet your horns." A riot of wild fist-fighting came then between the two gangs and for months around the Jones grocery store there was talk about which gang whipped the other.

After a fox-chase with horses, Uncle Jimmy Larkin was telling how his horse won the race, was the best horse in the world, and never drew a long breath; Abe didn't listen; Uncle Jimmy told it again, and Abe said, "Why don't you tell us how many short breaths he drew?" It raised a laugh on Jimmy, who jumped around threatening to fight, till Abe said quietly, "Now, Larkin, if you don't shut up I'll throw you in that water."

Asked by Farmer James Taylor if he could kill a hog, he answered, "If you will risk the hog I'll risk myself."

He had the pride of youth that resents the slur, the snub,

besides the riotous blood that has always led youth in reckless exploits. When he was cutting up didos one day at the Crawford farm-house, Mrs. Crawford asked, "What's going to become of you, Abe?" And with mockery of swagger, he answered, "Me? I'm going to be president of the United States."

Driving a horse at the mill, he was sending the whiplash over the nag and calling, "Gip up, you old hussy; git up, you old hussy." The horse let fly a hind foot that knocked down the big boy just as he yelled, "Git up." He lay bleeding, was taken home, washed, put to bed, and lay all night unconscious. As his eye winkers opened the next day and he came to, his tongue struggled and blurted, "You old hussy," thus finishing what he started to say before the knockdown.

V

Heroes Sung
and Unsung

from Paris-Underground

ETTA SHIBER

The English Pilot

[*Until the spring of 1940 American citizen Etta Shiber and her friend Kitty Beaurepos had chosen to stay in Paris in spite of the advance of German troops. Then, along with thousands of others, they found that their attempt to escape had come too late.*]

It was already dark when we reached the national road again, but we knew in advance we were coming to it, for we could hear the nerve-racking cacophony of the honking horns, at first faintly, and then louder and louder as we approached. We guided ourselves by the sound, for we had lost all sense of direction. We didn't know at what point we were rejoining the road, or how far we were from Paris.

We had reached a point about a hundred yards from the road when we heard a faint hum which rose swiftly in a fierce crescendo over our heads. With a jerk, Kitty stopped the car—so suddenly that I felt that she must have been expecting that sound and dreading it.

The hum became a roar, as the airplane passed by just ahead of us, and from the roar emerged the staccato tat-tat-tat of a machine gun. We could see the hulk of the plane in a denser black against the dark sky, and the flame spitting from the nozzles of its guns, as it swept over the crowded road, pouring death into the trapped ranks below.

In a matter of seconds, the crowded highway was emptied of its human freight. Terror-stricken drivers turned their cars off the road, into trees, into ditches, over the fields. Some of them overturned, and their occupants squirmed out and ran in panic from the road, or threw themselves into ditches. Only a few cars remained in the road, stalled, motionless. The figures in them were motionless, too. They had not joined the mad rush to get off the road because they were dead. They had been mowed down indiscriminately, men, women and children, by the sudden hail of death that had rained down upon them out of the sky.

Twenty minutes later several more planes swooped low over the road, but there was little for them to do. No one had attempted to get back on the highway. Only the stalled cars of the dead still remained for targets.

We had thrown ourselves into a roadside ditch with other refugees, and stayed there through the second attack. For some time, we didn't dare venture out. We remained lying in the dirt, apprehensively scanning the sky in the direction of Paris, wondering whether it was over, or whether more planes might suddenly roar down upon us if we emerged from our shelter.

I felt Kitty's hand squeeze mine. I looked towards her. Her eyes were wet with tears.

"Don't be afraid, Kitty," I said. "God will protect us."

Kitty shook her head.

"I'm not afraid. That's not why I'm crying. I can't help it when I think of those poor people—here, and in Poland, in Belgium, in Holland, the poor innocent refugees on whom the Boches turned their machine guns to clear the roads for their armies. I read about it in Paris, of course, but I didn't really believe it. I didn't want to believe it. I thought it was propaganda. I didn't think even German officers would be capable of ordering the massacre of innocent people. I didn't think German soldiers would be brutal enough to obey such orders. But it's true. We've seen it ourselves. We've seen them shooting down harmless, unarmed, helpless civilians!"

Kitty was silent for a moment. Then she added, almost under her breath, as though she were talking to herself:

"How does a young German flier feel, I wonder, when he opens fire on terror-stricken women and children—like us?"

All about us there was a ghostly silence. We knew that there were hundreds of people nearby, hugging the ground in fear like ourselves, but we might have been alone in this unknown open country. Then we heard a woman groaning somewhere in the dark, not far away. From her moans, we judged that she had been wounded. But no one offered to go to her aid. No one dared move.

It seemed ages before first one or two, then dozens of men and women began to creep cautiously out of the ditches. They stood up, looking first towards the sky, and began to collect their scattered belongings. Some of them stood aimlessly in the fields, as though at a loss what to do. They had been going somewhere, they didn't quite know where, running from a danger behind them. And now the danger had caught up to them. They stood still, trapped, deprived of motion, with nowhere to go, nothing to do. And we were trapped with them.

From the darkness the noise of many motors made itself heard; and suddenly, with a rush, the German Army was upon us.

They were motorcycle troops, rushing southward at breakneck speed, driving forward through the dark with complete assurance that the planes ahead of them would have swept the road clear, like great brooms. Without slowing up, they swung around the few stalled cars still standing motionless in the road.

There was something inhuman about those riders in their dark gray uniforms. They seemed like part of the machines they rode, as cold and as unfeeling. They looked neither to the right nor to the left as they roared by. I don't know what we had expected from the Germans, but certainly not this, certainly not that they would ignore our very presence. It was more fearsome than if they had dismounted from their motorcycles and arrested us, almost more fearsome than if they had fired on us. This passage of mounted automatons who seemed not to see us at all imbued us with a chill far greater than any we had felt even during the confused panic of the airplane attack. I thought I had been frightened then. It was nothing to the deep-buried fear that clutched at the pit of my stomach, and twisted and turned in my flesh.

But there was nothing we could do. We could only wait. We stood by our car, just before the point where the crossroad entered the highway, and watched.

Light armored cars followed the motorcycles. Sitting bolt upright in them were more lifeless statues, very young soldiers, almost boys. Stiff and morose, they were dragged forward by the iron monsters in which they rode like victims to a sacrifice rather than triumphant conquerors. Not one of them spared even a glance for the refugees who lined the road on both sides. They were whisked by, pawns in the game of war, seemingly devoid of any human feelings, of joy or of pity.

The remnants of a French regiment sat alongside the road across from us. Half an hour before, the men beside the road and the men rushing down it might have been fighting each other. But now the battle had been adjourned, and they did not deign even to notice one another. The French soldiers sat beside the road, smoking, watching the procession of their enemies pass without seeming to see them. Their uniforms were clean. It was obvious that they had not yet been in battle. Perhaps they had been on their way to a front which had now disappeared. They had been too late, and there was no point in fighting now. They simply sat there and stared through the German soldiers passing south. And the Germans, in turn, glared forward stiffly into the empty air ahead. Nothing could have increased the effect of unreality, of a nightmare from which we must soon awake before the tension became intolerable, more than this mutual ignoring of one army by the other.

The rumble of heavier engines filled the air, and shook the earth about us. The tanks were coming. The very air seemed to have come to life and to be shouting with brazen lungs. They burst upon us, not only down the main highway, but from the crossroads, roaring upon us from the route which we had followed through the night, mercifully too slowly to reach the road before the Nazi planes swept over it. They plowed across the fields. They seemed to be everywhere, to possess the whole earth about us.

It was an interminable parade which passed before our eyes, lasting all night, and then through the day. It was five o'clock in the afternoon before the road cleared. As the rear guard of the German Army passed down the road and disappeared in its own dust, it dropped men off behind it. Every two hundred yards, unfolding in a regular pattern behind the moving army, a German motorcyclist stopped, and took up his position. The military necessities had been satisfied for this region. Now civilians could be attended to. At last there was some one charged with looking out for us.

The nearest motorcyclist swept up to us, and stopped, one foot on the ground, holding his machine up at an angle as its motor coughed and spat.

"You will go back to Paris," he told us in excellent French.

"But we were going the other way," Kitty pleaded. "We want to go to Nice."

The German's words were polite, but there was a sneer on his lips as he answered:

"That, Madame, is the way we are going. You will go back to Paris."

What else could we do? We turned our car into the highway, and started back over the same road we had taken southward, ages ago, it seemed, in another existence. Once again we were in the same congested stream of traffic. We moved once more at the same snail's pace, though in the opposite direction. But there was a difference now. No one seemed to be in any hurry to arrive. When the road was blocked, and there was a long wait, no horns tooted, no one shouted at those ahead to get going. Every once in a while, the motorcycle guards, obeying an order passed down the line, hustled us all off the road, into the ditches or the fields, and another motorized column would roar down the vacant lane we had left. Then we could turn back into the road again—those of us who had not broken axles or turned over in the process—and a few miles farther on repeat the same action all over again.

We passed a group of unarmed French soldiers standing by the roadside, guarded by Germans with fixed bayonets. They looked frightened, unlike fighting men. They had been taken one by one out of passing cars in which they had sought to escape.

A car ahead of us was stopped, and a squad of Germans pulled out a young man in civilian clothes. He protested:

"What are you taking me for? I'm not a soldier."

A German shouted at him coarsely:

"*Maul halten!* Do you think we're fools? You can't escape just by putting on civilian clothes, you know. Get over there with the others."

And he was shoved into the group of forlorn frightened French prisoners.

"Look," Kitty said suddenly. "*English* prisoners!"

It was a very small group, standing by the roadside, hemmed in by German guards. Three of them wore the uniform of the R.A.F. The car in which they had tried to escape was standing in the ditch at the side of the road.

By evening we reached the roadside inn where we had learned of the fall of Paris on the southward trip. We were exhausted, ready to drop. But when the innkeeper, standing in the doorway, saw us pull up and stop, he motioned us away.

"I have nothing to give you," he said, "nothing at all. A million people have been through here in the last two days. What can you expect? They have eaten everything. There is nothing left, nothing."

I started to climb wearily back into the car, but Kitty touched me on the arm. She was incomparable in such situations.

"A cup of tea will be enough for us," she said, turning her most winsome smile on the innkeeper.

"*Pensez-vous!* I have no sugar," the innkeeper said, none too graciously.

"That doesn't matter," said Kitty. "We'll take it without sugar." And she marched straight in and sat down.

It worked. The innkeeper led us into an inner room, locked the door carefully behind us, and produced not only tea, but the sugar he had denied having. Perhaps it was the effect of Kitty's disarming smile which caused him later to confess that he had a small piece of salami and a little cheese left that we might have also.

It was the first food we had tasted in thirty-six hours. We were so exhausted and so hungry that we had no thought of discussing our predicament until we had finished. But then we began to talk; and at our first words the innkeeper asked:

"You are English?"

"I'm English," Kitty answered, "but I'm a French citizen now, since I married a Frenchman. My friend here is American."

"Then you can do something for me," the innkeeper said. "I don't speak English myself, and I have some one here who speaks only English. I can't make him understand me. Could you talk to him for me? Ask him how long he intends to stay. Tell him that I am very sorry, I don't want to ask him to leave—but there are Germans all around, they are hunting for Englishmen, and—you understand—it is dangerous for me. I am likely to get into trouble if he stays. Wait here a minute. I will bring him to you."

He left the room. Kitty and I looked at one another.

"An English soldier, no doubt," Kitty said. "He hasn't a chance of escaping, of course. They're sure to get him."

When the innkeeper returned, he was followed by a tall young man with reddish blond hair wearing a leather coat, beneath which the gray-blue uniform of the R.A.F. was visible. He was very young —barely twenty, it seemed. He came up to our table, smiling as calmly as though he were surrounded by friends, miles from any danger. He sat down with us, and told us in a few words who he was and how he had come to be there.

His name was William Gray. A pilot caught at Dunkirk, he had been unable to get to the evacuating ships and return to England. But with the aid of French peasants, he had managed to work his way through the German lines and had set out for the south of France, hoping to get below the territory held by the Germans. But they had moved faster than he had, and here they had caught up with him.

"I don't want to trouble you ladies," he said apologetically, "but if you would just tell this chap for me to be patient, that I will go as soon as he can get me some civilian clothes, I will be able to take care of myself after that."

"My poor friend," Kitty said, "civilian clothes won't do you any good. We've just come from the south, and we saw the Germans taking young men out of automobiles, uniforms or no uniforms. They'll take any one of military age. And as for you, who don't know a word of French—why, you couldn't walk ten steps without being caught."

The young flier stared at us incredulously. His face reflected disappointment and dismay.

"You think there's no chance? How about cutting across the fields?"

"Oh, that's just childish!" Kitty exclaimed, almost angrily. "The Germans are searching everywhere. They'll get you before you even reach a village."

The innkeeper had been standing in the doorway during this conversation, straining his ears as though he could understand by listening more closely. Now he broke in.

"What does he say?" he asked. "Is he going to go? I'm very sorry, you know—but really, you see how it is. I can't keep him here. They may come any minute. It is very dangerous."

"Have you any civilian clothes you can sell him?" Kitty asked.

"Never in the world!" the innkeeper cried excitedly. "*Quelle folie!* Tell him he must not put on civilian clothes. I am a good Frenchman, I hate the Germans and I respect the English, but that is something I can't do for him. It will mean his death if they catch him!"

We looked at the innkeeper in bewilderment.

"But don't you understand?" he hurried on, impatiently. "Explain this to him: if he is caught wearing his uniform, he will be treated as a prisoner of war. If he is in civilian clothes, he will be considered a spy. They will simply shoot him at once."

Kitty translated. Gray sat still for a moment. He hadn't thought of that.

"I guess they've got me," he said finally. He rose, with an embarrassed smile.

"I'm sorry I disturbed you, ladies. Will you do one more thing for me? Find out how much I owe. I'd better get out of here as soon as I can. If I'm going to be caught anyway, I'd better not involve any one else."

No translation was necessary. The innkeeper saw the Englishman take out his purse, and realized that he was about to be rid of his dangerous guest. Too happy at this relief to be interested in money, he pushed aside the Englishman's hand, indicating by gestures that he wanted no payment. Also in gestures, William Gray expressed his thanks, and moved, with uncertain step, towards the door.

"What are you going to do?" Kitty asked.

He turned, still smiling, a forced smile through which his weariness and despair showed only too plainly.

"I don't know," he answered, "but please don't worry about me. I'll be all right. I hope you'll excuse me for intruding on you."

I pressed Kitty's arm.

"Don't let him go," I whispered. Kitty looked at me in surprise. "Haven't you noticed," I went on, "how much he looks like Irving —the same nose, the same chin? He looks exactly as poor Irving did when he was twenty."

Kitty had known my brother well, before that awful day when we buried him in the Père Lachaise cemetery in Paris.

"If only for the sake of Irving's memory, we can't let this boy go," I begged. "We've got to get him out of this. We can't let the Germans get him."

"That's all very well," said Kitty, "but how can we prevent it? What can we do?"

"I have an idea," I went on. "Our car is just outside . . ."

"But you're crazy!" Kitty exclaimed. "Don't you remember how they stopped all the cars? They'd pick him up before we got half a mile away. You don't think the German military police will let us cart him off right under their noses, do you?"

"Wait a minute, Kitty," I said. "I've thought of that. How about our luggage compartment? If we take the trunk out, he can hide there."

"All the way to Paris?"

"Yes," I said, "all the way to Paris. He'll have a better chance of giving the Germans the slip in a big city than here. We'll get him to Paris, and then figure out what to do with him there."

Kitty beamed on me with that enchanting smile which I had come to love so much in the years we had spent together. Automatically, she took over command again. I vaguely suspected her of having thought of the same plan before I uttered a word, and having simply left it to me to express what both of us desired. She hurried into the outer room, where William Gray was standing at the window, peering cautiously out towards the road.

"I say, Mr. Gray," she said, "come back here a moment. We want to talk to you."

And with that sentence, we were launched upon an adventure which a week earlier we would have dismissed as impossibly fantastic. Yet it had come about so naturally that neither Kitty nor myself realized that we had projected ourselves into a new course from which we would not thereafter be able to escape. We had closed the door on our calm unruffled existence.

It was no easy job for William Gray to stow himself away in the luggage compartment of our car, but he had to admit that it couldn't have been better arranged as a hiding place if it had been built especially for that purpose. It didn't open from the outside, like most luggage compartments. On the contrary, the opening was from the interior of the car, behind the back seats.

He was unfortunately tall, but luckily thin. He pulled himself in somehow or other, his long legs doubled up under him, and grinned at our expressions, which must have indicated our doubt that any one could ride long in so cramped a position.

"Now don't you worry about me," he assured us. "I'm quite comfortable. If by any chance the Germans find me here, you must swear up and down that you never saw me before in your lives, and don't know how I got in here. I'll say that I slipped in while you were in the inn eating. That way you won't get into any trouble on my account—in case."

We closed the luggage compartment on our passenger, and were on our way. The highway had cleared up somewhat now, and we made reasonable progress. There were guards all along the road, and three times before we reached the Porte d'Orléans, the point from which we had left Paris, we were stopped, and asked to show our papers.

We held them out with trembling hands, and our hearts were in our mouths as the guards peered into the car. But none of them made any motion to look into the luggage compartment and each time we drove on again, hearts thumping, but bursting with relief.

At the Porte itself, a more elaborate control had been set up. A German soldier assigned to inspect our car threw open the door, pushed our baggage aside and scrutinized the interior carefully, using a flashlight to illuminate every corner. His hand grazed the luggage compartment, and I held my breath. But he made no move to open it. He turned to us, and said in perfect French:

"Well, ladies, your wanderings on the French highways are over —at least, if you can prove you live in Paris. Have you your papers?"

We produced our identity cards, which gave our Paris address. Satisfied, he waved us on.

As soon as we were out of hearing, Kitty turned to me with a self-satisfied chuckle.

"Those efficient Germans aren't so smart, after all," she laughed. "Imagine! Four of them, and not one thought to look into the luggage compartment!"

"Thank God they didn't," I replied. "But after all, it's not so surprising. With a sentry every two hundred yards along the road watching every one who moves, it probably never occurred to them that any one would have an opportunity to stow some one away. Besides, the military police are only common soldiers. They've probably never seen a luggage compartment opening into a car before, and haven't any idea there would be room for a man to hide in it."

"There isn't much," Kitty said. "If we have to stop again, you'd better take a look at the poor fellow to make sure he hasn't suffocated."

A muffled voice reassured us from within the luggage compartment.

"I'm perfectly all right," William Gray said. "The only thing that worries me is that I might get you into trouble."

"Hush," Kitty warned him. "Not another word. Some one might hear you."

Although we had made better time coming back than going, still it had taken us all night to reach Paris. By the time we had cleared the bottleneck of the Porte d'Orléans, where thousands of returning refugees like ourselves were having their papers checked by the German military police, it was broad daylight. Once out of the congestion about the gate, we were able to speed along the outer boulevards at a normal pace, for the first time since we had started out. All about us we saw the signs of the German occupation.

It was with a constriction of the heart that I saw the Eiffel Tower again, for at its top, where the French Tricolor had always whipped proudly to the breeze, the Nazi swastika now flew.

German military cars rushed past us. When we reached the bridge we wanted to take across the Seine we had a long wait, until a German motorized regiment had passed over it. We went by the Louvre, and there, too, we saw the swastika flying where the Tricolor should have been.

But as we swung through the Place de la Concorde and into the Champs-Elysées, I could not restrain the feeling of joy at being back in Paris, even under the Germans, which always gripped me whenever I returned from a trip to look up that magnificent stretch towards the beautiful silhouette of the Arc de Triomphe, shining at the top of its hill against the clear blue sky.

Beneath its vault, I knew, lay the body of the Unknown Soldier, guarded by the Eternal Flame. From this point, every year, the great military parades which commemorated the storming of the Bastille, July 14, the day of French independence, took their start. I remembered how, nearly a year ago, I had seen the French Army in all its impressive might march down this broad avenue, followed by tanks which shook the ground and made the air vibrate with their roar, while from the sky behind the Arc, 600 planes swooped down above the procession. And now that mighty army had been defeated, and the avenue over which Louis the Fourteenth's horses had pelted to Versailles, the avenue over which Napoleon's victorious forces had marched into the city, was filled with hurrying German military cars, the swastika painted on their sides . . .

We circled the Arc, and a moment later the car ground to a stop in front of 2, Rue Balny d'Avricourt—home!

"At last," Kitty said, cutting the motor. "Very good. Very, very good indeed."

I was panic-stricken at the idea of getting out of the car. Somehow it had seemed safer to be sitting in it. It was our fortress.

"What do we do now?" I asked faintly.

"We must be very careful," Kitty said. "We must be discreet, and

we must be on the alert every instant. Don't make any false moves
—just act natural."

"Do—do I get out first?" I gulped.

I sensed imaginary Nazis everywhere, waiting to pounce upon me
the moment I set foot on the ground. They might be watching us
from behind lamp posts, or around the corner, or from any window in
the street. They might even be waiting for us in the entrance, ready
to trap us as we came in.

"Wait!" Kitty whispered tensely.

A German military guard came marching down the street, surrounding a French soldier. They have probably been searching the houses,
I thought, looking for soldiers in hiding, and this is one of the poor
chaps they caught.

We remained in the car, motionless. I looked at Kitty, and she
seemed very pale. I wondered if she had just realized fully, as I had,
at that very moment, that this adventure of ours could be very dangerous for ourselves, that William Gray was not the only one of us
who risked being shot.

We waited for a few moments after the Germans had disappeared
around the corner.

Kitty turned towards the luggage compartment.

"Mr. Gray! Can you hear me?" she called softly.

"Yes," came his muffled voice.

"We are going to get out now. Button up your leather coat over
your uniform before you come out. I'll go first, then Etta, then you
slip out, follow us into the house and get into the elevator right
after us. Act naturally, and don't hesitate, whether we meet any one
or not. Don't say anything now. The street is clear. Here we go!"

Briskly, Kitty opened the car door and stepped out. If I had
worried about going first a moment ago, I was twice as frightened
now at the prospect of being left behind. I sprang out of the car
after Kitty and hurried across the sidewalk behind her. I heard the
door of the car slam shut, and I knew William Gray was just behind
me. I didn't dare look back. It was only a few steps across the sidewalk, but it seemed to take forever to cross it. Then we were in the
familiar entry of our home, and I felt better. We were in luck.
There was no one in the hall, and the elevator, of the self-service

type common in French apartment houses, was, for once, empty, and waiting on the ground floor.

We got in without losing a second, fearful that some other tenant might follow behind us. The doors swung shut, Kitty pressed the sixth floor button, and the elevator rumbled slowly upward. I held my breath. My nails were cutting into the palms of my hands. I didn't dare look at either of the others.

It seemed to me that the elevator took long enough to rise to the top of the Empire State Building. At last it jarred to a stop. Kitty stepped out, fitted her key into the lock, and pushed open our apartment door. We hurried in, and I threw myself against the door and pushed the safety bolt, in a state approaching panic. For a moment, I leaned against the door. My legs seemed too weak to support my weight. Then I tottered towards a chair and sat down. It was good to sit down, safe in my own apartment, surrounded by my own familiar belongings.

Kitty's nerves must have been better than mine. She threw herself into an armchair and laughed happily.

"There, you see, Etta, everything went off very neatly," she said. "Who would believe us if we told them that we had smuggled an English aviator past hundreds of German guards into Paris, and into our apartment?"

I was still shaken.

"Thank God for our good luck," I said. "Suppose we had met some one downstairs or in the elevator? I'm certainly glad that's over. I wouldn't go through it again for a million dollars."

I wonder what I would have done if I could have had a flash of the future when I spoke those words? I thought we had come to the end of our adventure. It was only beginning.

"Oh, it might not have been so bad even if some one had seen him," Kitty said. "They might not have noticed his uniform under that coat. By the way, what's become of him?"

William Gray appeared in the doorway.

"You know, I shouldn't have done this," he said. "I didn't realize —I shouldn't have let you take so much risk on my account. I really don't know what to say. I can't forgive myself for putting you in such a position."

He looked younger than ever in his embarrassment. The expression on his face showed his genuine deep concern.

"Now listen to me, young man," Kitty said firmly. "On the road, you were planning to tell any one who discovered you that you had crept into our car without our knowledge, and let us out of it that way. Well, you can't do that now. You're in our apartment, and no one is going to make the Germans believe, if they catch you, that we don't know you and have no idea how you got in. We're your accomplices now. We're all in this together, and there's no point in worrying about water that's gone over the dam. You're our guest. Make yourself at home, and forget about how we got into this pickle. What we have to do now is figure out how to get out of it."

And with that, she swept off to her own room to tidy up, humming a gay little melody which always came into her head when she felt particularly happy, and, above all, pleased with herself.

It was easy enough for Kitty to say that we had to find some way of getting out of our predicament, but it wasn't so simple to do. Here we were, two middle-aged respectable women of sheltered background, with an English pilot on our hands, in enemy territory, and our problem was to find out how he could escape and get back to England. We knew it could be done, we knew that some persons had done it, but we had no idea how to go about it.

I remembered the "underground railway" of pre-Civil War days, which spirited runaway slaves into the free states. I supposed some similar organization existed to help hidden English soldiers—but how could we get in touch with it? It didn't seem likely that any one in our quiet circle would know anything about it. We were baffled, completely at a loss. We didn't know where to turn, how to begin.

Meantime the Gestapo was conducting its search for hidden soldiers with characteristic thoroughness. House to house searches yielded many Frenchmen of military age, hiding with friends or relatives or even with complete strangers, who had taken them in just as we had taken William Gray in. Once in a while they also got an English civilian or soldier. We heard that they relished such captures particularly; so we knew that our guest would strike them as a particular prize—if they caught him.

We lived for a week in an atmosphere of almost constant terror, expecting daily that the Gestapo would get around to us. We were as careful as we could be. William never went near the window, never answered the telephone. We even refused to let him smoke his pipe, lest the odor should give him away. It irked him that he couldn't shave, since, of course, he had had nothing with him, and we didn't dare to make the unexplainable purchase of a razor.

Whenever the doorbell rang, William dashed to the bathroom and locked himself in. But we realized that this would be no good if the Germans really wished to search the apartment, and after a while he gave it up.

The possibility of a search was a real danger, not a fancy conjured up out of our fear. The Germans were doing it daily. They took a block at a time, shut off all the streets leading to it, and then went through it methodically, apartment by apartment, not forgetting the cellars and roofs, searching every nook and cranny.

It was very clear that if such a search occurred in our block, William would certainly be found—and we would be arrested along with him. As the searches continued, it became daily more evident that it was urgent to find a solution. Our immunity could not last forever.

But where could we turn for help?

Both of us had many friends in Paris, but most of them seemed to have gotten away earlier than we did, and were in the unoccupied zone. Kitty sat at the telephone for hours, dialling one number after the other, but always the regular distant hum told her that no one was at the other end of the line. Some of our friends had made no attempt to leave Paris; but, perhaps not very curiously, those who had been willing to stay behind though they knew the Germans were coming were not the ones we felt we could trust with our secret.

For by this time, the change had already taken place which split the French people into two groups—those who were pro-British and those who were anti-British, which was practically the same thing as saying those who were anti-Vichy and those who were pro-Vichy. Later, as the Germans taught the French to hate them, the pro-British element increased greatly; but in the opening days of the occupation, deceived by clever German propaganda and the studied and ordered politeness of the Germans, which masked their real intentions, many Frenchmen bowed to the act of Marshal Pétain in concluding an armistice with the Germans.

A formidable propaganda campaign was begun, attacking the pre-war régime of France, democracies in general, and the British in particular. The newspapers and the radio, all under German control, insisted day after day that the British were to blame for the defeat of France, that Britain had forced France into the war and then abandoned her to her fate when catastrophe threatened. The propagandists even went back into history, and brought out a popular-priced edition of the story of the trial of Jeanne d'Arc, to show that English perfidy had been exercised against France even then, when they burned a Frenchwoman who has since become a saint.

The continuous reiteration of this propaganda began to have its effect upon some Frenchmen. They had at first sought to explain the staggering blow which had been dealt them by some hitherto unsuspected military weakness of the French Army, or by the effect on the public morale of the broadcasts of Ferdonnet, the traitor of Stuttgart, who spoke nightly to France from Germany. But under the impact of German propaganda, Frenchmen began to discover a new scapegoat—the English. There were many of them who were ready to impute all the blame to them. And so France was divided into two camps, those who accepted this German theory which placed responsibility on the English, and those who fought against it.

Most of our acquaintances who had stayed in Paris belonged to the first group. Paris was still more or less deserted. Few persons had returned of their own free will. But once in a while we would meet some old friend in the street. If Kitty felt that he might prove sympathetic, she would hint that we had heard something about an English aviator in hiding, anxious to escape to England, hoping thus to find some one who might help us.

But the result was invariable. Always our friend's face would harden and his manner become cold. We would feel a sense of restraint between us. We knew that none of them would report us, but we knew also that they would do nothing to help us. They were afraid. We could understand that, for we were afraid too.

The only one who shared our secret was our Breton maid, Margot, who had been with Kitty for twelve years. We trusted her completely. When we returned to Paris, we sent word to her at her native village, to which she had gone some time before we left, and she returned to us immediately. She often heard our long conversations about the steps we thought of taking to help save William Gray. She never joined them, never mentioned him, but we knew she would not betray us.

Nothing useful came out of those long futile conversations. Through them, we arrived at only one positive conclusion. That was that we had not only the Germans, but also a certain group of Frenchmen, to fear. We had to be careful everywhere, with every one. It was not safe to assume that every Frenchman was automatically the enemy of the Germans who had conquered his country.

Fearful though we were for ourselves during this period, we could not fail to be touched by the behavior of William Gray. He was so tactful, so inconsolable that his presence was causing us so much concern, and so worried, not for himself, but for us, at the fact that there seemed to be no solution to the situation, that we felt more strongly than ever that we had done right in bringing him to Paris. More than ever, we felt that we must find some way to save him.

Once we caught him tiptoeing out of the door, dressed to leave, trying to relieve us of our troubles by removing from us the risk of his presence. Kitty pulled his leather jacket off herself, and scolded him like a little boy caught in some naughtiness.

"Besides," she ended, after a torrent of scolding, "that wouldn't have solved anything. They'd have caught you before you could get off this street. Do you think it would have been hard for them to find out where you came from? No, it's just no good, my young man. And whatever you may think, it isn't courageous either. It's unworthy of you, and it's unworthy of us."

"But really," William protested, "it's cowardly of me to stay here while my very presence is endangering you every day I remain."

With typical energy, Kitty put him in his place at once.

"I never heard such nonsense!" she snorted. "Cowardly, indeed! We're perfectly safe as long as you don't leave here. Who would think to look here for a British soldier? What's the use of all the trouble we've gone to already if you're not going to let us finish the job? Ungrateful brat!"

And she smiled broadly at the boy she was berating.

"Now let that be the last of that. You're staying here until we find out how to get you out of reach of the Germans. I don't know whether it will take a week or a month or the duration, but I do know one thing—we're not going to let you out of here until we know the Germans won't get you."

There was nothing William could do except give in. He went to his room with a heart-rending smile of gratitude on his worried boyish face. As the door closed behind him, Kitty turned towards me. I had thought she was exaggerating her emotion for William's benefit, but now I could see that she was still deeply agitated, profoundly troubled by what had just happened.

"Etta," she said, "we just *can't* let him go. I wouldn't have any peace of mind for the rest of my life. I hadn't told you before, because I didn't want to worry you unnecessarily, but I hear they're shooting all the British soldiers they catch now. They treat them as spies."

"How do you know?" I asked.

"Mr. Vuillemin told me. Of course, I don't know whether he was telling the truth or not, but what reason would he have to lie? He told me about one case in Belgium where the Germans rounded up a company of French soldiers. There was a British soldier with them. He had his uniform on, but he had some civilian clothes in a bag. He had intended to use them to escape. They lined up the Frenchmen and marched them off as prisoners of war, but they charged the Englishman with having civilian clothes because he was a spy, and shot him on the spot."

A sickening wave seemed to pass through me as I imagined the bullets of a firing squad tearing into the skull of the gentle boy in the next room.

"But, Kitty, you don't think they could treat William that way?"

"I'm afraid they could," Kitty said. "That story has been haunting me like a nightmare ever since Mr. Vuillemin told it to me—and you know he isn't the sort of peson to pass on mere rumors. Every time I think of it, I think of poor naïve William Gray, and I'm determined they shan't get the chance to murder him. That's why we mustn't let him slip out, Etta, even though he is willing to sacrifice himself for us. We've *got* to keep him from falling into the hands of the Germans."

But once again, it was easier said than done. Trains were running regularly now from Paris to the unoccupied zone, but there seemed to be no solution there. We could perhaps have gotten him a pass (for once the German administration established itself in Paris, anything could be had from it for a price, even a pass to the unoccupied zone), but an official pass was no guarantee he could get out. Inspection of papers at the border between the two zones was most severe, and the authorities did not hesitate to send a whole train back for the slightest irregularity. We heard of one train which was sent back to Paris three times before it was finally permitted to cross the border. And, of course, William did not speak French.

The more we heard about those trains, the surer we were that we dared not send him out of the occupied zone by that route. We learned that the Germans examined every compartment minutely, to make sure that nothing and nobody was hidden in it. Passengers were searched, uniformed female police being provided to inspect the women.

It was forbidden to carry any written document from one zone to the other, and the police made an especially rigid search for letters. They were described as arrogant, affecting contempt and disgust while they turned out the contents of trunks and handbags. They seemed to take special delight in ordering passengers to step off trains to the platform for further investigation when they reached the border at night, after every one had undressed and gone to bed in the sleepers. We were told that they showed a preference for ordering women in flimsy night dresses off the train in this fashion.

Even after inspections had been finished, trains were sometimes held for hours, without explanation, while the anxious passengers wondered what was wrong, and doubted if they would ever get safely out of German territory. Sometimes, though all papers were in order, the passengers would be told that the frontier was closed and the train couldn't go through. That usually meant a wait of several days.

That was the legal way of crossing the frontier. We were sure it would never do for William. He would have to get across it by stealth—and we had heard a thousand stories about that.

We had been told that persons crossing the demarcation line surreptitiously had to go on foot, being careful to avoid the guards on both sides of the border. At first, the penalty for being caught was only being returned to the zone you were trying to escape from. Then orders were given to open fire on anyone seen trying to get from one region into the other. Some persons were killed in this fashion, and those who were only wounded were sentenced to long terms in prison.

Yet men still risked their lives to get out of German-held territory nightly. They had to sacrifice all their belongings, for of course they could carry no baggage on a trip which might oblige them to walk as much as ten miles across rough country in pitch darkness. There were volunteer guides who would take them across, and sometimes sentinels could be bribed. But here, too, caution was necessary. Sometimes a guide would lead his charges straight into the arms of the Germans and collect a reward for his services. Or a sentry would accept a bribe—and then fire on the refugees who had paid him. Nobody could be trusted.

Many ingenious ruses were used to cross the line. In one village, for instance, there was a cemetery whose main gate opened into unoccupied territory. But in the rear wall was an old forgotten door which had not served for years; and that was in unoccupied territory. Inhabitants of the village at first were surprised to note a sudden increase in the number of mourners at local funerals. But they noted also that fewer mourners returned from the cemetery than went to it; and the old-timers recalled the disused door and realized that it was serving once more.

Another story we heard was that of a doctor whose house happened to straddle the line of demarcation. His practice increased enormously—for after seeing his patients, he let them go out by either the front or back door, without inquiring by which they had entered.

But none of these stories helped us, for naturally by the time they had become common knowledge, the Germans knew them, too. They had already arrested those concerned and plugged the leaks in the frontier by the time we heard about them. We couldn't find any one who knew about any such means of getting across the border which hadn't yet been discovered. Day after day, we ran up against a blank wall in our attempts to find out how to get William Gray out of danger.

Kitty was late for supper. Margot had prepared what she could. It wasn't much. We had discovered from bitter personal experience the truth of what we had been told, that wherever the Germans appeared, food disappeared. We had an extra disadvantage. We had three ration cards in the house—but four mouths to feed.

When Kitty breezed in, I could tell at once from the look on her face that it was good news which had detained her.

"Imagine, Etta!" she burst out, before she had even taken her hat off. "I've found some one who can help us! Do you remember Chancel, of the Gueules Cassées?"

I remembered him very well. He was a big husky chap, who had suffered a face wound in the last war. The men disfigured in that fashion had formed their own association, and called it Les Gueules Cassées (The Broken Mugs). Chancel held some official position in this group, exactly what I don't remember. We had met him at the Foyer du Soldat, where we had both worked before our attempt to get out of Paris.

"I ran into him on the subway," Kitty said. "I couldn't say very much to him there, of course, for you can never tell who may be listening. They say some Gestapo agents do nothing except ride back and forth on the subways, listening to everything that's said. But the few words we exchanged gave me the impression that he can and will help us. I trust him. He's a real Frenchman, one who won't ever compromise with the Germans. I made an appointment to see him tomorrow afternoon."

We were all cheered up by even this faint glimmering of hope, and we treated our scanty meal as though it were a gala feast. For the first time, I saw a smile on William's face which wasn't distorted by some other emotion—fear, or worry, or anxiety for us. He had been particularly depressed during the last few days, and it was good to see him care-free for once.

We sat together in the living room after dinner drinking our last treasured coffee, which Margot had brought out because she sensed that this special treat would coincide with our holiday mood. We didn't talk. The silence seemed soothing, and we sat quietly, sipping our coffee, and thinking, all of us, of that interview next day which we hoped—no, which we believed—would end our troubles.

And then the doorbell rang.

Today, as I write these lines, that strident peal is months behind me, but I feel again the chill which seized my whole body and the cold perspiration which started from every pore. I don't know why that particular ring should have sounded like the trump of doom, unless it was because I knew, deep down inside me, that we were basing our happiness on the most fragile of hopes; and so an equally fragile interruption could destroy it, and plunge me back at once into the abyss of fear where I had dwelt for the past week. Or perhaps it was that there was a sharp, aggressive, urgent quality about that ringing, bequeathed to it by the finger which pressed upon the button, arrogant and unfriendly.

I can still see the pale frightened face of Margot as she slipped into the room and closed the door behind her. She almost whispered, in a colorless voice:

"The Germans are here."

Kitty was the first to recover from the icy terror which gripped all of us.

"Soldiers?"

"No, civilians."

"It must be the Gestapo," Kitty gasped.

There was an instant of silence so intense that I could hear Kitty's heavy breathing. Then she swung to me:

"Quick! Take Bill to your room. Try to hide him somewhere." She cast a swift glance around the room.

"Take the third cup with you. Hurry!"

She shoved us in the direction of the door. As we went out, we heard her say, lifting her voice so that she could be heard outside, in a tone indicating impatience with a frightened servant:

"Don't be silly, Margot! Don't keep the gentlemen waiting. Bring them in here."

I was standing in the center of my room, straining my ears, trying to hear what Kitty was saying. I couldn't; but it seemed to me that they, in the next room, must be able to hear the beating of my heart. Each pulse sounded in my ears like the blow of a hammer.

William sat on the edge of the sofa, his head bent forward on his chest, his hands clenched. I wondered if he were praying. I remained standing only because I was petrified, my limbs too weak even to carry me to the sofa.

Kitty had told me to hide William. But how? Where? There wasn't even a closet in the room. The bathroom? Surely, if they searched at all, they would look there. What difference whether they found him here or there?

I stood still, immovable, thoughts and fears pursuing one another in my head in a mad torrent. Out of the vague indistinct familiarity of the objects about me, two of them suddenly took on sharpness and clarity as they caught my eye—the photographs, standing on my dresser, of the two men who had been dearest in the world to me— my husband, whom I had buried in New York, and my brother, who was resting here in Paris, in the cemetery of Père Lachaise.

In that ghastly moment, as if the two pictures had come to life, I could hear the very tones of their voices within me, and what they seemed to be saying was characteristic of what I had often heard them say in real life.

I imagined my husband's voice, as he would have said: "Well, Etta, you've gotten yourself into a pretty mess. But don't lose your head. There must be a way out."

And I seemed to hear my brother say, as he had said so often when he was alive:

"Don't worry, Etta. I'll fix everything up."

Even in my disarray, I could not help noticing again how much this picture of my brother looked like the young man sitting in anguish on the edge of the sofa, waiting for his executioners to come and lead him away to the firing squad. And suddenly I understood how my brother really was going to help us, how he was going to get us out of this dilemma.

I darted to the sofa, grasped William by the arm, started tearing at his clothes.

"Quick!" I whispered. "Get off your clothes, and into bed. Pretend you are very ill. Leave the talking to me."

Together we pulled off his outer clothing as I whispered my plan to him in quick short phrases. He was in bed in a matter of seconds. I tied a towel around his head—just in time. For at that moment. I heard Kitty calling:

"Etta, where are you? This gentleman wants to see your room."

As I came into the living room, it seemed to me that the piercing glance of the Gestapo agent bored right through me. But I was strengthened for the part I had to play by the slight amusement I was able to feel, even through my terror, at the short moustache with which he had slavishly copied his master. Somehow that made him seem less terrifying, reduced the fear always induced by the word "Gestapo."

He was not alone. Two other plainclothesmen were standing in the doorway. Behind them I could see Madame Beugler, our concierge, her suspicious eyes watching every move of the German. It was easy to see that he would get no help from her.

I admired the calm with which Kitty was conducting herself. She introduced me with a smile which only one who knew her as well as I did could have realized was forced.

"This is my very dear American friend, Mrs. Shiber," she said. "She has been living with me in Paris, and finds herself an unwitting victim of the war, far from home—like yourself."

I steeled myself to be as natural as possible, while I said:

"Come this way if you want to see my room. You'll have to excuse its appearance. My brother is in bed. He's quite ill. I'm afraid he may have contracted intestinal flu, there's so much of it in town now. I hope you won't have to disturb him."

I could see surprise on the faces of both Kitty and the concierge, but fortunately that Gestapo agent wasn't looking at them. I evaded their eyes, for fear I'd betray myself, but turned towards my room and opened the door for the policeman.

He stepped across the threshold. William made a realistic invalid, with his unshaven face and the towel about his head.

"It's all right, Irving," I said soothingly. "Don't try to talk." I turned to the agent. "This is my brother," I said.

The Gestapo man darted a single swift glance at the bed.

"His papers, please," he said curtly.

I opened the drawer in my bureau where I kept all documents— the drawer towards which it had seemed to me the eyes of my brother in the photograph were looking when, a few minutes ago, I had suddenly realized that there was a way out. I took out the red wallet which had remained undisturbed there ever since Irving's death, drew out his American passport and the green identity card issued to all foreigners in France by the police, and handed them over.

The Gestapo official flipped through the pages of the passport. He came to the picture of my brother, and flashed another quick glance towards the bed. I thanked God again for William's unshaven face, and also for the fact that the passport, issued some years back, carried a picture taken when Irving was nearer William's age.

The policeman closed the passport, and opened the identity card.

"This card has expired," he said. "Why wasn't it renewed?"

"We intended to go back to America, because of the war," I said. "We would have gone long ago, if his health had been better. It didn't seem worth renewing it under the circumstances."

I knew that unrenewed identity cards were not unusual. So, apparently, did the German. He handed the card back without comment, and asked for my papers. Those, I knew, were in order, and I breathed more freely. He checked them, returned them with a frigid word of thanks, and left the bedroom. I breathed again. Our ordeal was over!

But there I was wrong. I had not counted on the methodical technique of the Germans.

Back in the living room, the Gestapo officer said to one of his aides:

"The list of tenants."

He took it, looked through it carefully. Then he turned towards Madame Beugler:

"I do not find the name of Madame's brother on this list."

I was thunderstruck. This was something I had not thought of. My knees weakened again. After all my acting, I thought, after we had apparently succeeded, were we to be tripped up by this minute detail?

It was Kitty's turn to save the situation. Mme. Beugler was obviously confused and frightened. Kitty spoke up:

"Goodness, it's no crime to forget a name, is it? Irving isn't a regular tenant here, anyhow. He has only been here since he was ill and needed some one to take care of him."

Mme. Beugler rose nobly to the occasion.

"I'm sorry, sir," she said to the policeman. *"Je suis idiote—I* forgot about the gentleman. He never asked me for a certificate of domicile, so he isn't on my list."

I held my breath for a few seconds which seemed like an age.

The Nazi sat down slowly at the table, took out his fountain pen, and put on a pair of glasses, which he drew from his pocket. This might have made him seem less formidable also—but I was too frightened to think of that at the moment. What did he intend to write, I wondered? Perhaps a warrant for our arrest?

What he did was to take the list of tenants, and add to it, in his own writing, the name of my brother Irving!

It had worked! We were saved! I wanted to shout with joy, but we were not yet alone. One of the two assistants looked perfunctorily into the closets and bathroom—and I rejoiced that I hadn't tried to hide William.

When they declared themselves satisfied that we were innocent of concealing anything or anybody, the Gestapo agent picked up his hat, and the procession started out, inspecting the entry on the way. The door closed behind them. Kitty instinctively sprang to it, and pushed the bolt.

Now I no longer had any desire to shout with joy. I had suddenly gone limp inside. Kitty leaned her back against the door, and we looked into each other's eyes in silence. Next door we heard the loud long peal of the doorbell.

In the doorway of my room appeared a pale-faced unshaven young man in his underwear, a towel tied around his head.

"What happened?" asked William Gray.

Not until we were sure the Gestapo men had left the building did we dare sit down again around the small table in the living room, from which, half an hour earlier, we had been precipitated in an instant from bliss to terror.

Without a word from us, Margot brought in a bottle of champagne and three glasses. We clinked them solemnly together as we drank a silent toast to our escape.

"How in the world did it ever occur to you to pass William off as your brother, Etta?" Kitty asked. "Had you thought of it before?"

"No," I said. "The idea had never entered my head. It must have been the danger that inspired me—or Irving. I think it was Irving.

We have him to thank that we are not the prisoners of the Gestapo now."

And I told her of how Irving's photograph had caught my eye, and how I imagined that his voice had said he would help me.

"It's a miracle, Etta," Kitty said with conviction. "It's nothing short of a miracle. It's not so much that you thought of your brother's papers. The stupid thing is that we didn't think of that before, for you remember you were first attracted to William because he resembled your brother. The miracle is that that sharp-eyed Gestapo man didn't notice that the photograph on your bureau is a later picture of the man whose photo was on the passport—obviously a man twenty years older than William."

"I don't know how I looked," William said, "but I swear to you that while he was in the room I felt old enough to pass for my grandfather."

And with that, we all went off into peals of uncontrollable, almost hysterical, laughter, as our tortured nerves at last sought relief in merriment.

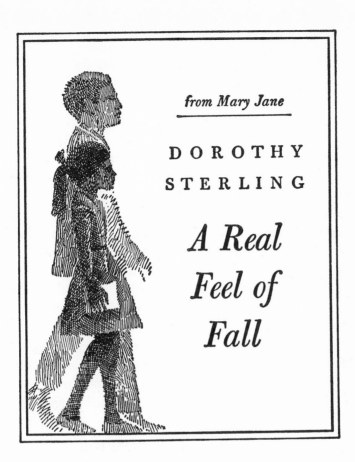

from Mary Jane

DOROTHY
STERLING

*A Real
Feel of
Fall*

I t was Mary Jane's last week on the farm. Purple asters were blooming in the fields. Katydids were singing their end-of-summer song. And Mamma had written that she was coming on Thursday to carry Mary Jane back home.

When Mary Jane was a little girl, too little to know about East and West and the earth turning on its axis, she thought that the sun rose on the road in front of Grampa's farm and set in the pine forests that covered the mountain slopes in the distance. In High Ridge where she lived most of the year, the sun never seemed to rise and set. It was just there, above the buildings on nice days and then, when it was time to go in for supper, it disappeared. Only you never saw it go. On the farm you could follow its course all day long.

When Mary Jane was a little girl, the whole family spent summers on Grampa's farm. Now Lou Ellen was a nurse in a hospital in the North, coming home only at Christmas time, and James was off studying to be a lawyer like Daddy. Now Mary Jane was big, big enough to know about the earth's rotation and to spend the summer on the farm alone with Grampa.

Grampa's farm was different from other farms. All the farmers nearby planted tobacco, but Grampa planted only what he liked—vegetables for the kitchen, corn for the chickens, and flowers to pleasure his eyes.

If the rabbits nibbled his cabbages, he just shrugged his shoulders. "They're entitled to a share for looking so pert when they zigzag across the grass," he said.

If the blue jays and redbirds and crows swooped down to eat his chicken feed, he put out more corn and sang a song that he'd learned when he was a boy. The two of them, Mary Jane and Grampa, would watch the birds eating and sing, off-key, but good and loud:

> "Hi, says the red bird sitting on a fence.
> Once I courted a handsome wench.
> She proved fickle and from me fled
> And ever since then my head's been red.
>
> "Hi, says the chicken hawk to the crow.
> If you aren't black, well I don't know;
> And ever since old Adam was born,
> You've been known for stealing corn.
>
> "Hi, says the black bird to the crow.
> What makes the white folks hate us so?
> Ever since old Adam was born
> It's been our trade to pull up corn.
>
> "Hi, says the crow to the chicken hawk.
> I understand your big loud talk;
> You'd like to dive and catch a hen,
> And I hope the farmer will shoot you then."

Grampa wouldn't even shoot chicken hawks. "Little bit of trouble they might cause with the chickens, that's nothing to the good they do feasting all year on grasshoppers and those mice your ma's so down on," he explained.

Mary Jane's mother, who'd been brought up in the city, shivered when she heard Grampa even talk about mice. "Better to be down on them than make pets of them, Pa Douglas," she retorted. "People say you open up your door in the winter and tell all the field mice, 'Come in and keep warm.' Why, they say you even feed the weeds in your garden."

Grampa chuckled his slow deep chuckle. He didn't mind Mamma's teasing. Besides, what she said about the weeds was true. Alongside proper garden flowers, roses and hollyhocks that everyone grew, he planted rows of dandelions and sky-blue chicory and frilly white Queen Anne's lace.

Planting weeds wasn't as crazy as it sounded. A long time ago when Grampa was teaching at the state agricultural college he found ways to make rubber from dandelions and oil from seeds of other wild plants. Even now, although he had retired from the college and didn't teach any more, he still liked experimenting with plants, seeing if he could make them bigger or bluer or good to eat.

All summer long while Grampa fussed with his flower garden Mary Jane fussed with his animals. Mornings, she led Sophie the cow from the barn to the pasture and evenings she brought her safely back home again. She'd have milked her, too, except that her fingers weren't strong enough yet. But she could feed the chickens and the pigs and the awkward, long-legged calf that Sophie had borne in the spring, and she could take care of Curly.

At the beginning of the summer Curly had been the runt of the pig litter, in danger of being crushed to death by a careless mother and starved by greedy brothers and sisters. Mary Jane had taken him from the pen and fed him milk from a baby's bottle and vegetables from his own dish. Now Curly was sleek and fat and spoiled and he followed Mary Jane all over the farm.

After supper, when Mary Jane and Grampa sat on the back stoop watching the distant mountains turn from green to blue to black, Curly came too. He put his front feet on the steps, grunting and straining until he'd climbed up after them. Instead of admiring the sunset, he poked his snout into Mary Jane's overalls pocket to hunt for more things to eat. Mary Jane scratched his head, right between the ears, while Grampa sang "Mary had a little pig." His voice rumbled along:

> "He followed her to school one day
> Which was against the rule.
> It made the children laugh and play
> To see a pig at school."

Mary Jane began to giggle. She laughed until Curly squealed and Grampa tapped his pipe on the porch rail.

"My singing's not all that funny," he protested. "Even *your* singing's not that funny."

"It's not the singing." Mary Jane giggled again. "It's just—well— I got to thinking about Wilson High. It has millions of steps in front, marble, I guess——"

"Limestone," Grampa corrected her.

"Millions of limestone steps, and there's me walking up them with Curly following. . . ." This time Mary Jane laughed until there were tears in the corners of her eyes.

Grampa sucked on his pipe, waiting until she was quiet. "Been meaning to ask you about Wilson. How come you decided to go there 'stead of to Douglass, where Lou Ellen and James did their studying?"

Mary Jane was surprised at the quesion. Grampa knew perfectly well that Woodrow Wilson High was the best high school in High Ridge, if not in the whole state. "Last spring, before we graduated from Dunbar, the superintendent of schools talked at our assembly. He said the high school would be integrated in September. Those children who were graduating, if we had good marks and all, we could go to Wilson if we wanted. Mamma and Daddy weren't so sure, but I knew right that day I was going to Wilson. And I am."

"Mmm." Grampa nodded. "Haven't said why."

"Because it's better than Douglass, that's why. Douglass has French, but Wilson has French and Latin. Douglass has just plain science— stuff I mostly know already. Wilson has physics and chemistry and biology. How'm I going to be a biologist if I don't go to Wilson?"

Grampa took the pipe out of his mouth and studied its bowl.

"Some people," he observed, "seem to think I'm a biologist and I never went to Wilson."

"Oh, Grampa." Mary Jane was impatient now. "Things have changed since you were a boy. I know about how you had to study with your speller tied to the handles of a plow. And about washing dishes and scrubbing floors and cooking for people to earn money to go to school. But that's not the modern way. Now everybody can go, only some schools are better. I feel like I've got a right to go to Wilson. Besides——" She hesitated, searching for the words. "Besides, I want to see if I can do as good work as they do."

"Think you can?"

Mary Jane's braids bounced on her shoulders as she nodded. "May be hard though."

"Probably be hard," Grampa agreed. "Any friends going along there with you?"

"There are three, four older kids transferring from Douglass to the high school, but the only ones going to junior high are Fred Jackson and me. I've known Fred all my life, but I wouldn't exactly call him a friend, him being a boy."

"I see." Grampa nodded once more.

Mary Jane wondered if he did see. He was asking practically the same questions Mamma and Daddy asked. "Likely you'll be lonesome," Mamma had said. "Only you and Fred in that great big school."

"Grownups!" Mary Jane burst out as if she were back home, arguing with Mamma. "Grownups think we just go to school to socialize. If I wanted to socialize I wouldn't have to go to school at all. I'm going to Wilson to get an education."

Said out loud like that, the words sounded big and brave. While she waited for Grampa to answer them, the sun dipped behind the mountains, leaving only a faint red glow on the distant peaks. Suddenly it was cold and dark on the stoop and Mary Jane shivered.

"Real feeling of fall in the air tonight," Grampa commented as he stood up, stretching. "You run put Curly to bed now and I'll get a fire started inside."

Curly had no intention of going to bed. He trotted alongside Mary Jane until they reached the barn. Then he refused to budge.

She had to get behind him and push hard to put him in the pen. After she locked the gate he squealed so pitifully that she stayed to scratch his head and comfort him.

Walking back to the house, she shook her head. Curly sure was spoiled. What was he going to do when she went home?

* * *

Mary Jane and Grampa never said another word about Wilson High. Not even when it was Last Night on the farm and she was bustling about packing her clothes and he was checking on her neck and ears and fingernails to make sure she was properly clean before Mamma came.

What with all the washing and the packing and the washing again, they had only a short time to remember everything that had happened during the summer and to give instructions about Curly and make jokes.

Grampa sang:

> "Oh to be a cricket
> In a dusty thistle thicket."

And Mary Jane sang:

> "The sow got the measles
> And she died in the spring."

And they both laughed because neither of them could carry a tune and neither of them cared.

"No more lazying yourself under the hickory tree," Grampa teased.

"No more cleaning out the chicken coop. You'll have to do some work now," Mary Jane answered back. Cleaning the chicken coop was the one farm job she didn't like.

No more Grampa—no more Curly—no more Sophie—until next summer. But Mary Jane didn't feel sad when Mamma arrived in the morning as they were putting away the breakfast dishes. Mamma looked so trim and young and pretty in a new cotton dress that Mary Jane was glad she'd packed away her overalls. It would be good to wear dresses for a change and look in store windows on Main Street and do all the city things that city children did. The farm was nice, but so was home.

While Grampa stuffed the back of the car with tomatoes and eggs and flowers and greens and Mamma opened the closets to see if she had forgotten anything, Mary Jane skipped out to the barnyard. Curly's corkscrew tail waggled like a dog's when she kissed him good-by—after first making sure that Mamma wasn't looking. Mamma was understanding about most things, but she just didn't approve of kissing pigs—or letting them kiss you back. Wiping off the wet spot that Curly's snout had left on her cheek, Mary Jane ran to the car.

Grampa said, "Write me, child, when you take a notion," and kissed her in the exact same place Curly had. She hugged him, sniffing at the flower in the buttonhole of his faded blue shirt, and she waved good-by out of the car window until Mamma took the turn at the crossroads. When she couldn't see Grampa any more, she settled back in her seat to think about High Ridge.

Mamma was full of scraps of news. Lou Ellen wrote that she was working on an interesting case. James hoped to get home for a weekend soon. Daddy had been busy with——

"Well, you'll see. It's a surprise for you."

No matter how hard Mary Jane begged, Mamma wouldn't tell the surprise. "You'll like it," she teased, "although these next couple days you won't have much chance to make use of it."

What in the world could "it" be? Mary Jane was trying so hard to guess that she scarcely paid attention as her mother told about all the things they would have to do at home in the next few days.

"Doctor . . . dentist . . . hairdresser . . ."

"Hairdresser? Whatever for?" Mary Jane sat up when Mamma said that. Her hair touched her shoulder blades when she unbraided it, and it was one of her ambitions to let it grow until it reached her waist. Like a princess in a storybook. Like Rapunzel, who let down her hair so the king's son could climb up to the castle where she was imprisoned.

"You're getting too big for pigtails," Mamma explained. "I've been studying the way the girls fix their hair now. Mostly they wear it short or in a pony tail. I thought cut it a little in front too, sort of fluffed up on your forehead and——"

"But, Mamma," Mary Jane protested. She reminded her mother that Gwen and Peggy and Laura and all her very best friends had braids. "And mine are the longest of anybody's."

She didn't tell her mother about the princess in the storybook, because Mamma would have thought that was silly, but she argued for a long time. And Mamma argued back, pointing out how much easier it would be to brush her hair in the morning if it were shorter.

"You're going to high school now," she said, "and the girls there set great store by how you look."

For a moment Mary Jane thought of asking if braids were all right for Douglass but not for Wilson High. Only that might start talk that she didn't want to hear. Besides, Mamma did know a lot more about fashions than she did and—well, not having braids would save time in the mornings, and well . . . Before they reached High Ridge she had agreed to the trip to the beauty parlor and was once more guessing about her surprise.

Everything at home looked small and trim and citified after the farm. Instead of scarlet trumpet vines climbing over weather-beaten shingles, there were gray stucco and shutters with fresh green paint and aluminum screen doors. Instead of barns and fields and chicken coop, there were rows of houses with tiny plots of grass in front and garages in back, each exactly alike for as far as you could see. Instead of oaks and hickories with spreading branches, there were spindly sidewalk trees with wrought-iron fences around them and privet hedges and scraggly hollies bunched against the porches.

But Mary Jane liked it. At home there were Mamma and Daddy and girls to play with, and stores and television. And upstairs in her bedroom there was the surprise.

The big old maple beds that she and Lou Ellen had always slept in were gone. In their place were day beds with broad bolsters to make them comfortable for sitting on. There were new bureaus built into the wall, and a desk with rows of drawers on either side and bookshelves above. And a real, honest-to-goodness dressing table with a mirror so that she wouldn't have to use the mirror in the bathroom when she fixed her hair. And a gooseneck lamp that could be used for studying at the desk or reading in bed.

Daddy had put up wallpaper with tiny bunches of flowers all over it, and Mamma had made a skirt for the dressing table and new curtains and pretty dark blue drapes that you closed by pulling a cord, like a stage curtain.

Mary Jane wanted to telephone Gwen and Peggy and Laura to come right over to see everything, but Mamma said no, there wasn't time.

"I want you to unpack while I fix supper. Daddy'll be home before you know it, and I'll have to hump some to get ready before he comes."

Mary Jane unpacked slowly. The bureau drawers smelled new and piny and she folded her clothes carefully as she put them away. Now that she was big and going to high school and had such a nice room she was going to be neat. No more kicking socks under the bed and leaving shoes in the middle of the floor and stuffing half-dirty sweaters in the drawers. Everything was going to be in its place the way Mamma wanted it to be.

By the time she was finished unpacking and had set the table, her regular job when she was home, she heard Daddy's key in the door. Then she forgot she was big and going to high school as she made a flying leap into his arms. Pretending that she was too heavy to hold, he dropped her on the couch.

"Let's get a good look at you," he said. "Your legs get longer by the minute."

"It's your forehead's getting longer," she teased. Truth to tell, Daddy was more than a little bit bald and didn't always like to be reminded of it. But tonight she could say anything without making him mad, because it was her first night home.

Supper was a First-Night-Home supper with steak and french fries and a three-layer cake with her favorite chocolate frosting.

"And no dandelion greens or wild chicory in the salad," Mamma pointed out. She didn't always approve of Grampa's cooking, especially when he experimented with wild plants. Mamma preferred proper food that came from the supermarket.

Mary Jane chattered away, telling about Sophie and the chickens and even about Curly. Although not "He followed her to school one day" and what Grampa said afterward. They filled her in on High Ridge news until long past time to clear the table.

Because it was First Night Home, Mamma excused her from helping with the dishes, and Mary Jane went into the living room to watch television. After two months away there were lots of programs to catch up on. It seemed like no time at all before Daddy said, "Time for bed, sugar," and she walked upstairs to sleep in her brand-new bed.

In the morning she had no chance to phone Gwen or Peggy or anybody. "Do you know all that we have to do today?" Mamma asked.

Mary Jane didn't know but she soon found out. Mamma bustled in and out of the department stores on Main Street, moving so quickly that Mary Jane had trouble keeping up with her. First a jacket, even though the old one that she'd gotten last spring was perfectly good, not too short in the sleeves or anything. Before she could stop to admire the new gray blazer, Mamma was in another department, studying racks and racks of skirts.

Mamma knew exactly what she wanted when it came to buying clothes. Sometimes the things that Mamma wanted weren't the ones that Mary Jane liked best. Mamma wouldn't even look at a felt skirt with little dog cutouts sewn all around. Instead, she picked out a charcoal gray without anything on it at all and a straight skirt in navy blue and sent Mary Jane into the dressing room to try them on. The straight skirt made her look grownup-tall, and when Mamma promised to buy a petticoat with a real hoop to wear under the gray one, Mary Jane gave up teasing for the skirt with the dogs.

Then Mamma picked out a white blouse and a blue shirt with a buttoned-down collar and cuffs that needed cuff links, just as if there weren't drawers full of blouses at home. Of course Mary Jane didn't remind her of this, because if Mamma felt like buying new clothes she certainly felt like wearing them.

Next to the blouse counter were the sweaters. This time Mary Jane saw exactly what *she* wanted—a red sweater of soft, soft wool. Tugging at Mamma's elbow, she begged her to buy it.

"Red? You can't wear red, child. You'll look terrible in it."

"Why can't I wear red?" Mary Jane asked. "Please, Mamma, please. It'll be fabulous with the gray skirt."

"No red." Mamma was positive.

"But I always wear red," Mary Jane argued. And she listed for her mother all the red clothes she owned—sweaters, blouses, even the jacket she'd gotten last spring.

"Why do you suppose I bought you the blazer? So you wouldn't wear that red jacket to school," Mamma interrupted. "You have to dress more carefully now that you're going to—to—high school."

"But Lou Ellen wore red sweaters when she went to high school," Mary Jane said, feeling as if she'd scored a point. Mamma always held Lou Ellen up to her as an example. Lou Ellen had done her lessons on time and hung up her clothes and kept her fingernails clean and——

"Only Lou Ellen didn't go to Wilson." Mamma sounded snappish now, as if she were tired. "That's just what they expect you to wear. Red or purple or some loud color, like a minstrel show."

Mary Jane wrinkled her forehead. This would take some thinking about. She didn't know what a minstrel show was and she didn't ask. But she dropped the sweater as if it had been a live coal and straggled after Mamma.

"Socks." Mamma consulted her list again. "They're wearing knee socks this year, those heavy ribbed ones."

Mary Jane wondered if the "they" who were wearing knee socks and straight skirts and shoulder-strap bags and dickies this year were the same "they" who expected her to wear loud colors. And was it also the same "they" who said that she and Mamma couldn't eat in any of the Main Street restaurants when they were hungry?

After "socks" and "pocketbook" and "dickies" and "petticoat" were crossed off the the shopping list, Mary Jane and Mamma walked around the corner to the parking lot. It was too far to go home, so they ate a picnic lunch in the car.

"Now for the shoe store," Mamma said as Mary Jane finished her sandwich, "and then we'll go to the beauty parlor."

Mary Jane had never in her whole life gotten more than one pair of shoes at a time, but today Mamma let her pick out two— rust-brown loafers and flats that looked like ballet slippers. She was so excited about the flats and Mamma's offer of stockings to go with them for dress-up that she stopped wondering about the "theys." For a while.

At the beauty parlor she squeezed her eyes closed so that she couldn't see the scissors as they traveled around her head. Clutching the arms of the chair, she refused to look at all until Miss Alice, the hairdresser, had trimmed the little fluff in front and brushed away the hairs from the back of her neck. When the haircut was over, Miss Alice turned the chair and held the mirror so that it showed the pony tail. Mary Jane had to admit that it did look nice. And much more grown up than the braids.

Miss Alice had known Mary Jane since she was a little girl, when she used to come in with Mamma and ride in the chairs until she was dizzy. Only now she called her "Miss Mary Jane" and shook hands as they said good-by.

"Up at the school, if they say mean things to you, just pay them no mind. Just go about your business," she advised.

Mamma frowned at Miss Alice, but she didn't say a word. In the car, riding home, she kept going over her list, making sure they hadn't forgotten anything. Mary Jane didn't say a word either. She was just plain weary, from the fluff on her forehead to the tips of her brandnew shoes.

After they carried all the packages up the stairs and spread them out on Lou Ellen's bed, Mamma looked them over approvingly.

"Least they won't be able to say you're not well dressed," she sighed.

"They" again. It gave Mary Jane a queer feeling in the pit of her stomach. Not a stomach-ache really, but a fluttery, butterfly-wings sort of feeling. As if something was going to happen. Only then Gwen telephoned and Peggy came over to see her new room and her new clothes, and the fluttery feeling went away.

*   *   *

Saturday morning while Mamma went off to market Daddy took Mary Jane to the dentist and the doctor. "It won't hurt a bit," the dentist promised, and it didn't, although he filled two cavities and made her practice the proper way to brush her teeth, not sideways, but up and down.

The doctor didn't hurt either. He told her to say "ah" and listened to her chest and weighed and measured her. When he was all done he squeezed the muscles in her arm.

"Strong as an ox," he announced. "This girl of yours, she ought to be able to handle things up at the school if they give her a hard time."

He was joking, of course, but Daddy didn't seem to like it. Neither did Mary Jane. She was getting a little bit tired of people talking about Wilson.

There had even been an article in the morning paper. "Six Negro children," it said, "will be the first of their race to enter a previously all-white school in High Ridge on Monday. They are enrolled in Woodrow Wilson High School, which has junior and senior high divisions in the same building."

Mary Jane cut it out carefully to put in the collection of things she was saving for her children, a collection that included second-grade spelling tests, a baby tooth, and her certificate of graduation from Dunbar. Mamma clipped it too, borrowing a paper from the lady next door, so that she could send it on to Lou Ellen.

Of course Lou Ellen knew all about Wilson already. When Mary Jane came home from the doctor's there was a package on the hall table, a package postmarked "Philadelphia" where Lou Ellen's hospital was. Inside the brown paper wrapping Mary Jane found a silk scarf of pale, pale blue. Last year her big sister had sent her red bows for her braids, this year a blue scarf to tie around her pony tail. Trust Lou Ellen to know!

Mary Jane ran upstairs to her new dressing table. She sat there for a long time, looking in the mirror and fooling with the scarf until she'd gotten it just right. Then she fluffed out the curls on her forehead with a comb, pleased with the way she looked.

This whole business—the new clothes and the present from Lou Ellen and the things the hairdresser and the doctor had said— reminded her of when she was six and had her tonsils out. For days ahead of time everyone was particularly nice to her. Mamma fixed her favorite foods and Daddy bought her a new doll, and even Mamma's sisters came over with toys. Afterward, when her throat hurt, they let her eat ice cream and no vegetables and watch television until real late at night.

The fuss people were making now, they acted as if going to Wilson was as bad as having tonsils out. "Only it's not," she told Gwen after lunch, when they sat down on the porch to play jacks. "Sure there'll be a few kids who'll be mean, it's talked about so much in their homes. But there were mean kids at Dunbar too. You know that. And after the first days, when I get used to it, it'll be all right."

"'Spect so." Gwen nodded. "Only I'm glad I'm not you. I mean, it's scary enough going to Douglass, just starting high school with those big kids and algebra and all."

"Nothing to be scared about." Feeling brave, Mary Jane tossed the ball way up and had to scramble across the floor to catch it.

"Mmm." Gwen was concentrating on scraping all ten jacks into her hand. "Mamma says she'd worry something awful if I was going to Wilson. She says she doesn't know how your mother can stand it."

"Mothers always have to have something to worry about," Mary Jane pointed out. "Mine didn't like it one bit either when Lou Ellen went North to nursing school. And the first time Daddy let James drive the car at night, she wouldn't even go to bed until he came home."

"Mmm," Gwen repeated. "Wonder if we'll be like that. When we're mothers."

"Probably," Mary Jane sighed. "I mean, when you get old, something just makes you worry, I guess."

Playing jacks and talking about mothers-are-all-alike helped to quiet the butterfly wings in Mary Jane's stomach. Especially when Mamma invited Gwen to stay for supper and afterward Daddy took them to the drive-in, where they saw a neat cowboy movie.

Sunday school the next morning was all right too. When she came home the house was full of roast-lamb-mint-sauce smells *and* uncles and aunts, each with a present for Mary Jane. Not toys like when she had her tonsils out, but a ball-point pen and cuff links for the new blue shirt and a schoolbag with millions of compartments and pockets.

The schoolbag was red plaid with red leather straps and a red leather handle. Mary Jane looked sidewise at Mamma, wondering whether she had noticed that Aunt Ruth didn't seem to know about "they"—or else didn't care. When she thanked her for the bag, Aunt Ruth said something surprising.

"It's me who ought to thank you. What you're doing will make it easier for my Jimmy and the others when they come along."

Mary Jane had never thought like that about going to high school. She was going to Wilson because it was a better school and she wanted to go. But Aunt Ruth made her feel special and important, as if she were an explorer or inventor or something. She was so pleased with herself and everybody else that she didn't grumble after dinner when Mamma asked her to take Jimmy to the playground while the ladies cleaned up and the men sat on the porch to smoke their cigars. So pleased that she pushed Jimmy in the swing about a billion times until her arms ached and Aunt Ruth came to call for him.

When the shadows of the houses grew long and skinny, she skipped home. Skipped slowly, because she was thinking about what to wear tomorrow and because that tonsils-coming-out-butterfly-wings feeling was starting up again.

At the supper table she was still trying to decide between the gray skirt and the navy blue and wondering what Mamma would say if she wore her flats to school, when she realized that Daddy was talking to her.

"Mary Jane"—he'd had to say it twice—"Mr. Jackson called before. He and Fred'll be here first thing in the morning."

"Whatever for?"

"We're going to carry you two to school." He sounded offhanded, but Mary Jane was so surprised that she dropped her fork on the floor and had to go to the kitchen to get a clean one.

Daddy always said, "God gave children legs to walk with, not for climbing into cars." Daddy never, never drove her anyplace unless it was miles away. And Wilson wasn't miles away—only five blocks. That was one of the reasons she'd wanted to go there—because it was nearer than Douglass.

Was this more "they" stuff? "They always carry their children to school. . . . You'll look terrible if you walk. . . ."? Only it couldn't be. "They" didn't drive their children to Wilson. Everyone walked there. She'd seen them walking and swinging their books and shouting to their friends, and so had Daddy, plenty of times.

The butterfly wings were beating so fast now that she could scarcely repeat, "Whatever for?"

"Chickadee." Daddy reached over to pat her hand. "While you were on the farm—there's been talk this summer—some people don't want colored going to Wilson High. Tomorrow—well, they might try to stop you. Mr. Jackson, Reverend Coleman, and I saw the police chief yesterday. He said we'd get protection, all we need. Said he doesn't want any trouble, and I believe him. But still——"

Mary Jane watched Mamma fiddling with her spoon, fiddling with her water glass. All grownups were worriers, she reminded herself. But suppose this time they were right. Suppose this time there really was something to worry about.

"Chickadee," Daddy continued, "if you wanted to change your mind and go to Douglass, there's nobody who'd fault you. Nobody at all. They'd understand."

Mary Jane shook her head, fighting to catch her breath, to keep back tears. Thinking about Aunt Ruth, and Grampa, who worked so hard to get his schooling, and Red Anne. "I'll go to Wilson," she managed to say, and nothing more.

Suddenly she wasn't hungry for dessert. Suddenly she was in a great hurry to go upstairs and put out her things for school. To go to her room and close the door and cry.

Only she was too big for tears. Instead of crying, she laid out her things for the morning the way Mamma liked her to do. Looking in the closet, she picked the gray skirt instead of the blue, because the hoop petticoat made her feel princessy and she wouldn't have to remember to hold her stomach in. Then a white blouse and gray knee socks and the loafers with shiny pennies under the flaps, pennies that Uncle Ben had given her that morning.

After that, she fixed her pocketbook. Wallet first, with the pictures of Lou Ellen and James and Grampa and her week's allowance. Comb, mirror, handkerchief, and even a fingernail file.

Last came the schoolbag. Pencils with needle-sharp points, the new ball-point pen, and an eraser that Daddy had brought from his office, a round one with a brush on the end for sweeping away the crumbs. The bag looked empty still, but tomorrow when she came home it would be bulging with books and notes and homework assignments.

Tomorrow. Long after Mamma had come in to check over her clothes and Daddy had said, "Jacksons'll be here at eight, so don't be a sleepyhead, hear?" she sat on her bed, wondering if she'd forgotten anything. Long after they'd kissed her good night, she watched the street light shining through her new drapes and thought about how it would be at Wilson High.

Mr. Jackson and Fred arrived at the Douglases' while Mary Jane was still eating breakfast. Tall Mr. Jackson making polite talk with Daddy while she spooned up her cereal, and Fred looking stiff and uncomfortable in a new suit and freshly shined shoes. Mary Jane almost wanted to giggle, to tell them all that it wouldn't hurt a bit. But she couldn't, because there was a lump in her throat, as if her tonsils had grown back.

Mamma had little frown lines on her forehead as she smoothed the lapels of Mary Jane's new blazer and straightened the bow on her pony tail and asked if she'd remembered to take a handkerchief.

"Now you be good and don't fret your teachers," she said. "Hear?"

It was the same thing she said every year on the first day of school. The same thing she used to tell Lou Ellen and James when they were little. Only people who knew Mamma well, like Mary Jane and Daddy, could have said there was anything different about her good-by kiss that showed this wasn't any ordinary first school day.

She stood on the porch, waving to them as they drove off. Mary Jane watched her through the back window of the car until she was only a blur. Fred, who had grown about a mile over the summer, was talking about basketball. He talked goals and fouls and dribbles steadily until Daddy parked the car across the street from school. Then Fred stopped—right in the middle of a sentence.

Mary Jane looked out to see what had made Fred stop talking.

The fluttery feeling traveled from her stomach to her chest to her throat, and she clutched her schoolbag with a perspiring hand.

"Man!" Fred whistled through his teeth.

Because across the street, in front of Wilson, there was a row of green and white police cars. And behind the cars there were millions of people. Men and women and children sitting on the low stone wall, swarming over the big lawn and crowding the broad limestone steps. Men and women and children shouting and talking until Daddy and Mr. Jackson and Fred and Mary Jane got out of the car, then putting their voices together for a thundering "Boo-o-o!"

For a moment Mary Jane thought about Curly following her to school and how frightened he'd be by the noise. Then she stopped thinking about anything at all. With Daddy and Mr. Jackson on the outside and Fred and Mary Jane in the middle like a sandwich, the four of them marched across the street.

On the school sidewalk, two policemen joined them. The policemen went first, clearing a path through the crowd, leading the way. It was as if they were marching in a parade.

Heads up. Eyes front. One-two-three-four.

Only instead of drums to keep time to there were screams.

A man, angry. "Go back to Africa!"

Mary Jane turned her head, trying to see who it was. What did he mean?

A woman, high-pitched—could it have been a woman? "Pull her black curls out!"

Mary Jane's scalp tingled as if someone were tugging at it. Automatically her hand jerked up toward her forehead, toward the little fluff she'd combed so carefully at her new dressing table that morning. Then Daddy caught her hand, squeezing it in his own.

Heads up. Eyes front. Eyes on the broad blue backs of the policemen.

They were on the steps now, the white steps that led to the open school door. The crowd, not people, but a crazy Thing of faces and open mouths, was behind them, roaring in their ears. The Thing moved closer, closer, until it seemed as if it were about to pounce. Mary Jane stifled a scream, and one of the policemen turned and shouted.

"Stand still. Move back!"

The Thing stood still, stepped back, turned into people again. In a way, that was worse, because the people were yelling at *her*, at Mary Jane Douglas, beloved daughter of Mamma and Daddy, baby sister of Lou Ellen and James. Mary Jane, who'd never had anything bad happen to her in her life, except to her tonsils, and even then the doctor didn't mean to hurt. They couldn't be screaming at her—but they were.

Daddy squeezed her hand again. Heads up. Eyes front. They were on the landing now, close to the door. A group of boys were chanting, for all the world as if they were at a football game:

> "Two-four-six-eight
> We ain't gonna integrate."

Two-four-six-eight. The four of them marched through the door and all the way down the corridor to the principal's office keeping time to the rhythm of the chant.

While they waited to meet Mrs. Davis, Daddy let go of her hand to give her a quick little hug. She looked up at him, her eyes round, black, startled. He looked down at her, straightening the bow on her pony tail, not neatly the way Mamma would do, but clumsily, like Dad. Mary Jane put down her schoolbag and straightened it all over again, as if fixing her bow was the most important thing in the whole world just then.

"Boy, that was rough," Fred whispered. "Look at my hand." When he held out his hand, it was trembling.

"Are you all right?" Daddy asked anxiously. "Should I take you home?"

Mary Jane shook her head. After the noise outside it was so quiet in the corridor that her ears buzzed. It was hard to speak around the lump in her throat. "I'm all right," she gulped. "You can go now."

But Daddy stayed until Mrs. Davis said "Hello" to all of them and introduced them to the other Negro children, three boys and a girl, who were entering the upper grades. When the warning bell rang, Daddy kissed her good-by and Mr. Jackson kissed Fred, who looked embarrassed but pleased just the same. After that it was definitely time for parents to leave and school to begin.

"Junior High Assembly," Mrs. Davis explained as she led them along winding corridors to the auditorium. "This is where you'll get your assignments to your home rooms."

In the big auditorium Mary Jane and Fred sat alone. Alone in the midst of a room full of boys and girls. Alone, as if they were on a desert island in the middle of the ocean.

Mrs. Davis gave a welcoming speech, saying how glad she was to greet all the new people and that she hoped everyone had had a restful summer so that they could buckle down to some good hard work this term. It was a nice speech. Mary Jane had heard Mrs. Buckley give one like it at Dunbar every fall.

After Mrs. Davis' talk, another teacher stood up to read the home-room assignments. She called boys and girls up to the front of the room, one after the other, to get their cards.

The A's, the B's, the C's. Fred looked down sympathetically as the teacher began on the D's. For a moment Mary Jane thought he was going to pat her hand. Only then he remembered that he was a boy and she was a girl and that patting hands just wasn't done, in school or out, first day or last, when you were twelve.

"Mary Jane Douglas." She shivered a little, even though she was still wearing her blazer. Slowly she stood up and walked down the aisle to the front of the room. Head up. Eyes front.

The room was so quiet that she could hear her own footsteps tapping on the floor, her new loafers with the good-luck pennies in them. Until, from somewhere behind her, there was a muffled chorus:

> "We don't want her
> You can have her.
> She's too black for me."

Mary Jane flushed, faltered, kept on walking. Her cheeks were burning as Mrs. Davis jumped up from her seat on the stage and sternly rapped for order.

"Disgraceful . . . no more of that . . . rude . . . won't permit . . ."

Words. Words that Mary Jane scarcely heard as she took her assignment card and walked back to her seat. Head up, eyes front, not listening, not seeing anything. Not even reading the card until Fred came back with his and they compared them. He was in home-room 127, she in room 124. Her home-room teacher was Miss Rousseau, the card said.

After all the assignments had been given out and the junior high had pledged allegiance and sung "Oh, say can you see," the boys and girls shuffled through the auditorium doors to the crisscross of corridors beyond. Everyone seemed to know where to go except Fred and Mary Jane. They stood there looking uncertainly at each other, when something surprising happened. At least Mary Jane *thought* it happened. Puzzling over it later, she wasn't sure that it hadn't been a dream.

A girl came up to them, a little girl with bright red cheeks and pale blond hair, and said that she was sorry about the crowd outside. "Can I help you find your way?" she asked. "My sister used to go here, so I know where the rooms are, sort of. It's awfully confusing if you don't."

Instead of answering, they showed her their cards. She led them up a flight of stairs and down a hall to their home rooms. Then she disappeared without even saying "Good-by."

Room 124 was pleasant and sunny, with high windows and movable desks and a green blackboard behind the teacher's chair. Not much different from the classrooms at Dunbar except for the color of the blackboard, and the desks which were brand-new.

Even Miss Rousseau looked like the Dunbar teachers. Ageless, the way teachers always seemed to be, not exactly pretty, but not ugly either. Like the Dunbar teachers, except that Miss Rousseau's skin was fair instead of brown and she talked with a funny sort of accent. She rolled her *r*'s and did things with her *th*'s in a way that Mary Jane had never heard before.

"Good morning." She smiled as Mary Jane hesitated in the doorway, not sure of what to do next.

A bell rang and Miss Rousseau started to assign seats. Alphabetical order again, which put Douglas in the second row, with a window on one side and a girl named Duncan on the other.

Only the girl named Duncan didn't sit down. Instead she marched up to the teacher's desk and loudly announced, "My mother said I wasn't to sit by *her*."

Miss Rousseau lifted her eyebrows. "In my class," she answered, "pupils sit where they are assigned." Calmly she continued to read out the names.

The girl named Duncan started to leave the room, then thought better of it. Without looking at Mary Jane, she slid her desk over until it was almost touching the one at her right. It stayed there until Miss Rousseau finished with her seating list.

"Now, Darlene." The teacher's voice was calm. "You can put your desk back in place."

Mumbling under her breath, Darlene obeyed. Through the entire period, however, she kept her head turned toward the door. If she *had* to sit next to Mary Jane, at least she wasn't going to look at her. For a crazy moment Mary Jane felt like giggling. Darlene was going to have an awful stiff neck by the end of the term.

The next minutes were busy ones. Miss Rousseau gave out schedule cards and locker numbers and explained about periods and bells and lunch and gym and not being late and bringing a note to the nurse if you were sick. Then the whole class trooped out to the hall to find their lockers and practice their combinations.

The combinations worked like the locks on safes. Two turns to the right. Stop at 27. One turn to the left. Stop at 14. Then right again until the lock clicked open when you reached 7. Mary Jane twirled and stopped and twirled and stopped until she knew her combination by heart. After she hung up her blazer on the hook inside the locker she went back to her home room.

There was another bell and still another, and regular classes began. Today was only a half day, so classes meant learning your teachers' names and getting your seat and your books. For first period Mary Jane stayed right where she was, alongside Darlene, because their class was French and Miss Rousseau taught it.

Miss Rousseau not only taught French, she *was* French, she told the class. Which explained the funny accent. At any other time Mary Jane, who had never met a person before who didn't come from North Carolina or Kentucky or Tennessee, would have been interested in someone from Paris, France, who said "ze" when she meant "the."

But not today when her head ached and the back of her neck felt sore and she couldn't swallow the lump in her throat no matter how hard she tried.

After French and more bells came English and more bells, then Arithmetic, History, and Science. Only History was called Social Studies now, and Arithmetic was Math. All of the classrooms looked like her home room, except Science, which had tables instead of desks and a sink in the back of the room, and Social Studies, which had Fred.

Mary Jane had never realized before how much she liked Fred until she saw his friendly, dark face when she entered the Social Studies room. While people were still finding their seats, he leaned forward to whisper in her ear.

"Already I've been kicked in the shins and had my books knocked out of my arm. Score, Wilson two, Jackson nothing. This keeps up, I'll get a complex or something. I'll begin to think they don't like me," he chuckled.

"Who did it?" Mary Jane's lips framed the words as the teacher called the class to order.

Fred shrugged his shoulders, the smile gone from his face. "Seems like all of them."

Mary Jane chewed her underlip as she copied the homework assignment from the board. "Columbus Finds a New World, pages 3–11." The next bell would mean Science, and then school would be over for the day. The bell after the next one would mean going outside to face that howling, hating crowd. Maybe, she thought, they wouldn't be there. Maybe they had forgotten and gone away. But after she'd taken her blazer from her locker and found Fred and then Daddy in the noisy vestibule, she knew that the crowd was still outside, still waiting.

Down the steps and across the lawn she walked, with the policemen leading and the voices screaming. Mean, hate-filled voices screeching in her ears. She blinked at the white light from a photographer's flash gun. She ducked when a stick glanced off her shoulder. But she wasn't what you'd really call hurt. She was still putting one foot in front of the other and squeezing Daddy's hand and trying not to listen to the roar of the crowd.

One-two-three-four, and they had crossed the street. One-two-three-four, and they were in the car. With the doors closed and the windows rolled up to shut out the noise.

It was the end of Mary Jane's first day in junior high.

STEPHEN LEACOCK

and

The Human Element in Mathematics

The student of arithmetic who has mastered the first four rules of his art, and successfully striven with money sums and fractions, finds himself confronted by an unbroken expanse of questions known as problems. These are short stories of adventure and industry with the end omitted, and though betraying a strong family resemblance, are not without a certain element of romance.

The characters in the plot of a problem are three people called A, B, and C. The form of the question is generally of this sort:

"A, B, and C do a certain piece of work. A can do as much work in one hour as B in two, or C in four. Find how long they work at it."

Or this:

"A, B, and C are employed to dig a ditch. A can dig as much in one hour as B can dig in two, and B can dig twice as fast as C. Find how long, etc., etc."

Or after this wise:

"A lays a wager that he can walk faster than B or C. A can walk half as fast again as B, and C is only an indifferent walker. Find how far, and so forth."

The occupations of A, B, and C are many and varied. In the older arithmetics they contented themselves with doing "a certain piece of work." This statement of the case, however, was found too sly and mysterious, or possibly lacking in romantic charm. It became the fashion to define the job more clearly and to set them at walking matches, ditch-digging, regattas, and piling cord wood. At times, they became commercial and entered into partnership, having with their old mystery a "certain" capital. Above all they revel in motion. When they tire of walking-matches—A rides on horseback, or borrows a bicycle and competes with his weaker-minded associates on foot. Now they race on locomotives; now they row; or again they become historical and engage stage-coaches; or at times they are aquatic and swim. If their occupation is actual work they prefer to pump water into cisterns, two of which leak through holes in the bottom and one of which is water-tight. A, of course, has the good one; he also takes the bicycle, and the best locomotive, and the right of swimming with the current. Whatever they do they put money on it, being all three sports. A always wins.

In the early chapters of the arithmetic, their identity is concealed under the names John, William, and Henry, and they wrangle over the division of marbles. In algebra they are often called X, Y, Z. But these are only their Christian names, and they are really the same people.

Now to one who has followed the history of these men through countless pages of problems, watched them in their leisure hours dallying with cord wood, and seen their panting sides heave in the full frenzy of filling a cistern with a leak in it, they become something more than mere symbols. They appear as creatures of flesh and blood, living men with their own passions, ambitions, and aspirations like the rest of us. Let us view them in turn. A is a full-blooded blustering fellow, of energetic temperament, hot-headed and strong-willed. It is he who proposes everything, challenges B to work, makes the bets, and bends the others to his will. He is a man of great physical strength and phenomenal endurance. He has been known to walk forty-eight hours at a stretch, and to pump ninety-six. His life is arduous and full of peril. A mistake in the working of a sum may keep him digging a fortnight without sleep. A repeating decimal in the answer might kill him.

B is a quiet, easy-going fellow, afraid of A and bullied by him, but very gentle and brotherly to little C, the weakling. He is quite in A's power, having lost all his money in bets.

Poor C is an undersized, frail man, with a plaintive face. Constant walking, digging, and pumping has broken his health and ruined his nervous system. His joyless life has driven him to drink and smoke more than is good for him, and his hand often shakes as he digs ditches. He has not the strength to work as the others can, in fact, as Hamlin Smith has said, "A can do more work in one hour than C in four."

The first time that ever I saw these men was one evening after a regatta. They had all been rowing in it, and it had transpired that A could row as much in one hour as B in two, or C in four. B and C had come in dead fagged and C was coughing badly. "Never mind, old fellow," I heard B say, "I'll fix you up on the sofa and get you some hot tea." Just then A came blustering in and shouted, "I say, you fellows, Hamlin Smith has shown me three cisterns in his garden and he says we can pump them until to-morrow night. I bet I can beat you both. Come on. You can pump in your rowing things, you know. Your cistern leaks a little, I think, C." I heard B growl that it was a dirty shame and that C was used up now, but they went, and presently I could tell from the sound of the water that A was pumping four times as fast as C.

For years after that I used to see them constantly about town and always busy. I never heard of any of them eating or sleeping. Then owing to a long absence from home, I lost sight of them. On my return I was surprised to no longer find A, B, and C at their accustomed tasks; on inquiry I heard that work in this line was now done by N, M, and O, and that some people were employing for algebraical jobs four foreigners called Alpha, Beta, Gamma, and Delta.

Now it chanced one day that I stumbled upon old D, in the little garden in front of his cottage, hoeing in the sun. D is an aged labouring man who used occasionally to be called in to help A, B, and C. "Did I know 'em, sir?" he answered, "why, I knowed 'em ever since they was little fellows in brackets. Master A, he were a fine lad, sir, though I always said, give me Master B for kind-heartedness-like. Many's the job as we've been on together, sir, though I never did no racing nor aught of that, but just the plain labour, as you might say. I'm getting a bit too old and stiff for it nowadays, sir—just scratch about in the garden here and grow a bit of a logarithm, or raise a common denominator or two. But Mr. Euclid he use me still for them propositions, he do."

From the garrulous old man I learned the melancholy end of my former acquaintances. Soon after I left town, he told me, C had been taken ill. It seems that A and B had been rowing on the river for a wager, and C had been running on the bank and then sat in a draught. Of course the bank had refused the draught and C was taken ill. A and B came home and found C lying helpless in bed. A shook him roughly and said, "Get up, C, we're going to pile wood." C looked so worn and pitiful that B said, "Look here, A, I won't stand this, he isn't fit to pile wood to-night." C smiled feebly and said, "Perhaps I might pile a little if I sat up in bed." Then B, thoroughly alarmed, said, "See here, A, I'm going to fetch a doctor; he's dying." A flared up and answered, "You've no money to fetch a doctor." "I'll reduce him to his lowest terms," B said firmly, "that'll fetch him." C's life might even then have been saved but they made a mistake about the medicine. It stood at the head of the bed on a bracket, and the nurse accidentally removed it from the bracket without changing the sign. After the fatal blunder C seems to have sunk rapidly. On the evening of the next day, as the shadows deepened in the little room, it was clear to all that the end was near. I think that even A was affected at the last as he stood with bowed head, aimlessly offering to bet with the doctor on C's laboured breathing. "A," whispered C, "I think I'm going fast." "How fast do you think you'll go, old man?" murmured A. "I don't know," said C, "but I'm going at any rate."—The end came soon after that. C rallied for a moment and asked for a certain piece of work that he had left downstairs. A put it in his arms and he expired. As his soul sped heavenward A watched its flight with melancholy admiration. B burst into a passionate flood of tears and sobbed, "Put away his little cistern and the rowing clothes he used to wear, I feel as if I could hardly ever dig again."— The funeral was plain and unostentatious. It differed in nothing from the ordinary, except that out of deference to sporting men and mathematicians, A engaged two hearses. Both vehicles started at the same time, B driving the one which bore the sable parallelopiped containing the last remains of his ill-fated friend. A on the box of the empty hearse generously consented to a handicap of a hundred yards, but arrived first at the cemetery by driving four times as fast as B. (Find the distance to the cemetery.) As the sarcophagus was lowered, the grave was surrounded by the broken figures of the first book of Euclid.—It was noticed that after the death of C, A became a changed man. He lost interest in racing with B, and dug but languidly. He finally gave up his work and settled down to live on the interest of his bets.—B never recovered from the shock of C's death; his grief preyed upon his intellect and it became deranged. He grew moody and spoke only in monosyllables. His disease became rapidly aggravated, and he presently spoke only in words whose spelling was regular and which presented no difficulty to the beginner. Realising his precarious condition he voluntarily submitted to be incarcerated in an asylum, where he abjured mathematics and devoted himself to writing the History of the Swiss Family Robinson in words of one syllable.

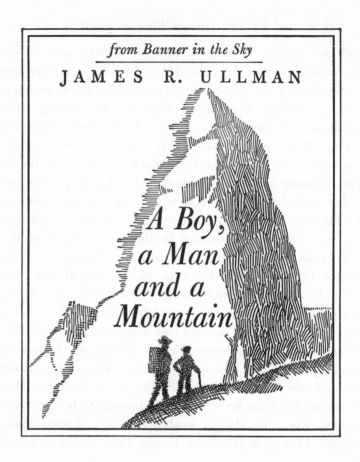

from Banner in the Sky

JAMES R. ULLMAN

A Boy,
a Man
and a
Mountain

[In the heart of the Swiss Alps, on the high frontier between earth and sky, stands one of the great mountains of the world. To men generally it is known as the Citadel, but the people of the valley beneath it seldom call it by that name. They call it the Rudisberg—Rudi's Mountain. And that is because, in the long-gone year of 1865, there lived in that valley a boy called Rudi Matt. . . .]

Most of the boys of the village were tall, broad and strongly built. Rudi was small and slim. But to make up for it, he was quick. In all his sixteen years he had probably never been quicker than on a certain summer morning when he slipped out the kitchen door of the Beau Site Hotel and into the alley beyond. When Teo Zurbriggen, the cook, turned from his stove to get a jar from the spice shelf, Rudi had been at his usual place, washing the breakfast dishes. But when, five seconds later, Old Teo turned back, his young helper was gone.

The cook muttered under his breath. But, almost at the same time, he smiled. He smiled because he knew what the boy was up to, and in his old heart he was glad.

Outside, Rudi did not follow the alley to the main street. He went in the other direction, came to a second alley, and ran quickly through the back part of the town. He made a wide detour around his mother's house; another around the house of his uncle, Franz Lerner. Fortunately he met no one who knew him—or at least who knew he was supposed to be working in the kitchen of the Beau Site.

Soon he came to the edge of the town and a roaring brook. Across the brook lay a footbridge; but, instead of using it, he worked his way upstream around a bend and then crossed over, leaping agilely from boulder to boulder. From the far side he looked back. Apparently no one had seen him. Scrambling up the bank, he plunged through a clump of bushes, skirted a barnyard and picked up a path through the meadows. Here, for the first time, he stopped running. There was no living thing to be seen except a herd of grazing cows. The only sound was the tinkling of their bells.

The meadows rolled gently, tilting upward, and their green slope was sprayed with wildflowers. The path crossed a fence, over a rickety stile, then bent and rejoined the brook; and now the cowbells faded and there was again the sound of rushing water. Rudi walked on. Three or four times he passed people going in the opposite direction, but they were only *Ausländer*—tourists—and nothing to worry about. Whatever guides were climbing that day were already high in the mountains. And any others who might have known and questioned him were back in the town or on their farms.

Rudi smiled at the passersby. "*Grüss Gott*," he said—"God's Greetings"—in the ancient salutation of the Alps. "*Grüss Gott*," they said in reply.

He was no longer hurrying. He walked with the slow, rhythmic pace of the mountain people, and, though the path was now steepening sharply, he felt no strain. His legs, his lungs, all of his slight wiry body, were doing what they did best; what they had been born to do. His feet, through the soles of his shoes, moulded themselves to each hump and crevice of the path. Arms and shoulders swung in easy balance. His breathing was steady, his heartbeat strong and even.

"A typical mountain boy," one would have said, seeing him at a distance. But then, coming closer, one would have seen that he was not typical at all. Partly, this was because of his slimness, his lightness of muscle and bone; but even more it was in his small, almost delicate features and his fair, pink-and-white complexion. Rudi Matt hated his complexion. In summer he exposed his face for hours to the burning sun, in winter he scrubbed it violently with snow, trying to make it brown and tough and weatherstained, as a mountain man's should be. But no stain appeared. No whisker sprouted. "Angel-face," the other boys called him. Or, rather, *had* called him, until they learned that his fists, though small, were useful. Most of the men of Kurtal had black hair. Rudi's was blond. Most of them had dark eyes. Rudi's were light—though exactly what color no one was quite sure. His mother called them hazel, but she saw them only when he was at home or around the village. When he left the village, when he climbed above it, they seemed to change, as the light changed. Looking up at the great peaks above the valley, they seemed to hold within themselves the gray of mountain rock, the blue of mountain sky.

Rudi Matt climbed on. Now that he was no longer afraid of being stopped, his heart was filled with peace and joy. Just why he had run off on this particular day he could not have said. He had had to —that was all. He had looked from the window of the hotel kitchen and seen the peaks that rimmed the valley rising vast and shining in the morning sun; and he could no more have stopped himself than he could have stopped breathing. A few minutes before, he had been a prisoner. Now he was free. He no longer looked backward—only up— as slowly the great mountain world unfolded before him.

The path bore away from the brook, zigzagged up the highest of the meadows and entered a forest. And here Rudi stopped. Beside the path, at the forest's edge, was a shrine. It was a tiny thing, no more than a rough wooden box nailed to one of the trees, and inside was a cross and a chipped image of the Virgin. Carved in the wood near the Virgin's feet was the name JOSEF MATT, and beneath it the dates, *1821–1850*.

Rudi had never known his father. It had been fifteen years since he had died. But every time in his life that the boy had come to this place he had stopped and prayed. He prayed now, kneeling in the soft moss before the shrine. Then he arose, crossed himself and climbed on through the forest.

A few minutes later he made a second stop. Leaving the path, he made his way between the trees to a large blue spruce and reached for the stout stick that was concealed in its branches. This was his *alpenstock*, the climber's staff he had made for himself, as a substitute for an ice-ax, which he did not own; and he kept it hidden here because he was afraid that if he took it home his mother or uncle might find it. It was a strong staff, almost five feet long, with a sharp point on one end and a crook on the other. And if it was nothing like the real *alpenstocks* and axes that Kronig, the smith, made at his forge in the village, at least it was better than nothing. As he hefted it now in his hand, feeling its familiar weight and balance, it was no longer merely a stick, but a part of himself.

He climbed on. For a while, still thinking of his father, he walked slowly and somberly, with his eyes on the ground. But this did not last long, for he was young and the sun was shining and he was doing what he most loved to do in all the world. He tilted his stick before him like a lance. He picked up stones and threw them at the trees. He threw back his head and yodeled and the high wild YOOOO–LEEEE–OOOOO–LAAAY–EEEEE rode the still air like a soaring bird.

The path twisted upward. Always upward. The forest was close around him; then a little less close; then not close at all. The great firs and spruces fell away, and he came out onto a slope of dwarf pine and scraggly, moss-hugging shrubs. Sitting on a boulder, he ate a bite of lunch. He had no knapsack, any more than he had an ice-ax, but he had managed to stuff a piece of bread and another of cheese into a pocket before bolting from the hotel kitchen, and, plain and cumbled though they were, they tasted better than any food he had ever eaten in the hotel or in his home.

His eyes moved down across the treetops to the valley. There was the white thread of the brook dividing it; on either side the meadows and farms; in the valley's center the town of Kurtal. He could see the main street, the square, the church, the Beau Site Hotel, where he worked, and the two other hotels beyond it. All three buildings were new; even Rudi could remember when they had not been there at all. Ten or twelve years before, Kurtal had been no more than a tiny farming village, lost in a deep Swiss valley. But while Rudi had grown, it had grown too. It had become what the *Ausländer* called a "resort." Each year, during the summer months, there were more and more visitors—people from the cities, people from England, France, Germany, and even from faraway America—coming up in the coaches from the lowlands. In the last few summers there had been so many of them that there was even talk of building a railway.

It was the mountains that brought them, of course: the tall white glorious mountains of the Alps. In the old days the people of the outside world had not been interested in the Alps; they had left them to those who had been born and lived there. But in Rudi's own lifetime all that had changed. The *Ausländer* had come: first in trickles, then in droves. They had moved up into the villages, into the high valleys, onto the glaciers, onto the peaks themselves. The sport, the craft, the adventure of mountaineering had been born. In every village, men whose ancestors through all history had been farmers and herdsmen were now farmers and herdsmen no longer, but Alpine guides. And the profession of guide was the proudest in the land. To be a member of the Company of Guides of Kurtal was the highest honor that a man could attain.

Men had not only come to the mountains. They had conquered them. A generation before, only a handful of peaks in the Alps had been climbed to the top, but now, in 1865, there were scarcely any that had *not* been. One by one, year after year, they had been attacked, besieged and taken. Mont Blanc, Monte Rosa, the Dom, the Weisshorn, the Schreckhorn, the Eiger, the Dent Blanche, the Lyskamm—all these and a hundred more, the whole great white host of the most famous mountains of Europe—had felt the boot nails of their conquerors in their summit snows.

All of them . . . *except one.*

Rudi Matt was no longer looking down into the valley. He was looking up and beyond it, and now slowly his eyes moved across the wide circle of the ranges. They moved over the meadows and forests, the glaciers and snowfields, the gorges and precipices, the ridges and peaks. They rested on the snowdome of Monte Rosa, the spire of the Wunderhorn (his father had first climbed it), the Rotalp (his uncle Franz), the soaring crest of the Weisshorn. Now at last he had turned completely; he was looking in the direction in which he had been climbing. And still his eyes moved on—and up—and up. The other mountains fell away. There was a gap, a deep gorge, a glacier. The earth seemed almost to be gathering itself together. It leaped upward.

And there it was. . . .

The Citadel!

It stood up like a monument: great, terrible—and alone. The other mountains were as nothing beside it. It rose in cliff upon cliff, ridge upon ridge, tower upon tower, until the sharp, curving wedge of its summit seemed to pierce the very heart of the sky. It was a pyramid built up out of a thousand parts—out of granite and limestone and snow and ice, out of glaciers, precipices, crags, ledges, spires, cornices—but so perfect was its vast shape, so harmonious the blending of its elements, that it appeared a single, an organic, almost a living thing. Rudi Matt had been born in its shadow. He had seen it every day of his life. He had stared up at it from the village, from the forests, from the glaciers on every side, until its every detail was fixed indelibly in his mind. But familiarity had not bred indifference. The years had not paled its magic. Instead, that magic had grown stronger, deeper. And on this day, as on every day in his life when he had looked up at it, Rudi Matt felt again the catch in his breath and the wild surging of his heart.

There it stood. The Citadel. The last unconquered summit of the Alps.

"It cannot be climbed," said the people of the valleys. In the past fifteen years no one had even tried to climb it. "It will never be climbed," they said.

No?

Now he was moving on again. He came to a stream, stopped and drank. A furry marmot watched him from a nearby boulder, whistled shrilly and disappeared. High above, a giant hawk whirled slowly through the still, blue air.

Beyond the stream was a fork in the path. The right-hand branch, plain and well trodden, led off toward the Dornelberg and the

Wunderhorn, two of the most popular peaks for climbing in the district. But it was not this branch that Rudi followed. Bearing left, he moved on along a barely visible trail that climbed upward toward the base of the Citadel. He was above treeline now. Even the dwarf pine and shrubs were gone—all grass and moss were gone—and the earth was a bare sweep of gravel and tumbled boulders. Among the boulders the going was tricky, for he had no proper nailed mountainboots; but his feet were nimble, his balance true, and, making deft use of his self-made staff, he climbed quickly and easily. When, after an hour, he turned and looked back, the rocky point where he had stopped to eat seemed almost as far below him as the village.

The world into which he had now come was one of stillness and desolation. There was the gray of rock, the white of snow, the blue of sky—and that was all there was. The only movement, anywhere, was that of his own body; the only sound the scraping of his own feet against the boulders. Yet Rudi was not conscious of loneliness. He was too used to being alone for that. Every one of the perhaps fifty times during the past two years that he had climbed up to the Citadel's glaciers, he had been alone, and he was now as familiar with this world, and as at home in it, as in the valley below. Pausing now and then, he stared at the mountain that towered gray and monstrous above him. Most of the people in the town believed it was the home of demons, who would destroy anyone who ventured onto its forbidden slopes. . . . Well, maybe. . . . But he, Rudi, was not yet within a mile of the mountain itself. And if any demons did, indeed, come down into the foothills, they would do so, he was certain, only under cover of night.

He looked up, and the sun was bright and golden in the zenith. The thin finger of cold, that for an instant had touched him, dwindled and was gone.

The slope steepened. The boulders grew larger. He had come to the terminal moraine of the Citadel's glacier—the great mass of tumbled, broken rock which all ice-sheets push and grind before them in their slow descent. Ten more minutes brought him to the top of the moraine, and now the glacier spread before him. Or, more accurately, two glaciers; for he had come out at a point, facing the Kurtal ridge of the Citadel, where its northern and eastern ice-streams met and joined. The one on the north, which was broader, rose to the pass between the Citadel and the Dornelberg and was known as the Dornel Glacier. The eastern one, called the Blue Glacier, was the steeper and climbed like a giant stairway to the saddle—or col—near the base of the Citadel's southeastern ridge. Beyond this col, invisible from where he stood, still another glacier dropped away on the south side of the mountain, toward the valley and village of Broli.

Rudi had ascended both glaciers. He had been to Broli. No less than five times, indeed, he had completely circled the base of the Citadel, climbing up one glacier and down another, traversing the cols and lower ridges, threading his way through the deep, trackless gorges beneath the mountain's western face. He had stared upward until his neck ached and his eyes swam. He had studied every ridge and cliff and ice-wall and ledge and chimney that could be seen from below. He knew more about the approaches to the Citadel than any guide in Kurtal. And yet he still did not know enough. Still he kept coming up to the glaciers to stare again, to study, to measure. To do this, he had played truant from school— even from church. Now he was running out on his job. Always it meant tears and pleas from his mother, often harsh words from his Uncle Franz. But he did not care. He kept coming back. Nothing in heaven or earth could have held him from coming back.

This time he went up the Blue Glacier. He had not particularly planned to, and just why he picked the Blue, rather than the Dornel, he could not have said. Later, thinking back to that day, he racked his memory for some sign, some motive or portent, that had been the reason for his choice. But he could never find one. He simply crossed the junction of the two icestreams, bore left, and climbed on toward the south . . . and his destiny.

Like all glaciers, the Blue was cut through by crevasses: deep splits and chasms caused by the pressures of the slow-moving ice. When hidden by snow these could be a great hazard to climbers; but on this midsummer day no snow had fallen in some time, the crevasses were plain to view, and there was no danger if one kept his eyes open and paid attention. Rudi zigzagged his way carefully upward. On the ice, of course, his smooth-soled shoes were even worse than on the boulders, but by skillful balancing and use of his stick he kept himself from slipping.

As he climbed, a black dot came into view on the high col ahead. This was an old hut, built many years before by the first explorers of the mountain, but now abandoned and all but forgotten by the people of the valleys. Rudi had twice spent nights there during his circuits of the Citadel, and he knew it well. But it was not there, specifically, that he was going now. He was not going anywhere, specifically, but only climbing, watching, studying. Every few paces now, he would stop and stare upward, motionless.

The east face of the Citadel rose above him like a battlement. Cliff upon cliff, it soared up from the glacier, its rock bulging and bristling, its walls veined with long streaks of ice. Far overhead, he could see a band of snow, which marked the mountain's first setback. Beyond it, the sloping walls disappeared for a space, only to bulge out again higher up—incredibly higher up—in a great gray thrust against the empty sky. So vast was it, so steep, so mighty, that it seemed more than a mere mass of rock and ice. More than a mere mountain. It seemed a new world rising up out of the old world that was its mother; a world with a life and a meaning of its own; beautiful and menacing, beckoning and unknown.

But it was not of beauty or terror that Rudi Matt was thinking as he gazed up at it now from the Blue Glacier. It was of a deep cleft, wide enough for a man's body, that slanted up the rock wall before him—and ended. Of a series of ledges, broad enough for a man's feet, that rose one above another toward the high belt of snow—and petered out. His eyes searched up and down, to the right and the left. He climbed on, stopped, and studied the next section of the face. Then he climbed on again.

He moved through absolute silence. Later in the day, when sun and melting snow had done their work, great rock-and-ice masses would break loose from the heights above and come roaring down the mountainside. But it was still too early for this. The Citadel rose up like a tower of iron. There was no movement anywhere. No stirring. No sound.

And then there was a sound. . . .

Rudi stood motionless. It was not the sound of the mountain, of falling rock and ice. It was a voice. He waited; he looked around him; every sense was straining. But he saw nothing. Nothing moved. It was his imagination, he thought: a trick of his mind, or of the stillness. Or was it—and now the cold finger of fear touched him again—was it the voice of a mountain demon?

He stood without breathing. And the sound came again. It seemed at the same time to come from nearby and far away. He waited. Once more it came. And then suddenly he knew where it came from. It was from beneath the ice. From a crevasse in the glacier.

He approached the nearest crevasse and called out. But there was no answer. He went on to a second. No answer. Again he waited and listened. Again the voice came, faintly. Straight ahead was a third chasm in the ice, and, advancing cautiously, he peered over the edge.

The crevasse was about six feet wide at the top and narrowed gradually as it went down. But how deep it was Rudi could not tell. After a few feet the blue walls of ice curved away at a sharp slant, and what was below the curve was hidden from sight.

"Hello!" Rudi called.

"Hello—" A voice answered from the depths.

"How far down are you?"

"I'm not sure. About twenty feet, I'd guess."

"On the bottom?"

"No. I can't even see the bottom. I was lucky and hit a ledge."

The voice spoke in German, but with a strange accent. Whoever was down there, Rudi knew, it was not one of the men of the valley.

"Are you hurt?" he called.

"Nothing broken—no," said the voice. "Just shaken up some. And cold."

"How long have you been there?"

"About three hours."

Rudi looked up and down the crevasse. He was thinking desperately of what he could do.

"Do you have a rope?" asked the voice.

"No."

"How many of you are there?"

"Only me."

There was a silence. When the voice spoke again, it was still quiet and under strict control. "Then you'll have to get help," it said.

Rudi didn't answer. To get down to Kurtal would take at least two hours, and for a party to climb back up would take three. By that time it would be night, and the man would have been in the crevasse for eight hours. He would be frozen to death.

"No," said Rudi, "it would take too long."

"What else is there to do?"

Rudi's eyes moved over the ice-walls: almost vertical, smooth as glass. "Have you an ax?" he asked.

"No. I lost it when I fell. It dropped to the bottom."

"Have you tried to climb?"

"Yes. But I can't get a hold."

There was another silence. Rudi's lips tightened, and when he spoke again his voice was strained. "I'll think of something," he cried. "I'll think of *something!*"

"Don't lose your head," the voice said. "The only way is to go down for help."

"But you'll—"

"Maybe. And maybe not. That's a chance we'll have to take."

The voice was as quiet as ever. And, hearing it, Rudi was suddenly ashamed. Here was he, safe on the glacier's surface, showing fear and despair, while the one below, facing almost certain death, remained calm and controlled. Whoever it was down there, it was a real man. A brave man.

Rudi drew in a long, slow breath. With his climbing-staff he felt down along the smooth surface of the ice-walls.

"Are you still there?" said the voice.

"Yes," he said.

"You had better go."

"Wait—"

Lying flat on the glacier, he leaned over the rim of the crevasse and lowered the staff as far as it would go. Its end came almost to the curve in the walls.

"Can you see it?" he asked.

"See what?" said the man.

Obviously he couldn't. Standing up, Rudi removed his jacket and tied it by one sleeve to the curved end of the staff. Then, holding the other end, he again lay prone and lowered his staff and jacket.

"Can you see it now?" he asked.

"Yes," said the man.

"How far above you is it?"

"About ten feet."

Again the staff came up. Rudi took off his shirt and tied one of its sleeves to the dangling sleeve of the jacket. This time, as he lay down, the ice bit, cold and rough, into his bare chest; but he scarcely noticed it. With his arms extended, all the shirt and half the jacket were out of sight beneath the curve in the crevasse.

"How near are you now?" he called.

"Not far," said the voice.

"Can you reach it?"

"I'm trying."

There was the sound of scraping boot-nails; of labored breathing. But no pull on the shirtsleeve down below.

"I can't make it," said the voice. It was fainter than before.

"Wait," said Rudi.

For the third time he raised the staff. He took off his trousers. He tied a trouser-leg to the loose sleeve of the shirt. Then he pulled, one by one, at all the knots he had made: between staff and jacket, jacket and shirt, shirt and trousers. He pulled until the blood pounded in his head and the knots were as tight as his strength could make them. This done, he stepped back from the crevasse to the point where his toes had rested when he lay flat. With feet and hands he kicked and scraped the ice until he had made two holes. Then, lying down as before, he dug his toes deep into them. He was naked now, except for his shoes, stockings and underpants. The cold rose from the ice into his blood and bones. He lowered the staff and knotted clothes like a sort of crazy fishing line.

The trousers, the shirt and half of the jacket passed out of sight. He was leaning over as far as he could.

"Can you reach it now?" he called.

"Yes," the voice answered.

"All right. Come on."

"You won't be able to hold me. I'll pull you in."

"No you won't."

He braced himself. The pull came. His toes went taut in their ice-holds and his hands tightened on the staff until the knuckles showed white. Again he could hear a scraping sound below, and he knew that the man was clawing his boots against the ice-wall, trying both to lever himself up and to take as much weight as possible off the improvised lifeline. But the wall obviously offered little help. Almost all his weight was on the lifeline. Suddenly there was a jerk, as one of the knots in the clothing slipped, and the staff was almost wrenched from Rudi's hands. But the knot held. And his hands held. He tried to call down, "All right?" but he had no breath for words. From below, the only sound was the scraping of boots on ice.

How long it went on Rudi could never have said. Perhaps only for a minute or so. But it seemed like hours. And then at last— at last—it happened. A hand came into view around the curve of the crevasse wall: a hand gripping the twisted fabric of his jacket, and then a second hand rising slowly above it. A head appeared. A pair of shoulders. A face was raised for an instant and then lowered. Again one hand moved slowly up past the other.

But Rudi no longer saw it, for now his eyes were shut tight with the strain. His teeth were clamped, the cords of his neck bulged, the muscles of his arm felt as if he were being drawn one by one from the bones that held them. He began to lose his toeholds. He was being dragged forward. Desperately, frantically, he dug in his feet, pressed his whole body down, as if he could make it part of the glacier. Though all but naked on the ice, he was pouring with sweat. Somehow he stopped the slipping. Somehow he held on. But now suddenly the strain was even worse, for the man had reached the lower end of the staff. The slight "give" of the stretched clothing was gone, and in its place, was rigid deadweight on a length of wood. The climber was close now.

But heavy. Indescribably heavy. Rudi's hands ached and burned, as if it were a rod of hot lead that they clung to. It was not a mere man he was holding, but a giant; or a block of granite. The pull was unendurable. The pain unendurable. He could hold on no longer. His hands were opening. It was all over.

And then it was over. The weight was gone. There was a scraping sound close beneath him; a hand on the rim of ice; a figure pulling itself up onto the lip of the crevasse. The man was beside Rudi, turning to him, staring at him.

"Why—you're just a boy!" he said in astonishment.

Rudi was too numb to move or speak. Taking the staff from him, the man pulled up the line of clothes, untied the knots and shook them out.

"Come on now. Quickly!" he said.

Pulling the boy to his feet, he helped him dress. Then he rubbed and pummeled him until at last Rudi felt the warmth of returning circulation.

"Better?" the man asked, smiling.

Rudi nodded. And finally he was able to speak again. "And you, sir," he said, "you are all right?"

The man nodded. He was warming himself now: flapping his arms and kicking his feet together. "A few minutes of sun and I'll be as good as new."

Nearby, a black boulder lay embedded in the glacial ice, and, going over to it, they sat down. The sunlight poured over them like a warm bath. Rudi slowly flexed his aching fingers and saw that the man was doing the same. And then the man had raised his eyes and was looking at him.

"It's a miracle how you did it," he said. "A boy of your size. All alone."

"It was nothing," Rudi murmured.

"Nothing?"

"I—I only—"

"Only saved my life," said the man.

For the first time, now, Rudi was really seeing him. He was a man of perhaps thirty, very tall and thin, and his face, too, was thin, with a big hawklike nose and a strong jutting chin.

His weather-browned cheeks were clean-shaven, his hair black, his eyes deep-set and gray. And when he spoke, his voice was still almost as quiet as when it had been muffled by the ice-walls of the crevasse. He is—what?—Rudi thought. Not Swiss, he knew. Not French or German. English, perhaps? Yes, English. . . . And then suddenly a deep excitement filled him, for he knew who the man was.

"You are Captain Winter?" he murmured.

"That's right."

"And I—I have saved—I mean—"

Rudi stopped in confusion, and the Englishman grinned. "You've saved," he said, smiling, "one of the worse imbeciles that ever walked on a glacier. An imbecile who was so busy looking up at a mountain that he couldn't even see what was at his feet."

Rudi was wordless—almost stunned. He looked at the man, and then away in embarrassment, and he could scarcely believe what had happened. The name of Captain John Winter was known through the length and breadth of the Alps. He was the foremost mountaineer of his day, and during the past ten years had made more first ascents of great peaks than any other man alive. Rudi had heard that he had come to Kurtal a few days before. He had hoped that at least he would see him in the hotel or walking by in the street. But actually to meet him—and in this way! To pull him from a crevasse—save him. . . . It was incredible!

Captain Winter was watching him. "And you, son," he asked. "What is your name?"

Somehow the boy got his voice back. "Rudi," he said. "Rudi Matt."

"Matt?" Now it was the man's turn to be impressed. "Not of the family of the great Josef Matt?"

"He was my father," Rudi said.

Captain Winter studied him with his gray eyes. Then he smiled again. "I should have known," he said. "A boy who could do what you've done—"

"Did you know my father, sir?"

"No, unfortunately I didn't. He was before my day. But ever since I was a boy I have heard of him. In twenty years no one has come to the Alps and not heard of the great guide, Josef Matt."

Rudi's heart swelled. He looked away. His eyes fixed on the vast mountain that rose before them, and then he saw that Captain Winter was watching it too.

Unconsciously the Englishman spoke his thoughts. "Your father was—" He caught himself and stopped.

"Yes," said Rudi softly, "he was killed on the Citadel."

There was a silence. Captain Winter reached into a pocket and brought out an unbroken bar of chocolate. "Lucky I fell on the other side," he grinned.

He broke the bar in two and handed half to Rudi.

"Oh no, sir, thank you. I couldn't."

"When I meet a boy your age who can't eat chocolate," said Winter, "I'll be glad to stay in a crevasse for good."

Rudi took it, and they sat munching. The sun was warm on their thawing bodies. Far above, it struck the cliffs and snowfields of the Citadel, so brightly that they had to squint against the glare.

Then there was Winter's quiet voice again. "What do you think, Rudi?"

"Think, sir?"

"Can it be climbed?"

"Climbed? The Citadel?"

"Your father thought so. Alone among all the guides of Switzerland, he thought so." There was another pause. "And I think so too," said Captain Winter.

The boy was peering again at the shining heights. And suddenly his heart was pounding so hard that he was sure the Englishman must be able to hear it. "Is—is that why you have come here, sir?" he asked. "To try to climb the Citadel?"

"Well, now—" Winter smiled. "It's not so simple, you know. For one thing, there's not a guide in the valley who would go with me."

"I have an uncle, sir. He is—"

"Yes, I know your uncle. Franz Lerner. He is the best in Kurtal, and I've spoken to him. But he would not go. Anything but that,

he said. Any other peak, any route, any venture. But not *that,*
he said. Not the Citadel."

"He remembers my father—"

"Yes, he remembers your father. They all remember him. And
while they love and respect his memory, they all think he was
crazy." Winter chuckled softly. "Now they think *I'm* crazy," he
added. "And maybe they're right too," he said.

"What will you do, sir?" asked Rudi. "Not try it alone?"

"No, that crazy I'm not." Winter slowly stroked his long jaw.
"I'm not certain what I'll do," he went on. "Perhaps I'll go over
to the next valley. To Broli. I've been told there is a guide there—
a man called Saxo. Do you know him?"

"Yes—Emil Saxo. I have never met him, but I have heard of
him. They say he is a very great guide."

"Well, I thought perhaps I'd go and talk with him. After a while.
But first I must reconnoitre some more. Make my plans. Pick the
route. If there *is* a route."

"Yes, there is! Of course there is!"

Rudi had not thought the words. They simply burst out from
him. And now again he was embarrassed as the man looked at him
curiously.

"So?" said Captain Winter. "That is interesting, Rudi. Tell me
why you think so."

"I have studied the Citadel many times, sir."

"Why?"

"Because—because—" He stopped. He couldn't say it.

"Because you want to climb it yourself?"

"I am not yet a grown man, sir. I know I cannot expect—"

"I wasn't a grown man either," said the Captain, "when I first
saw the Citadel. I was younger than you—only twelve—and my
parents had brought me here for a summer holiday. But I can still
remember how I felt when I looked up at it, and the promise I
made myself that some day I was going to climb it." He paused.
His eyes moved slowly upward. "Youth is the time for dreams,
boy," he murmured. "The trick is, when you get older, not to forget
them."

Rudi listened, spellbound. He had never heard anyone speak like that. He had not known a grown man could think and feel like that.

Then Winter asked:

"This east face, Rudi—what do you think of it?"

"Think of it, sir?"

"Could it be climbed?"

Rudi shook his head. "No, it is no good. The long chimney there—you see. It looks all right; it could be done. And to the left, the ledges"—he pointed—"they could be done too. But higher up, no. They stop. The chimney stops, and there is only smooth rock."

"What about the northeast ridge?"

"That is not good either."

"It's not so steep."

"No, it is not so steep," said Rudi. "But the rocks are bad. They slope out, with few places for holds."

"And the north face?"

Rudi talked on. About the north face, the west ridge, the southwest ridge. He talked quietly and thoughtfully, but with deep inner excitement, for this was the first time in his life that he had been able to speak to anyone of these things which he had thought and studied for so long. . . . And then suddenly he stopped, for he realized what he was doing. He, Rudi Matt, a boy of sixteen who worked in the kitchen of the Beau Site Hotel, was presuming to give his opinions to one of the greatest climbers in the world.

But Captain Winter had been listening intently. Sometimes he nodded. "Go on," he said now, as Rudi paused.

"But I am only—"

"Go on."

And Rudi went on . . .

"That doesn't leave much," said the captain a little later.

"No sir," said the boy.

"Only the southeast ridge."

"Yes sir."

"That was the way your father tried, wasn't it?"

"Yes sir."

"And you believe it's the *only* way?"

"Yes sir."

Captain Winter rubbed his jaw for a moment before speaking again. Then—"That also is very interesting to me, Rudi," he said quietly, "because it is what I believe too."

Later, they threaded their way down the Blue Glacier. For a while they moved in silence. Then Captain Winter asked:

"What do you do, Rudi?"

"Do, sir?"

"Are you an apprentice guide? A porter?"

Rudi swallowed. "No sir."

"What then?"

He could hardly say it. "A—a dishwasher."

"A dishwasher?"

"In the Beau Site Hotel. It is my mother, sir. Since my father died, you see, she is afraid—she does not want—" Rudi swallowed again. "I am to go into the hotel business," he murmured.

"Oh."

Again they moved on without speaking. It was now late afternoon, and behind them the stillness was broken by a great roaring, as sun-loosened rock and ice broke off from the heights of the Citadel.

When they reached the path Rudi spoke again, hesitantly. "Will you please do me a favor, sir," he asked.

"Of course," said Winter.

"Before we come to the town we will separate. And you will please not tell anyone that I have been up here today?"

The Englishman looked at him in astonishment. "Not tell anyone? You save my life, boy, and you want me to keep it a secret?"

"It was nothing, sir. Truly. And if you say that I have been in the mountains, my mother and uncle will hear, and I will be in trouble." Rudi's voice took on a note of urgency. "You will not do it, sir? You will promise—please?"

Winter put a hand on his shoulder. "Don't worry," he said. "I won't get you in trouble." Then he smiled and added: "Master Rudi Matt—dishwasher."

They walked down the path. The sun sank. Behind them, the mountain roared.

* * *

In the kitchen of the Beau Site Hotel old Teo Zurbriggen went about his work. He had long since finished up the breakfast dishes that Rudi had left half-washed, but meanwhile lunch had come and gone and a hundred new ones stood waiting for the suds. And for these Teo had no time, because he was busy cooking dinner.

Gretchen, the waitress, moved back and forth from the dining room. "The boy is a good-for-nothing," she snorted. "Running out and leaving his work."

"He did not run out," said Teo. "I have told you: his mother, Frau Matt, is sick and needs him. And besides," he added, "there are enough clean dishes for dinner."

Gretchen went back to the dining room, and Teo looked out the window. "The sun is low," he thought, "and he should be back soon. Even if he went all the way to the glaciers, he should be back soon."

Old Teo, they called him. He was not really so old; not more than perhaps fifty-five. But his brown skin was wrinkled, his hair almost white, his eyes pale and watery behind craggy brows. And also, he was a cripple. Fifteen years before, in the prime of his life, he had been one of the foremost guides of Kurtal—and the only one willing to accompany Josef Matt and his employer, Sir Edward Stephenson, on their famous attempt on the Citadel. Unlike the other two, he had been brought down alive, but so badly injured from a thirty-foot fall that his career as a mountain man was over. Even now, he walked with a deep limp. His left arm was half paralyzed and his shoulder hunched up against his neck. He had tried farming, until his wife died and he grew too lonely. Then he had worked at odd jobs around the town. And when the Beau Site was built he became its cook.

He was a good cook—but not a happy one. If it had not made it too dark for his work, he would have put blinds on the kitchen windows to shut out the sight of the soaring mountains.

There were footsteps in the alley outside. "Ah, there's the runaway," thought old Teo. But it wasn't. It was Rudi's uncle, Franz Lerner.

He was a big man—not tall, but broad and stoutly built—and his shoulders filled the doorway as he entered. His face, too, was broad, strong and square-cut, with weathered skin, a short fringe of beard and dark, slow-moving eyes. Indeed, everything about him was slow: his gait, his gestures, his speech. Slow and deliberate. Slow and powerful. He was dressed in rough guide's clothing and held a pipe between his teeth.

"*Grüss Gott*," he said to Teo.

"*Grüss Gott*," said the cook.

Franz looked around. "Where is the boy?"

"He is out. I—I sent him to the market."

"His mother wants him to do an errand before he comes home. She asked me to tell him."

"I will tell him when he comes back."

At that moment Gretchen the waitress reappeared. "Good evening," she said to Franz. "It is too bad your sister, the Widow Matt, is ill."

"Ill?"

"Why yes. Is she not? Old Teo said the boy had gone to—"

She looked questioningly at the cook. Franz looked at the cook. Then his eyes moved to the stacks of dirty dishes.

"So," he said. "It is *that* again."

Teo said nothing.

Franz took a step forward. "Is it not?" he demanded. "He has sneaked off again to the mountains."

Teo cleared his throat. "There were not many dishes," he murmured. "And besides, the day was so fine—"

"It is not a question of how many dishes. Or of the weather. It is that here is where he works. Where he belongs. Not wandering around in the mountains."

"I am not sure you are right," said Teo.

"What do you mean by that?"

Teo shrugged his twisted shoulders. "You cannot put out a fire by wishing it out. You cannot bottle the wind."

The two men stood facing each other. Gretchen went back into the dining room.

"If you cannot control him," said Franz, "I shall have to speak to Herr Hempel, the proprietor. Perhaps he should work in another part of the hotel."

"And perhaps he should not work in the hotel at all," said Teo.

"He *must* work in the hotel. It is his mother's wish. He is to be trained for the business."

"He is not a child any more. He cannot be made to do what he does not want to."

"And what he *does* want to—"

"—is to be a guide, of course. If not a full guide yet, at least a porter—an apprentice."

Franz shook his head. "He is not strong enough to be a guide. He is too small. And also too irresponsible." He pointed at the dirty dishes. "Look how he leaves things. How he shirks his work. What would he do in the mountains, where there are real problems and responsibilities?"

"At least he should have the chance to learn." Old Teo came closer and his voice grew lower. "You are a guide, Franz," he said. "When I was young, I too was a guide, and we know how such things are. He cannot stand to see the other boys going out as porters and helpers, learning to be guides, while he works in a kitchen like a girl or an old man. He is Josef Matt's son, and the mountains are in his blood."

"And what do you think is in my sister's blood?" Franz demanded. "A widow at twenty-three, with her husband killed on the Citadel. A widow left with a single child. Do you expect her to let him do as his father did? To die as his father died?" He brought a big hand down heavily on the table. "No. There have been enough guides in the family. And enough sorrow for one woman. This boy will learn a trade, a profession. Soon now he will go for training to a big hotel in Zurich. When he comes back he will be a clerk, then a manager; one day he may even be a proprietor. Something the family can be proud of."

Teo studied him with his pale old eyes. "It is for your sister that you speak now, Franz," he said quietly. "Not for yourself."

"What I speak is sense. And what I speak is what will be." Franz turned abruptly to the door. "I will go now and tell her about this thing."

He went out. Teo stood for a while at the window, watching the mountains and the setting sun. Then he went back to his oven. . . . "Whatever they do, it will be no use," he thought. "They will see. They will find out. You cannot bottle the wind. . . ."

Frau Matt's house was small and neat. And so was Frau Matt. As a young girl, when she married Josef Matt, she had been one of the beauties of Kurtal, and though the years of her widowhood had faded her, she was still, in her late thirties, an attractive, almost a pretty woman. She had not grown fat, as did so many of the village women as they neared middle age. She had the same fine features and light complexion as her son. She was known for the sweetness of her smile. But there was no smile on her face this summer evening, as she sat listening to her brother Franz.

"No," she said sadly, "old Teo does not seem able to control Rudi at all."

"He does not even *want* to control him," said Franz.

"When this summer is over it will be all right, I think. Now, at sixteen, he is wild and willful. But in the fall he will go to Zurich for his training. He will be away from the mountains. And when he comes back he will have interest and pride in his work."

Her brother nodded without speaking.

"You know what I want for him," she said. "How I have hoped and planned for him. You do not think I am wrong, Franz?"

"I think you must do as your heart tells you, Ilse."

"My heart—yes. But it is not just that. It is not of myself that I want to think, but of Rudi. So that he may have a good life. So that he may grow up and marry and have children, and not destroy it all by—"

She broke off. When she spoke again it was with a great effort to be calm and reasonable.

"If he were a different sort of boy—bigger and stronger—perhaps I would feel differently. But he is so small, so delicate."

"Yes," Franz agreed, "he is not built for the mountains."

"And he is so quick and bright. His manners are good. In the hotel business he can make a great success. If only he will stop wanting to be what he is not."

"It is when he thinks of his father that he wants to be a guide."

"Yes, of course—when he thinks of his father. . . . And then when I think of him. Of my own Josef. Of how young he was, how gay and proud. How he used to laugh when I worried about him—"

Frau Matt closed her eyes, and there was a silence in the room. Then the door opened and Rudi came in.

"Good evening, Mother," he said. "Good evening, Uncle."

The two looked at him without answering.

"Is something wrong?" he asked.

"Only that we were wondering," said Franz grimly, "if you were coming home at all tonight."

"It was very busy at the hotel today. There were many dirty dishes."

"Yes, I know. I saw them."

"You—you—" Rudi swallowed. "You mean you were there? It must have been while I was out on an errand."

"No doubt. And it must have been a very hard errand, considering what it did to your feet."

Rudi looked down at his shoes, scuffed by rocks and coated with the dust of the trail.

"Did—did old Teo say—"

"Your crony Teo told one lie after another. First to the waitress. Then to me. And now you are taking up where he left off."

Rudi was silent. His uncle stood up. "I am getting sick of these lies, boy," he said. "Good and sick of all this nonsense!"

Still Rudi said nothing.

"Well, what do you have to say for yourself?"

"I am sorry, Uncle."

"Sorry? Is that all? Sorry until the next time, when you do the same thing again."

"You promised me, Rudi," said Frau Matt gently.

The boy couldn't look at her. "Yes, Mother," he murmured.

"Why didn't you keep your promise?"

"I don't know."

"You don't know?"

"It—it is hard to explain. I did not mean to go—truly. I did not think of going at all. But when I stand there at the kitchen window, when I see the sun and the mountains—"

"I do not want to scold," his mother told him. "In all other things you are a good boy. Only in this do you disobey me and lie to me." She paused, studying her son's face. "I want you to be happy," she went on. "I want only to do what is right and good for you. In the hotel, and with Herr Hempel so interested in you, you will have such a fine future—the best of any boy in Kurtal. Can't you see how much better it is than the other? Than only climbing around on rocks and ice?"

"I have been a guide for twenty years," his uncle put in, "and look what it has got me. I do not have enough education even to speak to the fine visitors who now come here to Kurtal. I have not yet saved enough money to buy a dozen cows.

"Look what it has done for Teo Zurbriggen. He is crippled. He is poor. Soon you will have a fine career. You will be a business man, a gentleman. But he must work all his life in a kitchen."

There was a silence, and Rudi stared at the floor. "I will go now to the hotel," he murmured, "and finish the dishes."

But as he turned to leave there was a knock on the door.

"Come in," said his uncle.

And Captain Winter appeared.

"Ah—Franz," he said. "They told me at your house that I could find you here."

"It is an honor, my Captain. Sit down, please. This is my sister, Frau Matt."

Winter bowed respectfully. "The honor is mine, madam," he said, "to meet the widow of the great Josef Matt."

"And this is her son, Rudi," Franz said, as an afterthought.

The Englishman turned and looked at the boy, but he remembered his promise, and no sign of recognition showed on his face. "Hello, son," he said pleasantly. Then he turned back to Franz. "I just wanted to ask," he said, "if you're available for a climb tomorrow."

"Tomorrow? Yes, my Captain." Franz hesitated. "That is, if you do not mean—"

Winter smiled. "No, I don't mean the Citadel. I was thinking of the Wunderhorn. I know you've been on it often, and they say it's a good climb."

"Yes, it is good," Franz agreed.

"And that it gives a clear view of the Citadel."

"Yes, that is good too."

"Excellent. Suppose we leave tomorrow about noon. We can spend the night at the Blausee Hut and go on up the next morning. We'll need food and blankets, of course. It will probably be best to have a porter." He turned, as if struck by a sudden thought. "How about the youngster here?" he suggested, indicating Rudi. "He should do fine as a helper."

"No," said Franz. "No, my Captain. The boy is not available; he works elsewhere. But I will find a good man who—"

Rudi's voice cut suddenly across his uncle's. "Please!" The word was as if wrenched from his flesh. "Please! Just this once let me come, and I will show you what I can do!"

Franz shook his head. "It is not possible. Only now we have just talked of these things, and your mother does not—"

"But this is different, Uncle—with Captain Winter." Rudi's voice, his eyes, his whole body was pleading. "Captain Winter knows I can do it. He will tell you. Up on the glacier today he saw what I can do."

"On the glacier?" The guide's eyes moved to Winter. "You mean that he was with you, my Captain?"

"Oh, then they know—?" Winter glanced at Rudi.

"All we know," said Franz, "is that he went up into the mountains today. Leaving his work and defying his mother."

"But he told you nothing of what happened?"

"Happened?" Frau Matt repeated.

"No," said Franz, "he told us nothing."

"In that case," said Captain Winter quietly, "it will be my pleasure to tell you. Today, on the Blue Glacier, this boy saved my life."

"Saved—your—life?" breathed Frau Matt.

Franz stared at him. "What are you saying, my Captain?"

Winter told the story, and they listened in silence. Rudi listened too, feeling the blood slowly seeping into his cheeks and forehead, until it seemed to him that his whole face was on fire. Now and then he raised his eyes, but dropped them again almost instantly. And at last the Captain came to the end of the story.

Then he said: "What your son did, Frau Matt, was a very skillful and a very brave thing. There is no question but that I would be dead right now if he had not done it. I think his father, if he were alive today, would be proud of him."

Now the pounding in Rudi's head was so strong that he thought at any moment it might split right open. Through it, dimly, he was aware that his mother and uncle were no longer looking at Captain

Winter, but at him. Indeed, Franz was staring, almost as if he had never seen him before.

"When did you learn these things?" the guide asked.

"I—I didn't." The boy's voice was no more than a whisper. "I just did what seemed best."

"And you held the captain while he climbed up? All alone? With your own strength?"

"Yes, Uncle."

Winter crossed the room and put a hand on Rudi's shoulder. "Rudi told me," he said, "that he should not have been up in the mountains. But, as you see, it was very lucky for me that he was, and I beg you not to be angry with him. A boy who has done what he did deserves a reward, and I shall see that he gets it. But there's a reward *you* can give him that would be better than anything else." He paused and smiled at Frau Matt. "Let him come with us tomorrow on the Wunderhorn."

Franz started to speak, stopped, and looked at his sister. And now Captain Winter went over to her. "I think I know how you feel, Frau Matt," he said gently. "But, I promise you, there would be no danger. Your brother and I will be right there with him. And the Wunderhorn is not a difficult mountain."

Frau Matt looked at her hands. Then at last she looked up. . . . *"Please—please"* . . . Rudi murmured.

"What you have just told us—" his mother said to Winter. "What my boy has done—I am proud of him, of course. But—" she hesitated, "but there are things, my captain, that perhaps you do not understand. Rudi is not a mountain boy, you see. He is not to be a guide, but a hotel man. For years we have planned his career, and now he is serving his apprenticeship in the kitchen at the Beau Site." Casting about for straws, she found one and clutched it. "Every day he works there. The cook needs him. He cannot be spared."

Rudi leapt forward and knelt by his mother's chair. "Yes—yes, I can—truly, Mother." The words tumbled over one another. "Old Teo will let me go—I know he will—he has said so. And besides there is Toni Hassler—he spoke to me last week—he would work as my substitute—"

He had seized her hands and was looking pleadingly into her face. Frau Matt looked back at him for a moment, and then past him, at the two men who stood watching. "I know that Captain Winter is a great climber," she said at last. "If he asks this for you—if he feels it is all right—"

Winter nodded reassuringly.

"And if your uncle—"

"It is up to you, Ilse," said Franz.

Frau Matt was beaten. "Then—then," she said "—this time—this once—"

But when she tried to go on, she couldn't, because Rudi was covering her face with kisses.

When he reached the hotel kitchen there were two hundred dirty dishes waiting for him beside the tub. But for all he cared there could have been two thousand.

During the whole evening he broke only three.

PEARL S. BUCK

Little Red

Little Red was called Little, because his father was Big Red, and he was called Red because, like his father, he always wore something red. Big Red and Little Red, father and son, had always lived, since they were born, in a village on the edge of a small lake in the mountainous country of Lu, in the province of Kiangsi, in China.

The reason the two, father and son, so loved the color red was a simple one. Big Red had been the only son of his mother, and for that reason she kept him dressed in red until he was too big, and then she gave him a red kerchief to wear around his neck.

"I can see you a long way off," she always said, "because of the red kerchief."

So Big Red grew up wearing the red kerchief.

When Little Red was born, he looked exactly like his father, and his mother, who was a sweet and gentle woman, was the first to see this. She loved Big Red, and as a sign of her joy in the little son, she kept him dressed in red until he was too big, and then she gave him a red kerchief, but a little one.

"I can always see where you both are, father and son, Big and Little, with your red kerchiefs," she said.

It was true that when the farmers were working in their fields she could see her two, and when they went to town she could see them coming home, for when she looked out of the door there were the two spots of red, which were their kerchiefs.

They lived happily in the village until the Japanese came, and they never even imagined that someday an enemy would come and take their beautiful country. Some people might have called them poor, for no one in the village had ever seen an automobile, much less owned one, and the houses were small, and none of the fathers ever had much money in his pockets. On the other hand, some people would have called them rich, for they had good food to eat, rice and vegetables, and very fine fish, and chickens and pork, and certainly the best eggs. And they had clothes enough to keep them warm in winter, and in summer Little Red and his playmates went swimming in the ponds, or they climbed the mountains behind the village and spent the day exploring. In autumn they gathered chestnuts from the trees on the mountains and roasted them over charcoal. Altogether it was a good life.

When the Japanese came it changed so quickly that it was hard to believe that it was the same place. The village had been such a safe and pleasant one, where babies played in the street, and where mothers sat in the doorways sewing and watching and talking to one another and laughing at what their children did. As soon as school was over, the school children played in the street, too, and Little Red was always one of them. They played hopscotch and shuttlecock and toss-pennies, and then skipped home to early suppers, and if there were actors in town visiting, they might go to a play in the temple court afterward.

It was as pleasant as that one day, and the next day all was changed. The villagers had heard something about the war, of course. People in the village did not read newspapers, but they listened to other people traveling by, and they heard about the Japanese and how they wanted to take the whole of China. But almost as soon as they heard it, it really happened. For the next day the whole village was in confusion. An army of men came tramping through. Some of the men were on foot, but some rode in the cars which the village had never seen. Little Red happened to be home from school for lunch, and he had taken his bowl to the door and stood eating as fast as he could because he wanted to get back to school in time to play before afternoon work began. He was pushing rice and cabbage into his mouth with his chopsticks when suddenly he felt his father pull his shoulders, jerk him back, and slam the door shut and bar it.

Inside the house everything went wrong at once. His father dropped his bowl on the tile floor and broke it, his mother spilled the tea she was pouring, and the baby began to cry.

"The dwarfs are really here," Big Red gasped to Little Red's mother.

"You must run out of the back door up the mountain," she gasped back. "You should have gone yesterday with the other men, when we first heard the dwarfs were near."

"I did want to get the cabbage planted before I went away," he groaned, "so that if I didn't get back you would have something to eat with the rice."

Before anything could be done, there was a great noise and clatter at the door.

"Shall I open the door, Father?" Little Red asked.

Before anyone could open the door it crashed in, and there stood the strange men who were the Japanese. Big Red and Little Red and the mother and the baby could only stare at them. They were all terrified, and the baby was so frightened that he stopped crying, his mouth wide open.

"You," one of the men yelled at Big Red. He was an officer and he carried a sword as well as a pistol. "Come out here! We want able-bodied men to carry loads for us!"

The moment he spoke the soldiers behind him seized Big Red by the hands and legs and jerked him out in the street. There was already a long line of villagers tied together with ropes, and to this long line Little Red now saw his father tied too. He ran and clung to his father's waist, and his father bent and whispered in his ear, "Get back into the house, bar the door, and take care of your mother!"

He dared not disobey his father, and yet how could he bear to see him go? He obeyed and he disobeyed. He ran into the house, barred the door, and ran out the back door again. There from a distance he watched what happened to his father. The line of villagers was driven down the road like oxen, and the enemy soldiers whipped them if they went too slowly and pricked them with their bayonets. At the head of the line Little Red saw his father march steadfastly away southward. Hiding himself in the bushes, he followed until he was sure of their road, and then he ran home to tell his mother.

You can imagine how his mother cried when she heard what had happened to Big Red. She put the baby in his crib and sat down on a bench in the kitchen and cried and cried, wiping her eyes on her blue cotton apron.

"We will never see him again," she sobbed. "He is such a big strong man, he is so good, he is such a fine worker, they will never let him go. And now he is a prisoner! Oh, if I had only made him go to the mountains yesterday."

"What is in the mountains, Mother?" Little Red asked.

Then his mother told him, "In the mountains there are men from many villages gathering together in an army to fight the enemy. They wanted your father to come yesterday and lead them, and he promised to go as soon as the enemy drew near. This morning, even, he might have gone and been safe if he had not stayed to plant those wretched cabbages. How can I eat them now? They would choke me, for it is because of them he is taken prisoner."

Little Red listened to all of this and said nothing.

He was at this time twelve years old and he knew that there are times when it is better for a boy to listen and say nothing, especially when he is planning something very big. He let his mother cry until she was tired, and he held the baby when that small one began to fret, and he burned the grass under the caldron in the stove when his mother stopped crying after a long time and sighed and said, "Well, I suppose we must eat, even if he is gone. But you eat—I can't eat a thing."

She was rather astonished when he ate an unusually big supper, and she was inclined to be a little cross with him for it. "I am glad you have a big appetite," she said, "but I am surprised, when you know how your poor father is suffering."

He still said nothing. He went to bed very early and so did she, and they had not opened the door since he barred it shut at noon. The mother had cried so much that she went to sleep, although she had not thought she could. But Little Red did not sleep. In his bed he had put a bit of broken brick, and he lay with it in the middle of his back. He lay a long time thus, purposely to keep awake, and when at last he began to hear his mother breathe as though she were sound asleep he rose and made ready to carry out his plan. In his belt he thrust the kitchen chopping knife. In his red kerchief he tied some bread, rolls, and salted cabbage, and two hard-boiled salted duck eggs, which his mother always kept on hand. Then he felt in the broken teapot and took out half of the family money which they kept there. It was never very much, but he thought half would be enough for him in case he did not get home for a long time.

He wished that he could tell his mother where he was going, but she could not read, and there was no use in writing her a note. So he had to go without a word.

He opened the back door and slipped through. The moon was bright and better than any lamp, but he walked softly just the same. He had a long way to go and he set out swiftly and steadily southward. He knew exactly what he was going to do. He was going to find out where his father was, and with the knife he would cut the ropes that bound him and help him to get away.

He thought exactly how it would go. They would have to stop for the night somewhere. Probably the prisoners would all be lying on the ground. Of course they would be guarded by the soldiers. But he would creep forward carefully, making use of every shadow. Perhaps there might be a shadow over the moon by then to help him. Often enough clouds came out of the mountains in the night and spread up over the sky. But the sky was clear now.

He had never been out in the night alone before and he did not like it very well. The frogs were croaking loudly in the ponds, and a bird wailed out of a bamboo grove. But he went on. Two hours passed and he came at last to a village, where he hoped to find his father. It was empty. On the silent street every door was barred. His dream of finding Big Red there was only a dream.

He was so tired that for a moment he was discouraged. Where now should he turn?

But if they were going south, his reason told him, they would still be going south.

He got down on his knees and looked at the road in the bright moonlight. Like all the roads of that province, it had a stone path down the middle, made of flat stones from the mountains and polished smooth by people's feet. If many people had walked down the road today the dust would be tramped away and it would be a sign of which way his father had gone. Sure enough, the polished stone was smooth and clean of dust. He got up again and followed it. When the road forked he followed the one which was clean of dust upon its stone path. It led steadily south.

Now Little Red knew that if you keep going south far enough you reach the great river, and if the prisoners and his father reached the river they would be put on boats, and then there would be no way of following them, for the water could give him no hint and no clue. He began to run instead of walk, dogtrotting along on his tired feet.

I must take the nearest way to the river port! he thought.

He had been to the river port twice with his father, because that is where the fair is held every year, and he knew the way. But of course the gates of the city would be locked at such an hour, and a country boy with a red kerchief full of bread and cabbage and two duck eggs would certainly not be let in or even listened to if he knocked.

There's nothing to do but go around the city, Little Red now told himself.

So he went around the city to the river's edge and crawled along in the mud for a long way. The city wall came right down to the river, and he had to step into the water to get past, but he did that easily enough, and was indeed quite ready to swim if the water were deep. But at this season the river was low, and he was able to walk around the wall.

Now he knew that the boats were all tethered to iron rings fastened in the stones of the river wall on either side of steep stone steps that went to the river, and so to the steps he went. There was not a sign of anyone. The moonlight shone down on the wet steps, and the quiet boats bobbed up and down on the slight swell of the river, and the whole city slept.

He had a dreadful moment of dismay. Suppose they had not come here at all! Perhaps he had guessed entirely wrongly! Then he remembered that he had come around the city, and they perhaps would come another way. And he had come quickly, being alone, and they would come slowly. He sat down on a corner of the step and made himself very small, and waited. He was so hungry that although he tried not to, he felt compelled to eat a piece of the bread he had brought for his father, but he would not allow himself to eat one of the duck eggs.

Scarcely had he done this when he heard a loud noise in the city. Shots rang out in the night, men yelled and cursed, and he heard the heavy squeak of the city gates.

I am right, he thought wildly. I shall see my father! And he squeezed himself very small against the wet wall, into a shadow which the parapet just above his head cast down on the steps. The red kerchief of food he hid between his knees.

Sure enough, in a few minutes of heartbeats so loud that they sounded in his ears like drums, he saw the weary line of men drag themselves around the corner. His father was still at the head of them. He knew his father, for he held up his head, and besides there was the red kerchief about his neck, clearly to be seen in the white moonlight. It was all Little Red could do not to call out, not to press forward. But he knew this would never do. So he sat small and close in the shadow.

It was well he did, for now the soldiers rushed after the prisoners and herded them down the steps together, and Little Red lost sight of his father entirely. A soldier brushed past him as he hurried down to the boats, and for a moment he was terrified. The soldier looked down at him, saw him, and gave him a kick and then went on. Little Red sat motionless while the prisoners were pushed on the boats.

Now he was glad that his father was Big Red. For he watched the spot of red on the tall man who got into the boats with all the others. Then Little Red put down his kerchief but he kept the knife in his belt, and silently, as the boats left the shore, he crept down the steps. Into the water he went as cleanly and deeply as one of the river animals that live along the shores of rivers. He paddled softly after the boats and after the big man who sat on the edge of one of them, his red kerchief fluttering in the night wind.

The boats were rowboats, sampans, and small cargo boats, and the men to whom they belonged rowed slowly and unwillingly, knowing that they would get no pay for what they did. It was not too hard for Little Red to paddle along like a small dog and reach the side of the boat where Big Red sat, his head in his hands, tied to the other prisoners by the rope around his waist. Little Red dared not call. He hung onto the boat by one hand and with the other he reached for the knife and slipped it to his father's foot. Then he pounded lightly on that foot.

Big Red looked down from under his hands. He saw a kitchen knife—nothing else. Then he saw something bob up out of the water, a dark, wet little face. He could not see who it was, and before he looked again the head was bobbing away toward the shore.

For Little Red had very sensibly reasoned that he would go back and wait on the steps so that his father would have only himself to save. Purposely he did not let his father see who he was.

If he knows it is I, he thought, he will stay to see that I am all right and then maybe we'll both be caught.

So he took care of himself and dragged himself out of the river and sat on the steps, very wet and a little cold. The red kerchief was still there, to his joy, for he had been afraid a dog might find it. The food smelled delicious, and he had to be very stern with himself and not even open the kerchief lest he eat more of it. He simply sat and waited.

Big Red, when he saw the knife, could not imagine how it had got there. If he had believed in strange things as some people did, he would have said a river god had come to his help. He was so astonished that he was almost ready to believe it. But he knew that he must not waste time wondering. He took the knife, which was very sharp, and softly cut his ropes. Then quietly he laid it on the foot of the next man and slipped into the water without a ripple. It was easy enough, for the boat was so laden with prisoners that its side was almost level with the river. He sank under the water and began to swim, holding his breath as long as he could. And then one of those clouds came out of the mountains, as they so often did just before dawn, and covered the face of the setting moon. When he came up again he was quite safe. No one could have seen his dark head against the muddy water of the river.

Little Red sat in the darkness on the steps and shivered. Now he could not see his father and he must listen carefully. Yes, in a few moments he heard a man breathing heavily and trying not to breathe. He called out softly, "My father!"

There was no answer. The breathing stopped suddenly. His father was afraid. Little Red understood at once.

"Big Red!" he whispered loudly. "It is Little Red!"

"Little Red?" his father whispered. "Then where are you?"

Feeling for each other along the step, they found one another and each gave the other a big hug.

"Why, you Little Red," his father gasped in a whisper. "How did you come here?"

"I brought the kitchen knife," Little Red whispered back.

But Big Red did not stop while he listened. With the father's arm about his son's shoulder, they went around the city wall and struck over a narrow path to the hills. And all the time Little Red told his father exactly what had happened, and Big Red laughed and hugged Little Red and said over and over again, "You see why the enemy can never conquer our country—no country can be conquered whose boys are like you!"

When they had reached the mountains they went into a little cave and now they felt safe.

"Here is the food," Little Red said proudly. Then he felt he must tell the worst. "I did eat one piece of bread because I was so hungry," he confessed, "but I would not allow myself to have a duck egg."

His father took the kerchief and opened it and divided the food exactly into half. "You are a brave man," he said, "and brave men must eat. Moreover, they must share equally all that they have."

So they ate, and Little Red ate the duck egg, and it tasted even better than he had imagined.

"Now," his father said when they had eaten, "I must go up higher into the mountains and stay there."

"Oh," cried Little Red. "Let me come with you, Father!"

At this Big Red looked grave. "Who will look after the family?" he asked.

It was now Little Red who looked grave. "I should so much like to live in the mountains," he begged, "with you, Father! Because the baby keeps me awake at night when he cries."

His father laughed and clapped him on the shoulder. "Now," he said, "here's a compromise. You shall be the messenger between home and mountains. One night at home, one night in the mountains—how is that? Messengers we must have."

And that is how Little Red became what he is today, a messenger between the men on the plains and the men in the mountains. He stops often to see how his mother and the baby are, but he never stays more than one night. But sometimes by coaxing his father he stays a couple of nights and more in the mountains in an old ruined temple, where the villagers have made a fort. From there they go down into the valley and fight the enemy, and, as often as he can, Little Red tells them where the enemy is. He is too young to enlist, but how can Big Red do without him?

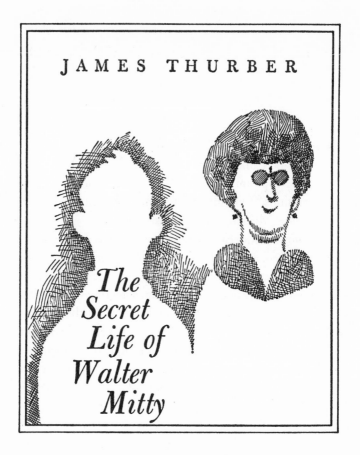

JAMES THURBER

The Secret Life of Walter Mitty

W e're going through!" The Commander's voice was like thin ice breaking. He wore his full-dress uniform, with the heavily braided white cap pulled down rakishly over one cold gray eye. "We can't make it, sir. It's spoiling for a hurricane, if you ask me." "I'm not asking you, Lieutenant Berg," said the Commander. "Throw on the power light! Rev her up to 8,500! We're going through!" The pounding of the cylinders increased: ta-pocketa-pocketa-pocketa-*pocketa-pocketa*. The Commander stared at the ice forming on the pilot window. He walked over and twisted a row of complicated dials. "Switch on No. 8 auxiliary!" he shouted. "Switch on No. 8 auxiliary!" repeated Lieutenant Berg. "Full strength in No. 3 turret!" shouted the Commander. "Full strength in No. 3 turret!" The crew, bending to their various tasks in the huge, hurtling eight-engined Navy hydroplane, looked at each other and grinned. "The Old Man'll get us through," they said to one another. "The Old Man ain't afraid of Hell!" . . .

"Not so fast! You're driving too fast!" said Mrs. Mitty. "What are you driving so fast for?"

"Hmm?" said Walter Mitty. He looked at his wife, in the seat beside him, with shocked astonishment. She seemed grossly unfamiliar, like a strange woman who had yelled at him in a crowd.

"You were up to fifty-five," she said. "You know I don't like to go more than forty. You were up to fifty-five." Walter Mitty drove on toward Waterbury in silence, the roaring of the SN202 through the worst storm in twenty years of Navy flying fading in the remote, intimate airways of his mind. "You're tensed up again," said Mrs. Mitty. "It's one of your days. I wish you'd let Dr. Renshaw look you over."

Walter Mitty stopped the car in front of the building where his wife went to have her hair done. "Remember to get those overshoes while I'm having my hair done," she said. "I don't need overshoes," said Mitty. She put her mirror back into her bag. "We've been all through that," she said, getting out of the car. "You're not a young man any longer." He raced the engine a little. "Why don't you wear your gloves? Have you lost your gloves?" Walter Mitty reached in a pocket and brought out the gloves. He put them on, but after she had turned and gone into the building and he had driven on to a red light, he took them off again. "Pick it up, brother!" snapped a cop as the light changed, and Mitty hastily pulled on his gloves and lurched ahead. He drove around the streets aimlessly for a time, and then he drove past the hospital on his way to the parking lot.

. . . "It's the millionaire banker, Wellington McMillan," said the pretty nurse. "Yes?" said Walter Mitty, removing his gloves slowly. "Who has the case?" "Dr. Renshaw and Dr. Benbow, but there are two specialists here, Dr. Remington from New York and Mr. Pritchard-Mitford from London. He flew over." A door opened down a long, cool corridor and Dr. Renshaw came out. He looked distraught and haggard. "Hello, Mitty," he said. "We're having the devil's own time with McMillan, the millionaire banker and close personal friend of Roosevelt. Obstreosis of the ductal tract. Tertiary. Wish you'd take a look at him." "Glad to," said Mitty.

In the operating room there were whispered introductions: "Dr. Remington, Dr. Mitty. Mr. Pritchard-Mitford, Dr. Mitty." "I've read your book on streptothricosis," said Pritchard-Mitford, shaking hands. "A brilliant performance, sir." "Thank you," said Walter Mitty. "Didn't know you were in the States, Mitty," grumbled Remington. "Coals to Newcastle, bringing Mitford and me up here for a tertiary." "You are very kind," said Mitty. A huge, complicated machine, connected to the operating table, with many tubes and wires, began at this moment to go pocketa-pocketa-pocketa. "The new anesthetizer is giving way!" shouted an interne. "There is no one in the East who knows how to fix it!" "Quiet, man!" said Mitty, in a low, cool voice. He sprang to the machine, which was now going pocketa-pocketa-queep-pocketa-queep. He began fingering delicately a row of glistening dials. "Give me a fountain pen!" he snapped. Someone handed him a fountain pen. He pulled a faulty piston out of the machine and inserted the pen in its place. "That will hold for ten minutes," he said. "Get on with the operation." A nurse hurried over and whispered to Renshaw, and Mitty saw the man turn pale. "Coreopsis has set in," said Renshaw nervously. "If you would take over, Mitty?" Mitty looked at him and at the craven figure of Benbow, who drank, and at the grave, uncertain faces of the two great specialists. "If you wish," he said. They slipped a white gown on him; he adjusted a mask and drew on thin gloves; nurses handed him shining . . .

"Back it up, Mac! Look out for that Buick!" Walter Mitty jammed on the brakes. "Wrong lane, Mac," said the parking-lot attendant, looking at Mitty closely. "Gee. Yeh," muttered Mitty. He began cautiously to back out of the lane marked "Exit Only." "Leave her sit there," said the attendant. "I'll put her away." Mitty got out of the car. "Hey, better leave the key." "Oh," said Mitty, handing the man the ignition key. The attendant vaulted into the car, backed it up with insolent skill, and put it where it belonged.

They're so damn cocky, thought Walter Mitty, walking along Main Street; they think they know everything. Once he had tried to take his chains off, outside New Milford, and he had got them wound around the axles. A man had had to come out in a wrecking car and unwind them, a young, grinning garageman. Since then Mrs. Mitty always made him drive to a garage to have the chains taken off. The next time, he thought, I'll wear my right arm in a sling; they won't grin at me then. I'll have my right arm in a sling and they'll see I couldn't possibly take the chains off myself. He kicked at the slush on the sidewalk. "Overshoes," he said to himself, and he began looking for a shoe store.

When he came out into the street again, with the overshoes in a box under his arm, Walter Mitty began to wonder what the other thing was his wife had told him to get. She had told him twice, before they set out from their house for Waterbury. In a way he hated these weekly trips to town—he was always getting something wrong. Kleenex, he thought, Squibb's, razor blades? No. Toothpaste, toothbrush, bicarbonate, carborundum, initiative and referendum? He gave it up. But she would remember it. "Where's the what's-its-name?" she would ask. "Don't tell me you forgot the what's-its-name." A newsboy went by shouting something about the Waterbury trial.

. . . "Perhaps this will refresh your memory." The District Attorney suddenly thrust a heavy automatic at the quiet figure on the witness stand. "Have you ever seen this before?" Walter Mitty took the gun and examined it expertly. "This is my Webley-Vickers 50.80," he said calmly. An excited buzz ran around the courtroom. The judge rapped for order. "You are a crack shot with any sort of firearms, I believe?" said the District Attorney, insinuatingly. "Objection!" shouted Mitty's attorney. "We have shown that the defendant could not have fired the shot. We have shown that he wore his right arm in a sling on the night of the fourteenth of July." Walter Mitty raised his hand briefly and the bickering attorneys were stilled. "With any known make of gun," he said evenly, "I could have killed Gregory Fitzhurst at three hundred feet *with my left hand*." Pandemonium broke loose in the courtroom. A woman's scream rose above the bedlam and suddenly a lovely, dark-haired girl was in Walter Mitty's arms. The District Attorney struck at her savagely. Without rising from his chair, Mitty let the man have it on the point of the chin. "You miserable cur!" . . .

"Puppy biscuit," said Walter Mitty. He stopped walking and the buildings of Waterbury rose up out of the misty courtroom and surrounded him again. A woman who was passing laughed. "He said 'Puppy biscuit,'" she said to her companion. "That man said 'Puppy biscuit' to himself." Walter Mitty hurried on. He went into an A & P, not the first one he came to but a smaller one farther up the street. "I want some biscuit for small, young dogs," he said to the clerk. "Any special brand, sir?" The greatest pistol shot in the world thought a moment. "It says 'Puppies Bark for It' on the box," said Walter Mitty.

His wife would be through at the hairdresser's in fifteen minutes, Mitty saw in looking at his watch, unless they had trouble drying it; sometimes they had trouble drying it. She didn't like to get to the hotel first; she would want him to be there waiting for her as usual. He found a big leather chair in the lobby, facing a window, and he put the overshoes and the puppy biscuit on the floor beside it. He picked up an old copy of *Liberty* and sank down into the chair. "Can Germany Conquer the World Through the Air?" Walter Mitty looked at the pictures of bombing planes and of ruined streets.

. . . "The cannonading has got the wind up in young Raleigh, sir," said the sergeant. Captain Mitty looked up at him through tousled hair. "Get him to bed," he said wearily. "With the others. I'll fly alone." "But you can't, sir," said the sergeant anxiously. "It takes two men to handle that bomber and the Archies are pounding hell out of the air. Von Richtman's circus is between here and Saulier." "Somebody's got to get that ammunition dump," said Mitty. "I'm going over. Spot of brandy?" He poured a drink for the sergeant and one for himself. War thundered and whined around the dugout and battered at the door. There was a rending of wood and splinters flew through the room. "A bit of a near thing," said Captain Mitty carelessly. "The box barrage is closing in," said the sergeant. "We only live once, Sergeant," said Mitty, with his faint, fleeting smile. "Or do we?" he poured another brandy and tossed it off. "I never see a man could hold his brandy like you, sir," said the sergeant. "Begging your pardon, sir," Captain Mitty stood up and strapped on his huge Webley-Vickers automatic. "It's forty kilometers through hell, sir," said the sergeant. Mitty finished one last brandy. "After all," he said softly, "what isn't?" The pounding of the cannon increased; there was the rat-tat-tatting of machine guns, and from somewhere came the menacing pocketa-pocketa-pocketa of the new flame-throwers. Walter Mitty walked to the door of the dugout humming "Auprès de Ma Blonde." He turned and waved to the sergeant. "Cheerio!" he said. . . .

Something struck his shoulder. "I've been looking all over this hotel for you," said Mrs. Mitty. "Why do you have to hide in this old chair? How did you expect me to find you?" "Things close in," said Walter Mitty vaguely. "What?" Mrs. Mitty said. "Did you get the what's-its-name? The puppy biscuit? What's in that box?" "Overshoes," said Mitty. "Couldn't you have put them on in the store?" "I was thinking," said Walter Mitty. "Does it ever occur to you that I am sometimes thinking?" She looked at him. "I'm going to take your temperature when I get you home," she said.

They went out through the revolving doors that made a faintly derisive whistling sound when you pushed them. It was two blocks to the parking lot. At the drugstore on the corner she said, "Wait here for me. I forgot something. I won't be a minute." She was more than a minute. Walter Mitty lighted a cigarette. It began to rain, rain with sleet in it. He stood up against the wall of the drugstore, smoking. . . . He put his shoulders back and his heels together. "To hell with the handkerchief," said Walter Mitty scornfully. He took one last drag on his cigarette and snapped it away. Then, with that faint, fleeting smile playing about his lips, he faced the firing squad; erect and motionless, proud and disdainful, Walter Mitty the Undefeated, inscrutable to the last.

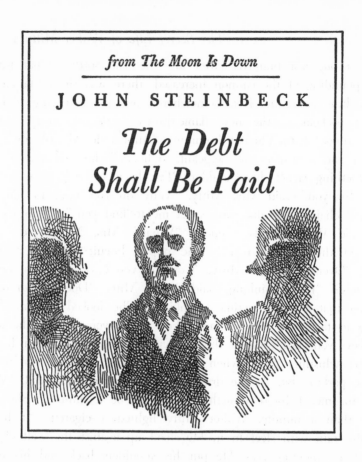

from The Moon Is Down

JOHN STEINBECK

The Debt Shall Be Paid

[*The Germans had occupied the town swiftly and efficiently. They needed its coal to supply the Axis armies. It should be a simple task, Colonel Lanser thought, to keep these unwarlike people subdued and manageable.*]

In the dark, clear night a white, half-withered moon brought little light. The wind was dry and singing over the snow, a quiet wind that blew steadily, evenly from the cold point of the Pole. Over the land the snow lay very deep and dry as sand. The houses snuggled down in the hollows of banked snow, and their windows were dark and shuttered against the cold, and only a little smoke rose from the banked fires.

In the town the footpaths were frozen hard and packed hard. And the streets were silent, too, except when the miserable, cold patrol came by. The houses were dark against the night, and a little lingering warmth remained in the houses against the morning. Near the mine entrance the guards watched the sky and trained their instruments on the sky and turned their listening-instruments against the sky, for it was a clear night for bombing. On nights like this the feathered steel spindles came whistling down and roared to splinters. The land would be visible from the sky tonight, even though the moon seemed to throw little light.

Down toward one end of the village, among the small houses, a dog complained about the cold and the loneliness. He raised his nose to his god and gave a long and fulsome account of the state of the world as it applied to him. He was a practiced singer with a full bell throat and great versatility of range and control. The six men of the patrol slogging dejectedly up and down the streets heard the singing of the dog, and one of the muffled soldiers said, "Seems to me he's getting worse every night. I suppose we ought to shoot him."

And another answered, "Why? Let him howl. He sounds good to me. I used to have a dog at home that howled. I never could break him. Yellow dog. I don't mind the howl. They took my dog when they took the others," he said factually, in a dull voice.

And the corporal said, "Couldn't have dogs eating up food that was needed."

"Oh, I'm not complaining. I know it was necessary. I can't plan the way the leaders do. It seems funny to me, though, that some people here have dogs, and they don't have even as much food as we have. They're pretty gaunt, though, dogs and people."

"They're fools," said the corporal. "That's why they lost so quickly. They can't plan the way we can."

"I wonder if we'll have dogs again after it's over," said the soldier. "I suppose we could get them from America or some place and start the breeds again. What kind of dogs do you suppose they have in America?"

"I don't know," said the corporal. "Probably dogs as crazy as everything else they have." And he went on, "Maybe dogs are no good, anyway. It might be just as well if we never bothered with them, except for police work."

"It might be," said the soldier. "I've heard the Leader doesn't like dogs. I've heard they make him itch and sneeze."

"You hear all kinds of things," the corporal said. "Listen!" The patrol stopped and from a great distance came the bee hum of planes.

"There they come," the corporal said. "Well, there aren't any lights. It's been two weeks, hasn't it, since they came before?"

"Twelve days," said the soldier.

The guards at the mine heard the high drone of the planes. "They're flying high," a sergeant said. And Captain Loft tilted his head back so that he could see under the rim of his helmet. "I judge over 20,000 feet," he said. "Maybe they're going on over."

"Aren't very many." The sergeant listened. "I don't think there are more than three of them. Shall I call the battery?"

"Just see they're alert, and then call Colonel Lanser—no, don't call him. Maybe they aren't coming here. They're nearly over and they haven't started to dive yet."

"Sounds to me like they're circling. I don't think there are more than two," the sergeant said.

In their beds the people heard the planes and they squirmed deep into their featherbeds and listened. In the palace of the Mayor the little sound awakened Colonel Lanser, and he turned over on his back and looked at the dark ceiling with wide-open eyes, and he held his breath to listen better and then his heart beat so that he could not hear as well as he could when he was breathing. Mayor Orden heard the planes in his sleep and they made a dream for him and he moved and whispered in his sleep.

High in the air the two bombers circled, mud-colored planes. They cut their throttles and soared, circling. And from the belly of each one tiny little objects dropped, hundreds of them, one after another. They plummeted a few feet and then little parachutes opened and drifted small packages silently and slowly downward toward the earth, and the planes raised their throttles and gained altitude, and then cut their throttles and circled again, and more of the little objects plummeted down, and then the planes turned and flew back in the direction from which they had come.

The tiny parachutes floated like thistledown and the breeze spread them out and distributed them as seeds on the ends of thistledown are distributed. They drifted so slowly and landed so gently that sometimes the ten-inch packages of dynamite stood upright in the snow, and the little parachutes folded gently down around them. They looked black against the snow. They landed in the white fields and among the woods of the hills and they landed in trees and hung down from the branches. Some of them landed on the housetops of the little town, some in the small front yards, and one landed and stood upright in the snow crown on top of the head of the village statue of St. Albert the Missionary.

One of the little parachutes came down in the street ahead of the patrol and the sergeant said, "Careful! It's a time bomb."

"It ain't big enough," a soldier said.

"Well, don't go near it." The sergeant had his flashlight out and he turned it on the object, a little parachute no bigger than a handkerchief, colored light blue, and hanging from it a package wrapped in blue paper.

"Now don't anybody touch it," the sergeant said. "Harry, you go down to the mine and get the captain. We'll keep an eye on this damn thing."

The late dawn came and the people moving out of their houses in the country saw the spots of blue against the snow. They went to them and picked them up. They unwrapped the paper and read the printed words. They saw the gift and suddenly each finder grew furtive, and he concealed the long tube under his coat and went to some secret place and hid the tube.

And word got to the children about the gift and they combed the countryside in a terrible Easter egg hunt, and when some lucky child saw the blue color, he rushed to the prize and opened it and then he hid the tube and told his parents about it. There were some people who were frightened, who turned the tubes over to the military, but they were not very many. And the soldiers scurried about the town in another Easter egg hunt, but they were not so good at it as the children were.

In the drawing-room of the palace of the Mayor the dining-table remained with the chairs about as it had been placed the day Alex Morden was shot. The room had not the grace it had when it was still the palace of the Mayor. The walls, bare of standing chairs, looked very blank. The table with a few papers scattered about on it made the room look like a business office. The clock on the mantel struck nine. It was a dark day now, overcast with clouds, for the dawn had brought the heavy snow clouds.

Annie came out of the Mayor's room; she swooped by the table and glanced at the papers that lay there. Captain Loft came in. He stopped in the doorway, seeing Annie.

"What are you doing here?" he demanded.

And Annie said sullenly, "Yes, sir."

"I said, what are you doing here?"

"I thought to clean up, sir."

"Let things alone, and go along."

And Annie said, "Yes, sir," and she waited until he was clear of the door, and she scuttled out.

Captain Loft turned back through the doorway and he said, "All right, bring it in." A soldier came through the door behind him, his rifle hung over his shoulder by a strap, and in his arms he held a number of the blue packages, and from the ends of the packages there dangled the little strings and pieces of blue cloth.

Loft said, "Put them on the table." The soldier gingerly laid the packages down. "Now go upstairs and report to Colonel Lanser that I'm here with the—things," and the soldier wheeled about and left the room.

Loft went to the table and picked up one of the packages, and his face wore a look of distaste. He held up the little blue cloth parachute, held it above his head and dropped it, and the cloth opened and the package floated to the floor. He picked up the package again and examined it.

Now Colonel Lanser came quickly into the room, followed by Major Hunter. Hunter was carrying a square of yellow paper in his hand. Lanser said, "Good morning, Captain," and he went to the head of the table and sat down. For a moment he looked at the little pile of tubes, and then he picked one up and held it in his hand. "Sit down, Hunter," he said. "Have you examined these?"

Hunter pulled out a chair and sat down. He looked at the yellow paper in his hand. "Not very carefully," he said. "There are three breaks in the railroad all within ten miles."

"Well, take a look at them and see what you think," Lanser said.

Hunter reached for a tube and stripped off the outer covering, and inside was a small package next to the tube. Hunter took out a knife and cut into the tube. Captain Loft looked over his shoulder. Then Hunter smelled the cut and rubbed his fingers together, and he said, "It's silly. It's commercial dynamite. I don't know what per cent of nitroglycerin until I test it." He looked at the end. "It has a regular dynamite cap, fulminate of mercury, and a fuse—about a minute, I suppose." He tossed the tube back onto the table. "It's very cheap and very simple," he said.

The colonel looked at Loft. "How many do you think were dropped?"

"I don't know, sir," said Loft. "We picked up about fifty of them, and about ninety parachutes they came in. For some reason the people leave the parachutes when they take the tubes, and then there are probably a lot we haven't found yet."

Lanser waved his hand. "It doesn't really matter," he said. "They can drop as many as they want. We can't stop it, and we can't use it against them, either. They haven't conquered anybody."

Loft said fiercely, "We can beat them off the face of the earth!"

Hunter was prying the copper cap out of the top of one of the sticks, and Lanser said, "Yes—we can do that. Have you looked at this wrapper, Hunter?"

"Not yet, I haven't had time."

"It's kind of devilish, this thing," said Colonel Lanser. "The wrapper is blue, so that it's easy to see. Unwrap the outer paper and here"—he picked up the small package—"here is a piece of chocolate. Everybody will be looking for it. I'll bet our own soldiers steal the chocolate. Why, the kids will be looking for them, like Easter eggs."

A soldier came in and laid a square of yellow paper in front of the colonel and retired, and Lanser glanced at it and laughed harshly. "Here's something for you, Hunter. Two more breaks in your line."

Hunter looked up from the copper cap he was examining, and he asked, "How general is this? Did they drop them everywhere?"

Lanser was puzzled. "Now, that's the funny thing. I've talked to the capital. This is the only place they've dropped them."

"What do you make of that?" Hunter asked.

"Well, it's hard to say. I think this is a test place. I suppose if it works here they'll use it all over, and if it doesn't work here they won't bother."

"What are you going to do?" Hunter asked.

"The capital orders me to stamp this out so ruthlessly that they won't drop it any place else."

Hunter said plaintively, "How am I going to mend five breaks in the railroad? I haven't rails right now for five breaks."

"You'll have to rip out some of the old sidings, I guess," said Lanser.

Hunter said, "That'll make a hell of a roadbed."

"Well, anyway, it will make a roadbed."

Major Hunter tossed the tube he had torn apart onto the pile, and Loft broke in, "We must stop this thing at once, sir. We must arrest and punish people who picked these things up, before they use them. We have to get busy so these people won't think we are weak."

Lanser was smiling at him, and he said, "Take it easy, Captain. Let's see what we have first, and then we'll think of remedies."

He took a new package from the pile and unwrapped it. He took the little piece of chocolate, tasted it, and he said, "This is a devilish thing. It's good chocolate, too. I can't even resist it myself. The prize in the grab-bag." Then he picked up the dynamite. "What do you think of this really, Hunter?"

"What I told you. It's very cheap and very effective for small jobs, dynamite with a cap and a one-minute fuse. It's good if you know how to use it. It's no good if you don't."

Lanser studied the print on the inside of the wrapper. "Have you read this?"

"Glanced at it," said Hunter.

"Well, I have read it, and I want you to listen to it carefully," said Lanser. He read from the paper, " 'To the unconquered people: Hide this. Do not expose yourself. You will need this later. It is a present from your friends to you and from you to the invader of your country. Do not try to do large things with it.' " He began to skip through the bill. "Now here, 'rails in the country.' And, 'work at night.' And, 'tie up transportation.' Now here, 'Instructions: rails. Place stick under rail close to the joint, and tight against a tie. Pack mud or hardbeaten snow around it so that it is firm.

When the fuse is lighted you have a slow count of sixty before it explodes.' "

He looked up at Hunter and Hunter said simply, "It works." Lanser looked back at his paper and he skipped through. " 'Bridges: Weaken, do not destroy.' And here, 'transmission poles,' and here, 'culverts, trucks.'" He laid the blue handbill down. "Well, there it is."

Loft said angrily, "We must do something! There must be a way to control this. What does headquarters say?"

Lanser pursed his lips and his fingers played with one of the tubes. "I could have told you what they'd say before they said it. I have the orders. 'Set booby traps and poison the chocolate.'" He paused for a moment and then he said, "Hunter, I'm a good, loyal man, but sometimes when I hear the brilliant ideas of headquarters, I wish I were a civilian, an old, crippled civilian. They always think they are dealing with stupid people. I don't say that this is a measure of their intelligence, do I?"

Hunter looked amused. "Do you?"

Lanser said sharply, "No, I don't. But what will happen? One man will pick up one of these and get blown to bits by our booby trap. One kid will eat chocolate and die of strychnine poisoning. And then?" He looked down at his hands. "They will poke them with poles, or lasso them, before they touch them. They will try the chocolate on the cat. Goddamn it, Major, these are intelligent people. Stupid traps won't catch them twice."

Loft cleared his throat. "Sir, this is defeatist talk," he said. "We must do something. Why do you suppose it was only dropped here, sir?"

And Lanser said, "For one of two reasons: either this town was picked at random or else there is communication between this town and the outside. We know that some of the young men have got away."

Loft repeated dully, "We must do something, sir."

Now Lanser turned on him. "Loft, I think I'll recommend you for the General Staff. You want to get to work before you even know what the problem is. This is a new kind of conquest. Always before, it was possible to disarm a people and keep them in ignorance. Now they listen to their radios and we can't stop them. We can't even find their radios."

A soldier looked in through the doorway. "Mr. Corell to see you, sir."

Lanser replied, "Tell him to wait." He continued to talk to Loft. "They read the handbills; weapons drop from the sky for them. Now it's dynamite, Captain. Pretty soon it may be grenades, and then poison."

Loft said anxiously, "They haven't dropped poison yet."

"No, but they will. Can you think what will happen to the morale of our men or even to you if the people had some of those little game darts, you know, those silly little things you throw at a target, the points coated perhaps with cyanide, silent, deadly little things that you couldn't hear coming, that would pierce the uniform and make no noise? And what if our men knew that arsenic was about? Would you or they drink or eat comfortably?"

Hunter said dryly, "Are you writing the enemy's campaign, Colonel?"

"No, I'm trying to anticipate it."

Loft said, "Sir, we sit here talking when we should be searching for this dynamite. If there is organization among these people, we have to find it, we have to stamp it out."

"Yes," said Lanser, "we have to stamp it out, ferociously, I suppose. You take a detail, Loft. Get Prackle to take one. I wish we had more junior officers. Tonder's getting killed didn't help us a bit. Why couldn't he let women alone?"

Loft said, "I don't like the way Lieutenant Prackle is acting, sir."

"What's he doing?"

"He isn't doing anything, but he's jumpy and he's gloomy."

"Yes," Lanser said, "I know. It's a thing I've talked about so much. You know," he said, "I might be a major-general if I hadn't talked about it so much. We trained our young men for victory and you've got to admit they're glorious in victory, but they don't quite know how to act in defeat. We told them they were brighter and braver than other young men. It was a kind of shock to them to find out that they aren't a bit braver or brighter than other young men."

Loft said harshly, "What do you mean by defeat? We are not defeated."

And Lanser looked coldly up at him for a long moment and did not speak, and finally Loft's eyes wavered, and he said, "Sir."

"Thank you," said Lanser.

"You don't demand it of the others, sir."

"They don't think about it, so it isn't an insult. When you leave it out, it's insulting."

"Yes, sir," said Loft.

"Go on, now, try to keep Prackle in hand. Start your search. I don't want any shooting unless there's an overt act, do you understand?"

"Yes, sir," said Loft, and he saluted formally and went out of the room.

Hunter regarded Colonel Lanser amusedly. "Weren't you rough on him?"

"I had to be. He's frightened. I know his kind. He has to be disciplined when he's afraid or he'll go to pieces. He relies on discipline the way other men rely on sympathy. I suppose you'd better get to your rails. You might as well expect that tonight is the time when they'll really blow them, though."

Hunter stood up and he said, "Yes. I suppose the orders are coming in from the capital?"

"Yes."

"Are they——"

"You know what they are," Lanser interrupted. "You know what they'd have to be. Take the leaders, shoot the leaders, take hostages, shoot the hostages, take more hostages, shoot them"—his voice had risen but now it sank almost to a whisper—"and the hatred growing and the hurt between us deeper and deeper."

Hunter hesitated. "Have they condemned any from the list of names?" and he motioned slightly toward the Mayor's bedroom.

Lanser shook his head. "No, not yet. They are just arrested so far."

Hunter said quietly, "Colonel, do you want me to recommend—maybe you're overtired, Colonel? Could I—you know—could I report that you're overtired?"

For a moment Lanser covered his eyes with his hand, and then his shoulders straightened and his face grew hard. "I'm not a civilian,

Hunter. We're short enough of officers already. You know that. Get to your work, Major. I have to see Corell."

Hunter smiled. He went to the door and opened it, and he said out of the door, "Yes, he's here," and over his shoulder he said to Lanser, "It's Prackle. He wants to see you."

"Send him in," said Lanser.

Prackle came in, his face sullen, belligerent. "Colonel Lanser, sir, I wish to——"

"Sit down," said Lanser. "Sit down and rest a moment. Be a good soldier, Lieutenant."

The stiffness went out of Prackle quickly. He sat down beside the table and rested his elbows on it. "I wish——"

And Lanser said, "Don't talk for a moment. I know what it is. You didn't think it would be this way, did you? You thought it would be rather nice."

"They hate us," Prackle said. "They hate us so much."

Lanser smiled. "I wonder if I know what it is. It takes young men to make good soldiers, and young men need young women, is that it?"

"Yes, that's it."

"Well," Lanser said kindly, "does she hate you?"

Prackle looked at him in amazement. "I don't know, sir. Sometimes I think she's only sorry."

"And you're pretty miserable?"

"I don't like it here, sir."

"No, you thought it would be fun, didn't you? Lieutenant Tonder went to pieces and then he went out and they got a knife in him. I could send you home. Do you want to be sent home, knowing we need you here?"

Prackle said uneasily, "No, sir, I don't."

"Good. Now I'll tell you, and I hope you'll understand it. You're not a man any more. You are a soldier. Your comfort is of no importance and, Lieutenant, your life isn't of much importance. If you live, you will have memories. That's about all you will have. Meanwhile you must take orders and carry them out. Most of the orders will be unpleasant, but that's not your business. I will not lie to you, Lieutenant. They should have trained you for this, and not for flower-strewn streets. They should have built your soul with truth, not led it along with lies." His voice grew hard. "But you took the job, Lieutenant. Will you stay with it or quit it? We can't take care of your soul."

Prackle stood up. "Thank you, sir."

"And the girl," Lanser continued, "the girl, Lieutenant, you may rape her, or protect her, or marry her—that is of no importance so long as you shoot her when it is ordered."

Prackle said wearily, "Yes, sir, thank you, sir."

"I assure you it is better to know. I assure you of that. It is better to know. Go now, Lieutenant, and if Corell is still waiting, send him in." And he watched Lieutenant Prackle out of the doorway.

When Mr. Corell came in, he was a changed man. His left arm was in a cast, and he was no longer the jovial, friendly, smiling Corell. His face was sharp and bitter, and his eyes squinted down like little dead pig's eyes.

"I should have come before, Colonel," he said, "but your lack of co-operation made me hesitant."

Lanser said, "You were waiting for a reply to your report, I remember."

"I was waiting for much more than that. You refused me a position of authority. You said I was valueless. You did not realize that I was in this town long before you were. You left the Mayor in his office, contrary to my advice."

Lanser said, "Without him here we might have had more disorder than we have."

"That is a matter of opinion," Corell said. "This man is a leader of a rebellious people."

"Nonsense," said Lanser; "he's just a simple man."

With his good hand Corell took a black notebook from his right pocket and opened it with his fingers. "You forgot, Colonel, that I had my sources, that I had been here a long time before you. I have to report to you that Mayor Orden has been in constant contact with every happening in this community. On the night when Lieutenant Tonder was murdered, he was in the house where the murder was committed. When the girl escaped to the hills, she stayed with one of his relatives. I traced her there, but she was gone. Whenever men have escaped, Orden has known about it and has helped them. And I even strongly suspect that he is somewhere in the picture of these little parachutes."

Lanser said eagerly, "But you can't prove it."

"No," Corell said, "I can't prove it. The first thing I know; the last I only suspect. Perhaps now you will be willing to listen to me."

Lanser said quietly, "What do you suggest?"

"These suggestions, Colonel, are a little stronger than suggestions. Orden must now be a hostage and his life must depend on the peacefulness of this community. His life must depend on the lighting of one single fuse on one single stick of dynamite."

He reached into his pocket again and brought out a little folding book, and he flipped it open and laid it in front of the colonel. "This, sir, was the answer to my report from headquarters. You will notice that it gives me certain authority."

Lanser looked at the little book and he spoke quietly. "You really did go over my head, didn't you?" He looked up at Corell with frank dislike in his eyes. "I heard you'd been injured. How did it happen?"

Corell said, "On the night when your lieutenant was murdered I was waylaid. The patrol saved me. Some of the townsmen escaped in my boat that night. Now, Colonel, must I express more strongly than I have that Mayor Orden must be held hostage?"

Lanser said, "He is here, he hasn't escaped. How can we hold him more hostage than we are?"

Suddenly in the distance there was a sound of an explosion, and both men looked around in the direction from which it came. Corell said, "There it is, Colonel, and you know perfectly well that if this experiment succeeds there will be dynamite in every invaded country."

Lanser repeated quietly, "What do you suggest?"

"Just what I have said. Orden must be held against rebellion."

"And if they rebel and we shoot Orden?"

"Then that little doctor is next; although he holds no position, he's next in authority in the town."

"But he holds no office."

"He has the confidence of the people."

"And when we shoot him, what then?"

"Then we have authority. Then rebellion will be broken. When we have killed the leaders, the rebellion will be broken."

Lanser asked quizzically, "Do you really think so?"

"It must be so."

Lanser shook his head slowly and then he called, "Sentry!" The door opened and a soldier appeared in the doorway. "Sergeant," said Lanser, "I have placed Mayor Orden under arrest, and I have placed Doctor Winter under arrest. You will see to it that Orden is guarded and you will bring Winter here immediately."

The sentry said, "Yes, sir."

Lanser looked up at Corell and he said, "You know, I hope you know what you're doing. I do hope you know what you're doing."

* * *

In the little town the news ran quickly. It was communicated by whispers in doorways, by quick, meaningful looks—"The Mayor's been arrested"—and through the town a little quiet jubilance ran, a fierce little jubilance, and people talked quietly together and went apart, and people going in to buy food leaned close to the clerks for a moment and a word passed between them.

The people went into the country, into the woods, searching for dynamite. And children playing in the snow found the dynamite, and by now even the children had their instructions. They opened the packages and ate the chocolate, and then they buried the dynamite in the snow and told their parents where it was.

Far out in the country a man picked up a tube and read the instructions and he said to himself, "I wonder if this works." He stood the tube up in the snow and lighted the fuse, and he ran back from it and counted, but his count was fast. It was sixty-eight before the dynamite exploded. He said, "It does work," and he went hurriedly about looking for more tubes.

Almost as though at a signal the people went into their houses and the doors were closed, the streets were quiet. At the mine the soldiers carefully searched every miner who went into the shaft, searched and researched, and the soldiers were nervous and rough and they spoke harshly to the miners. The miners looked coldly at them, and behind their eyes was a little fierce jubilance.

In the drawing-room of the palace of the Mayor the table had been cleaned up, and a soldier stood guard at Mayor Orden's bed-room door. Annie was on her knees in front of the coal grate, putting little pieces of coal on the fire. She looked up at the sentry standing in front of Mayor Orden's door and she said truculently, "Well, what are you going to do to him?" The soldier did not answer.

The outside door opened and another soldier came in, holding Doctor Winter by the arm. He closed the door behind Doctor Winter and stood against the door inside the room. Doctor Winter said, "Hello, Annie, how's His Excellency?"

And Annie pointed at the bedroom and said, "He's in there."

"He isn't ill?" Doctor Winter said.

"No, he didn't seem to be," said Annie. "I'll see if I can tell him you're here." She went to the sentry and spoke imperiously. "Tell His Excellency that Doctor Winter is here, do you hear me?"

The sentry did not answer and did not move, but behind him the door opened and Mayor Orden stood in the doorway. He ignored the sentry and brushed past him and stepped into the room. For a moment the sentry considered taking him back, and then he returned to his place beside the door. Orden said, "Thank you, Annie. Don't go too far away, will you? I might need you."

Annie said, "No, sir, I won't. Is Madame all right?"

"She's doing her hair. Do you want to see her, Annie?"

"Yes, sir," said Annie, and she brushed past the sentry, too, and went into the bedroom and shut the door.

Orden said, "Is there something you want, Doctor?"

Winter grinned sardonically and pointed over his shoulder to his guard. "Well, I guess I'm under arrest. My friend here brought me."

Orden said, "I suppose it was bound to come. What will they do now, I wonder?" And the two men looked at each other for a long time and each one knew what the other was thinking.

And then Orden continued as though he had been talking. "You know, I couldn't stop it if I wanted to."

"I know," said Winter, "but they don't know." And he went on with a thought he had been having. "A time-minded people," he said, "and the time is nearly up. They think that just because they have only one leader and one head, we are all like that.

They know that ten heads lopped off will destroy them, but we are a free people; we have as many heads as we have people, and in a time of need leaders pop up among us like mushrooms."

Orden put his hand on Winter's shoulder and he said, "Thank you. I knew it, but it's good to hear you say it. The little people won't go under, will they?" He searched Winter's face anxiously.

And the doctor reassured him, "Why, no, they won't. As a matter of fact, they will grow stronger with outside help."

The room was silent for a moment. The sentry shifted his position a little and his rifle clinked on a button.

Orden said, "I can talk to you, Doctor, and I probably won't be able to talk again. There are little shameful things in my mind." He coughed and glanced at the rigid soldier, but the soldier gave no sign of having heard. "I have been thinking of my own death. If they follow the usual course, they must kill me, and then they must kill you." And when Winter was silent, he said, "Mustn't they?"

"Yes, I guess so." Winter walked to one of the gilt chairs, and as he was about to sit down he noticed that its tapestry was torn, and he petted the seat with his fingers as though that would mend it. And he sat down gently because it was torn.

And Orden went on, "You know, I'm afraid. I have been thinking of ways to escape, to get out of it. I have been thinking of running away. I have been thinking of pleading for my life, and it makes me ashamed."

And Winter, looking up, said, "But you haven't done it."

"No, I haven't."

"And you won't do it."

Orden hesitated. "No, I won't. But I have thought of it."

And Winter said, gently, "How do you know everyone doesn't think of it? How do you know I haven't thought of it?"

"I wonder why they arrested you, too," Orden said. "I guess they will have to kill you, too."

"I guess so," said Winter. He rolled his thumbs and watched them tumble over and over.

"You know so." Orden was silent for a moment and then he said, "You know, Doctor, I am a little man and this is a little town, but there must be a spark in little men that can burst into flame. I am afraid, I am terribly afraid, and I thought of all the things I might do to save my own life, and then that went away, and sometimes now I feel a kind of exultation, as though I were bigger and better than I am, and do you know what I have been thinking, Doctor?" He smiled, remembering. "Do you remember in school, in the *Apology?* Do you remember Socrates says, 'Someone will say, "And are you not ashamed, Socrates, of a course of life which is likely to bring you to an untimely end?" To him I may fairly answer, "There you are mistaken: a man who is good for anything ought not to calculate the chance of living or dying; he ought only to consider whether he is doing right or wrong."'" Orden paused, trying to remember.

Doctor Winter sat tensely forward now, and he went on with it, "'Acting the part of a good man or of a bad.' I don't think you have it quite right. You never were a good scholar. You were wrong in the denunciation, too."

Orden chuckled. "Do you remember that?"

"Yes," said Winter, eagerly, "I remember it well. You forgot a line or a word. It was graduation, and you were so excited you forgot to tuck in your shirt-tail and your shirt-tail was out. You wondered why they laughed."

Orden smiled to himself, and his hand went secretly behind him and patrolled for a loose shirt-tail. "I was Socrates," he said, "and I denounced the School Board. How I denounced them! I bellowed it, and I could see them grow red."

Winter said, "They were holding their breaths to keep from laughing. Your shirt-tail was out."

Mayor Orden laughed. "How long ago? Forty years."

"Forty-six."

The sentry by the bedroom door moved quietly over to the sentry by the outside door. They spoke softly out of the corners of their mouths like children whispering in school. "How long you been on duty?"

"All night. Can't hardly keep my eyes open."

"Me too. Hear from your wife on the boat yesterday?"

"Yes! She said say hello to you. Said she heard you was wounded. She don't write much."

"Tell her I'm all right."

"Sure—when I write."

The Mayor raised his head and looked at the ceiling and he muttered, "Um—um—um. I wonder if I can remember—how does it go?"

And Winter prompted him, "'And now, O men——'"

And Orden said softly, "'And now, O men who have condemned me——'"

Colonel Lanser came quietly into the room; the sentries stiffened. Hearing the words, the colonel stopped and listened.

Orden looked at the ceiling, lost in trying to remember the old words. "'And now, O men who have condemned me,'" he said, "'I would fain prophesy to you—for I am about to die—and—in the hour of death—men are gifted with prophetic power. And I— prophesy to you who are my murderers—that immediately after my— my death——'"

And Winter stood up, saying, "'Departure.'"

Orden looked at him. "What?"

And Winter said, "The word is 'departure,' not 'death.' You made the same mistake before. You made that mistake forty-six years ago."

"No, it is death. It is death." Orden looked around and saw Colonel Lanser watching him. He asked, "Isn't it 'death'?"

Colonel Lanser said, "'Departure.' It is 'immediately after my departure.'"

Doctor Winter insisted, "You see, that's two against one. 'Departure' is the word. It is the same mistake you made before."

Then Orden looked straight ahead and his eyes were in his memory, seeing nothing outward. And he went on, "'I prophesy to you who are my murderers that immediately after my—departure punishment far heavier than you have inflicted on me will surely await you.'"

Winter nodded encouragingly, and Colonel Lanser nodded, and they seemed to be trying to help him to remember. And Orden went on, "'Me you have killed because you wanted to escape the accuser, and not to give an account of your lives—!'"

Lieutenant Prackle entered excitedly, crying, "Colonel Lanser!"

Colonel Lanser said, "Shh—" and he held out his hand to restrain him.

And Orden went on softly, "'But that will not be as you suppose; far otherwise.'" His voice grew stronger. "'For I say that there will be more accusers of you than there are now'"—he made a little gesture with his hand, a speech-making gesture—"'accusers whom hitherto I have restrained; and as they are younger they will be more inconsiderate with you, and you will be more offended at them.'" He frowned, trying to remember.

And Lieutenant Prackle said, "Colonel Lanser, we have found some men with dynamite."

And Lanser said, "Hush."

Orden continued. "'If you think that by killing men you can prevent someone from censuring your evil lives, you are mistaken.'" He frowned and thought and he looked at the ceiling, and he smiled embarrassedly and he said, "That's all I can remember. It is gone away from me."

And Doctor Winter said, "It's very good after forty-six years, and you weren't very good at it forty-six years ago."

Lieutenant Prackle broke in, "The men have dynamite, Colonel Lanser."

"Did you arrest them?"

"Yes, sir. Captain Loft and——"

Lanser said, "Tell Captain Loft to guard them." He recaptured himself and he advanced into the room and he said, "Orden, these things must stop."

And the Mayor smiled helplessly at him. "They cannot stop, sir."

Colonel Lanser said harshly, "I arrested you as a hostage for the good behavior of your people. Those are my orders."

"But that won't stop it," Orden said simply. "You don't understand. When I have become a hindrance to the people, they will do without me."

Lanser said, "Tell me truly what you think. If the people know you will be shot if they light another fuse, what will they do?"

The Mayor looked helplessly at Doctor Winter. And then the bedroom door opened and Madame came out, carrying the Mayor's chain of office in her hand. She said, "You forgot this."

Orden said, "What? Oh, yes," and he stooped his head and

Madame slipped the chain of office over his head, and he said, "Thank you, dear."

Madame complained, "You always forget it. You forget it all the time."

The Mayor looked at the end of the chain he held in his hand—the gold medallion with the insignia of his office carved on it. Lanser pressed him. "What will they do?"

"I don't know," said the Mayor. "I think they will light the fuse."

"Suppose you ask them not to?"

Winter said, "Colonel, this morning I saw a little boy building a snow man, while three grown soldiers watched to see that he did not caricature your leader. He made a pretty good likeness, too, before they destroyed it."

Lanser ignored the doctor. "Suppose you ask them not to?" he repeated.

Orden seemed half asleep; his eyes were drooped, and he tried to think. He said, "I am not a very brave man, sir. I think they will light it, anyway." He struggled with his speech. "I hope they will, but if I ask them not to, they will be sorry."

Madame said, "What is this all about?"

"Be quiet a moment, dear," the Mayor said.

"But you think they will light it?" Lanser insisted.

The Mayor spoke proudly. "Yes, they will light it. I have no choice of living or dying, you see, sir, but—I do have a choice of how I do it. If I tell them not to fight, they will be sorry, but they will fight. If I tell them to fight, they will be glad, and I who am not a very brave man will have made them a little braver." He smiled apologetically. "You see, it is an easy thing to do, since the end for me is the same."

Lanser said, "If you say yes, we can tell them you said no. We can tell them you begged for your life."

And Winter broke in angrily, "They would know. You do not keep secrets. One of your men got out of hand one night and he said the flies had conquered the flypaper, and now the whole nation knows his words. They have made a song of it. The flies have conquered the flypaper. You do not keep secrets, Colonel."

From the direction of the mine a whistle tooted shrilly. And a quick gust of wind sifted dry snow against the windows.

Orden fingered his gold medallion. He said quietly, "You see, sir, nothing can change it. You will be destroyed and driven out." His voice was very soft. "The people don't like to be conquered, sir, and so they will not be. Free men cannot start a war, but once it is started, they can fight on in defeat. Herd men, followers of a leader, cannot do that, and so it is always the herd men who win battles and the free men who win wars. You will find that is so, sir."

Lanser was erect and stiff. "My orders are clear. Eleven o'clock was the deadline. I have taken hostages. If there is violence, the hostages will be executed."

And Doctor Winter said to the colonel, "Will you carry out the orders, knowing they will fail?"

Lanser's face was tight. "I will carry out my orders no matter what they are, but I do think, sir, a proclamation from you might save many lives."

Madame broke in plaintively, "I wish you would tell me what all this nonsense is."

"It is nonsense, dear."

"But they can't arrest the Mayor," she explained to him.

Orden smiled at her. "No," he said, "they can't arrest the Mayor. The Mayor is an idea conceived by free men. It will escape arrest."

From the distance there was a sound of an explosion. And the echo of it rolled to the hills and back again. The whistle at the coal mine tooted a shrill, sharp warning. Orden stood very tensely for a moment and then he smiled. A second explosion roared—nearer this time and heavier—and its echo rolled back from the mountains. Orden looked at his watch and then he took his watch and chain and put them in Doctor Winter's hand. "How did it go about the flies?" he asked.

"The flies have conquered the flypaper," Winter said.

Orden called, "Annie!" The bedroom door opened instantly and the Mayor said, "Were you listening?"

"Yes, sir." Annie was embarrassed.

And now an explosion roared near by and there was a sound of splintering wood and breaking glass, and the door behind the sentries puffed open. And Orden said, "Annie, I want you to stay with Madame as long as she needs you. Don't leave her alone."

He put his arm around Madame and he kissed her on the forehead and then he moved slowly toward the door where Lieutenant Prackle stood. In the doorway he turned back to Doctor Winter. "Crito, I owe a cock to Asclepius," he said tenderly. "Will you remember to pay the debt?"

Winter closed his eyes for a moment before he answered, "The debt shall be paid."

Orden chuckled then. "I remembered that one. I didn't forget that one." He put his hand on Prackle's arm, and the lieutenant flinched away from him.

And Winter nodded slowly. "Yes, you remembered. The debt shall be paid."

VI

Possibly Impossible

RAY BRADBURY

The Fog Horn

Out there in the cold water, far from land, we waited every night for the coming of the fog, and it came, and we oiled the brass machinery and lit the fog light up in the stone tower. Feeling like two birds in the gray sky, McDunn and I sent the light touching out, red, then white, then red again, to eye the lonely ships. And if they did not see our light, then there was always our Voice, the great deep cry of our Fog Horn shuddering through the rags of mist to startle the gulls away like decks of scattered cards and make the waves turn high and foam.

"It's a lonely life, but you're used to it now, aren't you?" asked McDunn.

"Yes," I said. "You're a good talker, thank the Lord."

"Well, it's your turn on land tomorrow," he said, smiling, "to dance the ladies and drink gin."

"What do you think, McDunn, when I leave you out here alone?"

"On the mysteries of the sea." McDunn lit his pipe. It was a quarter past seven of a cold November evening, the heat on, the light switching its tail in two hundred directions, the Fog Horn bumbling in the high throat of the tower. There wasn't a town for a hundred miles down the coast, just a road which came lonely through dead country to the sea, with few cars on it, a stretch of two miles of cold water out to our rock, and rare few ships.

"The mysteries of the sea," said McDunn thoughtfully. "You know, the ocean's the biggest damned snowflake ever? It rolls and swells a thousand shapes and colors, no two alike. Strange. One night, years ago, I was here alone, when all of the fish of the sea surfaced out there. Something made them swim in and lie in the bay, sort of trembling and staring up at the tower light going red, white, red, white across them so I could see their funny eyes. I turned cold. They were like a big peacock's tail, moving out there until midnight. Then, without so much as a sound, they slipped away, the million of them was gone. I kind of think maybe, in some sort of way, they came all those miles to worship. Strange. But think how the tower must look to them, standing seventy feet above the water, the God-light flashing out from it, and the tower declaring itself with a monster voice. They never came back, those fish, but don't you think for a while they thought they were in the Presence?"

I shivered. I looked out at the long gray lawn of the sea stretching away into nothing and nowhere.

"Oh, the sea's full." McDunn puffed his pipe nervously, blinking. He had been nervous all day and hadn't said why. "For all our engines and so-called submarines, it'll be ten thousand centuries before we set foot on the real bottom of the sunken lands, in the fairy kingdoms there, and know *real* terror. Think of it, it's still the year 300,000 Before Christ down under there. While we've paraded around with trumpets, lopping off each other's countries and heads, they have been living beneath the sea twelve miles deep and cold in a time as old as the beard of a comet."

"Yes, it's an old world."

"Come on. I got something special I been saving up to tell you."

We ascended the eighty steps, talking and taking our time. At the top, McDunn switched off the room lights so there'd be no reflection in the plate glass. The great eye of the light was humming, turning easily in its oiled socket. The Fog Horn was blowing steadily, once every fifteen seconds.

"Sounds like an animal, don't it?" McDunn nodded to himself. "A big lonely animal crying in the night. Sitting here on the edge of ten billion years calling out to the Deeps, I'm here, I'm here, I'm here. And the Deeps *do* answer, yes, they do. You been here now for three months, Johnny, so I better prepare you. About this time of year," he said, studying the murk and fog, "something comes to visit the lighthouse."

"The swarms of fish like you said?"

"No, this is something else. I've put off telling you because you might think I'm daft. But tonight's the latest I can put it off, for if my calendar's marked right from last year, tonight's the night it comes. I won't go into detail, you'll have to see it yourself. Just sit down there. If you want, tomorrow you can pack your duffel and take the motorboat in to land and get your car parked there at the dinghy pier on the cape and drive on back to some little inland town and keep your lights burning nights, I won't question or blame you. It's happened three years now, and this is the only time anyone's been here with me to verify it. You wait and watch."

Half an hour passed with only a few whispers between us. When we grew tired waiting, McDunn began describing some of his ideas to me. He had some theories about the Fog Horn itself.

"One day many years ago a man walked along and stood in the sound of the ocean on a cold sunless shore and said, 'We need a voice to call across the water, to warn ships; I'll make one. I'll make a voice like all of time and all of the fog that ever was; I'll make a voice that is like an empty bed beside you all night long, and like an empty house when you open the door, and like trees in autumn with no leaves. A sound like the birds flying south, crying, and a sound like November wind and the sea on the hard, cold shore. I'll make a sound that's so alone that no one can miss it, that whoever hears it will weep in their souls, and hearths will seem warmer, and being inside will seem better to all who hear it in the distant towns. I'll make me a sound and an apparatus and they'll call it a Fog Horn and whoever hears it will know the sadness of eternity and the briefness of life.'"

The Fog Horn blew.

"I made up that story," said McDunn quietly, "to try to explain why this thing keeps coming back to the lighthouse every year. The Fog Horn calls it, I think, and it comes. . . ."

"But——" I said.

"Sssst!" said McDunn. "There!" He nodded out to the Deeps.

Something was swimming toward the lighthouse tower.

It was a cold night, as I have said; the high tower was cold, the light coming and going, and the Fog Horn calling and calling through the raveling mist. You couldn't see far and you couldn't see plain, but there was the deep sea moving on its way about the night earth, flat and quiet, the color of gray mud, and here were the two of us alone in the high tower, and there, far out at first, was a ripple, followed by a wave, a rising, a bubble, a bit of froth. And then, from the surface of the cold sea came a head, a large head, dark-colored, with immense eyes, and then a neck. And then—not a body—but more neck and more! The head rose a full forty feet above the water on a slender and beautiful dark neck. Only then did the body, like a little island of black coral and shells and crayfish, drip up from the subterranean. There was a flicker of tail. In all, from head to tip of tail, I estimated the monster at ninety or a hundred feet.

I don't know what I said. I said something.

"Steady, boy, steady," whispered McDunn.

"It's impossible!" I said.

"No, Johnny, *we're* impossible. *It's* like it always was ten million years ago. *It* hasn't changed. It's *us* and the land that've changed, become impossible. *Us!*"

It swam slowly and with a great dark majesty out in the icy waters, far away. The fog came and went about it, momentarily erasing its shape. One of the monster eyes caught and held and flashed back our immense light, red, white, red, white, like a disk held high and sending a message in primeval code. It was as silent as the fog through which it swam.

"It's a dinosaur of some sort!" I crouched down, holding to the stair rail.

"Yes, one of the tribe."

"But they died out!"

"No, only hid away in the Deeps. Deep, deep down in the deepest Deeps. Isn't *that* a word now, Johnny, a real word, it says so much: the Deeps. There's all the coldness and darkness and deepness in the world in a word like that."

"What'll we do?"

"Do? We got our job, we can't leave. Besides, we're safer here than in any boat trying to get to land. That thing's as big as a destroyer and almost as swift."

"But here, why does it come *here?*"

The next moment I had my answer.

The Fog Horn blew.

And the monster answered.

A cry came across a million years of water and mist. A cry so anguished and alone that it shuddered in my head and my body. The monster cried out at the tower. The Fog Horn blew. The monster roared again. The Fog Horn blew. The monster opened its great toothed mouth and the sound that came from it was the sound of the Fog Horn itself. Lonely and vast and far away. The sound of isolation, a viewless sea, a cold night, apartness. That was the sound.

"Now," whispered McDunn, "do you know why it comes here?"

I nodded.

"All year long, Johnny, that poor monster there lying far out, a thousand miles at sea, and twenty miles deep maybe, biding its time, perhaps it's a million years old, this one creature. Think of it, waiting a million years; could *you* wait that long? Maybe it's the last of its kind. I sort of think that's true. Anyway, here come men on land and build this lighthouse, five years ago. And set up their Fog Horn and sound it and sound it out toward the place where you bury yourself in sleep and sea memories of a world where there were thousands like yourself, but now you're alone, all alone in a world not made for you, a world where you have to hide.

"But the sound of the Fog Horn comes and goes, comes and goes, and you stir from the muddy bottom of the Deeps, and your eyes open like the lenses of two-foot cameras and you move, slow, slow, for you have the ocean sea on your shoulders, heavy. But that Fog Horn comes through a thousand miles of water, faint and familiar, and the furnace in your belly stokes up, and you begin to rise, slow,

slow. You feed yourself on great slakes of cod and minnow, on rivers of jellyfish, and you rise slow through the autumn months, through September when the fogs started, through October with more fog and the horn still calling you on, and then, late in November, after pressurizing yourself day by day, a few feet higher every hour, you are near the surface and still alive. You've got to go slow; if you surfaced all at once you'd explode. So it takes you all of three months to surface, and then a number of days to swim through the cold waters to the lighthouse. And there you are, out there, in the night, Johnny, the biggest damn monster in creation. And here's the lighthouse calling to you, with a long neck like your neck sticking way up out of the water, and a body like your body, and, most important of all, a voice like your voice. Do you understand now, Johnny, do you understand?"

The Fog Horn blew.

The monster answered.

I saw it all, I knew it all—the million years of waiting alone, for someone to come back who never came back. The million years of isolation at the bottom of the sea, the insanity of time there, while the skies cleared of reptile-birds, the swamps dried on the continental lands, the sloths and saber-tooths had their day and sank in tar pits, and men ran like white ants upon the hills.

The Fog Horn blew.

"Last year," said McDunn, "that creature swam round and round, round and round, all night. Not coming too near, puzzled, I'd say. Afraid, maybe. And a bit angry after coming all this way. But the next day, unexpectedly, the fog lifted, the sun came out fresh, the sky was as blue as a painting. And the monster swam off away from the heat and the silence and didn't come back. I suppose it's been brooding on it for a year now, thinking it over from every which way."

The monster was only a hundred yards off now, it and the Fog Horn crying at each other. As the lights hit them, the monster's eyes were fire and ice, fire and ice.

"That's life for you," said McDunn. "Someone always waiting for someone who never comes home. Always someone loving some thing more than that thing loves them. And after a while you want to destroy whatever that thing is, so it can't hurt you no more."

The monster was rushing at the lighthouse.

The Fog Horn blew.

"Let's see what happens," said McDunn.

He switched the Fog Horn off.

The ensuing minute of silence was so intense that we could hear our hearts pounding in the glassed area of the tower, could hear the slow greased turn of the light.

The monster stopped and froze. Its great lantern eyes blinked. Its mouth gaped. It gave a sort of rumble, like a volcano. It twitched its head this way and that, as if to seek the sounds now dwindled off into the fog. It peered at the lighthouse. It rumbled again. Then its eyes caught fire. It reared up, threshed the water, and rushed at the tower, its eyes filled with angry torment.

"McDunn!" I cried. "Switch on the horn!"

McDunn fumbled with the switch. But even as he flicked it on, the monster was rearing up. I had a glimpse of its gigantic paws, fishskin glittering in webs between the fingerlike projections, clawing at the tower. The huge eye on the right side of its anguished head glittered before me like a caldron into which I might drop, screaming. The tower shook. The Fog Horn cried; the monster cried. It seized the tower and gnashed at the glass, which shattered in upon us.

McDunn seized my arm. "Downstairs!"

The tower rocked, trembled, and started to give. The Fog Horn and the monster roared. We stumbled and half fell down the stairs. "Quick!"

We reached the bottom as the tower buckled down toward us. We ducked under the stairs into the small stone cellar. There were a thousand concussions as the rocks rained down; the Fog Horn stopped abruptly. The monster crashed upon the tower. The tower fell. We knelt together, McDunn and I, holding tight, while our world exploded.

Then it was over, and there was nothing but darkness and the wash of the sea on the raw stones.

That and the other sound.

"Listen," said McDunn quietly. "Listen."

We waited a moment. And then I began to hear it. First a great vacuumed sucking of air, and then the lament, the bewilderment, the loneliness of the great monster, folded over and upon us, above us, so that the sickening reek of its body filled the air, a stone's thickness away from our cellar. The monster gasped and cried. The tower was gone. The light was gone. The thing that had called to it across a million years was gone. And the monster was opening its mouth and sending out great sounds. The sounds of a Fog Horn, again and again. And ships far at sea, not finding the light, not seeing anything, but passing and hearing late that night, must've thought: There it is, the lonely sound, the Lonesome Bay horn. All's well. We've rounded the cape.

And so it went for the rest of that night.

The sun was hot and yellow the next afternoon when the rescuers came out to dig us from our stoned-under cellar.

"It fell apart, is all," said Mr. McDunn gravely. "We had a few bad knocks from the waves and it just crumbled." He pinched my arm.

There was nothing to see. The ocean was calm, the sky blue. The only thing was a great algaic stink from the green matter that covered the fallen tower stones and the shore rocks. Flies buzzed about. The ocean washed empty on the shore.

The next year they built a new lighthouse, but by that time I had a job in the little town and a wife and a good small warm house that glowed yellow on autumn nights, the doors locked, the chimney puffing smoke. As for McDunn, he was master of the new lighthouse, built to his own specifications, out of steel-reinforced concrete. "Just in case," he said.

The new lighthouse was ready in November. I drove down alone one evening late and parked my car and looked across the gray waters and listened to the new horn sounding, once, twice, three, four times a minute far out there, by itself.

The monster?

It never came back.

"It's gone away," said McDunn. "It's gone back to the Deeps. It's learned you can't love anything too much in this world. It's gone into the deepest Deeps to wait another million years. Ah, the poor thing! Waiting out there, and waiting out there, while man comes and goes on this pitiful little planet. Waiting and waiting."

I sat in my car, listening. I couldn't see the lighthouse or the light standing out in Lonesome Bay. I could only hear the Horn, the Horn, the Horn. It sounded like the monster calling.

I sat there wishing there was something I could say.

**MARY-ALICE
SCHNIRRING**

*Child's
Play*

Henry bent lower over the drawing-board as the twilight deepened. With a dark-red crayon, he filled in the outlines of another city; then, with a pen dipped in India ink, drew—rapidly and with remarkable delicacy and skill for a twelve-year-old—a temple, a palace, and a barracks; and sketched in hastily some ambiguous dwelling places. He muttered to himself as he worked.

"This'll keep old Charley Anderson in his place, I bet," was the tenor of his mumblings. "His barracks only have room for about two hundred warriors, and my Royal Guards can clean them up with one hand tied behind their backs. Anyway, the Thorvians are a bunch of sissies." In large letters, he labeled the city

"THORVIA," and sat back with a little smile on his face, wiggling his fingers to uncramp them.

A voice called from somewhere downstairs. "Hen-reeee. Hen-reeee! Your dinner is ready! Why aren't you ever around to help me set the table or anything, instead of sulking up in your room all the time? Why—" the voice trailed off into peevish, whining incoherencies. The boy stood up, scowling; but prepared, laggingly, to go downstairs. He paused, however, for one more look at the map.

It was drawn with remarkable precision. It appeared to be a map of a mountainous country, dominated by one large city, built on the top and upper slopes of the highest of the mountains. This city, marked "DRACO," was elaborately and painstakingly developed with the little India ink symbols. A truly magnificent palace was at its very heart; and around the palace, cunningly enough, were strong barracks, each with a watch-tower. Beyond these, again, was a very wide, bare, circular road, completely surrounding barracks, palace, gardens and all. Apparently the ruler of this kingdom had a healthy distrust of his subjects, or else expected, but was prepared for, an invasion.

The remainder of the map bore out the second theory; for Draco was the heart of a whole system of smaller cities, or states. Since each city had a palace (though none as impressive as the one in Draco), the effect was that of a feudal overlord, surrounded by lesser rulers. So, in fact, was the case. Henry, who dragged out a dreary existence with his aunt and uncle—an existence complicated by the limp which he would always have, as a souvenir of the accident in which his mother and father had been killed—had found that in order to make life with the other boys of his age bearable, he would have to make himself superior to them. Since any physical superiority was out of the question, his quick mind had found the way out.

As Kirwan, ruler of Draco and its subject states, Henry held a position of unquestioned authority among his fellows. More—the game had captured their imaginations to such an extent that former, and possibly healthier, pastimes were neglected. Billy Daniels (Fiero, Prince of Maglar); Donny Clark (Andrus of Ghuria); Joe Domenico

(Horvath of Balcur); and Robin Johnson (Duke Shira, of Friya), lived only for the campaigns against the Dog-Men of the Outer Mountains, the internecine wars that trouble Draconia with scarcely a let-up, and, of course, the political strife that was one of its chief *raisons-d'être*. In turn, each one had tried to out-maneuver Henry; but Kirwan, King of Draconia, had maintained his power against each of them, and his ascendancy over their minds at the same time. "The game," however, held even more sway over Henry than over the others. More and more, his life as Henry Booth seemed the game, and a very unpleasant and dull game, at that; while, as Kirwan, he lived in a dangerously brilliant world, of which every corner was twice as familiar to him as the drab surroundings of his Aunt Martha's and Uncle Joe's house.

Aunt Martha and Uncle Joe were not fond of Henry, to start with. He didn't act nicely at *all* to their dear little Charley (about to become ruler of Thorvia); and Charley such a bright little fellow—and so healthy! Imagine—100 pounds, and only eleven years old!

That, of course, was one way of looking at it—the Anderson's way. Henry's way was, quite simply, that Charley was a big overgrown slob of a boy, and a nasty little sneak and bully besides. Henry's views were actually far less biased than those of his aunt and uncle. In fact, the only reason for the creation of "Thorvia" was that Charley had prowled, and sneaked, and opened bureau drawers, and listened in corners to too good effect. Briefly, Charley knew too much, and, in his inimitable way, could break up the game with dreadful ease—but even his calculating, disagreeable little mind recognized its pull, and a Dukedom was the price of his cooperation.

All this passed vaguely and hastily through Kirwan's mind, as he lingered in the doorway, still under the spell of his own creation. It was Kirwan who frowned standing there, foreseeing trouble with his latest vassal-lord; it was Kirwan who suddenly went back to the drawing-board, took up the India ink again, and quickly sketched something in the southeastern corner of Thorvia. But it was Henry who dropped pen and ink nervously and ran to the door and down the stairs, at a repetition of the whining cry, "Hen-reeeeee!" from downstairs.

He sat through an unattractive meal of boiled potatoes, cabbage, and a very poor grade of chopped beef, topped off by a bread pudding that was mostly bread. What raisins there were, went to Charley, who had also engulfed the lion's share of the chopped beef. Quantity, not quality, was his motto; and glands alone were not responsible for the hundred pounds that were Charley.

The meal was enlivened by Aunt Martha's monologue, mostly based on Henry, and never complimentary to him; with variations on Charley's virtues and good, healthy appetite—so different from Henry, picking at his food, as if he shouldn't be grateful to his dear auntie and uncle who provided his food, at what expense no one knew; and look how Charley likes to play outdoors—not always frowsting in his room, when he wasn't in corners with those other boys—and just what was it they did, anyway? Aunt Martha thought that she and Mrs. Daniels and Mrs. Clark and Mrs. Domenico (though Mrs. Domenico was not really a lady, to Aunt Martha's way of thinking, though doubtless a good-hearted woman), and Mrs. Johnson ought to get together and find out just what was going on. You didn't see Aunt Martha's Charley—

Panic, that had been growing in Henry as this speech rose to its crisis, flowered into speech.

"It's—it's just a club, Aunt Martha," he stammered, rashly.

"Just a club!" she sniffed. "And what kind of a club is it that is too good for my Charley?"

Henry's panic subsided. This emergency had already been faced, and dealt with. He even smiled.

"Why, we elected Charley a member at the last meeting, Aunt Martha," he said, looking at Charley. Charley's face, which had worn a greasy, knowing smile, suddenly took on a look of surprise, mingled with disbelief. He stared at Henry.

"Ya did?" Astonishment and—yes, pleasure—even normal, little-boy pleasure, characterized his tone.

"Yes, Charley. You're a full-fledged member of—the club now. Tell you about it after dinner."

Aunt Martha was not going to give up quite so easily, although it was easy to see that she was mollified.

"Well, I want to know more about it before I let Charley join, anyway," she said firmly. But Uncle Joe for once stood up to her.

"Now, Martha—boys' clubs are secret. Can't expect 'em to tell you about what goes on. Leave the kids alone."

"Well, I can trust Charley," said Aunt Martha, fondly, giving in at last.

"I know Mother's little man wouldn't belong to any club that wasn't nice."

Charley smiled, as unpleasant a smile as Henry ever remembered seeing, even on Charley's face, and replied in a sick-sweet voice, "Yes, Mamma dear."

They rose from the table, and Charley grabbed Henry by the arm and pulled him outdoors, into the spring night.

"Hurry up!" he said, feverishly. "If ya didn't mean it, I'm gonna tell everybody the whole thing. Didja mean it, really? Have I got a kingdom of my own in Draconia? What's its name? Where is it? How big—"

Henry was Kirwan. "Quiet!" he said. "My lords and I meet in conference tonight. You will be inducted into our company as Duke of Thorvia. As is our custom, you may choose your own name by which you will henceforth be known to us in Draconia. Be ready at midnight." Shaking his arm loose from the fat, wet grasp of his newest Duke, King Kirwan limped away down the street.

At a quarter to twelve, Kirwan, King of Draconia, sat in the palace in the heart of Draco, his principal city, surrounded by his liege lords, the Prince Fiero of Maglar, Prince Andrus of Ghuria, Prince Horvath of Balcur, and Duke Shira of Friya. All of them looked troubled; Fiero and Shira downright furious.

"Kirwan," spoke up Fiero. "I crave leave to speak."

"Speak," said Kirwan, not looking up.

"I like not this new dukedom. It bounds Maglar all along my northeastern border, and this new Duke is a trouble-maker."

"And a slimy louse," said Duke Shira, fervently. "As the only other Duke of this company, one who has not yet attained his Princeship, I respectfully plead, O Kirwan, that you make him less than a Duke. I would not be akin to him even in title."

Kirwan looked up, finally. It was noticeable that his eyes blazed with excitement, mingled with a look of uncertainty. "Am I not your liege lord," he said, though not angrily. "And do you not trust me?"

"We trust you, Kirwan," said dark-eyed Horvath, who had not spoken before.

"But we know thisa new Duke is trouble-maker. We can control heem in Draconia, yes—but outside?"

For a moment, Kirwan hesitated; then he spoke slowly and hesitantly. "I think—I think I can control him outside, as well. I have a plan—"

The new Duke of Thorvia, Edric by name, was proving a trouble-maker. And Kirwan's liege lords, who had expected this, but believed that Kirwan could handle it, were becoming mutinous. First, Edric had shown a tendency to ridicule the whole secret life of Draconia; but after a couple of weeks, he had become as absorbed by it as the rest. Then, however, the greed that was the cornerstone of his whole character, had begun to come to the fore. The marvelously intricate details of the whole country—the peasants' huts, the different uniforms of the fighting men in the service of each ruler; their number and character—even their names; the strange flowers in the garden of the palace at Draco; the unpleasant call of a certain bird found only in the unexplored woods of Ghuria and the revolting characteristics of the pale fawn-colored mink-like animal that the Friyans had tried, unsuccessfully, to exterminate; Edric, with a surprising quickness, had learned them all, and even added to his fellow-lords' knowledge.

What puzzled Edric sometimes (or, rather, it puzzled Charley Anderson) was the fact that it did not seem to him that he invented the things. It seemed rather as if they had always been there, in the back of his mind, and had just come casually to the fore. Even more strange—and when Charley thought of it, he was uneasy; although to Edric it was more a sullen annoyance than a surprise—was that Kirwan knew still more than Edric and, once or twice, had corroborated Edric's descriptions with certain emendations—*which Edric somehow realized were correct.*

There was the night when Horvath had entertained them in his palace at Balcur. The Dog-Men had been quiescent for some weeks, and conversation was idly turning on the swamp-lands in the southeastern corner of Thorvia, unfamiliar territory, except for such features as Edric's palace, the barracks, and the peasants' huts, to most of the group. Edric was saying, "There must be mineral springs underground in the swamp. It—it sort of churns around, sometimes; but not always in the same place."

Kirwan had a small, secret smile on his face. "Not always the same place, no," he agreed. "But I think you will find always the same *sort* of place."

"Whatta you mean, the same sort of place?" Edric demanded, puzzled. "The whole swamp is the same sort of place. And I don't know why I should have to have a swamp in Thorvia—nobody else has. And this one has a nasty smell, somehow." He stopped short, realizing with an unexplained thrill of fear that it *did* have a nasty smell. But how could it have? And—how did he know it, and know that he wasn't "making it up?" His mind was so absorbed by this rather frightening problem that he almost missed Kirwan's answer.

"It only—er—churns around near those dark-purple waterlilies, doesn't it?" said Kirwan, mildly; yet with a gleam of almost uncontrollable excitement in his eyes. "What?" said Edric, and thought. "Yes," he said, and then with more conviction. "Yes. Only by the purple flowers." Then, jumping up, and with his voice shrill, "Why? What is it? You know what it is. How do you know?"

Kirwan cast down his eyes to the map, which he always took with him to the meetings. "Why, mineral springs, as you suggested," he answered. "That's what makes the swamp smell, probably, too. As for its only being near the flowers, why, it's the other way around. The flowers grow there because there's some quality in the springs that feeds them."

Edric was almost satisfied with this explanation. But back in his bed, later that night, Charley Anderson still lay awake, and thought, and thought. And his thoughts came to fruition a week later.

It was in the middle of a discussion at the dinner-table—the usual discussion of why Henry wasn't eating his lambstew, but this time flavored with the unusual spice of the fact that Charley was only picking at his.

"It's that dratted club of yours," pronounced Aunt Martha. "It's got to stop. You, Charley, you've been mooning around the house now almost as bad as Henry, for goodness knows how long. Just what is this club, anyway?"

Charley cast a sidelong look at Henry, who was looking at him with a strange expression—a waiting sort of look. Charley squirmed in his chair, uneasily. "Oh—it's just a club," he answered, sullenly. "Ya can't tell about it while you're in it. But they haven't been treating me right, and I think I'll resign—and then, Mamma, I'll tell you all about it." As he spoke the last words, he looked straight at Henry, with a sly, triumphant expression, that said even more plainly than words, "See? I have you in a cleft stick. Either you knuckle under to me, or—"

Henry looked back at him, with an unreadable gleam in his eyes. Or was it Kirwan who looked back at him? Charley—Edric—found himself unable to decide, but something made him say, quickly, "Of course, if they're nicer to me, I won't resign—and then I couldn't tell."

"There, Henry," said Aunt Martha. "I *knew* you were being mean to poor little Charley. You're jealous of him, that's what it is; because you're a cripple and he's a big strong, clever boy. Either you treat him right, or I'll break up that club of yours—and I mean it!"

Henry looked at his plate. His nostrils flared, but he said absolutely nothing for a minute. Then he looked up, his expression imitating perfectly that of a twelve-year-old boy who, while still sullen, has been forced into following a course of action repugnant to him. "Oh, all right!" he said. "We'll fix Charley up so he won't kick." And under his breath, he added, "Ever again."

That night Kirwan worked late with his fine-pointed drawing pen and the India ink. And when he had finished, the false dawn was just breaking; and showed, as he switched off his light, the addition he had made to his map in the southeastern corner of Thorvia. It was beautifully executed; a sluggish, somehow oily-looking creature. Drawn to the scale of the map, it was very large—in fact, almost half the size of the swamp itself. It had a disgusting appearance, and was so clearly limned that one could almost see it move. Henry had a distinct talent. He slept, then, with the little smile that had become almost a fixture, on his face.

"King Kirwan," said Duke Shira, "I crave the help of some Draconian fighting men."

Kirwan's eyebrows shot up. "So? Are not the Friyans content? Surely you do not expect trouble with your people?"

"No," said Shira. "The people are content, except for one thing—the woods are becoming increasingly full of khalders, and—you know why we must keep them down."

Kirwan nodded. Andrus of Ghuria, who had a tendency toward squeamishness, gulped a little, and looked unhappy, since the khalders, those pale fawn-colored animals that looked something like weasels, had habits that were better not thought of.

"The only thing is," said Kirwan, slowly, "that I have reason to believe I will need all my fighting men shortly. Why not ask Duke Edric for some of his forces?"

All eyes turned toward Edric, who sat, fatly, in his chair, with a smug smile. "Sure," he said, pleasantly, "I'll let you have half of them. But—I need more land, an' more influence. In fact, I think Kirwan ought to take over Thorvia, and I'll take Draco—and, of course, whatever goes with it."

The only one apparently unmoved in the middle of the resulting turmoil was Kirwan. "Quiet!" he said, loudly. And under the influence of his voice, they actually did quiet down.

"I have been expecting this," he said, unconcernedly. "But I am prepared for it. Edric—" he turned toward him suddenly. "Have you been down to the marsh lately?"

The fat Duke of Thorvia stirred uneasily. "What's that got to do with it?" he demanded. "Anyway, it's your headache now—Draco has no marsh," and he giggled. "And either I get Draco, and rule the whole bunch, or—you know."

"Know what?" demanded Fiero truculently. But Kirwan held up his hand.

"He means he'll destroy Draconia by—well, exposing it to the light," he said, indifferently; almost with amusement at his own joke. "But—Edric, have you noticed that the dark purple waterlilies have all withered?"

A peculiar look came over Edric's face. "What of it?" he asked, shrilly. "What's that got to do with it?"

Kirwan smiled. "Why, I would suggest that after we disband tonight, you go down to the swamp and—maybe you'll find out why it churns. It might be mineral springs, you know; and it would be interesting to find out what else it could be—wouldn't it?"

Edric's face looked ghastly. "I won't! You can't make me!" he cried. "I won't go near it!"

"You have to sleep," suggested Kirwan, still smiling. The others looked puzzled and frightened, but Edric looked dreadful. "I won't sleep!" he screamed. "I won't sleep!"

When they broke up, he was still muttering it.

At five o'clock in the morning, Kirwan sat up in bed. A look of anticipation, a listening look, was on his face, making it strangely unpleasant. His attic room was directly above Charley's large, airy bedroom; and sounds traveled upwards fairly plainly. An anomalous sound was reaching his ears now—a wet, squelchy, crawling sound. Suddenly, he heard a terrible cry.

As the sound of running feet, crying voices, and finally a dreadful scream from Auntie Martha, reached his ears, Kirwan turned over and went to sleep, smiling.

from The Borrowers

MARY NORTON

The Adventures of Pod

[*Everything about the Borrowers was secret. It wasn't until the Boy actually met a Borrower that both the "big people" and the Borrowers had to recognize each other's existence.*]

Mrs. May lived in two rooms in Kate's parents' house in London; she was, I think, some kind of relation. Her bedroom was on the first floor, and her sitting room was a room which, as part of the house, was called "the breakfast-room." Now breakfast-rooms are all right in the morning when the sun streams in on the toast and marmalade, but by afternoon they seem to vanish a little and to fill with a strange silvery light, their own twilight; there is a kind of sadness in them then, but as a child it was a sadness Kate liked. She would creep in to Mrs. May just before tea-time and Mrs. May would teach her to crochet.

Mrs. May was old, her joints were stiff, and she was—not strict exactly, but she had that inner certainty which does instead. Kate was never "wild" with Mrs. May, nor untidy, nor self-willed; and Mrs. May taught her many things besides crochet: how to wind wool into an egg-shaped ball; how to run-and-fell and plan a darn; how to tidy a drawer and to lay, like a blessing, above the contents, a sheet of rustling tissue against the dust.

"Where's your work, child?" asked Mrs. May one day, when Kate sat hunched and silent upon the hassock. "You mustn't sit there dreaming. Have you lost your tongue?"

"No," said Kate, pulling at her shoe button, "I've lost the crochet hook." They were making a bed-quilt—in woolen squares: there were thirty still to do. "I know where I put it," she went on hastily; "I put it on the bottom shelf of the bookcase just beside my bed."

"On the bottom shelf?" repeated Mrs. May, her own needle flicking steadily in the firelight. "Near the floor?"

"Yes," said Kate, "but I looked on the floor. Under the rug. Everywhere. The wool was still there though. Just where I'd left it."

"Oh dear," exclaimed Mrs. May lightly, "don't say they're in this house too!"

"That what are?" asked Kate.

"The Borrowers," said Mrs. May, and in the half light she seemed to smile.

Kate stared a little fearfully. "Are there such things?" she asked after a moment.

"As what?"

"As people, other people, living in a house who . . . borrow things?"

Mrs. May laid down her work. "What do you think?" she asked.

"I don't know," Kate said, pulling hard at her shoe button. "There can't be. And yet"—she raised her head—"and yet sometimes I think there must be."

"Why do you think there must be?" asked Mrs. May.

"Because of all the things that disappear. Safety pins, for instance. Factories go on making safety pins, and every day people go on buying safety pins and yet, somehow, there never is a safety pin just when you want one. Where are they all? Now, at this minute? Where do they go to? Take needles," she went on. "All the needles my mother ever bought—there must be hundreds—can't just be lying about this house."

"Not lying about the house, no," agreed Mrs. May.

"And all the other things we keep on buying. Again and again and again. Like pencils and match boxes and sealing-wax and hairpins and drawing pins and thimbles—"

"And hat pins," put in Mrs. May, "and blotting paper."

"Yes, blotting paper," agreed Kate, "but not hat pins."

"That's where you're wrong," said Mrs. May, and she picked up her work again. "There was a reason for hat pins."

Kate stared. "A reason?" she repeated. "I mean—what kind of a reason?"

"Well, there were two reasons really. A hat pin is a very useful weapon and"—Mrs. May laughed suddenly—"but it all sounds such nonsense and"—she hesitated—"it was so very long ago!"

"But tell me," said Kate, "tell me how you *know* about the hat pin. Did you ever see one?"

Mrs. May threw her a startled glance. "Well, yes—" she began.

"Not a hat pin," exclaimed Kate impatiently, "a—what-ever-you-called-them—a Borrower?"

Mrs. May drew a sharp breath. "No," she said quickly. "I never saw one."

"But someone else saw one," cried Kate, "and you know about it. I can see you do!"

"Hush," said Mrs. May, "no need to shout!" She gazed downwards at the upturned face and then she smiled and her eyes slid away into distance. "I had a brother—" she began uncertainly.

Kate knelt upon the hassock. "And he saw them!"

"I don't know," said Mrs. May, shaking her head, "I just don't know!" She smoothed out her work upon her knee. "He was such a tease. He told us so many things—my sister and me—impossible things. He was killed," she added gently, "many years ago now, on the North-West Frontier. He became colonel of his regiment. He died what they call 'a hero's death' . . ."

"Was he your only brother?"

"Yes, and he was our little brother. I think that was why"—

she thought for a moment, still smiling to herself—"yes, why he told us such impossible stories, such strange imaginings. He was jealous, I think, because we were older—and because we could read better. He wanted to impress us; he wanted, perhaps, to shock us. And yet"—she looked into the fire—"there was something about him —perhaps because we were brought up in India among mystery and magic and legend—something that made us think that he saw things that other people could not see; sometimes we'd know he was teasing, but at other times—well, we were not so sure. . . ." She leaned forward and, in her tidy way, brushed a fan of loose ashes under the grate, then, brush in hand, she stared again at the fire. "He wasn't a very strong little boy: the first time he came home from India he got rheumatic fever. He missed a whole term at school and was sent away to the country to get over it. To the house of a great-aunt. Later I went there myself. It was a strange old house. . . ." She hung up the brush on its brass hook and, dusting her hands on her handkerchief, she picked up her work. "Better light the lamp," she said.

"Not yet," begged Kate, leaning forward. "Please go on. Please tell me—"

"But I've told you."

"No, you haven't. This old house—wasn't that where he saw—he saw . . . ?"

Mrs. May laughed. "Where he saw the Borrowers? Yes, that's what he told us . . . what he'd have us believe. And, what's more, it seems that he didn't just see them but that he got to know them very well; that he became part of their lives, as it were; in fact, you might almost say that he became a borrower himself. . . ."

"Oh, *do* tell me. Please. Try to remember. Right from the very beginning!"

"But I do remember," said Mrs. May. "Oddly enough I remember it better than many real things which have happened. Perhaps it was a real thing. I just don't know. You see, on the way back to India my brother and I had to share a cabin—my sister used to sleep with our governess—and, on those very hot nights, often we couldn't sleep; and my brother would talk for hours and hours, going over old ground, repeating conversations, telling me details

again and again—wondering how they were and what they were
doing and—"

"They? Who were they—exactly?"

"Homily, Pod, and little Arrietty."

"Pod?"

"Yes, even their names were never quite right. They imagined
they had their own names—quite different from human names—
but with half an ear you could tell they were borrowed. Even
Uncle Hendreary's and Eggletina's. Everything they had was borrowed; they had nothing of their own at all. Nothing. In spite
of this, my brother said, they were touchy and conceited, and
thought they owned the world."

"How do you mean?"

"They thought human beings were just invented to do the dirty
work—great slaves put there for them to use. At least, that's what
they told each other. But my brother said that, underneath, he
thought they were frightened. It was because they were frightened,
he thought, that they had grown so small. Each generation had
become smaller and smaller, and more and more hidden. In the
olden days, it seems, and in some parts of England, our ancestors
talked quite openly about the 'little people.' "

"Yes," said Kate, "I know."

"Nowadays, I suppose," Mrs. May went on slowly, "if they exist
at all, you would only find them in houses which are old and
quiet and deep in the country—and where the human beings live
to a routine. Routine is their safeguard. They must know which
rooms are to be used and when. They do not stay long where
there are careless people, or unruly children, or certain household
pets.

"This particular old house, of course, was ideal—although as far
as some of them were concerned, a trifle cold and empty. Great-
Aunt Sophy was bedridden, through a hunting accident some twenty
years before, and as for other human beings there was only Mrs.
Driver the cook, Crampfurl the gardener, and, at rare intervals,
an odd housemaid or such. My brother, too, when he went there
after rheumatic fever, had to spend long hours in bed, and for
those first weeks it seems the Borrowers did not know of his
existence.

"He slept in the old night-nursery, beyond the schoolroom. The schoolroom, at that time, was sheeted and shrouded and filled with junk—odd trunks, a broken sewing-machine, a desk, a dressmaker's dummy, a table, some chairs, and a disused pianola—as the children who had used it, Great-Aunt Sophy's children, had long since grown up, married, died, or gone away. The night-nursery opened out of the schoolroom and, from his bed, my brother could see the oil painting of the battle of Waterloo which hung above the schoolroom fireplace and, on the wall, a corner cupboard with glass doors in which was set out, on hooks and shelves, a doll's tea-service—very delicate and old. At night, if the schoolroom door was open, he had a view down the lighted passage which led to the head of the stairs, and it would comfort him to see, each evening at dusk, Mrs. Driver appear at the head of the stairs and cross the passage carrying a tray for Aunt Sophy with Bath Oliver biscuits and the tall, cut-glass decanter of Fine Old Pale Madeira. On her way out Mrs. Driver would pause and lower the gas jet in the passage to a dim, blue flame, and then he would watch her as she stumped away downstairs, sinking slowly out of sight between the banisters.

"Under this passage, in the hall below, there was a clock, and through the night he would hear it strike the hours. It was a grandfather clock and very old. Mr. Frith of Leighton Buzzard came each month to wind it, as his father had come before him and his great-uncle before that. For eighty years, they said (and to Mr. Frith's certain knowledge), it had not stopped and, as far as anyone could tell, for as many years before that. The great thing was—that it must never be moved. It stood against the wainscot, and the stone flags around it had been washed so often that a little platform, my brother said, rose up inside.

"And, under this clock, below the wainscot, there was a hole. . . ."

*　　*　　*

It was Pod's hole—the keep of his fortress; the entrance to his home. Not that his home was anywhere near the clock: far from it—as you might say. There were yards of dark and dusty passageway, with wooden doors between the joists and metal gates against the mice. Pod used all kinds of things for these gates—a flat leaf of a folding cheese-grater, the hinged lid of a small cash-box, squares of pierced zinc from an old meat-safe, a wire fly-swatter. . . . "Not that I'm afraid of mice," Homily would say, "but I can't abide the smell." In vain Arrietty had begged for a little mouse of her own, a little blind mouse to bring up by hand—"like Eggletina had had." But Homily would bang with the pan lids and exclaim: "And look what happened to Eggletina!" "What," Arrietty would ask, "what did happen to Eggletina?" But no one would ever say.

It was only Pod who knew the way through the intersecting passages to the hole under the clock. And only Pod could open the gates. There were complicated clasps made of hairpins and safety pins of which Pod alone knew the secret. His wife and child led more sheltered lives in homelike apartments under the kitchen, far removed from the risks and dangers of the dreaded house above. But there was a grating in the brick wall of the house, just below the floor level of the kitchen above, through which Arrietty could see the garden—a piece of graveled path and a bank where crocus bloomed in spring; where blossom drifted from an unseen tree; and where later an azalea bush would flower; and where birds came—and pecked and flirted and sometimes fought. "The hours you waste on them birds," Homily would say, "and when there's a little job to be done you can never find the time. I was brought up in a house," Homily went on, "where there wasn't no grating, and we were all the happier for it. Now go off and get me the potato."

That was the day when Arrietty, rolling the potato before her from the storehouse down the dusty lane under the floor boards, kicked it ill-temperedly so that it rolled rather fast into their kitchen, where Homily was stooping over the stove.

"There you go again," exclaimed Homily, turning angrily; "nearly pushed me into the soup. And when I say 'potato' I don't mean the whole potato. Take the scissor, can't you, and cut off a slice."

"Didn't know how much you wanted," mumbled Arrietty, and Homily, snorting and sniffing, unhooked the blade and handle of half a pair of manicure scissors from a nail on the wall, and began to cut through the peel.

"You've ruined this potato," she grumbled. "You can't roll it back now in all that dust, not once it's been cut open."

"Oh, what does it matter?" said Arrietty. "There are plenty more."

"That's a nice way to talk. Plenty more. Do you realize," Homily went on gravely, laying down the half nail scissor, "that your poor father risks his life every time he borrows a potato?"

"I meant," said Arrietty, "that there are plenty more in the storeroom."

"Well, out of my way now," said Homily, bustling around again, "whatever you meant—and let me get the supper."

Arrietty wandered through the open door into the sitting room. Ah, the fire had been lighted and the room looked bright and cozy. Homily was proud of her sitting room: the walls had been papered with scraps of old letters out of waste-paper baskets, and Homily had arranged the handwriting sideways in vertical strips which ran from floor to ceiling. On the walls, repeated in various colors, hung several portraits of Queen Victoria as a girl; these were postage stamps, borrowed by Pod some years ago from the stamp box on the desk in the morning room. There was a lacquer trinket box, padded inside and with the lid open, which they used as a settle; and that useful stand-by—a chest of drawers made of match boxes. There was a round table with a red velvet cloth, which Pod had made from the wooden bottom of a pill box supported on the carved pedestal of a knight from the chest set. (This had caused a great deal of trouble upstairs when Aunt Sophy's eldest son, on a flying mid-week visit, had invited the vicar for "a game after dinner." Rosa Pickhatchet, who was housemaid at the time, gave in her notice. After she had left other things were found to be missing, and no one was engaged in her place. From that time onwards Mrs. Driver ruled supreme.) The knight itself—its bust, so to speak—stood on a column in the corner, where it looked very fine, and lent that air to the room which only statuary can give.

Beside the fire, in a tilted wooden bookcase, stood Arrietty's library. This was a set of those miniature volumes which the Victorians loved to print, but which to Arrietty seemed the size of very large church Bibles. There was Bryce's *Tom Thumb Gazetteer of the World*, including the last census; Bryce's *Tom Thumb Dictionary*, with short explanations of scientific, philosophical, literary, and technical terms; Bryce's *Tom Thumb Edition of the Comedies of William Shakespeare,* including a foreword on the author; another book, whose pages were all blank, called *Memoranda;* and, last but not least, Arrietty's favorite Bryce's *Tom Thumb Diary and Proverb Book,* with a saying for each day of the year and, as a preface, the life story of a little man called General Tom Thumb, who married a girl called Mercy Lavinia Bump. There was an engraving of their carriage and pair, with little horses—the size of mice. Arrietty was not a stupid girl. She knew that horses could not be as small as mice, but she did not realize that Tom Thumb, nearly two feet high, would seem a giant to a Borrower.

Arrietty had learned to read from these books, and to write by leaning sideways and copying out the writings on the walls. In spite of this, she did not always keep her diary, although on most days she would take the book out for the sake of the saying which sometimes would comfort her. Today it said: "You may go farther and fare worse," and, underneath: "Order of the Garter, instituted 1348." She carried the book to the fire and sat down with her feet on the hob.

"What are you doing, Arrietty?" called Homily from the kitchen.

"Writing my diary."

"Oh," exclaimed Homily shortly.

"What did you want?" asked Arrietty. She felt quite safe; Homily liked her to write; Homily encouraged any form of culture. Homily herself, poor ignorant creature, could not even say the alphabet. "Nothing. Nothing," said Homily crossly, banging away with the pan lids; "it'll do later."

Arrietty took out her pencil. It was a small white pencil, with a piece of silk cord attached, which had come off a dance program, but, even so, in Arrietty's hand, it looked like a rolling-pin.

"Arrietty!" called Homily again from the kitchen.

"Yes?"

"Put a little something on the fire, will you?"

Arrietty braced her muscles and heaved the book off her knees, and stood it upright on the floor. They kept the fuel, assorted slack and crumbled candle-grease, in a pewter mustard-pot, and shoveled it out with the spoon. Arrietty trickled only a few grains, tilting the mustard spoon, not to spoil the blaze. Then she stood there basking in the warmth. It was a charming fireplace, made by Arrietty's grandfather, with a cogwheel from the stables, part of an old cider-press. The spokes of the cogwheel stood out in starry rays, and the fire itself nestled in the center. Above there was a chimney-piece made from a small brass funnel, inverted. This, at one time, belonged to an oil lamp which matched it, and which stood, in the old days, on the hall table upstairs. An arrangement of pipes, from the spout of the funnel, carried the fumes into the kitchen flues above. The fire was laid with match-sticks and fed with assorted slack and, as it burned up, the iron would become hot, and Homily would simmer soup on the spokes in a silver thimble, and Arrietty would broil nuts. How cozy those winter evenings could be. Arrietty, her great book on her knees, sometimes reading aloud; Pod at his last (he was a shoemaker, and made button-boots out of kid gloves—now, alas, only for his family); and Homily, quiet at last, with her knitting.

Homily knitted their jerseys and stockings on black-headed pins, and, sometimes, on darning needles. A great reel of silk or cotton would stand, table high, beside her chair, and sometimes, if she pulled too sharply, the reel would tip up and roll away out of the open door into the dusty passage beyond, and Arrietty would be sent after it, to re-wind it carefully as she rolled it back.

The floor of the sitting room was carpeted with deep red blotting paper, which was warm and cozy, and soaked up the spills. Homily would renew it at intervals when it became available upstairs, but since Aunt Sophy had taken to her bed Mrs. Driver seldom thought of blotting paper unless, suddenly, there were guests. Homily liked things which saved washing because drying was difficult under the floor; water they had plenty, hot and cold, thanks to Pod's father who had tapped the pipes from the kitchen boiler. They bathed in a small tureen, which once had held *pâté de foie gras*. When you had wiped out your bath you were supposed to put the lid back, to stop people putting things in it. The soap, too, a great cake of it, hung on a nail in the scullery, and they scraped pieces off. Homily liked coal tar, but Pod and Arrietty preferred sandalwood.

"What are you doing now, Arrietty?" called Homily from the kitchen.

"Still writing my diary."

Once again Arrietty took hold of the book and heaved it back on to her knees. She licked the lead of her great pencil, and stared a moment, deep in thought. She allowed herself (when she did remember to write) one little line on each page because she would never—of this she was sure—have another diary, and if she could get twenty lines on each page the diary would last her twenty years. She had kept it for nearly two years already, and today, 22nd March, she read last year's entry: "Mother cross." She thought a while longer then, at last, she put ditto marks under "mother," and "worried" under "cross."

"What did you say you were doing, Arrietty?" called Homily from the kitchen.

Arrietty closed the book. "Nothing," she said.

"Then chop me up this onion, there's a good girl. Your father's late tonight. . . ."

Sighing, Arrietty put away her diary and went into the kitchen. She took the onion ring from Homily, and slung it lightly round her shoulders, while she foraged for a piece of razor blade. "Really, Arrietty," exclaimed Homily, "not on your clean jersey! Do you want to smell like a bit-bucket? Here, take the scissor—"

Arrietty stepped through the onion ring as though it were a child's hoop, and began to chop it into segments.

"Your father's late," muttered Homily again, "and it's my fault, as you might say. Oh dear, oh dear, I wish I hadn't—"

"Hadn't what?" asked Arrietty, her eyes watering. She sniffed loudly and longed to rub her nose on her sleeve.

Homily pushed back a thin lock of hair with a worried hand. She stared at Arrietty absently. "It's that tea cup you broke," she said.

"But that was days ago—" began Arrietty, blinking her eyelids, and she sniffed again.

"I know. I know. It's not you. It's me. It's not the breaking that matters, it's what I said to your father."

"What did you say to him?"

"Well, I just said—there's the rest of the service, I said—up there, where it always was, in the corner cupboard in the schoolroom."

"I don't see anything bad in that," said Arrietty as, one by one, she dropped the pieces of onion into the soup.

"But it's a high cupboard," exclaimed Homily. "You have to get up by the curtain. And your father at his age—" She sat down suddenly on a metal-topped champagne cork. "Oh, Arrietty, I wish I'd never mentioned it!"

"Don't worry," said Arrietty, "Papa knows what he can do." She pulled a rubber scent-bottle cork out of the hole in the hot-water pipe and let a trickle of scalding drops fall into the tin lid of an aspirin bottle. She added cold and began to wash her hands.

"Maybe," said Homily. "But I went on about it so. What's a tea cup! Your Uncle Hendreary never drank a thing that wasn't out of a common acorn cup, and he's lived to a ripe old age and had the strength to emigrate. My mother's family never had nothing but a little bone thimble which they shared around. But it's once you've *had* a tea cup, if you see what I mean. . . ."

"Yes," said Arrietty, drying her hands on a roller towel made out of surgical bandage.

"It's that curtain," cried Homily. "He can't climb a curtain at his age—not by the bobbles!"

"With his pin he could," said Arrietty.

"His pin! I led him into that one too! Take a hat pin, I told him, and tie a bit of name-tape to the head, and pull yourself upstairs. It was to borrow the emerald watch from Her bedroom for me to time the cooking." Homily's voice began to tremble. "Your mother's a wicked woman, Arrietty. Wicked and selfish, that's what she is!"

"You know what?" exclaimed Arrietty suddenly.

Homily brushed away a tear. "No," she said wanly, "what?"

"I could climb a curtain."

Homily rose up. "Arrietty, you dare stand there in cold blood and say a thing like that!"

"But I could! I could! I could borrow! I know I could!"

"Oh!" gasped Homily. "Oh, you wicked heathen girl! How can

you speak so!" and she crumpled up again on the cork stool. "So it's come to this!" she said.

"Now, Mother, please," begged Arrietty, "now, don't take on!"

"But don't you see, Arrietty . . ." gasped Homily; she stared down at the table at loss for words and then, at last, she raised a haggard face. "My poor child," she said, "don't speak like that of borrowing. You don't know—and, thank goodness, you never will know"—she dropped her voice to a fearful whisper—"what it's like upstairs. . . ."

Arrietty was silent. "What is it like?" she asked after a moment.

Homily wiped her face on her apron and smoothed back her hair. "Your Uncle Hendreary," she began, "Eggletina's father—" and then she paused. "Listen!" she said. "What's that?"

Echoing on the wood was a faint vibration—the sound of a distant click. "Your father!" exclaimed Homily. "Oh, look at me! Where's the comb?"

They had a comb: a little, silver, eighteenth-century eyebrow comb from the cabinet in the drawing room upstairs. Homily ran it through her hair and rinsed her poor red eyes and, when Pod came in, she was smiling and smoothing down her apron.

Pod came in slowly, his sack on his back; he leaned his hat pin, with its dangling name-tape, against the wall and, on the middle of the kitchen table, he placed a doll's tea cup; it was the size of a mixing bowl.

"Why, Pod—" began Homily.

"Got the saucer too," he said. He swung down the sack and untied the neck. "Here you are," he said, drawing out the saucer. "Matches it."

He had a round, currant-bunny sort of face; tonight it looked flabby.

"Oh, Pod," said Homily, "you do look queer. Are you all right?"

Pod sat down. "I'm fair enough," he said.

"You went up the curtain," said Homily. "Oh, Pod, you shouldn't have. It's shaken you—"

Pod made a strange face, his eyes swiveled round toward Arrietty. Homily stared at him, her mouth open, and then she turned. "Come along, Arrietty," she said briskly, "you pop off to bed, now, like a good girl, and I'll bring you some supper."

"Oh," said Arrietty, "can't I see the rest of the borrowings?"

"Your father's got nothing now. Only food. Off you pop to bed. You've seen the cup and saucer."

Arrietty went into the sitting room to put away her diary, and took some time fixing her candle on the upturned drawing pin which served as a holder.

"Whatever are you doing?" grumbled Homily. "Give it here. There, that's the way. Now off to bed and fold your clothes, mind."

"Good night, Papa," said Arrietty, kissing his flat white cheek.

"Careful of the light," he said mechanically, and watched her with his round eyes until she had closed the door.

"Now, Pod," said Homily, when they were alone, "tell me. What's the matter?"

Pod looked at her blankly. "I been 'seen,'" he said.

Homily put out a groping hand for the edge of the table; she grasped it and lowered herself slowly on to the stool. "Oh, Pod," she said.

There was silence between them. Pod stared at Homily and Homily stared at the table. After a while she raised her white face. "Badly?" she asked.

Pod moved restlessly. "I don't know about that badly. I been 'seen.' Ain't that bad enough?"

"No one," said Homily slowly, "hasn't never been 'seen' since Uncle Hendreary and he was the first they say for forty-five years." A thought struck her and she gripped the table. "It's no good, Pod, I won't emigrate!"

"No one's asked you to," said Pod.

"To go and live like Hendreary and Lupy in a badger's set! The other side of the world, that's where they say it is—all among the earthworms."

"It's two fields away, above the spinney," said Pod.

"Nuts, that's what they eat. And berries. I wouldn't wonder if they don't eat mice—"

"You've eaten mice yourself," Pod reminded her.

"All draughts and fresh air and the children growing up wild. Think of Arrietty!" said Homily. "Think of the way she's been brought up. An only child. She'd catch her death. It's different for Hendreary."

"Why?" asked Pod. "He's got four."

"That's why," explained Homily. "When you've got four, they're brought up rough. But never mind that now. . . . Who saw you?"

"A boy," said Pod.

"A what?" exclaimed Homily, staring.

"A boy." Pod sketched out a rough shape in the air with his hands. "You know, a boy."

"But there isn't—I mean, what sort of a boy?"

"I don't know what you mean 'what sort of a boy.' A boy in a night-shirt. A boy. You know what a boy is, don't you?"

"Yes," said Homily. "I know what a boy is. But there hasn't been a boy, not in this house, these twenty years."

"Well," said Pod, "there's one here now."

Homily stared at him in silence, and Pod met her eyes. "Where did he see you?" asked Homily at last.

"In the schoolroom."

"Oh," said Homily, "when you was getting the cup?"

"Yes," said Pod.

"Haven't you got eyes?" asked Homily. "Couldn't you have looked first?"

"There's never nobody in the schoolroom. And what's more," he went on, "there wasn't today."

"Then where was he?"

"In bed. In the night-nursery or whatever it's called. That's where he was. Sitting up in bed. With the doors open."

"Well, you could have looked in the nursery."

"How could I—halfway up the curtain!"

"Is that where you was?"

"Yes."

"With the cup?"

"Yes. I couldn't get up or down."

"Oh, Pod," wailed Homily, "I should never have let you go. Not at your age!"

"Now, look here," said Pod, "don't mistake me. I got up all right. Got up like a bird, as you might say, bobbles or no bobbles. But"—he leaned toward her—"afterwards—with the cup in me hand, if you see what I mean. . . ." He picked it up off the table. "You see, it's heavy like. You can hold it by the handle, like this . . . but it drops or droops, as you might say. You should take a cup like this in your two hands. A bit of cheese off a shelf, or an apple—well, I drop that . . . give it a push and it falls and I climbs down in me own time and picks it up. But with a cup—you see what I mean? And coming down, you got to watch your feet. And, as I say, some of the bobbles was missing. You didn't know what you could hold on to, not safely. . . ."

"Oh, Pod," said Homily, her eyes full of tears, "what did you do?"

"Well," said Pod, sitting back again, "he took the cup."

"What do you mean?" exclaimed Homily, aghast.

Pod avoided her eyes. "Well, he'd been sitting up in bed there watching me. I'd been on that curtain a good ten minutes, because the hall clock had just struck the quarter—"

"But how do you mean—'he took the cup'?"

"Well, he'd got out of bed and there he was standing, looking up. 'I'll take the cup,' he said."

"Oh!" gasped Homily, her eyes staring, "and you give it him?"

"He took it," said Pod, "ever so gentle. And then, when I was down, he give it me." Homily put her face in her hands. "Now don't take on," said Pod uneasily.

"He might have caught you," shuddered Homily in a stifled voice.

"Yes," said Pod, "but he just give me the cup. 'Here you are,' he said."

Homily raised her face. "What are we going to do?" she asked.

Pod sighed. "Well, there isn't nothing we can do. Except—"

"Oh, no," exclaimed Homily, "not that. Not emigrate. Not that, Pod, now I've got the house so nice and a clock and all."

"We could take the clock," said Pod.

"And Arrietty? What about her? She's not like those cousins. She can *read*, Pod, and sew a treat—"

"He don't know where we live," said Pod.

"But they look," exclaimed Homily. "Remember Hendreary! They got the cat and—"

"Now, now," said Pod, "don't bring up the past."

"But you've got to think of it! They got the cat and—"

"Yes," said Pod, "but Eggletina was different."

"How different? She was Arrietty's age."

"Well, they hadn't told her, you see. That's where they went wrong. They tried to make her believe that there wasn't nothing but was under the floor. They never told her about Mrs. Driver or Crampfurl. Least of all about cats."

"There wasn't any cat," Homily pointed out, "not till Hendreary was 'seen.'"

"Well, there was, then," said Pod. "You got to tell them, that's what I say, or they try to find out for themselves."

"Pod," said Homily solemnly, "we haven't told Arrietty."

"Oh, she knows," said Pod; he moved uncomfortably. "She's got her grating."

"She doesn't know about Eggletina. She doesn't know about being 'seen.'"

"Well," said Pod, "we'll tell her. We always said we would. There's no hurry."

Homily stood up. "Pod," she said, "we're going to tell her now."

ROBERT LAWSON

Mr. Wilmer's Strange Saturday

William Wilmer was twenty-nine years old before he discovered that he could converse with animals. In fact it happened on his twenty-ninth birthday and it made a great difference in his life. From then on, life became highly exciting and lots of fun. He was always a little sorry that he hadn't discovered his great gift sooner, because up to that time existence had been very dull indeed. However, as Mrs. Keeler, his landlady, always said—especially when she looked at her husband—"You can't expect everything," so Mr. Wilmer was quite content with the way things worked out.

William Wilmer's twenty-ninth birthday (it came on the nineteenth of April) started just the same as any other day. In fact each of his days, except Sunday, started just the same as every other day, and ended about the same. He wouldn't have remembered that it *was* his birthday, except that in the morning he had received the usual greeting card from his Aunt Edna in Peoria—Aunt Edna never failed to send one. There was always a picture of a bunch of flowers printed on it and the words BIRTHDAY GREETINGS TO A DEAR NEPHEW. And written in purple ink there was always the same message: *"You see I never forget, just like the elephant, ha! ha! Your loving* AUNT EDNA.*"*

Sometimes Mr. Wilmer wished she *would* forget, just for a change; and having once seen a snapshot of Aunt Edna he thought the elephant smile was rather unwisely chosen. However, he dutifully removed last year's card from the mirror over his bureau and stuck up the new one, where it would remain until next birthday.

This morning, just as every other morning, Mr. Wilmer walked three blocks across town and three blocks down, to where there was a bus stop. It was a beautiful spring morning, quite warm for the nineteenth of April, as Mr. and Mrs. Keeler had both remarked— twice. There had been a shower during the night and now little wisps of steam were rising from the sidewalk wherever the sun struck. An ice wagon rattled by, the driver whistling loudly. A little bird of some sort hopped about in a starved-looking tree and whistled back at him. William Wilmer had a strange, vague feeling that something unusual was stirring in the air today, that today something *different* was going to happen. It disturbed him a little, for he was so used to things being the same that the thought of any change was a bit frightening. "I guess it's just spring," he thought—and, recollecting the birthday card: "After all, twenty-nine isn't so *terribly* old."

The bus took him seven blocks crosstown and twelve down, to the subway station. At the newsstand there, just as every morning, he bought his copy of the *Daily Bleat* and a roll of Peppermint Patooties. On the subway train he sat in his regular front right-hand corner seat of the fourth car, took one Peppermint Patootie, and looked at the pictures of murderers, gunmen and politicians, as far as 72nd Street. At 72nd Street, as usual, he ate his second Patootie and turned to the comic page. There was always just time between 72nd Street and his stop to look at "Captain Super" and "Bring 'em Back Dead," fold the paper and put it in his pocket for Claude the elevator starter, straighten his hat and unwrap three Patooties for the Policeman's horse.

The Policeman always sat on his horse halfway up the first block from the subway station and for as many mornings as he could remember Mr. Wilmer had always stopped and given the horse three Peppermint Patooties. The horse had learned to recognize him (which few people ever did) and always pawed at the curb and stretched out his neck eagerly at his approach. It was the pleasantest thing in Mr. Wilmer's day; that and saying "Good morning" to that redheaded Miss Sweeney who sat four desks away from him at the office.

The Policeman had never appeared to notice Mr. Wilmer. He always sat up very straight, glaring at the traffic, but this morning he suddenly turned down a beefy, unpleasant face and growled, "Leave off feedin' the horse sugar."

Mr. Wilmer was stunned and quite terrified. It was the first time in his life that a Policeman had ever spoken to him. He could feel little prickles run up his spine, he burst into a sweat and his knees felt weak. He was conscious of the horse's whiskers tickling his hand, of the warm breath that was making the Patooties soft and sticky. Hastily he snatched back the offending offering and tried to speak, but his voice was husky and not very steady.

"Excuse me," he stammered, "I didn't know. It's—er—they're not really sugar. They're peppermint—er—Peppermint Patooties."

The Policeman had resumed his statue-like pose and was again glaring at the traffic. Without even bothering to look down he rumbled, "Peppermint or spearmint or potaties or patooties or sugar or salt—leave off feedin' the horse, that's all."

Burning with embarrassment William Wilmer stumbled away. His head was buzzing, his hand was stuck up with Peppermint Patooties, but he dared not throw them in the gutter—he remembered the signs: DO NOT LITTER YOUR STREETS. He tried to put them in his pocket, but they only gathered tufts of fuzz and stuck tighter.

As he hastened from the scene of his humiliation he suddenly heard a voice speaking. It was a small voice, very small and far away, but perfectly clear and distinct. "The big, bullnecked, ham-faced, overbearing bully," it was saying, "the stupid, selfish, heavy-bottomed brute! I'll get even with him, I'll fix him—"

Mr. Wilmer glanced back over his shoulder and was astonished to discover that there was no one anywhere near. There were only the Policeman, his red neck bulging over his collar, and the impatiently pawing horse. "That's queer," he thought, but he was so confused and upset that he did not realize how queer it really was.

He hurried into the lobby of the Safe, Sane and Colossal Insurance Company Building, forgot to give Claude the starter his copy of the *Daily Bleat*, and was rewarded for his thoughtlessness by having the elevator door slammed on his heel.

Ever since he had finished High School eleven years ago, William Wilmer had worked for the Safe, Sane and Colossal Insurance Company. The office where he spent his days was on the ninth floor of the S. S. & C. Building. It was a huge room, almost a block square and filled with rows of desks, very much like a schoolroom. There were seventeen aisles and six desks in each row between the aisles. Mr. Wilmer's desk was in the seventh row, second from the left of Aisle J. On each desk was either a typewriter or a calculating machine. Mr. Wilmer's desk had a calculator.

At night the machines were protected by covers of rubberized cloth and every morning punctually at 8:57 William Wilmer sat down at his desk, took off the cover, folded it neatly and placed it in the lower right-hand drawer of his desk. Then he pulled up his cuffs, eased his coat and started to work.

On the right-hand corner of his desk there was always waiting a square wire basket filled with long slips of pink, green or yellow paper on which were columns of figures. The figures on the pink slips were to be added, those on the green slips to be divided and the yellow ones subtracted. So all day Mr. Wilmer punched at the keys of his machine, adding, subtracting or dividing. The results came out on strips of white paper which he carefully placed in a wire basket on the *left*-hand corner of his desk. Punctually, every hour, an office boy brought a fresh basketful of pink, green and yellow slips and carried away the white ones. At 4:57 each afternoon a buzzer sounded, Mr. Wilmer pulled down his cuffs and coat sleeves, put the cover on his machine and went home.

It was not a very exciting life.

The only exciting thing was when he smiled good morning to that redheaded Miss Sweeney who sat four desks to the right of him across Aisle J. Her hair, although undeniably red, was soft and wavy. It looked as though it had been brushed a great deal, not just kinked up with cheap permanents like that of most of the other girls. Her eyes were deep blue, with black-lashed rims, and when she smiled her nose, which was extremely short, wrinkled in a most entrancing way. Her morning greeting made William Wilmer feel warm and happy for hours. He could punch cheerily at the keys of his machine and forget all about the Safe, Sane and Colossal Insurance Company and Mrs. Keeler's tiresome boardinghouse. He didn't quite know just what he *did* think about at those times, but they were very pleasant thoughts.

This morning however, his birthday morning, everything was wrong. He was still red and confused from the Policeman's rudeness. He removed the cover from his machine, placed it in the lower right-hand drawer, pulled up his cuffs, eased his coat and looked over to smile good morning to Miss Sweeney. She wasn't there.

He guessed at once that she was in one of the inner offices taking dictation and he was right, for soon she emerged from Mr. Twitch's office looking extremely angry, slammed her notebook on her desk and began hammering furiously at her typewriter without even glancing in Mr. Wilmer's direction.

"Oh well," he sighed, "I might have known it—everything's wrong this morning." He did not have to wonder why Miss Sweeney was mad; everyone who had any dealings with Mr. Twitch always came away angry.

Mr. A. Wellington Twitch was the Office Manager and was a thoroughly unpleasant creature. He wasn't much older than Mr. Wilmer, but he *looked* much older, for he was slightly bald and was becoming stout, a fact which he tried to conceal by always wearing tightly buttoned double-breasted coats. His neckties always matched his socks and the neatly pressed handkerchief which peeped from his breast pocket always matched the necktie. This handkerchief was only for show; the one he really used was carried in his trousers-pocket and was generally damp and not too clean, for Mr. Twitch usually had a cold in the head.

His full name was Arthur Wellington Twitch and it is conceivable, though not likely, that when he was young his mother called him Artie or his playmates called him "Art," but it seemed impossible now that he could have ever been called anything so affectionate. It seemed still more impossible that he could ever have had any play-mates.

William Wilmer was still thinking about what an unhappy morning it had been when he became aware that Mr. Twitch was standing beside his desk. He was twisting his little black mustache, a sure sign that he was preparing to be particularly nasty, and speaking in a loud voice so that everyone around could hear.

"Well, Wilmer," he was saying, "daydreaming again, I see. It's really a shame that our little duties here should interfere with your slumbers. Perhaps they will not—very much longer. Three mistakes this morning—three: two additions and one subtraction and in the amount of three dollars, eighty-seven cents."

Mr. Wilmer, hot and confused, tried to stammer something about being sorry, but Mr. Twitch was enjoying himself now and went on in a louder and more sneering tone.

"Of course, to a man of your financial standing the sum of three dollars, eighty-seven cents is practically nothing, a mere bagatelle, as it were, but I can assure you that the Safe, Sane and Colossal Insurance Company, Incorporated, does not share your views. Nor does the Safe, Sane and Colossal Company appreciate your innova-tions in the science of addition and subtraction; and what's more they're not going to put up with it. Now watch your step, my lad. One more mistake like this—just one—and you'll be out in the street. And I can tell you, jobs don't grow on trees these days."

As he strutted off one or two of the clerks tittered, but Miss Sweeney did not. She looked more angry than ever and it was some consolation to William Wilmer to see her nose wrinkle with distaste and the small tip of a very pink tongue protrude slightly at the re-treating back of A. Wellington Twitch.

She gave Mr. Wilmer a sweet and sympathetic smile, but he was too miserable now to be cheered by anything. It certainly was being a happy birthday! All he could do was to keep punching at the keys of his machine and wait for the noontime buzzer to buzz. He made several mistakes, but didn't know and didn't care.

This morning, it being Saturday, the office closed at noon. At 11:57 the office boys went up and down the aisles placing small envelopes on all the desks. William Wilmer put his in his pocket without even opening it. It was his weekly wage and he knew that it contained exactly $34.86, less Social Security, bond payments, Withholding Tax and so on.

As he emerged from the S. S. & C. Building he noticed that it was much warmer. Spring had really arrived and this made him feel even more depressed. He didn't care much for Saturday afternoons at any time, but in spring and summer he liked them even less. Everyone was always hurrying toward the stations and the ferries and the bus terminals. They were laden with bags, picnic baskets, tennis rackets, golf clubs, bathing suits and kodaks. He knew they were going to the beaches or to the country for week ends, but he didn't know anyone who would invite him to the country for a week end and he didn't care much for the beaches, he always got pushed around so much—besides, he sunburned very easily.

So he usually went to a movie on Saturday afternoon and to another one Saturday evening. Sundays were different, they were all right. Because then there were the Sunday papers to read and William Wilmer read every one of them from beginning to end. He read the news and the editorials, the scientific articles and the book reviews. He read the real estate advertisements, the Garden Section, the society notes and even the recipes and the funnies. But what he enjoyed most of all were the Vacation Travel Sections; he read every word of those. He read about cruises to the Caribbean and Nova Scotia and Labrador and Alaska. And about the Grand Canyon and Yellowstone Park, where you could feed the bears; about California and Florida. He liked to picture himself clad in immaculate white linens, stretched in a deck chair, while the ship plowed gently through soft tropical seas and the Southern Cross glowed warmly above the horizon.

Somehow in these imaginings that redheaded Miss Sweeney was always there too. He could picture just how well she would wear Southern resort clothes (he even picked out several outfits for her from the better advertisements) and how her coppery hair would seem even more burnished under a Southern sun and how her very short nose would wrinkle even more fascinatingly as she gazed with delight on the beauties of strange far places. Yes, Sundays were all right.

And then Sunday afternoons he always went over to the Zoo and looked at the animals. He didn't know much about animals, but he liked them. They were so powerful and lithe, yet so resigned to being shut up in cages. Somehow he felt a great kinship with them, for after all, his life in the Safe, Sane and Colossal Insurance Company office was pretty much the same as theirs. Only *they* didn't have any Mr. A. Wellington Twitch to boss them around. He was sure that none of the Zoo's keepers would ever dare be as mean as Mr. Twitch—some tiger or puma would have his leg off in a minute.

What with the spring and the warmth and the unpleasant events of the morning Mr. Wilmer was completely upset and out of sorts. Suddenly, with reckless self-abandon, he decided, "I think I'll go to the Zoo this afternoon instead of tomorrow." It was quite a grave change from the routine of eleven years of established habit, but he felt really desperate. Perhaps the quiet companionship of the animals would help restore his nerves, so without giving himself time to change his mind he hastily boarded a bus and went up to the Zoo.

There were fewer people about than he had expected. The sudden warm weather had made the animal houses seem unbearably stuffy and most people were sprawled on the lawns or messing around on the ponds. William Wilmer wandered through the Large Mammal House and paused in front of his favorite cage. The sign on it said AFRICAN LION (*Felis leo*)—and another sign said TOBY. Toby was Mr. Wilmer's favorite, for of all the animals he seemed the handsomest and most resigned. All day he lay with his proud yellow eyes staring fixedly into space, contemptuous alike of old ladies' poking umbrellas or children's tossed candies.

Today, however, he was restless. He paced and tossed and shook his head. He flopped down and stretched his legs, clawed at the floor and rose and paced again.

Mr. Wilmer hadn't noticed. He was still too upset to notice anything much. He kept seeing the Policeman's angry red face, he remembered the sticky Peppermint Patooties clasped in his hand. He could see Mr. Twitch twisting his little black mustache and hear his sarcastic, rasping voice.

He remembered, too, that other voice, that small faraway one that he had heard in the street when there was no one there but the Policeman and his horse. It was queer, that was; he couldn't imagine what it could have been.

And then he suddenly heard it again! It was the same voice or one very much like it, small and far away, but perfectly clear and distinct. It was saying, "Well, what have *you* got to be grumbling about?"

William Wilmer looked around to see who was talking, but for once, the Lion House was completely empty of people. There was no one at all, except himself and one Keeper, who was way down at the other end, sweeping and whistling softly; it couldn't be he. Astonished, he looked all around again and then noticed Toby's yellow eyes fixed intently on his face. At last it began to dawn on him that it was Toby speaking—speaking to him, and rather irritably. The great lips scarcely moved, the voice seemed to come from somewhere way inside. It seemed very small for a lion, but perfectly clear.

"Well," said Toby, "I asked, 'What have *you* to be grumbling about?'"

Mr. Wilmer didn't know quite how to answer. He knew Toby could not understand him if he just spoke in his ordinary voice. It ought to be that small faraway sound; far away and small, but clear and distinct. He tried very hard, he did funny little things with the muscles of his throat and suddenly it came! It came from somewhere way down deep, he didn't have to do anything with his lips or tongue, it just came out, small and far away, very much like Toby's or the Policeman's horse's, but a little thinner.

"Why I wasn't—er—grumbling—exactly," said William Wilmer with his new voice. "I was just sort of thinking and talking to myself, I guess. You see, it's been a very upsetting day. There was that unpleasant Policeman and Mr. Twitch—it was mostly Twitch I think that got me worked up—"

"Twitch," snorted Toby, "Twitch—what's a twitch to bother anybody? Young man, did you ever have a *twinge?*" He hitched himself closer to the bars. "Did you ever have a *pain?* A searing, blinding, red-hot spasm burning through your jaw and down the side of your neck like a bolt of slow lightning?" He hitched himself still closer. "Young man, did you ever have a TOOTHACHE?"

"Oh, yes indeed," said William sympathetically. "When I was in High School once I had a dreadful time. It was a wisdom tooth—infected—it was really terrible. I know how you must feel."

"You do *not*," answered Toby. "You can't have the faintest conception." He sniffed tolerantly and opened his mouth wide to show the rows of great glistening fangs. "'Terrible'!" he snorted. "What would *you* know about terrible, with those tiny little chips of teeth you have? Why this single one of mine, upper right eyetooth— that's the one that's giving me the agony—why that one tooth has more ivory in it than you have in your whole head, and that much more pain too.

"And the trouble is"—he banged the bars irritably—"the trouble is that these blithering idiots can't find out what's the matter with me."

"Why don't you tell them?" asked Mr. Wilmer. "Why don't you tell them, like you've just told me?"

"Tell them?" snapped Toby. "Don't you think I would if I could? It just happens that you're the first and only human I've seen since I was brought to this God-forsaken, dreary country who could understand Animal or speak Animal, the very first. Now if you would only tell them for me—" A fresh spasm of pain caused him to emit a series of heartrending roars.

Mr. Wilmer, politely waiting for the pain to pass, was suddenly conscious of the Keeper at his side.

"Now then, now then," said the Keeper. "Don't be bothering the animal. It's bad enough he is, let alone, what with something ailing him and nobody knowing what. Four days and nights he's been roaring and bellering and me not able to do anything for him, not even clean the cage, that ugly-tempered he is, and him that's usually a lamb."

"It's a toothache," said Mr. Wilmer. "The upper right eyetooth."

The Keeper regarded him severely. "Toothache is it?" he inquired. "Toothache you say—and in the upper right eyetooth? And just what might *you* be, to be telling *me* about his toothaches and eyeteeth? A mind reader perhaps, or maybe one of them Indian physics or swamis? Here's the Director been up with him two nights, and the State Veterinary, and him with his stethoscopes and X-rays and injections and all, and devil a thing can they find ailing poor Toby— and you to be telling me it's the toothache!"

"I'm sure it is," said Mr. Wilmer. "He just told me so. He said—"

"He *what?*" asked the Keeper slowly.

"He *said* it was the toothache—the upper right eyetooth. You see, we were talking about toothaches and how painful they can be and he said—"

The Keeper grasped Mr. Wilmer kindly, but firmly, by the elbow and started walking him toward the door, talking all the while in a soothing tone.

"Sure and it's a *very* hot day, unseasonable really and the sun real strong for this time in April. You wouldn't have been walking without your hat would you, or maybe have a drop of liquor under your belt, or two perhaps, it being Saturday afternoon and all? We'll just be stepping out into the good fresh air now, quiet-like and not making any disturbances—disturbances disturbs the animals, especially in this spring weather." They were outside now and the Keeper steered Mr. Wilmer toward a shady path. "Right down by the lake there," he said, "there'll be plenty of benches, cool and in the shade—sitting there awhile you'll likely feel better."

He went back toward the Lion House shaking his head. "Too bad," he said. "A nice lad he seemed, quiet and well-behaved. He didn't *look* nuts. It just goes to show—you never can tell."

William Wilmer did sit in the shade for a while and tried to collect his thoughts, but it was rather difficult. It had been a most confusing day and he felt very tired. He decided to go home to Mrs. Keeler's and retire right after dinner, he certainly didn't want to go to any movie. He felt as though he *were* a movie, a sort of one-man two-reel comedy.

*   *   *

Sunday morning Mr. Wilmer woke quite early. The soft breeze stirring his window curtains promised a day still warmer than yesterday, the air even *smelled* springlike. He decided to walk to the corner and get the Sunday papers before breakfast instead of afterward as he usually did. "My, I certainly am becoming unpredictable," he thought.

As he went down Mrs. Keeler's front steps it was almost like walking into a greenhouse, the morning was so balmy. Down the street two whitewings were flushing the pavement with a fire hose and whenever the stream splashed up from the curbing the early sun struck sparkles and rainbows in the dancing spray. The water ran clear and bubbling down the gutters with little brooklike gurglings.

The same feeling of something impending that had come over him yesterday morning was even stronger today. Certainly, plenty had happened yesterday, mostly unpleasant, but that business of hearing the Policeman's horse and talking with Toby had been very pleasant and most exciting, although quite mystifying. It seemed so long ago he wondered if all those things actually could have happened; it didn't seem possible, he must have imagined everything. Perhaps the Keeper at the Zoo *had* been right, it might have been the heat, or something he had eaten. Yet he could still hear those small, clear voices, he could remember exactly how he had done something queer with the muscles way down in his throat and how, without his even moving his lips or tongue, his own small, clear Animal voice had come out, perfectly distinct and understandable to Toby, although apparently inaudible to anyone else.

There was a milk wagon standing beside the curb. The big, dappled gray horse looked tired, his head hung sleepily. On a sudden impulse Mr. Wilmer decided to try out his new voice. He didn't see the driver anywhere, but he carefully clasped his hands behind his back; no use being called down again for feeding someone's horse.

Then William Wilmer did those strange little things with his throat muscles and the small, clear voice came out just as it had done yesterday. "Good morning," he said politely, "quite warm, isn't it?"

The horse opened one eye, fixing it wearily on Mr. Wilmer, and *his* voice came, much like Toby's but even more like the Policeman's horse's. "Morning," he grunted. "Got the time?"

Mr. Wilmer consulted his watch and announced that it was about 7:45.

"Half an hour more," said the horse, closing his eye again. "The rest of this block—down the Avenue—all the next block—down the Avenue—then back to the stables." He suddenly opened both eyes and stared sorrowfully at Mr. Wilmer. "Ever do any night work, young feller?" Without waiting for a reply, he snorted, "Well, don't!" and closed his eyes again.

The rattling of bottles announced the approach of the driver, and automatically, head hanging and eyes still closed, the old horse clopped along to the next building.

William Wilmer, standing in the deserted street, was swept by a great wave of elation and excitement. It *was* true! He *could* actually talk with animals!

He hurried home with the papers, his mind in a dazed whirl. This accomplishment promised to make life much more interesting; week ends would no longer be boring. . . . He didn't dream *how* interesting life was going to be.

At breakfast Mrs. Keeler inquired: "In early, weren't you? No movie?"

"No," answered Mr. Wilmer, "I was sort of tired, it was quite hot yesterday, and I just didn't feel like it."

Mr. Keeler, helping himself to a third cup of coffee, winked heavily. "Spring," he pronounced. "Ah, spring! In spring a young man's fancy—"

Mrs. Keeler quenched him with a glance. "You're not a young man," she said, "and Heaven knows you're not fancy—and as for spring, there's that bedspring in the third floor front you're to fix today, I'm glad you reminded me of it."

"Yes, my dear," said Mr. Keeler, wiping his walrus mustache with a loud swishing noise. "I was considering that, just as soon as I have glanced at the headlines." He picked up Mr. Wilmer's Sunday papers. "Ah, here's an interesting item—'Zoo's Prize Lion Suffering from Mysterious Ailment.'"

"Give Mr. Wilmer his own paper," Mrs. Keeler interrupted, "and get going."

Mr. Wilmer glanced at the front page and there, staring out with his patient eyes, was a large photograph of Toby. He began to read the article aloud: "Officials of the Central Zoo have been greatly concerned by the inexplicable illness of Toby, the Zoo's oldest and most prized lion. Dr. Wimpole, State Veterinary, has made several examinations and taken numerous blood tests without any result. X-ray photographs have failed to reveal the seat of the trouble. Carrington Carrington-Carr, Director of the Central Zoo, confesses himself completely baffled. Three eminent specialists, summoned last week from Johns Hopkins, recommended a diet of Vitamins A, E, I, O, U and sometimes Y, but the patient has shown no improvement. A further consultation of experts will take place this morning—"

"Why, that's silly!" Mr. Wilmer broke off. "It's only a toothache, upper right eyetooth; why, just yesterday he said—"

He became aware that both Mr. and Mrs. Keeler were eying him oddly. "And how," Mrs. Keeler inquired quietly, "and how would *you* know it was toothache—and upper right eyetooth at that—and *who* was it said just what?"

"Why, Toby," he began. "He said—" Then suddenly Mr. Wilmer remembered the Keeper at the Zoo yesterday. He remembered the queer way the Keeper had eyed him as he led him from the Lion House, and now saw that same look pass between Mr. and Mrs. Keeler.

"I—ah—don't remember," he stammered, hurriedly. "Do you know, I think I'll walk over to the Zoo this morning"—and he hastily retreated from the dining room.

Mrs. Keeler was lost in speculation as the front door closed. "Funny," she mused. "No movie last night and he always goes Saturdays, out for the papers before breakfast and he never does that, to the Zoo this morning and he always goes in the afternoon—"

"Spring, my dear," said Mr. Keeler, rummaging for the sporting page. "Spring—birds—flowers—Love, maybe."

"Love . . ." said Mrs. Keeler picking up the coffee pot and balancing it thoughtfully, as a discus thrower weighs his missile. "Spring . . . Spring, my love—and spring fast. Bedspring—third-floor front."

Mr. Keeler sprang.

As Mr. Wilmer entered the Park he heard a sound that seemed like distant thunder, but the sky was unusually blue and the sun shone warmly. "Must be building a new subway," he thought. As he neared the Lion House, however, he realized that the sound was the roaring of animals. All the lions and tigers, the leopards, panthers and pumas seemed to be holding forth at a great rate, but one set of roars was much louder and more thunderous than all the others. "Goodness, what a noise," said Mr. Wilmer, as he entered the building. It was empty of people, for the morning was still early.

He went straight to Toby's cage, only to find the bars covered by a large canvas sheet on which was hung a sign, CLOSED FOR REPAIRS. The loudest roars were coming from this cage, and between the roars Mr. Wilmer could hear men's voices and the shuffling of feet.

As he stood there two men came hurrying by. One was the Keeper who had escorted him out the day before, the other was a tall worried-looking man dressed in rough gray tweeds. The Keeper spied

Mr. Wilmer, paused, and then suddenly pounced on him with a glad cry.

"This is him," he shouted, above the roaring of the animals. "This is him, Mr. Carrington-Carr, this is the guy!"

The tall man removed an unlighted pipe from his mouth and inquired, "What guy, Gallagher?"

"The one I was after telling you about," cried the Keeper excitedly. "Him that said to me yesterday 'twas the toothache was bothering poor Toby; upper right eyetooth he said, didn't you now?" He shook Mr. Wilmer's arm. "Didn't you say 'twas the toothache?"

"Why yes, I did," answered Mr. Wilmer, slightly dazed by the noise and the Keeper's excitement.

The tall man extended his hand and smiled pleasantly. "My name is Carrington-Carr," he said. "Carrington Carrington-Carr, Director here. Keeper Gallagher has told us a rather odd story of your visit here yesterday and of your truly extraordinary diagnosis of Toby's trouble. Tell me now, just what was it led you to believe that it was toothache?"

Mr. Wilmer hesitated, he didn't want *everyone* to think he was crazy; but this man seemed pleasant and intelligent—perhaps he would understand. "Well—you see," he stammered, "he—er—that is—Toby *said* so. We were just sort of talking about things and he said that he had a terrible toothache, upper right eyetooth, and he said—I'm sorry, but his own words were: 'These blithering idiots can't find out what's the matter with me.'"

Mr. Carrington-Carr flashed a startled glance at the Keeper, but went on quietly. "If Toby possesses this remarkable linguistic ability, which we have certainly never noted, why do you suppose he didn't tell *us* his troubles?"

"Why—er—he said that I was the first person he had met who could understand Animal or talk Animal."

"Have you been aware of this great gift long?" the Director asked.

"No sir, I only discovered it yesterday," Mr. Wilmer answered. "It was a great surprise, I can assure you."

"I don't doubt that," said Mr. Carrington-Carr with a slight smile. "Tell me now, just how *does* one converse with an animal? Let us suppose, for a moment, that I am a lion; would you mind just saying 'Good morning' to me?"

"Certainly not," said William Wilmer. He did the strange little things with his throat muscles and heard his small, faraway, clear voice say, "Good morning, Mr. Carrington-Carr, nice day."

"Well, go ahead," said the Director.

"I have—I did," Mr. Wilmer answered. "I said 'Good morning, Mr. Carrington-Carr.'"

Again the Director exchanged glances with the Keeper. "I didn't hear anything, did you, Gallagher?"

"Devil a word," he answered. "I told you he was nuts."

"Perhaps if you really *were* a lion—" began Mr. Wilmer.

"Don't get fresh with the Director—" interrupted Gallagher, but Mr. Carrington-Carr silenced him.

"Nuts or not," he said, "or voices or no voices, the fact still remains that none of our precious experts had been able to discover what Toby's trouble was until at our consultation last night you mentioned this young man's seemingly fantastic story. As you remember, more in desperation than anything else, we took new X-rays of Toby's teeth, and discovered that the diagnosis was absolutely correct. It *is* toothache, and as far as we can tell, it *is* the upper right eyetooth, although we are not absolutely certain on this latter point.

"Come, let's find out," he ended suddenly and led the way through an office and into a narrow brick passage that ran back of the cages. It was a very narrow passage and they had to pass much too close to the bars for William Wilmer's comfort, for all the animals, excited by Toby's roars, were also roaring and pacing their cages excitedly. In the passage, back of Toby's cage, was a group of young men, many of whom carried cameras while the rest had notebooks. Mr. Wilmer judged they were newspaper reporters.

"Stand aside, boys, and leave the Director get by," shouted Mr. Gallagher; "and mind now, none of your flashlights till you get permission, the poor beast is excited enough as it is."

In the cage were several distinguished-looking gentlemen, most of them in surgeons' white coats. There were two Keepers, armed with heavy iron bars, and a table covered with a white cloth on which was spread an array of shiny surgical instruments. The sight of these made Mr. Wilmer feel somewhat sickish, so he turned his attention to the patient.

Poor Toby looked far from dignified or resigned. He was spread-eagled out on the floor; heavy ropes stretched from his paws to the four corners of the cage. A thick piece of wood was stuck between his jaws and lashed tightly with stout cords, but he managed to keep up a continual roaring and moaning in spite of the gag.

"Gentlemen," said Director Carrington-Carr, raising his hand for attention, "allow me to present Mr.—er—"

"Wilmer," said Mr. Wilmer, "William Wilmer."

"Gentlemen," went on the Director, "Mr. Wilmer is the young man whose uncannily accurate diagnosis enabled us to locate the seat of Toby's trouble. You will, of course, recollect Keeper Gallagher's extraordinary tale at our consultation last evening.

"Mr. Wilmer, it seems, by his own account, was enabled to accomplish this remarkable diagnosis by conversing with Toby in a private form of language with which very few humans are privileged to be conversant. In short, he talked to the lion and the lion told him what the trouble was."

At this a chorus of talk and laughter arose from the newsmen and even the dignified gentlemen in white coats smiled broadly.

"Pipe down, youse," Mr. Gallagher warned the reporters as he toyed with his iron bar, "or out you go."

Mr. Carrington-Carr motioned the scientists closer and continued: "We have not time, at the moment, to go into this remarkable phenomenon, if it is; that can come later. The important thing is that this young man's diagnosis has been, thus far, absolutely correct, as proven by our X-rays. He also says that the trouble is with the upper right eyetooth. Of this we have no proof and to pull the wrong tooth of an animal as valuable as this would be an extremely grave error. I therefore propose to allow Mr. Wilmer to converse quietly with Toby for a few moments and make as certain as is humanly possible that we are doing the right thing. It may help us and it certainly cannot do any harm."

William Wilmer knelt down and put his hand on Toby's feverish paw. He did the peculiar things with his throat muscles and heard his small, faraway voice say, "Well, Toby, they certainly have got you down."

Toby answered, *his* small voice much muffled by the gag. "How han I hawk wiv his ham hick in my mou?"

Mr. Wilmer looked up at the small ring of intent faces. "He says he can't talk well with that stick in his mouth. Could you take it out?"

Mr. Gallagher and another Keeper gingerly untied the lashings and Toby disgustedly spat out the heavy stick. "There, that's *less* bad," he grumbled. "*Now* what is it?"

Mr. Wilmer said, "Toby, these gentlemen have at last found out what your trouble is and they want to relieve it as quickly as possible, only they're not absolutely certain which tooth it is."

"I *told* you," Toby answered irritably. "I told you it was the upper right eyetooth; why didn't you tell *them?*"

"I tried to," apologized Mr. Wilmer, "I *did* try to, but they all thought I was crazy. Perhaps I'd better point it out to them, so there can't be any mistake. This is the one, isn't it?" And he placed his finger on the great gleaming fang. Toby emitted a roar that shook the building and brought down a small snowstorm of flaked paint from the ceiling.

"I guess that's the one all right," said Mr. Wilmer, turning to the Director and the attentive scientists.

They went to work at once. The stick was replaced and well tied. Two white-coated doctors shot huge syringes of anesthetic into Toby's gums; then, while the keepers held his head firmly, another doctor clamped a shiny pair of forceps on the upper right eyetooth. He struggled and wrestled and yanked while Toby's roars made the canvas screen flap as though in a summer wind. Finally, with a great heave and a piercing bellow, the tooth came out, followed by a rush of blood. Other doctors hastily closed in and examined the cavity with flashlights and magnifying glasses.

"He's right!" they chorused excitedly. "That *is* the one—badly ulcerated too!"

The exhausted doctor who had done the pulling advanced with the gory fang still clamped in his forceps. "Here it is, Mr. Wilmer," he cried. "That's the baby, you had it right."

But Mr. Wilmer wasn't there. At the first gush of blood he had quietly fainted and now lay flat on the floor, his head under the instrument table.

When he came to, he was in the Director's office. His hair was wet and his collar sopping, for Keeper Gallagher had helpfully tossed a bucket of water over him. His head was buzzing and his eyes dazzled by the continuous popping of flashlights. His nostrils were filled with the fumes of smelling salts and his ears with the shouts of the reporters and photographers: "Give us a smile now, Bud." "Look over here, attaboy." "What's your address?" "Where do you work?" "How's about a smile?" "When did you learn to talk the lingo?" "Married?" "Got a girl friend?"

William Wilmer answered their questions as well as he could, which wasn't very well, for he still felt dizzy and the flashlights made his head ache.

"How's about a few pictures with the animal?" asked one of the photographers, so they all trooped back to the cage. The ropes that held poor Toby had been eased so that he could lie more comfortably.

"Do you feel better?" Mr. Wilmer inquired anxiously.

"Ever so much better," replied Toby. "Pain's all gone. Jaw's sore though, probably have to eat mush and trash for a few days. I'm certainly grateful to you though."

"Don't mention it," Mr. Wilmer answered. "Sorry I couldn't have helped you sooner."

They took pictures of Mr. Wilmer sitting with his arm around Toby's neck, of Mr. Wilmer patting Toby, of Mr. Wilmer shaking hands with the Director, with the Keeper and with each of the scientific gentlemen.

"Come on, Daniel," called one of the photographers. "Let's have one with your hand in the lion's mouth." So Mr. Wilmer obligingly posed with his hand in Toby's mouth while Toby smiled pleasantly. However, when they demanded that he pose holding up the tooth, he began to turn green again and the Director called a halt.

They had lunch in the Director's office. It was a large, pleasant room looking out through the trees to the lake and it was a very good lunch too, but Mr. Wilmer didn't get a chance to eat much of it, for the scientists kept plying him with questions. Every time he tried to swallow anything one of them would place a stethoscope against his throat and listen. They listened to his head and his back and his chest, they shined flashlights in his eyes and looked in his ears through little silver funnels.

Each of them wanted William Wilmer to visit him in order to undergo more thorough investigation; and before the luncheon was over he had promised to go to Chicago, Boston, Battle Creek, Washington and Baltimore. He hadn't any idea of just how or when he could go, but the gentlemen were all so pleasant and eager that he couldn't refuse.

After lunch Director Carrington-Carr made a short speech.

"Gentlemen," he said, "we have today witnessed a most remarkable demonstration of something—we do not quite know what. Mr. Wilmer's belief in his ability to converse with animals is, I am sure, completely honest and sincere, and certainly seems to have been borne out by results in the case of Toby. However, as men of science it is, of course, our duty to be skeptical of *anything* new until it has been proved beyond the possibility of a doubt.

"I believe I have thought of a method by which we can test absolutely this gift of Mr. Wilmer's. I have here," and he held up a large ledger, "a complete life history of every animal in the Central Zoo; its age, birthplace, family tree, place of capture, date of arrival here, number of offspring, illnesses, operations and so on. This record is kept in my office safe and its contents are known only to me. It would seem a very simple matter to prove beyond all question this ability of our young friend, if we were to stroll about the grounds and allow him to interview various of the animals. If he can extract from them a few essential details of their private lives and if those details agree with our records, I can see no reason for doubting that he possesses some secret method, hitherto unknown to science, of communicating with the members of the animal kingdom. That is, of course, if Mr. Wilmer is willing to co-operate in this experiment."

"I'd be very glad to," said William Wilmer, struggling with a chocolate éclair, "very glad indeed."

It was quite an imposing group which set forth, all except Mr. Wilmer. His hair was still damp and stringy, his hat had been lost somewhere, and his collar was much the worse for wear. On his left walked Director Carrington-Carr and on his right Keeper Gallagher, carrying the official ledger. Behind them came the scientific gentlemen, in top hats and long coats, flanked by two guards to protect them from the crowd of newsmen and photographers. A great many small boys joined the procession, and several dogs and three nursemaids pushing baby carriages. A balloon seller and a peanut vender with his pushcart brought up the rear.

"We might try Lucy first," said Mr. Carrington-Carr. "Here she is, right here." Lucy was an Indian elephant. She eyed the group with pleasant interest and extended her trunk for peanuts. Keeper Gallagher fumbled in his pocket for peanuts with one hand while he tried to open the ledger with the other.

"Now, Mr. Wilmer," said the Director, as the scientific gentlemen gathered close and the guards shoved the crowd back, "suppose you just ask Lucy a few questions: date of birth, place of capture, date of arrival here—just a few. Take your time and don't be nervous."

"None of them flashlights now," Mr. Gallagher cautioned.

Mr. Wilmer *was* nervous, though; he couldn't help being. He had never spoken with an elephant before, and Lucy, although not especially large as elephants go, did loom up pretty imposingly.

He cleared his throat, did those funny little things with the muscles and in his small Animal voice said, "Good afternoon Miss Lucy, pleasant day isn't it?"

Lucy dropped Mr. Gallagher's peanuts, cocked up one ear and fixed her small twinkling eye on Mr. Wilmer. "Well, goodness gracious me!" she cried. "It certainly is pleasant to talk to someone; why, this is the first chance I've had since I left Burma, out there of course all the gentlemen know how to talk to us, even the little children do, and if there's one thing I love more than another it's talk. My, my, this *is* a pleasure. What did you say the name was?" —and extended her trunk.

"Wilmer," he answered, grasping the trunk cordially, "William Wilmer. You see," he went on hastily, for Lucy threatened to start chatting again, "I only discovered yesterday that I could talk with you people or I should have called on you sooner. But these gentlemen, Mr. Carrington-Carr, you're acquainted with him I suppose, and these scientists, don't quite believe I can do it—I can't quite believe it myself—and you could help me very much if you wouldn't mind answering a few questions."

"Not at all," replied Lucy pleasantly. "Delighted, I'm sure."

Mr. Wilmer looked at the Director. "What first?" he asked.

"Age," answered Carrington-Carr.

"Oh dear, I don't think I'd better ask that," Mr. Wilmer hesitated.

"You see she's a lady. Perhaps we'd better start with birthplace. Where were you born, Miss Lucy?"

Lucy closed her eyes and recited, "I was born in the jungle of northeast Burma, about twelve miles north of the village of Bding Bdang. The village is not far from the border of Assam."

Mr. Wilmer repeated this information to the Director, who was intently studying the ledger. He looked startled, but merely said, "Go on—date of capture."

"When were you captured, Miss Lucy?" inquired Mr. Wilmer.

"Well, 'captured' is hardly the word," Lucy replied with a sigh, "I was captivated, really. It was an extremely handsome elephant in the herd of one Dhingbat Dhong, a resident of the village. I just sort of wandered in and joined the herd. I was young and inexperienced, of course, scarcely forty-eight at the time. That was back in 1915—spring, naturally."

Mr. Wilmer relayed these facts to the Director, who looked still more startled. "Good Lord!" he murmured. "Go on—date of arrival at Zoo."

Mr. Wilmer was startled too, for glancing over Mr. Gallagher's shoulder he had caught a glimpse of these old entries in the ledger:—

BIRTHPLACE: Jungle of N. E. Burma.
PLACE OF CAPTURE: Bding Bdang.
DATE OF CAPTURE: April, 1915.
OWNER: Dhingbat Dhong.

"When did you arrive here at the Zoo, Miss Lucy?" he inquired.

Again she closed her eyes and thought back. "March 27, 1921, and a horrider day I've never known: rain, sleet and a chill that went through my bones like icewater. I thought then, 'What a nasty climate this is,' and I've never thought any differently. Don't you think it's a nasty climate, Mr. Wilmer?"

"Indeed I do," he agreed. "Terrible." The next question was "Any offspring?" but he decided to skip that one too; after all, he had been calling her "Miss."

"Have you had any illnesses or operations since being here, Miss Lucy?" he asked instead.

"Nothing but head colds," she replied. "I have those a great deal and you can't imagine how trying they can be with a nose the size of mine—not that it's unduly large, but still, five or six feet of nose is *something* when you have a cold in the head. The only serious thing was an infected toe. It was operated on a year ago last January, the sixteenth, I think. Dr. Wimpole did it, very skillful and a charming gentleman, but quite uneducated; I couldn't understand a word he said."

Mr. Wilmer retailed these details to Director Carrington-Carr, who said in a rather dazed way "Check." He closed the ledger, handed it to Keeper Gallagher, and turning to the scientists announced: "Gentlemen, believe it or not, every answer agrees with our records, absolutely. Shall we proceed?"

Before proceeding, however, the photographers had to have their inning. They took pictures of Mr. Wilmer shaking hands with Lucy, of Mr. Wilmer with Lucy's trunk around his neck, feeding Lucy a peanut, shaking hands with the Director, shaking hands with Keeper Gallagher, and of all the scientists shaking hands with each other.

Then they proceeded to the Crocodile House and Mr. Wilmer interviewed a crocodile with perfect results: every answer checked exactly with the records in the ledger. During the rest of the afternoon he questioned a camel, a hippopotamus, a wart hog, a boa constrictor, an eagle and an armadillo. As each question was answered correctly Mr. Carrington-Carr checked it off in the ledger, his astonishment growing steadily as in a dazed voice he automatically repeated, "Check . . . Check . . . Check." The amazement of the scientists also increased until they even ceased to argue with one another. Several times Keeper Gallagher was seen to cross himself.

The only upset came when Mr. Wilmer attempted to question a Siberian Bear. He was a great towering fellow and seemed friendly enough and eager to talk, but William Wilmer couldn't understand a word of what he said, although he repeated it several times. Puzzled, he turned to Mr. Carrington-Carr. "I just can't understand him," he said. "He keeps saying something that sounds like 'Ne *govoru po Angliski.'"*

"What was that?" one of the scientists asked quickly. William Wilmer repeated it as well as he could.

"Why that is Russian," the scientist explained excitedly. "That is Russian for 'No speak English.'"

"Glory be!" shouted Keeper Gallagher. "Of course it would be. He's only been here a week, come Monday. Just off the boat he is and how could the poor beast be learning to talk American in them few days?"

Director Carrington-Carr slammed the ledger shut and started toward the office. "Come, gentlemen," he said; "I think you will agree that this phenomenon has been proven beyond the shadow of a doubt."

When they were all back in the Director's office and the newsmen had been locked out, Mr. Carrington-Carr began: "Gentlemen, what we have just witnessed seems utterly fantastic, impossible, unbelievable—and yet—it seems to be true. I just do not know *what* to think—"

"*I* think," said William Wilmer weakly, "I'd like to go home."

The Director suddenly noticed that he was quite pale and seemed about to faint again. "Oh, I'm so sorry," he said hastily. "We really have put you through quite an exhausting day." He went to a cupboard and brought Mr. Wilmer a small glass of brandy. "Here, take this, it will do you good."

William Wilmer had never tasted brandy and he choked and sputtered considerably, but it did make him feel better.

"I'll drive the lad home," volunteered Keeper Gallagher. "I've got the jalopy here and I live only a few blocks above his address." He eyed the glass meaningly. "I've not had too easy a day meself, what with Toby and all."

William Wilmer vaguely remembered shaking hands with the Director and all the scientific gentlemen and being led kindly out to Mr. Gallagher's car. He climbed in and promptly went to sleep.

Later, he remembered being waked up at Mrs. Keeler's house; he remembered more flashlights and Mr. Gallagher's officious voice saying, "Make room there and leave the gentleman get to his bed. It's completely exhausted he is, what with conversing all day with the animals and confounding the scientific world and all."

He remembered hearing, as he wearily climbed the stairs to his room, Mr. Gallagher addressing Mr. and Mrs. Keeler. "Shure ma'am, the miracles I've seen and heard this day have me completely unstrung. A glass of beer maybe, to settle me nerves, and I'll tell you events will have your eyes popping out like hardboiled eggs."

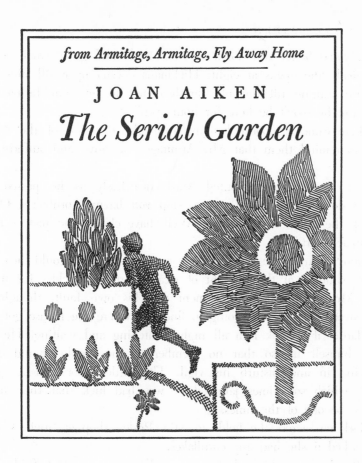

from Armitage, Armitage, Fly Away Home

JOAN AIKEN

The Serial Garden

"Cold rice pudding for breakfast?" said Mark, looking at it with disfavor.

"Don't be fussy," said his mother. "You're the only one who's complaining." This was unfair, for she and Mark were the only members of the family at table, Harriet having developed measles while staying with a school friend, while Mr. Armitage had somehow managed to lock himself in the larder. Mrs. Armitage never had anything but toast and marmalade for breakfast anyway.

Mark went on scowling at the chilly-looking pudding. It had come straight out of the fridge, which was not in the larder.

"If you don't like it," said Mrs. Armitage, "unless you want Daddy to pass you cornflakes through the larder ventilator, flake by flake, you'd better run down to Miss Pride and get a small packet of cereal. She opens at eight; Hickmans doesn't open till nine. It's no use waiting till the blacksmith comes to let your father out; I'm sure he won't be here for hours yet."

There came a gloomy banging from the direction of the larder, just to remind them that Mr. Armitage was alive and suffering in there.

"*You're* all right," shouted Mark heartlessly as he passed the larder door. "There's nothing to stop *you* having cornflakes. Oh, I forgot, the milk's in the fridge. Well, have cheese and pickles then. Or treacle tart."

Even through the zinc grating on the door he could hear his father shudder at the thought of treacle tart and pickles for breakfast. Mr. Armitage's imprisonment was his own fault, though; he had sworn that he was going to find out where the mouse got into the larder if it took him all night, watching and waiting. He had shut himself in, so that no member of the family should come bursting in and disturb his vigil. The larder door had a spring catch which sometimes jammed; it was bad luck that this turned out to be one of the times.

Mark ran across the fields to Miss Pride's shop at Sticks Corner and asked if she had any cornflakes.

"Oh, I don't think I have any left, dear," Miss Pride said woefully. "I'll have a look. . . . I think I sold the last packet a week ago Tuesday."

"What about the one in the window?"

"That's a dummy, dear."

Miss Pride's shop window was full of nasty, dingy old cardboard cartons with nothing inside them, and several empty display stands which had fallen down and never been propped up again. Inside the shop were a few small, tired-looking tins and jars, which had a worn and scratched appearance as if mice had tried them and given up. Miss Pride herself was small and wan, with yellowish gray hair; she rooted rather hopelessly in a pile of empty boxes. Mark's mother never bought any groceries from Miss Pride's if she could help it, since the day when she had found a label inside the foil wrapping of a cream cheese saying, "This cheese should be eaten before May 11, 1899."

"No cornflakes I'm afraid, dear."

"Any wheat crispies? Puffed corn? Rice nuts?"

"No, dear. Nothing left, only Brekkfast Brikks."

"Never heard of *them*," said Mark doubtfully.

"Or I've a jar of Ovo here. You spread it on bread. That's nice for breakfast," said Miss Pride, with a sudden burst of salesmanship. Mark thought the Ovo looked beastly, like yellow paint, so he took the packet of Brekkfast Brikks. At least it wasn't very big. . . . On the front of the box was a picture of a fat, repulsive, fair-haired boy, rather like the chubby Augustus, banging on his plate with his spoon.

"They look like tiny doormats," said Mrs. Armitage, as Mark shoveled some Brikks into the bowl.

"They taste like them too. Gosh," said Mark. "I must hurry or I'll be late for school. There's rather a nice cut-out garden on the back of the packet though; don't throw it away when it's empty, Mother. Good-by, Daddy," he shouted through the larder door, "hope Mr. Ellis comes soon to let you out." And he dashed off to catch the school bus.

At breakfast next morning Mark had a huge helping of Brekkfast Brikks and persuaded his father to try them.

"They taste just like esparto grass," said Mr. Armitage fretfully.

"Yes I know, but do take some more, Daddy. I want to cut out the model garden, it's so lovely."

"Rather pleasant, I must say. It looks like an eighteenth-century German engraving," his father agreed. "It certainly was a stroke of genius putting it on the packet. No one would ever buy these things to eat for pleasure. Pass me the sugar, please. And the cream. And the strawberries."

It was the half-term holiday, so after breakfast Mark was able to take the empty packet away to the playroom and get on with the job of cutting out the stone walls, the row of little trees, the fountain, the yew arch, the two green lawns, and the tiny clumps of brilliant flowers. He knew better than to "stick tabs in slots and secure with paste," as the directions suggested; he had made models from packets before and knew they always fell to pieces unless they were firmly bound together with transparent sticky tape.

It was a long, fiddling, pleasurable job.

Nobody interrupted him. Mrs. Armitage only cleaned the playroom once every six months or so, when she made a ferocious descent on it and tidied up the tape recorders, roller-skates, meteorological sets, and dismantled railway engines, and threw away countless old magazines, stringless tennis rackets, abandoned paintings, and unsuccessful models. There were always bitter complaints from Mark and Harriet; then they forgot and things piled up again till next time.

As Mark worked, his eye was caught by a verse on the outside of the packet:

> "Brekkfast Brikks to start the day
> Make you fit in every way.
> Children bang their plates with glee
> At Brekkfast Brikks for lunch and tea!
> Brekkfast Brikks for supper too
> Give peaceful sleep the whole night through."

"Blimey," thought Mark, sticking a cedar tree into the middle of the lawn and then bending a stone wall round at dotted lines A, B, C, and D. "I wouldn't want anything for breakfast, lunch, tea, and supper, not even Christmas pudding. Certainly not Brekkfast Brikks."

He propped a clump of gaudy scarlet flowers against the wall and stuck them in place.

The words of the rhyme kept coming into his head as he worked and presently he found that they went rather well to a tune that was running through his mind, and he began to hum, and then to sing; Mark often did this when he was alone and busy.

> "Brekkfast Brikks to sta–art the day,
> Ma–ake you fi–it in every way—

"Blow, where did I put that little bit of sticky tape? Oh, there it is.

> "Children bang their pla–ates with glee
> At Brekkfast Brikks for lunch and tea

"Slit gate with razor-blade, it says, but it'll have to be a penknife.

> "Brekkfast Brikks for supper toohoo
> Give peaceful sleep the whole night throughoo. . . .

"Hullo. That's funny," said Mark.

It was funny. The openwork iron gate he had just stuck in

position now suddenly towered above him. On either side, to right and left, ran the high stone wall, stretching away into foggy distance. Over the top of the wall he could see tall trees, yews and cypresses and others he didn't know.

"Well, that's the neatest trick I ever saw," said Mark. "I wonder if the gate will open?"

He chuckled as he tried it, thinking of the larder door. The gate did open, and he went through into the garden.

One of the things that had already struck him as he cut them out was that the flowers were not at all in the right proportions. But they were all the nicer for that. There were huge velvety violets and pansies the size of saucers; the hollyhocks were as big as dinner-plates and the turf was sprinkled with enormous daisies. The roses, on the other hand, were miniature, no bigger than cuff-buttons. There were real fish in the fountain, bright pink.

"*I* made all this," thought Mark, strolling along the mossy path to the yew arch. "Won't Harriet be surprised when she sees it. I wish she could see it now. I wonder what made it come alive like that?"

He passed through the yew arch as he said this and discovered that on the other side there was nothing but gray, foggy blackness. This, of course, was where his cardboard garden had ended. He turned through the archway and gazed with pride at a border of huge scarlet tropical flowers which were perhaps supposed to be geraniums but certainly hadn't turned out that way. "I know! Of course, it was the rhyme, the rhyme on the packet."

He recited it. Nothing happened. "Perhaps you have to sing it," he thought and (feeling a little foolish) he sang it through to the tune that fitted so well. At once, faster than blowing out a match, the garden drew itself together and shrank into its cardboard again, leaving Mark outside.

"What a marvelous hiding place it'll make when I don't want people to come bothering," he thought. He sang the spell once more, just to make sure that it worked, and there was the mossy wall, the stately iron gate, and the treetops. He stepped in and looked back. No playroom to be seen, only gray blankness.

At that moment he was startled by a tremendous clanging, the sort of sound the Trump of Doom would make if it was a dinner bell. "Blow," he thought. "I suppose that's lunch." He sang the spell for the fourth time; immediately he was in the playroom, and the garden was on the floor beside him, and Agnes was still ringing the dinner bell outside the door.

"All right, I heard," he shouted. "Just coming."

He glanced hurriedly over the remains of the packet to see if it bore any mention of the fact that the cut-out garden had magic properties. It did not. He did, however, learn that this was Section Three of the Beautiful Brekkfast Brikk Garden Series, and that Sections One, Two, Four, Five, and Six would be found on other packets. In case of difficulty in obtaining supplies, please write to Fruhstucksgeschirrziegelsteinindustrie (Great Britain), Lily Road, Shepherds Bush.

"Elevenpence a packet," Mark murmured to himself, going to lunch with unwashed hands. "Five elevens are thirty-five. Thirty-five pennies are—no, that's wrong. Fifty-five pence are four-and-sevenpence. Father, if I mow the lawn and carry coal every day for a month, can I have four shillings and sevenpence?"

"You don't want to buy another space-gun, do you?" said Mr. Armitage looking at him suspiciously. "Because one is quite enough in this family."

"No, it's not for a space gun, I swear."

"Oh, very well."

"And can I have the four-and-seven now?"

Mr. Armitage gave it reluctantly. "But that lawn has to be like velvet, mind," he said. "And if there's any falling off in the coal supply, I shall demand my money back."

"No, no, there won't be," Mark promised in reply. As soon as lunch was over, he dashed down to Miss Pride's. Was there a chance that she would have sections One, Two, Four, Five, and Six? He felt certain that no other shop had even heard of Brekkfast Brikks, so she was his only hope, apart from the address in Shepherds Bush.

"Oh, I don't know, I'm sure," Miss Pride said, sounding very doubtful—and more than a little surprised. "There might just be a couple on the bottom shelf—yes, here we are."

They were sections Four and Five, bent and dusty, but intact,

Mark saw with relief. "Don't you suppose you have any more anywhere?" he pleaded.

"I'll look in the cellar but I can't promise. I haven't had deliveries of any of these for a long time. Made by some foreign firm they were; people didn't seem very keen on them," Miss Pride said aggrievedly. She opened a door revealing a flight of damp stone stairs. Mark followed her down them like a bloodhound on the trail.

The cellar was a fearful confusion of mildewed, tattered, and toppling cartons, some full, some empty. Mark was nearly knocked cold by a shower of pilchards in tins, which he dislodged on to himself from the top of a heap of boxes. At last Miss Pride, with a cry of triumph, unearthed a little cache of Brekkfast Brikks, three packets which turned out to be the remaining sections, Six, One, and Two.

"There, isn't that a piece of luck now!" she said, looking quite faint with all the excitement. It was indeed rare for Miss Pride to sell as many as five packets of the same thing at one time.

Mark galloped home with his booty and met his father on the porch. Mr. Armitage let out a groan of dismay.

"I'd almost rather you'd bought a space gun," he said. Mark chanted in reply

> "Brekkfast Brikks for supper too
> Give peaceful sleep the whole night through."

"I don't want peaceful sleep," Mr. Armitage said. "I intend to spend tonight mouse-watching again. I'm tired of finding footprints in the Stilton."

During the next few days Mark's parents watched anxiously to see, Mr. Armitage said, whether Mark would start to sprout esparto grass instead of hair. For he doggedly ate Brekkfast Brikks for lunch, with soup, or sprinkled over his pudding; for tea, with jam, and for supper lightly fried in dripping, not to mention, of course, the immense helpings he had for breakfast with sugar and milk. Mr. Armitage for his part soon gave out; he said he wouldn't taste another Brekkfast Brikk even if it were wrapped in an inch-thick layer of *pâté de foie gras*. Mark regretted that Harriet, who was a handy and uncritical eater, was still away, convalescing from her measles with an aunt.

In two days the second packet was finished (sundial, paved garden, and espaliers). Mark cut it out, fastened it together, and joined it on to Section Three with trembling hands. Would the spell work for this section, too? He sang the rhyme in rather a quavering voice, but luckily the plywood door was shut and there was no one to hear him. Yes! The gate grew again above him, and when he opened it and ran across the lawn through the yew arch, he found himself in a flagged garden full of flowers like huge blue cabbages.

Mark stood hugging himself with satisfaction, and then began to wander about smelling the flowers, which had a spicy perfume most unlike any flower he could think of. Suddenly he pricked up his ears. Had he caught a sound? There! It was like somebody crying and seemed to come from the other side of the hedge. He ran to the next opening and looked through. Nothing: only gray mist and emptiness. But, unless he had imagined it, just before he got there, he thought his eye had caught the flash of white-and-gold draperies swishing past the gateway.

"Do you think Mark's all right?" Mrs. Armitage said to her husband next day. "He seems to be in such a dream all the time."

"Boy's gone clean off his rocker if you ask me," grumbled Mr. Armitage. "It's all these doormats he's eating. Can't be good to stuff your insides with moldy jute. Still I'm bound to say he's cut the lawn very decently and seems to be remembering the coal. I'd better take a day off from the office and drive you over to the shore for a picnic; sea air will do him good."

Mrs. Armitage suggested to Mark that he should slack off on the Brekkfast Brikks, but he was so horrified that she had to abandon the idea. But, she said, he was to run four times round the garden every morning before breakfast. Mark almost said, "Which garden?" but stopped just in time. He had cut out and completed another large lawn, with a lake and weeping willows, and on the far side of the lake had a tantalizing glimpse of a figure dressed in white and gold who moved away and was lost before he could get there.

After munching his way through the fourth packet, he was able to add on a broad grass walk bordered by curiously clipped trees.

At the end of the walk he could see the white-and-gold person, but when he ran to the spot, no one was there—the walk ended in the usual gray mist.

When he had finished and had cut out the fifth packet (an orchard), a terrible thing happened to him. For two days he could not remember the tune that worked the spell. He tried other tunes, but they were no use. He sat in the playroom singing till he was hoarse or silent with despair. Suppose he never remembered it again?

His mother shook her head at him that evening and said he looked as if he needed a dose. "It's lucky we're going to Shinglemud Bay for the day tomorrow," she said. "That ought to do you good."

"Oh, *blow*. I'd forgotten about that," Mark said. "Need I go?"

His mother stared at him in utter astonishment.

But in the middle of the night he remembered the right tune, leaped out of bed in a tremendous hurry, and ran down to the playroom without even waiting to put on his dressing gown and slippers.

The orchard was most wonderful, for instead of mere apples its trees bore oranges, lemons, limes and all sorts of tropical fruits whose names he did not know, and there were melons and pine-apples growing, and plantains and avocados. Better still, he saw the lady in her white and gold waiting at the end of an alley and was able to draw near enough to speak to her.

"Who are you?" she asked. She seemed very much astonished at the sight of him.

"My name's Mark Armitage," he said politely. "Is this your garden?"

Close to, he saw that she was really very grand indeed. Her dress was white satin embroidered with pearls, and swept the ground; she had a gold scarf and her hair, dressed high and powdered, was confined in a small gold-and-pearl tiara. Her face was rather plain, pink with a long nose, but she had a kind expression and beautiful gray eyes.

"Indeed it is," she announced with hauteur. "I am Princess Sophia Maria Louisa of Saxe-Hoffenpoffen-und-Hamster. What are you doing here, pray?"

"Well," Mark explained cautiously, "it seemed to come about through singing a tune."

"Indeed. That is most interesting. Did the tune, perhaps, go like this?"

The princess hummed a few bars.

"That's it! How did you know?"

"Why, you foolish boy, it was I who put the spell on the garden, to make it come alive when the tune is played or sung."

"I say!" Mark was full of admiration. "Can you do spells as well as being a princess?"

She drew herself up. "Naturally! At the court of Saxe-Hoffen-poffen, where I was educated, all princesses were taught a little magic, not so much as to be vulgar, just enough to get out of social difficulties."

"Jolly useful," Mark said, "How did you work the spell for the garden, then?"

"Why, you see," (the princess was obviously delighted to have somebody to talk to; she sat on a stone seat and patted it, inviting Mark to do likewise) "I had the misfortune to fall in love with Herr Rudolf, the Court Kapellmeister, who taught me music. Oh, he was so kind and handsome! And he was most talented, but my father, of course, would not hear of my marrying him because he was only a common person."

"So what did you do?"

"I arranged to vanish, of course. Rudi had given me a beautiful book with many pictures of gardens. My father kept strict watch to see I did not run away, so I used to slip between the pages of the book when I wanted to be alone. Then, when we decided to marry, I asked my maid to take the book to Rudi. And I sent him a note telling him to play the tune when he received the book. But I believe that spiteful Gertrud must have played me false and never taken the book, for more than fifty years have now passed and I have been here all alone, waiting in the garden, and Rudi has never come. Oh, Rudi, Rudi," she exclaimed, wringing her hands and crying a little, "where can you be? It is so long—so long!"

"Fifty years," Mark said kindly, reckoning that must make her nearly seventy. "I must say you don't look it."

"Of course I do not, dumbhead. For me, I make it that time

does not touch me. But tell me, how did you know the tune that works the spell? It was taught me by my dear Rudi."

"I'm not sure where I picked it up," Mark confessed. "For all I know it may be one of the Top Ten. I'll ask my music teacher, he's sure to know. Perhaps he'll have heard of your Rudolf too."

Privately Mark feared that Rudolf might very well have died by now, but he did not like to depress Princess Sophia Maria by such a suggestion, so he bade her a polite good night, promising to come back as soon as he could with another section of the garden and any news he could pick up.

He planned to go and see Mr. Johansen, his music teacher, next morning, but he had forgotten the family trip to the beach. There was just time to scribble a hasty post card to the British office of Fruhstucksgeschirrziegelsteinindustrie, asking them if they could inform him from what source they had obtained the pictures used on the packets of Brekkfast Brikks. Then Mr. Armitage drove his wife and son to Shinglemud Bay, gloomily prophesying wet weather.

In fact, the weather turned out fine, and Mark found it quite restful to swim and play beach cricket and eat ham sandwiches and lie in the sun. For he had been struck by a horrid thought: suppose he should forget the tune again when he was inside the garden— would he be stuck there, like Father in the larder? It was a lovely place to go and wander at will, but somehow he didn't fancy spending the next fifty years there with Princess Sophia Maria. Would she oblige him by singing the spell if he forgot it, or would she be too keen on company to let him go? He was not inclined to take any chances.

It was late when they arrived home, too late, Mark thought, to disturb Mr. Johansen, who was elderly and kept early hours. Mark ate a huge helping of sardines on Brekkfast Brikks for supper—he was dying to finish Section Six—but did not visit the garden that night.

Next morning's breakfast (Brikks with hot milk for a change) finished the last packet—and just as well, for the larder mouse, which Mr. Armitage still had not caught, was discovered to have nibbled the bottom left-hand corner of the packet, slightly damaging an ornamental grotto in a grove of lime trees. Rather worried about this, Mark decided to make up the last section straightaway, in case the magic had been affected. By now he was becoming very skillful at the tiny fiddling task of cutting out the little tabs and slipping them into the little slots; the job did not take long to finish. Mark attached Section Six to Section Five and then, drawing a deep breath, sang the incantation once more. With immense relief he watched the mossy wall and rusty gate grow out of the playroom floor; all was well.

He raced across the lawn, round the lake, along the avenue, through the orchard, and into the lime grove. The scent of the lime flowers was sweeter than a cake baking.

Princess Sophia Maria came towards him from the grotto, looking slightly put out.

"Good morning!" she greeted Mark. "Do you bring me any news?"

"I haven't been to see my music teacher yet," Mark confessed. "I was a bit anxious because there was a hole."

"Ach, yes, a hole in the grotto! I have just been looking. Some wild beast must have made its way in, and I am afraid it may come again. See, it has made tracks like those of a big bear." She showed him some enormous footprints in the soft sand of the grotto floor. Mark stopped up the hole with prickly branches and promised to bring a dog when he next came, though he felt fairly sure the mouse would not return.

"I can borrow a dog from my teacher—he has plenty. I'll be back in an hour or so—see you then," he said.

"*Auf Wiedersehen*, my dear young friend."

Mark ran along the village street to Mr. Johansen's house, Houndshaven Cottage. He knew better than to knock at the door because Mr. Johansen would be either practicing his violin or out in the barn at the back, and in any case the sound of barking was generally loud enough to drown any noise short of gunfire.

Besides giving music lessons at Mark's school, Mr. Johansen kept a guest house for dogs whose owners were abroad or on holiday. He was extremely kind to the guests and did his best to make them feel at home in every way, finding out from their owners what were their favorite foods, and letting them sleep on his own bed, turn about. He spent all his spare time with them, talking to them and playing either his violin or long playing records of domestic sounds likely to appeal to the canine fancy—such as knives being sharpened, cars starting up, and children playing ball games.

Mark could hear Mr. Johansen playing Brahms' lullaby in the barn, so he went out there; the music was making some of the more susceptible inmates feel homesick: howls, sympathetic moans, and long shuddering sighs came from the numerous comfortably carpeted cubicles all the way down the barn.

Mr. Johansen reached the end of the piece as Mark entered. He put down his fiddle and smiled welcomingly.

"Ach, how *gut!* It is the young Mark."

"Hullo, sir."

"You know," confided Mr. Johansen, "I play to many audiences in my life all over the world, but never anywhere do I get such a response as from zese dear doggies—it is really remarkable. But come in, come into ze house and have some coffee cake."

Mr. Johansen was a gentle, white-haired elderly man; he walked slowly with a slight stoop and had a kindly sad face with large dark eyes. He looked rather like some sort of dog himself, Mark always thought, perhaps a collie or a long-haired dachshund.

"Sir," Mark said, "if I whistle a tune to you, can you write it down for me?"

"Why, yes, I shall be most happy," Mr. Johansen said, pouring coffee for both of them.

So Mark whistled his tune once more; as he came to the end, he was surprised to see the music master's eyes fill with tears, which slowly began to trickle down his thin cheeks.

"It recalls my youth, zat piece," he explained, wiping the tears away and rapidly scribbling crotchets and minims on a piece of music paper. "Many times I am whistling it myself—it is wissout doubt from me you learn it—but always it is reminding me of how happy I was long ago when I wrote it."

"You *wrote* that tune?" Mark said, much excited.

"Why yes. What is so strange in zat? Many, many tunes haf I written."

"Well—" Mark said, "I won't tell you just yet in case I'm mistaken —I'll have to see somebody else first. Do you mind if I dash off right away? Oh, and might I borrow a dog—preferably a good ratter?"

"In zat case, better have my dear Lotta—alzough she is so old she is ze best of zem all," Mr. Johansen said proudly. Lotta was his own dog, an enormous shaggy lumbering animal with a tail like a palm tree and feet the size of electric polishers; she was reputed to be of incalculable age; Mr. Johansen called her his strudel hound. She knew Mark well and came along with him quite biddably, though it was rather like leading a mammoth.

Luckily his mother, refreshed by her day at the sea, was heavily engaged with Agnes the maid in spring cleaning. Furniture was being shoved about, and everyone was too busy to notice Mark and Lotta slip into the playroom.

A letter addressed to Mark lay among the clutter on the table; he opened and read it while Lotta foraged happily among the piles of magazines and tennis nets and cricket hats and rusting electronic equipment, managing to upset several things and increase the general state of huggermugger in the room.

> Dear Sir, (the letter said—it was from Messrs. Digit, Digit, & Rule, a firm of chartered accountants)—We are in receipt of your inquiry as to the source of pictures on packets of Brekkfast Brikks. We are pleased to inform you that these were reproduced from the illustrations of a little-known 18th-century German work, *Steinbergen's Gartenbuch.* Unfortunately the only known remaining copy of this book was burnt in the disastrous fire which destroyed the factory and premises of Messrs. Fruhstucksgeschirrziegelsteinindustrie two months ago. The firm has now gone into liquidation and we are winding up their effects.
>
> *Yours faithfully,*
> P. J. Zero, Gen. Sec.

"*Steinbergen's Gartenbuch,*" Mark thought. "That must have been the book that Princess Sophia used for the spell—probably the same copy. Oh, well, since it's burned, it's lucky the pictures were reproduced on the Brekkfast Brikks packets. Come on, Lotta, let's go and find a nice princess then. Good girl! Rats! Chase 'em!"

He sang the spell and Lotta, all enthusiasm, followed him into the garden.

They did not have to go far before they saw the princess—she was sitting sunning herself on the rim of the fountain. But what happened then was unexpected. Lotta let out the most extraordinary cry—whine, bark, and howl all in one—and hurled herself towards the princess like a rocket.

"Hey! Look out! Lotta! *Heel!*" Mark shouted in alarm. But Lotta, with her great paws on the princess' shoulders, had about a yard of salmon-pink tongue out, and was washing the princess' face all over with frantic affection.

The princess was just as excited. "Lotta, Lotta! She knows me, it's dear Lotta, it must be! Where did you get her?" she cried to Mark, hugging the enormous dog, whose tail was going round faster than a turbo prop.

"Why, she belongs to my music master, Mr. Johansen, and it's he who made up the tune," Mark said.

The princess turned quite white and had to sit down on the fountain's rim again.

"*Johansen?* Rudolf Johansen? My Rudi! At last! After all these years! Oh, run, run, and fetch him immediately, please! Immediately!"

Mark hesitated a moment.

"Please make haste!" she besought him. "Why do you wait?"

"It's only— Well, you won't be surprised if he's quite *old,* will you? Remember he hasn't been in a garden keeping young like you."

"All that will change," the princess said confidently. "He has only to eat the fruit of the garden. Why, look at Lotta—when she was a puppy, for a joke I gave her a fig from this tree, and you can see she is a puppy still, though she must be older than any other dog in the world! Oh, please hurry to bring Rudi here."

"Why don't you come with me to his house?"

"That would not be correct etiquette," she said with dignity. "After all, I *am* royal."

"Okay," said Mark. "I'll fetch him. Hope he doesn't think I'm crackers."

"Give him this." The princess took off a locket on a gold chain. It had a miniature of a romantically handsome young man with dark curling hair. "My Rudi," she explained fondly. Mark could just trace a faint resemblance to Mr. Johansen.

He took the locket and hurried away. At the gate something made him look back: the princess and Lotta were sitting at the edge of the fountain, side by side. The princess had an arm round Lotta's neck; with the other hand she waved to him, just a little.

"Hurry!" she called again.

Mark made his way out of the house, through the spring-cleaning chaos, and flew down the village to Houndshaven Cottage. Mr. Johansen was in the house this time, boiling up a noisome mass of meat and bones for the dogs' dinner. Mark said nothing at all, just handed him the locket. He took one look at it and staggered, putting his hand to his heart; anxiously, Mark led him to a chair.

"Are you all right, sir?"

"Yes, yes! It was only ze shock. Where did you get ziss, my boy?"

So Mark told him.

Surprisingly, Mr. Johansen did not find anything odd about the story; he nodded his head several times as Mark related the various points.

"Yes, yes, her letter, I have it still—" he pulled out a worn little scrap of paper, "but ze *Gartenbuch* it reached me never. Zat wicked Gertrud must haf sold it to some bookseller who sold it to Frustucksgeschirrziegelsteinindustrie. And so she has been waiting all ziss time! My poor little Sophie!"

"Are you strong enough to come to her now?" Mark asked.

"*Natürlich!* But first we must give ze dogs zeir dinner; zey must not go hungry."

So they fed the dogs, which was a long job as there were at least sixty and each had a different diet, including some very odd preferences like Swiss roll spread with Marmite and yeast pills wrapped in slices of caramel. Privately, Mark thought the dogs were a bit spoiled, but Mr. Johansen was very careful to see that each visitor had just what it fancied.

"After all, zey are not mine! Must I not take good care of zem?"

At least two hours had gone by before the last willow-pattern plate was licked clean and they were free to go. Mark made rings round Mr. Johansen all the way up the village; the music master limped quietly along, smiling a little; from time to time he said, "Gently, my friend. We do not run a race. Remember I am an old man."

That was just what Mark did remember. He longed to see Mr. Johansen young and happy once more.

The chaos in the Armitage house had changed its location: the front hall was now clean, tidy, and damp; the rumpus of vacuuming had shifted to the playroom. With a black hollow of apprehension in his middle, Mark ran through the open door and stopped, aghast. All the toys, tools, weapons, boxes, magazines, and bits of machinery had been rammed into the cupboards; the floor where his garden had been laid out was bare. Mrs. Armitage was in the playroom taking down the curtains.

"*Mother!* Where's my Brekkfast Brikks garden?"

"Oh, darling, you didn't want it, did you? It was all dusty, I thought you'd finished with it. I'm afraid I've burned it in the furnace. Really you *must* try not to let this room get into such a clutter, it's perfectly disgraceful. Why, hullo, Mr. Johansen," she added in embarrassment. "I didn't see you, I'm afraid you've called at the worst possible moment. But I'm sure you'll understand how it is at spring-cleaning time."

She rolled up her bundle of curtains, glancing worriedly at Mr. Johansen; he looked rather odd, she thought. But he gave her his tired, gentle smile, and said,

"Why, yes, Mrs. Armitage, I understand, I understand very well. Come, Mark. We have no business here, you can see."

Speechlessly, Mark followed him. What was there to say?

"Never mind," Mrs. Armitage called after Mark. "The Rice Nuts pack has a helicopter on it."

Every week in *The Times* newspaper you will see this advertisement:

BREKKFAST BRIKKS PACKETS. £100
offered for any in good condition,
whether empty or full.

So, if you have any, you know where to send them.

But Mark is growing anxious; none have come in yet, and every day Mr. Johansen seems a little thinner and more elderly. Besides, what will the princess be thinking?

VII

Anteaters, Otters, and Others

from *Three Tickets to Adventure*

GERALD DURRELL

*After
the
Anteater*

To capture a giant anteater had been one of our main objectives in going to the Rupununi, for we had heard that they were much easier to catch in the grassland than in the forests of Guiana. For three days after our arrival at Karanambo we did nothing but talk and think about anteaters, until eventually McTurk promised to see what he could do. One morning just after breakfast a short, squat Amerindian materialized in front of the house in the disconcertingly silent way these people do. He had a bronze, Mongolian-looking face, and his dark slitlike eyes were saved from being crafty by the shy twinkle in them. He was dressed quite simply in the remains of a shirt and pants, and on his sleek black head was perched an absurd pixie hat constructed out of what once had been velvet. To anyone who had been expecting a fierce warrior, clad in a vivid feather headdress and daubed with tribal signs of clay, he would have been a great disappointment. As it was, he had an air of dour confidence about him, which I found comforting.

"This is Francis," said McTurk, waving at the apparition. "I think he knows where you might find an anteater."

We could not have greeted Francis more delightedly if he had known the whereabouts of a large reef of gold. And we discovered after some questioning that Francis *had* known where an anteater was, having seen one some three days before, but whether it was still there or not was another matter. McTurk suggested that Francis should go and see, and, if the creature was still hanging around, he would come and fetch us and we would have a try at catching it. Francis smiled shyly and agreed to the plan. He went off and returned the next morning to say that he had been successful. He had found where the anteater was living, and was willing to lead us there the next day.

"How are we to reach the place?" I asked McTurk.

"On horses, of course," he answered. "It's no use going in the jeep; you'll have to crisscross about the savanna a good bit, and the jeep's no use for that sort of thing."

I turned to Bob. "Can you ride?" I inquired hopefully.

"Well, I've been *on* a horse, if that's what you mean," said Bob cautiously, and then hastily added, "only a very quiet one, of course."

"If we have nice docile mounts I expect we can manage," I said to McTurk.

"Oh, I'll pick you out a pair of quiet animals," said McTurk, and he went off with Francis to arrange the details. Later he told us that we were to meet Francis and the horses the following morning at a spot about two miles away. From there we were to strike out into the unknown.

The grassland was a lovely golden-green in the first rays of the sun when we set off, bumping our way in the jeep towards the distant line of trees that was the place of rendezvous. The sky was a delicate jay's-wing blue, and high above us two minute hawks circled slowly, searching the vast grassland for their breakfast. Dragonflies, vivid as fireworks, shot across the swerving nose of the jeep, and the warm wind of our progress stirred and tumbled the fawn dust of the track into a swirling cloud behind us. McTurk, holding the steering wheel negligently with one hand and using the other to cram his hat more firmly on his head, leaned across and began to tell me something, shouting to make himself heard above the roar of the engine and the wind.

"This Indian—Francis. Thought I'd warn you—apt to be a bit queer. Gets excited—sort of fits, I think. Says the world turns around inside his head. No reason why today—thought I'd warn you. Quite harmless, of course."

"Are you sure he's harmless?" I roared back, aware of a sinking feeling in the pit of my stomach.

"Oh, quite harmless, definitely."

"What's all this?" Bob asked from the back seat.

"McTurk says Francis has fits," I said soothingly.

"Has what?" shouted Bob.

"Fits."

"*Fits?*"

Yes, you know—goes a bit queer in the head sometimes. But McTurk says he's quite harmless."

"My God!" said Bob sepulchrally, lying back in his seat and closing his eyes, an expression of extreme martyrdom on his face.

We reached the trees, and there, squatting on the ground, was Francis, his pixie hat tilted at a rakish angle. Behind him stood the horses in a dejected half-circle, heads drooping and reins dangling. They were clad in high-pommelled and extremely uncomfortable-looking saddles. We extricated ourselves from the jeep and greeted Francis with slightly strained joviality. McTurk wished us good hunting, turned the jeep, and started off with a roar that sent all the horses onto their hind legs, stirrups and bits jangling. Francis calmed them somewhat and led them forward for our inspection. We gazed at our mounts, and they gazed back with equal suspicion.

"Which one are you going to have?" I asked Bob.

"I don't suppose it'll make much difference," he said, "but I'll have the brown one with the cast in its eye."

That left me with a large grey that appeared to have a good deal of mule in its make-up. I addressed it in what I hoped was a cheerful voice and stepped up to its side, whereupon it waltzed sideways and showed the whites of its eyes.

"Good boy," I crooned huskily, trying to get my foot into the stirrup.

"It's not a he, it's a she," said Bob helpfully.

I at last managed to hoist myself on to my mount's bony back, and I gathered up the reins hastily. Bob's beast seemed more tractable, letting him get mounted before showing any signs of restiveness. Once he was planted in the saddle, however, it proceeded to walk backwards, quite slowly but with grim determination, and would, I think, have gone on until it reached the Brazilian border if its progress had not been halted by a large prickly bush. It stopped dead and refused to move.

By this time Francis had mounted his grim black horse and was jogging off down the path, so with an effort I pulled my mount over and followed him. Bob's cries of encouragement to his steed grew faint in the distance. We rounded a corner, and he became lost to view. Presently he caught up with us, his horse cleverly executing a movement that was a cross between a walk and a trot, while Bob jolted in the saddle, red in the face, clutching in one hand a large twig with which he belaboured the creature's backside whenever he could spare a hand to do so. I reined in and watched his progress with interest.

"How does it feel?" I inquired as he passed.

He gave me an awful look. "It—would—be—all right," he replied, speaking between jolts, "if—he—would—only move—properly."

"Wait a second," I said helpfully, "and I'll come up behind and give him a slap."

From behind, Bob and his steed looked as though they were performing an intricate Latin rumba. I kicked my mount into a trot, and as I drew level with the waggling rump of the animal in front I gathered up my reins and leaned over to give it a slap. Up till then my horse's actions had been exemplary, but now she decided that I was making a sly and dastardly attack on her for no reason at all, so she gathered herself into a bunch and leaped forward with the alacrity of a grasshopper. I had a quick glimpse of Bob's surprised face, and then we were shooting down the path towards Francis. As we drew level with him he turned in his saddle and grinned broadly. He chirruped to his horse, flapped the reins on its neck, and before I realized what was happening we were galloping neck and neck down the path, Francis uttering strange guttural yelps to his mount to encourage it to further efforts.

"Francis!" I yelled. "This is not a race! I'm trying to stop—*stop!*"

The idea slowly took root in our guide's mind, and a look of acute disappointment spread over his face. Reluctantly he drew in his horse, and to my infinite relief mine also slowed down. We stopped and waited until Bob danced up on his animal, and then I worked out a new arrangement. Francis was to lead, Bob was to follow him, and I was to bring up the rear and thus keep Bob's steed up to the mark. So, at a gentle walk, we continued on our way.

The sun was now very hot, and the savanna stretched away before us, shimmering in its rays—mile upon mile of grassland, green, gold, and brown, and in the distance, it seemed at the very rim of the world, a line of humpbacked mountains of pale greeny-blue. There was no life to be seen on this ocean of grass; the only moving things were ourselves and our shadows. For over two hours we rode through the knee-high grass, led by Francis, who was slouching at ease in his saddle, his hat over his eyes, apparently asleep. The monotony of the view and the hot sun made us sleepy, and we followed our guide's example and dozed.

Suddenly I opened my eyes and found to my surprise that the flat savanna had produced a hollow, a great oval crater with gently sloping sides. In the centre was a reed-fringed lake, its banks covered with a scattering of stunted bushes. As we skirted the lake everything seemed suddenly to come to life: a small cayman slid into the smooth waters with hardly a ripple; ten jabiru storks marched solemnly along the farther shore, gazing down their long beaks in a meditative way; the bushes were full of tiny birds, twittering and fluttering.

"Bob, wake up and enjoy the fauna," I suggested. He peered sleepily from under the brim of his hat, said, "Um," as intelligently as he could, and went back to sleep again.

Two emerald-green lizards darted across the path between my horse's slowly plodding hoofs, so intent on each other that they never noticed us. A diminutive kingfisher dropped from a branch into the lake and flew up to its perch again with something in its beak. Gold and black dragonflies zoomed about the reeds and hovered over the tiny pink orchids that bloomed like a mist over the swampy ground. On a battered tree stump sat a pair of black vultures; they watched us with a macabre hopefulness that was far from reassuring in view of our guide's mental condition. We rode past the lake and headed once more across the grassland, and the twittering of the birds faded and died behind us. Then there was only the steady swish of our horses' legs pushing through the grass. I went to sleep.

I was awakened by my horse's ambling to a standstill. I found that Francis had also awakened and was sitting on his horse, surveying the area like a battered Napoleon. In front of us the land lay flat as a chessboard; on our left the ground rose gently, the slope covered with great clumps of grass and stunted bushes. I rode up alongside our guide and looked at him inquiringly. He waved a brown hand and gestured at the country. I presumed that we had arrived at anteater territory.

"What is it?" Bob asked.

"I think this is where he saw the anteater."

Francis, we had been assured, could speak English, and now was the great moment when he was to give us the details of the chase. Looking me squarely in the eye, he proceeded to utter a series of sounds which, for sheer incomprehensibility, I have rarely heard equalled. He repeated them twice while I listened carefully, but still I could not make out a single word that seemed at all familiar. I turned to Bob, who had been easing himself painfully up and down in the saddle and taking no part in this exchange.

"Didn't you say you could speak an Indian dialect?"

"Well, yes. But those were Indians in Paraguay, and I don't think it's anything like Munchi."

"Can you remember any?"

"Yes, I think so. Just a smattering."

"Well, have a shot at trying to understand what Francis is saying."

"Isn't he speaking English?" asked Bob in surprise.

"For all I can make of it he might be speaking Patagonian. Go on, Francis, say it again."

Francis, with a long-suffering air, repeated his little speech. Both listened carefully, with a frown on his face. "No," he said at last, "I can't make anything of it. It's certainly not English."

We looked at Francis, and he looked pityingly back at us. Soon, however, an idea occurred to him, and with many gestures and shrill cries he at last managed to explain what he was getting at. This was the place where he had seen the anteater. Somewhere in this area it was probably asleep—here he folded his hands against his cheek, closed his eyes, and uttered loud snores. We were to spread out into a line and beat through the undergrowth, making as much noise as possible.

So we spread out at thirty-yard intervals and urged our steeds through the long grass with loud cries and yodellings. Francis, away on my right, was giving a very fair imitation of a pack of hounds in full cry, while on my left I could hear Bob singing snatches of "Loch Lomond," interspersed with shrill screeches of "Shoo!"—a combination guaranteed to flush any anteater. Thus we progressed for about half a mile, until my throat was sore with shouting and I was beginning to wonder if there really had been an anteater there, or if, indeed, there were any anteaters in Guiana at all. My cries lost their first rich quality and became more like the depressed cawing of a lone crow.

Suddenly Francis utter a piercing and triumphant cry, and I could see a dark shape bobbing through the long grass in front of his horse. I turned my steed and rode towards it as fast as I could, yelling to Bob as I did so. My horse staggered wildly over the tussocks of grass and the deep heat cracks in the soil as I urged her on. The dark shape burst from the cover of the long grass and started off across a comparatively grassless plain at a rolling gallop, and I saw that it was indeed an anteater, and a bigger one than any I had seen in captivity. It travelled across the plain at remarkable speed, its great icicle-shaped head swinging from side to side, and its shaggy tail streaming out behind it like a pennant. Francis was in hot pursuit, uncoiling his lasso as he rode, and cheering his horse on with wild, staccato cries. I had by now extricated my horse from the long grass, and I headed her towards the anteater, but no sooner did she catch sight of our quarry than she decided she did not like it and turned and made off in the opposite direction with speed and determination. It took all my strength to turn her, for her mouth was like a bucket, but eventually I managed to gain a certain control over her. Even so, we approached the fray in a circular and crablike fashion. I was just in time to see Francis gallop alongside the anteater, and, after whirling his lasso, drop it over the beast's head. It was a bad throw, for the noose slipped right over the anteater's head, and the animal simply cantered straight through it, swerved wildly, and headed back towards the long grass. Francis was forced to pause, haul in his rope, and recoil it, and meanwhile the quarry was heading at full speed for thick undergrowth, in which it would be impossible for Francis to use his lasso. Urging my reluctant mount forward, I succeeded in heading the anteater off, and steering it back onto the plain, and by keeping my horse at a brisk canter I found I could stay alongside the animal.

The anteater galloped on over the plain, hissing and snorting down its long nose, its stunted little legs thumping on the sun-baked earth. Francis caught us up again, spun his rope round two or three times, and dropped it neatly over the animal's forequarters, pulling the noose tight as it reached the anteater's waist. He was off his horse in a second, and, hanging grimly to the rope, was dragged across the grass by the enraged anteater. I asked Bob to hold the horses, and joined Francis on the end of the rope. The anteater had incredible strength in its thick bow legs and shaggy body, and the two of us had all we could do to bring it to a standstill. Francis, the sweat pouring down his face, peered around; then he uttered a grunt and pointed behind me. Looking round, I saw a small tree growing about a hundred yards away, the only one for miles. Gasping and panting, we managed to chivvy the anteater towards it. When we at length arrived at the tree we succeeded in getting another loop of rope round the angry animal's body, and then we proceeded to tie the loose end to the trunk of the tree. Just as we were tying the last knot Francis looked up into the branches and gave a warning yelp. Looking up, I saw about two feet above my head a wasps' nest the size of a football, with the entire colony clinging to the outside and looking extremely irritated, to say the least. The anteater's struggles were making the small tree sway as though struck by a hurricane, and the movement was not appreciated by the wasps. Francis and I backed away silently and hurriedly. At our retreat the anteater decided to have a short rest before getting down to the stern work of removing the ropes. The tree stopped swaying, and the wasps settled down again.

We made our way back to where Bob was holding the horses and unpacked the various items we had brought with us to capture the anteater: two large sacks, a ball of thick twine, and some lengths of stout cord. Armed with these and a murderous-looking jackknife belonging to Francis, we again approached the tree. We were just in time to see the anteater shake itself free of the last loop of rope and waddle off across the savanna. I was only too pleased to leave Francis to disentangle his lasso from the wasp-infested tree, while I pursued the quarry on foot, rapidly tying a slipknot in a piece of cord as I ran. I dashed up alongside the creature and flung my makeshift lasso at its head. I missed. I tried again, with the same result. This went on for some time, until the anteater became a trifle tired of my attentions. It suddenly skidded to a standstill, turned, and rose up on its hind legs, facing me. I also halted, and examined it warily, particularly the great six-inch claws with which its front feet were armed. It snuffled at me, quivering its long nose, its tiny boot-button eyes daring me to come a step nearer. I walked round it in a circumspect manner, and it revolved also, keeping its claws well to the fore. I made a rather halfhearted attempt to throw the noose over its head, but it greeted this with such a violent waving of claws and enraged, snuffling hisses that I desisted and waited for Francis to bring his lasso. I made a mental note that seeing an animal behind bars in a well-regulated zoo is quite a different matter from trying to catch one with a short length of cord. In the distance I could see Francis still trying to disentangle his lasso from the tree without bringing the wasps down about his ears.

The anteater sat down on its tail and proceeded solemnly to brush bits of grass off its nose with its large curved claws. I had noticed that each time it hissed or snuffled a stream of saliva dribbled from its mouth and hung in long, glutinous strands like a thick spiderweb. As the beast galloped across the plain this sticky saliva trailed on the ground and collected bits of grass and twig. Each time the anteater tossed its head in anger these strands of saliva and their debris were flapped onto its nose and shoulders, where they stuck like glue. Now it had come to the conclusion that this armistice was an ideal moment for a quick wash and brush-up. Having cleaned its long grey nose to its satisfaction, it then rubbed its shoulders on the grass to free them from the adhesive saliva. Then it rose to its feet, gave an absurdly doglike shake, and plodded off towards the long grass as slowly and calmly as though such things as human beings with lassos had never entered its life. At this moment Francis joined me, out of breath but unstung, carrying his rope. We started after the anteater, which was still shuffling along in a slow, nonchalant way. Hearing our approach, it sat down again and watched us in a resigned fashion. With two of us, it was at a distinct disadvantage, and while I attracted its attention Francis crept up behind it, threw the noose over its shoulders, and pulled it tight round its waist. The anteater was off again in a moment, dashing across the grass and dragging us with it. For half an hour we struggled back and forth across the savanna, but at last we succeeded in getting so many ropes around the beast that it could not move. Then we thrust it, trussed up and immobile as a Christmas turkey, into the largest sack and sat down to have a much needed cigarette, feeling rather pleased with ourselves.

But then another snag developed. The horses were unanimous in their disapproval when we tried to hoist the sackful of anteater onto their backs. Their alarm was increased by the anteater, which uttered loud and prolonged hisses every time we staggered up to the horses with it. We made several attempts, but had to give up, for the horses showed every symptom of a collective nervous breakdown. After a good deal of thought Francis indicated that the only way out of the difficulty was for me to lead his horse while he followed, carrying the anteater on his back. I was a bit doubtful whether he would succeed, as the sack was extremely heavy and we were a good eight or nine miles from Karanambo. But I helped him to get the sack onto his back, and we set off. Francis struggled along bravely, the sweat pouring off him, his burden making things as difficult as possible by wriggling violently. The heat of the afternoon sun was intense, and there was no breeze to fan the brow of our anteater-carrier. He began to mutter to himself. Soon he was lagging fifty yards behind.

We progressed a tortuous half-mile, and Bob turned round to have a look. "What's the matter with Francis?" he asked in astonishment.

Turning round, I saw that our guide had put the anteater down and was walking round and round it, talking to it violently and waving his arms.

"I have a horrible feeling that the world's turning round on him," I said.

"*What?*"

"That's what he says happens when he has a fit."

"Good God!" said Bob, really startled. "I hope you know the way back from here."

"No, I don't. Anyway, hang on to his horse a second, and I'll go back and see what's happening."

I cantered back to where Francis was having his long conversation with the anteater. My arrival did not interrupt him; he did not even look up. From the expression on his face and his wild gesticulations I gathered that he was going into the subject of the anteater's ancestors with all the thoroughness allowed by the Munchi dialect. The object of his abuse was gazing up at him unmoved, blowing a few gentle bubbles from its nose. Presently, having exhausted his vocabulary, Francis stopped talking and looked at me sorrowfully.

"What's the matter, Francis?" I asked soothingly and rather fatuously, since it was perfectly obvious what was the matter. Francis drew a deep breath and then let forth a torrent of speech at me. I listened carefully, but all I could understand was the oft-repeated word "draftball," which, whatever it meant, struck me as having nothing whatsoever to do with the matter in hand. After some considerable time I gathered that what Francis wanted us to do was this: someone was to stay with the anteater while the other two rode to the outstation—a distant speck on the horizon he pointed out to me—to procure this very necessary item, a draftball. Hoping we would find someone at the outstation who had a greater command of English, I agreed to the suggestion and helped him carry the anteater into the shade of some nearby bushes. Then I rode back to explain to Bob.

"You'll have to stay here with the anteater while Francis and I ride back to the outstation for a draftball," I said.

"A draughtboard?" asked Bob in amazement. "What the devil for?"

"Not a draughtboard, a draftball," I corrected airily.

"And what is a draftball?"

"I haven't the faintest idea. Some form of transport, I imagine."

"Is this your idea, or did Francis think it up?"

"Francis. He seems to think it's the only way."

"Yes, but what *is* a draftball?"

"My dear chap, I'm no linguist; some form of cart, I think. Anyway there will be other people at the outstation, and I can enlist their aid."

"By which time I shall have died of thirst or been disembowelled by the anteater," said Bob bitterly. "What a wonderful idea."

"Nonsense, the anteater's perfectly safe in his sack, and I'll bring you a drink from the outstation."

"If you reach the outstation. For all you know, Francis, in his present mental condition, might take you on a four-day jaunt over the Brazilian border. Oh, well, I suppose I shall have to sacrifice myself once again for the sake of your collecting."

As I rode off with Francis, Bob shouted after us, "I should like to point out that I came to Guiana to *paint,* not play nursemaid to a blasted anteater—*and don't forget that drink!*"

I prefer not to remember the ride to the outstation. Francis made his horse go like the wind, and mine, obviously under the impression that we were going home for good, followed suit. It seemed as if we rode forever, but at last I heard dogs barking, and we galloped in at a gate and drew up in front of a long, low white house in a manner I have rarely seen equalled outside a Western film. I half expected a sign informing me that we had arrived at the Gold Dust Saloon. A delightful old Amerindian appeared and greeted me in Spanish. I grinned stupidly and followed him into the blessed cool and shade of the house. Two wild-looking youths and a handsome girl were seated on the low wall of the room; one of the youths was engaged in splitting up a stick of sugar cane and dropping the bits to three naked infants who sprawled on the floor. I seated myself on a low wooden form, and presently the girl brought me a most welcome cup of coffee, and while I drank it the old man conducted a long conversation with me in a mixture of English and very in-

ferior Spanish. Presently Francis reappeared and led me outside to a
field, where grazed a large and very obvious bull.

"Draftball," said Francis, pointing.

I went inside and had more coffee while the bull was being
saddled, and then, before mounting my horse again, I got the old
man to give me a bottle of water for Bob. We said good-bye, mounted
our steeds, and rode through the gate.

"Where's the draft-bull?" I asked Francis.

He pointed. I saw the bull cantering heavily over the savanna,
and perched on his back was a woman who later proved to be
Francis's wife, her long dark hair flowing in the wind, looking from
that distance not unlike a brunette Lady Godiva.

By taking a short cut across the savanna we arrived back well in
advance of the bull. We found things in chaos. The anteater had
freed both its front legs by some gigantic effort and had then ripped
open the sack and crawled half out of it. When we arrived it was
dashing round in a circle, wearing the sack on its hindquarters like an
ill-fitting pair of shorts, with Bob in hot pursuit. After recapturing the
beast and pushing it into a new sack, I soothed Bob by producing the
bottle of water, and after this lukewarm refreshment he recovered
enough to tell me what had happened since we left him. As soon as
we were out of sight his horse, which he had thought was securely
tied to a small bush, had wandered off and refused to be caught for
some time. Bob pursued it over the savanna, mouthing endearments,
and eventually succeeded in catching it. When he got back he found
that the anteater had broken out of the sack and was trying to undo
the ropes. Hot and angry, Bob forced it back into the sack, only to
find that the horse had wandered off again. This apparently went on
for a long time; at one point the monotony was relieved slightly by
the arrival of a herd of longhorned cattle that stood around watching
Bob's efforts in a supercilious and slightly belligerent way. Bob said
he would not have minded their presence so much if bulls had not
seemed so predominant in the herd. Eventually they drifted off, and
Bob was making yet another sortie after the anteater when we appeared.

"The world," he said, "was just starting to turn round on me when
you all arrived."

Just at that moment Francis's wife appeared, galloping across the grass on the bull, and Bob watched her approach with bulging eyes. "What is *that?*" he asked in tones of awe. "Can you see it too?"

"That, my dear fellow, is the draftball, procured at considerable expense to rescue us."

Bob lay back in the grass and closed his eyes. "I've seen quite enough of bulls today to last me a lifetime," he said. "I refuse to help you load the anteater on to that creature. I shall lie here until you have been gored to death, and then I'll ride quietly home."

So Francis, his wife, and I loaded the snorting anteater on to the bull's broad and stoical back. Then we levered our aching bodies on to the horses again and set off on the long trail back to Karanambo. The sun hung for a brief moment over the distant rim of mountains, flooding the savanna with a glorious green twilight, and then it was dark. In the gloom the burrowing owls called softly to one another, and as we passed the lake a pair of white egrets skimmed its surface like shooting stars. We were dead tired and aching in every limb. Our horses stumbled frequently, nearly sending us over their heads. The stars came out, and still we plodded on over the endless grass, not knowing in which direction we were travelling and not caring very much. A pale chip of moon rose, silvering the grass and making the draft-bull look huge and misshapen in its light, like some great, heavy-breathing, prehistoric monster moving across the gloom of a newly formed world. I dozed uncomfortably, jogging back and forth in my saddle. Occasionally Bob's horse stumbled, and I heard him curse fluently as the jerk stabbed the pommell of the saddle into his long-suffering abdomen.

Presently I noticed a pale light flickering through some trees ahead of us, vanishing and reappearing like a will-o'-the-wisp. It was very small and wan in comparison to the gigantic stars that seemed to hang only a few feet above our heads.

"Bob," I called, "I think those are the lights of the jeep."

"Praise the Lord!" said Bob fervently. "If you only knew how I long to get off this saddle!"

The lights of the jeep grew brighter, and we could hear the throb of its engine. It rounded the trees, bathing us in the cold beam of its headlights, and the horses bobbed and bucked, but in a very tired and dispirited manner. We dismounted and hobbled towards the car.

"What luck?" asked McTurk from the gloom.

"We got a big male," I replied with a certain amount of vanity.

"And we've had a *lovely* day," said Bob.

McTurk chuckled. We sat down and had a smoke, and presently the prehistoric monster staggered into the glare of the headlights, and we unloaded the anteater from his back. The precious creature was then placed in the jeep on a bed of sacks, and we scrambled in beside it, having turned our horses loose on the savanna to find their way back to the outstation. The anteater awoke suddenly as the jeep started, and began to thrash about. I held its long nose in a firm grip, for I knew that a bang on the metal sides of the jeep would kill it as surely as a bullet would.

"Where are you going to keep it?" asked McTurk.

The thought had not occurred to me before. I realized suddenly that we had no cages and no wood to make them. Moreover, we could not obtain any. But it would take more than this sobering thought to destroy my delight in having captured the anteater.

"We'll have to tether it somehow," I said airily.

McTurk grunted.

When we got back to the house we unloaded the beast and unwound the yards of rope and sacking that enveloped it. Then with McTurk's aid, we fashioned a rope harness and placed it round the anteater's shoulders. To this was attached a long piece of rope, which we tied to a shade tree in the compound. Beyond giving the animal a drink of water I did nothing for it that night, for I wanted to get it onto a substitute food straight away, and I felt it would be more likely to eat if it was really hungry.

Getting an animal onto a substitute food is one of the most difficult and worrying jobs a collector has to face. It is necessary when you obtain a creature, such as the anteater, that has a very restricted diet in the wild state—it might be a certain kind of leaf or fruit, a particular kind of fish, or something equally tricky. Only very rarely can this diet be supplied when the animal reaches England, and the collector's job is to teach his specimen to eat something else, something that *can* be supplied by the zoo to which the animal is going. So you have to concoct a palatable substitute food that the creature will eat, enjoy, and thrive on. With some beasts it is a very difficult job, this changing over of diets, for you stand the risk of the substitute's disagreeing with the creature and making it ill. If this happens you may lose it. Some beasts are very stubborn and go on refusing the substitute until, in despair, you are forced to let them go. Others fall on the substitute the first time it is offered and feed off it greedily. Sometimes you get this contradictory attitude in two members of the same species.

The substitute for the anteater consisted of three pints of milk with two raw eggs and a pound or so of finely minced raw beef mixed in, the whole thing being topped off with three drops of cod-liver oil. I prepared this mixture early the next morning, and when it was ready I broke open the nearest termites' nest and scattered a thick layer of these creatures on the surface of the milk. Then I carried the bowl out to the anteater.

He was lying curled up on his side under the tree, completely covered by his tail, which was spread over him like an enormous ostrich feather. It hid his body and nose from view, and from a distance it made him look like a pile of grey grass. When you see these animals in the zoo you never realize how useful their great tails are. On the open savanna, curled up between two tussocks of grass, its tail spread over it like an umbrella, the anteater is sheltered from all but the very worst weather.

When the animal heard me approaching he snorted in alarm, whipped back his tail, and rose onto his hind legs, ready to do battle. I put the bowl down in front of him, offered up a brief prayer that he would not be difficult, and retreated to watch. He shambled over to the bowl and sniffed loudly round the rim. Then he plunged the tip of his nose into the milk, and his long gray snakelike tongue began to whip in and out of the mixture. He did not pause once until he had emptied the bowl, and I stood and watched him with incredulous delight.

Anteaters belong to a group of animals that do not possess teeth; instead they are furnished with sticky saliva and a long tongue with which to pick up their food—a tongue that acts on the principle of flypaper. So each time the anteater whipped his tongue back into his mouth it carried with it a certain amount of egg, milk, and chopped meat. Even by this laborious method it did not take him long to clean up the mixture, and when he had finished he sniffed around the bowl for some time to make sure he had not overlooked any. Then he lay down, curled himself up, spread his tail over himself like a tent, and sank into a contented sleep. From that moment on he was little or no trouble to look after.

Some weeks later, when we were back in Georgetown, we got a mate for Amos, as we called him. A pair of slim, well-dressed East Indians arrived one morning in a sleek new car and asked us if we wanted a barim (the local name for the giant anteater). When we replied that we certainly did they calmly opened the trunk of the car, and inside, tied up with masses of rope, was a full-grown female anteater. As a conjuring trick this was considerably more impressive than producing a rabbit out of a hat. However, the creature was exhausted and had several nasty cuts on her body and legs; we were a bit doubtful whether she would survive. But after some first aid to her wounds, and a long drink, she revived enough to attack us all in a very determined manner, and we thought she was well enough to be introduced to Amos.

Amos was living in a spacious pen under trees. When we opened the door of his pen and introduced the pointed nose of his bride-to-be he greeted her with such an ungentlemanly display of hissings, snufflings, and waving of claws that we hastily removed her to safety. Then we divided Amos's pen with a row of stakes and put the female next door to him. They could see and smell each other through this division, and we hoped that constant sniffing would bring about a more tender feeling on the part of Amos.

The first day the female worried us by refusing the substitute food completely. She would not even sample it. The next day I had an idea, and I pushed Amos's feeding bowl right up against the dividing fence at breakfast time. As soon as the female saw—and heard—him eating his meal she went across to investigate. Obviously Amos was enjoying whatever it was, so she poked her long tongue through the bars and into his bowl. Within ten minutes they had finished the food. Every day after that we were treated to the touching sight of Amos and his wife-to-be, separated by bars, feeding lovingly out of the same bowl. Eventually she learned to eat out of her own dish, but she always preferred to feed with Amos if she could.

When I landed Amos and his wife at Liverpool and saw them driven off to the zoo they were destined for, I felt considerable pride at having landed them safely, for anteaters are not the easiest of creatures to keep in captivity.

SHEILA BURNFORD

Three Set Out

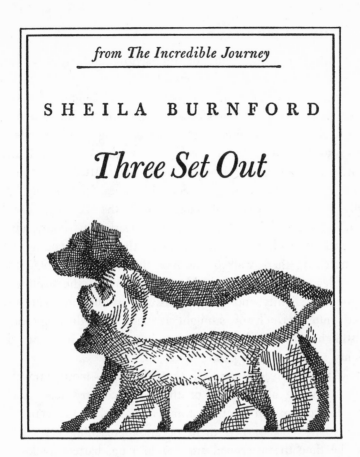

[*The two dogs and the cat had been left with a friend of the family while their owners were away on vacation. The three should have been all right when the man also went away for a few days, leaving them in the care of his housekeeper. But the note was blown from the table, so no one missed them when the animals set off for their much-loved home. They had only instinct to guide them across hundreds of miles of Canadian wilderness.*]

They had kept a fairly steady pace for the first hour or so, falling into an order which was not to vary for many miles or days; the Labrador ran always by the left shoulder of the old dog, for the bull terrier was very nearly blind in the left eye, and they jogged along fairly steadily together—the bull terrier with his odd, rolling, sailorlike gait, and the Labrador in a slow lope. Some ten yards behind came the cat, whose attention was frequently distracted, when he would stop for a few minutes and then catch up again.

But, in between these halts, he ran swiftly and steadily, his long slim body and tail low to the ground.

When it was obvious that the old dog was flagging, the Labrador turned off the quiet, graveled road and into the shade of a pinewood beside a clear, fast-running creek. The old dog drank deeply, standing up to his chest in the cold water; the cat picked his way delicately to the edge of an overhanging rock. Afterwards they rested in the deep pine needles under the trees, the terrier panting heavily with his eyes half closed, and the cat busy with his eternal washing. They lay there for nearly an hour, until the sun struck through the branches above them. The young dog rose and stretched, then walked towards the road. The old dog rose too, stiff-legged, his head low. He walked toward the waiting Labrador, limping slightly and wagging his tail at the cat, who suddenly danced into a patch of sunlight, struck at a drifting leaf, then ran straight at the dogs, swerving at the last moment, and as suddenly sitting down again.

They trotted steadily on, all that afternoon—mostly traveling on the grassy verge at the side of the quiet country road; sometimes in the low overgrown ditch that ran alongside, if the acute hearing of the young dog warned them of an approaching car.

By the time the afternoon sun lay in long, barred shadows across the road, the cat was still traveling in smooth, swift bursts, and the young dog was comparatively fresh. But the old dog was very weary, and his pace had dropped to a limping walk. They turned off the road into the bush at the side, and walked slowly through a clearing in the trees, pushing their way through the tangled undergrowth at the far end. They came out upon a small open place where a giant spruce had crashed to the ground and left a hollow where the roots had been, filled now with drifted dry leaves and spruce needles.

The late afternoon sun slanted through the branches overhead, and it looked invitingly snug and secure. The old dog stood for a minute, his heavy head hanging, and his tired body swaying slightly, then lay down on his side in the hollow. The cat, after a good deal of wary observation, made a little hollow among the spruce needles and curled around in it, purring softly. The young dog disappeared into the undergrowth and reappeared presently, his smooth coat dripping water, to lie down a little away apart from the others.

The old dog continued to pant exhaustedly for a long time, one hind leg shaking badly, until his eyes closed at last, the labored breaths came further and further apart, and he was sleeping—still, save for an occasional long shudder.

Later on, when darkness fell, the young dog moved over and stretched out closely at his side and the cat stalked over to lie between his paws; and so, warmed and comforted by their closeness, the old dog slept, momentarily unconscious of his aching, tired body or his hunger.

In the nearby hills a timber wolf howled mournfully; owls called and answered and glided silently by with great outspread wings; and there were faint whispers of movement and small rustling noises around all through the night. Once an eerie wail like a baby's crying woke the old dog and brought him shivering and whining to his feet; but it was only a porcupine, who scrambled noisily and clumsily down a nearby tree trunk and waddled away, still crying softly. When he lay down again the cat was gone from his side—another small night hunter slipping through the unquiet shadows that froze to stillness at his passing.

The young dog slept in fitful, uneasy starts, his muscles twitching, constantly lifting his head and growling softly. Once he sprang to his feet with a full-throated roar which brought a sudden splash in the distance, then silence—and who knows what else unknown, unseen or unheard passed through his mind to disturb him further? Only one thing was clear and certain—that at all costs he was going home, home to his own beloved master. Home lay to the west, his instinct told him; but he could not leave the other two—so somehow he must take them with him, all the way.

In the cold hour before dawn, the bull terrier woke, then staggered painfully to his feet. He was trembling with cold and was extremely hungry and thirsty. He walked stiffly in the direction of the pool nearby, passing on his way the cat, who was crouched over something held between his paws. The terrier heard a crunching sound as the cat's jaws moved, and, wagging his tail in interest, moved over to investigate. The cat regarded him distantly, then stalked away, leaving the carcass; but to the terrier it was a disappointing mess of feathers only. He drank long and deeply at the pool and on his return tried the feathers again, for he was ravenous; but they stuck in his gullet and he retched them out. He nibbled at some stalks of grass, then, delicately, his lips rolled back over his teeth, picked a few overripe raspberries from a low bush. He had always liked to eat domestic raspberries this way, and although the taste was reassuringly familiar, it did nothing to appease his hunger. He was pleased to see the young dog appear presently; he wagged his tail and licked the other's face, then followed resignedly when a move was made towards the direction of the road. They were followed a few moments later by the cat, who was still licking his lips after his feathery breakfast.

In the gray light of dawn the trio continued down the side of the road until they reached a point where it took a right-angled turn. Here they hesitated before a disused logging trail that led westward from the side of the road, its entrance almost concealed by overhanging branches. The leader lifted his head and appeared almost as though he were searching for the scent of something, some reassurance; and apparently he found it, for he led his companions up the trail between the overhanging trees. The going here was softer; the middle was overgrown with grass and the ruts on either side were full of dead leaves. The close-growing trees which almost met overhead would afford more shade when the sun rose higher. These were all considerations that the old dog needed, for he had been tired today even before he started, and his pace was already considerably slower.

Both dogs were very hungry and watched enviously when the cat caught and killed a chipmunk while they were resting by a stream in the middle of the day. But when the old dog advanced with a hopeful wag of his tail, the cat, growling, retreated into the bushes with his prey. Puzzled and disappointed, the terrier sat listening to the crunching sounds inside the bushes, saliva running from his mouth.

A few minutes later the cat emerged and sat down, daintily cleaning his whiskers. The old dog licked the black Siamese face with his panting tongue and was affectionately patted on the nose in return. Restless with hunger, he wandered up the banks of the creek, investigating every rock and hollow, pushing his hopeful nose through tunnels of withered sedge and into the yielding earth of molehills. Sadly he lay down by an unrewarding blueberry bush, drew his paws down tightly over his blackened face, then licked the dirt off them.

The young dog, too, was hungry; but he would have to be on the verge of starvation before the barriers of deep-rooted Labrador heredity would be broken down. For generations his ancestors had been bred to retrieve without harming, and there was nothing of the hunter in his make-up; as yet, any killing was abhorrent to him. He drank deeply at the stream and urged his companions on.

The trail ran high over the crest of this hilly, wooded country, and the surrounding countryside below was filled with an overwhelming beauty of color; the reds and vermilions of the occasional maples; pale birch, and yellow poplar, and here and there the scarlet clusters of mountain ash berries against a rich dark-green background of spruce and pine and cedar.

Several times they passed log ramps built into the side of the hill, picking their way across the deep ruts left by the timber sleighs below; and sometimes they passed derelict buildings in rank, overgrown clearings, old stables for the bush horses and living quarters for the men who had worked there a generation ago. The windows were broken and sagging and weeds were growing up between the floorboards, and even one old rusted cookstove had fireweed springing from the firebox. The animals, strangely enough, did not like these evidences of human occupation and skirted them as far as possible, hair raised along their backs.

Late in the afternoon the old dog's pace had slowed down to a stumbling walk, and it seemed as if only sheer determination were keeping him on his feet at all. He was dizzy and swaying, and his heart was pounding. The cat must have sensed this general failing, for he now walked steadily beside the dogs, very close to his tottering old friend, and uttered plaintive worried bleats. Finally, the old dog came to a standstill by a deep rut half-filled with muddy water. He stood there as if he had not even the strength to step around it; his head sagged, and his whole body was trembling. Then, as he tried to lap the water, his legs seemed to crumple under him and he collapsed, half in and half out of the rut. His eyes were closed, and his body moved only to the long, shallow, shuddering breaths that came at widening intervals. Soon he lay completely limp and still. The young dog became frantic now: he whined, as he scratched at the edge of the rut, then nudged and pushed with his nose, doing everything in his power to rouse the huddled, unresponsive body. Again and again he barked, and the cat growled softly and continuously, walking back and forth and rubbing his whole length against the dirty, muddied head. There was no response to their attention. The old dog lay unconscious and remote.

The two animals grew silent, and sat by his side, disturbed and uneasy; until at last they turned and left him, neither looking back—the Labrador disappearing into the bushes where the crack of broken branches marked his progress farther and farther away; the cat stalking a partridge which had appeared at the side of the trail some hundred yards away and was pecking unconcernedly at the sandy dirt. But at the shrill warning of a squirrel, it flew off across the trail with a sudden whirr into the trees, while the cat was still some distance away. Undaunted, still licking his lips in anticipation, the cat continued around a bend in the trail in search of another, and was lost to sight.

The shadows lengthened across the deserted track, and the evening wind sighed down it to sweep a flurry of whispering leaves across the rut, their brown brittleness light as a benison as they drifted across the unheeding white form. The curious squirrel peered in bright-eyed wonder from a nearby tree, clucking softly to itself. A shrew ran halfway across, paused and ran back; and there was a soft sound of wings as a whisky-jack landed and swayed to and fro on a birch branch, tilting his head to one side as he looked down and called to his mate to come and join him. The wind died away—a sudden hush descended.

Suddenly, there was a sound of a heavy body pushing through the undergrowth, accompanied by a sharp cracking of branches, and the spell was broken. Chattering shrilly in alarm and excitement, the squirrel ran up the trunk of the tree and the whisky-jacks flew off. Now onto the trail on all fours scampered a half-grown bear cub, round furry ears pricked and small deep-set eyes alight with curiosity in the sharp little face as he beheld the old dog. There was a grunting snuffling sound in the bush behind the cub: his mother was investigating a rotten tree stump. The cub stood for a moment and then hesitantly advanced toward the rut where the terrier lay. He sniffed around, wrinkling his facile nose at the unfamiliar smell, then reached out a long curved black paw and tapped the white head. For a moment the mists of unconsciousness cleared and the old dog opened his eyes, aware of danger. The cub sprang back in alarm and watched from a safe distance. Seeing that there was no further movement, he loped back and cuffed again with his paw, this time harder, and watched for a response. Only enough strength was left in the old dog for a valiant baring of his teeth. He snarled faintly with pain and hatred when his shoulder was raked by the wicked claws of the excited cub, and made an attempt to struggle to his feet. The smell of the drawn blood excited the cub further; he straddled the dog's body and started to play with the long white tail, nibbling at the end like a child with a new toy. But there was no response: all conscious effort drained, the old dog no longer felt any pain or indignity. He lay as though asleep, his eyes veiled and unseeing, his lip still curled in a snarl.

Around the bend in the trail, dragging a large dead partridge by the wing, came the cat. The wing sprang back softly from his mouth as he gazed transfixed at the scene before him. In one split second a terrible transformation took place; his blue eyes glittered hugely and evilly in the black masked face, and every hair on the wheat-colored body stood upright so that he appeared twice his real size; even the chocolate-colored tail puffed up as it switched from side to side. He crouched low to the ground, tensed and ready, and uttered a high, ear-splitting scream; and, as the startled cub turned, the cat sprang.

He landed on the back of the dark furred neck, clinging with his monkeylike hind legs while he raked his claws across the cub's eyes. Again and again he raked with the terrible talons, hissing and spitting in murderous devilry until the cub was screaming in pain and fear, blinded with blood, making ineffectual brushing movements with his paws to dislodge the unseen horror on his back. His screams were answered by a thunderous roar as the huge black she-bear crashed through the bushes and rushed to the cub. She swiped at the clinging cat with a tremendous paw; but the cat was too quick for her and with a hiss of fury leaped to the ground and disappeared behind a tree. The unfortunate cub's head received the full force of the blow and he was sent spinning across the track into the bushes. In a blind, frustrated rage, maddened by the cries of her cub, the mother turned for something on which to vent her fury, and saw the still figure of the old dog. Even as she lumbered snarling towards him the cat distracted her attention with a sudden leap to the side of the track. The bear halted, then reared up to full height for attack, red eyes glinting savagely, neck upstretched and head weaving from side to side in a menacing, snakelike way. The cat uttered another banshee scream and stepped forward with a stiff-legged, sideways movement, his squinting, terrible eyes fixed on his enormous adversary. Something like fear or indecision crept into the bear's eyes as the cat advanced; she shuffled back a step with lowered head. Slow, deliberate, purposeful, the cat came on—again the bear retreated, bewildered by the tactics of this terrible small animal, distraught by her cub's whimpering, slowly falling back before the relentless inch-by-inch advance. Now the cat stopped and crouched low, lashing his tail from side to side—the bear stopped too, shifting her weight uneasily before the spring that must follow, longing to decamp but afraid to turn her back. A sudden crackle of undergrowth turned the huge animal into a statue, rigid with apprehension—and when a great dog sprang out of the bush and stood beside the cat, teeth bared and snarling, every hair on his russet back and ruff erect, she dropped to all fours, turned swiftly and fled towards her cub. There was a last growl of desperate bravado from the bush and a whimpering cry; then the sounds of the bears' escape receded in the distance. Finally all was quiet again; the curious squirrel leaped from his ringside seat and scrambled farther down the trunk of the tree.

The cat shrank back to his normal size. His eyes regained their usual cool, detached look. He shook each paw distastefully in turn, glanced briefly at the limp, muddied bundle by his feet, blood oozing from four deep parallel gashes on the shoulder, then turned and sauntered slowly down the track towards his partridge.

The young dog nosed his friend all over, his lips wrinkling at the rank bear smell, then attempted to stanch the wounds with his rough tongue. He scratched fresh leaves over the bloodstained ones, then barked by the old dog's head; but there was no response, and at last he lay down panting on the grass. His eyes were uneasy and watchful, the hairs still stood upright in a ridge on his back, and from time to time he whined in perplexity. He watched the cat drag a large gray bird almost up to the nose of the unconscious dog, then slowly and deliberately begin to tear at the bird's flesh. He growled softly, but the cat ignored him and continued his tearing and eating. Presently, the enticing smell of raw, warm meat filtered through into the old dog's senses. He opened one eye and gave an appreciative sniff. The effect was galvanizing: his muddied half-chewed tail stirred and he raised his shoulders, then his forelegs, with a convulsive effort, like an old work horse getting up after a fall.

He was a pitiful sight—the half of his body that had lain in the rut was black and soaking, while the other was streaked and stained with blood. He looked like some grotesque harlequin. He trembled violently and uncontrollably throughout the length of his body, but in the sunken depths of the slanted black-currant eyes there was a faint gleam of interest—which increased as he pushed his nose into the still-warm bundle of soft gray feathers. This time there was no growling rebuff over the prey: instead, the cat sat down a few yards away, studiedly aloof and indifferent, then painstakingly washed down the length of his tail. When the end twitched he pinned it down with a paw.

The old dog ate, crunching the bones ravenously with his blunt teeth. Even as his companions watched him, a miraculous strength slowly seeped back into his body. He dozed for a while, a feather hanging from his mouth, then woke again to finish the last morsel. By nightfall he was able to walk over to the soft grass at the side of the track, where he lay down and blinked happily at his companions, wagging his pitiful tail. The Labrador lay down beside him, and licked the wounded shoulder.

An hour or two later the purring cat joined them, carelessly dropping another succulent morsel by his old friend's nose. This was a deer mouse, a little creature with big eyes and long hind legs like a miniature kangaroo. It was swallowed with a satisfying gulp, and soon the old dog slept.

But the cat purring against his chest and the young dog curled at his back were wakeful and alert most of the remaining night; neither moved from his side.

Hunger was now the ruling instinct in the Labrador and it drove him out to forage in the early dawn. He was desperate enough to try some deer droppings, but spat them out immediately in disgust. While he was drinking from a marsh pool still covered with lily pads, he saw a frog staring at him with goggle eyes from a small stone: measuring the distance carefully, he sprang and caught it in the air as it leaped to safety. It disappeared down his throat in one crunch and he looked around happily for more. But an hour's patient search rewarded him with only two, so he returned to his companions. They had apparently eaten, for there were feathers and fur scattered around and both were licking their lips. But something warned him not to urge his old companion on. The terrier was still utterly exhausted, and in addition had lost a lot of blood from the gashes suffered at the cub's claws the day before. These were stiff and black with blood, and had a tendency to open and bleed slightly with any movement, so all that day he lay peacefully in the warm fall sunshine on the grass sleeping, eating what the cat provided, and wagging his tail whenever one of the others came near.

The young dog spent most of the day still occupied with his ceaseless foraging for food. By evening he was desperate, but his luck turned when a rabbit, already changing to its white winter coat, suddenly started up from the long grass and swerved across his path. Head down, tail flying, the young dog gave chase, swerving and turning in pursuit, but always the rabbit was just out of reach of his hungry jaws. At last, he put all his strength into one violent lunge and felt the warm pulsating prize in his mouth. The generations fell away, and the years of training never to sink teeth into feathers or fur; for a moment the Labrador looked almost wolflike as he tore at the warm flesh and bolted it down in ravenous gulps.

They slept in the same place that night and most of the following day, and the weather mercifully continued warm and sunny. By the third day the old dog seemed almost recovered and the wounds were closed. He had spent most of the day ambling around and sleeping, so that by now he seemed almost frisky and quite eager to walk a little.

So, in the late afternoon, they left the place which had been their home for three days and trotted slowly along the track together again. By the time the moon rose they had traveled several miles, and they had come to the edge of a small lake which the track skirted.

A moose was standing in the water among the lily pads on the far shore, his great antlered head and humped neck silhouetted clearly against the pale moon. He took no notice of the strange animals across the water but thrust his head again and again under the water, raising it high in the air after each immersion, and arching his neck. Two or three water hens swam out from the reeds, a little crested grebe popped up like a jack-in-the-box, in the water beside them, and the spreading ripples of their wake caught the light of the moon. As the three sat, ears pricked, they watched the moose squelch slowly out of the muddy water, shake himself, and turn, cantering up the bank out of sight.

The young dog turned his head suddenly, his nose twitching, for his keen scent had caught a distant whiff of wood smoke, and of something else—something unidentifiable. . . . Seconds later, the old dog caught the scent too, and started to his feet, snuffing and questioning with his nose. His thin whippy tail began to sweep to and fro and a bright gleam appeared in the slanted black-currant eyes. Somewhere, not too far away, were human beings—his world: he could not mistake their message—or refuse their invitation—they were undoubtedly cooking something. He trotted off determinedly in the direction of the tantalizing smell. The young dog followed somewhat reluctantly, and for once the cat passed them both; a little moon-mad perhaps, for he lay in wait to dart and strike, then streaked back into the shadows, only to reappear a second later in an elaborate stalk of their tails. Both dogs ignored him.

The scent on the evening breeze was a fragrant compound of roasting rice, wild-duck stew and wood smoke. When the animals looked down from a hill, tantalized and hungry, they saw six or seven fires in the clearing below—their flames lighting up a semi-circle of tents and conical birch-bark shelters against a dark background of trees; flickering over the canoes drawn up on the edge of a wild rice marsh and dying redly in the black waters beyond; and throwing into ruddy relief the high, flat planes of brown Ojibway faces gathered around the centers of warmth and brightness.

The men were a colorful lot in jeans and bright plaid shirts, but the women were dressed in somber colors. Two young boys, the only children there, were going from fire to fire shaking grain in shallow pans and stirring it with paddles as it parched. One man in long soft moccasins stood in a shallow pit trampling husks, half his weight supported on a log frame. Some of the band lay back from the fires, smoking and watching idly, talking softly among themselves; while others still ate, ladling the fragrant contents of a black iron pot onto tin plates. Every now and then one of them would throw a bone back over a shoulder into the bush, and the watching animals gazed hungrily after. A woman stood at the edge of the clearing pouring grain from one bark platter to another, and the loose chaff drifted off on the slight wind like smoke.

The old dog saw nothing of this, but his ears and nose supplied all that he needed to know: he could contain himself no longer and picked his way carefully down the hillside, for his shoulder still pained him. Halfway down he sneezed violently in an eddy of chaff. One of the boys by the fire looked up at the sound, his hand closing on a stone, but the woman nearby spoke sharply, and he waited, watching intently.

The old dog limped out of the shadows and into the ring of firelight, confident, friendly, and sure of his welcome; his tail wagging his whole stern ingratiatingly, ears and lips laid back in his nightmarish grimace. There was a stunned silence—broken by a wail of terror from the smaller boy, who flung himself at his mother—and then a quick excited chatter from the Indians. The old dog was rather offended and uncertain for a moment, but he made hopefully for the nearest boy, who retreated, nervously clutching his stone. But again the woman rebuked her son, and at the sharpness of her tone the old dog stopped, crestfallen. She laid down her basket then, and walked quickly across the ring of firelight, stooping down to look more closely. She spoke some soft words of reassurance, then patted his head gently and smiled at him. The old dog leaned against her and whipped his tail against her black stockings, happy to be in contact with a human being again. She crouched down beside him to run her fingers lightly over his ears and back, and when he licked her face appreciatively, she laughed. At this, the two little boys drew nearer to the dog and the rest of the band gathered around. Soon the old dog was where he most loved to be—the center of attention among some human beings. He made the most of it and played to an appreciative audience; when one of the men tossed him a chunk of meat he sat up painfully on his hindquarters and begged for more, waving one paw in the air. This sent the Indians into paroxysms of laughter, and he had to repeat his performance time and time again, until he was tired and lay down, panting but happy.

The Indian woman stroked him gently in reward, then ladled some of the meat from the pot onto the grass. The old dog limped towards it; but before he ate he looked up in the direction of the hillside where he had left his two companions.

A small stone rebounded from rock to rock, then rolled into the sudden silence that followed.

When a long-legged, blue-eyed cat appeared out of the darkness, paused, then filled the clearing with a strident plaintive voice before walking up to the dog and calmly taking a piece of meat from him, the Indians laughed until they were speechless and hiccupping. The two little boys rolled on the ground, kicking their heels in an abandonment of mirth, while the cat chewed his meat unmoved; but this was the kind of behavior the bull terrier understood, and he joined in the fun. But he rolled so enthusiastically that the wounds reopened: when he got to his feet again his white coat was stained with blood.

All this time the young dog crouched on the hillside, motionless and watchful, although every driving, urgent nerve in his body fretted and strained at the delay. He watched the cat, well-fed and content, curl himself on the lap of one of the sleepy children by the fire; he heard the faint note of derision in some of the

Indians' voices as a little, bent, ancient crone addressed them in earnest and impassioned tones before hobbling over to the dog to examine his shoulder as he lay peacefully before the fire. She threw some cattail roots into a boiling pot of water, soaked some moss in the liquid, and pressed it against the dark gashes. The old dog did not move; only his tail beat slowly. When she had finished, she scooped some more meat onto a piece of birchbark and set it on the grass before the dog; and the silent watcher above licked his lips and sat up, but still he did not move from his place.

But when the fires began to burn low and the Indians made preparations for the night, and still his companions showed no signs of moving, the young dog grew restless. He skirted the camp, moving like a shadow through the trees on the hill behind, until he came out upon the lake's shore a quarter of a mile upwind of the camp. Then he barked sharply and imperatively several times.

The effect was like an alarm bell on the other two. The cat sprang from the arms of the sleepy little Indian boy and ran towards the old dog, who was already on his feet, blinking and peering around rather confusedly. The cat gave a guttural yowl, then deliberately ran ahead, looking back as he paused beyond the range of firelight. The old dog shook himself resignedly and walked slowly after—reluctant to leave the warmth of the fire. The Indians watched impassively and silently and made no move to stop him. Only the woman who had first befriended him called out softly, in the tongue of her people, a farewell to the traveler.

The dog halted at the treeline beside the cat and looked back, but the commanding, summoning bark was heard again, and together the two passed out of sight and into the blackness of the night.

That night they became immortal, had they known or cared, for the ancient woman had recognized the old dog at once by his color and companion: he was the White Dog of the Ojibways, the virtuous White Dog of Omen, whose appearance heralds either disaster or good fortune. The Spirits had sent him, hungry and wounded, to test tribal hospitality; and for benevolent proof to the skeptical they had chosen a cat as his companion—for what *mortal* dog would suffer a cat to rob him of his meat? He had been made welcome, fed and succored: the omen would prove fortunate.

from The Silent World

J. Y. COUSTEAU
with Frederic Dumas

Shark Close-Ups

On a goggle dive at Djerba Island off Tunisia in 1939 I met sharks underwater for the first time. They were magnificent gun-metal creatures, eight feet long, that swam in pairs behind their servant remoras. I was uneasy with fear, but I calmed somewhat when I saw the reaction of my diving companion, Simone. She was scared. The sharks passed on haughtily.

The Djerba sharks were entered in a shark casebook I kept religiously until we went to the Red Sea in 1951, where sharks appeared in such numbers that my census lost value. From the data, covering over a hundred shark encounters with many varieties, I can offer two conclusions: The better acquainted we become with sharks, the less we know them, and one can never tell what a shark is going to do.

Man is separated from the shark by an abyss of time. The fish still lives in the late Mesozoic, when the rocks were made: it has changed but little in perhaps three hundred million years. Across the gulf of ages, which evolved other marine creatures, the relentless, indestructible shark has come without need of evolution, the oldest killer, armed for the fray of existence in the beginning.

One sunny day in the open sea between the islands of Boavista and Maio, in the Cape Verde group, a long Atlantic swell beat on an exposed reef and sent walls of flume high into the air. Such a sight is the dread of hydrographers, who mark it off sternly to warn the mariner. But the *Élie Monnier* was attracted to such spots. We anchored by the dangerous reef to dive from the steeply rolling deck into the wild sea. Where there is a reef, there is abundant life.

Small sharks came when we dropped anchor. The crew broke out tuna hooks and took ten of them in as many minutes. When we went overside for a camera dive, there were only two sharks left in the water. Under the racing swell we watched them strike the hooks and thrash their way through the surface. Down in the reef we found the savage population of the open ocean, including some extremely large nurse sharks, a class that is not supposed to be harmful to man. We saw three sharks sleeping in rocky caverns. The camera demanded lively sharks. Dumas and Tailliez swam into the caves and pulled their tails to wake them. The sharks came out and vanished into the blue, playing their bit parts competently.

We saw a fifteen-foot nurse shark. I summoned Didi and conveyed to him in sign language that he would be permitted to relax our neutrality toward sharks and take a crack at this one with his super-harpoon gun. It had a six-foot spear with an explosive head and three hundred pounds of traction in its elastic bands. Dumas fired straight down at a distance of twelve feet. The four-pound harpoon struck the shark's head and, two seconds later, the harpoon tip exploded. We were severely shaken. There was some pain involved.

The shark continued to swim away, imperturbably, with the spear sticking from its head like a flagstaff. After a few strokes the harpoon shaft fell to the bottom and the shark moved on. We swam after it as fast as we could to see what would happen. The shark showed every sign of normal movement, accelerated gradually and vanished.

The only conclusion we could draw was that the harpoon went clear through the head and exploded externally, because no internal organ could survive a blast that nearly incapacitated us six harpoon lengths away. Even so, taking such a burst a few inches from the head demonstrated the extraordinary vitality of sharks.

One day we were finishing a movie sequence on trigger fish when Dumas and I were galvanized with ice-cold terror. It is a reaction unpleasant enough on land, and very lonely in the water. What we saw made us feel that naked men really do not belong under the sea.

At a distance of forty feet there appeared from the gray haze the lead-white bulk of a twenty-five-foot *Carcharodon carcharias*, the only shark species that all specialists agree is a confirmed maneater. Dumas, my bodyguard, closed in beside me. The brute was swimming lazily. In that moment I thought that at least he would have a belly-ache on our three-cylinder lungs.

Then, the shark saw us. His reaction was the last conceivable one. In pure fright, the monster voided a cloud of excrement and departed at an incredible speed.

Dumas and I looked at each other and burst into nervous laughter. The self-confidence we gained that day led us to a foolish negligence. We abandoned the bodyguard system and all measures of safety. Further meetings with sharp-nosed sharks, tiger sharks, mackerel sharks, and ground sharks, inflated our sense of shark mastery. They all ran from us. After several weeks in the Cape Verdes, we were ready to state flatly that all sharks were cowards. They were so pusillanimous they wouldn't hold still to be filmed.

One day I was on the bridge, watching the little spark jiggle up and down on the echo-sound tape, sketching the profile of the sea floor nine thousand feet below the open Atlantic off Africa. There was the usual faint signal of the deep scattering layer twelve hundred feet down. The deep scattering layer is an astounding new problem of oceanography, a mystifying physical mezzanine hovering above the bedrock of the sea. It is recorded at two to three hundred fathoms in the daytime and it ascends toward the surface at night.

The phenomenon rises and falls with the cycle of sun and dark, leading some scientists to believe it is a dense blanket of living organisms, so vast as to tilt the imagination. As I watched the enigmatic scrawls, the stylus began to enter three distinct spurs on the tape, three separate scattering layers, one above the other. I was lost in whirling ideas, watching the spark etch the lowest and heaviest layer, when I heard shouts from the deck, "Whales!" A herd of sluggish bottlenosed whales surrounded the Élie Monnier.

In the clear water we studied the big dark forms. Their heads were round and glossy with bulbous foreheads, the "bottle" which gives them their name. When a whale broke the surface, it spouted and the rest of the body followed softly, stretching in relaxation. The whale's lips were curved in a fixed smile with tiny eyes close to the tucks of the lips, a roguish visage for such a formidable creature. Dumas skinned down to the harpoon platform under the bow while I stuck a film magazine in the underwater camera. The whales were back from a dive. One emerged twelve feet from Dumas. He threw the harpoon with all his might. The shaft struck near the pectoral fin and blood started. The animal sounded in an easy rhythm and we paid out a hundred yards of harpoon line, tied to a heavy gray buoy. The buoy was swept away in the water—the whale was well hooked. The other whales lay unperturbed around the Élie Monnier.

We saw Dumas's harpoon sticking out of the water; then it, the whale and buoy disappeared. Dumas climbed the mast with binoculars. I kept the ship among the whales, thinking they would not abandon a wounded comrade. Time passed.

Libera, the keen-eyed radio man, spotted the buoy and there was the whale, seemingly unhurt, with the harpoon protruding like a toothpick. Dumas hit the whale twice with dum-dum bullets. Red water washed on the backs of the faithful herd, as it gathered around the stricken one. We struggled for an hour to pick up the buoy and tie the harpoon line to the Élie Monnier.

A relatively small bottlenosed whale, heavily wounded, was tethered to the ship. We were out of sight of land, with fifteen hundred fathoms of water under the keel, and the whale herd diving and spouting around the ship. Tailliez and I entered the water to follow the harpoon line to the agonized animal.

The water was an exceptional clear turquoise blue. We followed the line a few feet under the surface, and came upon the whale. Thin streams of blood jetted horizontally from the bullet holes. I swam toward three other bottlenoses. As I neared them, they turned up their flukes and sounded. It was the first time I had been under water to actually see them diving and I understood the old whaler's word, "sound." They did not dive obliquely as porpoises often do. They sped straight down, perfectly vertical. I followed them down a hundred feet. A fifteen-foot shark passed way below me, probably attracted by the whale's blood. Beyond sight was the deep scattering layer; down there a herd of leviathans grazed; more sharks roamed. Above in the sun's silvery light was Tailliez and a big whale dying. Reluctantly I returned to the ship.

Back on deck I changed into another lung and strapped a tablet of cupric acetate on an ankle and one on my belt. When this chemical dissolves in water it is supposed to repulse sharks. Dumas was to pass a noose over the whale's tail, while I filmed. Just after we went under he saw a big shark, but it was gone before I answered his shout. We swam under the keel of the ship and located the harpoon line.

A few lengths down the line in a depth of fifteen feet we sighted an eight-foot shark of a species we had never before seen. He was impressively neat, light gray, sleek, a real collector's item. A ten-inch fish with vertical black-and-white stripes accompanied him a few inches above his back, one of the famous pilot fish. We boldly swam toward the shark, confident that he would run as all the others had. He did not retreat. We drew within ten feet of him, and saw all around the shark an escort of tiny striped pilots three or four inches long.

They were not following him; they seemed part of him. A thumb-nail of a pilot fish wriggled just ahead of the shark's snout, miraculously staying in place as the beast advanced. He probably found there a compressibility wave that held him. If he tumbled out of it, he would be hopelessly left behind. It was some time before we realized that the shark and his courtiers were not scared of us.

Sea legends hold that the shark has poor eyesight and pilot fish guide him to the prey, in order to take crumbs from his table. Scientists today tend to pooh-pooh the attribution of the pilot as a seeing-eye dog, although dissection has confirmed the low vision of sharks. Our experiences lead us to believe they probably see as well as we do.

The handsome gray was not apprehensive. I was happy to have such an opportunity to film a shark, although, as the first wonder passed, a sense of danger came to our hearts. Shark and company slowly circled us. I became the film director, making signs to Dumas, who was co-starred with the shark. Dumas obligingly swam in front of the beast and along behind it. He lingered at the tail and reached out his hand. He grasped the tip of the caudal fin, undecided about giving it a good pull. That would break the dreamy rhythm and make a good shot, but it might also bring the teeth snapping back at him. Dumas released the tail and pursued the shark round and round. I was whirling in the center of the game, busy framing Dumas. He was swimming as hard as he could to keep up with the almost motionless animal. The shark made no hostile move nor did he flee, but his hard little eyes were on us.

I tried to identify the species. The tail was quite asymmetrical, with an unusually long top, or heterocercal caudal fin. He had huge pectorals, and the large dorsal fin was rounded with a big white patch on it. In outline and marking he resembled no shark we had seen or studied.

The shark had gradually led us down to sixty feet. Dumas pointed down. From the visibility limit of the abyss, two more sharks climbed toward us. They were fifteen-footers, slender, steel-blue animals with a more savage appearance. They leveled off below us. They carried no pilot fish.

Our old friend, the gray shark, was getting closer to us, tightening his slowly revolving cordon. But he still seemed manageable. He turned reliably in his clockwise prowl and the pilots held their stations. The blue pair from the abyss hung back, leaving the affair to the first comer. We revolved inside the ring, watching the gray, and tried to keep the blues located at the same time. We never found them in the same place twice.

Below the blue sharks there appeared great tunas with long fins. Perhaps they had been there since the beginning, but it was the first time we noticed them. Above us flying fish gamboled, adding a discordant touch of gaiety to what was becoming a tragedy for us. Dumas and I ransacked our memories for advices on how to frighten off sharks. "Gesticulate wildly," said a lifeguard. We flailed our arms. The gray did not falter. "Give 'em a flood of bubbles," said a helmet diver. Dumas waited until the shark had reached his nearest point and released a heavy exhalation. The shark did not react. "Shout as loud as you can," said Hans Hass. We hooted until our voices cracked.

The shark appeared deaf. *"Cupric acetate tablets fastened to leg and belt will keep sharks away if you go into the drink,"* said an Air Force briefing officer. Our friend swam through the copper-stained water without a wink. His cold, tranquil eye appraised us. He seemed to know what he wanted, and he was in no hurry.

A small dreadful thing occurred. The tiny pilot fish on the shark's snout tumbled off his station and wriggled to Dumas. It was a long journey for the little fellow, quite long enough for us to speculate on his purpose. The mite butterflied in front of Dumas's mask. Dumas shook his head as if to dodge a mosquito. The little pilot fluttered happily, moving with the mask, inside which Dumas focused in cross-eyed agony.

Instinctively I felt my comrade move close to me, and I saw his hand held out clutching his belt knife. Beyond the camera and the knife, the gray shark retreated some distance, turned, and glided at us head-on.

We did not believe in knifing sharks, but the final moment had come, when knife and camera were all we had. I had my hand on the camera button and it was running, without my knowledge that I was filming the oncoming beast. The flat snout grew larger and there was only the head. I was flooded with anger. With all my strength I thrust the camera and banged his muzzle. I felt the wash of a heavy body flashing past and the shark was twelve feet away, circling us as slowly as before, unharmed and expressionless. I thought, *Why in hell doesn't he go to the whale? The nice juicy whale. What did we ever do to him?*

The blue sharks now climbed up and joined us. Dumas and I decided to take a chance on the surface. We swam up and thrust our masks out of the water. The *Élie Monnier* was three hundred yards away, under the wind. We waved wildly and saw no reply from the ship. We believed that floating on the surface with one's head out of the water is the classic method of being eaten away. Hanging there, one's legs could be plucked like bananas. I looked down. The three sharks were rising toward us in a concerted attack.

We dived and faced them. The sharks resumed the circling maneuver. As long as we were a fathom or two down, they hesitated to approach. It would have been an excellent idea for us to navigate toward the ship. However, without landmarks, or a wrist compass, we could not follow course.

Dumas and I took a position with each man's head watching the other man's flippers, in the theory that the sharks preferred to strike at feet. Dumas made quick spurts to the surface to wave his arms for a few seconds. We evolved a system of taking turns for brief appeals on the surface, while the low man pulled his knees up against his chest and watched the sharks. A blue closed in on Dumas's feet while he was above. I yelled. Dumas turned over and resolutely faced the shark. The beast broke off and went back to the circle. When we went up to look we were dizzy and disoriented from spinning around under water, and had to revolve our heads like a lighthouse beacon to find the *Élie Monnier*. We saw no evidence that our shipmates had spied us.

We were nearing exhaustion, and cold was claiming the outer layers of our bodies. I reckoned we had been down over a half hour. Any moment we expected the constriction of air in our mouthpieces, a sign that the air supply nears exhaustion. When it came, we would reach behind our backs and turn the emergency supply valve. There was five minutes' worth of air in the emergency ration. When that was gone, we could abandon our mouthpieces and make mask dives, holding our breath. That would quicken the pace, redouble the drain on our strength, and leave us facing tireless, indestructible creatures that never needed breath. The movements of the sharks grew agitated. They ran around us, working all their strong propulsive fins, turned down and disappeared. We could not believe it. Dumas and I stared at each other. A shadow fell across us. We looked up and saw the hull of the *Élie Monier's* launch. Our mates had seen our signals and had located our bubbles. The sharks ran when they saw the launch.

We flopped into the boat, weak and shaken. The crew were as distraught as we were. The ship had lost sight of our bubbles and drifted away. We could not believe what they told us; we had been in the water only twenty minutes. The camera was jammed by contact with the shark's nose.

On board the *Élie Monnier*, Dumas grabbed a rifle and jumped into the small boat to visit the whale. He found it faintly alive. We saw a brown body separate from the whale and speed away, a shark.

Dumas rowed around to the whale's head and gave the *coup de grâce*, point-blank with a dum-dum bullet. The head sank with the mouth open, streaming bubbles from the blowhole. Sharks twisted in the red water, striking furiously at the whale. Dumas plunged his hands in the red froth and fastened a noose to the tail, which is what he had started out to do when we were diverted by our friend.

We hoisted the whale aboard and were impressed by the moon-shaped shark bites. The inch-thick leather of the whale had been scooped out cleanly, without rips, ten or fifteen pounds of blubber at a bite. The sharks had waited until we were cheated away from them before they struck the easy prey.

The whale became Surgeon Longet's biggest dissection. He swept his scalpel down the belly. Out on deck burst a slimy avalanche of undigested three-pound squids, many of them intact, almost alive. In the recesses of the stomach were thousands of black squid beaks. My mind leaped back to the fathogram of the deep scattering layer. The coincidence of the whale's lunch and the lines drawn on the fathogram may have been entirely fortuitous. It was not strict proof. But I could not dispel an unscientific picture of that dark gloaming of the scattering layer twelve hundred feet down, and whales crashing into a meadow writhing with a million arms of squids.

Standing for Dakar we met a porpoise herd. Dumas harpooned one in the back. It swam like a dog on a tether, surrounded by the pack. The mammals demonstrated a decided sense of solidarity. Save that the whale was now a porpoise. Dumas and Tailliez dived into a re-enactment of the previous drama. This time the dinghy carefully followed their air bubbles.

I watched the porpoise swimming on its leash like a bait goat a lion hunter has tied to a stake. The sharks went for the porpoise. It was cruelty to an animal but we were involved with a serious study of sharks, and had to carry it out.

The sharks circled the porpoise as they had circled us. We stood on deck remarking on the cowardice of sharks, beasts as powerful as anything on earth, indifferent to pain, and splendidly equipped as killers. Yet the brutes timidly waited to attack. Attack was too good a word for them. The porpoise had no weapons and he was dying in a circle of bullies.

At nightfall Dumas sent a *coup de grâce* into the porpoise. When it was dead, a shark passed closely by the mammal, and left entrails in the water. The other sharks passed across the porpoise, muddying the sea with blood. There was no striking and biting. The sharks spooned away the solid flesh like warm butter, without interrupting their speed.

Sharks have never attacked us with resolution, unless the overtures of our friend and the two blues may be called pressing an attack. Without being at all certain, we suppose that sharks more boldly strike objects floating on the surface. It is there that the beast finds its usual meals, sick or injured fish and garbage thrown from ships. The sharks we have met took a long time surveying submerged men. A diver is an animal they may sense to be dangerous. Aqualung bubbles may also be a deterrent.

After seeing sharks swim on unshaken with harpoons through the head, deep spear gashes on the body and even after sharp explosions near their brains, we place no reliance in knives as defensive arms. We believe better protection is our "shark billy," a stout wooden staff four feet long, studded with nail tips at the business end. It is employed, somewhat in the manner of the lion tamer's chair, by thrusting the studs into the hide of an approaching shark. The nails keep the billy from sliding off the slippery leather, but do not penetrate far enough to irritate the animal. The diver may thus hold a shark at his proper distance. We carried shark billies on wrist thongs during hundreds of dives in the Red Sea, where sharks were commonplace. We have never had occasion to apply the billy, and it may prove to be merely another theoretical defense against the creature which has eluded man's understanding.

from the Autobiography of Lincoln Steffens

L I N C O L N
S T E F F E N S

A Boy on
Horseback

M y life on horseback from the age of eight to fifteen was a happy one, free, independent, full of romance, adventure, and learning, of a sort. Whether my father had any theory about it or was moved only by my prayers I do not know. But he did have some ideas. He took away my saddle, for example. My mother protested that I had suffered enough, but he insisted and he gave me reasons, some for himself, some for me. He said I would be a better horseman if I learned to ride without stirrups and a saddle horn to keep my balance. The Indians all rode bareback, and the Comanches, the best horsemen on the plains, used to attack, clinging out of sight to the far side of their horses and shooting under their necks.

"We had to shoot a Comanche's horse to get the fellow," he said, "and even then the devil would drop behind his dead pony and shoot at us over the carcass."

I consented finally to having my beautiful saddle hung high in the harness room until I could sit my horse securely. The result was that I came to prefer to ride bareback and used the saddle only for show or for games and work that needed stirrups and a horn, as in picking up things off a box on the ground or handling cattle (calves) with a rope.

That, however, was but one detail. I had begun about that time to play boys' games: marbles, tops, baseball, football, and I can see now my father stopping on his way home to watch us. He used to wag his head; he said nothing to me, but I knew he did not like those games. I think now that he thought there was some gambling in them, and he had reason to dread gambling. It was a vice that hung over from the mining days in California, and the new businessmen were against it. They could not have it stopped because "Frank" Rhodes, the political boss, was the keeper of a famous gambling house; he protected businessmen, but also he protected his own business. They could not fight Frank too openly, but they lost money and they lost clerks and cashiers through the gambling hells. My father had had to discharge a favorite bookkeeper on account of his heavy play at the gaming tables. He may have given me the pony to keep me from gambling games or to get me off the streets and out into the country. There was another result, however, which he did not foresee.

After that blessed pony loped into my life, I never played those trading games which, as I see them now, are the leads not merely to gambling but to business. For there goes on among boys an active trade in marbles, tops, knives, and all the other tools and properties of boyhood. A born trader finds himself in them, and the others learn to like to trade. My theory is that those games are the first lessons in business: they cultivate the instinct to beat the other fellows on 'Change and so quicken their predatory wits. Desirable or no, I never got that training; I never had any interest in, I have always had a distaste for business, and this my father did not intend. I remember how disappointed he was later when he offered to stay in his business till I could succeed him and I rejected the "great opportunity" with quick scorn—'Business! Never."

My pony carried me away not only from business but from the herd also and the herding habits of mind. The tendency of the human animal to think what others think, say what the mob says, do what the leaders command, and, generally, go with the crowd, is drilled in deep at school, where the playground has its fashions, laws, customs, and tyrannies just as Main Street has. I missed that. I never played "follow the leader," never submitted to the ideals and the discipline of the campus or, for that matter, of the faculty; and so, ever since, I have been able to buy stocks during a panic, sell when the public was buying; I could not always face, but I could turn my back on, public opinion. I think I learned this when, as a boy on horseback, my interest was not in the campus; it was beyond it; and I was dependent upon, not the majority of boys, but myself and the small minority group that happened to have horses.

I began riding alone. When I mounted my pony the morning after I got him I knew no other boys that had horses, and I did not think of anybody else. I had a world before me. I felt lifted up to another plane, with a wider range. I could explore regions I had not been able to reach on foot. Sacramento is protected from high water in the rivers by levees which send the overflow off to flood other counties. I had visited these levees on foot and wondered what was beyond them. Now I could ride over them and the bridges to—anywhere, I thought. The whole world was open to me. I need not imagine it any more, I could go and see.

I was up early to water, feed, and clean the pony before breakfast. That meal, essential for the horse, was of no importance to me. I slighted it. My father, cautioning me not to work a horse till he had fed fully, said I had plenty of time to eat myself. But I could not eat. I was too excited, too eager, and when I was free to rise from the table I ran out to see if the pony was through his breakfast. He wasn't. I watched him; he was in no hurry. I urged him a bit, but he only lost time looking around at me curiously, and then slowly resumed his meal. My sisters came out to see me off, and one of them rebuked my impatience with a crude imitation of a grown-up.

"The *pony* eats like a gentleman," she said, as if I cared about gentlemen. Something my father had said hit me harder. He said that teamsters, vaqueros, and Indians fed more and longer when they were in a hurry to get off on a long, hard run than on other days; they foresaw that they must be "fortified with food." It took nerve, he admitted, to eat that way, but those fellows had nerve. They could control their animals so perfectly because they had self-control. They didn't force a horse, even in a pursuit. They changed the gait often and went long stretches at a walk. And they could shoot straight, especially in a fight or a battle, because they never became fidgety.

I didn't know it then, but I can see now, of course, that my father was using my horse to educate me, and he had an advantage over the schoolteachers; he was bringing me up to my own ideals; he was teaching me the things my heroes knew and I wanted to learn. My mother did not understand that. When she came out to the stable, I was anticipating the end of the pony's meal by putting on his saddle blanket and surcingle, and telling my sisters where I was going.

"Don't ride too far the first day," she said. "You will get hungry and sore."

Awful! But I got away at last, and I rode—in all directions. Intending to do one levee that day, and the others in succession the next two days, I rode over them all that morning. I rode over the first one to the American River, and I was disappointed. The general character of the earth's surface did not change much even in that great distance and the change was for the worse—sand and muddy brush. I turned back and rode over the opposite levee, and I could hardly believe it—the land on the other side was like the land on this side. I rode into town again and went across the bridge over the Sacramento River to Yolo County, and that was not different. By that time I was hungry, very hungry, and I came home. Also I was a little hot and uncomfortable in the seat. I was late for lunch, but my mother had kept things warm for me, good things, and she did not ask me very bad questions. Where had I gone? I told her that. What had I seen? I could not tell her that. I had gone to the horizon and seen nothing new, but I did not know that myself well enough to report it to anybody else. Nor could I answer her inquiry for the cause of my depression. Only I denied that I was sore, as she suggested. No, no, not that. I had fed my horse and rubbed him down; when I had eaten I went out and watered and walked him. Then I cleaned him until my sisters came home, and then we all cleaned him.

The next day I was sore, so sore I could hardly sit or walk, but having lied about it, I had to prove it; so I rode off again, in pain, but bravely as a cowboy or an Indian taking torture; only I did not go far. I stopped, dismounted, and let my pony feed on some grass under the trees of East Park. I lay there, and no, I did not think; I imagined things. I imagined myself as all sorts of persons, a cowboy, a trapper, a soldier, a knight, a crusader—I fancied myself as the hero of every story I had read. Not all on this one day. From the day my pony came to me I seem to have spent many, many hours, playing around in my imagination, which became the most active faculty of my mind. For, as I say, I was alone much of the time. I learned to like to be alone, and that pleasure I come back to always, even now. When I am tired of the crowd I go off somewhere by myself and have a good time inside my mind.

As a boy I would ride far, far away to some spot, give my pony a long rope to swing round on, and let him feed on the grass, while I sat and did nothing but muse. I read a great deal. Finding that books fed my fancies, I would take one along, and finding a quiet nook, I read. And my reading always gave me something to be. I liked to change the hero I was to the same thing on horseback, and once wholly in the part, I would remount my pony and be Napoleon, or Richard the Lionhearted, or Byron, so completely that any actual happening would wake me up dazed as from a dreaming sleep. Dream people lived or lay in wait for me in the brush across the river, so that the empty spaces beyond my old horizon, the levee, became not only interesting but fascinating with dread or glory, and populated with Persons.

"Hey, Kid! Don't swim the river there. The rapids'll sweep you clean to San Francisco."

I looked up. It was the bridge-tender, the man that walked the trestle over the American River after every train to put out fires started on the dry sleepers by live coals dropped from the locomotives. I respected a man that filled a responsible place like his, but I slid into the water, swam alongshore, came out, and dressed. I could not tell him that Byron swam the Hellespont, which was harder to do than to cross the American at that point; and I did not like to confess that I had a trap set on the other side where the Chinamen had their peanut farm and represented the Saracens to me. When I was dressed, the trestle-walker bade me meet him at the end of the trestle.

I did, and a friendship was well started. He didn't scold me, he praised my swimming, but he said that the current was strong at that place and that it wasn't brave, it was foolish, to go in there. "A boy oughtn't to do what a man wouldn't do." He asked me some questions, my name, age, where I lived, where my father's business was. He felt over and approved my pony. I asked him how he could walk so fast on the trestle, having no planks to go on, and stepping from one sleeper to the other.

"Oh," he said, "I can walk 'em fast now because I walked 'em slow at first."

I wanted to try. He took my hand and made me walk slowly, one by one, until I was over my nervousness. When I could do it alone, he invited me to his watchman's cabin, about one-third of the way across. I went, he following. When we reached his little house we sat down, and we had, man to man, a nice, long talk, which became so confidential that I trusted him with the information that I was a trapper and had my traps set for beavers all up and down the river. And my faith was not misplaced. He didn't say that there were no beavers in that river; we both knew there weren't, and we both knew that that didn't matter. All he said was that he was a gold miner himself—and expected to strike it rich some day.

"I don't work at it much," he admitted. "Mostly I tend bridge. But in between trains, when I ain't got a thing to do, I think about it. I think how I came west to find a fat claim and work it and get rich, so I write home that that's what I'm doing, prospectin', and I am, too, and sometimes I play I have struck it and I go home and I spend my money."

After that I caught more beavers, and he and I spent my profits my way. Yes, and after that he struck it richer than ever, and him and me, we went back east and we just blew in his money his way. It was fun. I got a bad name from this. There were grown-ups who said I was a "fearful liar," and no doubt I was unconvincing sometimes. My father asked me questions, and I told him about my bridge-tender. I said that my bridge-tender could run as fast as a train on the trestle, and my father gave me a talking-to, for telling such a whopper. I felt so bad about it that I told the bridge-tender.

He thought a moment and then he said, "The next time your

father is to take a train out this way, tell me, and tell him to be on the rear platform."

The next time my father was to take a train that crossed the trestle, I told him what to do, and I went out to my bridge-tender. He climbed down off the trestle, disappeared into the brush, and came back with a few ripe cantaloupes. We waited till the train came. Now trains had to go slow on that trestle, and as the locomotive passed, the bridge-tender held up a melon to the engineer and said something about "easy does it." So when the train passed, the bridge-tender jumped out after it and ran and ran; and he caught up to the rear car and he handed that melon to my father, who waved to him and then took off his hat to me.

The bridge-tender and me, we were awful proud. We talked about it and laughed. "That'll fix him," the bridge-tender said, and he wished we could get just one beaver to show 'em. "I'd give good money if I could buy one somewheres."

But I had no trouble about the beavers. Men scoffed, and some boys did at first, but I soon had all my crowd setting and watching traps in the river. And we had a war, too. There was that peanut farm run by the Chinamen who were Turks and Saracens. We boys were crusaders, knights. So when we used to swim over to steal the peanuts, we either got peanuts, which were good, or we had a battle with the Saracens, which was better. They came at us with clods of earth, which they threw. We fired back, and when they came too near we dived into the river, and ducking and diving, swam home to the Christian shore.

My crowd was small and of very slow growth. They were all fellows I met on horseback, an odd lot. First—and last—there was Hjalmar Bergman, a Swedish boy. His father, a potter, and his mother lived in a hut out on the outskirts of the town; they spoke no English and were very poor. Hjalmar had a horse because his father, who had received it in payment of a debt, had no use for it. Black Bess, as I renamed her, was a big mare, high spirited, but well trained in the cattle game. Whenever any dangerous work had to be done the vaqueros would borrow Black Bess, and we boys would go with her and see the fun. Jake Short, who was the best cowboy in town those days, knew Bess well; and she knew him or his business. Once there was a "loco" (mad) steer in a field that had to be shot.

We sat on the fence and watched Jake ride out on Bess with his big Colt revolver ready. When Bess caught sight of the steer coming head down at them, she halted, braced herself, and stood fast, moving only to keep facing the crazy beef. Jake dropped the reins, settled his hips to the left in his saddle, and leaned far forward on the right side. The steer came madly on till he was within ten feet of them; then Jake fired and Black Bess leaped bodily to the left, letting the steer fall upon the spot where she had stood. Jake jumped down and finished the steer, and there stood Bess just where he had left her.

"That's what I call a hoss," he said to Hjalmar, and I was proud. Bess was Hjalmar's hoss, but she was in our crowd.

There were other boys with horses, all sorts of boys and all sorts of horses, but mostly they were boys and horses that belonged in one way or another to the cattle and the butchering business. Will Cluness, the doctor's son, had a pony "just to ride," but he didn't go with us much; he preferred marbles, tops, and the other games on the ground. I invented or adapted games to horse play; Will liked some of them. Hide-and-seek, for example. We found a long, straight stretch of road in old East Park, with paths and brush and trees beside it. There, at the end of a run of, say, an eighth of a mile, we drew a line across the road. The boy who was "it" held his horse on the line while the rest of us scattered into the woods. "It" called out now and then—"Ready?"—until there was no answer; then he rode where he thought we might be. He took care to keep behind him a clear run to the home line, but he had to hunt for us or the sight of us on our horses. Our game was to ride out of sight around him and make a dash for home. If he saw one of us or a horse he recognized he shouted the rider's name, pointed, and, turning, ran his horse for home base. The named rider would start at the same instant, and there was a race.

The horses soon learned this game and would start for home so suddenly at the sight of "it" that their boy was sometimes left behind. I was hiding under a tree one day when my pony saw the white horse of Ernie Southworth, who was "it"; he leaped forward, banging me against a limb of the tree; I clutched the limb, and the pony darted out of the woods, met "it" on the road, raced him, and won. We had a dispute whether the rider had to be on his horse at the finish, and it happened so often that the horse came in alone that we made a rule: a horse, with or without his rider, won or lost the race.

But Will soon tired of this and our other games. He could not fight Saracens that were really only Chinamen, and he held it in great contempt to set traps for beavers that did not exist. There were other boys like that. They were realists, I would say now; practical men. I learned to play with such boys, too, but I preferred the fellows that were able to help create a world of our own and live in it.

I took men into my crowd, too; especially horsemen. The other fellows did not; they said that grown-ups laughed at and spoiled every game. And that was true in the main. But I knew men like the bridge-tender who could play, and there was Jake Stortz, a German who lived and had his barn on the block back of my stable. Jake had the city street-cleaning contract, and he was a fireman and a truckman. He had lots of horses. His wife, a barefooted peasant woman, took care of the horses, and she and Jake were my advisers in the care, feeding, and handling of my pony. Jake let me be a fireman. He put a bit on my pony's halter, as he did on one of his own horses, arranged it so that you could with one movement snap it into the horse's mouth, untie, clear, mount him bareback, and so start for a fire the moment the whistle blew. At first I had to ride to the fire with Jake, and he would not wait a second for me, but I soon learned the signals and where to head for. I beat Jake to the fire sometimes, and the firemen knew it. "Where's Jake?" they'd call to me when I dashed up alone.

The first time there was a fire when I was at the dinner table, I upset my chair and frightened the whole family, but I got out and away so fast that nobody could say a word till I came home an hour or so later. Then I had to explain; my father spoke to Jake, and there was no trouble. I could go to fires any time except when I was in school or in bed, and my mother made me a fireman's red shirt.

* * *

Colonel Carter gave me a colt. I had my pony, and my father meanwhile had bought a pair of black carriage horses and a cow, all of which I had to attend to when we had no "man." And servants were hard to get and keep in those days; the women married, and the men soon quit service to seize opportunities always opening. My hands were pretty full, and so was the stable. But Colonel Carter seemed to think that he had promised me a horse. He had not; I would have known it if he had. No matter. He thought he had, and maybe he did promise himself to give me one. That was enough. The kind of man that led immigrant trains across the continent and delivered them safe, sound, and together where he promised would keep his word. One day he drove over from Stockton, leading a two-year-old which he brought to our front door and turned over to me as mine. Such a horse!

She was a cream-colored mare with a black forelock, mane, and tail and a black stripe along the middle of her back. Tall, slender, high spirited. I thought then—I think now that she was the most beautiful of horses. Colonel Carter had bred and reared her with me and my uses in mind. She was a careful cross of a mustang mare and a thoroughbred stallion, with the stamina of the wild horse and the speed and grace of the racer. And she had a sense of fun. As Colonel Carter got down out of his buggy and went up to her, she snorted, reared, flung her head high in the air, and, coming down beside him, tucked her nose affectionately under his arm.

"I have handled her a lot," he said. "She is kind as a kitten, but she is as sensitive as a lady. You can spoil her by one mistake. If you ever lose your temper, if you ever abuse her, she will be ruined forever. And she is unbroken. I might have had her broken to ride for you, but I didn't want to. I want you to do it. I have taught her to lead, as you see; had to, to get her over here. But here she is, an unbroken colt; yours. You take and you break her. You're only a boy, but if you break this colt right, you'll be a man—a young man, but a man. And I'll tell you how."

Now, out west, as everybody knows, they break in a horse by riding out to him in his wild state, lassoing, throwing, and saddling him; then they let him up, frightened and shocked, with a yelling broncho buster astride of him. The wild beast bucks, the cowboy drives his spurs into him, and off they go, jumping, kicking, rearing, falling, till by the weight of the man, the lash, and the rowels, the horse is broken—in body and spirit. This was not the way I was to break my colt.

"You must break her to ride without her ever knowing it," Colonel Carter said. "You feed and you clean her—you; not the stableman. You lead her out to water and to walk. You put her on a long rope and let her play, calling her to you and gently pulling on the rope. Then you turn her loose in the grass lot there and, when she has romped till tired, call her. If she won't come, leave her. When she wants water or food, she will run to your call, and you will pet and feed and care for her." He went on for half an hour, advising me in great detail how to proceed. I wanted to begin right away. He laughed. He let me lead her around to the stable, water her, and put her in the stable and feed her.

There I saw my pony. My father, sisters, and Colonel Carter saw me stop and look at my pony.

"What'll you do with him?" one of my sisters asked. I was bewildered for a moment. What should I do with the little red horse? I decided at once.

"You can have him," I said to my sisters.

"No," said Colonel Carter, "not yet. You can give your sisters the pony by and by, but you'll need him till you have taught the colt to carry you and a saddle—months; and you must not hurry. You must learn patience, and you will if you give the colt time to learn it, too. Patience and control. You can't control a young horse unless you can control yourself. Can you shoot?" he asked suddenly.

I couldn't. I had a gun and I had used it some, but it was a rifle, and I could not bring down with it such game as there was around Sacramento—birds and hares. Colonel Carter looked at my father, and I caught the look. So did my father. I soon had a shotgun. But at the time Colonel Carter turned to me and said:

"Can't shoot straight, eh? Do you know what that means? That means that you can't control a gun, and that means that you can't control yourself, your eye, your hands, your nerves. You are wriggling now. I tell you that a good shot is always a good man. He may be a 'bad man' too, but he is quiet, strong, steady in speech, gait, and mind. No matter, though. If you break in this colt right, if you teach her her paces, she will teach you to shoot and be quiet."

He went off downtown with my father, and I started away with my colt. I fed, I led, I cleaned her, gently, as if she were made of glass;

she was playful and willing, a delight. When Colonel Carter came home with my father for supper, he questioned me.

"You should not have worked her today," he said. "She has come all the way from Stockton and must be tired. Yes, yes, she would not show fatigue; too fine for that, and too young to be wise. You have got to think for her, consider her as you would your sisters."

Sisters! I thought; I had never considered my sisters. I did not say that, but Colonel Carter laughed and nodded to my sisters. It was just as if he had read my thought. But he went on to draw on my imagination a centaur; the colt as a horse's body—me, a boy, as the head and brains of one united creature. I liked that. I would be that. I and the colt: a centaur.

After Colonel Carter was gone home I went to work on my new horse. The old one, the pony, I used only for business: to go to fires, to see my friends, run errands, and go hunting with my new shotgun. But the game that had all my attention was the breaking in of the colt, the beautiful cream-colored mare, who soon knew me—and my pockets. I carried sugar to reward her when she did right, and she discovered where I carried it; so did the pony, and when I was busy they would push their noses into my pockets, both of which were torn down a good deal of the time. But the colt learned. I taught her to run around a circle, turn and go the other way at a signal. My sisters helped me. I held the long rope and the whip (for signaling), while one of the girls led the colt; it was hard work for them, but they took it in turns. One would lead the colt round and round till I snapped the whip; then she would turn, turning the colt, till the colt did it all by herself. And she was very quick. She shook hands with each of her four feet. She let us run under her, back and forth. She was slow only to carry me. Following Colonel Carter's instructions, I began by laying my arm or a surcingle over her back. If she trembled, I drew it slowly off. When she could abide it, I tried buckling it, tighter and tighter. I laid over her, too, a blanket, folded at first, then open, and, at last, I slipped up on her myself, sat there a second, and as she trembled, slid off. My sisters held her for me, and when I could get up and sit there a moment or two, I tied her at a block, and we, my sisters and I, made a procession of mounting and dismounting. She soon got used to this and would let us slide off over her rump, but it was a long, long time before she would carry me.

That we practiced by leading her along a high curb where I could get on as she walked, ride a few steps, and then, as she felt me and crouched, slip off. She never did learn to carry a girl on her back; my sisters had to lead her while I rode. This was not purposeful. I don't know just how it happened, but I do remember the first time I rode on my colt all the way around the lot and how, when I put one of the girls up, she refused to repeat. She shuddered, shook, and frightened them off.

While we were breaking in the colt a circus came to town. The ring was across the street from our house. Wonderful! I lived in that circus for a week. I saw the show but once, but I marked the horse trainers, and in the mornings when they were not too busy I told them about my colt, showed her to them, and asked them how to train her to do circus tricks. With their hints I taught the colt to stand up on her hind legs, kneel, lie down, and balance on a small box. This last was easier than it looked. I put her first on a low big box and taught her to turn on it; then got a little smaller box upon which she repeated what she did on the big one. By and by we had her so that she would step up on a high box so small that her four feet were almost touching, and there also she would turn.

The circus man gave me one hint that was worth all the other tricks put together. "You catch her doing something of herself that looks good," he said, "and then you keep her at it." It was thus that I taught her to bow to people. The first day I rode her out onto the streets was a proud one for me and for the colt, too, apparently. She did not walk, she danced; perhaps she was excited, nervous; anyhow I liked the way she threw up her head, champed at the bit, and went dancing, prancing down the street. Everybody stopped to watch us, and so, when she began to sober down, I picked her up again with heel and rein, saying, "Here's people, Lady," and she would show off to my delight. By constant repetition I had her so trained that she would single-foot, head down, along a country road till we came to a house or a group of people. Then I'd say, "People, Lady," and up would go her head, and her feet would dance.

But the trick that set the town talking was her bowing to anyone I spoke to. "Lennie Steffens' horse bows to you," people said, and she did. I never told how it was done; by accident. Dogs used to run out at us, and the colt enjoyed it; she kicked at them sometimes with both hind hoofs. I joined her in the game, and being able to look behind more conveniently than she could, I watched the dogs until they were in range, then gave the colt a signal to kick. "Kick, gal," I'd say, and tap her ribs with my heel. We used to get dogs together that way; the colt would kick them over and over and leave them yelping in the road. Well, one day when I met a girl I knew I lifted my hat, probably muttered a "Good day," and I must have touched the colt with my heel. Anyway, she dropped her head and kicked— not much; there was no dog near, so she had responded to my un-expected signal by what looked like a bow. I caught the idea and kept her at it. Whenever I wanted to bow to a girl or anybody else, instead of saying "Good day," I muttered "Kick, gal," spurred her lightly, and—the whole centaur bowed and was covered with glory and conceit.

Yes, conceit. I was full of it, and the colt was quite as bad. One day my chum Hjalmar came into town on his Black Bess, blanketed. She had had a great fistule cut out of her shoulder and had to be kept warm. I expected to see her weak and dull, but no, the good old mare was champing and dancing, like my colt.

"What is it makes her so?" I asked, and Hjalmar said he didn't know, but he thought she was proud of the blanket. A great idea. I had a gaudy horse blanket. I put it on the colt and I could hardly hold her. We rode down the main street together, both horses and both boys, so full of vanity that everybody stopped to smile. We thought they admired, and maybe they did. But some boys on the street gave us another angle. They, too, stopped and looked, and as we passed, one of them said, "Think you're hell, don't you?"

Spoilsport!

We did, as a matter of fact; we thought we were hell. The recogni-tion of it dashed us for a moment; not for long, and the horses paid no heed. We pranced, the black and the yellow, all the way down J Street, up K Street, and agreed that we'd do it again, often. Only, I said, we wouldn't use blankets. If the horses were proud of a blanket, they'd be proud of anything unusually conspicuous. We tried a flower next time. I fixed a big rose on my colts' bridle just under her ear and it was great—she pranced downtown with her head turned, literally, to show off her flower. We had to change the decoration from time to time, put on a ribbon, or a bell, or a feather, but, really, it was not necessary for my horse. Old Black Bess needed an incentive to act up, but all I had to do to my horse was to pick up the reins, touch her with my heel, and say, "People"; she would dance from one side of the street to the other, asking to be admired. As she was. As we were.

I would ride down to my father's store, jump off my prancing colt in the middle of the street, and run up into the shop. The colt, free, would stop short, turn, and follow me right up on the sidewalk, unless I bade her wait. If anyone approached her while I was gone, she would snort, rear, and strike. No stranger could get near her. She became a frightened, frightening animal, and yet when I came into sight she would run to me, put her head down, and as I straddled her neck, she would throw up her head and pitch me into my seat, facing backward, of course. I whirled around right, and off we'd go, the vainest boy and the proudest horse in the State.

"Hey, give me a ride, will you?" some boy would ask.

"Sure," I'd say, and jump down and watch that boy try to catch and mount my colt. He couldn't. Once a cowboy wanted to try her and he caught her; he dodged her forefeet, grabbed the reins, and in one spring was on her back. I never did that again. My colt reared, then bucked, and, as the cowboy kept his seat, she shuddered, sank to the ground, and rolled over. He slipped aside and would have risen with her, but I was alarmed and begged him not to. She got up at my touch and followed me so close that she stepped on my heel and hurt me. The cowboy saw the point.

"If I were you, kid," he said, "I'd never let anybody mount that colt. She's too good."

That, I think, was the only mistake I made in the rearing of Colonel Carter's gift horse. My father differed from me. He discovered another error or sin, and thrashed me for it. My practice was to work hard on a trick, privately, and when it was perfect, let him see it. I would have the horse out in our vacant lot doing it as he came home to supper. One evening, as he approached the house, I was standing, whip in hand, while the colt, quite free, was stepping carefully over the bodies of a lot of girls, all my sisters and all their girl friends. (Grace Gallatin, later Mrs. Thompson-Seton, was among them.) My father did not express the admiration I expected; he was frightened and furious. "Stop that," he called, and he came running around into the lot, took the whip, and lashed me with it. I tried to explain; the girls tried to help me explain.

I had seen in the circus a horse that stepped thus over a row of prostrate clowns. It looked dangerous for the clowns, but the trainer had told me how to do it. You begin with logs, laid out a certain distance apart; the horse walks over them under your lead, and whenever he touches one you rebuke him. By and by he will learn to step with such care that he never trips. Then you substitute clowns. I had no clowns, but I did get logs, and with the girls helping, we taught the colt to step over the obstacles even at a trot. Walking, she touched nothing. All ready thus with the logs, I had my sisters lie down in the grass, and again and again the colt stepped over and among them. None was ever touched. My father would not listen to any of this; he just walloped me, and when he was tired or satisfied and I was in tears, I blubbered a short excuse: "They were only girls." And he whipped me some more.

My father was not given to whipping; he did it very seldom, but he did it hard when he did it at all. My mother was just the opposite. She did not whip me, but she often smacked me, and she had a most annoying habit of thumping me on the head with her thimbled finger. This I resented more than my father's thoroughgoing thrashings, and I can tell why now. I would be playing Napoleon and as I was reviewing my Old Guard, she would crack my skull with that thimble. No doubt I was in the way; it took a lot of furniture and sisters to represent properly a victorious army; and you might think as my mother did that a thimble is a small weapon. But imagine Napoleon at the height of his power, the ruler of the world on parade, getting a sharp rap on his crown from a woman's thimble. No. My father's way was more appropriate. It was hard. "I'll attend to you in the morning," he would say, and I lay awake wondering which of my crimes he had discovered. I know what it is to be sentenced to be shot at sunrise. And it hurt, in the morning, when he was not angry but very fresh and strong. But you see, he walloped me in my own person; he never humiliated Napoleon or my knighthood, as my mother did. And I learned something from his discipline, something useful.

I learned what tyranny is and the pain of being misunderstood and wronged, or, if you please, understood and set right; they are pretty much the same. He and most parents and teachers do not break in their boys as carefully as I broke in my colt. They haven't the time that I had, and they have not some other incentives I had. I saw this that day when I rubbed my sore legs. He had to explain to my indignant mother what had happened. When he had told it his way, I gave my version: how long and cautiously I had been teaching my horse to walk over logs and girls. And having shown how sure I was of myself and the colt, while my mother was boring into his silence with one of her reproachful looks, I said something that hit my father hard.

"I taught the colt that trick, I have taught her all that you see she knows, without whipping her. I have never struck her; not once. Colonel Carter said I mustn't, and I haven't."

And my mother, backing me up, gave him a rap: "There," she said, "I told you so." He walked off, looking like a thimble-rapped Napoleon.

from My Zoo Family

HELEN MARTINI
A Houseful of Lions and Tigers

I was married in 1932 and two years later I looked forward to starting a family. Like every prospective mother, I dreamed and planned—sewing, buying and preparing. The thought of failure never entered my mind. But I was not to have a family of my own, though for years I went from one hospital to another seeking the reason. Fortunately, I found my doctor's advice to find a hobby very easy to follow—I made my home my hobby. I had always been fond of cooking, so with my kitchen as a workshop and cookbooks as weapons, I concentrated on making dishes that my husband, blessed with a good appetite, found it easy to praise.

My husband, Fred, was a jeweler by trade. He was less fortunate than I in that he could never make his work his hobby as I had made mine. Fred's hobby had no connection whatever with his job. On week ends and holidays, all thoughts of glittering stones tucked away, he gave himself up to being the proud owner of twelve canaries, one parrot, a dog of no particular breed and a starling that had fallen out of the nest.

Starlings, when they are raised from babies, make very interesting pets and with patience, of which Fred has plenty, can be taught to come to the hand or perch on your shoulder. This young starling would immediately fly to the bathroom when released from his cage, perch on the edge of the bathtub and beg, by giving several shrill whistles, for us to run the water. Above everything he enjoyed his daily bath. Then having finished, he would fly from the tub to Fred's shoulder and groom each feather with his bill until he was thoroughly dry. Among other little tricks, he learned to open a set of miniature drawers in search of his favorite tidbits.

The parrot was an old female; her gentleness with men was really amazing, but women had to keep their distance. During the weekdays she would allow me to clean her cage and feed her, but during holidays and week ends I dared not even look in her direction. Polly was definitely Fred's pet, and no amount of kindness on my part would change her mind. She was a bird of many accomplishments, and she fascinated me as she did all of our friends.

The truth is that I enjoyed Fred's pets as much as he did.

Many times as we strolled through the Bronx Zoo, which was just a stone's throw from our house, Fred would look longingly at keepers attending to their charges. "I wish I had a job like that," he would say, and I knew in my heart that he meant it, but with the coming of Monday morning he was back among the busy throngs of Maiden Lane.

It is not easy to give up work you are accustomed to for work that is entirely different. Most men with so unconventional a longing would stifle it and live their lives in frustration, but not my husband.

One day, after coming home from a visit to the Zoo, I found myself saying: "If working in the Zoo would bring you happiness, why not try to get a job there? Look at the fun we could have. Every day would be like our week ends."

The more we talked and thought of the idea, the more excited we both became. Before retiring that night, I already felt as if Fred had secured the job, and I knew that he was feeling the same way.

On Monday morning Fred was awake and up long before his usual time. Even the parrot sensed the excitement in the apartment and, not wanting to be left out, gave several loud screams every few minutes which could be heard throughout the house.

Good fortune took Fred's hand that morning because when he arrived at the Park he learned from one of the keepers that several older men were retiring and that maybe a few new men would be hired to replace them. I have often wished that I could have seen Fred's face just then. He told me that he walked to the Administration Building but I am more inclined to believe that he did a little running.

When he returned home after his interview, I won't say that he looked discouraged, but on the other hand he was not his happy self. The next day he went off to his work at the usual time while I hurried up the housework in order to have more time to prepare some of his favorite dishes. No matter what little worry Fred had, the aroma of a freshly baked cake could always make him smile. All that day I prayed for good fortune to look our way. The next day was the same, and the next. Finally, after a week had gone by, I began to be as discouraged as Fred was, thinking that maybe a jeweler just didn't have the qualifications. I never left the house from ten to five— these being the hours the Park was open. What with watching for the mailman and listening for the phone, I was as jumpy as a mouse.

On a Tuesday morning, two weeks after Fred filed his application, the phone rang. Fred was wanted at the Park the next morning. Long after I hung up the receiver those words rang in my ears. How I ever managed to do anything the rest of the day is a mystery. I was tempted to phone Fred the news, but hesitated as I thought of the fun it would be to tell him in person. When he finally did arrive it was unnecessary for me to say even a word. Fred knew immediately, the moment he saw my face. Nevertheless he wanted to hear over and over again every little detail of the conversation.

Fred's departure for the Park the next morning left me a little worried; thoughts of his getting hurt in some way kept creeping into my mind. Several times during the day I actually heard myself praying. Five o'clock finally came, but it did not bring Fred. By five-thirty I thought of strolling over to the entrance of the Park and taking a quick look around. When six o'clock came I determined to do just that. My stroll, however, was more like a run and I was thoroughly winded when I arrived at the entrance to see, a short distance down the road, three men talking earnestly. One was unmistakably Fred. Quickly I returned home so that Fred would never know I had acted so foolishly.

When he rushed into the house a few minutes later, his first words were: "I've got to find out something about snakes."

"Are you going to work in the Reptile House?" I asked.

"I did today," he replied. Later he explained that he was to be a relief keeper, so would work from day to day where he was needed.

Snakes had never appealed to me, not that I disliked them, but rather that I had never heard any good about them.

While Fred ate his dinner, I busied myself searching through our books, marking the pages on snakes. As soon as dinner was over, the books were spread on the kitchen table, and while Fred read I noted down information to be followed up by further reading. It was almost midnight before Fred was ready to close his books and answer my eager questions.

The following day Fred worked on the deer ranges, which sent us back to our books for more knowledge. And so it went. Every day brought the study of some new animals, and every night when Fred returned home I would greet him with "What is new in the Zoo?" Very soon I was so fascinated by this new interest that I was in danger of neglecting my cooking. I began looking for short cuts in preparing dinner so as to give me more time for reading.

Almost before we realized it a year had passed by. Fred had worked in every building in the Park with the exception of the Bird House, and had helped care for every kind of animal. Then one night he came home looking particularly jovial. I knew at a glance that he had good news to report, never dreaming how good the news would be. From now on he was to be in sole charge of the Lion House and Sea Lion exhibit. Many old-time keepers a great deal more experienced than Fred had waited five to ten years before acquiring a building of their own. His interest and hard work were being well rewarded.

Every night now, when Fred came home, our talk was about his big cats and his sea lions. I was always amused to hear him tell about a pair of Bengal tigers. The male was a very old fellow who probably, in his younger days, had suffered from a bad case of rickets. At any rate, his hind legs were very weak and any walking he did was an effort. His back, instead of being straight as a tiger's should be, had a decided curve to it, and the only teeth he possessed were worn down to his gums. But regardless of all his miseries, Prince was perfectly happy with his young mate, Jenny, the finest specimen of Bengal tiger anyone would want to see. Her movements were as light and agile as a leopard's and her temper as quick as a shrew's.

Shortly after Fred took charge of the Lion House, the General Curator suggested that he mate Bruno and Lady, a pair of African lions, to see if this time a litter of cubs could be raised successfully. They had produced a fine litter once before, but due to Lady's highly nervous disposition she had neglected them and they had died. Perhaps a second try would be more successful.

A large wooden box was built to fit her den and the door leading from her den to the cage was left open to assure her from the beginning that she would have a place to go for complete privacy and comfort.

From 100 to 106 days is the gestation period for a lioness. Shortly after two months had passed, Bruno was separated from Lady as an extra precaution against injury. She showed no uneasiness at the separation. As a matter of fact, she began to spend a little more time in her den, which gave Fred hope that all was well and he would soon have the exhibit he so much wanted—a lioness with her cubs.

In the evenings now, after finishing his dinner, Fred would go back to the Lion House to see how Lady was getting on. Returning from a visit one night, he told me that he had heard a faint cry coming from Lady's den. She had not come out during the time he was there so it was difficult to be sure. He could have peeked into her den from an adjoining den but, knowing how nervous she was, he decided to wait until morning.

Sure enough, the next night Fred reported that his suspicions had been right. One cub had been born, but whether Lady was caring for it or not was unknown.

Fred left for work early the following morning. Then at ten o'clock, while I was busy putting the house in order, I heard his familiar ring. I never worried any more when he came home late, knowing that he was probably busy with some little chore he hadn't time for during the day. But his coming home early almost drove me to panic. I was relieved beyond words when I opened the door to see him all in one piece. To my surprise he was carrying an animal traveling case.

"Will you help me, Helen," he almost pleaded.

"Why of course," I responded. "What is it you want me to do, and what on earth have you got there?"

"It's the lion cub," he said, and he laid the case on the kitchen table. "I have already told the General Curator that you would be happy to take care of him."

"But Fred, I have never even seen a lion cub, let alone fed one."

"I know," Fred replied. "Just do for him what you would do for a human baby."

Quickly, Fred opened the lid of the case. The thought that here was the king of beasts never entered my mind as I gazed down at the completely helpless little creature. Without thought of fear I reached down and picked him up. From lack of care, his soft fluffy coat of very light tan hair was wet and stained.

I spread a blanket on the kitchen floor so that I could work without danger of his falling, and with the aid of a sponge and some mild soap and warm water I gave him his first bath. While doing so I named him Douglas MacArthur. When thoroughly groomed, his coat was as fluffy and soft as a lamb's. His hind parts showed small spots of light brown, and down the center of his back was a faint light brown stripe. His eyes were sealed. When he opened his large mouth with the intention of letting out a roar, he went through all the motions a grown lion goes through—only to utter a husky cry.

Next I measured him with my sewing tape. From tip of nose to tip of tail he was twenty-one and one-half inches. Weighing him on the kitchen scale was managed by putting him in one of my roasting pans. He weighed exactly three pounds.

A cardboard carton that groceries had come in was lined with bath towels to make a perfect bed for this strange baby. I placed it away from all drafts, in a corner of the kitchen, and while Fred stood guard I rummaged through a hope chest in the cellar for nursing bottles and blankets that had been stored away years before for a very different kind of infant.

Back in the kitchen once more, I prepared some evaporated milk and tested it on the back of my hand. My kitchen began to look like my neighbor's on her first day home from the hospital, and I was blissfully happy. Then I sat down on the floor by the sleeping box. By this time MacArthur was complaining in no uncertain terms that he was very hungry and would someone please hurry. I gingerly picked him up, not sure just how to hold him. He quickly solved the problem for me, however, by cradling in the crook of my arm. This was wonderful, as it left my other hand free. Now to get him to open his mouth, I rubbed the bottle nipple along his lips, to no avail. He kept his mouth tightly closed. I kept moistening his lips with a little of the milk to see if that would entice him, but he still refused to nurse.

"Supposing you were to put him on the floor, Helen," Fred suggested.

So I placed him on a large blanket spread on the floor. This gave me the advantage of two hands to work with, but trying to keep him still long enough to place the nipple firmly in his mouth was another problem.

Lion cubs cannot stand up on all fours when they are born, but they do flounder about by pulling and pushing with their weak limbs. They seem to be all body and head as they fumble about blindly, depending upon their keen sense of smell to keep them safe at their mother's side. Instinctively, this little fellow felt out of place among humans. There was no smell of safety here. His only desire was to get away.

By now Fred was down on the floor with me, trying to keep MacArthur in one spot while I tried to force the nipple into his mouth. Scrubbing or waxing floors is a tiring task, but this was positively back-breaking. After an hour or so I decided that there must be some other way, so once more I put the cub in his box. Fred, who weighs around 185 pounds, was even more exhausted than I.

"What are you going to do?" Fred asked in a worried voice.

"I don't know," I confessed, "but something besides crawl around on the floor."

As I sat down in Fred's favorite easy chair I had an idea. "If I were to put a pillow in my lap," I suggested, "the cub would have a more comfortable place to lie, and maybe he would relax."

The ruse worked. MacArthur seemed to enjoy the softness of the pillow, for I had no sooner put the nipple in his mouth than he began to suck. In a matter of minutes he had the three ounces consumed. This time when I put him back in his sleeping box, he curled his little legs under him and went to sleep.

The lion cub, when nursing from his mother, pushes alternately with his right and left front pads, thereby regulating the flow of milk. MacArthur instinctively did the same when nursing from the bottle. Lion cubs' claws are exceedingly sharp and unsheathed at birth, and remain so until they are able to stand on all fours.

MacArthur quickly established his new feeding schedule. He woke up exactly three hours from the first feeding, and once more I took my place in Fred's easy chair. He was now convinced that the milk was good and he immediately began pushing with his front paws. His sharp little claws left their mark each time they came in touch with my hand, so that I soon bore many scratches which I looked upon profoundly as badges of success.

The cub demanded a great deal of attention at this early stage; what with keeping him clean and comfortable and feeding him every three hours, I had little time for anything else.

The parrot resented the new arrival from the beginning, and our poor dog refused to come into the house. Fred solved the problem by taking all his pets down to his parents' home. We had often done this before when we had gone on vacation. Like Fred, his parents had a great liking for animals, so our pets were happy.

MacArthur's eyes began to crack open on the eleventh day but were not fully opened until the fifteenth, and even then he could only distinguish light from darkness. He did not have good vision until he was twenty-one days old. That was a great day, when he took his first stumbling steps on all fours. His incisor teeth, which had made their appearance at the same time that his eyes began to open, were now more noticeable.

Each day he became stronger on his legs, and at the age of five weeks, weighing seven pounds, he was able to run and play with anything that came within his reach. He took great delight in holding on to my ankle when I was trying to walk, forcing me to drag him along as I went gingerly about my chores. If I wanted to keep him busy while I did my housework, I had only to take off my shoe and give it to him. It became his favorite play toy. When he was tired playing with it, he would curl up next to it and go to sleep.

I no longer had to pick him up at feeding time; I had merely to sit in any chair and that was his cue to crawl up to my lap. When I put a harness on him he would follow me anywhere as obediently as a dog.

He was such a pleasure to have in the house that I began to hope the officials of the Zoo would forget that a lion cub had been born. But always, when Fred came home, he brought news that everyone was keenly interested in the cub's progress and very anxious to see him.

One night I thought the time had come to lose him, but when I finally pieced together what Fred was telling me, it turned out that the officials merely wanted me to bring the cub to the Park for a radio broadcast.

"Immediately after the broadcast you can bring him back home," Fred repeated, to make sure that I did not misunderstand him.

To prepare him for the broadcast, in which a number of Zoo animals were to participate, I decorated MacArthur's harness with red, white and blue ribbon and several lapel buttons that bore the picture of his famous namesake. At the Park, however, as everyone clamored to pet him, I realized that he needed no decorations at all. His willingness to tumble and play with all comers won everyone's heart as well as the vote of popularity. It also started a discussion about adopting him as a mascot for the famous Bronx Children's Zoo.

The Children's Zoo is a wonderful child's world, a unique zoo within a zoo, where the child rules supreme and adults alone are not admitted. It is a regular Mother Goose storybook come to life with a real, live Pussy-in-the-Well, Ba Ba Black Sheep, and all the rest, even a Noah's Ark, complete in every detail.

The moment the Superintendent of the Children's Zoo saw the lion cub that day, she began pleading to have him for exhibit. And somehow, as I watched her stroke him fondly, the thought of giving him up was not so awful. I had no doubt of his being well cared for, and he certainly would receive a lot of attention. Attention was what the lion cub loved.

The broadcast gave the lion cub so much notoriety that it was impossible to expect to keep him hidden away in an apartment much longer. There were many requests to see him. And then one night when he was two months old Fred came home to tell me that he would have to take the cub with him in the morning. At this time MacArthur was still accustomed to drinking his milk from a bottle in spite of my desperate efforts to get him to lap from a pan, and I worried that he would not accommodate himself to the Zoo routine. But Fred said, "Don't worry. Most of the animals in the Children's Zoo are fed with a bottle. Children love to watch them nursing."

Fred also reminded me that it would be only a matter of a few months when MacArthur would be transferred to the Lion House to be under his personal supervision. "And by that time, Helen," he teased, "he will be ready to gnaw on a large shank bone."

The next morning I tried hard to smile as I watched Fred ride off with MacArthur. In the days that followed I went about my housework secretly hoping that another animal would need caring for and would come to take MacArthur's place. I didn't visit him as often as I wanted to, thinking that perhaps the sight of me would make him discontented with his new home. Instead, I depended upon Fred to give me news of him along with his nightly cheery account of the happenings at the Zoo.

Before the year was up we had proof of the old saying that if you wish hard enough and long enough your wish will come true. Fred came home one day with the surprising news that Jenny, the spry and active mate of poor old Prince, was expecting a litter.

There was no way of predicting what kind of mother Jenny would be, but she had an unpromising record. Ever since her arrival in the Zoo she had been full of surprises. Her first show of temperament had been years ago when she was introduced to a Siberian tiger and was so contrary that for safety's sake they had to be separated. Later they tried to mate her with a magnificent male of her own species, but again she was so savage that she was removed to a cage by herself. Not until she got her first glimpse of poor old Prince did she show any signs of gentleness. What it was that attracted Jenny to

Prince will always be a mystery. It certainly was not his youth, nor his physique. Nevertheless, for Jenny it was love at first sight. On making his acquaintance Jenny spent the entire day grooming him. Prince was rapturous with joy at this attention and Jenny, from that day on, was like a lamb.

Still there was a question whether she would welcome cubs.

Fred made sure, during her months of gestation, that she received plenty of extra nourishment in the form of cod-liver oil, bone meal and milk. In her den, to which she had access, were plenty of straw and a wooden box for extra comfort. Shortly before her confinement, Prince was enticed from the cage he shared with her to one next door. At this he complained bitterly and showed his unhappiness by refusing all forms of food. It took days of gentle coaxing before he finally did relent and eat, and then only in Fred's presence. If Fred walked away while he was eating, Prince would leave the food and go sulk in a corner. In a week or so, however, he was back to normal although he still called piteously for Jenny to return.

Finally, one day a cry from Jenny's den announced that she was giving birth. This is always a big event in the Zoo, and the entire staff rejoiced that at last they were successful in breeding a pair of tigers.

From the cry Fred was convinced that there was only one cub. The crying continued all day, and a second day, while Jenny remained in her den. There was nothing to do but wait. On the third day the crying stopped.

The complete silence was worse than the crying, for it suggested that the cub was dead. It was so nerveracking, in fact, that the General Curator decided the den would have to be examined. The examination showed that one cub had been born and had starved to death—not from lack of care, however. Jenny had done her best but did not have the milk to feed her offspring. Many times in captivity this happens to the finest of animals. Of course, it was an awful disappointment.

First Lady and now Jenny had failed. It seemed fruitless to hope that we would have better success in future with the breeding of lions or tigers. Prince, however, failing to understand the misfortune, continued his pathetic calling for Jenny. Mr. Lee S. Crandall, the

General Curator, a man who cannot stand to have any creature in his domain unhappy, decided that Prince and Jenny deserved a second chance. Who knew? Jenny had shown her willingness to accept motherhood. Perhaps she would be able to nurse the next cubs.

Fred was delighted with this decision, and once more I dared to hope that I would be called upon in the role of foster mother.

About the middle of January, 1944, at the annual meeting of the New York Zoological Society, Mr. Crandall asked me if I would be ready with my nursing bottles in case the tigress needed help with her young. Would I! The event was expected around early February, gestation period for a tigress being from 100 to 105 days.

My apartment window held me like a magnet these days. I knew that the arrival of Mr. Crandall's car would mean he was bringing the cubs. Sure enough, on February 8, at exactly eleven in the morning, Mr. Crandall's car rounded the corner. I was so excited that I forgot to press the buzzer in answer to the ringing of the bell, which meant that Fred, who was carrying the precious bundle, had to stop and fumble for his key.

Arriving in my warm kitchen, Fred handed over to me a tiger cub he had carefully wrapped in his fleece-lined Park coat to protect it from the first bitter cold of the season. It was one of a litter of three but Mr. Crandall had left the others with their mother on the chance that she could nurse them. Fred and Mr. Crandall watched with intense interest as I removed the wrappings and placed the cub in one of several boxes I had provided for the emergency. Each box, measuring twenty inches square, was well lined and bedded with warm woolen receiving blankets. Mr. Crandall was actually beaming as he looked down at the tiny creature and commented on its distinctive markings. His face alone told me what we were doing now was far more important to the New York Zoological Society than the raising of a lion cub. Lions breed freely in captivity, tigers do not. And if they succeed in bearing young the cubs often die shortly afterward or develop rickets, which makes them useless for exhibition purposes. The cub measured twenty inches from the tip of his nose to the tip of his tail. Placing him in the same roasting pan and on the same kitchen scale used for MacArthur, we found him to weigh two pounds, eight ounces. All this information Mr. Crandall carefully jotted down in his notebook for the official Zoo record.

I knew that Mr. Crandall was anxious to see the result of the first feeding so from a large pot on the stove I took a sterilized bottle and filled it with three ounces of evaporated milk formula. Then, picking up the little tiger, I took my position in Fred's easy chair. If I had a moment's panic at the thought of his not accepting the milk, it was quickly dispelled as tiny bubbles of air made their appearance in the nursing bottle.

Mr. Crandall smiled broadly. "Well," he said as he donned his coat, "no point in my staying any longer, everything seems to be under control."

So off he went, accompanied by Fred, to see how Jenny's other two cubs were making out.

All the rest of the day I watched my charge with the anxiousness of a mother with her first-born. Every time he turned I was right there to make sure that he was not smothering. The three-hour feeding schedule kept him happy. He had instinctively snarled at me when I first picked him up. Now, however, after his second feeding, he purred when I touched him. Tiger cubs purr, whereas lion cubs do not, and this little sign of affection pleased me no end.

The next day, while I went joyfully about my house caring for the new arrival, a great deal of excitement and activity was going on in the Zoo. Once more an examination of Jenny's den was to take place, a procedure which called for great caution so as not to excite the mother or give her cause to suspect that her cubs were in danger.

The chains operating all den doors in the Lion House are located in a long passageway in the cellar. The dens, directly above, connect inside and outside cages of the Lion House, while inner or side doors to the dens are accessible from the passageway by means of a twelve-foot ladder.

The first step was to coax Jenny from her den away from her cubs. This called for the services of two men: one upstairs to entice Jenny through the door by means of a large juicy steak, the other downstairs in the passageway to manipulate the chain that would close the door the moment she left the den. Everything went well, and as soon as Jenny was safely locked in the cage the ladder was raised to position and the inner door to the den was opened. It is only on rare occasions that those side doors are used, because if in the shifting operation anything goes wrong and the animal still has access to his den, with the opening of this door to the passageway he can spring down on the men below.

Never in the history of the Park had so many officials gathered at one time in this narrow passageway. Fred, wearing a pair of new cotton gloves well scented with the essence of tiger so that no odor of man would be left, climbed the ladder. The door was opened and Fred lifted out two lovely cubs. They were examined by Dr. Leonard J. Goss, Veterinarian of the New York Zoological Park, who identified them as a male and a female. It was decided to leave the male with the mother for another day, but the female was given to Fred, who wrapped it in heated towels and after weighing it in at the Zoo hospital rushed it over to our warm apartment.

I now had a pair of tigers and my joy was complete. The first one I named Raniganj, after a city in the province of Bengal, India, where the tiger has his home. The second one I named Dacca, after another city in the same province. I placed Dacca alongside Raniganj in a box similar to his, then heated some milk and filled the nursing bottle. The moment I put the nipple to her lips she opened her mouth and sucked vigorously. She was so hungry that she would have taken twice the quantity offered and I had to force her to rest between gulps.

Fred was at the Park now almost continuously, watching Jenny but not daring to inspect her den for fear of alarming her. On the evening of February 10 he noticed that the cub's cry was growing weaker. All night he listened and by nine the next morning the crying had stopped altogether. Once more the officials gathered in chain alley to examine Jenny's den.

This time Fred found an emaciated little creature, cold and almost motionless. Without stopping to have it weighed, he hurried home with it and deposited it on the kitchen floor, saying, "He's in a pretty bad way, Helen."

He was indeed very weak and cold and his little tongue was dry around the edge. For a moment I was panic-stricken, until I thought of my electric heating pad. Adjusting it to a high temperature, I placed it underneath him and when it was quite warm I turned it to low. For two and one-half hours I tried squeezing warm milk into his mouth. But though his body soon began to wriggle weakly, he was far too weak to suck. He had used up all his strength crying for three days.

By the end of six hours I had managed to get a few mouthfuls down him and I was rewarded by a faint but steady cry and the pushing of his front paws, which meant that his interest in food was reviving. Soon after this he began drawing on the nipple. Now I could relax. I named this thin tiger Rajpur, after another city in the province of Bengal.

The tigers were born at a time when New York was experiencing one of its severest winters and a fuel shortage. Very little snow fell, which made the cold even more penetrating. Fred and I occupied then as now the third floor, formerly the attic, of a very old three-family frame house on a private road off Southern Boulevard that seems to have been pushed back and forgotten. Its low ceilings give it the appearance of a doll's house, and in other ways its dimensions are exactly suited to a person of small stature like myself. The kitchen, which is the first room you enter, is large and airy and the bedroom—also large—affords a magnificent view of the Bronx Zoo.

The place is unique and at that time held only one drawback for us. The landlady, an elderly woman who took great pride in her small backyard garden, did not encourage animals in the house and I had no illusions that she would welcome three tiger cubs, however small. That first twenty-four hours before reporters found us and the secret was out were a nightmare.

Unlike the tiger mother, I had to feed each one separately and I tried to do it immediately the baby started crying so that the noise would not reach our landlady's ears. As they drew the milk slowly from the nipple, one feeding usually lasted approximately forty-five minutes—and by that time one or both of the others had often wakened and started whimpering. When that happened, I sang or in some way made a noise to drown them out.

All went well until three o'clock in the morning, when the three decided to cry at once for their bottle. Any attempt to sing at such an hour would only add to the disturbance, so while Fred nervously tried to feed one, I worked on a second, while the third bawled at the top of his lungs. Finally, just as we expected, we heard the landlady moving about downstairs. Knowing that she would soon be on her way up, I decided in desperation to go down and if possible head her off.

"Is there anything the matter?" she asked as we met at the bottom of the stairs.

Not a thing, I assured her. We just had some company staying overnight.

Satisfied, the poor soul went back to her apartment. At least she could finish her night's rest before discovering that her home had been turned into an annex of the Zoo.

The next day, of course, the truth was out. Overnight my usually quiet apartment became the center of national interest. Reporters and photographers came from every paper and syndicate, each hopeful of getting something a little different from what the other fellow had, and all as thrilled as I was myself. Their coming roused the entire neighborhood until everyone along the street was zoo-minded and the talk was of nothing but tigers.

Could they be raised in a New York apartment? And would they grow up to become ferocious and devour us?

The answers would not be revealed immediately. The little eyes were still sealed shut and it would be a week or so before the gums showed signs of teeth. Kindness was the only weapon I would ever use in dealing with my charges, and I believed then as now that when unkindness and distrust are absent ferocity has a slim chance of taking root.

As for the landlady, she was determined to keep her distance until a way of solving the problem presented itself.

After a week of my constant care the tiger babies had doubled their weight to four pounds each. I, on the other hand, had lost an average of one pound a day and was beginning to show the effects of broken sleep. For melting the pounds away I recommended the raising of tigers as more effective than any diet or exercise.

At the age of two weeks their soft blue eyes were fully opened and incisor teeth almost too small to be seen had made their appearance. They were still too weak to walk and too young to take any interest in their surroundings, although their ears, which bore the characteristic white spot of the tiger and had been folded over at birth, would now perk up at any unusual sound.

When the cubs were sixteen days old, Raniganj lost his appetite and showed signs of a digestive disturbance. Finally, to get anything into him at all I had to resort to a medicine dropper. This meant holding him in my arms almost constantly, putting him down in his box only when I had to feed the other two. After four days, the veterinarian who had been visiting the cubs every morning decided to inject Raniganj with feline antiserum in lieu of a blood transfusion. Amazingly, within fifteen minutes Raniganj was crawling around in his box, crying for food. To watch him once more drawing vigorously on his rubber nipple made me feel as if the sun had come out after a week of rain.

His illness left Raniganj thoroughly spoiled, and he now steadfastly refused to be put in his box to sleep. Using a trick that had worked with MacArthur, the lion cub, I made a bed for him from several pieces of my clothing; but though this always contented him temporarily, he still demanded the greater part of my time. He was slowly earning the name of "little crosspatch."

By the end of a month all three cubs were walking and tumbling around their sleeping boxes, and it was obvious that they now needed a larger place in which to exercise. This created another problem, because the weather was still very cold, and I was afraid to put them on the floor. Then a relative, hearing of my plight, donated her baby's outgrown playpen. After Fred had sealed it on all sides with strips of thin plywood to protect the tigers from drafts and also to prevent them from sliding between the rails, it made an ideal place for them to romp.

Day by day they were becoming more and more playful. Rajpur weighed nine pounds now and Raniganj seven pounds, eight ounces, though he had been heavier than Rajpur before his unfortunate sickness. Dacca, the little female, was eight pounds, six ounces, and chock-full of dynamite. Even at this age they were remarkably different in temperament. Raniganj, probably because of the way he had been pampered, was definitely contrary, squalling, biting and scratching whenever any infant wish was balked. Rajpur was fat and indolent, willing to accept whatever came, especially food. Dacca was a regular little female—happy, bright and mischievous and always ready to defend herself against her brothers.

To watch the three of them at play was endlessly fascinating. They would box each others' faces with their fat little oversized paws; then they would start a game of wrestling, rolling on top of each other and trying to keep one another down. Rajpur was always good-natured about having the other two roll on him, but Raniganj would struggle and cry if he got pinned down, and when he wriggled free he would reward his tormentors with a nip and a snarl, which invariably set off another rough-and-tumble. Raniganj enjoyed the game only when he was winning; and often I had to pick him up and put him back in his box, with a rubber ball and one of my shoes. Little Dacca, on the other hand, never tired of teasing her brothers to wake up and play, and she was always the leader in the rough-and-tumble that followed.

When the tiger cubs were thirty-six days old, they began to get curious about what was going on outside their playpen. Most of their time and energy now was spent trying to climb to the top of its plywood walls, and when they succeeded, they would look over at me and cry to be picked up. A few days of this completely wore down my resistance and I gave them the liberty of the kitchen floor. They could walk very well, and even run after a fashion, but they were still clumsy and occasionally would tumble over in their effort to get ahead of me.

From this point on it was useless for me to try to get any work done around the house. As long as I was with them and they could nip my ankles in between their play, all was well. But if I went into the living room and closed the French door behind me, it would cause them great distress. They could see me through the glass panels and would line up and look at me, crying for me to come out. Always, when I went back to the kitchen, they would greet me as if I had been gone a lifetime, purring and all trying to climb into my arms at the same time.

The first time I let them into the living room—they were then forty-four days old—they had a field day, climbing up and down on the couch and chairs, and romping on the rug. Then they began stalking one another from behind the chairs; cautiously they would creep up in back of their prey, ears down, ready for attack. They would even stalk me when my back was turned. If I looked it became no fun, so I always made believe I did not see them. When one of the little tigers gained his objective, which was usually my ankle, he would nuzzle it, purring and rolling over in sheer delight.

By the end of two months their curiosity knew no limit. Dacca in particular seemed never to tire of exploring every nook and corner of my spacious kitchen. A tiger is very keen even at this early stage. From the day I first let them into the kitchen, cupboards and doors had been the chief targets of their curiosity. I had only to open the pantry door and they were right there, trying to push their way in. Now they would all three watch me closely when I went to a closet or cupboard, and if I failed to close the door securely, one of them surely would hook it open with his sharp little claws.

Dacca, the female, was the most active of the three, sleeping only when she was completely exhausted, while Rajpur, who now weighed twelve pounds, two ounces, would sleep whenever the opportunity afforded. Raniganj too had gained steadily, and weighed eleven pounds, four ounces, but he still complained about everything. It was perfectly all right for him to bite on Dacca's tail, but if Dacca or Rajpur bit or played with his tail he would snarl at them and run to me for protection. Or if Dacca and Rajpur were playing with a ball, he would watch his chance to take it away from them and bring it to me. My mistake, of course, was in always letting him have it while I got something more attractive for Rajpur and Dacca.

The cubs were clever enough at this stage (two and one-half months) to realize that the ringing of the bell meant the opening of the kitchen door, and they would line up ready to pounce in play at the visitor. Soon they began to recognize people and to form definite likes and dislikes. If you showed any fear of them they would stand at a safe distance and eye you cautiously. Later, given the opportunity, they would get behind you and nip you for being no fun. There was one photographer in particular they were very fond of, who never seemed to tire of their antics. How he ever managed to get a picture of them I don't know, for while two would attract his attention from the front, the other would circle around in back of him. When it came to mischief, it seemed to me they worked in perfect harmony.

I learned, for instance, not to run after a cub who stole a pot cover from the pantry, as Rajpur did one day, and leave the other two unwatched. I was expecting company that day and was about at my wit's end trying to keep the house tidy. After chasing Rajpur through the other rooms to salvage the cover, I returned to the kitchen to find that Raniganj and Dacca had everything in the pantry out on the floor, including potatoes, clothespins, pie plates and flour sifter. Another day, as I was washing some clothes in the bathroom tub, Raniganj got his head caught behind a radiator pipe in another room. While I was busy rescuing him, Dacca and Rajpur got into the bathroom—and when I went back they were having the time of their lives boxing one another in the tub of wash. It was then, incidentally, that I realized how fond tigers are of water.

The cubs soon learned that the living room couch was much more comfortable than their wooden sleeping boxes, and they would curl up together with a look of bliss that was as effective as a sign saying "Please do not disturb." The couch was their prize possession. Climbing up its sides made their legs and bodies strong, and tumbling off taught them caution. Small scatter rugs that I had selected carefully and always taken much pride in were now at their disposal as trains. They enjoyed nothing more than to have me pull them through the rooms while all three hung on for dear life. Later they would play tug-of-war for possession of a rug. One day while I was doing this for the benefit of several newsreelmen, Fred came home for lunch. The sound of his hearty laughter as he watched me run back and forth through the rooms with the cameraman close at my heels anxious not to miss a detail of this hilarious scene is something I shall always remember.

More than once the cubs' antics caused me embarrassment, such as the time a very well-dressed gentleman, unfamiliar with the ways of tigers, came to visit, laying his expensive hat on a chair. I failed to notice it, but quick little Dacca did not. It was not until the man was about to leave that I discovered the crumpled mess that had once been a well-made hat. He assured me that it did not matter, but his feeble smile said clearly that it did. Then there was the time a lady draped a mink coat over the living room couch. Thinking, I suppose, that it was just another luxury designed for them, the cubs pounced on it, fighting tooth and nail for its possession. Before I was able to rescue it, small pieces of fur were flying through the air that had not come from the tigers' backs.

It was April now, but the weather was still cold and the three tigers were still nursing from a bottle. All my attempts to get them to lap milk or to take a little meat had failed. I had first tried to wean them from the bottle when they were six weeks old, but without success. The question of how they should take their milk, however, was as nothing compared to the question of when they should begin to eat meat. A mother tiger solves the problem readily enough by dragging in a choice bit of entrails at just the right moment. But what tells the mother tiger when that moment is? One day, along about the middle of April, I gave each cub a tiny ball of raw chopped meat. They liked it very much, but all became violently sick; poor Rajpur went into a coma, from which I thought he would never emerge. All night I watched him, and all night he lay still. His usual affectionate purr was absent. Several times, as I gently turned him over, I became panic-stricken thinking that perhaps he was already dead. Raniganj and Dacca continued throughout the night to vomit and cry pitifully.

As the night wore on, I made a solemn promise to myself that if they lived through this siege never would I even show them meat again. It was ten o'clock the next morning, and Fred had already left for the Park, as heartbroken as I, when I saw Rajpur's little head sticking out over the top of his sleeping box. He had managed to crawl up the side and hold on to the edge with his paws, and was looking at me and purring to be picked up. Almost afraid to believe my eyes, I ran over to him and lifted him out. He was very weak, however, and when I once more put him back in his box he made no effort to move. Knowing how anxious Fred and the Park officials would be, I picked up my coat and ran down the block to the nearest phone. Not until I saw the storekeeper's puzzled expression did I realize that in spite of the bitter cold I had neglected to put my coat on and was still carrying it on my arm.

After this experience, I allowed the cubs to content themselves with the nursing bottle and the word "meat" was not mentioned in my house for many a day.

I now had three thoroughly spoiled young tigers to cope with, for thinking remorsefully always of their narrow squeak, I let them get away with all kinds of deviltry. Never in my life will I forget the expression on Rajpur's face the day that he discovered he had committed no crime in pulling open a cupboard door. Knowing that there was nothing there to hurt him, I sat quietly and allowed him to investigate the wonder. First he reached in with his fat little paw and touched a pot; then he looked over at me and purred, to see if I were going to scold him. Next he cautiously moved in a little farther and poked a little harder, looking back at me as he did so. Suddenly realizing that I was making no attempt to pull him back or scold him, he began pulling the saucepans out, one by one. Dacca and Raniganj, who had been busy in the next room boxing and wrestling, discovered that their brother had struck gold. Quicker than one can say "Jack Robinson," Dacca had hurtled over him and was in the far corner of the cupboard, pushing out the things that Rajpur had overlooked. Raniganj, after careful scrutiny, decided to take possession of everything that came tumbling out. Their antics that day left me weary from laughing.

Finally, when they were about three months old and better able to digest meat, I gave each one a small rib bone with a very tiny sliver of meat attached to it. To my astonishment the cubs licked and nibbled until the bones were like polished ivory. And there were no ill effects whatever. After that, Fred brought three little bones home from the Park every day, and gradually I left more and more meat on them. Eventually, I once more introduced a small amount of chopped meat, mixed with cod-liver oil, dicalcium and bone meal as a precaution against rickets. (I'd been giving them ten drops of Vi-Penta ever since they were a month old.) On this diet they throve, and I was confident at last that I was on the right road.

from Ring of Bright Water

GAVIN MAXWELL

Mijbil

[*While on a trip to the Middle East, Gavin Maxwell became interested in otters and acquired a young one, intending to raise it as a pet. Unfortunately the animal Chahala died shortly afterward, but Maxwell had fallen in love with otters and immediately began to search for another.*]

The night that Chahala died we reached Al Azair, Ezra's tomb, on the Tigris. From there Wilfred Thesiger and I were both going to Basra to collect and answer our mail from Europe before setting off together again. At the Consulate-General at Basra we found that Wilfred's mail had arrived but that mine had not.

'I cabled to England, and when, three days later, nothing had happened, I tried to telephone. The call had to be booked twenty-four hours in advance, and could be arranged only for a single hour in the day, an hour during which, owing to the difference in time, no one in London was likely to be available. On the first day the line was out of order; on the second the exchange was closed for a religious holiday. On the third day there was another breakdown. I arranged to join Thesiger at Abd el Nebi's *mudhif* in a week's time, and he left.

'Two days before the date of our rendezvous I returned to the Consulate-General late in the afternoon, after several hours' absence, to find that my mail had arrived. I carried it to my bedroom to read, and there squatting on the floor were two Marsh Arabs; beside them lay a sack that squirmed from time to time.

'They handed me a note from Thesiger. "Here is your otter, a male and weaned. I feel you may want to take it to London—it would be a handful in the *tarada*. It is the one I originally heard of, but the sheikhs were after it, so they said it was dead. Give Ajram a letter to me saying it has arrived safely—he has taken Kathia's place. . . ." '

With the opening of that sack began a phase of my life that in the essential sense has not yet ended, and may, for all I know, not end before I do. It is, in effect, a thraldom to otters, an otter fixation, that I have since found to be shared by most other people who have ever owned one.

The creature that emerged, not greatly disconcerted, from this sack on to the spacious tiled floor of the Consulate bedroom did not at that moment resemble anything so much as a very small medievally-conceived dragon. From the head to the tip of the tail he was coated with symmetrical pointed scales of mud armour, between whose tips was visible a soft velvet fur like that of a chocolate-brown mole. He shook himself, and I half expected this aggressive camouflage to disintegrate into a cloud of dust, but it remained unaffected by his manoeuvre, and in fact it was not for another month that I contrived to remove the last of it and see him, as it were, in his true colours.

Yet even on that first day I recognized that he was an otter of a species that I had never seen in the flesh, resembling only a curious otter skin that I had bought from the Arabs in one of the marsh villages. Mijbil, as I called the new otter, after a sheikh with whom we had recently been staying and whose name had intrigued me with a conjured picture of a platypus-like creature, was, in fact, of a race previously unknown to science, and was at length christened by zoologists, from examination of the skin and of himself, *Lutrogale perspicillata maxwelli,* or Maxwell's otter. This circumstance, perhaps, influenced on my side the intensity of the emotional relationship between us, for I became, during a year of his constant and violently affectionate companionship, fonder of him than of almost any human being, and to write of him in the past tense makes me feel as desolate as one who has lost an only child. For a year and five days he was about my bed and my bath spying out all my ways, and though I now have another otter no whit less friendly and fascinating, there will never be another Mijbil.

For the first twenty-four hours Mijbil was neither hostile nor friendly; he was simply aloof and indifferent, choosing to sleep on the floor as far from my bed as possible, and to accept food and water as though they were things that had appeared before him without human assistance. The food presented a problem, for it did not immediately occur to me that the Marsh Arabs had almost certainly fed him on rice scraps only supplemented by such portions of fish as are inedible to humans. The Consul-General sent out a servant to buy fish, but this servant's return coincided with a visit from Robert Angorly, a British-educated Christian Iraqi who was the Crown Prince's game warden and entertained a passionate interest in natural history. Angorly told me that none of the fishes that had been bought was safe for an animal, for they had been poisoned with digitalis, which, though harmless to a human in this quantity, he felt certain would be dangerous to a young otter. He offered to obtain me a daily supply of fish that had been taken with nets, and thereafter he brought every day half a dozen or so small reddish fish from the Tigris. These Mijbil consumed with gusto, holding them upright between his forepaws, tail end uppermost, and eating them like a stick of Edinburgh rock, always with five crunches of the left-hand side of the jaw alternating with five crunches on the right.

It was fortunate that I had recently met Angorly, for otherwise Mijbil might at once have gone the way of Chahala and for the same reason. Angorly had called at the Consulate-General during the time that I had been waiting for my mail from Europe, and had invited me to a day's duck shooting on the Crown Prince's fabulous marshes, an experience that nobody can ever have again, for now the hated Crown Prince is as dead as only a mob gone berserk could make him, and of my friend Angorly, whom I cannot believe ever to have taken much interest in anything political, there has been no word since the revolution.

Of the duck shoot my most enduring memory is of a great cloud of pink flamingos flying at head height to my butt, and of the rank upon rank of crimson and white wings rustling low over my head. Duck there were in thousands, but if the Crown Prince ever killed many from that butt he was a better man than I. It stood quite alone in a great waste of unbroken water that stretched away for a mile or more in all directions; its sides were no more than waist high, and in the centre of it was a wooden seat, at the right of which pretention stood an object like a bird-table, whose tray was designed to hold eight unopened boxes of twenty-five cartridges. It held them, and the broad scarlet patch that they formed flared a warning to every duck that came within two hundred yards. I was the cynosure of every bird's eye in the place. The floor of the butt was six inches under water, so the cartridges remained where they were, and the duck did not. After some five hours I was rescued from my indignity, and Angorly and I between us took home some hundred and fifty duck, of which I had contributed a meagre third. But the flamingoes were magnificent.

The otter and I enjoyed the Consul-General's long-suffering hospitality for a fortnight. The second night Mijbil came on to my bed in the small hours and remained asleep in the crook of my knees until the servant brought tea in the morning, and during that day he began to lose his apathy and take a keen, much too keen, interest in his surroundings. I fashioned a collar, or rather a body-belt, for him, and took him on a lead to the bathroom, where for half an hour he went wild with joy in the water, plunging and rolling in it, shooting up and down the length of the bath underwater, and making enough slosh and splash for a hippo. This, I was to learn, is a characteristic of otters; every drop of water must be, so to speak, extended and spread about the place; a bowl must at once be overturned, or, if it will not overturn, be sat in and sploshed in until it overflows. Water must be kept on the move and made to do things; when static it is as wasted and provoking as a buried talent.

It was only two days later that he escaped from my bedroom as

I entered it, and I turned to see his tail disappearing round the bend of the corridor that led to the bathroom. By the time I had caught up with him he was up on the end of the bath and fumbling at the chromium taps with his paws. I watched, amazed by this early exhibition of an intelligence I had not yet guessed; in less than a minute he had turned the tap far enough to produce a dribble of water, and, after a moment or two of distraction at his success, achieved the full flow. (He had, in fact, been fortunate to turn the tap the right way; on subsequent occasions he would as often as not try with great violence to screw it up still tighter, chittering with irritation and disappointment at its failure to co-operate.)

The Consulate had a big walled garden in which I exercised him, and, within it, a high-netted tennis court. In this enclosure I established after a few days that he would follow me without a lead and come to me when I called his name. By the end of a week he had accepted me in a relationship of dependence, and with this security established he began to display the principal otter characteristic of perpetual play. Very few species of animal habitually play after they are adult; they are concerned with eating, sleeping, or procreating, or with the means to one or other of these ends. But otters are one of the few exceptions to this rule; right through their lives they spend much of their time in play that does not even require a partner. In the wild state they will play alone for hours with any convenient floating object in the water, pulling it down to let it bob up again, or throwing it with a jerk of the head so that it lands with a splash and becomes a quarry to be pursued. No doubt in their holts they lie on their backs and play, too, as my otters have, with small objects that they can roll between their paws and pass from palm to palm, for at Camusfeàrna all the sea holts contain a profusion of small shells and round stones that can only have been carried in for toys.

Mij would spend hours shuffling a rubber ball round the room like a four-footed soccer player using all four feet to dribble the ball, and he could also throw it, with a powerful flick of the neck, to a surprising height and distance. These games he would play either by himself or with me, but the really steady play of an otter, the time-filling play born of a sense of well-being and a full stomach, seems to me to be when the otter lies on its back and juggles with small objects between its paws. This they do with an extraordinarily concentrated absorption and dexterity, as though a conjuror were trying to perfect some trick, as though in this play there were some goal that the human observer could not guess. Later, marbles became Mij's favourite toys for this pastime—for pastime it is, without any anthropomorphizing—and he would lie on his back rolling two or more of them up and down his wide, flat belly without ever dropping one to the floor, or, with forepaws upstretched, rolling them between his palms for minutes on end.

Even during that first fortnight in Basra I learnt a lot of Mij's language, a language largely shared, I have discovered, by many other races of otter, though with curious variations in usage. The sounds are widely different in range. The simplest is the call note, which has been much the same in all the otters I have come across; it is a short, anxious, penetrating, though not loud, mixture between a whistle and a chirp. There is also a query, used at closer quarters; Mij would enter a room, for instance, and ask whether there was anyone in it by the word 'Ha!', uttered in a loud, harsh whisper. If he saw preparations being made to take him out or to the bath, he would stand at the door making a musical bubbling sound interspersed with chirps; but it was the chirp, in all its permutations and combinations of high and low, from the single querulous note to a continuous flow of chitter, that was Mij's main means of vocal communication. He had one other note unlike any of these, a high, snarling caterwaul, a sort of screaming wail, that meant unequivocally that he was very angry, and if provoked further would bite. He bit, in anger as opposed to nips in excitable play, four times during the year that I had him. Each of these occasions was memorable in the highest degree, though I was only once at the receiving end.

An otter's jaws are, of course, enormously powerful—indeed the whole animal is of strength almost unbelievable in a creature of its size—and those jaws are equipped with teeth to crunch into instant pulp fish heads that seem as hard as stone. Like a puppy that nibbles and gnaws one's hands because he has so few other outlets for his feelings, otters seem to find the use of their mouths the most natural outlet for expression; knowing as I do their enormous crushing power I can appreciate what efforts my otters have made to be gentle in play, but their playful nips are gauged, perhaps, to the sensitivity of an otter's, rather than a human, skin. Mij used to look hurt and surprised when scolded for what must have seemed to him the most meticulous gentleness, and though after a time he learned to be as soft mouthed as a sucking dove with me he remained all his life somewhat over-excitably good-humoured and hail-fellow-well-bit with strangers.

The days passed peacefully at Basra, but I dreaded dismally the unpostponable prospect of transporting Mij to England, and to his ultimate destination, Camusfeàrna. B.O.A.C. would not fly livestock at all, and there was then no other line to London. Finally I booked a Trans-World flight to Paris, with a doubtful Air France booking on the same evening to London. Trans-World insisted that Mij should be packed into a box of not more than eighteen inches square, and that this box must be personal luggage, to be carried on the floor at my feet.

Mij's body was at that time perhaps a little over a foot long and his tail another foot; the designing of this box employed many anxious hours for myself and the ever-helpful Robert Angorly, and finally he had the container constructed by craftsmen of his acquaintance. The box was delivered on the afternoon before my departure on a 9.15 p.m. flight. It was zinc-lined, and divided into two compartments, one for sleeping and one for the relief of nature, and it appeared to my inexperienced eye as nearly ideal as could be contrived.

Dinner was at eight, and I thought that it would be as well to put Mij into the box an hour before we left, so that he would become accustomed to it before the jolting of the journey began to upset him. I manoeuvred him into it, not without difficulty, and he seemed peaceful when I left him in the dark for a hurried meal.

But when I returned, with only barely time for the Consulate car to reach the airport for the flight, I was confronted with an appalling spectacle. There was complete silence from inside the box, but from its airholes and the chinks around the hinged lid, blood had trickled and dried on the white wood. I whipped off the padlock and tore open the lid, and Mij, exhausted and blood-spattered, whimpered and tried to climb up my leg. He had torn the zinc lining to shreds, scratching his mouth, his nose and his paws, and had left it jutting in spiky ribbons all around the walls and the floor of the box. When I had removed the last of it, so that there were no cutting edges left, it was just ten minutes until the time of the flight, and the airport was five miles distant. It was hard to bring myself to put the miserable Mij back into that box, that now represented to him a torture chamber, but I forced myself to do it, slamming the lid down on my fingers as I closed it before he could make his escape. Then began a journey the like of which I hope I shall never know again.

I sat in the back of the car with the box beside me as the Arab driver tore through the streets of Basra like a ricochetting bullet. Donkeys reared, bicycles swerved wildly, out in the suburbs goats stampeded and poultry found unguessed powers of flight. Mij cried unceasingly in the box, and both of us were hurled to and fro and up and down like drinks in a cocktail shaker. Exactly as we drew to a screeching stop before the airport entrance I heard a splintering sound from the box beside me, and saw Mij's nose force up the lid. He had summoned all the strength in his small body and torn one of the hinges clean out of the wood.

The aircraft was waiting to take off; as I was rushed through the customs by infuriated officials I was trying all the time to hold down the lid of the box with one hand, and with the other, using a screwdriver purloined from the driver, to force back the screws into the splintered wood. But I knew that it could be no more than a temporary measure at best, and my imagination boggled at the thought of the next twenty-four hours.

It was perhaps my only stroke of fortune that the seat booked for me was at the extreme front of the aircraft, so that I had a bulkhead before me instead of another seat. The other passengers, a remarkable cross-section of the orient and occident, stared curiously as the dishevelled late arrival struggled up the gangway with a horrifyingly vocal Charles Addams-like box, and knowing for just what a short time it could remain closed I was on tenterhooks to see what manner of passenger would be my immediate neighbour. I had a moment of real dismay when I saw her to be an elegantly dressed and *soignée* American woman in early middle age. Such a one, I thought, would have little sympathy or tolerance for the draggled and dirty otter cub that would so soon and so inevitably be in her midst. For the moment the lid held, and as I sat down and fastened my safety belt there seemed to be a temporary silence from within.

The port engines roared, and then the starboard and the aircraft trembled and teetered against the tug of her propellers, and then we were taxiing out to take off, and I reflected that whatever was to happen now there could be no escape from it, for the next stop was Cairo. Ten minutes later we were flying westwards over the great marshes that had been Mij's home, and peering downward into the dark I could see the glint of their waters beneath the moon.

I had brought a brief-case full of old newspapers and a parcel of fish, and with these scant resources I prepared myself to withstand a siege. I arranged newspapers to cover all the floor around my feet, rang for the air hostess, and asked her to keep the fish in a cool place. I have retained the most profound admiration for that air hostess, and in subsequent sieges and skirmishes with otters in public places I have found my thoughts turning towards her as a man's mind turns to water in desert wastes. She was the very queen of her kind. I took her into my confidence; the events of the last half hour together with the prospect of the next twenty-four had shaken my equilibrium a little, and I daresay I was not too coherent, but she took it all in her graceful sheer nylon stride, and she received the ill-wrapped fish into her shapely hands as though I were travelling royalty depositing a jewel case with her for safe keeping. Then she turned and spoke with her country-woman on my left. Would I not prefer, she then enquired, to have my pet on my knee? The animal would surely feel happier there, and my neighbour had no objection. I could have kissed her hand in the depth of my gratitude. But, not knowing otters, I was quite unprepared for what followed.

I unlocked the padlock and opened the lid, and Mij was out like a flash. He dodged my fumbling hands with an eel-like wriggle and disappeared at high speed down the fuselage of the aircraft. As I tried to get into the gangway I could follow his progress among the passengers by a wave of disturbance amongst them not unlike that caused by the passage of a stoat through a hen run. There were squawks and shrieks and a flapping of travelling-coats, and half-way down the fuselage a woman stood up on her seat screaming out, 'A rat! A rat!' Then the air hostess reached her, and within a matter of seconds she was seated again and smiling benignly. That goddess, I believe, could have controlled a panic-stricken crowd single-handed.

By now I was in the gangway myself, and, catching sight of Mij's tail disappearing beneath the legs of a portly white-turbaned Indian, I tried a flying tackle, landing flat on my face. I missed Mij's tail, but found myself grasping the sandalled foot of the Indian's female companion; furthermore my face was inexplicably covered in curry. I staggered up babbling inarticulate apology, and the Indian gave me a long silent stare, so utterly expressionless that even in my hypersensitive mood I could deduce from it no meaning whatsoever. I was, however, glad to observe that something, possibly the curry, had won over the bulk of my fellow passengers, and that they were regarding me now as a harmless clown rather than as a dangerous lunatic. The air hostess stepped into the breach once more.

'Perhaps,' she said with the most charming smile, 'it would be better if you resumed your seat, and I will find the animal and bring it to you.' She would probably have said the same had Mij been an escaped rogue elephant. I explained that Mij, being lost and frightened, might bite a stranger, but she did not think so. I returned to my seat.

I heard the ripple of flight and pursuit passing up and down the body of the aircraft behind me, but I could see little. I was craning my neck back over the seat trying to follow the hunt when suddenly I heard from my feet a distressed chitter of recognition and welcome, and Mij bounded on to my knee and began to nuzzle my face and neck. In all the strange world of the aircraft I was the only familiar thing to be found, and in that first spontaneous return was sown the seed of the absolute trust that he accorded me for the rest of his life.

For the next hour or two he slept in my lap, descending from time to time for copious evacuations upon the newspaper at my feet, and each time I had, with an unrehearsed legerdemain, to spirit this out of sight and replace it with fresh newspaper. Whenever he appeared restless I rang for fish and water, for I had a feeling that, like the storyteller of the Arabian Nights, if I failed to keep him entertained retribution would fall upon me.

Otters are extremely bad at doing nothing. That is to say that they cannot, as a dog does, lie still and awake; they are either asleep or entirely absorbed in play or other activity. If there is no acceptable toy, or if they are in a mood of frustration, they will, apparently with the utmost good humour, set about laying the land waste. There is, I am convinced, something positively provoking to an otter about order and tidiness in any form, and the greater the state of confusion that they can create about them the more contented they feel. A room is not properly habitable to them until they have turned everything upside down; cushions must be thrown to the floor from sofas and armchairs, books pulled out of bookcases, wastepaper baskets overturned and the rubbish spread as widely as possible, drawers opened and contents shovelled out and scattered. The appearance of such a room where an otter has been given free rein resembles nothing so much as the aftermath of a burglar's hurried search for some minute and valuable object that he has believed to be hidden. I had never really appreciated the meaning of the word ransacked until I saw what an otter could do in this way.

This aspect of an otter's behaviour is certainly due in part to an intense inquisitiveness that belongs traditionally to a mongoose, but which would put any mongoose to shame. An otter must find out everything and have a hand in everything; but most of all he must know what lies inside any man-made container or beyond any man-made obstruction. This, combined with an uncanny mechanical sense of how to get things open—a sense, indeed of statics and dynamics in general—makes it much safer to remove valuables altogether rather than to challenge the otter's ingenuity by inventive obstructions. But in those days I had all this to learn.

We had been flying for perhaps five hours, and must, I thought, be nearing Cairo, when one of these moods descended upon Mijbil. It opened comparatively innocuously, with an assault upon the newspapers spread carefully round my feet, and in a minute or two the place looked like a street upon which royalty has been given a ticker-tape welcome. Then he turned his attentions to the box, where his sleeping compartment was filled with fine wood-shavings. First he put his head and shoulders in and began to throw these out backwards at enormous speed; then he got in bodily and lay on his back, using all four feet in a pedalling motion to hoist out the remainder. I was doing my best to cope with the litter, but it was like a ship's pumps working against a leak too great for them, and I was hopelessly behind in the race when he turned his attention to my neighbour's canvas Trans-World travel bag on the floor beside him. The zipper gave him pause for no more than seconds; by chance, in all likelihood, he yanked it back and was in head first, throwing out magazines, handkerchiefs, gloves, bottles of pills, tins of ear-plugs and all the personal paraphernalia of long-distance air travel. By the grace of God my neighbour was sleeping profoundly; I managed, unobserved, to haul

Mij out by the tail and cram the things back somehow. I hoped that she might leave the aircraft at Cairo, before the outrage was discovered, and to my infinite relief she did so. I was still grappling with Mij when the instruction lights came on as we circled the city, and then we were down on the tarmac with forty minutes to wait.

I think it was at Cairo that I realized what a complex and—to me at that time—unpredictable creature I had acquired. I left the aircraft last, and during all the time that we were grounded he was no more trouble than a well-behaved Pekinese dog. I put the lead on him and exercised him round the edge of the airfield; there were jet air-craft landing and taking off with an appalling din all around us, but he gave no sign of noticing them at all. He trotted along at my side, stopping as a dog does to investigate small smells in the grass, and when I went into the refreshment room for a drink he sat down at my feet as if this were the only life to which he was accustomed.

On our way back to the aircraft an Egyptian official hazarded the first of the many guesses as to his identity that I was to hear during the subsequent months. 'What you got there?' he asked. 'An ermine?'

My troubles really began at Paris, an interminable time later. Mij had slept from time to time, but I had not closed an eye, and it was by now more than thirty-six hours since I had even dozed. I had to change airports, and, since I knew that Mij could slip his body strap with the least struggle, there was no alternative to putting him back into his box. In its present form, however, the box was useless, for one hinge was dangling unattached from the lid.

Half an hour out from Paris I rang for the last time for fish and water, and explained my predicament to the air hostess. She went for-ward to the crew's quarters, and returned after a few minutes saying that one of the crew would come and nail down the box and rope it for me. She warned me at the same time that Air France's regulations differed from those of Trans-World, and that from Paris onward the box would have to travel freight and not in the passenger portion of the aircraft.

Mij was sleeping on his back inside my jacket, and I had to steel myself to betray his trust, to force him back into that hateful prison and listen to his pathetic cries as he was nailed up in what had become to me suddenly reminiscent of a coffin. There is a little-understood factor that is responsible for the deaths of many wild animals in shipment; it is generally known as 'travel shock', and the exact causes have yet to be determined. Personally I do not question that it is closely akin to the 'voluntary dying' of which Africans have long been reputed to be capable; life has become no longer tolerable, and the animal *chooses*, quite unconsciously no doubt, to die. It was travel shock that I was afraid might kill Mijbil inside that box, which to him represented a circumstance more terrible than any he had experienced, and I would be unable even to give him the reassuring smell of my hand through the breathing-holes.

We disembarked in torrential rain that formed puddles and lakes all over the tarmac and had reduced my thin, semi-tropical suit to a sodden pulp before even I had entered the bus that was to take me and the three other London-bound passengers across Paris to Orly Airport. I clung to the unwieldy box all this time, in the hope of reducing Mij's unavoidable period of despair after I became separated from it; together with the personal impedimenta that I could not well lose sight of it rendered movement almost impossible, and I felt near to voluntary death myself.

After an hour's wait at Orly, during which Mij's cries had given place to a terrifying silence, I and my three companions were hustled into an aircraft. Mij was wrested from me and disappeared into the darkness on a luggage transporter.

When we arrived at Amsterdam instead of London the company was profusely apologetic. There was no flight to London for a further fifty-five minutes.

I had lost sight of Mij's box altogether and no one seemed to have a very clear idea of what had happened to any of the luggage belonging to the four London-bound passengers. A helpful official suggested that it might still be in Paris, as it must be clearly labelled London and not Amsterdam.

I went to the Air France office and let the tattered shreds of my self-control fly to the winds. In my soaking and dishevelled condition I cannot have cut a very impressive figure, but my anger soared above these handicaps like an eagle on the wind. I said that I was transporting to London a live animal worth many thousands of pounds, that unless it was traced immediately it would die, and I would sue the Company and broadcast their inefficiency throughout the world. The official was under crossfire, for at my elbow an American business man was also threatening legal action. When the shindy was at its height another official arrived and said calmly that our luggage was now aboard a B.E.A. plane due for take-off in seven minutes, and would we kindly take our seats in the bus.

We deflated slowly. Muttering, 'I guess I'm going to cast my personal eyes on that baggage before I get air-borne again. They can't make a displaced person out of me', my American companion spoke for all of us waifs. So we cast our personal eyes into the freight compartment, and there was Mij's box, quite silent in a corner.

It was the small hours of the morning when we reached London Airport. I had cabled London from Amsterdam, and there was a hired car to meet me, but there was one more contretemps before I reached the haven of my flat. In all my travels I have never, but for that once, been required by the British Customs to open a single bag or to do more than state that I carried no goods liable to duty. It was, of course, my fault; the extreme fatigue and nervous tension of the journey had destroyed my diplomacy. I was, for whichever reason, so tired that I could hardly stand, and to the proffered *pro forma* and the question, 'Have you read this?' I replied, with extreme testiness and foolishness, 'Yes—hundreds of times.'

'And you have nothing to declare?'

'Nothing.'

'How long have you been out of this country?'

'About three months.'

'And during that time you have acquired nothing?'

'Nothing but what is on the list I have given you.' (This comprised my few purchases in Iraq; two uncured otter skins, a Marsh Arab's dagger, three cushion covers woven by the Beni Lam tribe, and one live otter.)

He seemed momentarily at a loss, but he had retired only *pour mieux sauter*. The attack, when it came, was utterly unexpected.

'Where did you get that watch?'

I could have kicked myself. Two days before, when playing water games with Mijbil in the bath, I had forgotten to screw in the winding handle of my Rolex Oyster, and it had, not unnaturally, stopped. I had gone into Basra and bought, for twelve shillings and sixpence, an outrageous time-piece that made a noise like castanets. It had stopped twice, unprovoked, during the journey.

I explained, but I had already lost face. I produced my own watch from a pocket, and added that I should be grateful if he would confiscate the replacement forthwith.

'It is not a question of confiscation,' he said, 'there is a fine for failing to declare dutiable goods. And now may I please examine that Rolex?'

It took another quarter of an hour to persuade him that the Rolex was not contraband; then he began to search my luggage. No corner was left unexplored; Mijbil himself could not have done better, and when he had finished none of the cases would close. Then he turned to the last item on my list, one live otter. He pondered this in silence for perhaps a minute. Then, 'You have with you a live otter?' I said that I very much doubted whether it was still alive, but that it had been when at Paris.

'If the animal is dead there will be no duty payable on the un-cured skin; if it is alive it is, of course, subject to the quarantine regulations.'

I had taken the trouble to check this point before leaving Iraq, and at last I was on firm ground. I told him that I knew there to be no quarantine regulations, and that since he had now cleared my luggage I proposed to leave with the otter; if he tried to detain me I would hold him legally responsible for the death of a valuable animal.

Just how long this battle would have lasted I do not know, for at that moment he was relieved by an official who was as helpful as he had been hostile, as benign as he had been bellicose. Within three minutes the box and all my luggage had been loaded on to the waiting car and we were on the last lap of the journey. What meant still more to me was that from the box there now came a faint enquiring chitter and a rustle of wood shavings.

Mijbil had in fact displayed a characteristic shared, I believe, by many animals; an apparent step, as it were, on the road to travel-shock death, but in fact a powerful buffer against it. Many animals seem to me to be able to go into a deep sleep, a coma, almost, as a voluntary act independent of exhaustion; it is an escape mechanism that comes into operation when the animal's inventiveness in the face of adversity has failed to ameliorate its circumstances. I have seen it very occasionally in trapped animals; an arctic fox in Finmark, captive by the leg for no more than an hour, a badger in a Surrey wood, a common house mouse in a box trap. It is, of course, almost a norm, too, of animals kept in too cramped quarters in zoos and in pet stores. I came to recognize it later in Mij when he travelled in cars, a thing he hated; after a few minutes of frenzy he would curl himself into a tight ball and banish entirely the distasteful world about him.

On that first day that he arrived in England he had, I think, been in just such a barricaded state ever since the lid of the box was nailed down before reaching Paris; back, for all one may know, among the familiar scenes of his Tigris swamps, or perhaps in a negative, imageless world where the medulla had taken over respiration and the forebrain rested in a state bordering upon catalepsy.

He was wide awake once more by the time we reached my flat, and when I had the driver paid off and the door closed behind me I felt a moment of deep emotional satisfaction, almost of triumph, that I had after all brought back a live otter cub from Iraq to London, and that Camusfeàrna was less than six hundred miles distant from me.

I prised open the lid of the box, and Mijbil clambered out into my arms to greet me with a frenzy of affection that I felt I had hardly merited.

VIII

Quests and Discoveries

SEAN O'FAOLAIN

The Trout

One of the first places Julia always ran to when they arrived in G— was The Dark Walk. It is a laurel walk, very old; almost gone wild; a lofty midnight tunnel of smooth, sinewy branches. Underfoot the tough brown leaves are never dry enough to crackle: there is always a suggestion of damp and cool trickle.

She raced right into it. For the first few yards she always had the memory of the sun behind her, then she felt the dusk closing swiftly down on her so that she screamed with pleasure and raced on to reach the light at the far end; and it was always just a little too long in coming so that she emerged gasping, clasping her hands, laughing, drinking in the sun. When she was filled with the heat and glare she would turn and consider the ordeal again.

This year she had the extra joy of showing it to her small brother, and of terrifying him as well as herself. And for him the fear lasted longer because his legs were so short and she had gone out at the far end while he was still screaming and racing.

When they had done this many times they came back to the house to tell everybody that they had done it. He boasted. She mocked. They squabbled.

"Cry babby!"

"You were afraid yourself, so there!"

"I won't take you any more."

"You're a big pig."

"I hate you."

Tears were threatening, so somebody said, "Did you see the well?" She opened her eyes at that and held up her long lovely neck suspiciously and decided to be incredulous. She was twelve and at that age little girls are beginning to suspect most stories: they have already found out too many, from Santa Claus to the stork. How could there be a well! In The Dark Walk? That she had visited year after year? Haughtily she said, "Nonsense."

But she went back, pretending to be going somewhere else, and she found a hole scooped in the rock at the side of the walk, choked with damp leaves, so shrouded by ferns that she uncovered it only after much searching. At the back of this little cavern there was about a quart of water. In the water she suddenly perceived a panting trout. She rushed for Stephen and dragged him to see, and they were both so excited that they were no longer afraid of the darkness as they hunched down and peered in at the fish panting in his tiny prison, his silver stomach going up and down like an engine.

Nobody knew how the trout got there. Even old Martin in the kitchen garden laughed and refused to believe that it was there, or pretended not to believe, until she forced him to come down and see. Kneeling and pushing back his tattered old cap he peered in.

"Be cripes, you're right. How the divil in hell did that fella get there?"

She stared at him suspiciously.

"You knew?" she accused; but he said, "The divil a' know," and reached down to lift it out. Convinced she hauled him back. If she had found it, then it was her trout.

Her mother suggested that a bird had carried the spawn. Her father thought that in the winter a small streamlet might have carried it down there as a baby, and it had been safe until the summer came and the water began to dry up. She said, "I see," and went back to look again and consider the matter in private. Her brother remained behind, wanting to hear the whole story of the trout, not really interested in the actual trout but much interested in the story which his mummy began to make up for him on the lines of, "So one day Daddy Trout and Mammy Trout . . ." When he retailed it to her she said, "Pooh."

It troubled her that the trout was always in the same position; he had no room to turn; all the time the silver belly went up and down; otherwise he was motionless. She wondered what he ate, and in between visits to Joey Pony and the boat, and a bathe to get cool, she thought of his hunger. She brought him down bits of dough; once she brought him a worm. He ignored the food. He just went on panting. Hunched over him she thought how all the winter, while she was at school, he had been in there. All the winter, in The Dark Walk, all day, all night, floating around alone. She drew the leaf of her hat down around her ears and chin and stared. She was still thinking of it as she lay in bed.

It was late June, the longest day of the year. The sun had sat still for a week, burning up the world. Although it was after ten o'clock it was still bright and still hot. She lay on her back under a single sheet, with her long legs spread, trying to keep cool. She could see the D of the moon through the fir tree—they slept on the ground floor. Before they went to bed her mummy had told Stephen the story of the trout again, and she, in her bed, had resolutely presented her back to them and read her book. But she had kept one ear cocked.

"And so, in the end, this naughty fish who would not stay at home got bigger and bigger and bigger, and the water got smaller and smaller. . . ."

Passionately she had whirled and cried, "Mummy, don't make it a horrible old moral story!" Her mummy had brought in a fairy godmother then, who sent lots of rain, and filled the well, and a stream poured out and the trout floated away down to the river below. Staring at the moon she knew that there are no such things as fairy godmothers and that the trout, down in The Dark Walk, was panting like an engine. She heard somebody unwind a fishing reel. Would the *beasts* fish him out?

She sat up. Stephen was a hot lump of sleep, lazy thing. The Dark Walk would be full of little scraps of moon. She leaped up and looked out the window, and somehow it was not so lightsome now that she saw the dim mountains far away and the black firs against the breathing land and heard a dog say *bark-bark*. Quietly she lifted the ewer of water and climbed out the window and scuttled along the cool but cruel gravel down to the maw of the tunnel. Her pajamas were very short so that when she splashed water it wet her ankles. She peered into the tunnel. Something alive rustled inside there. She raced in, and up and down she raced, and flurried, and cried aloud, "Oh, gosh, I can't find it," and then at last she did. Kneeling down in the damp she put her hand into the slimy hole. When the body lashed they were both mad with fright. But she gripped him and shoved him into the ewer and raced, with her teeth ground, out to the other end of the tunnel and down the steep paths to the river's edge.

All the time she could feel him lashing his tail against the side of the ewer. She was afraid he would jump right out. The gravel cut into her soles until she came to the cool ooze of the river's bank where the moon mice on the water crept into her feet. She poured out, watching until he plopped. For a second he was visible in the water. She hoped he was not dizzy. Then all she saw was the glimmer of the moon in the silent-flowing river, the dark firs, the dim mountains, and the radiant pointed face laughing down at her out of the empty sky.

She scuttled up the hill, in the window, plonked down the ewer, and flew through the air like a bird into bed. The dog said *bark-bark*. She heard the fishing reel whirring. She hugged herself and giggled. Like a river of joy her holiday spread before her.

In the morning Stephen rushed to her, shouting that "he" was gone, and asking "where" and "how." Lifting her nose in the air she said superciliously, "Fairy godmother, I suppose?" and strolled away patting the palms of her hands.

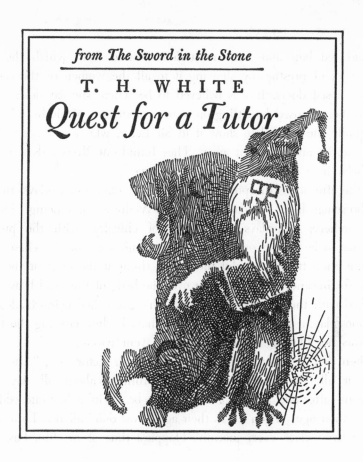

from The Sword in the Stone

T. H. WHITE
Quest for a Tutor

On Mondays, Wednesdays and Fridays it was Court Hand and Summulae Logicales, while the rest of the week it was the Organon, Repetition and Astrology. The governess was always getting muddled with her astrolabe, and when she got specially muddled she would take it out on the Wart by rapping his knuckles. She did not rap Kay's knuckles, because when Kay grew older he would be Sir Kay, the master of the estate. The Wart was called the Wart because it more or less rhymed with Art, which was short for his real name. Kay had given him the nickname. Kay was not called anything but Kay, as he was too dignified to have a nickname and would have flown into a passion if anybody had tried to give him one. The govern-

ess had red hair and some mysterious wound from which she de-
rived a lot of prestige by showing it to all the women of the castle,
behind closed doors. It was believed to be where she sat down, and
to have been caused by sitting on some armour at a picnic by mistake.
Eventually she offered to show it to Sir Ector, who was Kay's father,
had hysterics and was sent away. They found out afterwards that she
had been in a lunatic hospital for three years.

In the afternoons the programme was: Mondays and Fridays, tilting
and horsemanship; Tuesdays, hawking; Wednesdays, fencing; Thurs-
days, archery; Saturdays, the theory of chivalry, with the proper
measures to be blown on all occasions, terminology of the chase and
hunting etiquette. If you did the wrong thing at the mort or the un-
doing, for instance, you were bent over the body of the dead beast and
smacked with the flat side of a sword. This was called being bladed. It
was horseplay, a sort of joke like being shaved when crossing the line.
Kay was not bladed, although he often went wrong.

When they had got rid of the governess, Sir Ector said, "After all,
damn it all, we can't have the boys runnin' about all day like
hooligans—after all, damn it all? Ought to be havin' a first-rate eddication, at their age. When I was their age I was doin' all this Latin and
stuff at five o'clock every mornin'. Happiest time of me life. Pass the
port."

Sir Grummore Grummursum, who was staying the night because he
had been benighted out questin' after a specially long run, said that
when he was their age he was swished every mornin' because he
would go hawkin' instead of learnin'. He attributed to this weakness
the fact that he could never get beyond the Future Simple of Utor.
It was a third of the way down the left-hand leaf, he said. He thought
it was leaf ninety-seven. He passed the port.

Sir Ector said, "Had a good quest today?"

Sir Grummore said, "Oh, not so bad. Rattlin' good day, in fact.
Found a chap called Sir Bruce Saunce Pité choppin' off a maiden's
head in Weedon Bushes, ran him to Mixbury Plantation in the Bices-
ter, where he doubled back, and lost him in Wicken Wood. Must
have been a good twenty-five miles as he ran."

"A straight-necked 'un," said Sir Ector.

"But about these boys and all this Latin and that," added the old gentleman. "Amo, amas, you know, and runnin' about like hooligans: what would you advise?"

"Ah," said Sir Grummore, laying his finger by his nose and winking at the bottle, "that takes a deal of thinkin' about, if you don't mind my sayin' so."

"Don't mind at all," said Sir Ector. "Very kind of you to say anythin'. Much obliged, I'm sure. Help yourself to port."

"Good port this."

"Get it from a friend of mine."

"But about these boys," said Sir Grummore. "How many of them are there, do you know?"

"Two," said Sir Ector, "counting them both, that is."

"Couldn't send them to Eton, I suppose?" inquired Sir Grummore cautiously. "Long way and all that, we know."

It was not really Eton that he mentioned, for the College of Blessed Mary was not founded until 1440, but it was a place of the same sort. Also they were drinking Metheglyn, not Port, but by mentioning the modern wine it is easier to give you the feel.

"Isn't so much the distance," said Sir Ector, "but that giant What's-'is-name is in the way. Have to pass through his country, you understand."

"What is his name?"

"Can't recollect it at the moment, not for the life of me. Fellow that lives by the Burbly Water."

"Galapas," said Sir Grummore.

"That's the very chap."

"The only other thing," said Sir Grummore, "is to have a tutor."

"You mean a fellow who teaches you."

"That's it," said Sir Grummore. "A tutor, you know, a fellow who teaches you."

"Have some more port," said Sir Ector. "You need it after all this questin'."

"Splendid day," said Sir Grummore. "Only they never seem to kill nowadays. Run twenty-five miles and then mark to ground or lose him altogether. The worst is when you start a fresh quest."

"We kill all our giants cubbin'," said Sir Ector. "After that they give you a fine run, but get away."

"Run out of scent," said Sir Grummore, "I dare say. It's always the same with these big giants in a big country. They run out of scent."

"But even if you was to have a tutor," said Sir Ector, "I don't see how you would get him."

"Advertise," said Sir Grummore.

"I have advertised," said Sir Ector. "It was cried by the *Humberland Newsman and Cardoile Advertiser.*"

"The only other way," said Sir Grummore, "is to start a quest."

"You mean a quest for a tutor," explained Sir Ector.

"That's it."

"Hic, Haec, Hoc," said Sir Ector. "Have some more of this drink, whatever it calls itself."

"Hunc," said Sir Grummore.

So it was decided. When Grummore Grummursum had gone home next day, Sir Ector tied a knot in his handkerchief to remember to start a quest for a tutor as soon as he had time to do so, and, as he was not sure how to set about it, he told the boys what Sir Grummore had suggested and warned them not to be hooligans meanwhile. Then they went hay-making.

It was July, and every able-bodied man and woman on the estate worked during that month in the field, under Sir Ector's direction. In any case the boys would have been excused from being eddicated just then.

Sir Ector's castle stood in an enormous clearing in a still more enormous forest. It had a courtyard and a moat with pike in it. The moat was crossed by a fortified stone bridge which ended half-way across it. The other half was covered by a wooden drawbridge which was wound up every night. As soon as you had crossed the drawbridge you were at the top of the village street—it had only one street—and this extended for about half a mile, with thatched houses of wattle and daub on either side of it. The street divided the clearing into two huge fields, that on the left being cultivated in hundreds of long narrow strips, while that on the right ran down to a river and was used as pasture. Half of the right-hand field was fenced off for hay.

It was July, and real July weather, such as they had in Old England. Everybody went bright brown, like Red Indians, with startling teeth and flashing eyes. The dogs moved about with their tongues hanging out, or lay panting in bits of shade, while the farm horses sweated

through their coats and flicked their tails and tried to kick the horse-
flies off their bellies with their great hind hoofs. In the pasture field
the cows were on the gad, and could be seen galloping about with
their tails in the air, which made Sir Ector angry.

Sir Ector stood on the top of a rick, whence he could see what everybody was doing, and shouted commands all over the two-hundred-
acre field, and grew purple in the face. The best mowers mowed
away in a line where the grass was still uncut, their scythes roaring in
the strong sunlight. The women raked the dry hay together in long
strips with wooden rakes, and the two boys with pitchforks followed up on either side of the strip, turning the hay inwards so that
it lay well for picking up. Then the great carts followed, rumbling
with their spiked wooden wheels, drawn by horses or slow white
oxen. One man stood on top of the cart to receive the hay and
direct operations, while one man walked on either side picking up
what the boys had prepared and throwing it to him with a fork.
The cart was led down the lane between two lines of hay, and was
loaded in strict rotation from the front poles to the back, the man
on top calling out in a stern voice where he wanted each fork to
be pitched. The loaders grumbled at the boys for not having laid the
hay properly and threatened to tan them when they caught them, if
they got left behind.

When the wagon was loaded, it was drawn to Sir Ector's rick and
pitched to him. It came up easily because it had been loaded sys-
tematically—not like modern hay—and Sir Ector scrambled about on
top, getting in the way of his assistants, who did the real work, and
stamping and perspiring and scratching about with his fork and trying
to make the rick grow straight and shouting that it would all fall down
as soon as the west winds came.

The Wart loved hay-making, and was good at it. Kay, who was two
years older, generally stood on the edge of the bundle which he was
trying to pick up, with the result that he worked twice as hard as the
Wart for only half the result. But he hated to be beaten at anything,
and used to fight away with the wretched hay—which he loathed like
poison—until he was quite sick.

The day after Sir Grummore's visit was sweltering for the men who
toiled from milking to milking and then again till sunset in their battle
with the sultry element. For the hay was an element to them, like sea

or air, in which they bathed and plunged themselves and which they even breathed in. The seeds and small scraps stuck in their hair, their mouths, their nostrils, and worked, tickling, inside their clothes. They did not wear many clothes, and the shadows between their sliding muscles were blue on the nut-brown skins. Those who feared thunder had felt ill that morning.

In the afternoon the storm broke. Sir Ector kept them at it till the great flashes were right overhead, and then, with the sky as dark as night, the rain came hurling against them so that they were drenched at once and could not see a hundred yards. The boys lay crouched under the wagons, wrapped in hay to keep their wet bodies warm against the now cold wind, and all joked with one another while heaven fell. Kay was shivering, though not with cold, but he joked like the others because he would not show he was afraid. At the last and greatest thunderbolt every man startled involuntarily, and each saw the other startle, until they laughed away their shame.

But that was the end of the hay-making and the beginning of play. The boys were sent home to change their clothes. The old dame who had been their nurse fetched dry jerkins out of a press, and scolded them for catching their deaths, and denounced Sir Ector for keeping on so long. Then they slipped their heads into the laundered shirts, and ran out to the refreshed and sparkling court.

"I vote we take Cully and see if we can get some rabbits in the chase," cried the Wart.

"The rabbits will not be out in this wet," said Kay sarcastically; delighted to have caught him over natural history.

"Oh, come on. It will soon be dry."

"I must carry Cully, then."

Kay insisted on carrying the goshawk and flying her, when they went hawking together. This he had a right to do, not only because he was older than the Wart but also because he was Sir Ector's proper son. The Wart was not a proper son. He did not understand this, but it made him feel unhappy, because Kay seemed to regard it as making him inferior in some way. Also it was different not having a father and mother, and Kay had taught him that being different was wrong. Nobody talked to him about it, but he thought about it when he was alone, and was distressed. He did not like people to bring it up. Since the other boy always did bring it up when a question of precedence arose, he had got into the habit of giving in at once before it could be mentioned. Besides, he admired Kay and was a born follower. He was a hero-worshipper.

"Come on, then," cried the Wart, and they scampered off toward the Mews, turning a few cartwheels on the way.

The Mews was one of the most important parts of the castle, next to the stables and the kennels. It was opposite to the solar, and faced south. The outside windows had to be small, for reasons of fortification, but the windows which looked inward to the courtyard were big and sunny. The windows had close vertical slats nailed down them, but no horizontal ones. There was no glass, but to keep the hawks from draughts there was horn in the small windows. At one end of the Mews there was a little fireplace and a kind of snuggery, like the place in a saddle-room where the grooms sit to clean their tack on wet nights after fox-hunting. Here there were a couple of stools, a cauldron, a bench with all sorts of small knives and surgical instruments, and some shelves with pots on them. The pots were labelled Cardamum, Ginger, Barley Sugar, Wrangle, For a Snurt, For the Craye, Vertigo, etc. There were leather skins hanging up, which had been snipped about as pieces were cut out of them for jesses, hoods or leashes. On a neat row of nails there were Indian bells and swivels and silver varvels, each with Ector cut on. A special shelf, and the most beautiful of all, held the hoods: very old cracked rufter hoods which had been made for birds before Kay was born, tiny hoods for the merlins, small hoods for tiercels, splendid new hoods which had been knocked up to pass away the long winter evenings. All the hoods, except the rufters, were made in Sir Ector's colours: white leather with red baize at the sides and a bunch of blue-grey plumes on top, made out of the hackle feathers of herons. On the bench there was a jumble of oddments such as are to be found in every workshop, bits of cord, wire, metal, tools, some bread and cheese which the mice had been at, a leather bottle, some frayed gauntlets for the left hand, nails, bits of sacking, a couple of lures and some rough tallies scratched on the wood. These read: Conays IIIIII, Harn IIIIII, etc. They were not spelled very well.

Right down the length of the room, with the afternoon sun shining full on them, there ran the screen perches to which the birds were tied. There were two little merlins which had only just been taking up from hacking, an old peregrine who was not much use in this wooded country but who was kept for appearances, a kestrel on which the boys had learned the rudiments of falconry, a spar-hawk which Sir Ector was kind enough to keep for the parish priest, and, caged off in a special apartment of his own at the far end, there was the tiercel goshawk Cully.

The Mews was neatly kept, with sawdust on the floor to absorb the mutes, and the castings taken up every day. Sir Ector visited the place each morning at seven o'clock and the two austringers stood at attention outside the door. If they had forgotten to brush their hair he confined them to barracks. They took no notice.

Kay put on one of the left-hand gauntlets and called Cully from the perch—but Cully, with all his feathers close-set and malevolent, glared at him with a mad marigold eye and refused to come. So Kay took him up.

"Do you think we ought to fly him?" asked the Wart doubtfully. "Deep in the moult like this?"

"Of course we can fly him, you ninny," said Kay. "He only wants to be carried a bit, that's all."

So they went out across the hay-field, noting how the carefully raked hay was now sodden again and losing its goodness, into the chase where the trees began to grow, far apart as yet and parklike, but gradually crowding into the forest shade. The conies had hundreds of buries under these trees, so close together that the problem was not to find a rabbit, but to find a rabbit far enough away from its hole.

"Hob says that we must not fly Cully till he has roused at least twice," said the Wart.

"Hob does not know anything about it. Nobody can tell whether a hawk is fit to fly except the man who is carrying it.

"Hob is only a villein anyway," added Kay, and began to undo the leash and swivel from the jesses.

When he felt the trappings being taken off him, so that he was in hunting order, Cully did make some movements as if to rouse. He raised his chest, his shoulder coverts and the soft feathers of his thighs. But at the last moment he thought better or worse of it and subsided without the rattle. This movement of the hawk's made the Wart itch to carry him. He yearned to take him away from Kay and set him to rights himself. He felt certain that he could get Cully into a good

temper by scratching his feet and softly teasing his breast feathers upward, if only he were allowed to do it himself, instead of having to
plod along behind with the stupid lure. But he knew how annoying
it must be for the elder boy to be continually subjected to advice, and
so he held his peace. Just as in modern shooting, you must never offer
criticism to the man in command, so in hawking it was important that
no outside advice should be allowed to disturb the judgment of the
austringer.

"So-ho!" cried Kay, throwing his arm upward to give the hawk a
better take-off, and a rabbit was scooting across the close-nibbled turf
in front of them, and Cully was in the air. The movement had surprised the Wart, the rabbit and the hawk, all three, and all three hung
a moment in surprise. Then the great wings of the aerial assassin
began to row the air, but reluctant and undecided. The rabbit vanished
in a hidden hole. Up went the hawk, swooping like a child flung high
in a swing, until the wings folded and he was sitting in a tree. Cully
looked down at his masters, opened his beak in an angry pant of failure, and remained motionless. The two hearts stood still.

* * *

A good while later, when they had been whistling and luring and
following the disturbed and sulky hawk from tree to tree, Kay lost his
temper.

"Let him go, then," he said. "He is no use anyway."

"Oh, we could not leave him," cried the Wart. "What would
Hob say?"

"It is my hawk, not Hob's," exclaimed Kay furiously. "What does it
matter what Hob says? He is a servant."

"But Hob made Cully. It is all right for us to lose him, because we
did not have to sit up with him three nights and carry him all day and
all that. But we can't lose Hob's hawk. It would be beastly."

"Serve him right, then. He is a fool and it is a rotten hawk. Who
wants a rotten stupid hawk? You had better stay yourself, if you are so
keen on it. I am going home."

"I will stay," said the Wart sadly, "if you will send Hob when you
get there."

Kay began walking off in the wrong direction, raging in his heart because he knew that he had flown the bird when he was not properly in yarak, and the Wart had to shout after him the right way. Then the latter sat down under the tree and looked up at Cully like a cat watching a sparrow, with his heart beating fast.

It was well enough for Kay, who was not really keen on hawking except in so far as it was the proper occupation for a boy in his station of life, but the Wart had some of the falconer's feelings and knew that a lost hawk was the greatest possible calamity. He knew that Hob had worked on Cully for fourteen hours a day to teach him his trade, and that his work had been like Jacob's struggle with the angel. When Cully was lost a part of Hob would be lost too. The Wart did not dare to face the look of reproach which would be in the falconer's eye, after all that he had tried to teach them.

What was he to do? He had better sit still, leaving the lure on the ground, so that Cully could settle down and come in his own time. But Cully had no intention of doing this. He had been given a generous gorge the night before, and he was not hungry. The hot day had put him in a bad temper. The waving and whistling of the boys below, and their pursuit of him from tree to tree, had disturbed his never powerful brains. Now he did not quite know what he wanted to do, but it was not what anyone else wanted. He thought perhaps it would be nice to kill something, from spite.

A long time after that, the Wart was on the verge of the true forest, and Cully was inside it. In a series of infuriating removes they had come nearer and nearer, till they were further from the castle than the boy had ever been, and now they had reached it quite.

Wart would not have been frightened of an English forest nowadays, but the great jungle of Old England was a different matter. It was not only that there were wild boars in it, whose sounders would at this season be furiously rooting about, nor that one of the surviving wolves might be slinking behind any tree, with pale eyes and slavering chops. The mad and wicked animals were not the only inhabitants of the crowded gloom. When men themselves became wicked they took refuge there, outlaws cunning and bloody as the gore-crow, and as persecuted. The Wart thought particularly of a man named Wat, whose name the cottagers used to frighten their children with. He had once lived in Sir Ector's village and the Wart could remember him. He squinted, had no nose, and was weak in his wits. The children threw stones at him. One day he turned on the children and caught one and made a snarly noise and bit off his nose too. Then he ran into the forest. They threw stones at the child with no nose, now, but Wat was supposed to be in the forest still, running on all fours and dressed in skins.

There were magicians in the forest also in those legendary days, as well as strange animals not known to modern works of natural history. There were regular bands of Saxon outlaws—not like Wat— who lived together and wore green and shot with arrows which never missed. There were even a few dragons, though these were small ones, which lived under stones and could hiss like a kettle.

Added to this, there was the fact that it was getting dark. The forest was trackless and nobody in the village knew what was on the other side. The evening hush had fallen, and the high trees stood looking at Wart without a sound.

He felt that it would be safer to go home, while he still knew where he was—but he had a stout heart, and did not want to give in. He understood that once Cully had slept in freedom for a whole night he would be wild again and irreclaimable. Cully was a passager. But if the poor Wart could only mark him to roost, and if Hob would only arrive then with a dark lantern, they might still take him that night by climbing the tree, while he was sleepy and muddled with the light. The boy could see more or less where the hawk had perched, about a hundred yards within the thick trees, because the home-going rooks of evening were mobbing that place.

He made a mark on one of the trees outside the forest, hoping that it might help him to find his way back, and then began to fight his way into the undergrowth as best he might. He heard by the rooks that Cully had immediately moved further off.

The night fell still as the small boy struggled with the brambles. But he went on doggedly, listening with all his ears, and Cully's evasions became sleepier and shorter until at last, before the utter darkness fell, he could see the hunched shoulders in a tree above him against the sky. Wart sat down under the tree, so as not to disturb the bird any further as it went to sleep, and Cully, standing on one leg, ignored his existence.

"Perhaps," said the Wart to himself, "even if Hob does not come, and I do not see how he can very well follow me in this trackless woodland now, I shall be able to climb up by myself at about midnight, and bring Cully down. He might stay there at about midnight because he ought to be asleep by then. I could speak to him softly by name, so that he thought it was just the usual person coming to take him up while hooded. I shall have to climb very quietly. Then, if I do get him, I shall have to find my way home, and the drawbridge will be up. But perhaps somebody will wait for me, for Kay will have told them I am out. I wonder which way it was? I wish Kay had not gone."

He snuggled down between the roots of the tree, trying to find a comfortable place where the hard wood did not stick into his shoulder-blades.

"I think the way was behind that big spruce with the spike top. I ought to try to remember which side of me the sun is setting, so that when it rises I may keep it on the same side going home. Did something move under that spruce tree, I wonder? Oh, I wish I may not meet that old wild Wat and have my nose bitten off! How aggravating Cully looks, standing there on one leg as if there was nothing the matter."

At this there was a quick whirr and a smack and the Wart found an arrow sticking in the tree between the fingers of his right hand. He snatched his hand away, thinking he had been stung by something, before he noticed it was an arrow. Then everything went slow. He had time to notice quite carefully what sort of an arrow it was, and how it had driven three inches into the solid wood. It was a black arrow with yellow bands round it, like a wasp, and its cock feather was yellow. The two others were black. They were dyed goose feathers.

The Wart found that, although he was frightened of the danger of the forest before it happened, once he was in it he was not frightened any more. He got up quickly—but it seemed to him slowly—and went behind the other side of the tree. As he did this, another arrow came whirr and frump, but this one buried all except its feathers in the grass, and stayed still, as if it had never moved.

On the other side of the tree he found a waste of bracken, six foot high. This was splendid cover, but it betrayed his whereabouts by rustling. He heard another arrow hiss through the fronds, and what seemed to be a man's voice cursing, but it was not very near. Then he heard the man, or whatever it was, running about in the bracken. It was reluctant to fire any more arrows because they were valuable things and would certainly get lost in the undergrowth. Wart went like a snake, like a coney, like a silent owl. He was small and the creature had no chance against him at this game. In five minutes he was safe.

The assassin searched for his arrows and went away grumbling—but the Wart realized that, even if he was safe from the archer, he had lost his way and his hawk. He had not the faintest idea where he was. He lay down for half an hour, pressed under the fallen tree where he had hidden, to give time for the thing to go right away and for his own heart to cease thundering. It had begun beating like this as soon as he knew that he had got away.

"Oh," thought he, "now I am truly lost, and now there is almost no alternative except to have my nose bitten off, or to be pierced right through with one of those waspy arrows, or to be eaten by a hissing dragon or a wolf or a wild boar or a magician—if magicians do eat boys, which I expect they do. Now I may well wish that I had been good, and not angered the governess when she got muddled with her astrolabe, and had loved my dear guardian Sir Ector as much as he deserved."

At these melancholy thoughts, and especially at the recollection of kind Sir Ector with his pitchfork and his red nose, the poor Wart's eyes became full of tears and he lay most desolate beneath the tree.

The sun finished the last rays of its lingering good-bye, and the moon rose in awful majesty over the silver tree-tops, before he dared to stand. Then he got up, and dusted the twigs out of his jerkin, and wandered off forlorn, taking the easiest way and trusting himself to God. He had been walking like this for about half an hour, and sometimes feeling more cheerful—because it really was very cool and lovely in the summer forest by moonlight—when he came upon the most beautiful thing that he had seen in his short life so far.

There was a clearing in the forest, a wide sward of moonlit grass, and the white rays shone full upon the tree trunks on the opposite side. These trees were beeches, whose trunks are always more beautiful in a pearly light, and among the beeches there was the smallest movement and a silvery clink. Before the clink there were just the beeches, but immediately afterward there was a knight in full armour, standing still and silent and unearthly, among the majestic trunks. He was mounted on an enormous white horse that stood as rapt as its master, and he carried in his right hand, with its butt resting on the stirrup, a high, smooth jousting lance, which stood up among the tree stumps, higher and higher, till it was outlined against the velvet sky. All was moonlit, all silver, too beautiful to describe.

The Wart did not know what to do. He did not know whether it would be safe to go up to this knight, for there were so many terrible things in the forest that even the knight might be a ghost. Most ghostly he looked, too, as he hoved meditating on the confines of the gloom. Eventually the boy made up his mind that even if it were a ghost, it would be the ghost of a knight, and knights were bound by their vows to help people in distress.

"Excuse me," he said, when he was right under the mysterious figure, "but can you tell me the way back to Sir Ector's castle?"

At this the ghost jumped, so that it nearly fell off its horse, and gave out a muffled baaa through its visor, like a sheep.

"Excuse me," began the Wart again, and stopped, terrified, in the middle of his speech.

For the ghost lifted up its visor, revealing two enormous eyes frosted like ice; exclaimed in an anxious voice, "What, what?"; took off its eyes —which turned out to be horn-rimmed spectacles, fogged by being inside the helmet; tried to wipe them on the horse's mane—which only made them worse; lifted both hands above its head and tried to wipe them on its plume; dropped its lance; dropped the spectacles; got off the horse to search for them—the visor shutting in the process; lifted its visor; bent down for the spectacles; stood up again as the visor shut once more, and exclaimed in a plaintive voice, "Oh, dear!"

The Wart found the spectacles, wiped them, and gave them to the ghost, who immediately put them on (the visor shut at once) and began scrambling back on its horse for dear life. When it was there it held out its hand for the lance, which the Wart handed up, and, feeling all secure, opened the visor with its left hand, and held it open. It peered at the boy with one hand up—like a lost mariner searching for land—and exclaimed, "Ah-hah! Whom have we here, what?"

"Please," said the Wart, "I am a boy whose guardian is Sir Ector."

"Charming fellah," said the Knight. "Never met him in me life."

"Can you tell me the way back to his castle?"

"Faintest idea. Stranger in these parts meself."

"I am lost," said the Wart.

"Funny thing that. Now I have been lost for seventeen years.

"Name of King Pellinore," continued the Knight. "May have heard of me, what?" The visor shut with a pop, like an echo to the What, but was opened again immediately. "Seventeen years ago, come Michaelmas, and been after the Questing Beast ever since. Boring, very."

"I should think it would be," said the Wart, who had never heard of King Pellinore, nor of the Questing Beast, but he felt that this was the safest thing to say in the circumstances.

"It is the Burden of the Pellinores," said the King proudly. "Only a Pellinore can catch it—that is, of course, or his next of kin. Train all the Pellinores with that idea in mind. Limited eddication, rather. Fewmets, and all that."

"I know what fewmets are," said the boy with interest. "They are the droppings of the beast pursued. The harborer keeps them in his horn, to show to his master, and can tell by them whether it is a warrantable beast or otherwise, and what state it is in."

"Intelligent child," remarked the King. "Very. Now I carry fewmets about with me practically all the time.

"Insanitary habit," he added, beginning to look dejected, "and quite pointless. Only one Questing Beast, you know, so there can't be any question whether she is warrantable or not."

Here his visor began to droop so much that the Wart decided he had better forget his own troubles and try to cheer his companion, by asking questions on the one subject about which he seemed qualified to speak. Even talking to a lost royalty was better than being alone in the wood.

"What does the Questing Beast look like?"

"Ah, we call it the Beast Glatisant, you know," replied the monarch, assuming a learned air and beginning to speak quite volubly. "Now the Beast Glatisant, or, as we say in English, the Questing Beast—you may call it either," he added graciously—"this Beast has the head of a serpent, ah, and the body of a libbard, the haunches of a lion, and he is footed like a hart. Wherever this beast goes he makes a noise in his belly as it had been the noise of thirty couple of hounds questing.

"Except when he is drinking, of course," added the King.

"It must be a dreadful kind of monster," said the Wart, looking about him anxiously.

"A dreadful monster," repeated the King. "It is the Beast Glatisant."

"And how do you follow it?"

This seemed to be the wrong question, for Pellinore began to look even more depressed.

"I have a brachet," he said sadly. "There she is, over there."

The Wart looked in the direction which had been indicated with a despondent thumb, and saw a lot of rope wound round a tree. The other end of the rope was tied to King Pellinore's saddle.

"I do not see her very well."

"Wound herself round the other side, I dare say. She always goes the opposite way from me."

The Wart went over to the tree and found a large white dog scratching herself for fleas. As soon as she saw the Wart, she began wagging her whole body, grinning vacuously, and panting in her efforts to lick his face, in spite of the cord. She was too tangled up to move.

"It's quite a good brachet," said King Pellinore, "only it pants so, and gets wound round things, and goes the opposite way. What with that and the visor, what, I sometimes don't know which way to turn."

"Why don't you let her loose?" asked the Wart. "She would follow the Beast just as well like that."

"She goes right away then, you see, and I don't see her sometimes for a week.

"Gets a bit lonely without her," added the King, "following the Beast about, and never knowing where one is. Makes a bit of company, you know."

"She seems to have a friendly nature."

"Too friendly. Sometimes I doubt whether she is really chasing the Beast at all."

"What does she do when she sees it?"

"Nothing."

"Oh, well," said the Wart. "I dare say she will get to be interested in it after a time."

"It is eight months, anyway, since we saw the Beast at all."

The poor fellow's voice had grown sadder and sadder since the beginning of the conversation, and now he definitely began to snuffle. "It is the curse of the Pellinores," he exclaimed. "Always mollocking about after that beastly Beast. What on earth use is she, anyway? First you have to stop to unwind the brachet, then your visor falls down, then you can't see through your spectacles. Nowhere to sleep, never know where you are. Rheumatism in the winter, sunstroke in the summer. All this horrid armour takes hours to put on. When it is on it's either frying or freezing, and it gets rusty. You have to sit up all night polishing the stuff. Oh, how I do wish I had a nice house of my own to live in, a house with beds in it and real pillows and sheets. If I was rich that's what I would buy. A nice bed with a nice pillow and a nice sheet that you could lie in, and then I would put this beastly horse in a meadow and tell that beastly brachet to run away and play, and throw all this beastly armour out of the window, and let the beastly Beast go and chase himself—that I would."

"If you could show me the way home," said the Wart craftily, "I am sure Sir Ector would put you up in a bed for the night."

"Do you really mean it?" cried the King. "In a bed?"

"A feather bed."

King Pellinore's eyes grew round as saucers. "A feather bed!" he repeated slowly. "Would it have pillows?"

"Down pillows."

"Down pillows!" whispered the King, holding his breath. And then, letting it out in one rush, "What a lovely house your gentleman must have!"

"I do not think it is more than two hours away," said the Wart, following up his advantage.

"And did this gentleman really send you out to invite me in?" (He had forgotten about the Wart being lost.) "How nice of him, how very nice of him, I do think, what?"

"He will be pleased to see us," said the Wart truthfully.

"Oh, how nice of him," exclaimed the King again, beginning to bustle about with his various trappings. "And what a lovely gentleman he must be, to have a feather bed!

"I suppose I should have to share it with somebody?" he added doubtfully.

"You could have one of your own."

"A feather bed of one's very own, with sheets and a pillow—perhaps even two pillows, or a pillow and a bolster—and no need to get up in time for breakfast! Does your guardian get up in time for breakfast?"

"Never," said the Wart.

"Fleas in the bed?"

"Not one."

"Well!" said King Pellinore. "It does sound too nice for words, I must say. A feather bed and none of those fewmets for ever so long. How long did you say it would take us to get there?"

"Two hours," said the Wart—but he had to shout the second of these words, for the sounds were drowned in his mouth by a noise which had that moment arisen close beside them.

"What was that?" exclaimed the Wart.

"Hark!" cried the King.

"Mercy!"

"It is the Beast!"

And immediately the loving huntsman had forgotten everything else, but was busied about his task. He wiped his spectacles upon the seat of his trousers, the only accessible piece of cloth about him, while the belling and bloody cry arose all round. He balanced them on the end of his long nose, just before the visor automatically clapped to. He clutched his jousting lance in his right hand, and galloped off in the direction of the noise. He was brought up short by the rope which was wound round the tree—the vacuous brachet meanwhile giving a melancholy yelp—and fell off his horse with a tremendous clang. In a second he was up again—the Wart was convinced that the spectacles must be broken—and hopping round the white horse with one foot in the stirrup. The girths stood the test and he was in the saddle somehow, with his jousting lance between his legs, and then he was galloping round and round the tree, in the opposite direction to the one in which the bracket had wound herself up. He went round three times too often, the brachet meanwhile running and yelping the other way, and then, after four or five back casts, they were both free of the obstruction. "Yoicks, what!" cried King Pellinore, waving his lance in the air, and swaying excitedly in the saddle. Then he disappeared into the gloom of the forest, with the unfortunate hound trailing behind him at the other end of the cord.

The boy slept well in the woodland nest where he had laid himself down, in that kind of thin but refreshing sleep which people have when they begin to lie out of doors. At first he only dipped below the surface of sleep, and skimmed along like a salmon in shallow water, so close to the surface that he fancied himself in air. He thought himself awake when he was already asleep. He saw the stars above his face, whirling on their silent and sleepless axis, and the leaves of the trees rustling against them, and he heard small changes in the grass. These little noises of footsteps and soft-fringed wing-beats and stealthy bellies drawn over the grass blades or rattling against the bracken at first frightened or interested him, so that he moved to see what they were (but never saw), then soothed him, so that he no longer cared to see what they were but trusted them to be themselves, and finally left him altogether as he swam down deeper and deeper, nuzzling into the scented turf, into the warm ground, into the unending waters under the earth.

It had been difficult to go to sleep in the bright summer moonlight, but once he was there it was not difficult to stay. The sun came early, causing him to turn over in protest, but in going to sleep he had learned to vanquish light, and now the light could not rewake him. It was nine o'clock, five hours after daylight, before he rolled over, opened his eyes, and was awake at once. He was hungry.

The Wart had heard about people who lived on berries, but this did not seem practical at the moment, because it was July, and there were none. He found two wild strawberries and ate them greedily. They tasted nicer than anything, so that he wished there were more. Then he wished it was April, so that he could find some birds' eggs and eat those, or that he had not lost his goshawk Cully, so that the hawk could catch him a rabbit which he would cook by rubbing two sticks together like the base Indian. But he had lost Cully, or he would not have lost himself, and probably the sticks would not have lighted in any case. He decided that he could not have gone more than three or four miles from home, and that the best thing he could do would be to sit still and listen. Then he might hear the noise of the haymakers, if he were lucky with the wind, and he could hearken his way to the castle by that.

What he did hear was a faint clanking noise, which made him think that King Pellinore must be after the Questing Beast again,

close by. Only the noise was so regular and single in intention that
it made him think of King Pellinore doing some special action, with
great patience and concentration—trying to scratch his back without
taking off his armour, for instance. He went toward the noise.

There was a clearing in the forest, and in this clearing there was
a snug cottage built of stone. It was a cottage, although the Wart
could not notice this at the time, which was divided into two bits.
The main bit was the hall or every-purpose room, which was high
because it extended from floor to roof, and this room had a fire
on the floor whose smoke came out eventually from a hole in the
thatch of the roof. The other half of the cottage was divided into
two rooms by a horizontal floor which made the top half into a
bedroom and study, while the bottom half served for a larder, storeroom, stable and barn. A white donkey lived in this downstairs room,
and a ladder led to the one upstairs.

There was a well in front of the cottage, and the metallic noise
which the Wart had heard was caused by a very old gentleman who
was drawing water out of it by means of a handle and chain.

Clank, clank, clank, went the chain, until the bucket hit the lip of
the well, and "Drat the whole thing!" said the old gentleman. "You
would think that after all these years of study you could do better
for yourself than a by-our-lady well with a by-our-lady bucket,
whatever the by-our-lady cost.

"By this and by that," added the old gentleman, heaving his
bucket out of the well with a malevolent glance, "why can't they
get us the electric light and company's water?"

He was dressed in a flowing gown with fur tippets which had the
signs of the zodiac embroidered over it, with various cabalistic signs,
such as triangles with eyes in them, queer crosses, leaves of trees,
bones of birds and animals, and a planetarium whose stars shone like
bits of looking-glass with the sun on them. He had a pointed hat
like a dunce's cap, or like the headgear worn by ladies of that time,
except that the ladies were accustomed to have a bit of veil floating
from the top of it. He also had a wand of lignum vitae, which he
had laid down in the grass beside him, and a pair of horn-rimmed
spectacles like those of King Pellinore. They were unusual spectacles,
being without ear pieces, but shaped rather like scissors or like the
antennae of the tarantula wasp.

"Excuse me, sir," said the Wart, "but can you tell me the way to Sir Ector's castle, if you don't mind?"

The aged gentleman put down his bucket and looked at him. "Your name would be the Wart."

"Yes, sir, please, sir."

"My name," said the old man, "is Merlyn."

"How do you do?"

"How do."

When these formalities had been concluded, the Wart had leisure to look at him more closely. The magician was staring at him with a kind of unwinking and benevolent curiosity which made him feel that it would not be at all rude to stare back, no ruder than it would be to stare at one of his guardian's cows who happened to be thinking about his personality as she leaned her head over a gate.

Merlyn had a long white beard and long white moustaches which hung down on either side of it. Close inspection showed that he was far from clean. It was not that he had dirty fingernails, or anything like that, but some large bird seemed to have been nesting in his hair. The Wart was familiar with the nests of Spar-hark and Gos, the crazy conglomerations of sticks and oddments which had been taken over from squirrels or crows, and he knew how the twigs and the tree foot were splashed with white mutes, old bones, muddy feathers and castings. This was the impression which he got from Merlyn. The old man was streaked with droppings over his shoulders, among the stars and triangles of his gown, and a large spider was slowly lowering itself from the tip of his hat, as he gazed and slowly blinked at the little boy in front of him. He had a worried expression, as though he were trying to remember some name which began with Chol but which was pronounced in quite a different way, possibly Menzies or was it Dalziel? His mild blue eyes, very big and round under the tarantula spectacles, gradually filmed and clouded over as he gazed at the boy, and then he turned his head away with a resigned expression, as though it was all too much for him after all.

"Do you like peaches?"

"Very much indeed," said the Wart, and his mouth began to water so that it was full of sweet, soft liquid.

"They are scarcely in season," said the old man reprovingly, and he walked off in the direction of the cottage.

The Wart followed after, since this was the simplest thing to do, and offered to carry the bucket (which seemed to please Merlyn, who gave it to him) and waited while he counted the keys—while he muttered and mislaid them and dropped them in the grass. Finally, when they had got their way into the black and white home with as much trouble as if they were burgling it, he climbed up the ladder after his host and found himself in the upstairs room.

It was the most marvellous room that he had ever been in.

There was a real corkindrill hanging from the rafters, very life-like and horrible with glass eyes and scaly tail stretched out behind it. When its master came into the room it winked one eye in salutation, although it was stuffed. There were thousands of brown books in leather bindings, some chained to the book-shelves and others propped against each other as if they had had too much to drink and did not really trust themselves. These gave out a smell of must and solid brownness which was most secure. Then there was stuffed birds, popinjays, and maggot-pies and king-fishers, and peacocks with all their feathers but two, and tiny birds like beetles, and a reputed phoenix which smelt of incense and cinnamon. It could not have been a real phoenix, because there is only one of these at a time. Over by the mantelpiece there was a fox's mask, with GRAFTON, BUCK-INGHAM TO DAVENTRY, 2 HRS 20 MINS written under it, and also a forty-pound salmon with AWE, 43 MIN., BULLDOG written under it, and a very life-like basilisk with CROWHURST OTTER HOUNDS in Roman print. There were several boars' tusks and the claws of tigers and libbards mounted in symmetrical patterns, and a big head of Ovis Poli, six live grass snakes in a kind of aquarium, some nests of the solitary wasp nicely set up in a glass cylinder, an ordinary beehive whose inhabitants went in and out of the window unmolested, two young hedgehogs in cotton wool, a pair of badgers which immediately began to cry Yik-Yik-Yik-Yik in loud voices as soon as the magician appeared, twenty boxes which contained stick caterpillars and sixths of the puss-moth, and even an oleander that was worth sixpence—all feeding on the appropriate leaves—a guncase with all sorts of weapons which would not be invented for half a thousand years, a rod-box ditto, a chest of drawers full of salmon flies which had been tied by Merlyn himself, another chest whose drawers were labelled Mandragora, Mandrake, Old

Man's Beard, etc., a bunch of turkey feathers and goose-quills for making pens, an astrolabe, twelve pairs of boots, a dozen purse-nets, three dozen rabbit wires, twelve corkscrews, some ants' nests between two glass plates, ink-bottles of every possible colour from red to violet, darning-needles, a gold medal for being the best scholar at Winchester, four or five recorders, a nest of field mice all alive-o, two skulls, plenty of cut glass, Venetian glass, Bristol glass and a bottle of Mastic varnish, some satsuma china and some cloisonné, the fourteenth edition of the Encyclopaedia Britannica (marred as it was by the sensationalism of the popular plates), two paint-boxes (one oil, one watercolour), three globes of the known geographical world, a few fossils, the stuffed head of a cameleopard, six pismires, some glass retorts with cauldrons, bunsen burners, etc., and a complete set of cigarette cards depicting wild fowl by Peter Scott.

Merlyn took off his pointed hat when he came into this chamber, because it was too high for the roof, and immediately there was a scamper in one of the dark corners and a flap of soft wings, and a tawny owl was sitting on the black skull-cap which protected the top of his head.

"Oh, what a lovely owl!" cried the Wart.

But when he went up to it and held out his hand, the owl grew half as tall again, stood up as stiff as a poker, closed its eyes so that there was only the smallest slit to peep through—as you are in the habit of doing when told to shut your eyes at hide-and-seek—and said in a doubtful voice:

"There is no owl."

Then it shut its eyes entirely and looked the other way.

"It is only a boy," said Merlyn.

"There is no boy," said the owl hopefully, without turning round.

The Wart was so startled by finding that the owl could talk that he forgot his manners and came closer still. At this the bird became so nervous that it made a mess on Merlyn's head—the whole room was quite white with droppings—and flew off to perch on the farthest tip of the corkindrill's tail, out of reach.

"We see so little company," explained the magician, wiping his head with half a worn-out pair of pyjamas which he kept for that purpose, "that Archimedes is a little shy of strangers. Come, Archimedes, I want you to meet a friend of mine called Wart."

Here he held out his hand to the owl, who came waddling like a goose along the corkindrill's back—he waddled with this rolling gait so as to keep his tail from being damaged—and hopped down to Merlyn's finger with every sign of reluctance.

"Hold out your finger and put it behind his legs. No, lift it up under his train."

When the Wart had done this, Merlyn moved the owl gently backward, so that the boy's finger pressed against its legs from behind, and it either had to step back on the finger or get pushed off its balance altogether. It stepped back. The Wart stood there delighted, while the furry feet held tight on his finger and the sharp claws pricked his skin.

"Say how d'you do properly," said Merlyn.

"I will not," said Archimedes, looking the other way and holding tight.

"Oh, he *is* lovely," said the Wart again. "Have you had him long?"

"Archimedes has stayed with me since he was small, indeed since he had a tiny head like a chicken's."

"I wish he would talk to me."

"Perhaps if you were to give him this mouse here, politely, he might learn to know you better."

Merlyn took a dead mouse out of his skull-cap—"I always keep them there, and worms too, for fishing. I find it most convenient"— and handed it to the Wart, who held it out rather gingerly toward Archimedes. The nutty curved beak looked as if it were capable of doing damage, but Archimedes looked closely at the mouse, blinked at the Wart, moved nearer on the finger, closed his eyes and leaned forward. He stood there with closed eyes and an expression of rapture on his face, as if he were saying Grace, and then, with the absurdest sideways nibble, took the morsel so gently that he would not have broken a soap bubble. He remained leaning forward with closed eyes, with the mouse suspended from his beak, as if he were not sure what to do with it. Then he lifted his right foot—he was right-handed, though people say only men are—and took hold of the mouse. He held it up like a boy holding a stick of rock or a constable with his truncheon, looked at it, nibbled its tail. He turned it round so that it was head first, for the Wart had offered it the wrong way round, and gave one gulp. He looked round at the company with the tail hanging out of the corner of his mouth—as much as to say, "I wish you would not all stare at me so"—turned his head away, politely swallowed the tail, scratched his sailor's beard with his left toe, and began to ruffle out his feathers.

"Let him alone," said Merlyn. "Perhaps he does not want to be friends with you until he knows what you are like. With owls, it is never easy-come and easy-go."

"Perhaps he will sit on my shoulder," said the Wart, and with that he instinctively lowered his hand, so that the owl, who liked to be as high as possible, ran up the slope and stood shyly beside his ear.

"Now breakfast," said Merlyn.

The Wart saw that the most perfect breakfast was laid out neatly for two, on a table before the window. There were peaches. There were also melons, strawberries and cream, rusks, brown trout piping hot, grilled perch which were much nicer, chicken devilled enough to burn one's mouth out, kidneys and mushrooms on toast, fricassee, curry, and a choice of boiling coffee or best chocolate made with cream in large cups.

"Have some mustard," said the magician, when they had got to the kidneys.

The mustard-pot got up and walked over to his plate on thin silver legs that waddled like the owl's. Then it uncurled its handles and one handle lifted its lid with exaggerated courtesy while the other helped him to a generous spoonful.

"Oh, I love the mustard-pot!" cried the Wart. "Wherever did you get it?"

At this the pot beamed all over its face and began to strut a bit, but Merlyn rapped it on the head with a teaspoon, so that it sat down and shut up at once.

"It is not a bad pot," he said grudgingly. "Only it is inclined to give itself airs."

The Wart was so much impressed by the kindness of the old man, and particularly by the lovely things which he possessed, that he hardly liked to ask him personal questions. It seemed politer to sit still and to speak when he was spoken to. But Merlyn did not speak much, and when he did speak it was never in questions, so that the Wart had little opportunity for conversation. At last his curiosity got the better of him, and he asked something which had been puzzling him for some time.

"Would you mind if I ask you a question?"

"It is what I am for."

"How did you know to set breakfast for two?"

The old gentleman leaned back in his chair and lighted an enormous meerschaum pipe—Good gracious, he breathes fire, thought the Wart, who had never heard of tobacco—before he was ready to reply. Then he looked puzzled, took off his skullcap—three mice fell out—and scratched in the middle of his bald head.

"Have you ever tried to draw in a looking-glass?" he asked.

"I don't think I have."

"Looking-glass," said Merlyn, holding out his hand. Immediately there was a tiny lady's vanity-glass in his hand.

"Not that kind, you fool," he said angrily. "I want one big enough to shave in."

The vanity-glass vanished, and in its place there was a shaving mirror about a foot square. He then demanded pencil and paper in quick succession; got an unsharpened pencil and the *Morning Post*; sent them back; got a fountain pen with no ink in it and six reams of brown paper suitable for parcels; sent them back; flew into a passion in which he said by-our-lady quite often, and ended up with a carbon pencil and some cigarette papers which he said would have to do.

He put one of the papers in front of the glass and made five dots.

"Now," he said, "I want you to join those five dots up to make a W, looking only in the glass."

The Wart took the pen and tried to do as he was bid.

"Well, it is not bad," said the magician doubtfully, "and in a way it does look a bit like an M."

Then he fell into a reverie, stroking his beard, breathing fire, and staring at the paper.

"About the breakfast?"

"Ah, yes. How did I know to set breakfast for two? That was why I showed you the looking-glass. Now ordinary people are born forwards in Time, if you understand what I mean, and nearly everything in the world goes forward too. This makes it quite easy for the ordinary people to live, just as it would be easy to join those five dots into a W if you were allowed to look at them forwards, instead of backwards and inside out. But I unfortunately was born at the wrong end of Time, and I have to live backwards from in front, while surrounded by a lot of people living forwards from behind. Some people call it having second sight."

He stopped talking and looked at the Wart in an anxious way. "Have I told you this before?"

"No, we only met about half an hour ago."

"So little time to pass?" said Merlyn, and a big tear ran down to the end of his nose. He wiped it off with his pyjamas and added anxiously, "Am I going to tell it you again?"

"I do not know," said the Wart, "unless you have not finished telling me yet."

"You see, one gets confused with Time, when it is like that. All one's tenses get muddled, for one thing. If you know what is *going* to happen to people, and not what *has* happened to them, it makes it difficult to prevent it happening, if you don't want it to have happened, if you see what I mean? Like drawing in a mirror."

The Wart did not quite see, but was just going to say that he was sorry for Merlyn if these things made him unhappy, when he felt a curious sensation at his ear. "Don't jump," said the old man, just as he was going to do so, and the Wart sat still. Archimedes, who had been standing forgotten on his shoulder all this time, was gently touching himself against him. His beak was right against the lobe of the ear, which its bristles made to tickle, and suddenly a soft hoarse voice whispered, "How d'you do," so that it sounded right inside his head.

"Oh, owl!" cried the Wart, forgetting about Merlyn's troubles instantly. "Look, he has decided to talk to me!"

The Wart gently leaned his head against the smooth feathers, and the tawny owl, taking the rim of his ear in its beak, quickly nibbled right round it with the smallest nibbles.

"I shall call him Archie!"

"I trust you will do nothing of the sort," exclaimed Merlyn instantly, in a stern and angry voice, and the owl withdrew to the farthest corner of his shoulder.

"Is it wrong?"

"You might as well call me Wol, or Olly," said the owl sourly, "and have done with it.

"Or Bubbles," it added in a bitter voice.

Merlyn took the Wart's hand and said kindly, "You are young, and do not understand these things. But you will learn that owls are the most courteous, single-hearted and faithful creatures living. You must never be familiar, rude or vulgar with them, or make them look ridiculous. Their mother is Athene, the goddess of wisdom, and, although they are often ready to play the buffoon to amuse you, such conduct is the prerogative of the truly wise. No owl can possibly be called Archie."

"I am sorry, owl," said the Wart.

"And I am sorry, boy," said the owl. "I can see that you spoke in ignorance, and I bitterly regret that I should have been so petty as to take offence where none was intended."

The owl really did regret it, and looked so remorseful that Merlyn had to put on a cheerful manner and change the conversation.

"Well," said he, "now that we have finished breakfast, I think it is high time that we should all three find our way back to Sir Ector.

"Excuse me a moment," he added as an afterthought, and, turning round to the breakfast things, he pointed a knobbly finger at them and said in a stern voice, "Wash up."

At this all the china and cutlery scrambled down off the table, the cloth emptied the crumbs out of the window, and the napkins folded themselves up. All ran off down the ladder, to where Merlyn had left the bucket, and there was such a noise and yelling as if a lot of children had been let out of school. Merlyn went to the door and shouted, "Mind, nobody is to get broken." But his voice was entirely drowned in shrill squeals, splashes, and cries of "My, it is cold," "I shan't stay in long," "Look out, you'll break me," or "Come on, let's duck the teapot."

"Are you really coming all the way home with me?" asked the Wart, who could hardly believe the good news.

"Why not? How else can I be your tutor?"

At this the Wart's eyes grew rounder and rounder, until they were about as big as the owl's who was sitting on his shoulder, and his face got redder and redder, and a breath seemed to gather itself beneath his heart.

"My!" exclaimed the Wart, while his eyes sparkled with excitement at the discovery. "I must have been on a Quest!"

The Wart started talking before he was half-way over the drawbridge. "Look who I have brought," he said. "Look! I have been on a Quest! I was shot at with three arrows. They had black and yellow stripes. The owl is called Archimedes. I saw King Pellinore. This is my tutor, Merlyn. I went on a Quest for him. He was after the Questing Beast. I mean King Pellinore. It was terrible in the forest. Merlyn made the plates wash up. Hallo, Hob. Look, we have got Cully."

Hob just looked at the Wart, but so proudly that the Wart went quite red. It was such a pleasure to be back home again with all his friends, and everything achieved.

Hob said gruffly, "Ah, master, us shall make an austringer of 'ee yet."

He came for Cully, as if he could not keep his hands off him longer, but he patted the Wart too, fondling them both because he was not sure which he was gladder to see back. He took Cully on his own fist, reassuming him like a lame man putting on his accustomed wooden leg, after it had been lost.

"Merlyn caught him," said the Wart. "He sent Archimedes to look for him on the way home. Then Archimedes told us that he had been and killed a pigeon and was eating it. We went and frightened him off. After that, Merlyn stuck six of the tail feathers round the pigeon in a circle, and made a loop in a long piece of string to go round the feathers. He tied one end to a stick in the ground, and we went away behind a bush with the other end. He said he would not use magic. He said you could not use magic in Great Arts, just as it would be unfair to make a great statue by magic. You have to cut it out with a chisel, you see. Then Cully came down to finish the pigeon, and we pulled the string, and the loop slipped over the feathers and caught him round the legs. He was angry! But we gave him the pigeon."

Hob made a duty to Merlyn, who returned it courteously. They

looked upon one another with grave affection, knowing each other
to be masters of the same trade. When they could be alone together
they would talk about falconry, although Hob was naturally a silent
man. Meanwhile they must wait their time.

"Oh, Kay," cried the Wart, as the latter appeared with their
nurse and other delighted welcomers. "Look, I have got a magician
for our tutor. He has a mustard-pot that walks."

"I am glad you are back," said Kay.

"Alas, where did you sleep, Master Art?" exclaimed the nurse.
"Look at your clean jerkin all muddied and torn. Such a turn as
you gave us, I really don't know. But look at your poor hair with all
them twigs in it. Oh, my own random, wicked little lamb."

Sir Ector came bustling out with his greaves on back to front, and
kissed the Wart on both cheeks. "Well, well, well," he exclaimed
moistly. "Here we are again, hey? What the devil have we been
doin', hey? Settin' the whole household upside down."

But inside himself he was proud of the Wart for staying out after a
hawk, and prouder still to see that he had got it, for all the while
Hob held the bird in the air for everybody to see.

"Oh, sir," said the Wart, "I have been on that quest you said for
a tutor, and I have found him. Please, he is this gentleman here,
and he is called Merlyn. He has got some badgers and hedgehogs
and mice and ants and things on this white donkey here, because
we could not leave them behind to starve. He is a great magician, and
can make things come out of the air."

"Ah, a magician," said Sir Ector, putting on his glasses and
looking closely at Merlyn. "White magic, I hope?"

"Assuredly," said Merlyn, who stood patiently among the throng
with his arms folded in his necromantic gown, while Archimedes
sat very stiff and elongated on the top of his head.

"Ought to have some testimonials," said Sir Ector doubtfully. "It's
usual."

"Testimonials," said Merlyn, holding out his hand.

Instantly there were some heavy tablets in it, signed by Aristotle,
a parchment signed by Hecate, and some typewritten duplicates
signed by the Master of Trinity, who could not remember having
met him. All these gave Merlyn an excellent character.

"He had 'em up his sleeve," said Sir Ector wisely. "Can you do anything else?"

"Tree," said Merlyn. At once there was an enormous mulberry growing in the middle of the courtyard, with its luscious blue fruits ready to patter down. This was all the more remarkable, since mulberries only became popular in the days of Cromwell.

"They do it with mirrors," said Sir Ector.

"Snow," said Merlyn. "And an umbrella," he added hastily.

Before they could turn round, the copper sky of summer had assumed a cold and lowering bronze, while the biggest white flakes that ever were seen were floating about them and settling on the battlements. An inch of snow had fallen before they could speak, and all were trembling with the wintry blast. Sir Ector's nose was blue, and had an icicle hanging from the end of it, while all except Merlyn had a ledge of snow upon their shoulders. Merlyn stood in the middle, holding his umbrella high because of the owl.

"It's done by hypnotism," said Ector, with chattering teeth. "Like those wallahs from the Indies.

"But that'll do," he added hastily, "that'll do very well. I'm sure you'll make an excellent tutor for teachin' these boys."

The snow stopped immediately and the sun came out—"Enough to give a body a pewmonia," said the nurse, "or to frighten the elastic commissioners"—while Merlyn folded up his umbrella and handed it back to the air, which received it.

"Imagine the boy doin' a quest like that by himself," exclaimed Sir Ector. "Well, well, well! Wonders never cease."

"I do not think much of it as a quest," said Kay. "He only went after the hawk, after all."

"And got the hawk, Master Kay," said Hob reprovingly.

"Oh, well," said Kay, "I bet the old man caught it for him."

"Kay," said Merlyn, suddenly terrible, "thou wast ever a proud and ill-tongued speaker, and a misfortunate one. Thy sorrow will come from thine own mouth."

At this everybody felt uncomfortable, and Kay, instead of flying into his usual passion, hung his head. He was not at all an unpleasant person really, but clever, quick, proud, passionate and ambitious. He was one of those people who would be neither a follower nor a leader, but only an aspiring heart, impatient in the failing body which imprisoned it. Merlyn repented of his rudeness at once. He made a little silver hunting-knife come out of the air, which he gave him to put things right. The knob of the handle was made of the skull of a stoat, oiled and polished like ivory, and Kay loved it.

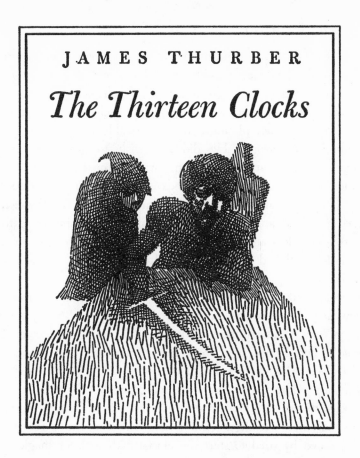

JAMES THURBER

The Thirteen Clocks

Once upon a time, in a gloomy castle on a lonely hill, where
there were thirteen clocks that wouldn't go, there lived a cold,
aggressive Duke, and his niece, the Princess Saralinda. She was warm
in every wind and weather, but he was always cold. His hands were
as cold as his smile and almost as cold as his heart. He wore gloves
when he was asleep, and he wore gloves when he was awake, which
made it difficult for him to pick up pins or coins or the kernels of
nuts, or to tear the wings from nightingales. He was six feet four,
and forty-six, and even colder than he thought he was. One eye
wore a velvet patch; the other glittered through a monocle, which
made half his body seem closer to you than the other half. He had
lost one eye when he was twelve, for he was fond of peering into

nests and lairs in search of birds and animals to maul. One afternoon, a mother shrike had mauled him first. His nights were spent in evil dreams, and his days were given to wicked schemes.

Wickedly scheming, he would limp and cackle through the cold corridors of the castle, planning new impossible feats for the suitors of Saralinda to perform. He did not wish to give her hand in marriage, since her hand was the only warm hand in the castle. Even the hands of his watch and the hands of all the thirteen clocks were frozen. They had all frozen at the same time, on a snowy night, seven years before, and after that it was always ten minutes to five in the castle. Travelers and mariners would look up at the gloomy castle on the lonely hill and say, "Time lies frozen there. It's always Then. It's never Now."

The cold Duke was afraid of Now, for Now has warmth and urgency, and Then is dead and buried. Now might bring a certain knight of gay and shining courage—"But, no!" the cold Duke muttered. "The Prince will break himself against a new and awful labor: a place too high to reach, a thing too far to find, a burden too heavy to lift." The Duke was afraid of Now, but he tampered with the clocks to see if they would go, out of a strange perversity, praying that they wouldn't. Tinkers and tinkerers and a few wizards who happened by tried to start the clocks with tools or magic words, or by shaking them and cursing, but nothing whirred or ticked. The clocks were dead, and in the end, brooding on it, the Duke decided he had murdered time, slain it with his sword, and wiped his bloody blade upon its beard and left it lying there, bleeding hours and minutes, its springs uncoiled and sprawling, its pendulum disintegrating.

The Duke limped because his legs were of different lengths. The right one had outgrown the left because, when he was young, he had spent his mornings place-kicking pups and punting kittens. He would say to a suitor, "What is the difference in the length of my legs?" and if the youth replied, "Why, one is shorter than the other," the Duke would run him through with the sword he carried in his swordcane and feed him to the geese. The suitor was supposed to say, "Why, one is longer than the other." Many a prince had been run through for naming the wrong difference. Others had been slain for offenses equally trivial: trampling the Duke's camellias, failing to praise his wines, staring too long at his gloves, gazing too long at his niece. Those who survived his scorn and sword were given incredible labors to perform in order to win his niece's hand, the only warm hand in the castle, where time had frozen to death at ten minutes to five one snowy night. They were told to cut a slice of moon, or change the ocean into wine. They were set to finding things that never were, and building things that could not be. They came and tried and failed and disappeared and never came again. And some, as I have said, were slain, for using names that start with X, or dropping spoons, or wearing rings, or speaking disrespectfully of sin.

The castle and the Duke grew colder, and Saralinda, as a princess will, even in a place where time lies frozen, became a little older, but only a little older. She was nearly twenty-one the day a prince, disguised as a minstrel, came singing to the town that lay below the castle. He called himself Xingu, which was not his name, and dangerous, since the name began with X—and still does. He was, quite properly, a thing of shreds and patches, a ragged minstrel, singing for pennies and the love of singing. Xingu, as he so rashly called himself, was the youngest son of a powerful king, but he had grown weary of rich attire and banquets and tournaments and the available princesses of his own realm, and yearned to find in a far land the maiden of his dreams, singing as he went, learning the life of the lowly, and possibly slaying a dragon here and there.

At the sign of the Silver Swan, in the town below the castle, where taverners, travelers, tale-tellers, tosspots, troublemakers, and other townspeople were gathered, he heard of Saralinda, loveliest princess on all the thousand islands of the ocean seas. "If you can turn the rain to silver, she is yours," a taverner leered.

"If you can slay the thorny Boar of Borythorn, she is yours," grinned a traveler. "But there is no thorny Boar of Borythorn, which makes it hard."

"What makes it even harder is her uncle's scorn and sword," sneered a tale-teller. "He will slit you from your guggle to your zatch."

"The Duke is seven feet, nine inches tall, and only twenty-eight years old, or in his prime," a tosspot gurgled. "His hand is cold enough to stop a clock, and strong enough to choke a bull, and swift enough to catch the wind. He breaks up minstrels in his soup, like crackers."

"Our minstrel here will warm the old man's heart with song, dazzle him with jewels and gold," a troublemaker simpered. "He'll trample on the Duke's camellias, spill his wine, and blunt his sword, and say his name begins with X, and in the end the Duke will say, 'Take Saralinda, with my blessing, O lordly Prince of Rags and Tags, O rider of the sun!'"

The troublemaker weighed eighteen stone, but the minstrel picked him up and tossed him in the air and caught him and set him down again. Then he paid his due and left the Swan.

"I've seen that youth before," the traveler mused, staring after Xingu, "but he was neither ragamuffin then, nor minstrel. Now let me see, where was it?"

"In his soup," the tosspot said, "like crackers."

II

Outside the tavern the night was lighted by a rocking yellow moon that held a white star in its horn. In the gloomy castle on the hill a lantern gleamed and darkened, came and went, as if the gaunt Duke stalked from room to room, stabbing bats and spiders, killing mice. "Dazzle the Duke with jewels," the minstrel said aloud. "There's something in it somewhere, but what it is and where, I cannot think." He wondered if the Duke would order him to cause a fall of purple snow, or make a table out of sawdust, or merely slit him from his guggle to his zatch, and say to Saralinda, "There he lies, your latest fool, a nameless minstrel. I'll have my varlets feed him to the geese." The minstrel shuddered in the moonlight, wondering where his zatch and guggle were. He wondered how and why and when he could invade the castle. A duke was never known to ask a ragged minstrel to his table, or set a task for him to do, or let him meet a princess. "I'll think of some way," thought the Prince. "I'll think of something."

The hour was late, and revelers began to reel and stagger home from inns and taverns, none in rags, and none in tags, and some in velvet gowns. One third of the dogs in town began to bark. The minstrel took his lute from his shoulder and improvised a song. He had thought of something.

> "Hark, hark, the dogs do bark,
> But only one in three.
> They bark at those in velvet gowns,
> They never bark at me."

A tale-teller, tottering home to bed, laughed at the song, and troublemakers and tosspots began to gather and listen.

> "The Duke is fond of velvet gowns,
> He'll ask you all to tea.
> But I'm in rags, and I'm in tags,
> He'll never send for me."

The townspeople crowded around the minstrel, laughing and cheering. "He's a bold one, Rags is, makin' songs about the Duke!" giggled a strutfurrow who had joined the crowd. The minstrel went on singing.

> "Hark, hark, the dogs do bark,
> The Duke is fond of kittens.
> He likes to take their insides out,
> And use their fur for mittens."

The crowd fell silent in awe and wonder, for the townspeople knew the Duke had slain eleven men for merely staring at his hands, hands that were gloved in velvet gloves, bright with rubies and with diamonds. Fearing to be seen in the doomed and desperate company of the mad minstrel, the revelers slunk off to their homes to tell their wives. Only the traveler, who thought he had seen the singer some otherwhere and time, lingered to warn him of his peril. "I've seen you shining in the lists," he said, "or toppling knights in battle, or breaking men in two like crackers. You must be Tristram's son, or Lancelot's, or are you Tyne or Tora?"

"A wandering minstrel, I," the minstrel said, "a thing of shreds and zatches." He bit his tongue in consternation at the slip it made.

"Even if you were the mighty Zorn of Zorna," said the man, "you could not escape the fury of the Duke. He'll slit you from your guggle to your zatch, from here to here." He touched the minstrel's stomach and his throat.

"I now know what to guard," the minstrel sighed.

A black figure in velvet mask and hood and cloak disappeared behind a tree. "The cold Duke's spy-in-chief," the traveler said, "a man named Whisper. Tomorrow he will die." The minstrel waited. "He'll die because, to name your sins, he'll have to mention mittens. I leave at once for other lands, since I have mentioned mittens." He sighed. "You'll never live to wed his niece. You'll only die to feed his geese. Goodbye, good night, and sorry."

The traveler vanished, like a fly in the mouth of a frog, and the minstrel was left alone in the dark, deserted street. Somewhere a clock dropped a stony chime into the night. The minstrel began to sing again. A soft finger touched his shoulder and he turned to see a little man smiling in the moonlight. He wore an indescribable hat, his eyes were wide and astonished, as if everything were happening for the first time, and he had a dark, describable beard. "If you have nothing better than your songs," he said, "you are somewhat less than much, and only a little more than anything."

"I manage in my fashion," the minstrel said, and he strummed his lute and sang.

> "Hark, hark, the dogs do bark,
>   The cravens are going to bed.
>   Some will rise and greet the sun,
>   But Whisper will be dead."

The old man lost his smile.

"Who are you?" the minstrel asked.

"I am the Golux," said the Golux, proudly, "the only Golux in the world, and not a mere Device."

"You resemble one," the minstrel said, "as Saralinda resembles the rose."

"I resemble only half the things I say I don't," the Golux said. "The other half resemble me." He sighed. "I must always be on hand when people are in peril."

"My peril is my own," the minstrel said.

"Half of it is yours and half is Saralinda's."

"I hadn't thought of that," the minstrel said. "I place my faith in you, and where you lead, I follow."

"Not so fast," the Golux said. "Half the places I have been to, never were. I make things up. Half the things I say are there cannot be found. When I was young I told a tale of buried gold, and men from leagues around dug in the woods. I dug myself."

"But why?"

"I thought the tale of treasure might be true."

"You said you made it up."

"I know I did, but then I didn't know I had. I forget things, too." The minstrel felt a vague uncertainty. "I make mistakes, but I am on the side of Good," the Golux said, "by accident and happenchance. I had high hopes of being Evil when I was two, but in my youth I came upon a firefly burning in a spider's web. I saved the victim's life."

"The firefly's?" said the minstrel.

"The spider's. The blinking arsonist had set the web on fire." The minstrel's uncertainty increased, but as he thought to slip away, a deep bell sounded in the castle and many lights appeared, and voices shouted orders and commands. A stream of lanterns started flowing down the darkness. "The Duke has heard your songs," the Golux said. "The fat is in the fire, the die is cast, the jig is up, the goose is cooked, and the cat is out of the bag."

"My hour has struck," the minstrel said. They heard a faint and distant rasping sound, as if a blade of steel were being sharpened on a stone.

"The Duke prepares to feed you to his geese," the Golux said. "We must invent a tale to stay his hand."

"What manner of tale?" the minstrel asked.

"A tale," the Golux said, "to make the Duke believe that slaying you would light a light in someone else's heart. He hates a light in people's hearts. So you must say a certain prince and princess can't be wed until the evening of the second day after the Duke has fed you to his geese."

"I wish that you would not keep saying that," the minstrel said.

"The tale sounds true," the Golux said, "and very like a witch's spell. The Duke has awe of witches' spells. I'm certain he will stay his hand, I think."

The sound of tramping feet came near and nearer. The iron guards of the Duke closed in, their lanterns gleaming and their spears and armor. "Halt!" There was a clang and clanking.

"Do not arrest my friend," the youth implored.

"What friend?" the captain growled.

The minstrel looked around him and about, but there was no one there. A guard guffawed and said, "Maybe he's seen the Golux."

"There isn't any Golux. I have been to school, and know," the captain said. The minstrel's uncertainty increased again. "Fall in!" the captain bawled. "Dress up that line."

"You heard him. Dress it up," the sergeant said. They marched the minstrel to the dungeon in the castle. A stream of lantern light flowed slowly up the hill.

III

It was morning. The cold Duke gazed out a window of the castle, as if he were watching flowers in bloom or flying birds. He was watching his varlets feeding Whisper to the geese. He turned away and took three limps and stared at the minstrel, standing in the great hall of the castle, both hands bound behind him. "What manner of prince is this you speak of, and what manner of maiden does he love, to use a word that makes no sense and has no point?" His voice sounded like iron dropped on velvet.

"A noble prince, a noble lady," the minstrel said. "When they are wed a million people will be glad."

The Duke took his sword out of his swordcane and stared at it. He limped across and faced his captive, and touched his guggle softly with the point, and touched his zatch, and sighed and frowned, and put the sword away. "We shall think of some amusing task for you to do," he said. "I do not like your tricks and guile. I think there is no prince or maiden who would wed if I should slay you, but I am neither sure nor certain." He grinned and said again, "We'll think of some amusing task for you to do."

"But I am not a prince," the minstrel said, "and only princes may aspire to Saralinda's hand."

The cold Duke kept on grinning. "Why, then we'll make a prince of you," he said. "The prince of Rags and Jingles." He clapped his gloves together and two varlets appeared without a word or sound. "Take him to his dungeon," said the Duke. "Feed him water without bread, and bread without water."

The varlets were taking the minstrel out of the great hall when down the marble stairs the Princess Saralinda floated like a cloud. The Duke's eye gleamed like crystal. The minstrel gazed in wonder. The Princess Saralinda was tall, with freesias in her dark hair, and she wore serenity brightly like the rainbow. It was not easy to tell her mouth from the rose, or her brow from the white lilac. Her voice was faraway music, and her eyes were candles burning on a tranquil night. She moved across the room like wind in violets, and her laughter sparkled on the air, which, from her presence, gained a faint and undreamed fragrance. The Prince was frozen by her beauty, but not cold, and the Duke, who was cold but not frozen, held up the palms of his gloves, as if she were a fire at which to warm his hands. The minstrel saw the blood come warmly to the lame man's cheeks. "This thing of rags and tags and tatters will play our little game," he told his niece, his voice like iron on velvet.

"I wish him well," the Princess said.

The minstrel broke his bonds and took her hand in his, but it was slashed away by the swift cane of the Duke. "Take him to his dungeon now," he said. He stared coldly at the minstrel through his monocle. "You'll find the most amusing bats and spiders there."

"I wish him well," the Princess said again, and the varlets took the minstrel to his dungeon.

When the great iron door of the dungeon clanked behind the minstrel, he found himself alone in blackness. A spider, swinging on a strand of web, swung back and forth. The zickering of bats was echoed by the walls. The minstrel took a step, avoiding snakes, and something squirmed. "Take care," the Golux said, "you're on my foot."

"Why are you here?" the minstrel cried.

"I forgot something. I forgot about the task the Duke will set you."

The minstrel thought of swimming lakes too wide to swim, of turning liquids into stone, or finding boneless creatures made of bone. "How came you here?" he asked. "And can you leave?"

"I never know," the Golux said. "My mother was a witch, but rather mediocre in her way. When she tried to turn a thing to gold, it turned to clay; and when she changed her rivals into fish, all she ever got was mermaids." The minstrel's heart was insecure. "My father was a wizard," said his friend, "who often cast his spells upon himself, when he was in his cups. Strike a light or light a lantern! Something I have hold of has no head."

The minstrel shuddered. "The task," he said. "You came to tell me."

"I did? Oh, yes. My father lacked the power of concentration, and that is bad for monks and priests, and worse for wizards. Listen. Tell the Duke that you will hunt the Boar, or travel thrice around the moon, or turn November into June. Implore him not to send you out to find a thousand jewels."

"And then?"

"And then he'll send you out to find a thousand jewels."

"But I am poor!" the minstrel cried.

"Come, come," the Golux said. "You're Zorn of Zorna. I had it from a traveler I met. It came to him as he was leaving town. Your father's casks and coffers shine with rubies and with sapphires."

"My father lives in Zorna," said the Prince, "and it would take me nine and ninety days: three and thirty days to go, and three and thirty days to come back here."

"That's six and sixty."

"It always takes my father three and thirty days to make decisions," said the Prince. "In spells and labors a certain time is always set, and I might be at sea when mine expires."

"That's another problem for another day," the Golux said. "Time is for dragonflies and angels. The former live too little and the latter live too long."

Zorn of Zorna thought awhile and said, "The task seems strange and simple."

"There are no jewels," the Golux said, "within the reach and ranges of this island, except the gems here in this castle. The Duke knows not that you are Zorn of Zorna. He thinks you are a minstrel without a penny or a moonstone. He's fond of jewels. You've seen them on his gloves."

The Prince stepped on a turtle. "The Duke has spies," he said, "who may know who I am."

The Golux sighed. "I may be wrong," he said, "but we must risk and try it."

The Prince sighed in his turn. "I wish you could be surer."

"I wish I could," the Golux said. "My mother was born, I regret to say, only partly in a caul. I've saved a score of princes in my time. I cannot save them all." Something that would have been purple, if there had been light to see it by, scuttled across the floor. "The Duke might give me only thirty days, or forty-two, to find a thousand jewels," said Zorn of Zorna. "Why should he give me ninety-nine?"

"The way I figure it," the Golux said, "is this. The longer the labor lasts, the longer lasts his gloating. He loves to gloat, you know."

The Prince sat down beside a toad. "My father may have lost his jewels," he said, "or given them away."

"I thought of that," the Golux said. "But I have other plans than one. Right now we have to sleep."

They found a corner without creatures and slept until the town clock struck the midnight hour.

Chains clanked and rattled, and the great iron door began to move. "The Duke has sent for you again," the Golux said. "Be careful what you say and what you do."

The great iron door began to open slowly. "When shall I see you next?" Zorn whispered. There was no answer. The Prince groped around in the dark and felt a thing very like a cat, and touched the thing without a head, but he could not find the Golux.

The great iron door was open wide now and the dungeon filled with lantern light.

"The Duke commands your presence," growled a guard. "What was *that*?"

"What was what?"

"I know not," said the guard. "I thought I heard the sound of someone laughing."

"Is the Duke afraid of laughter?" asked the Prince.

"The Duke is not afraid of anything. Not even," said the guard, "the Todal."

"The Todal?"

"The Todal."

"What's the Todal?"

A lock of the guard's hair turned white and his teeth began to chatter. "The Todal looks like a blob of glup," he said. "It makes a sound like rabbits screaming, and smells of old, unopened rooms. It's waiting for the Duke to fail in some endeavor, such as setting you a task that you can do."

"And if he sets me one, and I succeed?" the Prince inquired.

"The Blob will glup him," said the guard. "It's an agent of the devil, sent to punish evildoers for having done less evil than they should. I talk too much. Come on. The Duke is waiting."

IV

The Duke sat at one end of a black oak table in the black oak room, lighted by flaming torches that threw red gleams on shields and lances. The Duke's gloves sparkled when he moved his hands. He stared moodily through his monocle at young Prince Zorn. The Duke sneered, which made him even colder. "So you would hunt the Boar," he said, "or travel thrice around the moon, or turn November into June." He laughed, and a torch went out. "Saralinda in November turns November into June. A cow can travel thrice around the moon, or even more. And *anyone* can merely *hunt* the Boar. I have another plan for you. I thought it up myself last night, while I was killing mice. I'll send you out to find a thousand jewels and bring them back."

The Prince turned pale, or tried to. "A wandering minstrel, I," he said, "a thing of—"

"Rubies and sapphires." The Duke's chuckle sounded like ice cackling in a cauldron. "For you are Zorn of Zorna," he whispered, softly. "Your father's casks and vaults and coffers shine with jewels. In six and sixty days you could sail to Zorna and return."

"It always takes my father three and thirty days to make decisions," cried the Prince.

The Duke grinned. "That is what I wanted to know, my naïve Prince," he said. "Then you would have me give you nine and ninety days?"

"That would be fair," the Prince replied. "But how do you know that I am Zorn?"

"I have a spy named Hark," the Duke explained, "who found your princely raiment in your quarters in the town and brought it here, with certain signs and seals and signatures, revealing who you are. Go put the raiment on." He pointed at a flight of iron stairs. "You'll find it in a chamber on whose door a star is turning black. Don it and return. I'll think of beetles while you're gone, and things like that." The Duke limped to his chair and sat down again, and the Prince started up the iron stairs, wondering where the Golux was. He stopped and turned and said, "You will not give me nine and ninety days. How many, then?" The Duke sneered. "I'll think of a lovely number," he said. "Go on."

When Zorn came back he wore his royal attire, but the Duke's spies had sealed his sword, so that he could not draw it. The Duke sat staring at a man who wore a velvet mask and cloak and hood. "This is Hark," he said, "and this is Listen." He gestured with his cane at nothing.

"There's no one there," said Zorn.

"Listen is invisible," the Duke explained. "Listen can be heard, but never seen. They are here to learn the mark and measure of your task. I give you nine and ninety hours, not nine and ninety days, to find a thousand jewels and bring them here. When you return, the clocks must all be striking five."

"The clocks here in the castle?" asked the Prince. "The thirteen clocks?"

"The clocks here in the castle," said the Duke, "the thirteen clocks."

The Prince looked at the two clocks on the walls. Their hands pointed to ten minutes of five. "The hands are frozen," said the Prince. "The clocks are dead."

"Precisely," said the Duke, "and what is more, which makes your task a charming one, there are no jewels that could be found within the space of nine and ninety hours, except those in my vaults, and these." He held his gloves up and they sparkled.

"A pretty task," said Hark.

"Ingenious," said the voice of Listen.

"I thought you'd like it," said the Duke. "Unseal his sword." Invisible hands unsealed the Prince's sword.

"And if I should succeed?" asked Zorn.

The Duke waved a gloved hand at the iron stairs, and Zorn saw Saralinda standing there. "I wish him well," she said, and her uncle laughed and looked at Zorn. "I hired a witch," he said, "to cast a tiny spell upon her. When she is in my presence, all that she can say is this: 'I wish him well.' You like it?"

"A clever spell," said Hark.

"An awful spell," the voice of Listen said.

The Prince and Princess spoke a silent language with their eyes, until the Duke cried, "Go!" and Saralinda vanished up the stairs.

"And if I fail?" asked Zorn.

The Duke removed his sword from his swordcane and ran his glove along the blade. "I'll slit you from your guggle to your zatch, and feed you to the Todal."

"I've heard of it," said Zorn.

The Duke smiled. "You've only heard of half of it," he said. "The other half is worse. It's made of lip. It feels as if it had been dead at least a dozen days, but it moves about like monkeys and like shadows." The Prince took out his sword and put it back. "The Todal can't be killed," the Duke said, softly.

"It gleeps," said Hark.

"What's gleeping?" asked the Prince.

The Duke and Hark and Listen laughed. "Time is wasting, Prince," the Duke reminded him. "Already you have only eight and ninety hours. I wish you every strangest kind of luck." A wide oak door suddenly opened at the end of the room, and the Prince saw lightning and midnight and falling rain. "One last word and warning," said the Duke. "I would not trust the Golux overfar. He cannot tell what can be from what can't. He seldom knows what should be from what is."

The Prince glanced at Hark and at the Duke, and at a spot where he thought Listen stood. "When all the clocks are striking five," he said, and left the room. The laughter of the Duke and Hark and Listen followed him out the door and down the stairs and into the darkness. When he had gone a few steps from the castle, he looked up at a lighted window and thought he saw the Princess Saralinda standing there. A rose fell at his feet, and as he picked it up, the laughter of the Duke and Hark and Listen increased inside the black oak room and died away.

v

The Prince had gone but a short way from the castle when he felt a gentle finger touch his elbow. "It is the Golux," said the Golux, proudly. "The only Golux in the world."

The Prince was in no mood for the old man's gaiety and cheer. The Golux did not seem wonderful to him now, and even his indescribable hat was suddenly describable. "The Duke thinks you are not so wise as he thinks you think you are," he said.

The Golux smiled. "I think he is not so wise as he thinks I think he is," he said. "I was there. I know the terms. I had thought that only dragonflies and angels think of time, never having been an angel or a dragonfly."

"How were you there?" the Prince said in surprise.

"I am Listen," the Golux said, "or at any rate, he thinks I am. Never trust a spy you cannot see. The Duke is lamer than I am old, and I am shorter than he is cold, but it comes to you with some surprise that I am wiser than he is wise."

The Prince's courage began to return. "I think you are the most remarkable man in the world," he said.

"Who thought not so a moment since, knows not the apple from the quince," the Golux said. He scowled. "We now have only eight and ninety *hours* to find a thousand gems," he said.

"You said that you had other plans than one," the Prince reminded him.

"What plans?" the Golux asked.

"You didn't say," said Zorn.

The Golux closed his eyes and clasped his hands. "There was a treasure ship that sank, not more than forty hours from here," he said. "But, come to think of it, the Duke ransacked the ship and stole the jewels."

"So much," sighed Zorn, "for that."

The Golux thought again. "If there were hail," he said, "and we could stain the hail with blood, it might turn into rubies."

"There is no hail," said Zorn.

The Golux sighed. "So much," he said, "for that."

"The task is hard," said Zorn, "and can't be done."

"I can do a score of things that can't be done," the Golux said. "I can find a thing I cannot see and see a thing I cannot find. The first is time, the second is a spot before my eyes. I can feel a thing I cannot touch and touch a thing I cannot feel. The first is sad and sorry, the second is your heart. What would you do without me? Say 'nothing.'"

"Nothing," said the Prince.

"Good. Then you're helpless and I'll help you. I said I had another plan than one, and I have just remembered what it is. There is a woman on this isle, who'd have some eight and eighty years, and she is gifted with the strangest gift of all. For when she weeps, what do you think she weeps?"

"Tears," said Zorn.

"Jewels," said the Golux.

The Prince stared at him. "But that is too remarkable to be," he said.

"I don't see why," the Golux said. "Even the lowly oyster makes his pearls without the use of eyes or hands or any tools, and pearls are jewels. The oyster is a blob of glup, but a woman is a woman."

The Prince thought of the Todal and felt a small cold feeling in his guggle. "Where does this wondrous woman dwell?" he asked.

The old man groaned. "Over mountain, over stream, by the way of storm and thunder, in a hut so high or deep—I never can remember which—the naked eye can't see it." He stood up. "We must be on our way," he said. "It will take us ninety hours, or more or less, to go and come. It's this way, or it's that way. Make up my mind."

"How can I?" asked the Prince. "You have a rose," the Golux said. "Hold it in your hand." The Prince took out the rose and held it in his hand, and its stem slowly turned and stopped. "It's this way," cried the Golux, and they started off in the direction the stem of the rose had pointed out. "I will tell you the tale of Hagga," said the Golux.

When Hagga was eleven (he began) and picking cherries in the woods one day, and asphodel, she came upon the good King Gwain of Yarrow with his foot caught in a wolf trap. "Weep for me, maiden," said the King, "for I am ludicrous and laughable, with my foot caught in this trap. I am no longer ert, for I have lost my ertia. By twiddling my fingers or clapping my hands, I have often changed the fate of men, but now I cannot get my foot lose from this thing."

"I have no time for tears," the maiden said. She knew the secret of the trap, and was about to free the fettered foot, when a farmer from a near-by farm began to laugh. The King beshrewed him and his wife, and turned them into grasshoppers, creatures that look as if their feet were caught in traps, even when they aren't.

"Lo, the maid has freed my foot," the King exulted, seeing that she had, "but it is numb, and feels like someone else's foot, not mine." The maiden took off his shoe and rubbed his foot, until it felt like his and he could put it down. And for her kindness the grateful King gave her the power to weep jewels when she wept, instead of tears. When the people learned of the strange gift the King had given Hagga, they came from leagues around, by night and day, in warm and winter weather, to make her sad and sorry. Nothing tragic happened but she heard of it and wept. People came with heavy hearts and left with pearls and rubies. Paths were paved with pearls, and rivers ran with rubies. Children played with sapphires in the streets, and dogs chewed opals. Every peacock had at least nine diamonds in its gizzard, and one, cut open on St. Wistow's Day, had thirty-eight. The price of stones and pebbles rose, the price of gems declined, until, by making Hagga weep, you could be hanged and fined. In the end, the jewels were melted, in a frightful fire, by order of the King. "I will make her weep myself, one day each year," the King decreed, "and thus and hence, the flow of gems will make some sense, and have some point and balance." But alas, and but alack, the maid could weep no more at any tale of tragedy or tribulation. Damsels killed by dragons left her cold, and broken hearts, and children lost, and love denied. She never wept by day or night, in warm or winter weather. She grew to be sixteen, and twenty-six, and thirty-four, and forty-eight, and fifty-two, and now she waits, at eighty-eight, for me and you. "I hope," the Golux said, "that this is true. I make things up, you know."

The young Prince sighed and said, "I know you do. If Hagga weeps no more, why should she weep for you?"

The Golux thought it over. "I feel that she is frail and fragile. I trust that she is sad and sorry. I hope that she is neither dead nor dying. I'll think of something very sad to tell her. Very sad and lonely. Take out your rose, I think we're lost."

They had become tangled in brambles by now, and the trees of the forest they had entered were tall and thick. Thorns began to tear the Prince's raiment. Lightning flashed and thunder rolled, and all paths vanished. The Prince took out the rose and held it in his hand. The stem began to turn and twist, and pointed.

"Around this way," the Golux said. "It's lighter here." He found a narrow path that led straight onward. As they walked along the path, the Golux leading, they met a Jackadandy, whose clothes were torn and tattered.

"I told my tales to Hagga," said the man; "but Hagga weeps no more. I told her tales of lovers lost in April. I told her tales of maidens dead in June. I told her tales of princes fed to geese. I even told her how I lost my youngest niece."

"This is sad," the Golux said, "and getting sadder."

"The way is long," the torn man said, "and getting longer. The road goes uphill all the way, and even farther. I wish you luck," he said. "You'll need it." He disappeared in brambles.

The only light in the forest came from lightning, and when it flashed they watched the rose and followed where it pointed. This brought them, on the second day, into a valley. They saw a Jack-o'-lent approaching, his clothes all torn and tattered. "I told my tales to Hagga," said the man, "but Hagga weeps no more. I told her tales of lovers lost at sea and drowned in fountains. I told her tales of babies lost in woods and lost on mountains. She wept not," said the Jack-o'-lent. "The way is dark, and getting darker. The hut is high and even higher. I wish you luck. There is none." He vanished in the briars.

The brambles and the thorns grew thick and thicker in a ticking thicket of bickering crickets. Farther along and stronger, bonged the gongs of a throng of frogs, green and vivid on their lily pads. From the sky came the crying of flies, and the pilgrims leaped over a bleating sheep creeping knee-deep in a sleepy stream, in which swift and slippery snakes slid and slithered silkily, whispering sinful secrets.

A comet whistled through the sky, and by its light they saw the hut of Hagga high on Hagga's hill. "If she is dead, there may be strangers there," the Golux said.

"How many hours do we have left?" the Prince demanded.

"If we can make her weep within the hour," the Golux said, "we'll barely make it."

"I hope that she's alive and sad," said Zorn.

"I feel that she has died," the Golux sighed. "I feel it in my stomach. You better carry me. I'm weary."

Zorn of Zorna picked the Golux up and carried him.

VI

It was cold on Hagga's hill, and fresh with furrows where the dragging points of stars had plowed the fields. A peasant in a purple smock stalked the smoking furrows, sowing seeds. There was a smell, the Golux thought, a little like Forever in the air, but mixed with something faint and less enduring, possibly the fragrance of a flower. "There's no light in her window," the Golux said, "and it is dark and getting darker."

"There's no smoke in her chimney," said the Prince, "and it is cold and getting colder."

The Golux barely breathed and said, "What worries me the most is that spider's web there on the door, that stretches from the hinges to the latch."

The young Prince felt a hollow feeling in his zatch. "Knock on her door," the Golux said, his voice so high it quavered. He crossed his fingers and kept them crossed, and Zorn knocked on the door. No one answered. "Knock again," the Golux cried, and Prince Zorn knocked again.

Hagga was there. She came to the door and stared at them, a woman neither dead or dying, and clearly only thirty-eight or thirty-nine. The Golux had missed her age by fifty years, as old men often do. "Weep for us," the Golux cried, "or else this Prince will never wed his Princess."

"I have no tears," said Hagga. "Once I wept when ships were overdue, or brooks ran dry, or tangerines were overripe, or sheep got something in their eye. I weep no more," said Hagga. Her eyes were dry as deserts and her mouth seemed made of stone. "I have turned a thousand persons gemless from my door. Come in," she said. "I weep no more."

The room was dark and held a table and a chair, and in one corner something like a chest, made of oak and bound with brass. The Golux smiled and then looked sad, and said, "I have tales to make a hangman weep, and tales to bring a tear of sorrow to a monster's eye. I have tales that would disturb a dragon's sleep, and even make the Todal sigh."

At the mention of the Todal, Hagga's hair turned gray. "Once I wept when maids were married underneath the April moon. I weep no more when maids are buried, even in the month of June."

"You have the emotions of a fish," said the Golux, irritably. He sat on the floor and told her tales of the death of kings, and kindred things, and little children choked by rings.

"I have no tears," said Hagga.

He told her tales of the frogs in the forum, and the toads in the rice that destroyed the poppycockalorum and the cockahoopatrice.

"I weep no more," said Hagga.

"Look," the Golux said, "and listen! The Princess Saralinda will never wed this youth until the day he lays a thousand jewels upon a certain table."

"I would weep for Saralinda," Hagga sighed, "if I were able."

The Prince had wandered to the oaken chest. He seized its cover with his hand and threw it open. A radiance filled the room and lit the darkest corners. Inside the chest there were at least ten thousand jewels of the very sort and kind the Duke demanded. Diamonds flared and rubies glowed, and sapphires burned and emeralds seemed on fire. They looked at Hagga. "These are the jewels of laughter," Hagga said. "I woke up fourteen days ago to find them on my bed. I had laughed until I wept at something in my sleep." The Golux grabbed a gleaming handful of the gems, and then another, crowing with delight. "Put them back," said Hagga. "For there's a thing that you must know, concerning jewels of laughter. They always turn again to tears a fortnight after. It has been a fortnight, to the day and minute, since I took the pretties to this chest and put them in it."

Even as they watched, the light and color died. The diamonds dimmed, the emeralds went out, and the jewels of Hagga's laughter turned to tears, with a little sound like sighing. There was nothing in the chest but limpid liquid, leering up at them and winking. "You must think," the Golux cried. "You must think of what you laughed at in your sleep."

Hagga's eyes were blank. "I do not know, for this was fourteen days ago."

"Think!" the Golux said.

"Think!" said Zorn of Zorna.

Hagga frowned and said, "I never can remember dreams."

The Golux clasped his hands behind his back and thought it over. "As I remember and recall," he said, "the jewels of sorrow last forever. Such was the gift and power the good Gwain gave you. What was he doing, by the way, so many leagues from Yarrow?"

"Hunting," Hagga said. "Wolves, as I recall it."

The Golux scowled. "I am a man of logic, in my way. What happened on that awful day, to make him value sorrow over and above the gift of laughter? Why have these jewels turned to tears a fortnight after?"

"There was a farmer from a near-by farm, who laughed," said Hagga. "'On second thought,' the good King said, 'I will amend and modify the gift I gave you. The jewels of sorrow will last beyond all measure, but may the jewels of laughter give you little pleasure.'"

The Golux groaned. "If there's one thing in the world I hate," he said, "it is amendments." His eyes turned bright and brighter, and he clapped his hands. "I will make her laugh until she weeps," he said.

The Golux told her funny tales of things that were and had been, but Hagga's eyes were dry as quartz and her mouth seemed made of agate. "I laugh at nothing that has been," she said, "or is."

The Golux smiled. "Then we will think of things that will be, and aren't now, and never were. I'll think of something," and he thought, and thought of something.

> "A dehoy who was terribly hobble,
> Cast only stones that were cobble
> And bats that were ding,
> From a shot that was sling,
> But never hit inks that were bobble."

Hagga laughed until she wept, and seven moonstones trickled down her cheek and clattered on the floor. "She's weeping semiprecious stones!" the Golux wailed. He tried again:

> "There was an old coddle so molly,
> He talked in a glot that was poly,
> His gaws were so gew
> That his laps became dew,
> And he ate only pops that were lolly."

Hagga laughed until she wept, and seven brilliants trickled down her cheek and clattered on the floor. "Rhinestones!" groaned the Golux. "Now she's weeping costume jewelry!"

The young Prince tried his hand at telling tales of laughter, but for his pains he got a shower of tourmaline, a cat's-eye, and a flux of pearls. "The Duke hates pearls," the Golux moaned. "He thinks they're made by fish."

It grew darker in the room and they could scarcely see. The starlight and the moon were gone. They stood there, still as statues. The Golux cleared his throat. The Prince uncrossed his arms and crossed them. And then, without a rhyme or reason, out of time and out of season, Hagga laughed and kept on laughing. No one had said a word, no one had told a tale. It might have been the hooting of an owl. It might have been the crawling of a snail. But Hagga laughed and kept on laughing, and precious jewels twinkled down her cheek and sparkled on the floor, until the hut was ankle-deep in diamonds and in rubies. The Golux counted out a thousand and put them in a velvet sack that he had brought along. "I wish that she had laughed," he sighed, "at something I had said."

Zorn of Zorna took her hand. "God keep you warm in winter," said the Prince, "and cool in summer."

"Farewell," the Golux said, "and thank you."

Hagga laughed and kept on laughing, and sapphires burned upon the floor and lit the Golux toward the door.

"How many hours are left us now?" the young Prince cried. "It's odd," the Golux muttered to himself. "I could have sworn that she had died. This is the only time my stomach ever lied."

"How many hours are left us now?" the Prince implored.

Hagga sat upon the chest and kept on laughing.

"I should say," the Golux said, "that we have only forty left, but it is downhill all the way."

They went out into the moonless night and peered about them in the dark.

"I think it's this way," the Golux said, and they went the way he thought it was.

"What about the clocks?" demanded Zorn.

The Golux exhaled a sorry breath. "That's another problem for another hour," he said.

Inside the hut, something red and larger than a ruby glowed among the jewels and Hagga picked it up. "A rose," she said. "They must have dropped it."

VII

In the black oak room the yellow torches flared and crackled on the walls, and their fire burned on the lances and the shields. The Duke's gloves glittered. "How goes the night?" he gnarled.

"The moon is down," said Hark. "I have not heard the clocks."

"You'll never hear them!" screamed the Duke. "I slew time in this castle many a cold and snowy year ago."

Hark stared at him emptily and seemed to be chewing something. "Time froze here. Someone left the windows open."

"Bah!" The Duke sat down at the far end of the table, stood up again, and limped about. "It bled hours and minutes on the floor. I saw it with my eye." Hark kept on chewing something. Outside the Gothic windows thunder growled. An owl flew by.

"There are no jewels," roared the Duke. "They'll have to bring me pebbles from the sea or mica from the meadows." He gave his awful laugh. "How goes the night?" he asked again.

"I have been counting off and on," said Hark, "and I should say they have some forty minutes left."

"They'll never make it!" the cold Duke screamed. "I hope they drowned, or broke their legs, or lost their way." He came so close to Hark their noses almost touched. "Where were they going?" he whispered harshly.

Hark stepped backward seven steps. "I met a Jackadandy, some seven hours ago," he said. "They passed him on their way to Hagga's hill. Do you remember Hagga, and have you thought of her?"

The Duke's loud laughter rang the shields.

"Hagga weeps no more," he said. "Hagga has no tears. She did not even weep when she was told about the children locked up in my tower."

"I hated that," said Hark.

"I liked it," said the Duke. "No child can sleep in my camellias." He began to limp again and stared out at the night. "Where is Listen?" he demanded.

"He followed them," said Hark, "the Golux and the Prince."

"I do not trust him," growled the Duke. "I like a spy that I can see. Let me have men about me that are visible." He shouted "Listen!" up the stairs, and "Listen!" out the windows, but no one answered. "I'm cold," he rasped.

"You always are."

"I'm colder," snarled the Duke, "and never tell me what I always am!" He took his sword out and slashed at nothing and at silence. "I miss Whisper."

"You fed him to the geese," said Hark. "They seemed to like him."

"Silence! What was that?"

"What did it sound like?"

"Like princes stealing up the stairs, like Saralinda leaving." The Duke limped to the iron stairs and slashed again at silence and at nothing. "What does he feel like? Have you felt him?"

"Listen? He's five feet high," said Hark. "He has a beard, and something on his head I can't describe."

"The Golux!" shrieked the Duke. "You felt the Golux! I hired him as a spy and didn't know it."

A purple ball with gold stars on it came slowly bouncing down the iron stairs and winked and twinkled, like a naked child saluting priests. "What insolence is this?" the Duke demanded. "What *is* that thing?"

"A ball," said Hark.

"I know that!" screamed the Duke. "But why? What does its ghastly presence signify?"

"It looks to me," said Hark, "very like a ball the Golux and those children used to play with."

"They're on his side!" The Duke was apoplectic. "Their ghosts are on his side."

"He has a lot of friends," said Hark.

"Silence!" roared the Duke. "He knows not what is dead from what is dying, or where he's been from where he's going, or striking clocks from clocks that never strike."

"What makes me think he does?" The spy stopped chewing. Something very much like nothing anyone had seen before came trotting down the stairs and crossed the room.

"What is that?" the Duke asked, palely.

"I don't know what it is," said Hark, "but it's the only one there ever was."

The Duke's gloved hands shook and shimmered. "I'll throw them up for grabs betwixt the Todal and the geese! I'll lock them in the dungeon with the thing without a head!" At the mention of the Todal, Hark's velvet mask turned gray. The Duke's eye twisted upward in its socket. "I'll slay them all!" he said. "This sweetheart and her suitor, this cross-eyed clown! You hear me?"

"Yes," said Hark, "but there are rules and rites and rituals, older than the sound of bells and snow on mountains."

"Go on," the Duke said, softly, looking up the stairs.

"You must let them have their time and turn to make the castle clocks strike five."

"The castle clocks were murdered," said the Duke. "I killed time here myself one snowy morning. You still can see the old brown stains, where seconds bled to death, here on my sleeve." He laughed. "What else?" he asked.

"You know as well as I," said Hark. "The Prince must have his turn and time to lay a thousand jewels there on the table."

"And if he does?"

"He wins the hand of Princess Saralinda."

"The only warm hand in the castle," said the Duke. "Who loses Saralinda loses fire. I mean the fire of the setting suns, and not the cold and cheerless flame of jewels. Her eyes are candles burning in a shrine. Her feet appear to me as doves. Her fingers bloom upon her breast like flowers."

"This is scarcely the way," said Hark, "to speak of one's own niece."

"She's not my niece! I stole her! I stole her from the castle of a king! I snatched her from the bosom of a sleeping queen. I still bear on my hands the marks of where she bit me."

"The Queen?" asked Hark.

"The Princess," roared the Duke.

"Who was the King?" asked Hark.

His master scowled. "I never knew," he said. "My ship was beached upon an island in a storm. There was no moon or any star. No lights were in the castle."

"How could you find the Princess then?" asked Hark.

"She had a radiance," said the Duke. "She shone there like a star upon her mother's breast. I knew I had to have that splendor in my castle. I mean to keep her here till she is twenty-one. The day she is, I'll wed her, and that day is tomorrow."

"Why haven't you before?" asked Hark. "This castle is your kingdom."

The Duke smiled and showed his upper teeth. "Because her nurse turned out to be a witch who cast a spell upon me."

"What were its terms?" asked Hark.

"I cannot wed her till the day she's twenty-one, and that day is tomorrow."

"You said that once before."

"I must keep her in a chamber where she is safe from me. I've done that."

"I like that part," said Hark.

"I hate it," snarled the Duke. "I must give and grant the right to any prince to seek her hand in marriage. I've done that, too." He sat down at the table.

"In spells of this sort," Hark said, chewing, "one always finds a chink or loophole, by means of which the right and perfect prince can win her hand in spite of any task you set him. How did the witch announce that part of it?"

"Like this. 'She can be saved, and you destroyed, only by a prince whose name begins with X and doesn't.' There is no prince whose name begins with X and doesn't."

Hark's mask slipped off and he put it back again, but not before the Duke saw laughter in his eyes. "This prince," said Hark, "is Zorn of Zorna, but to your terror and distaste, he once posed as a minstrel. His name was Xingu then and wasn't. This is the prince whose name begins with X and doesn't."

The Duke's sword had begun to shake. "Nobody ever tells me anything," he whispered to himself.

Another ball came bouncing down the stairs, a black ball stamped with scarlet owls. The cold Duke watched it roll across the floor. "What impudence is this?" he cried.

Hark walked to the stairs and listened, and turned and said, "There's someone up there."

"It's the children!" croaked the Duke.

"The children are dead," said Hark, "and the sound I heard was made by living feet."

"How much time is left them?" cried the Duke.

"Half an hour, I think," said Hark.

"I'll have their guggles on my sword for playing games with me!" The Duke started up the stairs and stopped. "They're up there, all of them. Call out the guards," he barked.

"The guards are guarding the clocks," said Hark. "You wanted it that way. There are eleven guards, and each one guards a clock. You and I are guarding *these.*" He pointed at the two clocks on the walls. "You wanted it that way."

"Call out the guards," the Duke repeated, and his agent called the guards. They trooped into the room like engines. The Duke limped up the stairs, his drawn sword shining. "Follow me!" he cried. "Another game's afoot! I'll slay the Golux and the Prince, and marry Saralinda!" He led the way. The guards ramped up the stairs like engines. Hark smiled, and chewed again, and followed.

The black oak room was silent for a space of seven seconds. Then a secret door swung open in a wall. The Golux slipped into the room. The Princess followed. His hands were raw and red from climbing vines to Saralinda's chamber. "How could you find the castle in the dark without my rose?" she asked. "He would not let me burn a torch."

"You lighted up your window like a star, and we could see the castle from afar," the Golux said. "Our time is marked in minutes. Start the clocks!"

"I cannot start the clocks," the Princess said.

They heard the sound of fighting far above. "He faces thirteen men," she cried, "and that is hard."

"We face thirteen clocks," the Golux said, "and that is harder. Start the clocks!"

"How can I start the clocks?" the Princess wailed.

"Your hand is warmer than the snow is cold," the Golux said. "Touch the first clock with your hand." The Princess touched it. Nothing happened. "Again!" Saralinda held her hand against the clock and nothing happened. "We are ruined," said the Golux simply, and Saralinda's heart stood still.

She cried, "Use magic!"

"I have no magic to depend on," groaned the Golux. "Try the other clock."

The Princess tried the other clock and nothing happened. "Use logic, then!" she cried. In the secret walls they heard the Iron Guards pounding after Zorn, and coming close.

"Now let me see," the Golux said. "If you can touch the clocks and never start them, then you can start the clocks and never touch them. That's logic, as I know and use it. Hold your hand this far away. Now that far. Closer! Now a little farther back. A little farther. There! I think you have it! Do not move!"

The clogged and rigid works of the clock began to whir. They heard a tick and then a ticking. The Princess Saralinda fled from room to room, like wind in clover, and held her hand the proper distance from the clocks. Something like a vulture spread its wings and left the castle. "That was Then," the Golux said.

"It's Now!" cried Saralinda.

A morning glory that had never opened, opened in the courtyard. A cock that never crowed, began to crow. The light of morning stained the windows, and in the walls the cold Duke moaned, "I hear the sound of time. And yet I slew it, and wiped my bloody sword upon its beard." He thought that Zorn of Zorna had escaped the guards. His sword kept whining in the blackness, and once he slashed his own left knee—he thought it was the Golux. "Come out, you crooning knave!" he cried. "Stand forward, Zorn of Zorna!"

"He's not here," said the spy.

They heard the savage clash of swords. "They've got him!" squealed the Duke. "Eleven men to one!"

"You may have heard of Galahad," said Hark, "whose strength was as the strength of ten."

"That leaves one man to get him," cried the Duke. "I count on Krang, the strongest guard I have, the finest fencer in the world, save one. An unknown prince in armor vanquished him a year ago, somewhere on an island. No one else can do it."

"The unknown prince," said Hark, "was Zorn of Zorna."

"I'll slay him then myself!" The Duke's voice rose and echoed down the dark and secret stairs. "I slew time with the bloody hand that grips your arm, and time is greater far than Zorn of Zorna!"

Hark began to chew again. "No mortal man can murder time,"

he said, "and even if he could, there's something else: a clockwork in a maiden's heart, that strikes the hours of youth and love, and knows the southward swan from winter snow, and summer afternoons from tulip time."

"You sicken me with your chocolate chatter," snarled the Duke. "Your tongue is made of candy. I'll slay this ragged prince, if Krang has missed him. If there were light, I'd show you on my sleeves the old brown stains of seconds, where they bled and died. I slew time in these gloomy halls, and wiped my bloody blade—"

"Ah, shut up," said Hark. "You are the most aggressive villain in the world. I always meant to tell you that. I said it and I'm glad."

"Silence," roared the Duke. "Where are we?" They stumbled down the secret stairs.

"This is the hidden door," said Hark, "that leads into the oak room."

"Open," roared the Duke, his sword gripped in his hand. Hark groped and found the secret knob.

VIII

The black oak room was bright with flaming torches, but brighter with the light of Saralinda. The cold eye of the Duke was dazzled by the gleaming of a thousand jewels that sparkled on the table. His ears were filled with chiming as the clocks began to strike.

"One!" said Hark.

"Two!" cried Zorn of Zorna.

"Three!" the Duke's voice almost whispered.

"Four!" sighed Saralinda.

"Five!" the Golux crowed, and pointed at the table. "The task is done, the terms are met," he said.

The Duke's cold eye slowly moved around the room. "Where are my guards?" he croaked, "and where is Krang, the greatest of them all?"

"I lured them to the tower," said Zorn, "and locked them in. The one that's tied in knots is Krang."

The Duke glared at the jewels on the table. "They're false!" he said. "They must be colored pebbles!" He picked one up, and saw that it was real, and put it down again.

"The task is done," said Hark, "the terms are met."

"Not until I count them," said the Duke. "If there be only one that isn't here, I wed the Princess Saralinda on the morrow." The figures in the room were still and he could hear their breathing.

"What a gruesome way to treat one's niece," the Golux cried.

"She's not my niece," the lame man sneered. "I stole her from a king." He showed his lower teeth. "We all have flaws," he said, "and mine is being wicked." He sat down at the table and began to count the gems.

"Who is my father then?" the Princess cried.

The spy's black eyebrows rose. "I thought the Golux told you, but then, of course, he never could remember things."

"Especially," the Golux said, "the names of kings."

"Your father," said the spy, "is good King Gwain of Yarrow."

"I knew that once," the Golux said, "but I forgot it." He turned to Saralinda. "Then the gift your father gave to Hagga has operated in the end to make you happy."

The Duke looked up and bared his teeth. "The tale is much too tidy for my taste," he snarled. "I hate it." He went on counting.

"It's neat," said Hark, "and, to *my* taste, refreshing." He moved his mask. His eyes were bright and jolly. "If I may introduce myself," he said, "I am a servant of the King, the good King Gwain of Yarrow."

"That," the Golux said, "I didn't know. You could have saved the Princess many years ago."

The servant of the King looked sad, and said, "This part I always hate to tell, but I was under a witch's spell."

"I weary of witches," the Golux said, "with due respect to Mother."

The Duke's smile showed his upper teeth. "I cannot even trust the spies I see," he muttered. His eye moved glassily around and saw the Golux. "You mere Device!" he gnarled. "You platitude! You Golux ex machina!"

"Quiet, please," the Golux said, "you gleaming thief."

"Nine hundred ninety-eight." The Duke was counting. "Nine hundred ninety-nine." He had counted all the jewels, and put them in a sack. There was none left on the table. He gave them all a look of horrid glee. "The Princess," said the Duke, "belongs to me."

A deathly silence filled the room. The Golux turned a little pale and his hand began to shake. He remembered something in the dark, coming down from Hagga's hill, that struck against his ankle, a sapphire or a ruby that had fallen from the sack. "One thousand," groaned the Duke, in a tone of vast surprise. A diamond had fallen from his glove, the left one, and no one but the Golux saw it fall. The Duke stood up and sneered. "What are you waiting for?" he shrieked. "Depart! If you be gone forever, it will not be long enough! If you return no more, then it will be too soon!" He slowly turned to Zorn. "What kind of knots?" he snarled.

"Turk's head," the young Prince said. "I learned them from my sister."

"Begone!" the cold Duke screamed again, and bathed his hands in rubies. "My jewels," he croaked, "will last forever." The Golux, who had never tittered, tittered. The great doors of the oak room opened, and they left the cold Duke standing there, up to his wrists in diamonds.

"Yarrow," said the Prince, "is halfway on our journey." They stood outside the castle.

"You'll need these," said the Golux. He held the reins of two white horses. "Your ship lies in the harbor. It sails within the hour."

"It sails at midnight," Hark corrected him.

"I can't remember everything," the Golux said. "My father's clocks were always slow. He also lacked the power of concentration."

Zorn helped the Princess to her saddle. She gazed a last time at the castle. "A fair wind stands for Yarrow," said the Prince.

The Golux gazed a last time at the Princess. "Keep warm," he said. "Ride close together. Remember laughter. You'll need it even in the blessed isles of Ever After."

"There are no horses in the stables," mused the Prince. "Whence came these white ones?"

"The Golux has a lot of friends," said Hark. "I guess they give him horses when he needs them. But on the other hand, he may have made them up. He makes things up, you know."

"I know he does," sighed Zorn of Zorna. "You sail for Yarrow with us?"

"I must stay a fortnight longer," Hark replied. "So runs my witch's spell. It will give me time to tidy up, and untie Krang as well."

They looked around for the old Device, but he was there no longer. "Where has he gone?" cried Saralinda.

"Oh," said Hark, "he knows a lot of places."

"Give him," Saralinda said, "my love, and this." Hark took the rose.

The two white horses snorted snowy mist in the cool green glade that led down to the harbor. A fair wind stood for Yarrow and, looking far to sea, the Princess Saralinda thought she saw, as people often think they see, on clear and windless days, the distant shining shores of Ever After. Your guess is quite as good as mine (there are a lot of things that shine) but I have always thought she did, and I will always think so.

EPILOGUE

A fortnight later, the Duke was gloating over his jewels in the oak room when they suddenly turned to tears, with a little sound like sighing. The fringes of his glowing gloves were stained with Hagga's laughter. He staggered to his feet and drew his sword, and shouted, "Whisper!" In the courtyard of the castle six startled geese stopped hunting snails and looked up at the oak room. "What slish is *this?*" exclaimed the Duke, disgusted by the pool of melted gems leering on the table. His monocle fell, and he slashed his sword at silence and at nothing. Something moved across the room, like monkeys and like shadows. The torches on the walls went out, the two clocks stopped, and the room grew colder. There was a smell of old, unopened rooms and the sound of rabbits screaming. "Come on, you blob of glup," the cold Duke roared. "You may frighten octopi to death, you gibbous spawn of hate and thunder, but not the Duke of Coffin Castle!" He sneered. "Now that my precious gems have turned to thlup, living on, alone and cold, is not my fondest wish! On guard, you musty sofa!" The Todal gleeped. There was a stifled shriek and silence.

When Hark came into the room, holding a lighted lantern above his head, there was no one there. The Duke's sword lay gleaming on the floor, and from the table dripped the jewels of Hagga's laughter, that never last forever, like the jewels of sorrow, but turn again to tears a fortnight after. Hark stepped on something that squutched beneath his foot and flobbed against the wall. He picked it up and held it near the lantern. It was the small black ball stamped with scarlet owls. The last spy of the Duke of Coffin Castle, alone and lonely in the gloomy room, thought he heard, from somewhere far away, the sound of someone laughing.

SAKI

Tobermory

It was a chill, rain-washed afternoon of a late August day, that indefinite season when partridges are still in security or cold storage, and there is nothing to hunt—unless one is bounded on the north by the Bristol Channel, in which case one may lawfully gallop after fat red stags. Lady Blemley's house-party was not bounded on the north by the Bristol Channel, hence there was a full gathering of her guests round the tea-table on this particular afternoon. And, in spite of the blankness of the season and the triteness of the occasion, there was no trace in the company of that fatigued restlessness which means a dread of the pianola and a subdued hankering for auction bridge. The undisguised open-mouthed attention of the entire party was fixed on the homely negative personality of Mr. Cornelius

Appin. Of all her guests, he was the one who had come to Lady
Blemley with the vaguest reputation. Some one had said he was
"clever," and he had got his invitation in the moderate expectation, on
the part of his hostess, that some portion at least of his cleverness
would be contributed to the general entertainment. Until tea-time
that day she had been unable to discover in what direction, if any,
his cleverness lay. He was neither a wit nor a croquet champion, a
hypnotic force nor a begetter of amateur theatricals. Neither did his
exterior suggest the sort of man in whom women are willing to
pardon a generous measure of mental deficiency. He had subsided
into mere Mr. Appin, and the Cornelius seemed a piece of transparent baptismal bluff. And now he was claiming to have launched on
the world a discovery beside which the invention of gunpowder, of
the printing-press, and of steam locomotion were inconsiderable trifles.
Science had made bewildering strides in many directions during recent
decades, but this thing seemed to belong to the domain of miracle
rather than to scientific achievement.

"And do you really ask us to believe," Sir Wilfrid was saying,
"that you have discovered a means for instructing animals in the
art of human speech, and that dear old Tobermory has proved your
first successful pupil?"

"It is a problem at which I have worked for the last seventeen years," said Mr. Appin, "but only during the last eight or
nine months have I been rewarded with glimmerings of success.
Of course I have experimented with thousands of animals, but
latterly only with cats, those wonderful creatures which have as-
similated themselves so marvellously with our civilization while retaining all their highly developed feral instincts. Here and there
among cats one comes across an outstanding superior intellect, just
as one does among the ruck of human beings, and when I made
the acquaintance of Tobermory a week ago I saw at once that I
was in contact with a 'Beyond-cat' of extraordinary intelligence. I
had gone far along the road to success in recent experiments; with
Tobermory, as you call him, I have reached the goal."

Mr. Appin concluded his remarkable statement in a voice which
he strove to divest of a triumphant inflection. No one said "Rats,"
though Clovis's lips moved in a monosyllabic contortion which probably invoked those rodents of disbelief.

"And do you mean to say," asked Miss Resker, after a slight pause, "that you have taught Tobermory to say and understand easy sentences of one syllable?"

"My dear Miss Resker," said the wonder-worker patiently, "one teaches little children and savages and backward adults in that piecemeal fashion; when one has once solved the problem of making a beginning with an animal of highly developed intelligence one has no need for those halting methods. Tobermory can speak our language with perfect correctness."

This time Clovis very distinctly said, "Beyond-rats!" Sir Wilfrid was more polite, but equally sceptical.

"Hadn't we better have the cat in and judge for ourselves?" suggested Lady Blemley.

Sir Wilfrid went in search of the animal, and the company settled themselves down to the languid expectation of witnessing some more or less adroit drawing-room ventriloquism.

In a minute Sir Wilfrid was back in the room, his face white beneath its tan and his eyes dilated with excitement.

"By Gad, it's true!"

His agitation was unmistakably genuine, and his hearers started forward in a thrill of awakened interest.

Collapsing into an armchair he continued breathlessly: "I found him dozing in the smoking-room, and called out to him to come for his tea. He blinked at me in his usual way, and I said, 'Come on, Toby; don't keep us waiting'; and, by Gad! he drawled out in a most horribly natural voice that he'd come when he dashed well pleased! I nearly jumped out of my skin!"

Appin had preached to absolutely incredulous hearers; Sir Wilfrid's statement carried instant conviction. A Babel-like chorus of startled exclamation arose, amid which the scientist sat mutely enjoying the first fruit of his stupendous discovery.

In the midst of the clamour Tobermory entered the room and made his way with velvet tread and studied unconcern across to the group seated round the tea-table.

A sudden hush of awkwardness and constraint fell on the company. Somehow there seemed an element of embarrassment in addressing on equal terms a domestic cat of acknowledged mental ability.

"Will you have some milk, Tobermory?" asked Lady Blemley in a rather strained voice.

"I don't mind if I do," was the response, couched in a tone of even indifference. A shiver of suppressed excitement went through the listeners, and Lady Blemley might be excused for pouring out the saucerful of milk rather unsteadily.

"I'm afraid I've spilt a good deal of it," she said apologetically.

"After all, it's not my Axminster," was Tobermory's rejoinder.

Another silence fell on the group, and then Miss Resker, in her best district-visitor manner, asked if the human language had been difficult to learn. Tobermory looked squarely at her for a moment and then fixed his gaze serenely on the middle distance. It was obvious that boring questions lay outside his scheme of life.

"What do you think of human intelligence?" asked Mavis Pellington lamely.

"Of whose intelligence in particular?" asked Tobermory coldly.

"Oh, well, mine for instance," said Mavis, with a feeble laugh.

"You put me in an embarrassing position," said Tobermory, whose tone and attitude certainly did not suggest a shred of embarrassment. "When your inclusion in this house-party was suggested Sir Wilfrid protested that you were the most brainless woman of his acquaintance, and that there was a wide distinction between hospitality and the care of the feeble-minded. Lady Blemley replied that your lack of brain-power was the precise quality which had earned you your invitation, as you were the only person she could think of who might be idiotic enough to buy their old car. You know, the one they call 'The Envy of Sisyphus,' because it goes quite nicely up-hill if you push it."

Lady Blemley's protestations would have had greater effect if she had not casually suggested to Mavis only that morning that the car in question would be just the thing for her down at her Devonshire home.

Major Barfield plunged in heavily to effect a diversion.

"How about your carryings-on with the tortoise-shell puss up at the stables, eh?"

The moment he had said it every one realized the blunder.

"One does not usually discuss these matters in public," said Tobermory frigidly. "From a slight observation of your ways since you've been in this house I should imagine you'd find it inconvenient if I were to shift the conversation on to your own little affairs."

The panic which ensued was not confined to the Major.

"Would you like to go and see if cook has got your dinner ready?" suggested Lady Blemley hurriedly, affecting to ignore the fact that it wanted at least two hours to Tobermory's dinner-time.

"Thanks," said Tobermory, "not quite so soon after my tea. I don't want to die of indigestion."

"Cats have nine lives, you know," said Sir Wilfrid heartily.

"Possibly," answered Tobermory; "but only one liver."

"Adelaide!" said Mrs. Cornett, "do you mean to encourage that cat to go out and gossip about us in the servants' hall?"

The panic had indeed become general. A narrow ornamental balustrade ran in front of most of the bedroom windows at the Towers, and it was recalled with dismay that this had formed a favourite promenade for Tobermory at all hours, whence he could watch the pigeons—and heaven knew what else besides. If he intended to become reminiscent in his present outspoken strain the effect would be something more than disconcerting. Mrs. Cornett, who spent much time at her toilet table, and whose complexion was reputed to be of a nomadic though punctual disposition, looked as ill at ease as the Major. Miss Scrawen, who wrote fiercely sensuous poetry and led a blameless life, merely displayed irritation; if you are methodical and virtuous in private you don't necessarily want every one to know it. Bertie van Tahn, who was so depraved at seventeen that he had long ago given up trying to be any worse, turned a dull shade of gardenia white, but he did not commit the error of dashing out of the room like Odo Finsberry, a young gentleman who was understood to be reading for the Church and who was possibly disturbed at the thought of scandals he might hear concerning other people. Clovis had the presence of mind to maintain a composed exterior; privately he was calculating how long it would take to procure a box of fancy mice through the agency of the *Exchange and Mart* as a species of hush-money.

Even in a delicate situation like the present, Agnes Resker could not endure to remain too long in the background.

"Why did I ever come down here?" she asked dramatically.

Tobermory immediately accepted the opening.

"Judging by what you said to Mrs. Cornett on the croquetlawn yesterday, you were out for food. You described the Blemleys as the dullest people to stay with that you knew, but said they were clever enough to employ a first-rate cook; otherwise they'd find it difficult to get any one to come down a second time."

"There's not a word of truth in it! I appeal to Mrs. Cornett—" exclaimed the discomfited Agnes.

"Mrs. Cornett repeated your remark afterwards to Bertie van Tahn," continued Tobermory, "and said, 'That woman is a regular Hunger Marcher; she'd go anywhere for four square meals a day,' and Bertie van Tahn said—"

At this point the chronicle mercifully ceased. Tobermory had caught a glimpse of the big yellow Tom from the Rectory working his way through the shrubbery towards the stable wing. In a flash he had vanished through the open French window.

With the disappearance of his too brilliant pupil Cornelius Appin found himself beset by a hurricane of bitter upbraiding, anxious inquiry, and frightened entreaty. The responsibility for the situation lay with him, and he must prevent matters from becoming worse. Could Tobermory impart his dangerous gift to other cats? was the first question he had to answer. It was possible, he replied, that he might have initiated his intimate friend the stable puss into his new accomplishment, but it was unlikely that his teaching could have taken a wider range as yet.

"Then," said Mrs. Cornett, "Tobermory may be a valuable cat and a great pet; but I'm sure you'll agree, Adelaide, that both he and the stable cat must be done away with without delay."

"You don't suppose I've enjoyed the last quarter of an hour, do you?" said Lady Blemley bitterly. "My husband and I are very fond of Tobermory—at least, we were before this horrible accomplishment was infused into him; but now, of course, the only thing is to have him destroyed as soon as possible."

"We can put some strychnine in the scraps he always gets at dinner-time," said Sir Wilfrid, "and I will go and drown the stable cat myself. The coachman will be very sore at losing his pet, but I'll say a very catching form of mange has broken out in both cats and we're afraid of it spreading to the kennels."

"But my great discovery!" expostulated Mr. Appin; "after all my years of research and experiment—"

"You can go and experiment on the short-horns at the farm, who are under proper control," said Mrs. Cornett, "or the elephants at the Zoological Gardens. They're said to be highly intelligent, and they have this recommendation, that they don't come creeping about our bedrooms and under chairs, and so forth."

An archangel ecstatically proclaiming the Millennium, and then finding that it clashed unpardonably with Henley and would have to be indefinitely postponed, could hardly have felt more crestfallen than Cornelius Appin at the reception of his wonderful achievement. Public opinion, however, was against him—in fact, had the general voice been consulted on the subject it is probable that a strong minority vote would have been in favour of including him in the strychnine diet.

Defective train arrangements and a nervous desire to see matters brought to a finish prevented an immediate dispersal of the party, but dinner that evening was not a social success. Sir Wilfrid had had rather a trying time with the stable cat and subsequently with the coachman. Agnes Resker ostentatiously limited her repast to a morsel of dry toast, which she bit as though it were a personal enemy; while Mavis Pellington maintained a vindictive silence throughout the meal. Lady Blemley kept up a flow of what she hoped was conversation, but her attention was fixed on the doorway. A plateful of carefully dosed fish scraps was in readiness on the sideboard, but sweets and savoury and dessert went their way, and no Tobermory appeared either in the dining-room or kitchen.

The sepulchral dinner was cheerful compared with the subsequent vigil in the smoking-room. Eating and drinking had at least supplied a distraction and cloak to the prevailing embarrassment. Bridge was out of the question in the general tension of nerves and tempers, and after Odo Finsberry had given a lugubrious rendering of "Mélisande in the Wood" to a frigid audience, music was tacitly avoided. At eleven the servants went to bed, announcing that the small window in the pantry had been left open as usual for Tobermory's private use. The guests read steadily through the current batch of magazines, and fell back gradually on the "Badminton Library" and bound volumes of *Punch*. Lady Blemley made periodic visits to the pantry, returning each time with an expression of listless depression which forestalled questioning.

At two o'clock Clovis broke the dominating silence.

"He won't turn up tonight. He's probably in the local newspaper office at the present moment, dictating the first instalment of his reminiscences. Lady What's-her-name's book won't be in it. It will be the event of the day."

Having made this contribution to the general cheerfulness, Clovis went to bed. At long intervals the various members of the house-party followed his example.

The servants taking round the early tea made a uniform announcement in reply to a uniform question. Tobermory had not returned.

Breakfast was, if anything, a more unpleasant function than dinner had been, but before its conclusion the situation was relieved. Tobermory's corpse was brought in from the shrubbery, where a gardener had just discovered it. From the bites on his throat and the yellow fur which coated his claws it was evident that he had fallen in unequal combat with the big Tom from the Rectory.

By midday most of the guests had quitted the Towers, and after lunch Lady Blemley had sufficiently recovered her spirits to write an extremely nasty letter to the Rectory about the loss of her valuable pet.

Tobermory had been Appin's one successful pupil, and he was destined to have no successor. A few weeks later an elephant in the Dresden Zoological Garden, which had shown no previous signs of irritability, broke loose and killed an Englishman who had apparently been teasing it. The victim's name was variously reported in the papers as Oppin and Eppelin, but his front name was faithfully rendered Cornelius.

"If he was trying German irregular verbs on the poor beast," said Clovis, "he deserved all he got."

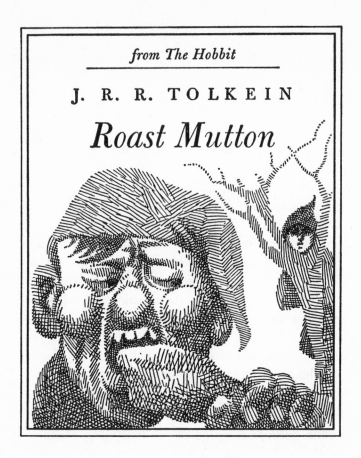

J. R. R. TOLKEIN

Roast Mutton

[*As most people know, hobbits are small folk with furry feet who are fond of a comfortable life and their own firesides. The respectable hobbit Bilbo Baggins would never quite understand why he had consented to help the dwarf Thorin and his companions in their quest for a vanished treasure, especially not on the morning after they and the wizard Gandalf had spent an evening in his hobbit-hole and nearly eaten him out of house and home without so much as a thank-you.*]

Up jumped Bilbo, and putting on his dressing-gown went into the dining-room. There he saw nobody, but all the signs of a large and hurried breakfast. There was a fearful mess in the room, and piles of unwashed crocks in the kitchen. Nearly every pot and pan he possessed seemed to have been used. The washing-up was so dismally real that Bilbo was forced to believe the party of the night before had not been part of his bad dreams, as he had rather hoped. Indeed he was really relieved after all to think that they had all gone without him, and without bothering to wake him up ("but with never a thank-you" he thought); and yet in a way he could not help feeling just a trifle disappointed. The feeling surprised him.

"Don't be a fool, Bilbo Baggins!" he said to himself, "thinking of dragons and all that outlandish nonsense at your age!" So he put on an apron, lit fires, boiled water, and washed up. Then he had a nice little breakfast in the kitchen before turning out the dining-room. By that time the sun was shining; and the front door was open, letting in a warm spring breeze. Bilbo began to whistle loudly and to forget about the night before. In fact he was just sitting down to a nice little second breakfast in the dining-room by the open window, when in walked Gandalf.

"My dear fellow," said he, "whenever *are* you going to come? What about *an early start?*—and here you are having breakfast, or whatever you call it, at half past ten! They left you the message, because they could not wait."

"What message?" said poor Mr. Baggins all in a fluster.

"Great Elephants!" said Gandalf, "you are not at all yourself this morning—you have never dusted the mantelpiece!"

"What's that got to do with it? I have had enough to do with washing up for fourteen!"

"If you had dusted the mantelpiece, you would have found this just under the clock," said Gandalf, handing Bilbo a note (written, of course, on his own note-paper).

This is what he read:

> "Thorin and Company to Burglar Bilbo greeting! For your hospitality our sincerest thanks, and for your offer of professional assistance our grateful acceptance. Terms: cash on delivery, up to and not exceeding one fourteenth of total profits (if any); all traveling expenses guaranteed in any event; funeral expenses to be defrayed by us or our representatives, if occasion arises and the matter is not otherwise arranged for.
>
> "Thinking it unnecessary to disturb your esteemed repose, we have proceeded in advance to make requisite preparations, and shall await your respected person at the Green Dragon Inn, Bywater, at 11 a.m. sharp. Trusting that you will be *punctual*,
>
> "We have the honour to remain
> "Yours deeply
> "Thorin & Co."

"That leaves you just ten minutes. You will have to run," said Gandalf.

"But—," said Bilbo.

"No time for it," said the wizard.

"But—," said Bilbo again.

"No time for that either! Off you go!"

To the end of his days Bilbo could never remember how he found himself outside, without a hat, a walking-stick or any money, or anything that he usually took when he went out; leaving his second breakfast half-finished and quite unwashed-up, pushing his keys into Gandalf's hands, and running as fast as his furry feet could carry him down the lane, past the great Mill, across The Water, and so for a whole mile or more.

Very puffed he was, when he got to Bywater just on the stroke of eleven, and found he had come without a pocket-handkerchief!

"Bravo!" said Balin who was standing at the inn door looking out for him.

Just then all the others came round the corner of the road from the village. They were on ponies, and each pony was slung about with all kinds of baggages, packages, parcels, and paraphernalia. There was a very small pony, apparently for Bilbo.

"Up you two get, and off we go!" said Thorin.

"I'm awfully sorry," said Bilbo, "but I have come without my hat, and I have left my pocket-handkerchief behind, and I haven't got any money. I didn't get your note until after 10.45 to be precise."

"Don't be precise," said Dwalin, "and don't worry! You will have to manage without pocket-handkerchiefs, and a good many other things, before you get to the journey's end. As for a hat, I have got a spare hood and cloak in my luggage."

That's how they all came to start, jogging off from the inn one fine morning just before May, on laden ponies; and Bilbo was wearing a dark-green hood (a little weather-stained) and a dark-green cloak borrowed from Dwalin. They were too large for him, and he looked rather comic. What his father Bungo would have thought of him, I daren't think. His only comfort was he couldn't be mistaken for a dwarf, as he had no beard.

They hadn't been riding very long, when up came Gandalf very splendid on a white horse. He had brought a lot of pocket-handkerchiefs, and Bilbo's pipe and tobacco. So after that the party went along very merrily, and they told stories or sang songs as they rode forward all day, except of course when they stopped for meals. These didn't come quite as often as Bilbo would have liked them, but still he began to feel that adventures were not so bad after all.

Things went on like this for quite a long while. There was a good deal of wide respectable country to pass through, inhabited by decent respectable folk, men or hobbits or elves or what not, with good roads, an inn or two, and every now and then a dwarf, or a tinker, or a farmer ambling by on business. But after a time they came to places where people spoke strangely, and sang songs Bilbo had never heard before. Inns were rare and not good, the roads were worse, and there were hills in the distance rising higher and higher. There were castles on some of the hills, and many looked as if they had not been built for any good purpose. Also the weather which had often been as good as May can be, even in tales and legends, took a nasty turn.

"To think it is June the first tomorrow," grumbled Bilbo, as he splashed along behind the others in a very muddy track. It was after tea-time; it was pouring with rain, and had been all day; his hood was dripping into his eyes, his cloak was full of water; the pony was tired and stumbled on stones; the others were too grumpy to talk. "And I'm sure the rain has got into the dry clothes and into the food-bags," thought Bilbo. "Bother burgling and everything to do with it! I wish I was at home in my nice hole by the fire, with the kettle just beginning to sing!" It was not the last time that he wished that!

Still the dwarves jogged on, never turning round or taking any notice of the hobbit. Somewhere behind the grey clouds the sun must have gone down, for it began to get dark. Wind got up, and the willows along the river-bank bent and sighed. I don't know what river it was, a rushing red one, swollen with the rains of the last few days, that came down from the hills and mountains in front of them.

Soon it was nearly dark. The winds broke up the grey clouds, and a waning moon appeared above the hills between the flying rags. Then they stopped, and Thorin muttered something about supper, "and where shall we get a dry patch to sleep on?"

Not until then did they notice that Gandalf was missing. So far he had come all the way with them, never saying if he was in the adventure or merely keeping them company for a while. He had eaten most, talked most, and laughed most. But now he simply was not there at all!

"Just when a wizard would have been most useful, too," groaned Dori and Nori (who shared the hobbit's views about regular meals, plenty and often).

They decided in the end that they would have to camp where they were. So far they had not camped before on this journey, and though they knew that they soon would have to camp regularly, when they were among the Misty Mountains and far from the lands of respectable people, it seemed a bad wet evening to begin on. They moved to a clump of trees, and though it was drier under them, the wind shook the rain off the leaves, and the drip, drip, was most annoying. Also the mischief seemed to have got into the fire. Dwarves can make a fire almost anywhere out of almost anything, wind or no wind; but they could not do it that night, not even Oin and Gloin, who were specially good at it.

Then one of the ponies took fright at nothing and bolted. He got into the river before they could catch him; and before they could get him out again, Fili and Kili were nearly drowned, and all the baggage that he carried was washed away off him. Of course it was mostly food, and there was mighty little left for supper, and less for breakfast.

There they all sat glum and wet and muttering, while Oin and Gloin went on trying to light the fire, and quarrelling about it. Bilbo was sadly reflecting that adventures are not all pony-riders in May-sunshine, when Balin, who was always their look-out man, said: "There's a light over there!" There was a hill some way off with trees on it, pretty thick in parts. Out of the dark mass of the trees they could now see a light shining, a reddish comfortable-looking light, as it might be a fire or torches twinkling.

When they had looked at it for some while, they fell to arguing. Some said "no" and some said "yes." Some said they could but go and see, and anything was better than little supper, less breakfast, and wet clothes all the night.

Others said: "These parts are none too well known, and are too near the mountains. Policemen never come so far, and the map-makers have not reached this country yet. They have seldom even heard of the king round here, and the less inquisitive you are as you go along, the less trouble you are likely to find." Some said: "After all there are fourteen of us." Others said: "Where has Gandalf got to?" This remark was repeated by everybody. Then the rain began to pour down worse than ever, and Oin and Gloin began to fight.

That settled it. "After all we have got a burglar with us," they said; and so they made off, leading their ponies (with all due and proper caution) in the direction of the light. They came to the hill and were soon in the wood. Up the hill they went; but there was no proper path to be seen, such as might lead to a house or a farm; and do what they could they made a deal of rustling and crackling and creaking (and a good deal of grumbling and dratting), as they went through the trees in the pitch dark.

Suddenly the red light shone out very bright through the tree-trunks not far ahead.

"Now it is the burglar's turn," they said, meaning Bilbo. "You must go on and find out all about that light, and what it is for, and if all is perfectly safe and canny," said Thorin to the hobbit. "Now scuttle off, and come back quick, if all is well. If not, come back if you can! If you can't, hoot twice like a barn-owl and once like a screech-owl, and we will do what we can."

Off Bilbo had to go, before he could explain that he could not hoot even once like any kind of owl any more than fly like a bat. But at any rate hobbits can move quietly in woods, absolutely quietly. They take a pride in it, and Bilbo had sniffed more than once at what he called "all this dwarvish racket," as they went along, though I don't suppose you or I would have noticed anything at all on a windy night, not if the whole cavalcade had passed two feet off. As for Bilbo walking primly towards the red light, I don't suppose even a weasel would have stirred a whisker at it. So, naturally, he got right up to the fire—for fire it was—without disturbing anyone. And this is what he saw.

Three very large persons sitting round a very large fire of beech-logs. They were toasting mutton on long spits of wood, and licking the gravy off their fingers. There was a fine toothsome smell. Also there was a barrel of good drink at hand, and they were drinking out of jugs. But they were trolls. Obviously trolls. Even Bilbo, in spite of his sheltered life, could see that: from the great heavy faces of them, and their size, and the shape of their legs, not to mention their language, which was not drawing-room fashion at all, at all.

"Mutton yesterday, mutton today, and blimey, if it don't look like mutton again tomorrer," said one of the trolls.

"Never a blinking bit of manflesh have we had for long enough," said a second. "What the 'ell William was a-thinkin' of to bring us into these parts at all, beats me—and the drink runnin' short, what's more," he said jogging the elbow of William, who was taking a pull at his jug.

William choked, "Shut yer mouth!" he said as soon as he could. "Yer can't expect folk to stop here for ever just to be et by you and Bert. You've et a village and a half between yer, since we come down from the mountains. How much more d'yer want? And time's been up our way, when yer'd have said 'thank yer Bill' for a nice bit o' fat valley mutton like what this is." He took a big bite off a sheep's leg he was toasting, and wiped his lips on his sleeve.

Yes, I am afraid trolls do behave like that, even those with only one head each. After hearing all this Bilbo ought to have done something at once. Either he should have gone back quietly and warned his friends that there were three fair-sized trolls at hand in a nasty mood, quite likely to try toasted dwarf, or even pony, for a change; or else he should have done a bit of good quick burgling. A really first-class and legendary burglar would at this point have picked the trolls' pockets—it is nearly always worthwhile, if you can manage it—, pinched the very mutton off the spits, purloined the beer, and walked off without their noticing him. Others more practical but with less professional pride would perhaps have stuck a dagger into each of them before they observed it. Then the night could have been spent cheerily.

Bilbo knew it. He had read of a good many things he had never seen or done. He was very much alarmed, as well as disgusted; he wished himself a hundred miles away, and yet—and yet somehow he could not go straight back to Thorin and Company emptyhanded. So he stood and hesitated in the shadows. Of the various burglarious proceedings he had heard of picking the trolls' pockets seemed the least difficult, so at last he crept behind a tree just behind William.

Bert and Tom went off to the barrel. William was having another drink. Then Bilbo plucked up courage and put his little hand in

William's enormous pocket. There was a purse in it, as big as a bag to Bilbo. "Ha!" thought he warming to his new work as he lifted it carefully out, "this is a beginning!"

It was! Trolls' purses are the mischief, and this was no exception. "'Ere, 'oo are you?" it squeaked, as it left the pocket; and William turned round at once and grabbed Bilbo by the neck, before he could duck behind the tree.

"Blimey, Bert, look what I've copped!" said William.

"What is it?" said the others coming up.

"Lumme, if I knows! What are yer?"

"Bilbo Baggins, a bur—a hobbit," said poor Bilbo, shaking all over, and wondering how to make owl-noises before they throttled him.

"A burrahobbit?" said they a bit startled. Trolls are slow in the uptake, and mighty suspicious about anything new to them.

"What's a burrahobbit got to do with my pocket, anyways?" said William.

"And can yer cook 'em?" said Tom.

"Yer can try," said Bert, picking up a skewer.

"He wouldn't make above a mouthful," said William, who had already had a fine supper, "not when he was skinned and boned."

"P'raps there are more like him round about, and we might make a pie," said Bert. "Here you, are there any more of your sort a-sneakin' in these here woods, yer nassty little rabbit," said he looking at the hobbit's furry feet; and he picked him up by the toes and shook him.

"Yes, lots," said Bilbo, before he remembered not to give his friends away. "No none at all, not one," he said immediately afterwards.

"What d'yer mean?" said Bert, holding him right way up, by the hair this time.

"What I say," said Bilbo gasping. "And please don't cook me, kind sirs! I am a good cook myself, and cook better than I cook, if you see what I mean. I'll cook beautifully for you, a perfectly beautiful breakfast for you, if only you won't have me for supper."

"Poor little blighter," said William (I told you he had already had as much supper as he could hold; also he had had lots of beer). "Poor little blighter! Let him go!"

"Not till he says what he means by *lots* and *none at all*."

said Bert. "I don't want to have me throat cut in me sleep! Hold his toes in the fire, till he talks!"

"You're a fat fool, William," said Bert, "as I've said afore this evening."

"And you're a lout!"

"And I won't take that from you, Bill Huggins," says Bert, and puts his fist in William's eye.

Then there was a gorgeous row. Bilbo had just enough wits left, when they dropped him on the ground, to scramble out of the way of their feet, before they were fighting like dogs, and calling one another all sorts of perfectly true and applicable names in very loud voices. Soon they were locked in one another's arms, and rolling nearly into the fire kicking and thumping, while Tom whacked at them both with a branch to bring them to their senses—and that of course only made them madder than ever.

That would have been the time for Bilbo to have left. But his poor little feet had been very squashed in Bert's big paw, and he had no breath in his body, and his head was going round; so there he lay for a while panting, just outside the circle of firelight.

Right in the middle of the fight up came Balin. The dwarves had heard noises from a distance, and after waiting for some time for Bilbo to come back, or to hoot like an owl, they started off one by one to creep towards the light as quietly as they could. No sooner did Tom see Balin come into the light than he gave an awful howl. Trolls simply detest the very sight of dwarves (uncooked). Bert and Bill stopped fighting immediately, and "a sack, Tom, quick!" they said, before Balin, who was wondering where in all this commotion Bilbo was, knew what was happening, a sack was over his head, and he was down.

"There's more to come yet," said Tom, "or I'm mighty mistook. Lots and none at all, it is," said he. "No burrahobbits, but lots of these here dwarves. That's about the shape of it!"

"I reckon you're right," said Bert, "and we'd best get out of the light."

And so they did. With sacks in their hands, that they used for carrying off mutton and other plunder, they waited in the shadows. As each dwarf came up and looked at the fire, and the spilled jugs, and the gnawed mutton, in surprise, pop! went a nasty smelly sack over his head, and he was down. Soon Dwalin lay by Balin, and Fili and Kili together, and Dori and Nori and Ori all in a heap, and Oin and Gloin and Bifur and Bofur and Bombur piled uncomfortably near the fire.

"That'll teach 'em," said Tom; for Bifur and Bombur had given a lot of trouble, and fought like mad, as dwarves will when cornered.

Thorin came last—and he was not caught unawares. He came expecting mischief, and didn't need to see his friends' legs sticking out of sacks to tell him that things were not all well. He stood outside in the shadows some way off, and said: "What's all this trouble? Who has been knocking my people about?"

"It's trolls!" said Bilbo from behind a tree. They had forgotten all about him. "They're hiding in the bushes with sacks," said he.

"O! are they?" said Thorin, and he jumped forward to the fire, before they could leap on him. He caught up a big branch all on fire at one end; and Bert got that end in his eye before he could step aside. That put him out of the battle for a bit. Bilbo did his best. He caught hold of Tom's leg—as well as he could, it was thick as a young tree-trunk—but he was sent spinning up into the top of some bushes, when Tom kicked the sparks up in Thorin's face.

Tom got the branch in his teeth for that, and lost one of the front ones. It made him howl, I can tell you. But just at that moment William came up behind and popped a sack right over Thorin's head and down to his toes. And so the fight ended. A nice pickle they were all in now: all neatly tied up in sacks, with three angry trolls (and two with burns and bashes to remember) sitting by them, arguing whether they should roast them slowly, or mince them fine and boil them, or just sit on them one by one and squash them into jelly: and Bilbo up in a bush, with his clothes and his skin torn, not daring to move for fear they should hear him.

It was just then that Gandalf came back. But no one saw him. The trolls had just decided to roast the dwarves now and eat them later—that was Bert's idea, and after a lot of argument they had all agreed to it.

"No good roasting 'em now, it'd take all night," said a voice. Bert thought it was William's.

"Don't start the argument all over again, Bill," he said, "or it *will* take all night."

"Who's a-arguing?" said William, who thought it was Bert that had spoken.

"You are," said Bert.

"You're a liar," said William; and so the argument began all over again. In the end they decided to mince them fine and boil them. So they got a great black pot, and they took out their knives.

"No good boiling 'em! We ain't got no water, and it's a long way to the well and all," said a voice. Bert and William thought it was Tom's.

"Shut up!" said they, "or we'll never have done. And yer can fetch the water yerself, if yer say any more."

"Shut up yerself!" said Tom, who thought it was William's voice. "Who's arguing but you, I'd like to know."

"You're a booby," said William.

"Booby yerself!" said Tom.

And so the argument began all over again, and went on hotter than ever, until at last they decided to sit on the sacks one by one and squash them, and boil them next time.

"Who shall we sit on first?" said the voice.

"Better sit on the last fellow first," said Bert, whose eye had been damaged by Thorin. He thought Tom was talking.

"Don't talk to yerself!" said Tom. "But if you wants to sit on the last one, sit on him. Which is he?"

"The one with the yellow stockings," said Bert.

"Nonsense, the one with the grey stockings," said a voice like William's.

"I made sure it was yellow," said Bert.

"Yellow it was," said William.

"Then what did yer say it was grey for?" said Bert.

"I never did. Tom said it."

"That I never did!" said Tom. "It was you."

"Two to one, so shut yer mouth!" said Bert.

"Who are you a-talkin' to?" said William.

"Now stop it!" said Tom and Bert together. "The night's gettin' on, and dawn comes early. Let's get on with it!"

"Dawn take you all, and be stone to you!" said a voice that

sounded like William's. But it wasn't. For just at that moment the light came over the hill, and there was a mighty twitter in the branches. William never spoke for he stood turned to stone as he stooped; and Bert and Tom were stuck like rocks as they looked at him. And there they stand to this day, all alone, unless the birds perch on them; for trolls, as you probably know, must be underground before dawn, or they go back to the stuff of the mountains they are made of, and never move again. That is what had happened to Bert and Tom and William.

"Excellent!" said Gandalf, as he stepped from behind the bushes, and helped Bilbo to climb down out of a thorn-tree. Then Bilbo understood. It was the wizard's voice that had kept the trolls bickering and quarrelling, until the light came and made an end of them.

The next thing was to untie the sacks and let out the dwarves. They were nearly suffocated, and very annoyed: they had not at all enjoyed lying there listening to the trolls making plans for roasting them and squashing them and mincing them. They had to hear Bilbo's account of what had happened to him twice over, before they were satisfied.

"Silly time to go practising burglary and pocket-picking," said Bombur, "when what we wanted was fire and food!"

"And that's just what you wouldn't have got of those fellows without a struggle, in any case," said Gandalf. "Anyhow you are wasting time now. Don't you realize that the trolls must have a cave or a hole dug somewhere near to hide from the sun in? We must look into it!"

They searched about, and soon found the marks of trolls' stony boots going away through the trees. They followed the tracks up the hill, until hidden by bushes they came on a big door of stone leading to a cave. But they could not open it, not though they all pushed while Gandalf tried various incantations.

"Would this be any good?" asked Bilbo, when they were getting tired and angry. "I found it on the ground where the trolls had their fight." He held out a largish key, though no doubt William had thought it very small and secret. It must have fallen out of his pocket, very luckily, before he was turned to stone.

"Why on earth didn't you mention it before?" they cried. Gandalf grabbed it and fitted it into the key-hole. Then the stone door swung back with one big push, and they all went inside. There were bones on the floor and a nasty smell was in the air; but there was a good deal of food jumbled carelessly on shelves and on the ground, among an untidy litter of plunder, of all sorts from brass buttons to pots full of gold coins standing in a corner. There were lots of clothes, too, hanging on the walls—too small for trolls, I am afraid they belonged to victims—and among them were several swords of various makes, shapes, and sizes. Two caught their eyes particularly, because of their beautiful scabbards and jewelled hilts.

Gandalf and Thorin each took one of these; and Bilbo took a knife in a leather sheath. It would have made only a tiny pocket-knife for a troll, but it was as good as a short sword for the hobbit.

"These look like good blades," said the wizard, half drawing them and looking at them curiously. "They were not made by any troll, nor by any smith among men in these parts and days; but if we can read the runes on them, we shall know more about them."

"Let's get out of this horrible smell!" said Fili. So they carried out the pots of coins, and such food as was untouched and looked fit to eat, also one barrel of ale which was still full. By that time they felt like breakfast, and being very hungry they did not turn their noses up at what they had got from the trolls' larder. Their own provisions were very scanty. Now they had bread and cheese, and plenty of ale, and bacon to toast in the embers of the fire.

After that they slept, for their night had been disturbed; and they did nothing more till the afternoon. Then they brought up their ponies, and carried away the pots of gold, and buried them very secretly not far from the track by the river, putting a great many spells over them, just in case they ever had the chance to come back and recover them. When that was done, they all mounted once more, and jogged along again on the path towards the East.

"Where did you go to, if I may ask?" said Thorin to Gandalf as they rode along.

"To look ahead," said he.

"And what brought you back in the nick of time?"

"Looking behind," said he.

"Exactly!" said Thorin; "but could you be more plain?"

"I went on to spy out our road. It will soon become dangerous and difficult. Also I was anxious about replenishing our small stock of provisions. I had not gone very far, however, when I met a couple of friends of mine from Riverdell."

"Where's that?" asked Bilbo.

"Don't interrupt!" said Gandalf. "You will get there in a few days now, if we're lucky, and find out all about it. As I was saying I met two of Elrond's people. They were hurrying along for fear of the trolls. It was they who told me that three of them had come down from the mountains and settled in the woods not far from the road; they had frightened everyone away from the district, and they way-laid strangers.

"I immediately had a feeling that I was wanted back. Looking behind I saw a fire in the distance and made for it. So now you know. Please be more careful, next time, or we shall never get anywhere!"

"Thank you!" said Thorin.

from To Kill a Mockingbird

HARPER LEE

Ol' One-Shot

Atticus was feeble: he was nearly fifty. When Jem and I asked him why he was so old, he said he got started late, which we felt reflected upon his abilities and manliness. He was much older than the parents of our school contemporaries, and there was nothing Jem or I could say about him when our classmates said, "*My* father—"

Jem was football crazy. Atticus was never too tired to play keep-away, but when Jem wanted to tackle him Atticus would say, "I'm too old for that, son."

Our father didn't do anything. He worked in an office, not in a drugstore. Atticus did not drive a dump-truck for the county, he was not the sheriff, he did not farm, work in a garage, or do anything that could possibly arouse the admiration of anyone.

Besides that, he wore glasses. He was nearly blind in his left eye, and said left eyes were the tribal curse of the Finches. Whenever he wanted to see something well, he turned his head and looked from his right eye.

He did not do the things our schoolmates' fathers did: he never went hunting, he did not play poker or fish or drink or smoke. He sat in the livingroom and read.

With these attributes, however, he would not remain as inconspicuous as we wished him to: that year, the school buzzed with talk about him defending Tom Robinson, none of which was complimentary. After my bout with Cecil Jacobs when I committed myself to a policy of cowardice, word got around that Scout Finch wouldn't fight any more, her daddy wouldn't let her. This was not entirely correct: I wouldn't fight publicly for Atticus, but the family was private ground. I would fight anyone from a third cousin upwards tooth and nail. Francis Hancock, for example, knew that.

When he gave us our air-rifles Atticus wouldn't teach us to shoot. Uncle Jack instructed us in the rudiments thereof; he said Atticus wasn't interested in guns. Atticus said to Jem one day, "I'd rather you shot at tin cans in the back yard, but I know you'll go after birds. Shoot all the bluejays you want, if you can hit 'em, but remember it's a sin to kill a mockingbird."

That was the only time I ever heard Atticus say it was a sin to do something, and I asked Miss Maudie about it.

"Your father's right," she said. "Mockingbirds don't do one thing but make music for us to enjoy. They don't eat up people's gardens, don't nest in corncribs, they don't do one thing but sing their hearts out for us. That's why it's a sin to kill a mockingbird."

"Miss Maudie, this is an old neighborhood, ain't it?"

"Been here longer than the town."

"Nome, I mean the folks on our street are all old. Jem and me's the only children around here. Mrs. Dubose is close on to a hundred and Miss Rachel's old and so are you and Atticus."

"I don't call fifty very old," said Miss Maudie tartly. "Not being wheeled around yet, am I? Neither's your father. But I must say Providence was kind enough to burn down that old mausoleum of mine, I'm too old to keep it up—maybe you're right, Jean Louise, this is a settled neighborhood. You've never been around young folks much, have you?"

"Yessum, at school."

"I mean young grown-ups. You're lucky, you know. You and Jem have the benefit of your father's age. If your father was thirty you'd find life quite different."

"I sure would. Atticus can't do anything. . . ."

"You'd be surprised," said Miss Maudie. "There's life in him yet."

"What can he do?"

"Well, he can make somebody's will so airtight can't anybody meddle with it."

"Shoot . . ."

"Well, did you know he's the best checker-player in this town? Why, down at the Landing when we were coming up, Atticus Finch could beat everybody on both sides of the river."

"Good Lord, Miss Maudie, Jem and me beat him all the time."

"It's about time you found out it's because he lets you. Did you know he can play a Jew's Harp?"

This modest accomplishment served to make me even more ashamed of him.

"Well . . ." she said.

"Well what, Miss Maudie?"

"Well nothing. Nothing—it seems with all that you'd be proud of him. Can't everybody play a Jew's Harp. Now keep out of the way of the carpenters. You'd better go home, I'll be in my azaleas and can't watch you. Plank might hit you."

I went to the back yard and found Jem plugging away at a tin can, which seemed stupid with all the bluejays around. I returned to the front yard and busied myself for two hours erecting a complicated breastworks at the side of the porch, consisting of a tire, an orange crate, the laundry hamper, the porch chairs, and a small U.S. flag Jem gave me from a popcorn box.

When Atticus came home to dinner he found me crouched down aiming across the street. "What are you shooting at?"

"Miss Maudie's rear end."

Atticus turned and saw my generous target bending over her bushes. He pushed his hat to the back of his head and crossed the street. "Maudie," he called, "I thought I'd better warn you. You're in considerable peril."

Miss Maudie straightened up and looked toward me. She said, "Atticus, you are a devil from hell."

When Atticus returned he told me to break camp. "Don't you ever let me catch you pointing that gun at anybody again," he said.

I wished my father was a devil from hell. I sounded out Calpurnia on the subject. "Mr. Finch? Why, he can do lots of things."

"Like what?" I asked.

Calpurnia scratched her head. "Well, I don't rightly know," she said.

Jem underlined it when he asked Atticus if he was going out for the Methodists and Atticus said he'd break his neck if he did, he was just too old for that sort of thing. The Methodists were trying to pay off their church mortgage, and had challenged the Baptists to a game of touch football. Everybody in town's father was playing, it seemed, except Atticus. Jem said he didn't even want to go, but he was unable to resist football in any form, and he stood gloomily on the sidelines with Atticus and me watching Cecil Jacobs's father make touchdowns for the Baptists.

One Saturday Jem and I decided to go exploring with our air-rifles to see if we could find a rabbit or a squirrel. We had gone about five hundred yards beyond the Radley Place when I noticed Jem squinting at something down the street. He had turned his head to one side and was looking out of the corners of his eyes.

"Whatcha looking at?"

"That old dog down yonder," he said.

"That's old Tim Johnson, ain't it?"

"Yeah."

Tim Johnson was the property of Mr. Harry Johnson who drove the Mobile bus and lived on the southern edge of town. Tim was a liver-colored bird dog, the pet of Maycomb.

"What's he doing?"

"I don't know, Scout. We better go home."

"Aw Jem, it's February."

"I don't care, I'm gonna tell Cal."

We raced home and ran to the kitchen.

"Cal," said Jem, "can you come down the sidewalk a minute?"

"What for, Jem? I can't come down the sidewalk every time you want me."

"There's somethin' wrong with an old dog down yonder."

Calpurnia sighed. "I can't wrap up any dog's foot now. There's some gauze in the bathroom, go get it and do it yourself."

Jem shook his head. "He's sick, Cal. Something's wrong with him."

"What's he doin', trying to catch his tail?"

"No, he's doin' like this."

Jem gulped like a goldfish, hunched his shoulders and twitched his torso. "He's goin' like that, only not like he means to."

"Are you telling me a story, Jem Finch?" Calpurnia's voice hardened.

"No Cal, I swear I'm not."

"Was he runnin'?"

"No, he's just moseyin' along, so slow you can't hardly tell it. He's comin' this way."

Calpurnia rinsed her hands and followed Jem into the yard. "I don't see any dog," she said.

She followed us beyond the Radley Place and looked where Jem pointed. Tim Johnson was not much more than a speck in the distance, but he was closer to us. He walked erratically, as if his right legs were shorter than his left legs. He reminded me of a car stuck in a sand-bed.

"He's gone lopsided," said Jem.

Calpurnia stared, then grabbed us by the shoulders and ran us home. She shut the wood door behind us, went to the telephone and shouted, "Gimme Mr. Finch's office!"

"Mr. Finch!" she shouted. "This is Cal. I swear to God there's a mad dog down the street a piece—he's comin' this way, yes sir, he's—Mr. Finch, I declare he is—old Tim Johnson, yes sir . . . yessir . . . yes—"

She hung up and shook her head when we tried to ask her what Atticus had said. She rattled the telephone hook and said, "Miss Eula May—now ma'am, I'm through talkin' to Mr. Finch, please don't connect me no more—listen, Miss Eula May, can you call Miss Rachel and Miss Stephanie Crawford and whoever's got a phone on this street and tell 'em a mad dog's comin'? Please ma'am!"

Calpurnia listened. "I know it's February, Miss Eula May, but I know a mad dog when I see one. Please ma'am hurry!"

Calpurnia asked Jem, "Radleys got a phone?"

Jem looked in the book and said no. "They won't come out anyway, Cal."

"I don't care, I'm gonna tell 'em."

She ran to the front porch, Jem and I at her heels. "You stay in that house!" she yelled.

Calpurnia's message had been received by the neighborhood. Every wood door within our range of vision was closed tight. We saw no trace of Tim Johnson. We watched Calpurnia running toward the Radley Place, holding her skirt and apron above her knees. She went up to the front steps and banged on the door. She got no answer, and she shouted, "Mr. Nathan, Mr. Arthur, mad dog's comin'! Mad dog's comin'!"

"She's supposed to go around in back," I said.

Jem shook his head. "Don't make any difference now," he said.

Calpurnia pounded on the door in vain. No one acknowledged her warning; no one seemed to have heard it.

As Calpurnia sprinted to the back porch a black Ford swung into the driveway. Atticus and Mr. Heck Tate got out.

Mr. Heck Tate was the sheriff of Maycomb County. He was as tall as Atticus, but thinner. He was long-nosed, wore boots with shiny metal eye-holes, boot pants and a lumber jacket. His belt had a row of bullets sticking in it. He carried a heavy rifle. When he and Atticus reached the porch, Jem opened the door.

"Stay inside, son," said Atticus. "Where is he, Cal?"

"He oughta be here by now," said Calpurnia, pointing down the street.

"Not runnin', is he?" asked Mr. Tate.

"Naw sir, he's in the twitchin' stage, Mr. Heck."

"Should we go after him, Heck?" asked Atticus.

"We better wait, Mr. Finch. They usually go in a straight line, but you never can tell. He might follow the curve—hope he does or he'll go straight in the Radley back yard. Let's wait a minute."

"Don't think he'll get in the Radley yard," said Atticus. "Fence'll stop him. He'll probably follow the road. . . ."

I thought mad dogs foamed at the mouth, galloped, leaped and lunged at throats, and I thought they did it in August. Had Tim Johnson behaved thus, I would have been less frightened.

Nothing is more deadly than a deserted, waiting street. The trees were still, the mockingbirds were silent, the carpenters at Miss Maudie's house had vanished. I heard Mr. Tate sniff, then blow his nose. I saw him shift his gun to the crook of his arm. I saw Miss Stephanie Crawford's face framed in the glass window of her front door. Miss Maudie appeared and stood beside her. Atticus put his foot on the rung of a chair and rubbed his hand slowly down the side of his thigh.

"There he is," he said softly.

Tim Johnson came into sight, walking dazedly in the inner rim of the curve parallel to the Radley house.

"Look at him," whispered Jem. "Mr. Heck said they walked in a straight line. He can't even stay in the road."

"He looks more sick than anything," I said.

"Let anything get in front of him and he'll come straight at it."

Mr. Tate put his hand to his forehead and leaned forward. "He's got it all right, Mr. Finch."

Tim Johnson was advancing at a snail's pace, but he was not playing or sniffing at foliage: he seemed dedicated to one course and motivated by an invisible force that was inching him toward us. We could see him shiver like a horse shedding flies; his jaw opened and shut; he was alist, but he was being pulled gradually toward us.

"He's lookin' for a place to die," said Jem.

Mr. Tate turned around. "He's far from dead, Jem, he hasn't got started yet."

Tim Johnson reached the side street that ran in front of the Radley Place, and what remained of his poor mind made him pause and seem to consider which road he would take. He made a few hesitant steps and stopped in front of the Radley gate; then he tried to turn around, but was having difficulty.

Atticus said, "He's within range, Heck. You better get him now before he goes down the side street—Lord knows who's around the corner. Go inside, Cal."

Calpurnia opened the screen door, latched it behind her, then unlatched it and held onto the hook. She tried to block Jem and me with her body, but we looked out from beneath her arms.

"Take him, Mr. Finch." Mr. Tate handed the rifle to Atticus; Jem and I nearly fainted.

"Don't waste time, Heck," said Atticus. "Go on."

"Mr. Finch, this is a one-shot job."

Atticus shook his head vehemently: "Don't just stand there, Heck! He won't wait all day for you—"

"For God's sake, Mr. Finch, look where he is! Miss and you'll go straight into the Radley house! I can't shoot that well and you know it!"

"I haven't shot a gun in thirty years—"

Mr. Tate almost threw the rifle at Atticus. "I'd feel mighty comfortable if you did now," he said.

In a fog, Jem and I watched our father take the gun and walk out into the middle of the street. He walked quickly, but I thought he moved like an underwater swimmer: time had slowed to a nauseating crawl.

When Atticus raised his glasses Calpurnia murmured, "Sweet Jesus help him," and put her hands to her cheeks.

Atticus pushed his glasses to his forehead; they slipped down, and he dropped them in the street. In the silence, I heard them crack. Atticus rubbed his eyes and chin; we saw him blink hard.

In front of the Radley gate, Tim Johnson had made up what was left of his mind. He had finally turned himself around, to pursue his original course up our street. He made two steps forward, then stopped and raised his head. We saw his body go rigid.

With movements so swift they seemed simultaneous, Atticus's hand yanked a ball-tipped lever as he brought the gun to his shoulder.

The rifle cracked. Tim Johnson leaped, flopped over and crumpled on the sidewalk in a brown-and-white heap. He didn't know what hit him.

Mr. Tate jumped off the porch and ran to the Radley Place. He stopped in front of the dog, squatted, turned around and tapped his finger on his forehead above his left eye. "You were a little to the right, Mr. Finch," he called.

"Always was," answered Atticus. "If I had my 'druthers I'd take a shotgun."

He stooped and picked up his glasses, ground the broken lenses to powder under his heel, and went to Mr. Tate and stood looking down at Tim Johnson.

Doors opened one by one, and the neighborhood slowly came alive. Miss Maudie walked along the steps with Miss Stephanie Crawford.

Jem was paralyzed. I pinched him to get him moving, but when Atticus saw us coming he called, "Stay where you are."

When Mr. Tate and Atticus returned to the yard, Mr. Tate was smiling. "I'll have Zeebo collect him," he said. "You haven't forgot much, Mr. Finch. They say it never leaves you."

Atticus was silent.

"Atticus?" said Jem.

"Yes?"

"Nothin'."

"I saw that, One-Shot Finch!"

Atticus wheeled around and faced Miss Maudie. They looked at one another without saying anything, and Atticus got into the sheriff's car. "Come here," he said to Jem. "Don't you go near that dog, you understand? Don't go near him, he's just as dangerous dead as alive."

"Yes, sir," said Jem. "Atticus—"

"What, son?"

"Nothing."

"What's the matter with you, boy, can't you talk?" said Mr. Tate, grinning at Jem. "Didn't you know your daddy's—"

"Hush, Heck," said Atticus, "let's go back to town."

When they drove away, Jem and I went to Miss Stephanie's front steps. We sat waiting for Zeebo to arrive in the garbage truck.

Jem sat in numb confusion, and Miss Stephanie said, "Uh, uh, uh, who'da thought of a mad dog in February? Maybe he wadn't mad, maybe he was just crazy. I'd hate to see Harry Johnson's face when he gets in from the Mobile run and finds Atticus Finch's shot his dog. Bet he was just full of fleas from somewhere—"

Miss Maudie said Miss Stephanie'd be singing a different tune if Tim Johnson was still coming up the street, that they'd find out soon enough, they'd send his head to Montgomery.

Jem became vaguely articulate: "'d you see him, Scout? 'd you see him just standin' there? . . . 'n' all of a sudden he just relaxed all over, an' it looked like that gun was a part of him . . . an' he did it so quick, like . . . I hafta aim for ten minutes 'fore I can hit somethin'. . . ."

Miss Maudie grinned wickedly. "Well now, Miss Jean Louise," she said, "still think your father can't do anything? Still ashamed of him?"

"Nome," I said meekly.

"Forgot to tell you the other day that besides playing the Jew's Harp, Atticus Finch was the deadest shot in Maycomb County in his time."

"Dead shot . . ." echoed Jem.

"That's what I said, Jem Finch. Guess you'll change *your* tune now. The very idea, didn't you know his nickname was Ol' One-Shot when he was a boy? Why, down at the Landing when he was coming up, if he shot fifteen times and hit fourteen doves he'd complain about wasting ammunition."

"He never said anything about that," Jem muttered.

"Never said anything about it, did he?"

"No ma'am."

"Wonder why he never goes huntin' now," I said.

"Maybe I can tell you," said Miss Maudie. "If your father's anything, he's civilized in his heart. Marksmanship's a gift of God, a talent—oh, you have to practice to make it perfect, but shootin's different from playing the piano or the like. I think maybe he put his gun down when he realized that God had given him an unfair advantage over most living things. I guess he decided he wouldn't shoot till he had to, and he had to today."

"Looks like he'd be proud of it," I said.

"People in their right minds never take pride in their talents," said Miss Maudie.

We saw Zeebo drive up. He took a pitchfork from the back of the garbage truck and gingerly lifted Tim Johnson. He pitched the dog onto the truck, then poured something from a gallon jug on and around the spot where Tim fell. "Don't yawl come over here for a while," he called.

When we went home I told Jem we'd really have something to talk about at school on Monday. Jem turned on me.

"Don't say anything about it, Scout," he said.

"What? I certainly am. Ain't everybody's daddy the deadest shot in Maycomb County."

Jem said, "I reckon if he'd wanted us to know it, he'da told us. If he was proud of it, he'da told us."

"Maybe it just slipped his mind," I said.

"Naw, Scout, it's something you wouldn't understand. Atticus is real old, but I wouldn't care if he couldn't do anything—I wouldn't care if he couldn't do a blessed thing."

Jem picked up a rock and threw it jubilantly at the carhouse. Running after it, he called back: "Atticus is a gentleman, just like me!"

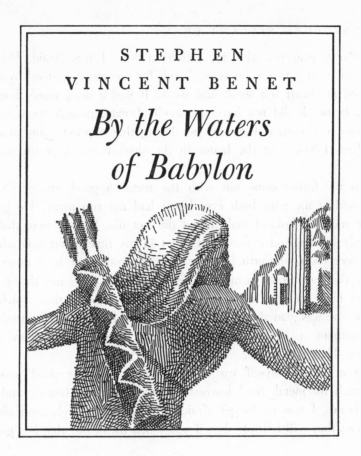

STEPHEN VINCENT BENET

By the Waters of Babylon

The north and the west and the south are good hunting ground, but it is forbidden to go east. It is forbidden to go to any of Dead Places except to search for metal and then he who touches the metal must be a priest or the son of a priest. Afterwards, both the man and the metal must be purified. These are the rules and the laws; they are well made. It is forbidden to cross the great river and look upon the place that was the Place of the Gods—this is most strictly forbidden. We do not even say its name though we know its name. It is there that spirits live, and demons—it is there that there are the ashes of the Great Burning. These things are forbidden—they have been forbidden since the beginning of time.

My father is a priest; I am the son of a priest. I have been in the

Dead Places near us, with my father—at first, I was afraid. When my father went into the house to search for the metal, I stood by the door and my heart felt small and weak. It was a dead man's house, a spirit house. It did not have the smell of man, though there were old bones in a corner. But it is not fitting that a priest's son should show fear. I looked at the bones in the shadow and kept my voice still.

Then my father came out with the metal—a good, strong piece. He looked at me with both eyes but I had not run away. He gave me the metal to hold—I took it and did not die. So he knew that I was truly his son and would be a priest in my time. That was when I was very young—nevertheless, my brothers would not have done it, though they are good hunters. After that, they gave me the good piece of meat and the warm corner by the fire. My father watched over me—he was glad that I should be a priest. But when I boasted or wept without a reason, he punished me more strictly than my brothers. That was right.

After a time, I myself was allowed to go into the dead houses and search for metal. So I learned the ways of those houses—and if I saw bones, I was no longer afraid. The bones are light and old—sometimes they will fall into dust if you touch them. But that is a great sin.

I was taught the chants and the spells—I was taught how to stop the running of blood from a wound and many secrets. A priest must know many secrets—that was what my father said. If the hunters think we do all things by chants and spells, they may believe so—it does not hurt them. I was taught how to read in the old books and how to make the old writings—that was hard and took a long time. My knowledge made me happy—it was like a fire in my heart. Most of all, I liked to hear of the Old Days and the stories of the gods. I asked myself many questions that I could not answer, but it was good to ask them. At night, I would lie awake and listen to the wind—it seemed to me that it was the voice of the gods as they flew through the air.

We are not ignorant like the Forest People—our women spin wool on the wheel, our priests wear a white robe. We do not eat grubs from the tree, we have not forgotten the old writings, although they are hard to understand. Nevertheless, my knowledge and my lack of knowledge burned in me—I wished to know more. When I was a man at last, I came to my father and said, "It is time for me to go on my journey. Give me your leave."

He looked at me for a long time, stroking his beard, then he said at last, "Yes. It is time." That night, in the house of the priesthood, I asked for and received purification. My body hurt but my spirit was a cool stone. It was my father himself who questioned me about my dreams.

He bade me look into the smoke of the fire and see—I saw and told what I saw. It was what I have always seen—a river, and, beyond it, a great Dead Place and in it the gods walking. I have always thought about that. His eyes were stern when I told him—he was no longer my father but a priest. He said, "This is a strong dream."

"It is mine," I said, while the smoke waved and my head felt light. They were singing the Star song in the outer chamber and it was like the buzzing of bees in my head.

He asked me how the gods were dressed and I told him how they were dressed. We know how they were dressed from the book, but I saw them as if they were before me. When I had finished, he threw the sticks three times and studied them as they fell.

"This is a very strong dream," he said. "It may eat you up."

"I am not afraid," I said and looked at him with both eyes. My voice sounded thin in my ears but that was because of the smoke.

He touched me on the breast and the forehead. He gave me the bow and the three arrows.

"Take them," he said. "It is forbidden to travel east. It is forbidden to cross the river. It is forbidden to go to the Place of the Gods. All these things are forbidden."

"All these things are forbidden," I said, but it was my voice that spoke and not my spirit. He looked at me again.

"My son," he said. "Once I had young dreams. If your dreams do not eat you up, you may be a great priest. If they eat you, you are still my son. Now go on your journey."

I went fasting, as is the law. My body hurt but not my heart. When the dawn came, I was out of sight of the village. I prayed and purified myself, waiting for a sign. The sign was an eagle. It flew east.

Sometimes signs are sent by bad spirits. I waited again on the flat rock, fasting, taking no food. I was very still—I could feel the sky above me and the earth beneath. I waited till the sun was beginning to sink. Then three deer passed in the valley, going east—they did not wind me or see me. There was a white fawn with them—a very great sign.

I followed them, at a distance, waiting for what would happen. My heart was troubled about going east, yet I knew that I must go. My head hummed with my fasting—I did not even see the panther spring upon the white fawn. But, before I knew it, the bow was in my hand. I shouted and the panther lifted his head from the fawn. It is not easy to kill a panther with one arrow but the arrow went through his eye and into his brain. He died as he tried to spring—he rolled over, tearing at the ground. Then I knew I was meant to go east—I knew that was my journey. When the night came, I made my fire and roasted meat.

It is eight suns' journey to the east and a man passes by many Dead Places. The Forest People are afraid of them but I am not. Once I made my fire on the edge of a Dead Place at night and, next morning, in the dead house, I found a good knife, little rusted. That was small to what came afterward but it made my heart feel big. Always when I looked for game, it was in front of my arrow, and twice I passed hunting parties of the Forest People without their knowing. So I knew my magic was strong and my journey clean, in spite of the law.

Toward the setting of the eighth sun, I came to the banks of the great river. It was half-a-day's journey after I had left the god-road— we do not use the god-roads now for they are falling apart into great blocks of stone, and the forest is safer going. A long way off, I had seen the water through trees but the trees were thick. At last, I came out upon an open place at the top of a cliff. There was the great river below, like a giant in the sun. It is very long, very wide. It could eat all the streams we know and still be thirsty. Its name is Ou-dis-sun, the Sacred, the Long. No man of my tribe had seen it, not even my father, the priest. It was magic and I prayed.

Then I raised my eyes and looked south. It was there, the Place of the Gods.

How can I tell what it was like—you do not know. It was there, in the red light, and they were too big to be houses. It was there with the red light upon it, mighty and ruined. I knew that in another moment the gods would see me. I covered my eyes with my hands and crept back into the forest.

Surely, that was enough to do, and live. Surely it was enough to spend the night upon the cliff. The Forest People themselves do not come near. Yet, all through the night, I knew that I should have to cross the river and walk in the places of the gods, although the gods ate me up. My magic did not help me at all and yet there was a fire in my bowels, a fire in my mind. When the sun rose, I thought, "My journey has been clean. Now I will go home from my journey." But, even as I thought so, I knew I could not. If I went to the Place of the Gods, I would surely die, but, if I did not go, I could never be at peace with my spirit again. It is better to lose one's life than one's spirit, if one is a priest and the son of a priest.

Nevertheless, as I made the raft, the tears ran out of my eyes. The Forest People could have killed me without fight, if they had come upon me then, but they did not come. When the raft was made, I said the sayings for the dead and painted myself for death. My heart was cold as a frog and my knees like water, but the burning in my mind would not let me have peace. As I pushed the raft from the shore, I began my death song—I had the right. It was a fine song.

"I am John, son of John," I sang. "My people are the Hill People.
    They are the men.
I go into the Dead Places but I am not slain.
I take the metal from the Dead Places but I am not blasted.
I travel upon the god-roads and am not afraid. E-yah! I have killed
    the panther, I have killed the fawn!
E-yah! I have come to the great river. No man has come there
    before.
It is forbidden to go east, but I have gone, forbidden to go on the
    great river, but I am there.
Open your hearts, you spirits, and hear my song.
    Now I go to the Place of the Gods, I shall not return.
My body is painted for death and my limbs weak, but my heart is
    big as I go to the Place of the Gods!"

All the same, when I came to the Place of the Gods, I was afraid, afraid. The current of the great river is very strong—it gripped my raft with its hands. That was magic, for the river itself is wide and calm. I could feel evil spirits about me, in the bright morning; I could feel their breath on my neck as I was swept down the stream. Never have I been so much alone—I tried to think of my knowledge, but it was a squirrel's heap of winter nuts. There was no strength in my knowledge any more and I felt small and naked as a new-hatched bird—alone upon the great river, the servant of the gods.

Yet, after a while, my eyes were opened and I saw. I saw both banks of the river—I saw that once there had been god-roads across it, though now they were broken and fallen like broken vines. Very great they were, and wonderful and broken—broken in the time of the Great Burning when the fire fell out of the sky. And always the current took me nearer to the Place of the Gods, and the huge ruins rose before my eyes.

I do not know the customs of rivers—we are the People of the Hills. I tried to guide my raft with the pole but it spun around. I thought the river meant to take me past the Place of the Gods and out into the Bitter Water of the legends. I grew angry then—my heart felt strong. I said aloud, "I am a priest and the son of a priest!" The gods heard me—they showed me how to paddle with the pole on one side of the raft. The current changed itself—I drew near to the Place of the Gods.

When I was very near, my raft struck and turned over. I can swim in our lakes—I swam to the shore. There was a great spike of rusted metal sticking out into the river—I hauled myself up upon it and sat there, panting. I had saved my bow and two arrows and the knife I found in the Dead Place but that was all. My raft went whirling downstream toward the Bitter Water. I looked after it, and thought if it had trod me under, at least I would be safely dead. Nevertheless, when I had dried my bowstring and re-strung it, I walked forward to the Place of the Gods.

It felt like ground underfoot; it did not burn me. It is not true what some of the tales say, that the ground there burns forever, for I have been there. Here and there were the marks and stains of the Great Burning, on the ruins, that is true. But they were old marks and old stains. It is not true either, what some of our priests say, that it is an island covered with fogs and enchantments. It is not. It is a great Dead Place—greater than any Dead Place we know. Everywhere in it there are god-roads, though most are cracked and broken. Everywhere there are the ruins of the high towers of the gods.

How shall I tell what I saw? I went carefully, my strung bow in my hand, my skin ready for danger. There should have been the wailings of spirits and the shrieks of demons, but there were not. It was very silent and sunny where I had landed—the wind and the rain and the birds that drop seeds had done their work—the grass grew in the cracks of the broken stone. It is a fair island—no wonder the gods built there. If I had come there, a god, I also would have built.

How shall I tell what I saw? The towers are not all broken—here and there one still stands, like a great tree in a forest, and the birds nest high. But the towers themselves look blind, for the gods are gone. I saw a fish-hawk, catching fish in the river. I saw a little dance of white butterflies over a great heap of broken stones and columns. I went there and looked about me—there was a carved stone with cut-letters, broken in half. I can read letters but I could not understand these. They said UBTREAS. There was also the shattered image of a man or a god. It had been made of white stone and he wore his hair tied back like a woman's. His name was ASHING, as I read on the cracked half of a stone. I thought it wise to pray to ASHING, though I do not know that god.

How shall I tell what I saw? There was no smell of man left, on stone or metal. Nor were there many trees in that wilderness of stone. There are many pigeons, nesting and dropping in the towers—the gods must have loved them, or, perhaps, they used them for sacrifices. There are wild cats that roam the god-roads, green-eyed, unafraid of man. At night they wail like demons but they are not demons. The wild dogs are more dangerous, for they hunt in a pack, but them I did not meet till later. Everywhere there are the carved stones, carved with magical numbers or words.

I went North—I did not try to hide myself. When a god or a demon saw me, then I would die, but meanwhile I was no longer afraid. My hunger for knowledge burned in me—there was so much that I could not understand. After a while, I knew that my belly was hungry. I could have hunted for my meat, but I did not hunt. It is known that the gods did not hunt as we do—they got their food from enchanted boxes and jars. Sometimes these are still found in the Dead Places—once, when I was a child and foolish, I opened such a jar and tasted it and found the food sweet. But my father found out and punished me for it strictly, for, often, that food is death. Now, though, I had long gone past what was forbidden, and I entered the likeliest towers, looking for the food of the gods.

I found it at last in the ruins of a great temple in the mid-city. A mighty temple it must have been, for the roof was painted like the sky at night with its stars—that much I could see, though the colors were faint and dim. It went down into great caves and tunnels— perhaps they kept their slaves there. But when I started to climb down, I heard the squeaking of rats, so I did not go—rats are unclean, and there must have been many tribes of them, from the squeaking. But near there, I found food, in the heart of a ruin, behind a door that still opened. I ate only the fruits from the jars—they had a very sweet taste. There was drink, too, in bottles of glass—the drink of the gods was strong and made my head swim. After I had eaten and drunk, I slept on the top of a stone, my bow at my side.

When I woke, the sun was low. Looking down from where I lay, I saw a dog sitting on his haunches. His tongue was hanging out of his mouth; he looked as if he were laughing. He was a big dog, with a gray-brown coat, as big as a wolf. I sprang up and shouted at him but he did not move—he just sat there as if he were laughing. I did not like that. When I reached for a stone to throw, he moved swiftly out of the way of the stone. He was not afraid of me; he looked at me as if I were meat. No doubt I could have killed him with an arrow, but I did not know if there were others. Moreover, night was falling.

I looked about me—not far away there was a great, broken god-road, leading North. The towers were high enough, but not so high, and while many of the dead-houses were wrecked, there were some that stood. I went toward this god-road, keeping to the heights of the ruins, while the dog followed. When I had reached the god-road, I saw that there were others behind him. If I had slept later, they would have come upon me asleep and torn out my throat. As it was, they were sure enough of me; they did not hurry. When I went into the dead-house, they kept watch at the entrance—doubtless they thought they would have a fine hunt. But a dog cannot open a door and I knew, from the books, that the gods did not like to live on the ground but on high.

I had just found a door I could open when the dogs decided to rush. Ha! They were surprised when I shut the door in their faces—it was a good door, of strong metal. I could hear their foolish baying beyond it but I did not stop to answer them. I was in darkness—I found stairs and climbed. There were many stairs, turning around till my head was dizzy. At the top was another door—I found the knob and opened it. I was in a long small chamber—on one side of it was a bronze door that could not be opened, for it had no handle. Perhaps there was a magic word to open it but I did not have the word. I turned to the door in the opposite side of the wall. The lock of it was broken and I opened it and went in.

Within, there was a place of great riches. The god who lived there must have been a powerful god. The first room was a small ante-room—I waited there for some time, telling the spirits of the place that I came in peace and not as a robber. When it seemed to me that they had had time to hear me, I went on. Ah, what riches! Few, even, of the windows had been broken—it was all as it had been. The great windows that looked over the city had not been broken at all though they were dusty and streaked with many years. There were coverings on the floors, the colors not greatly faded, and the chairs were soft and deep. There were pictures upon the walls, very strange, very wonderful—I remember one of a bunch of flowers in a jar—if you came close to it, you could see nothing but bits of color, but if you stood away from it, the flowers might have been picked yesterday. It made my heart feel strange to look at this picture—and to look at the figure of a bird, in some hard clay, on a table and see it so like our birds. Everywhere there were books and writings, many in tongues that I could not read. The god who lived there must have been a wise god and full of knowledge. I felt I had right there, as I sought knowledge also.

Nevertheless, it was strange. There was a washing-place but no water—perhaps the gods washed in air. There was a cooking-place but no wood, and though there was a machine to cook food, there was no place to put fire in it. Nor were there candles or lamps— there were things that looked like lamps but they had neither oil nor wick. All these things were magic, but I touched them and lived—the magic had gone out of them. Let me tell one thing to show. In the washing-place, a thing said "Hot" but it was not hot to the touch—another thing said "Cold" but it was not cold. This must have been a strong magic but the magic was gone. I do not understand—they had ways—I wish that I knew.

It was close and dry and dusty in their house of the gods. I have said the magic was gone but that is not true—it had gone from the magic things but it had not gone from the place. I felt the spirits about me, weighing upon me. Nor had I ever slept in a Dead Place before—and yet, tonight, I must sleep there. When I thought of it, my tongue felt dry in my throat, in spite of my wish for knowledge. Almost I would have gone down again and faced the dogs, but I did not.

I had not gone through all the rooms when the darkness fell. When it fell, I went back to the big room looking over the city and made fire. There was a place to make fire and a box with wood in it, though I do not think they cooked there. I wrapped myself in a floor-covering and slept in front of the fire—I was very tired.

Now I tell what is very strong magic. I woke in the midst of the night. When I woke, the fire had gone out and I was cold. It seemed to me that all around me there were whisperings and voices. I closed my eyes to shut them out. Some will say that I slept again, but I do not think that I slept. I could feel the spirits drawing my spirit out of my body as a fish is drawn on a line.

Why should I lie about it? I am a priest and the son of a priest. If there are spirits, as they say, in the small Dead Places near us, what spirits must there not be in that great Place of the Gods? And would not they wish to speak? After such long years? I know that I felt myself drawn as a fish is drawn on a line. I had stepped out of my body—I could see my body asleep in front of the cold fire, but it was not I. I was drawn to look out upon the city of the gods.

It should have been dark, for it was night, but it was not dark. Everywhere there were lights—lines of light—circles and blurs of light —ten thousand torches would not have been the same. The sky itself was alight—you could barely see the stars for the glow in the sky. I thought to myself "This is strong magic" and trembled. There was a roaring in my ears like the rushing of rivers. Then my eyes grew used to the light and my ears to the sound. I knew that I was seeing the city as it had been when the gods were alive.

That was a sight indeed—yes, that was a sight: I could not have seen it in the body—my body would have died. Everywhere went the gods, on foot and in chariots—there were gods beyond number and counting and their chariots blocked the streets. They had turned night to day for their pleasure—they did not sleep with the sun. The noise of their coming and going was the noise of many waters. It was magic what they could do—it was magic what they did.

I looked out of another window—the great vines of their bridges were mended and the god-roads went East and West. Restless, restless, were the gods and always in motion! They burrowed tunnels under rivers—they flew in the air. With unbelievable tools they did giant works—no part of the earth was safe from them, for, if they wished for a thing, they summoned it from the other side of the world. And always, as they labored and rested, as they feasted and made love, there was a drum in their ears—the pulse of the giant city, beating and beating like a man's heart.

Were they happy? What is happiness to the gods? They were great, they were mighty, they were wonderful and terrible. As I looked upon them and their magic, I felt like a child—but a little more, it seemed to me, and they would pull down the moon from the sky. I saw them with wisdom beyond wisdom and knowledge beyond knowledge. And yet not all they did was well done—even I could see that—and yet their wisdom could not but grow until all was peace.

Then I saw their fate come upon them and that was terrible past speech. It came upon them as they walked the streets of their city. I have been in the fights with the Forest People—I have seen men die. But this was not like that. When gods war with gods, they use weapons we do not know. It was fire falling out of the sky and a mist that poisoned. It was the time of the Great Burning and the Destruction. They ran about like ants in the streets of their city— poor gods, poor gods! Then the towers began to fall. A few escaped— yes, a few. The legends tell it. But, even after the city had become a Dead Place, for many years the poison was still in the ground. I saw it happen, I saw the last of them die. It was darkness over the broken city and I wept.

All this, I saw. I saw it as I have told it, though not in the body. When I woke in the morning, I was hungry, but I did not think first of my hunger for my heart was perplexed and confused. I knew the reason for the Dead Places but I did not see why it had happened. It seemed to me it should not have happened, with all the magic they had. I went through the house looking for an answer. There was so much in the house I could not understand—and yet I am a priest and the son of a priest. It was like being on one side of the great river, at night, with no light to show the way.

Then I saw the dead god. He was sitting in his chair, by the window, in a room I had not entered before and, for the first moment, I thought that he was alive. Then I saw the skin on the back of his hand—it was like dry leather. The room was shut, hot and dry—no doubt that had kept him as he was. At first I was afraid to approach him—then the fear left me. He was sitting looking out over the city— he was dressed in the clothes of the gods. His age was neither young nor old—I could not tell his age. But there was wisdom in his face and great sadness. You could see that he would have not run away. He had sat at his window, watching his city die—then he himself had died. But it is better to lose one's life than one's spirit—and you could see from the face that his spirit had not been lost. I knew, that, if I touched him, he would fall into dust—and yet, there was something unconquered in the face.

That is all of my story, for then I knew he was a man—I knew then that they had been men, neither gods nor demons. It is a great knowledge, hard to tell and believe. They were men —they went a dark road, but they were men. I had no fear after that—I had no fear going home, though twice I fought off the dogs and once I was hunted for two days by the Forest People. When I saw my father again, I prayed and was purified. He touched my lips and my breast, he said, "You went away a boy. You come back a man and a priest." I said, "Father, they were men! I have been in the Place of the Gods and seen it! Now slay me, if it is the law—but still I know they were men."

He looked at me out of both eyes. He said, "The law is not always the same shape—you have done what you have done. I could not have done it in my time, but you come after me. Tell!"

I told and he listened. After that, I wished to tell all the people but he showed me otherwise. He said, "Truth is a hard deer to hunt. If you eat too much truth at once, you may die of the truth. It was not idly that our fathers forbade the Dead Places." He was right—it is better the truth should come little by little. I have learned that, being a priest. Perhaps, in the old days, they ate knowledge too fast.

Nevertheless, we make a beginning. It is not for the metal alone we go to the Dead Places now—there are the books and the writings. They are hard to learn. And the magic tools are broken—but we can look at them and wonder. At least, we make a beginning. And, when I am chief priest we shall go beyond the great river. We shall go to the Place of the Gods—the place newyork—not one man but a company. We shall look for the images of the gods and find the god ASHING and the others—the gods Lincoln and Biltmore and Moses. But they were men who built the city, not gods or demons. They were men. I remember the dead man's face. They were men who were here before us. We must build again.

Biographical Notes

JOAN AIKEN, daughter of the American writer Conrad Aiken, was born in Rye, Sussex, England. She has engaged in a variety of professions including copywriting and editing and has written two novels for adults in addition to the three children's books which chronicle events during the reign of the mythical King James III, *The Wolves of Willoughby Chase, Black Hearts in Battersea,* and *Nightbirds on Nantucket,* and a volume of short stories.

LUDWIG BEMELMANS (1898–1962) was born in the Austrian Tyrol and came to the United States at sixteen to work in hotel management. He was the author of several books of personal reminiscence.

STEPHEN VINCENT BENÉT (1898–1943) came of one of New York's "first families of writers" and never followed any other profession. He wrote successfully in many forms, and his books include short stories such as *Thirteen O'Clock* and *Tales Before Midnight,* shorter poems such as *Young Adventure* and *Tiger Joy,* and the long narrative poem *John Brown's Body,* which won him the Pulitzer Prize for poetry in 1929.

RAY BRADBURY (1920–   ) was born in Waukegan, Illinois, and became interested in science fiction through the medium of the Buck Rogers comic strip. Since the age of twenty-one, he has written volumes of science fiction short stories which have secured him a position of eminence in the field. Among his books are *The Martian Chronicles, The Golden Apples of the Sun,* and *Fahrenheit 451.*

HEYWOOD BROUN (1888–1939) was born in New York and began his career as a sportswriter with the New York *Morning Telegraph.* He stayed with newspapers all his life, eventually writing a syndicated column, "It Seems to Me," as well as novels, essays, and a musical comedy. For a short time he was an active member of the Socialist Party. He founded the American Newspaper Guild, of which he was president until his death.

PEARL S. BUCK (1892–   ) was born in West Virginia, the daughter of missionaries, but raised in China. Her novel *The Good Earth* won the Pulitzer Prize; she received the Howells medal of American Academy of Arts and Letters in 1935; the Nobel Prize in 1938. Her concern with the land and people of the Orient has been reflected in her interest in international relief work as well as in her novels and short stories.

SHEILA BURNFORD was born in Scotland. She married a pediatrician and now lives in Ontario. During the war she was a V.A.D. in Royal Naval Hospitals, and after the war an ambulance driver. Moreover, she has a pilot's license and is a good marksman. In her best-selling book *The Incredible Journey*, the cat and bull terrier are based on real animals.

TRUMAN CAPOTE (1924–   ) spent most of his childhood in the Deep South, the locale of many of his stories. At seventeen, he left school and began to write seriously, first in New Orleans and then in New York, where he was hailed as a prodigy after the publication of *Other Voices, Other Rooms* in 1948. Since that time he has produced many novels and volumes of short stories as well as the "nonfiction novel" *In Cold Blood.*

JACQUES YVES COUSTEAU is a Frenchman whose interest in the world beneath the sea has led him to pioneer in the development of the aqualung, underwater archaeology, and experiments in prolonged submersion. In *The Silent World* and *World Without Sun* he has written fascinatingly of his experiences.

GERALD DURRELL has spent a lifetime surrounded by animals. His career as an animal collector has led him into many strange corners of the world about which he has written in his numerous books, among which are *The Bafut Beagles, Three Tickets to Adventure* and *Two in the Bush.*

F. SCOTT FITZGERALD (1896–1940), born in St. Paul, Minnesota, was sent east by his parents, first to prep school in New Jersey and later to Princeton University. After a tour of duty with the Army during World War I, he returned to New York City where he sold his first short stories. He then returned to St. Paul to finish his first novel, *This Side of Paradise.* In the ensuing years, he published several more novels, among them *The Great Gatsby,* considered by critics to be his finest work, and *Tender Is the Night,* before his untimely death in 1940.

LOUISE FITZHUGH was born in Memphis, Tennessee, and has lived in Washington, D.C., France, and Italy. She attended Bard College and Cooper Union. The critics were divided over her first book for children, *Harriet the Spy,* although in the year that it was published, 1964, the New York *Times* listed it as one of "The Year's Best Juveniles." A year earlier Miss Fitzhugh exhibited paintings in New York; in 1961 she illustrated *Suzuki Beane.* Her most recent book is *The Long Secret.*

ESTHER FORBES (1894–   ) was born in Westborough, Massachusetts, and was for several years an employee of the Boston publishing firm of

Houghton, Mifflin. She has written several novels with historical settings, among them a biography of Paul Revere, which won the Pulitzer Prize for history in 1943, and *Johnny Tremain*, a Newbery Medal winner (1944).

PAUL GALLICO (1897–   ) born and educated in New York City, began his career as a concert pianist but later switched to journalism. His interests in animals, sports, and the supernatural are reflected in many of his books, among which are *The Golden People*, *The Snow Goose*, *The Abandoned*, and *Love of Seven Dolls*, from which he wrote the screenplay for the movie *Lili*.

FRANK B. GILBRETH, JR., and ERNESTINE GILBRETH CAREY, two of the twelve children who appear in *Cheaper by the Dozen*, described the adventures of their family in Montclair, New Jersey, in that well-loved autobiographical book. In real life, their parents were among the first industrial engineers.

RUMER GODDEN (1907–   ), though born in Sussex, England, was brought up in India and later returned to England to go to school. Both countries have served as settings for her many novels, among which are *An Episode of Sparrows*, *The Greengage Summer*, *The River*, and *Kingfishers Catch Fire*.

GRAHAM GREENE (1904–   ), was born in London and has led an outwardly quiet life, while at the same time devoting himself to writing. After his conversion to Catholicism, he incorporated his faith into his writing and is one of the foremost Catholic writers today. His major works include *The Quiet American* and *The Power and the Glory*.

ERNEST HEMINGWAY (1898–1961) was born in Oak Park, Illinois. Soon after finishing high school, he went to Italy as an ambulance driver in the First World War. In 1920 he traveled to the Far East and settled in Paris the following year, where he published his first books. His earthy, direct prose style deeply influenced the development of many writers both in Europe and in the United States, and his stature as a writer was recognized when he received both the Pulitzer Prize (1953) and the Nobel Prize for Literature (1954). Some of his major books are *The Sun Also Rises*, *For Whom the Bell Tolls*, and *The Old Man and the Sea*.

O. HENRY (1862–1910), born William Sydney Porter, grew up in Greensboro, North Carolina. He left school at fifteen and went to Texas where he lived on a ranch, picked up a little French, Spanish, and German, and finally got a job at a bank. Suddenly, Porter was accused of embezzlement and was summoned to Austin to stand trial. Instead, he left the country, traveling part of the time on money stolen by Al Jennings, a famous outlaw. At thirty-five, he suddenly returned upon hearing that his wife was ill. He was tried and sentenced to five years in prison. After his release he spent most of his life in New York City, where he wrote as many as sixty-five stories in a year.

JAMES HILTON (1900–1954) was born in Leigh, Lancashire. He wrote his first novel, *Catharine Herself*, during his first undergraduate year at Cambridge but did not achieve success until he wrote *Good-bye, Mr. Chips* (1934), which became a best seller. That book carried *Lost Horizon* (1933) into the best-seller world, and both were made into films. Hilton lived in the United States from 1935 until his death.

SHIRLEY JACKSON (1919–1965) spent her married years in Vermont with her husband, critic Stanley Edgar Hyman, and their four children. Her works include both novels and short stories, ranging from the macabre to the witty and irreverent. They include *Life Among the Savages, The Lottery and Other Stories, We Have Always Lived in the Castle,* and *The Haunting of Hill House.*

ROBERT LAWSON (1892–   ) was born in New York City and spent most of his early career as an illustrator of children's books. It was not until 1938 that he began writing for his own illustrations, a course which brought him the Caldecott Medal in 1940 for *They Were Strong and Good* and the Newbery Medal in 1944 for *Rabbit Hill.* Some of his other books are *Smeller Martin, Mr. Revere and I,* and *Mr. Wilmer.*

STEPHEN LEACOCK (1869–1944), a Canadian, spent much of his professional life as a professor of economics at McGill University. As an author, he produced several books of humorous essays and volumes of economic and political theory.

HARPER LEE was brought up in the American South, which served as the locale for her first novel *To Kill a Mockingbird.* The book was on the best-seller list for over a year and a half and won the Pulitzer Prize. It was also the only novel chosen by four major book clubs.

LIN YUTANG (1895–   ) was born in China, studied in Shanghai, at Harvard in the United States, and in Leipzig. As a young man he became involved in internal Chinese politics but later modified his political position and left the country for residence in the United States and France. He served briefly with UNESCO in 1948. His many novels and volumes of short stories include *The Importance of Living* and *Famous Chinese Short Stories Retold.*

GAVIN MAXWELL is a Scotsman and journalist who has become known as a faithful and highly vocal devotee of otters. His regard for these engaging creatures and his love of the wild highland countryside show clearly in his best-selling books *A Ring of Bright Water* and *The Rocks Remain.*

HELEN MARTINI, a Bronx housewife, found herself one day in an unusual situation. Her husband Fred, a keeper in the lion house at the Bronx Zoo, telephoned to say he was bringing home some newborn lion cubs whose mother refused to care for them. The experiences which began for her that day are described in her book *My Zoo Family.*

C. AUBREY MENEN (1912–   ) was born in London and educated in English schools. His father was a high-caste Indian and his mother a nationalistic Irishwoman. Menen's first recognition as a writer came while he was a student at University College, London, when H. G. Wells gave Menen permission to dramatize Wells's book, *Shape of Things to Come.* In 1939 he left for India, where, after the outbreak of war, he supervised war publicity for the radio. In 1946, he again returned to India to organize the production of documentary and educational films. He is the author of many novels as well as books of autobiography and philosophy.

HECTOR HUGH MUNRO (1870–1916) who became famous as a short story writer under the name of Saki, was born in Burma but educated in England by relatives. After a short stint with the Burma police force (in which his father had served) he returned to England and took up journalism. He was killed in France during service with the 22nd Royal Fusiliers during World War I.

E. NESBIT (1858–1924) was one of six children in a London family. She early decided on a literary career but it was not until she was in her forties that she began to write for children and achieved success. Some of her best-known books are *Five Children and It, The Wouldbegoods,* and *The Treasure Seekers.*

EMILY NEVILLE was born in Connecticut. After graduating from Bryn Mawr, she worked as a copy girl for New York newspapers and married a newspaperman. They have five children. Mrs. Neville lives in New York City. *It's Like This, Cat,* her first novel for young adults, won the Newbery Medal in 1964.

MARY NORTON says in a letter opening *The Borrowers* that she was nearsighted before "The Powers That Were" discovered she needed glasses. The blurred world she explored with her four brothers—two older, two younger—until boarding school, and glasses. At school she found security even during the war years 1914–18. She writes that by just before the Second World War, people were forced to live as mythical men had in her childhood dreams.

SEAN O'FAOLAIN (1900–   ) is an Irishman whose first writing was done in Gaelic and who took an active part in the Irish Revolution and its accompanying Celtic revival. A novelist, biographer, and short story writer, he is best known for his ability to evoke the Irish atmosphere and background.

MARY RENAULT, born in London, went to Oxford to become a teacher but decided she preferred writing. Trained for three years in nursing, she wrote *Promise of Love* but returned to nursing when the war came, writing her next three books while off duty. She settled in Natal in South Africa before political problems made that area known internationally and later traveled in Greece for three months gathering material which later appeared in her brilliant historical novels *The King Must Die, The Bull from the Sea,* and others.

CARL SANDBURG (1878–1967) was the son of a Swedish blacksmith. Sandburg was an admirer of Walt Whitman and became himself a voice of the American people with his volume *The People, Yes.* His biography of Lincoln won the Pulitzer Prize in history in 1940 and he augmented his income by reading his own poetry and singing American folk songs. At his death he was one of America's best-known, best-loved, and most influential voices.

SAKI (see Munro, Hector Hugh).

WILLIAM SAROYAN (1908–   ) came of an Armenian family and was born in Fresno, California. After his father died (when Saroyan was two years old) he lived in an orphanage for several years. By the time he quit school, he had finished the second year of junior high school and had read every book in the school library. His first story appeared in 1933. The following year, he published *The Daring Young Man on the Flying Trapeze,* which was an instant success. Since then he has written many more short stories, novels, and plays. One of his most popular novels is *The Human Comedy* (1942), and his best known plays are *My Heart's in the Highlands* (1939) and *The Time of Your Life* (1940), for which he received a Pulitzer Prize which he refused to accept. He even wrote a best selling song, "Come On-a My House," which made all the top-forty charts in 1951.

MARY-ALICE SCHNIRRING is a successful writer of science fiction.

ETTA SHIBER, an American widow, was one of the many people who were trapped in Paris by the rapid advance of the German army in World War II. And like many others also, she found herself involved in the operations of the French underground. Discovered and arrested, Mrs. Shiber spent many rigorous months in a Nazi prison until she was exchanged shortly before the end of the war. She wrote of her fantastic experience in *Paris—Underground.*

MIKHAIL SHOLOKHOV (1905–   ) is a citizen of the Soviet Union, where he lives in the small town of Veshenskaya. As a teen-ager, he took an active part in the Russian Revolution, the events of which play a major part in many of his novels and stories. He is best known for *And Quiet Flows the Don* and *Tales of the Don* and was awarded the Nobel Prize for Literature in 1965.

LINCOLN STEFFENS (1866–1936) was a Californian best known as a political writer and flagbearer for sensational, unsuccessful, or controversial causes. His *Autobiography* gives a vivid picture of a colorful personality and remains his best known work.

JOHN STEINBECK (1902–   ) was born in California and studied marine biology at Stanford. His first three books were failures, and during the early portion of his career the fish he caught in Monterey Bay helped feed himself and his wife. However, in 1938 *The Grapes of Wrath*, called "the *Uncle Tom's Cabin* of the twentieth century," won the Pulitzer Prize, putting him on the road to commercial as well as artistic success. His other best sellers include *Tortilla Flat, Of Mice and Men, The Red Pony*, and *The Moon Is Down*. He received the Nobel Prize for Literature in 1962.

DOROTHY STERLING (1913–   ) was born in New York and has lived most of her life in the city and its suburbs. In addition to raising a family and taking an active part in the Civil Rights movement, she has written twenty-three books for children.

DYLAN THOMAS (1914–1953) born in Wales, was still a teen-ager when his first poems were published. He received the Oscar Blumenthal Prize from *Poetry* in 1938 and produced his autobiography, *Portrait of the Artist as a Young Dog* in 1940. His dramatic poetry readings were very popular in the U.S.A., and it was during one such tour that he died at the age of thirty-nine.

JAMES THURBER (1894–1961) was born in Columbus, Ohio, and began his literary career as a newspaper reporter. Thereafter he produced a steady stream of short stories, personal reminiscences, humorous essays, cartoons, and children's stories. One of the latter, *Many Moons,* was awarded the Caldecott Medal in 1944.

J[OHN] R[ONALD] R[EUEL] TOLKEIN (1892–   ) is an Englishman who has devoted most of his professional career to the study and teaching of Anglo-Saxon. Many of the creatures, customs, and trappings of Anglo-Saxon mythology appear in his four volumes which describe the fictional history of Middle Earth: *The Hobbit, The Fellowship of the Ring, The Two Towers,* and *The Return of the King.*

UNA TROY was born in Fermoy, County Cork, Ireland, during the exciting years of the Irish Revolution. She began her literary career in high school where she wrote tragic novels during study hours. After her graduation and marriage she continued to write, producing novels of political satire. Recently she has turned to humor and the Irish countryside and people she knows so well. Her books include *Mount Prospect, Dead Star's Light* (under a pseudonym), *We Are Seven,* and *The Other End of the Bridge.*

JAMES RAMSEY ULLMAN (1907–   ) is a New Yorker whose wide travel experience is reflected in his novels. A lover of mountains, he has visited and climbed in Brazil, Hawaii, Russia, South Africa, the Alps, and the Andes. Since 1949 he has made his home in Bermuda. Among his books are *The White Tower, River of the Sun,* and *Banner in the Sky.*

EVELYN WAUGH (1903–   ) comes of a prominent English literary family. After attending Oxford University and a London art school he settled down to writing and produced many satirical novels of English life among which are *Vile Bodies, Decline and Fall,* and *Brideshead Revisited.* He has also written biography and travel books.

E[LWYN] B[ROOKS] WHITE (1899–   ) was born in Mt. Vernon, New York, and has spent much of his life in New York City, being a frequent contributor to *The New Yorker.* In addition to his two books for children *Charlotte's Web* and Newbery Medal winner *Stuart Little,* he is the author of several volumes of humorous and critical essays, among which are *One Man's Meat* and *Here Is New York.*

T[ERENCE] H[ANBURY] WHITE (1906–   ), though born in India, was educated in England where he has lived ever since. His early works (written in the intervals of teaching school) were unsuccessful, but in 1938 his *The Sword in the Stone* became a Book-of-the-Month Club Selection, giving him a wide audience on both sides of the Atlantic. Since then he has completed the trilogy of which that was the first volume, calling it *The Once and Future King.* Others of his books are *Mistress Masham's Repose, The Goshawk,* and *The Book of Beasts.*

ABOUT THE AUTHOR

Georgess McHargue is the pseudonym of an unknown author who is at present employed by a large New York publishing house.